I come away with connection. I come away with catharsis. I come away feeling like I've been danced, drummed or jammed, like I'm the instrument that's been played, and that is awesome. Katy G. To me, live music, as a continuous happening, is incredible—it never, ever ends. Kendall D. Ever since I was a little girl, I have always loved all types of music. I was always drawn to rock and roll ... Kerry W. Every show was like a family reunion, as well as a new adventure. Leslie L. It's the ultimate release to be standing in a field, on a hill, on a floor in an indoor arena ... you name it, and just dancing as if you were five years old again. Lindsey H. My body is another instrument in my live music experience. It is my relationship to the music made visual. I feel most free when I am dancing. Lisa O. I leave a live music experience with clarity. It's about immersing myself and letting go of the daily grind. It's about creating space and openness to re-remember or re-learn or re-realize whatever lesson is needed in that moment. Molly B. Everyone has someone they like to be near at a show—a lover, a crew, a companion, a buddy. I like to be near to the band. We have a relationship now. They're my friends. We interact. We make each other smile and laugh. We dance together. I miss that when I'm not up front. Olivia M. Everything inevitably just devolves into a giant primordial jam ... Those are the times we're really reminded of why we do what we do in the larger context of the earth and nature. Pearl C. It feels like coming home. That's my tribe and it's where I want to be. Phyllis K. I love being there with my friends and seeing new music that people tell me I will love. Rachel B. Dancing takes me to my happy place. I feel confident, sexy, lose all my insecurities, and feel at peace with myself when I dance. Robyn S. At a festival, I want to radiate energy and good vibes, and dressing as bright as possible is a huge part of that. Sarah C. Music makes me better when I'm good and good when I'm blue. Shannon Dancing, laughing, spinning in circles for hours, or just laying in the grass and taking everything in. For me, live music is the greatest escape. Sydney C.

Hippie Chick

A Tale of Love, Devotion & Surrender

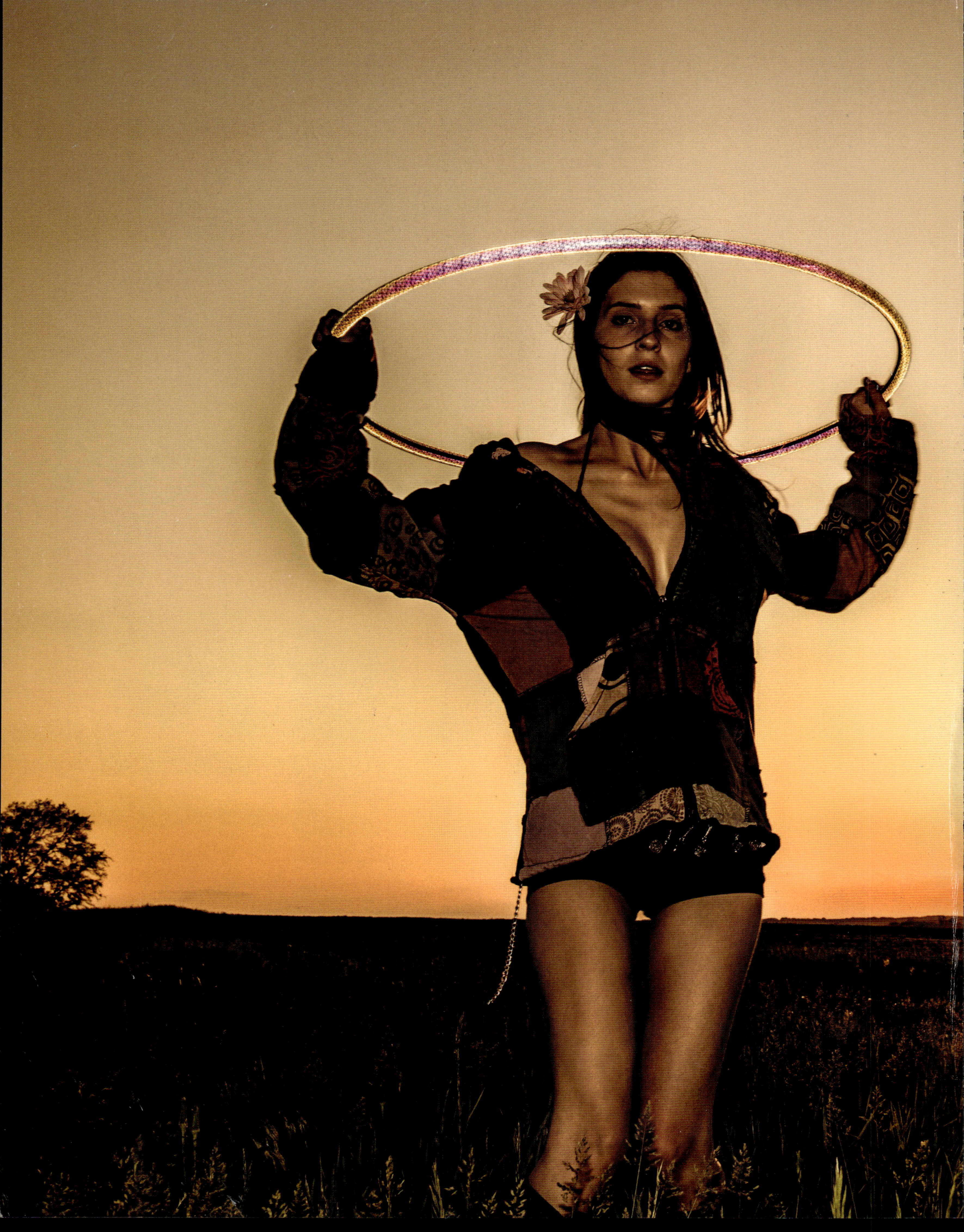

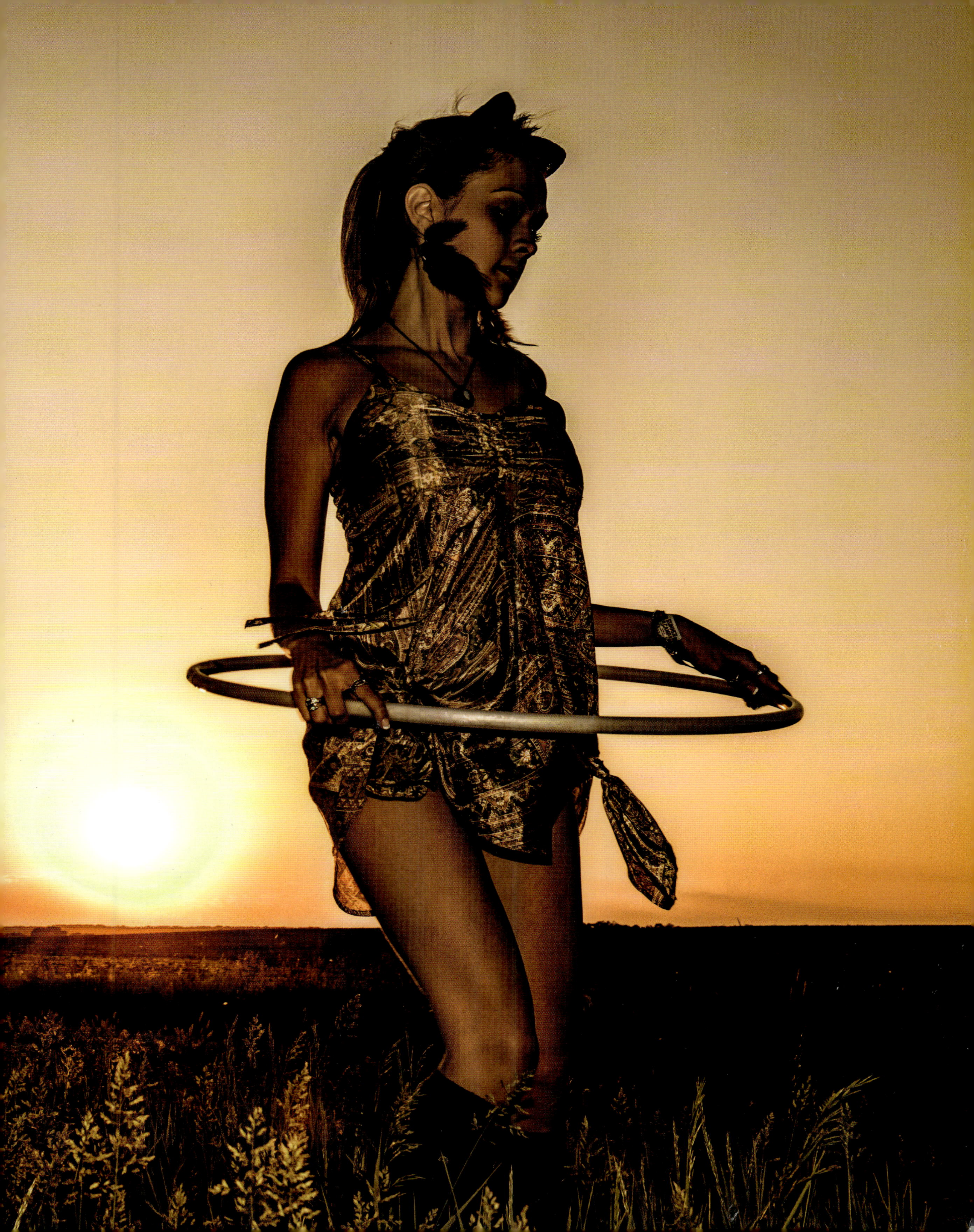

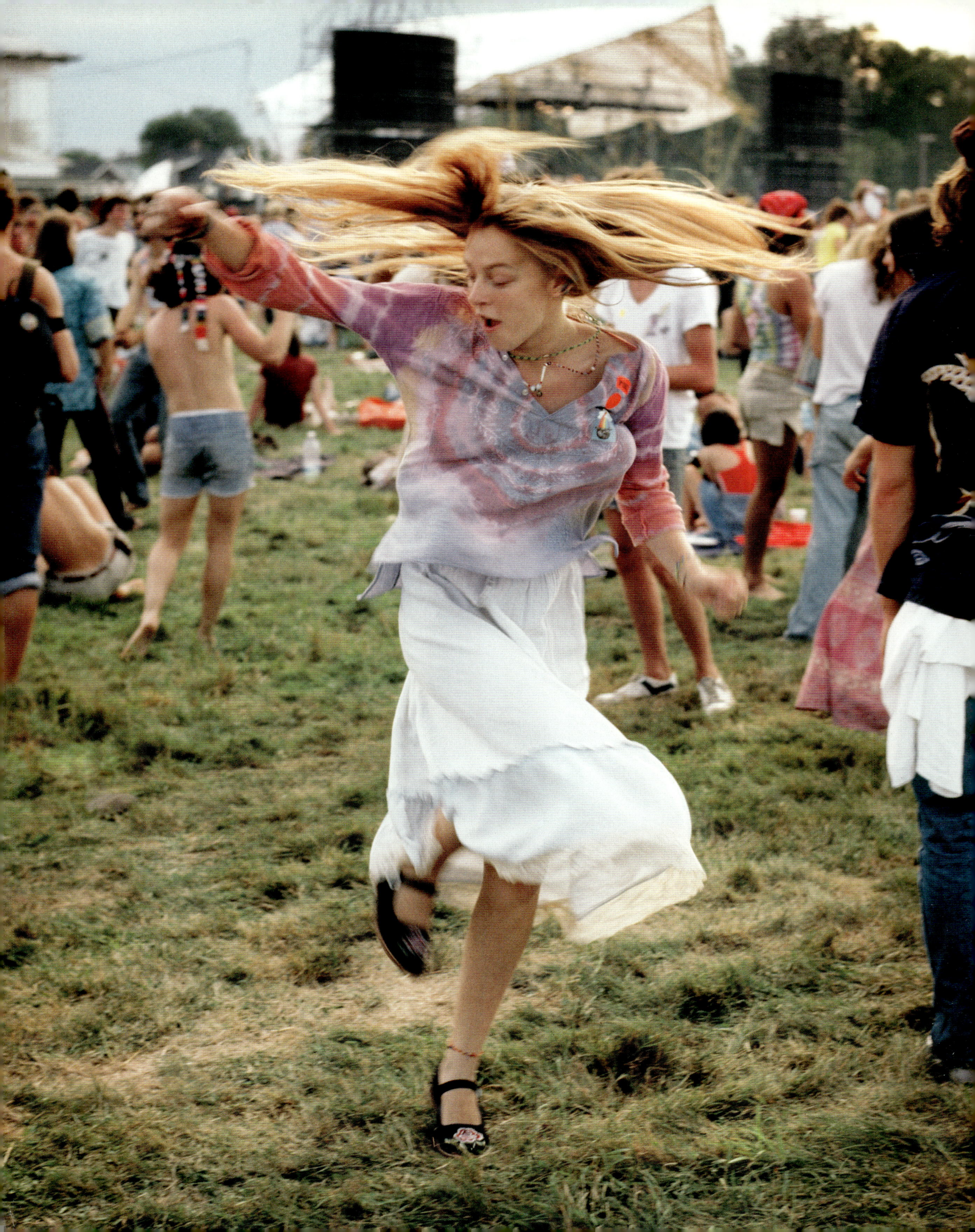

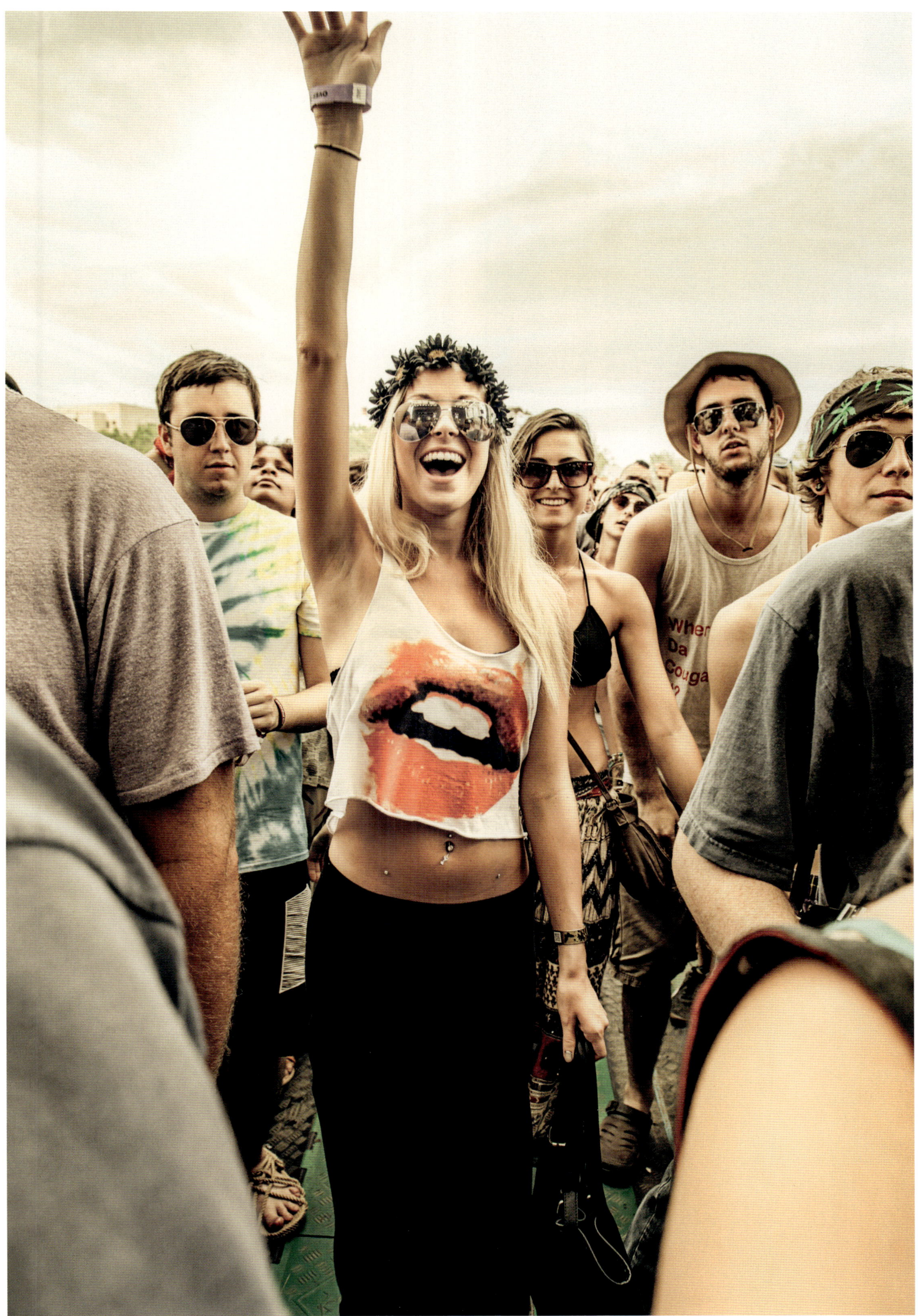

This book is dedicated to my #1 hippie chicks, Laurie Bienstock & Ricki Blakesberg.

"Without love in a dream it will never come true..." What started out thirty-five years ago with myself, a camera, and a bunch of like-minded souls on the road following the Grateful Dead, has now become Hippie Chick. I always knew there was something incredibly special about photographing the women who blazed the trail with fashion, passion, and inspiration, fueling the scene and the music! Hippie Chick began as a passing thought, evolving into an idea, then reality, through the enthusiastic blessings and validation of social media.

A simple message from a woman calling herself "Festival Girl" asking my permission to re-post a photo on her Instagram account has blossomed into a creative collaboration propelled by a mutual, burning desire to share the story of this tribe. This is visual anthropology, but without the words of Edith Johnson, I am not sure if this book would be a true record of the modern-day hippie chick! Thank you, Edith, for pouring your heart and soul into this project! Francie Greene, my creative partner with JAM, is back again with her fine skills as art director and designer, molding this book in to an object of beauty. I love our workflow and appreciate our many hours discussing how to make this book perfect! Ben Kautt, your skills with that computer are what really make my work stand out! Thank you for many years of creativity, brilliance, and technology! Grace Slick and Grace Potter, your powerful words added so much color and depth to this project. It means so much to me that you both could see this book was worthy of your participation! Other folks who need to be thanked and recognized include Carrie Lombardi, Emily Sevin, Tracey Diamond, Nate Erwin, Alison Tavel, China Isler, and Scott Hann. My family, Laurie Bienstock, Ricki Blakesberg, Sam Blakesberg, Bill and Joan Blakesberg, and always thanks to my dad, who gave his camera to a 16-year-old kid and set him free...and of course all the rest of my family. Thank you to hippie chicks—past, present, and future—for enriching the live music scene and being the muse to my lens.

All of the early photos from this book were taken at Grateful Dead concerts, so thank you to the good ol' Grateful Dead for changing so many of our lives and inspiring all the next generation bands that continue to energize the hippie chicks of yesterday, today, and tomorrow. Many of the recent photos were taken at festivals that I love! Thank you Summer Camp Music Festival, moe.down, Gathering of the Vibes, High Sierra Music Festival, Lockn' Music Festival, Hardly Strictly Bluegrass, Horning's Hideout, New Orleans Jazz and Heritage Festival, and Mountain Jam. Venues include the Greek Theatre – Berkeley, Fox Theater – Oakland, Bill Graham Civic Auditorium, Fox Theatre – Boulder, Ogden Theatre – Denver, The Fillmore – SF, Terrapin Crossroads, Sweetwater Music Hall, Capitol Theatre – Port Chester, Brooklyn Bowl, Crystal Bay Casino, Red Rocks Amphitheatre, The Mishawaka, Best Buy Theater – NYC, Great American Music Hall, and the Stanley Hotel! These venues are our temples and I thank them for being a part of the magic created, and for providing me with a space to capture that lightning in a bottle. Thanks to all the team members who run these festivals and venues. Your hospitality is appreciated and acknowledged.
I am so grateful. #savedbyrockandroll

Jay Blakesberg
San Francisco, June 2015

Editor's Note

Eighty-one women responded to our series of interview questions about their experiences in live music. The candidates were chosen among personal friends, friends of friends, fixtures on the scene, industry professionals, music forum members, rock and roll wives (or family), and notable women Jay or I spotted at shows. The result of these exchanges was hundreds of pages of anecdotes, memories, and opinions. We are honored that these women shared with us so generously. From their words, we curated a small selection of quotes to accompany Jay's images and provide a sense of what it means to be a hippie chick. Not all interviewees are visually represented in this book. When the woman quoted on a given page is featured in its accompanying image, we have indicated so in parentheses.

Edith Johnson
San Francisco, June 2015

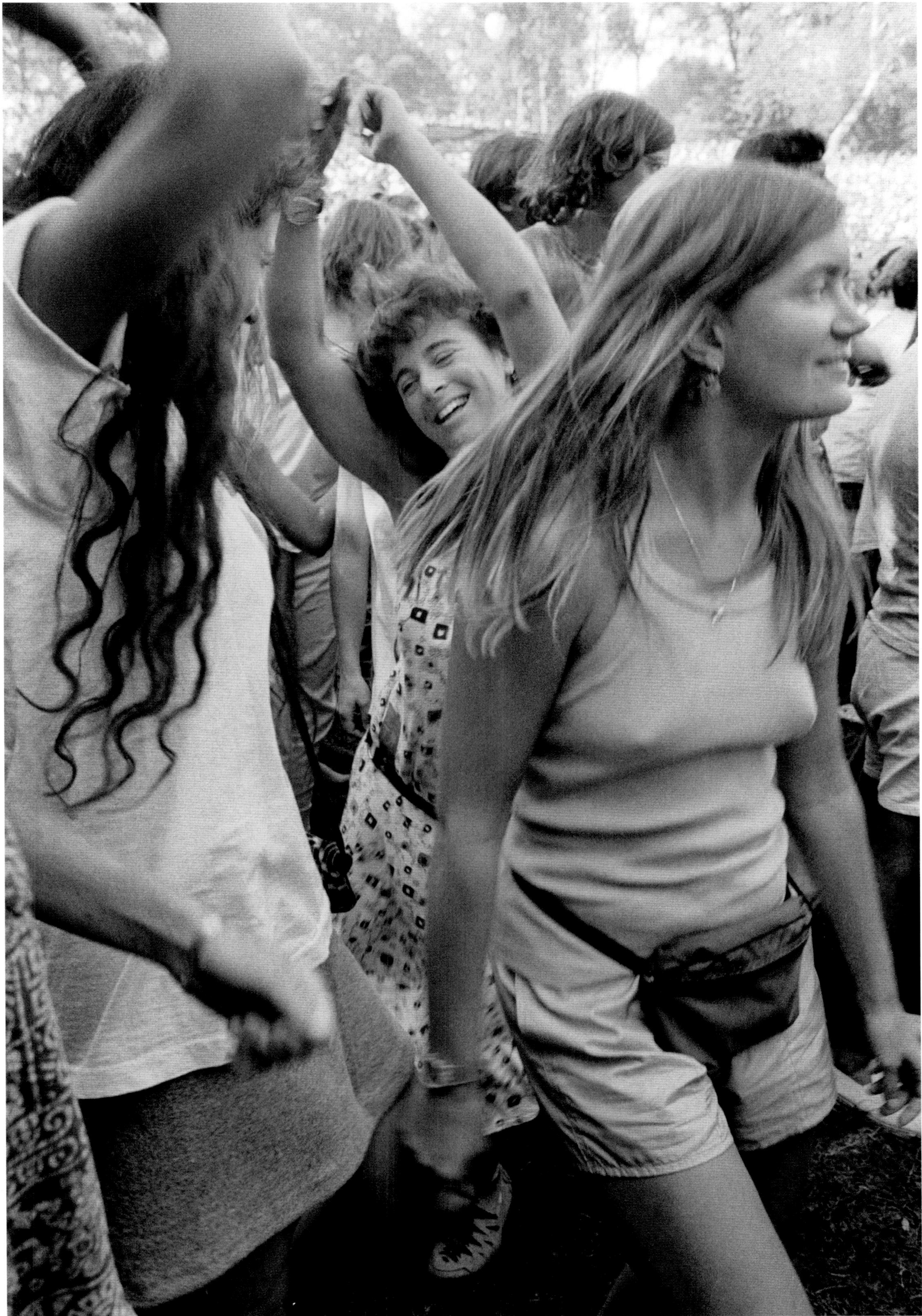

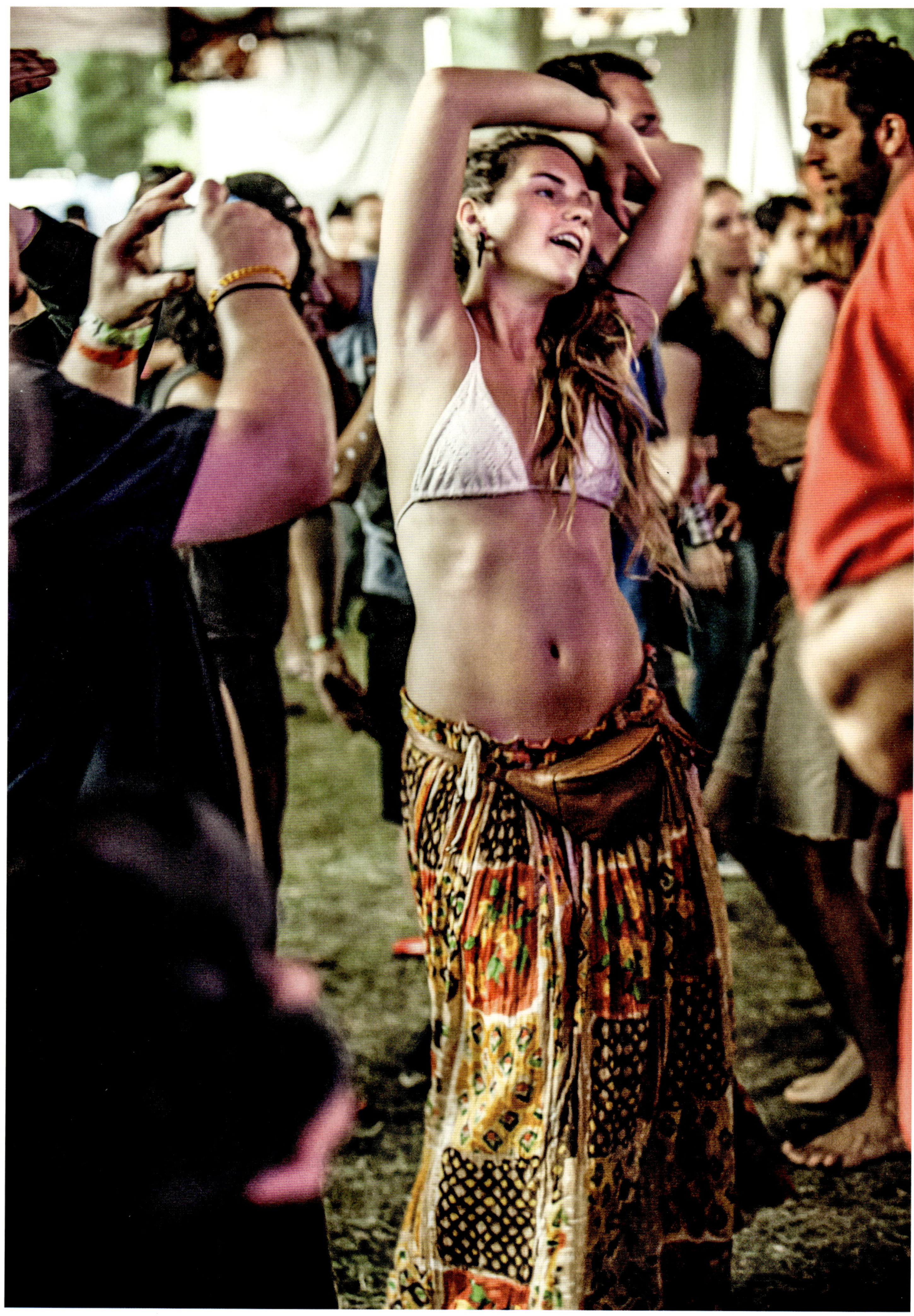

Hippie Chick

A Tale of Love, Devotion & Surrender

Photographs by Jay Blakesberg

Written & Edited by Edith Johnson

Foreword by Grace Slick

Afterword by Grace Potter

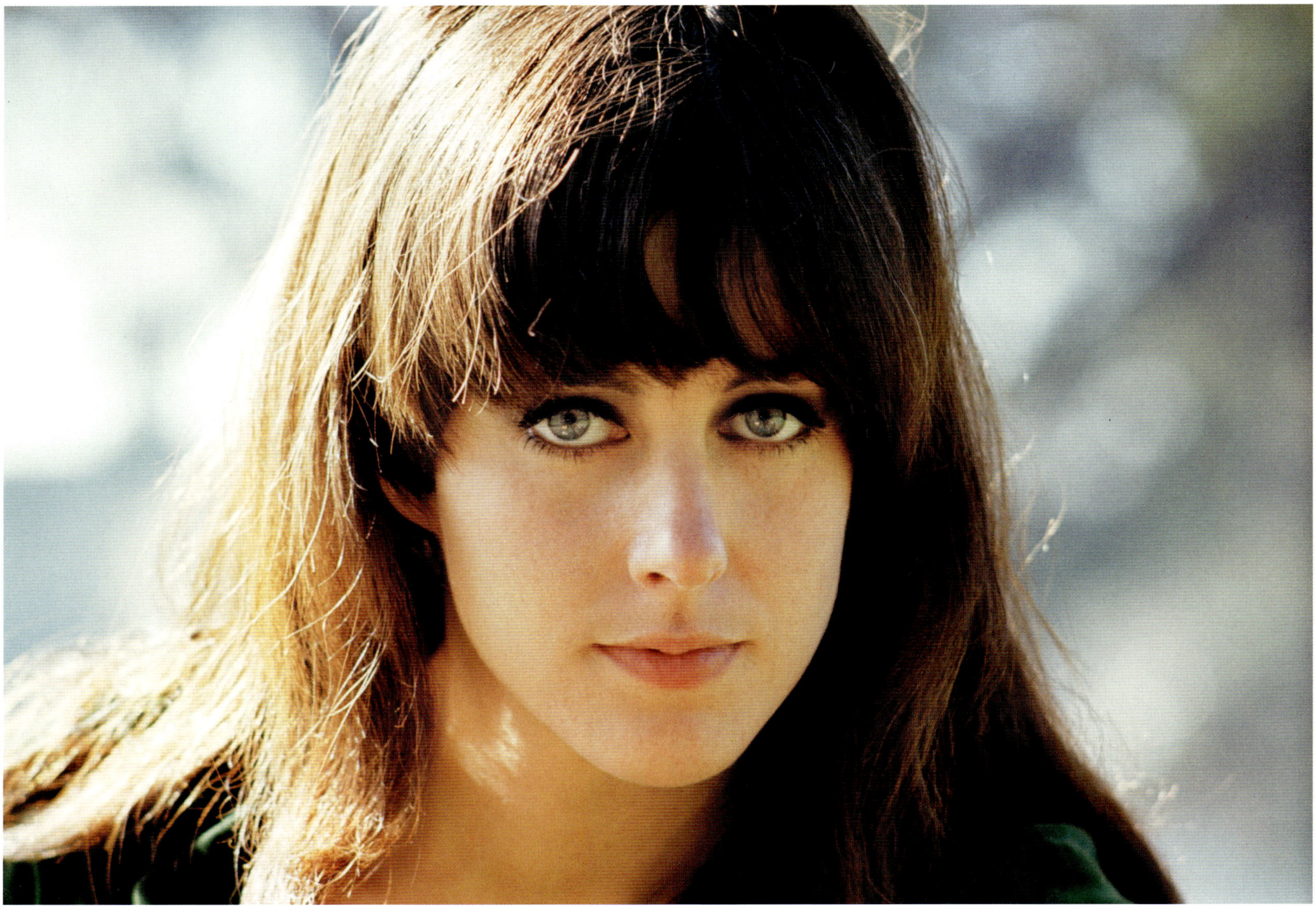

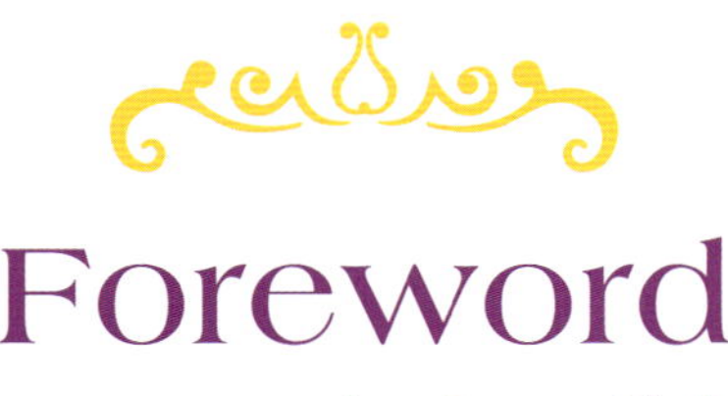

Foreword

by Grace Slick

What limits? We don't need no stinking limits.

And like a beautiful contagion, it caught on—a constant sense of blooming, unfolding, becoming. Push the beige aside and bring on the colors. Literal and figurative amplifications. Paint your wagon, paint your flag, paint your face. Money was not a priority; it was just useful in trade. Free made everybody feel good. Free music in the park, free food, free clothes, free speech, free love. Free created an even field. No special hierarchy.

Replace the word "effort" with "thrive." You can see it in the smiles, the unrestricted dancing, and whenever possible, clothing optional. Personal expression transcended the boundaries of any nominal shared identity. Collective names like "hippie" or "beat" feel incomplete because within those groups were individuals, each as unique in her (or his) existence as a comet or a mountain or a snowflake.

Because we had the benefit of the best public school systems before or since, we learned to differentiate between blind adherence to outdated social mores and the natural progress of change. A generation finding its own artistic morph. We had a choice of lifestyles. We could emulate the freedom of discovery enjoyed by nineteenth-century artists like Sergei Diaghilev, Gertrude Stein, and Picasso, who turned the art world on its head. Or we could adopt the aproned monotony of '50s icon June Cleaver.

We chose to manifest our dreams rather than follow a pre-set norm. We chose to fly rather than crawl. We chose to experiment rather than walk through someone else's flat world. A lot of young women I've talked to lately say they wish they had been alive in the '60s. I am most grateful to have been in my twenties during that time. There were no foreigners, only interesting differences in style and color. Other cultures offered new gifts to feed your senses and yes, "feed your head."

It sounds kind of idyllic, but remember, we didn't have Jon Stewart, Stephen Colbert, and Bill Maher to translate CNN for us. We had to figure out how fucked things really were on our own. Amid all the deaths—MLK, JFK, RFK, and the boys in Vietnam—we held out hope that through love and music, we could stop the violence that our parents perpetuated. Everything needed an overhaul. So the hippie chicks began the cleanup.

Some chicks shifted the domestic scene with chemical-free homemade food, handmade clothes, and hand-carved furnishings. Others made fantastic pre- and post-concert lives for the musicians, or were musicians themselves. Some hippie chicks changed the job environment by educating co-workers about acceptable wages, overtime pay, insurance, and equal pay for equal work. Hippie chicks worked in the political pits running for office or helping pro-change candidates realize their objectives. Many of us turned to the non-violent Buddhist practices—away from conventional western religions, which rang false with hypocrisy.

Sunrise
Surprise
Civilized Man
You were keeper to me
Now your animal is free
And you're free to die
You're old and your hands are gray
You're old, go home and stay
We've all heard your dirty stories
Two thousand years
Two thousand years
Two thousand years
Of your god damned glory

Angry song lyrics I wrote echoing some of the more indignant feelings of the era about the ignorant deceptions of previous generations. More than four decades later, they still resonate. It was, and will be again, a wonderful breakout point for hippie chicks and guys to sprout wings and jump the fences.

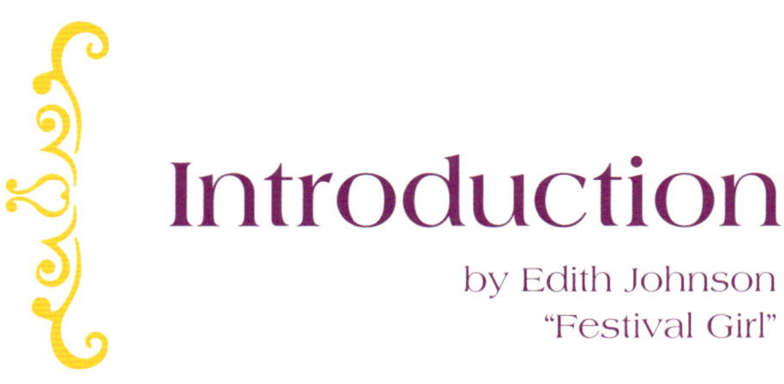

Introduction

by Edith Johnson
"Festival Girl"

> Stay right here 'cause these are the good old days.
>
> Carly Simon, "Anticipation"

Like many a modern-day hippie chick, I came to the scene through the music of my parents. The eldest of three daughters, I lacked a cool older sibling to show me the way. Instead, I relied on cues from my California-born, Utah-transplant parents: a maniac-on-the-dance-floor mother who embodied "long hair, don't care" well before that phrase was even uttered and a poet father—disguised as a lawyer—whose massive collection of music and its memorabilia is only surpassed in vastness by his undying love of it. So, with a free spirit and an aesthete at the helm, I was raised to worship at the altar of rock and roll. Classic rock and roll.

Essentially, my sisters and I were groomed to be groupies. My upbringing precludes me from ever being able to consider "the 'G' word"—as Miss Pamela once called it—a dirty word. In my house, we cared about the music and the artists or groups behind it. We were taught to emotionally invest in the personal triumphs and setbacks of every band my father loved. Heart-wrenching Hall of Fame induction speeches made us cry; comeback stories overwhelmed us with joy; and lyrics or jams were analyzed, admired, contextualized, and ultimately absorbed into the center of our souls. We wondered if anyone were as wise as Joni or as deep as Neil. Robert Hunter was as revered as Robert Frost; listening to *Who's Next* on infinite repeat was considered a productive use of time; and traveling "to the beat of a different drum," like Linda, was held up as the exemplar of freewheeling femininity.

By the time I hit adolescence (or vice versa), I was steeped in the songs of a bygone era. Even my earliest foray into music outside my parents' influence was backward looking: I spent my first allowance on a cassette tape of Bob Marley's *Legend*. Reggae was my first real love, in many ways, because it was my own. I devoted myself to it with the same reverence my parents taught me to accord to rock and roll. They initiated me into live music with a Paul Simon show and, a few months later, I initiated my dad into a glimpse of my future by dragging him to the Reggae Sunsplash festival. Bob took his place on my bedroom wall next to my treasured Jim Morrison "American Poet" poster, and three was good company for most of my teens.

Twenty-something wanderlust took me the way of the Lizard King, which is to say I ended up ambling around the streets of Paris with no particular direction home. By then, digitalization of music was ubiquitous and—for better or (mainly) for worse—I was able to bring thousands of songs with me without hundreds of Case Logics. Still preoccupied with the past, my travel companions included all my rock and reggae favorites, plus some golden age rap, the only music in my collection that approximated my own generation. I spent more time in my earbuds than out at shows; more time discussing music and disseminating playlists than exploring it "en live."

After half a decade roaming the rue Saint-André-des-Arts feeling "unfettered and alive," something called me back stateside. It took nearly as long to figure out that the source of the call was contained in different lyrics from the same Joni song. What I didn't know when I first returned was that I came home to fulfill my dharma. That is, I came home to support live music. Significantly, my return coincided with another one that, at the time, held no special meaning for me. Phish had reunited at Hampton and, in turn, my sister had reunited with her favorite band. The following year, I found myself in the middle of a three-night run at the Greek Theatre in Berkeley. And I mean that literally. I found myself. Like so many who passed (way) before me, my first Phish show was the first day of the rest of my life.

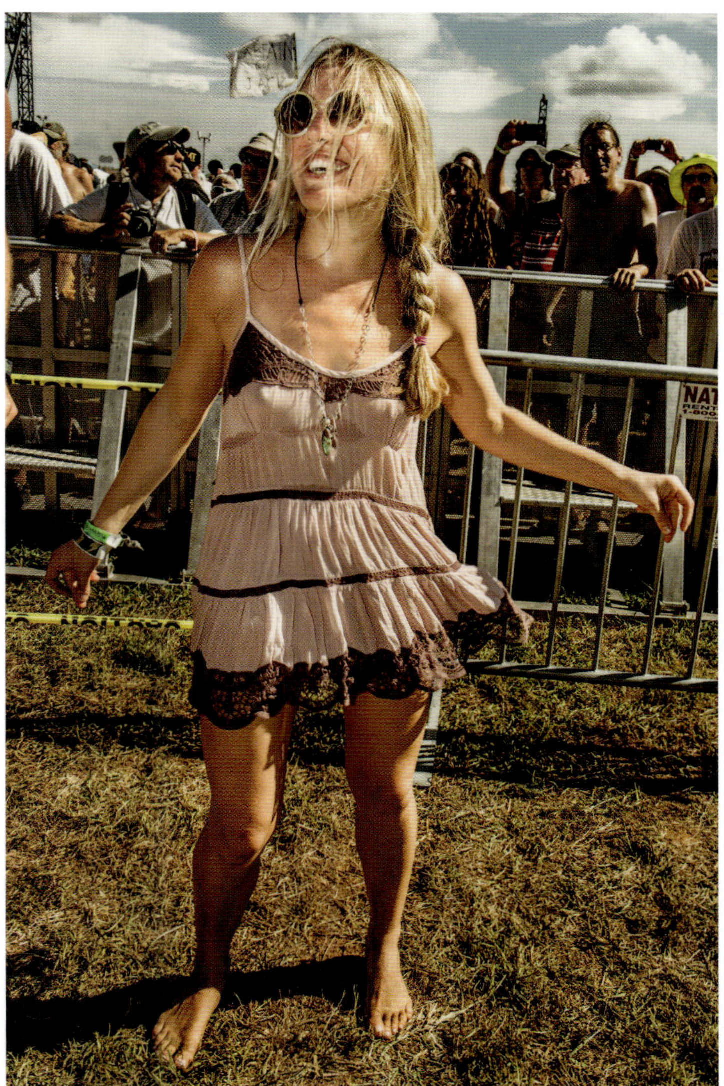

Funny, yet fitting, that it took a band from back when to bring me into the now. Although I came to Phish over a quarter century into their career, it was new music to my ears. What it did for me was help me feel a feeling I forgot: discovery. I remembered the sensations that filled my youth and made me fall in love with the sounds I had since canonized to the exclusion of others. Instead of wondering about what I'd missed, I set out to see what was happening. I became a genre-promiscuous, live music chasing festival girl, and I haven't looked back since.

The call back home had actually been a calling, and that calling was a cosmic command to stoke "the star-maker machinery." To me, that has come to mean so much more than materially supporting the business of music and its creation through purchasing albums and show tickets. It is a full-time, full-on surrender to each live music experience while I'm in it. I give it all I've got, and I've come to realize I'm not alone. Far from it. There is a whole constellation of star stokers, gypsy souls, and hippie chicks; fearless women with open hearts, minds, and ears, listening and living to be rocked. Thanks to Jay's photography, a great many of these goddesses grace the pages of this book.

Here's what I know: I am a badge-wearing, card-carrying hippie chick, and I am honored to be part of the broader community of amazing women documented here in words and images. My story is every hippie chick's story, and our story is music. Though the details are different, our tale is the same—one of love, devotion, and surrender. This trifecta of qualities also comprises the name of a 1973 Santana/Mahavishnu Orchestra album dedicated to Coltrane and inspired by the teachings of an Indian mystic. Perhaps, if you burn sage and listen to it backward while viewing this book, these photographs will come to life. But I have a better idea. Go out and see music. The best show isn't the next show, and it certainly isn't one behind us. As the wonderful Penny Lane once observed, "It's all happening." That's right, dear reader. And it's all happening now.

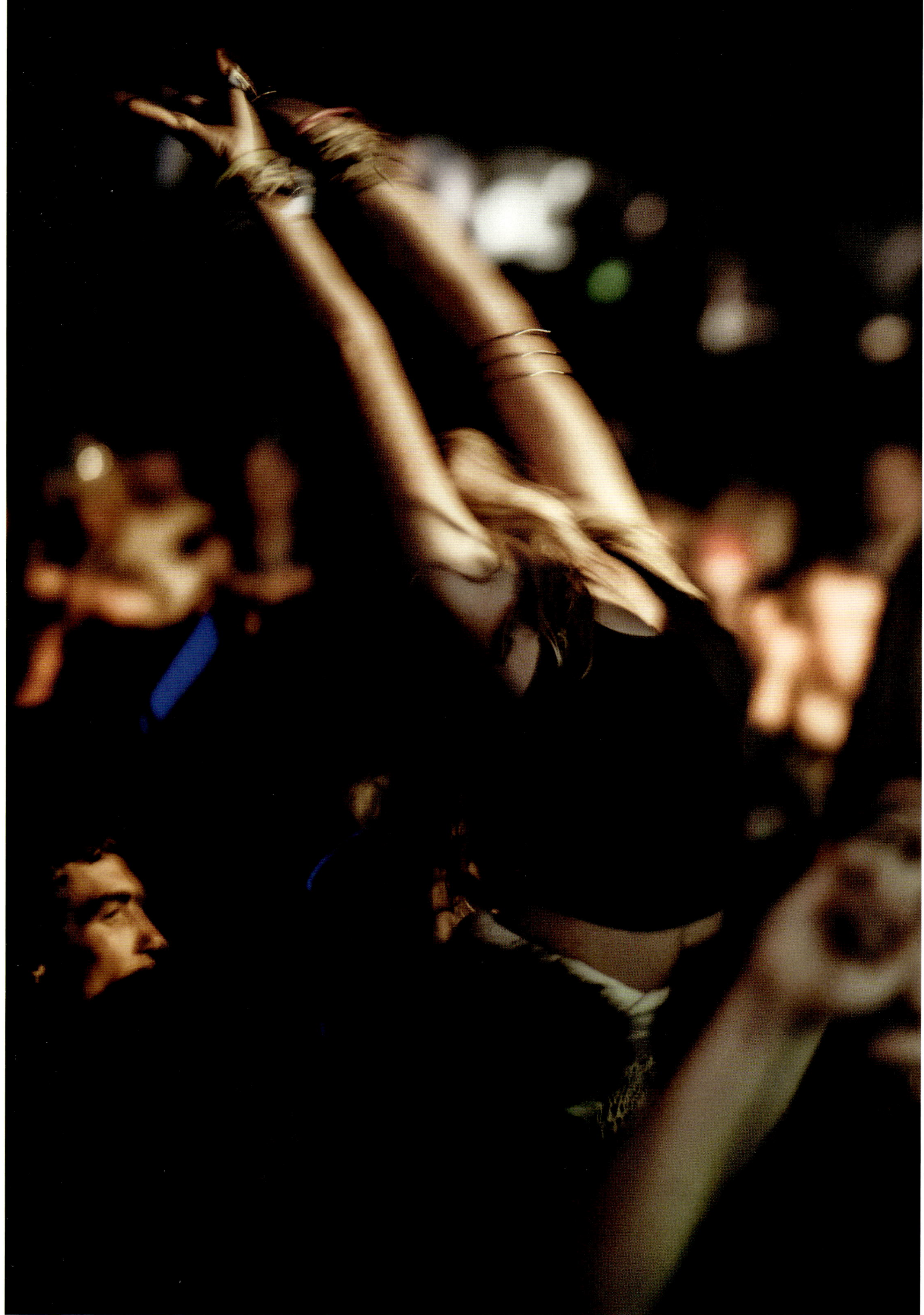

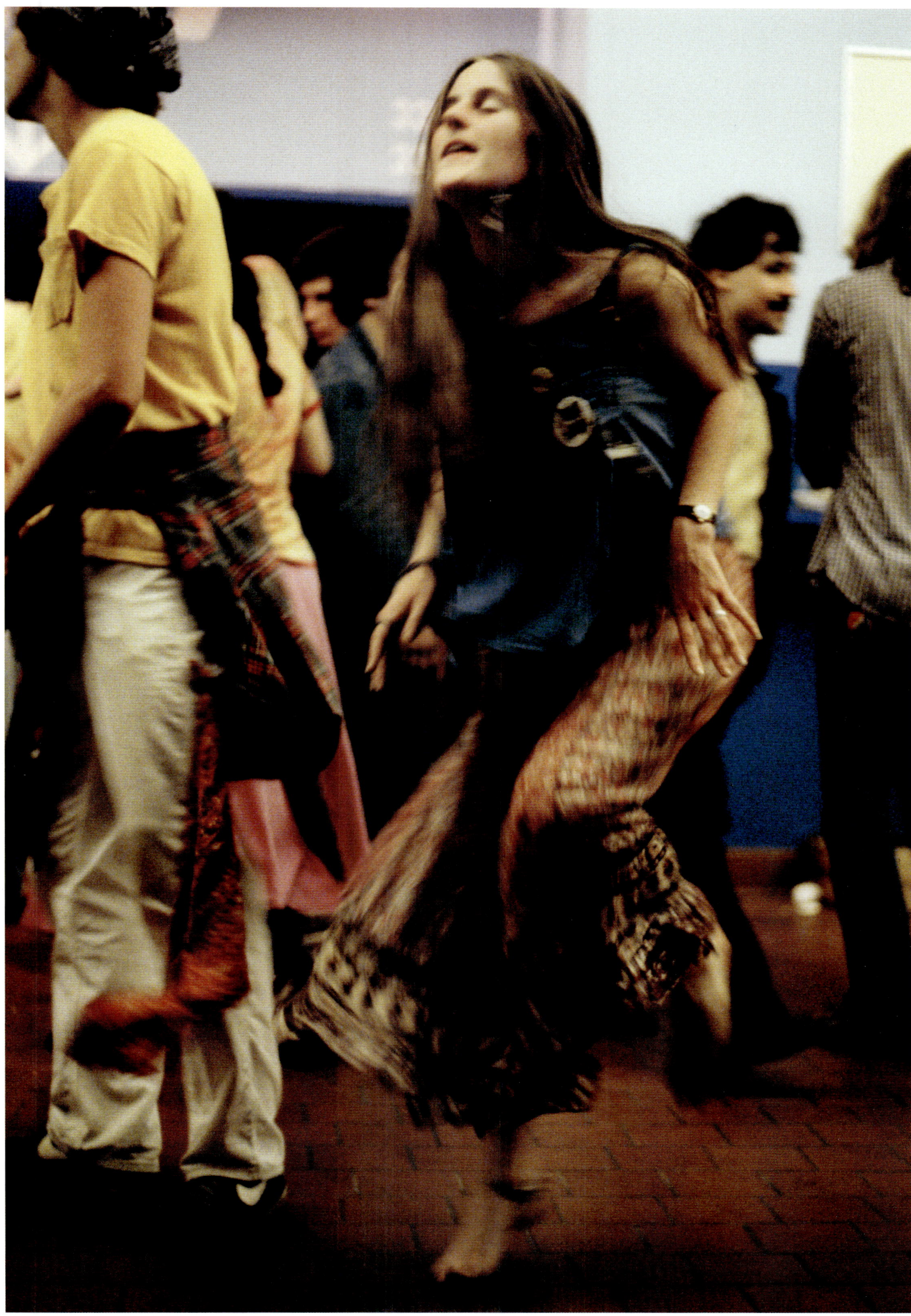

Love

Lord, you know it makes me high when you turn your love my way ...
The Allman Brothers Band, "Blue Sky"

Music is LOVE. It's more than a soundtrack buzzing and whirring in the background of life; it's the entire show. It's the divine spark flickering from soul to soul, connecting us to one another, to ourselves, and to the heartbeat of the universe. Music lives in the moment, but lingers long after—evanescent, yet everlasting. We can't pin it down and we don't need to. It flows within us and without us. It's everywhere; it's everything; it's all we need. It lights our path, offering a constant, cosmic companion on the eternal highway. In its company, we discover—and rediscover—who we truly are.

Music is part of our essential nature. We have a deep, primal need to sing, dance, play, and create. It's instinctual and yet, in this mechanized modern world, it's easy to forget. In the presence of music that moves us, our senses engage and emotions intensify. It pulses through our veins and attunes us to the rhythms of our hearts. When we finally get on the bus, we are able to recognize our own humanness—our need to feel, express, and relate. We are drawn into intimate accord with others traveling along the same vibration. These are our people.

How music touches us, how we experience it, is as unique as a thumbprint. No two people have the same trip; no one person has the same trip twice. There are infinite roads to the music we love. It can start slowly, a casual acquaintance that becomes a trusted friend over several encounters (or listens). It can smolder and burn, something we once caught a glimpse of and are dying to learn more about. It can come out of the blue and stone us with such astonishing force that everything else seems to evaporate, setting a new standard for all that follows.

Like love at first sight, love at first listen can strike when we least expect it. An innocent introduction by a friend, a detour to a new radio frequency, even an aimless stroll can bring us a song that feels like a soul mate. In live music, the likelihood of falling upon—and falling for—something new is inherent. Show serendipity. Concert kismet. That meant-to-be click, when we fall into sync with a sequence of sounds, favors an open mind and open heart. Floating freely from stage to stage and show to show, unburdened by expectation, makes room for any hippie chick to be swept off her feet.

It's sonic chemistry. Sweet alchemy. Our spirits stir and we are magnetized in the direction of the music. We receive it sensually before perceiving it intellectually. We feel it. It plugs straight into our souls, tuning us in and turning us on. We want to get closer. We want to bask in its radiance and stay warm in its glow. We choose to be together; to collaborate. The crowd's love expands toward the music and toward each other. The musicians receive it and reflect it back in a powerful, amplified state. It loops and cycles between us, an unbroken chain of euphoric energy.

Waves of exhilaration wash over us. We yearn for total submersion. Whether a dewy new romance or a love as old as dirt, the prospect of a live show fills us with the beautiful buzz of anticipation. Our hearts race and our temperatures rise. We get butterflies. This is it. Every note, every song, every jam, every show is a one-way journey into the present. We buy the ticket; we take the ride. We catapult through space and time. We rise. We fall. We spin. We stall ... We never want it to end. This is what we have waited for. We are complete.

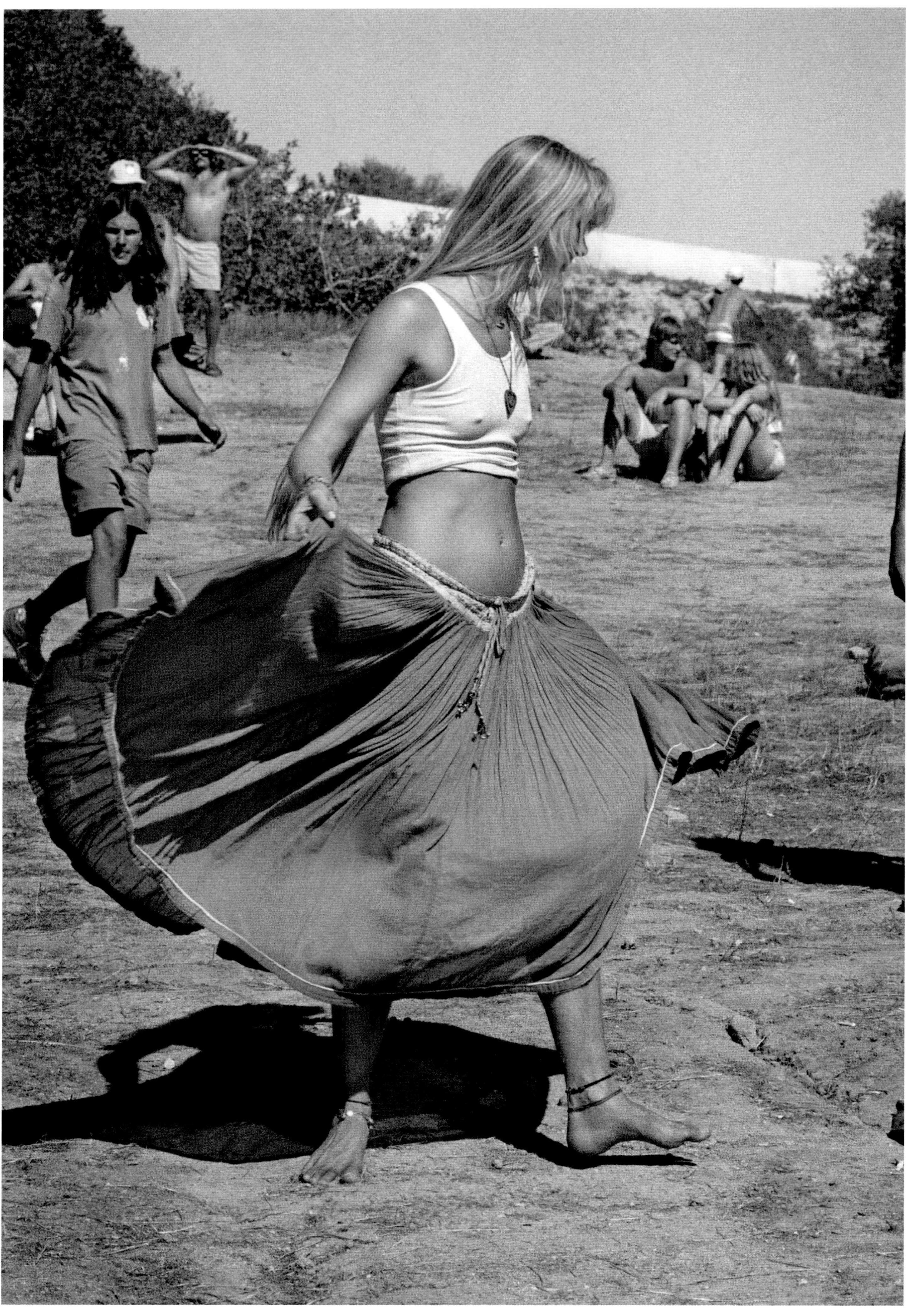

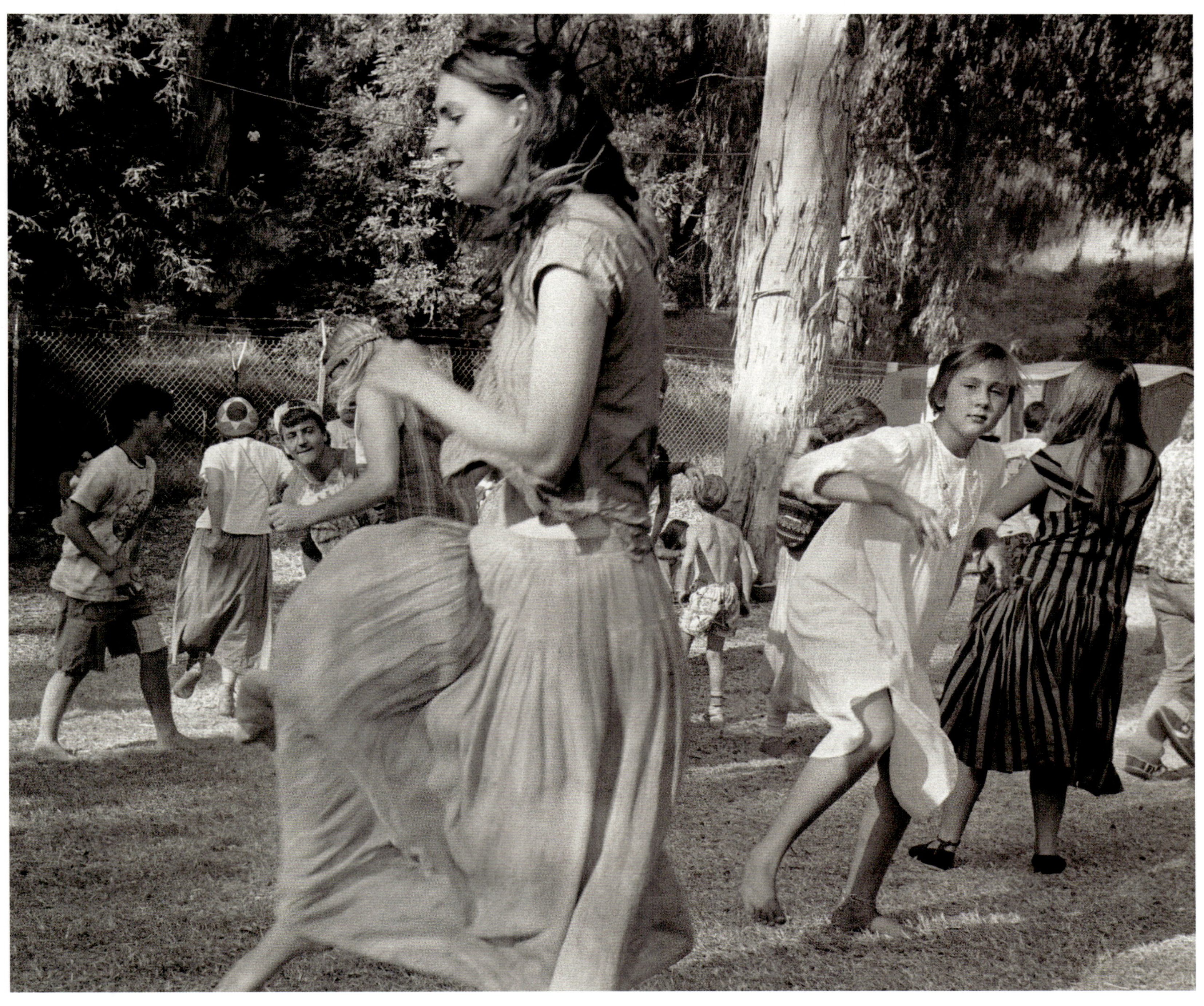

Connect to the rhythm and find beauty. Forget about everything else and just let the sound fill you and the music move you. Susie M.

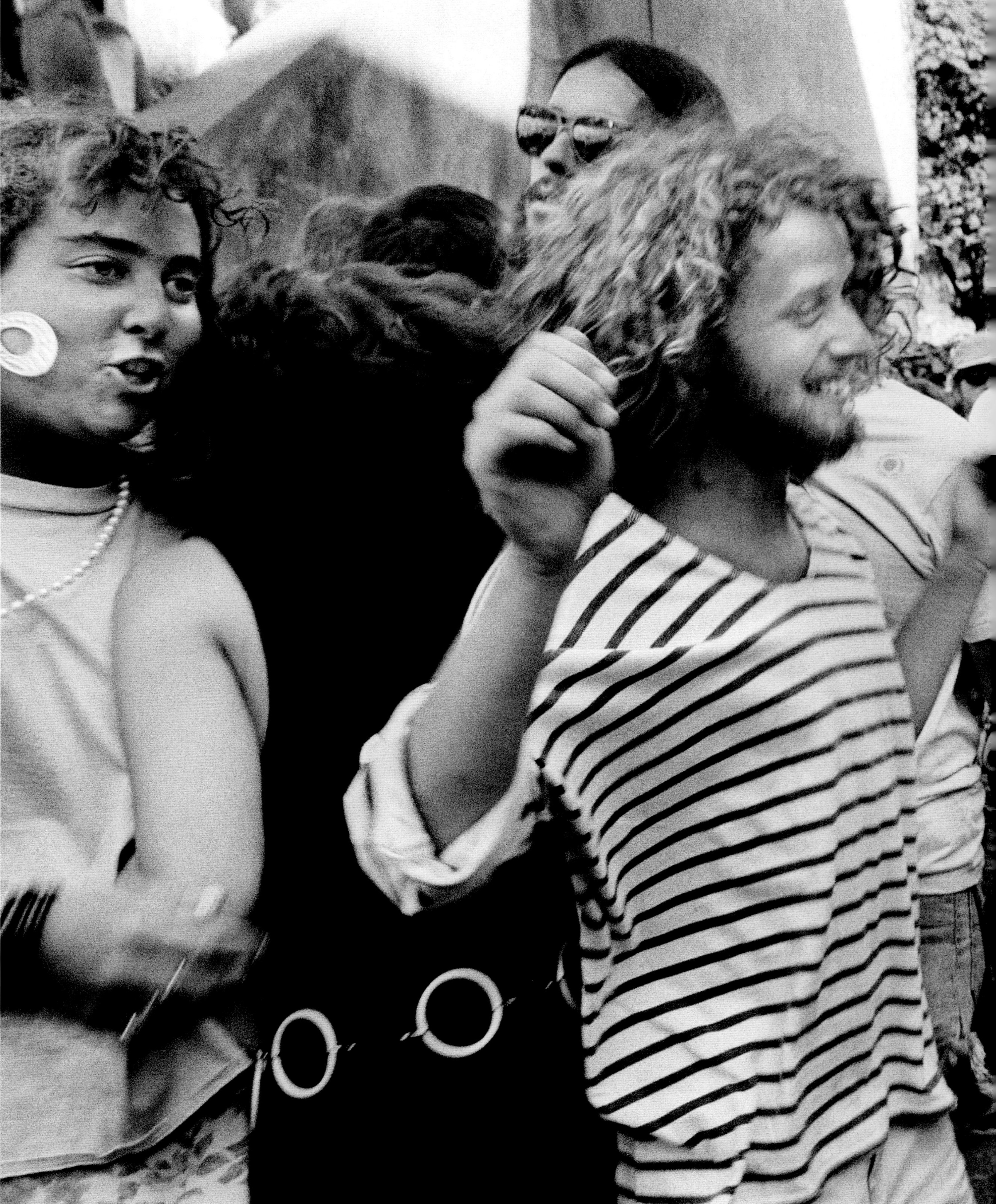

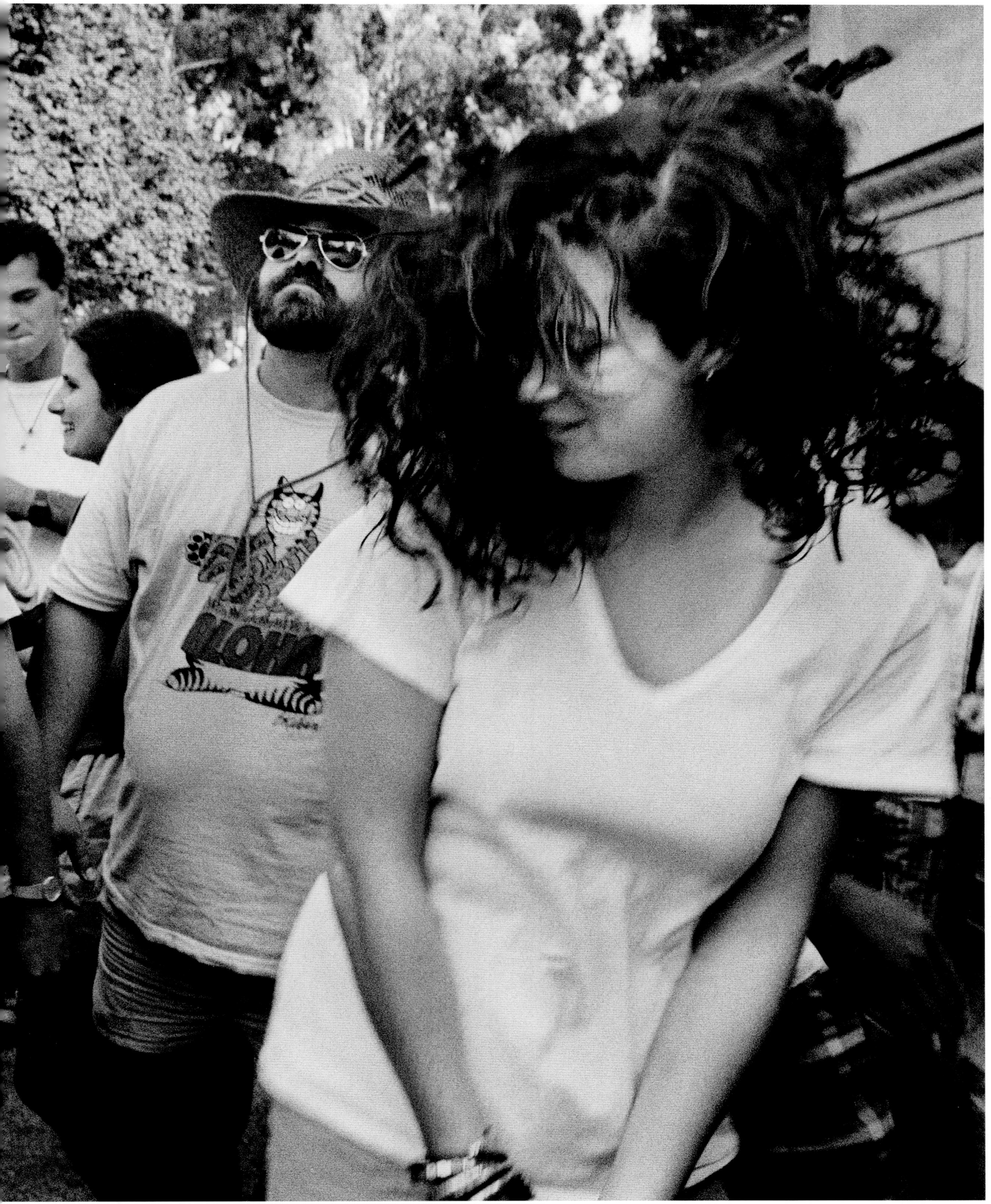

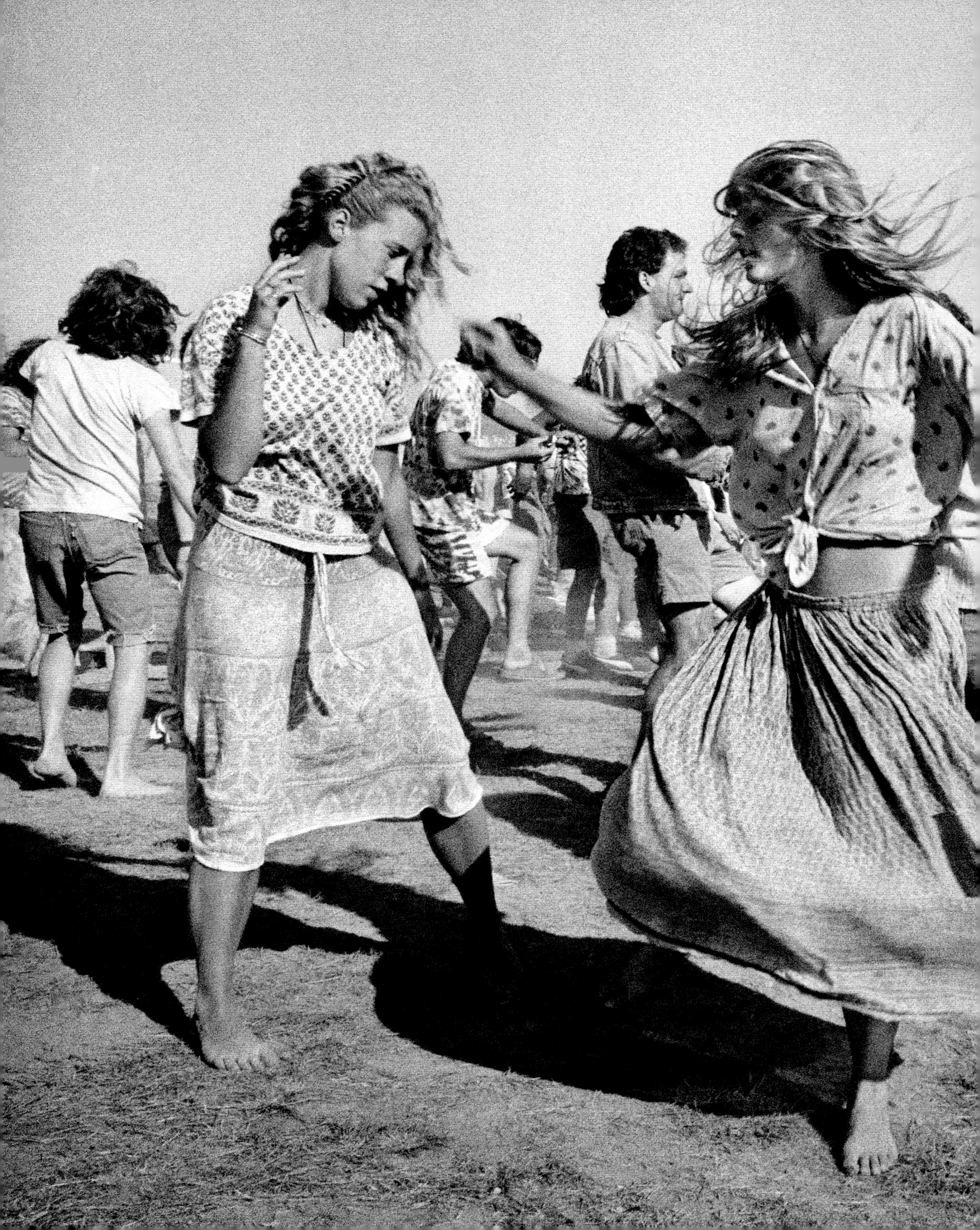

I love to be anonymous yet connected to thousands of people who are there chasing the same high that music brings me. Molly N.

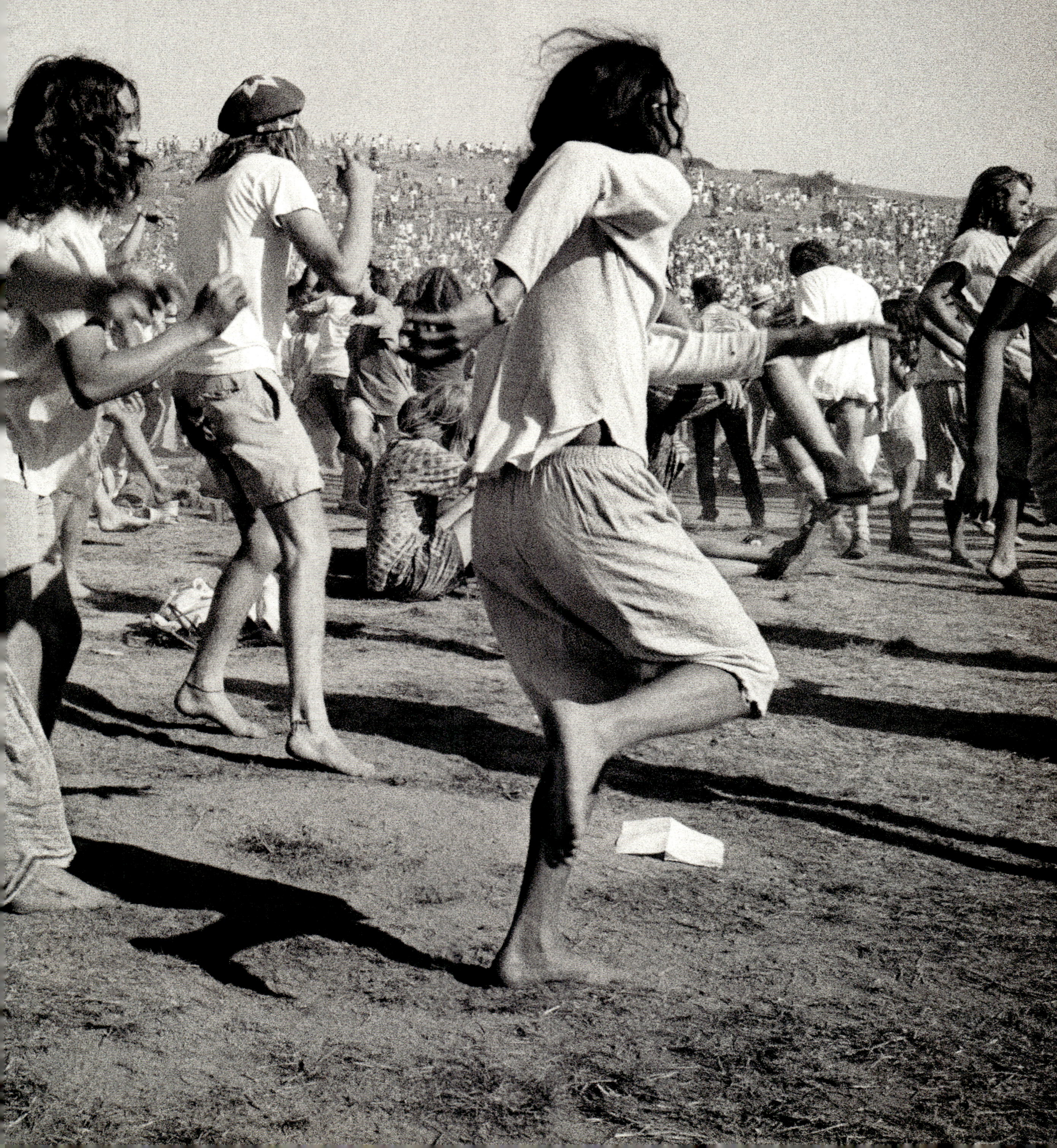

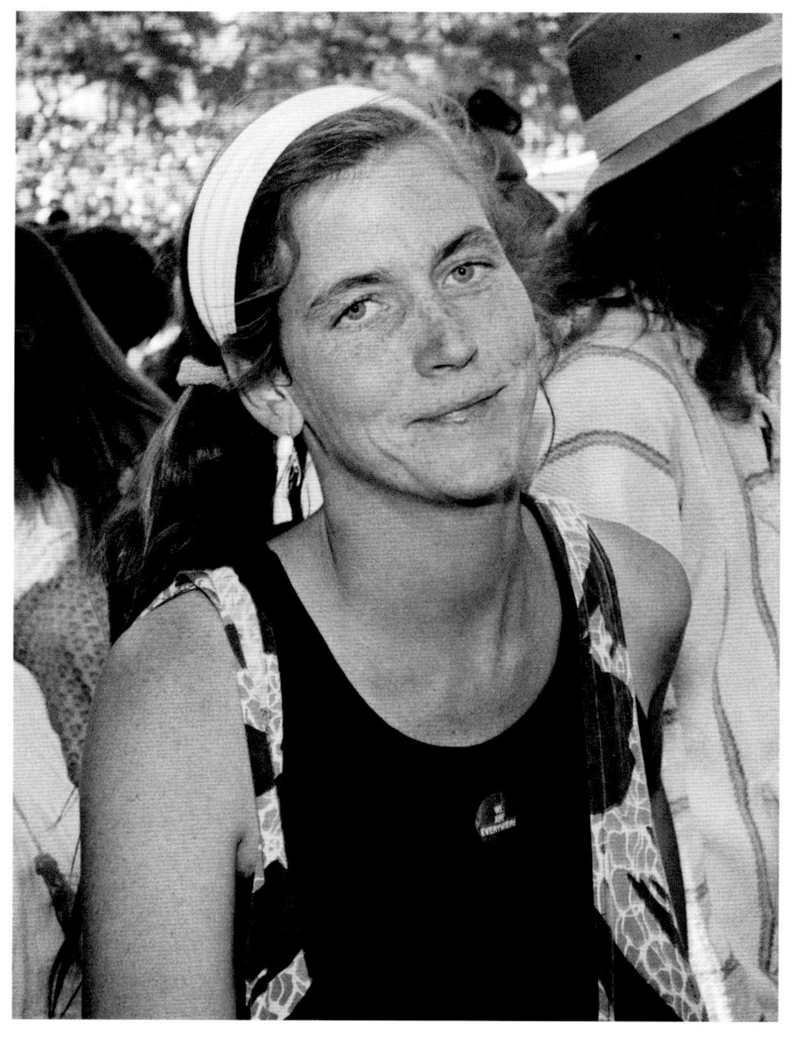

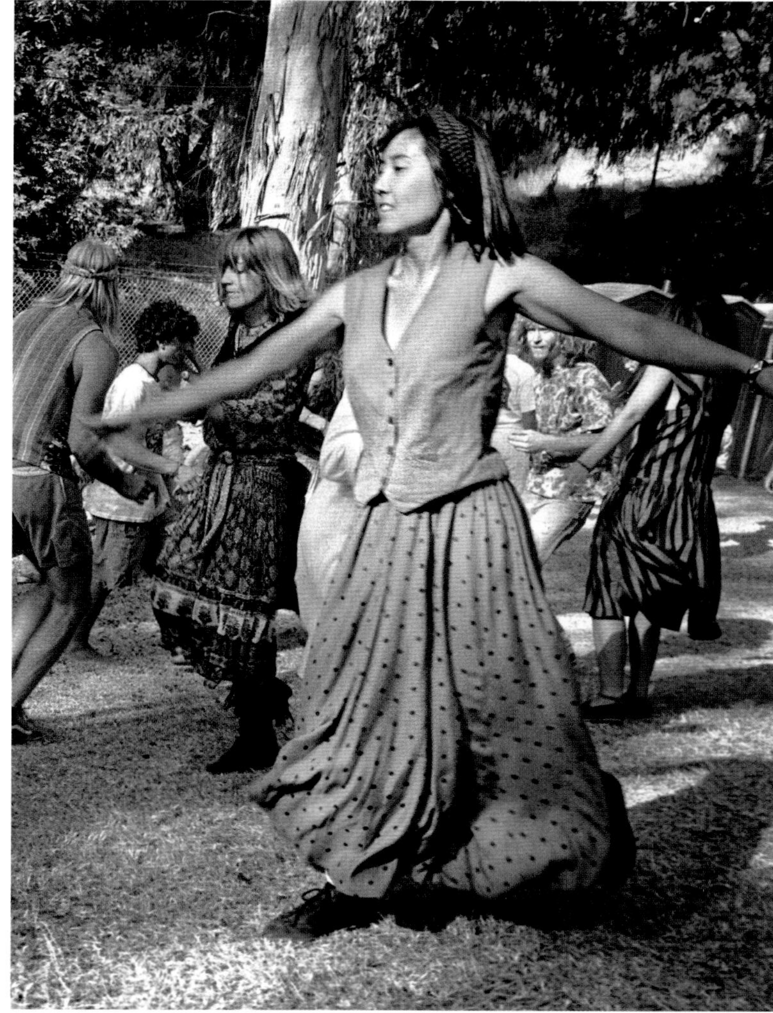

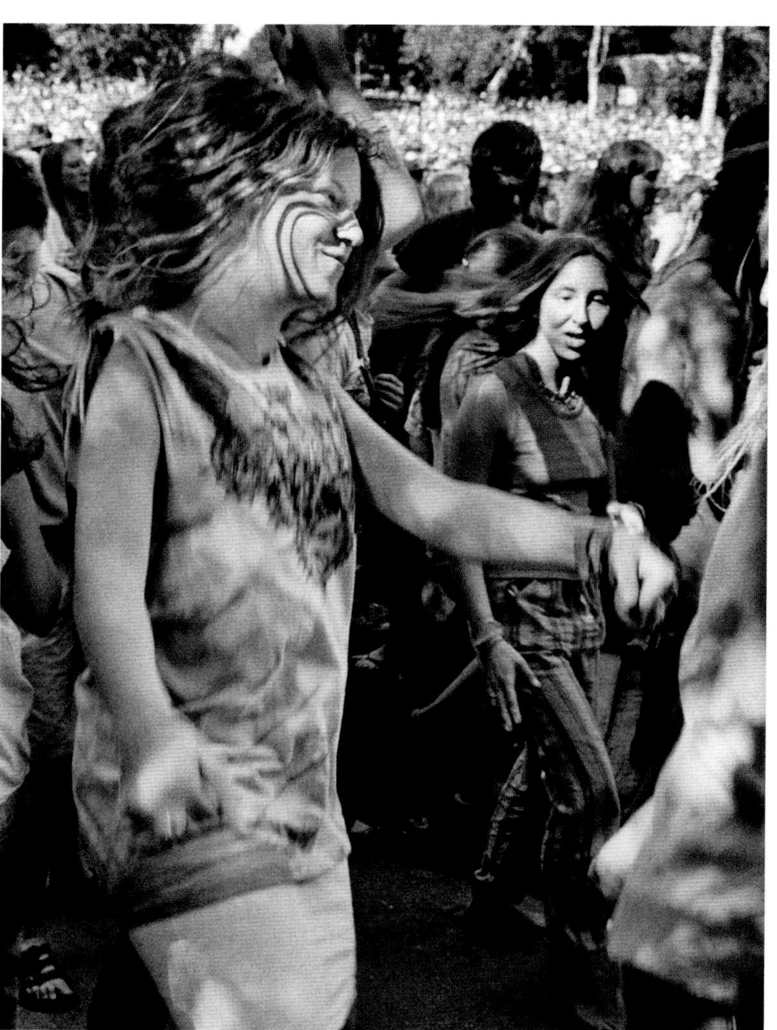

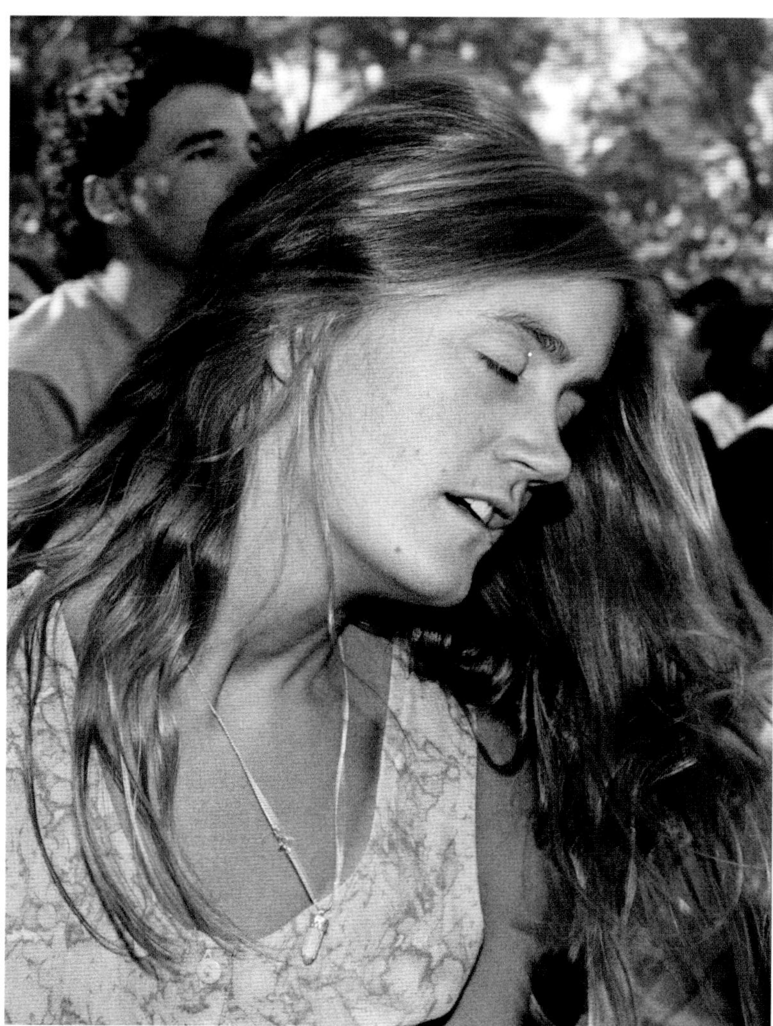

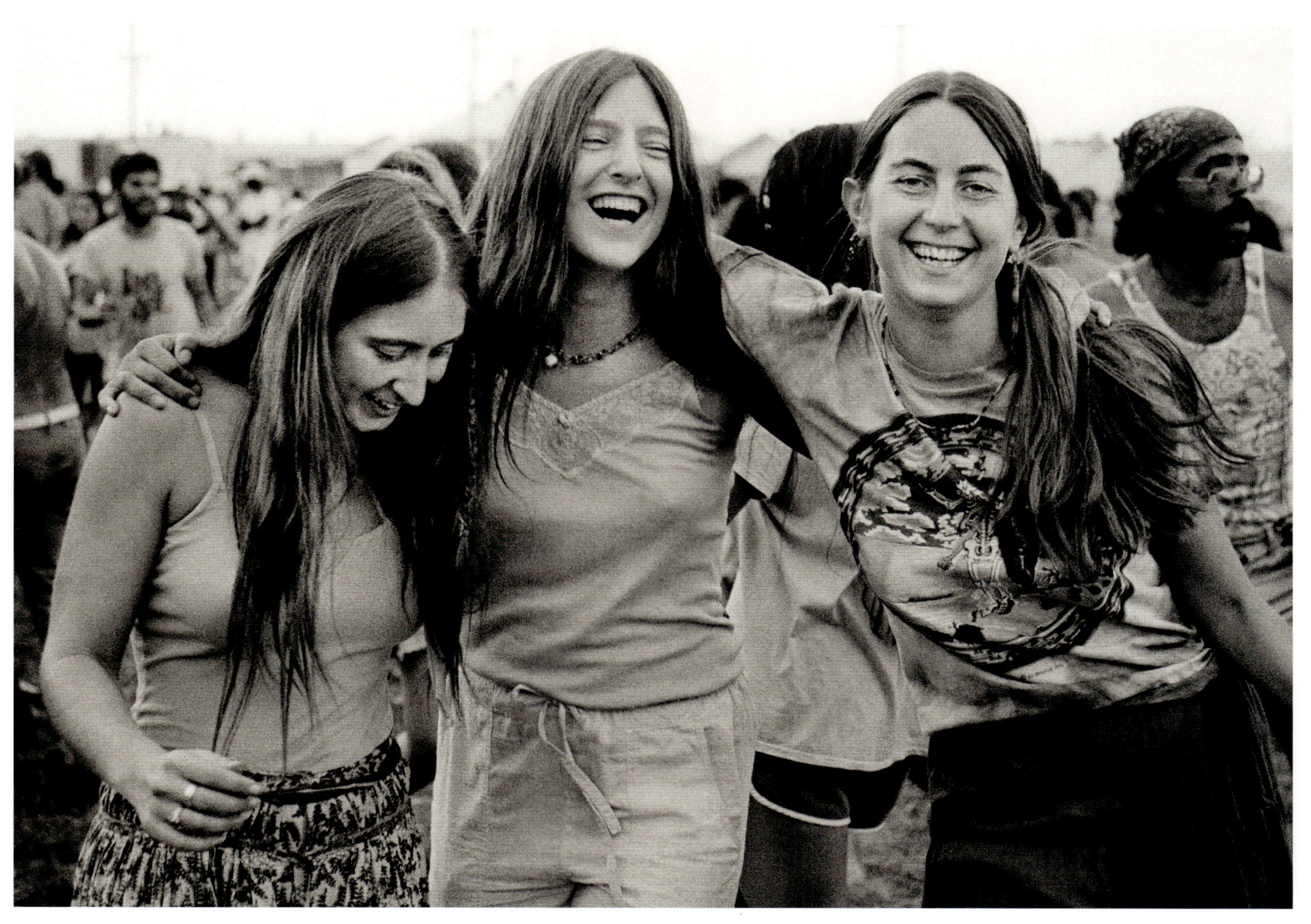

Festivals are an incredible chance to make a deeper connection to the music and to the people who love the music as much as you do. A chance to escape from life for a few days and be one with nature, to wear your most fun things, be whoever you want to be, and do whatever you feel, always. Kara A.

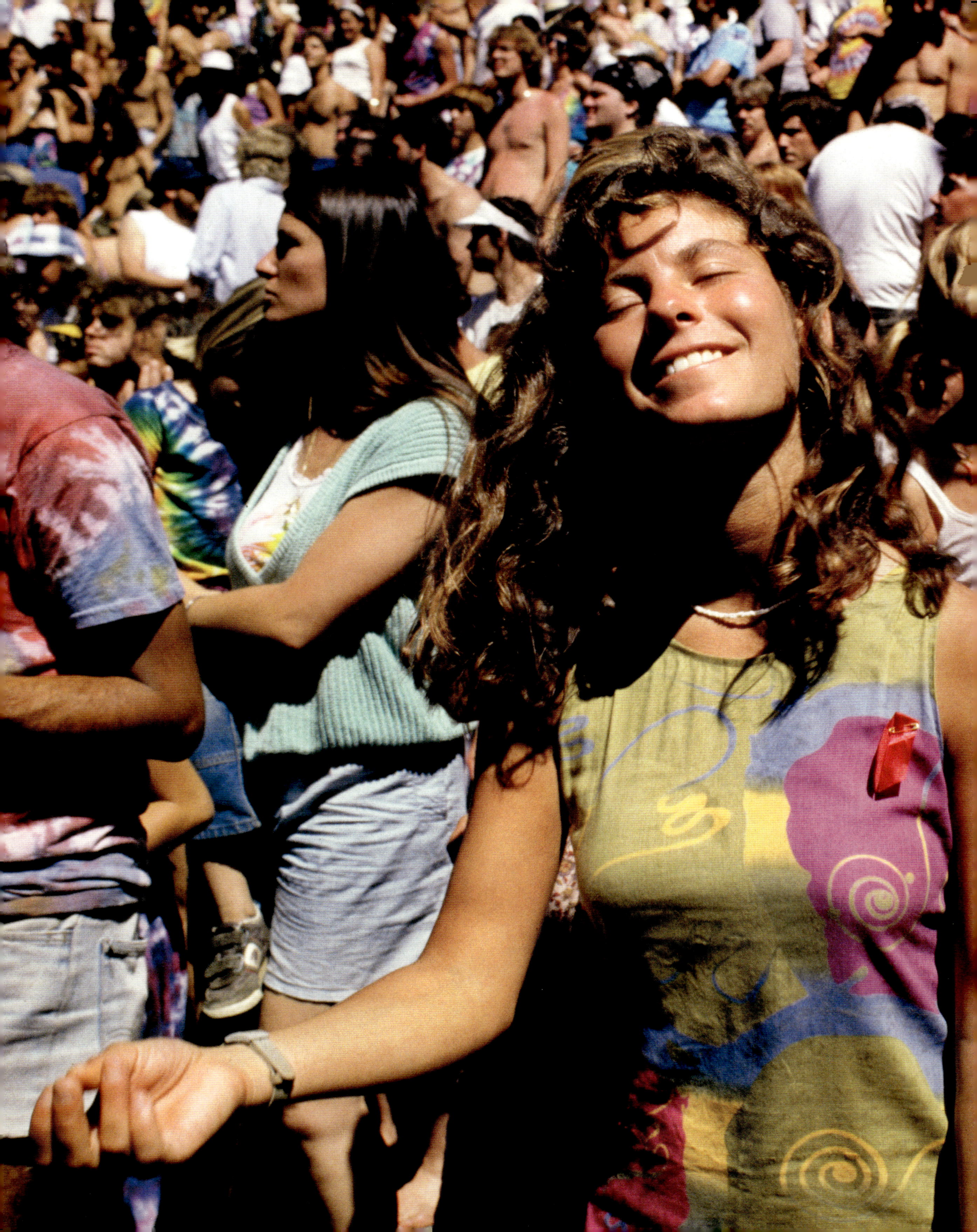

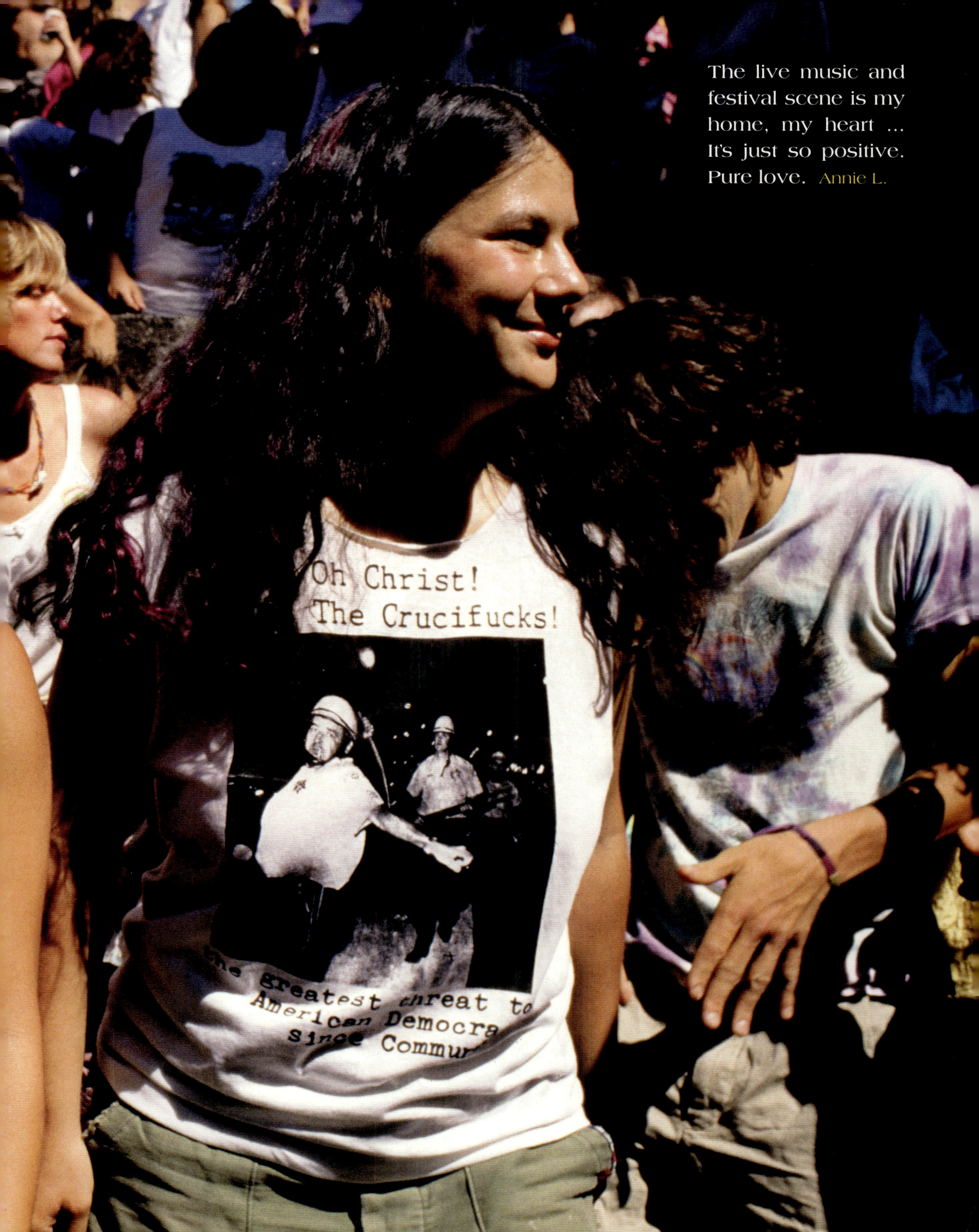

The live music and festival scene is my home, my heart ... It's just so positive. Pure love. Annie L.

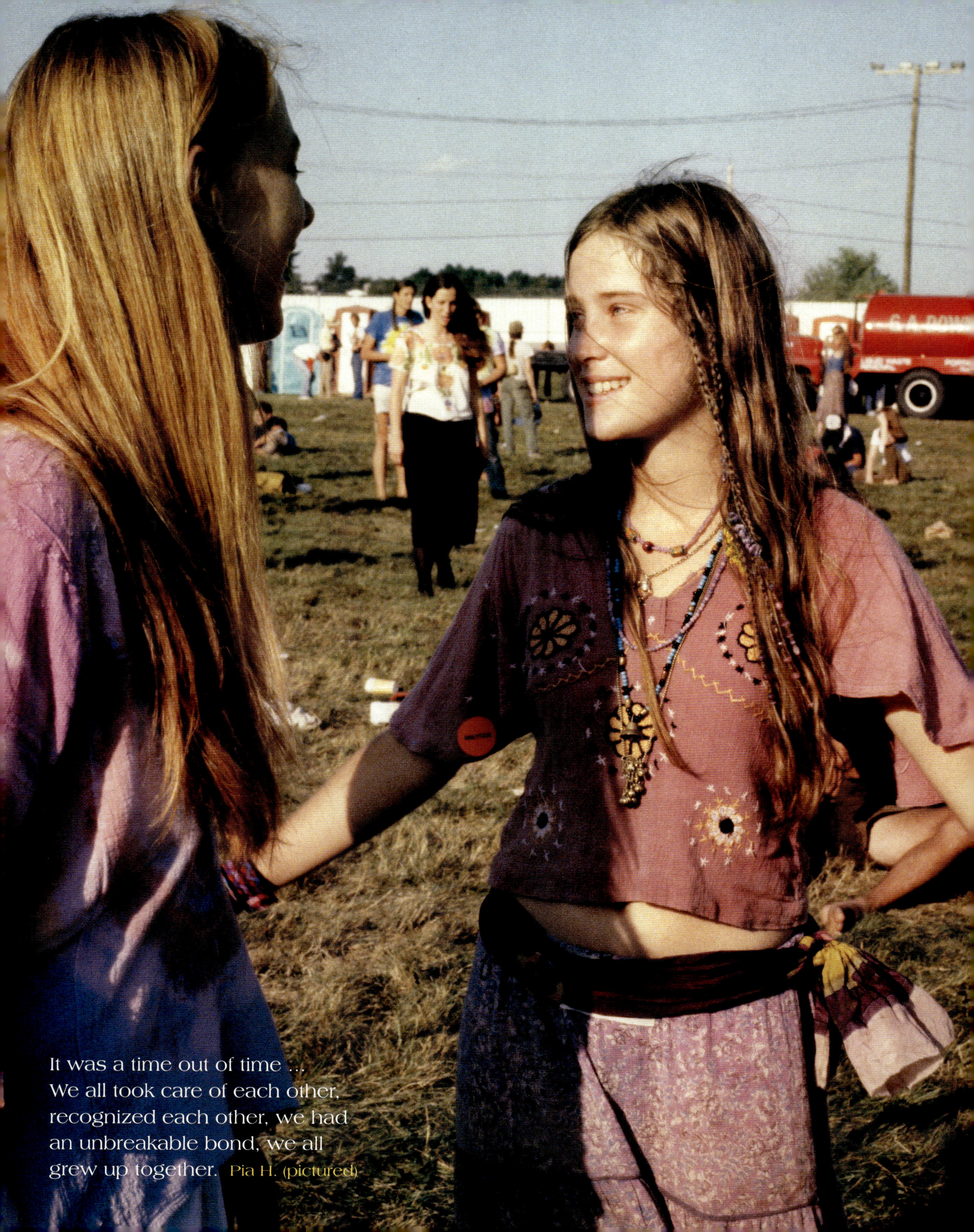

It was a time out of time ...
We all took care of each other,
recognized each other, we had
an unbreakable bond, we all
grew up together. Pia H. (pictured)

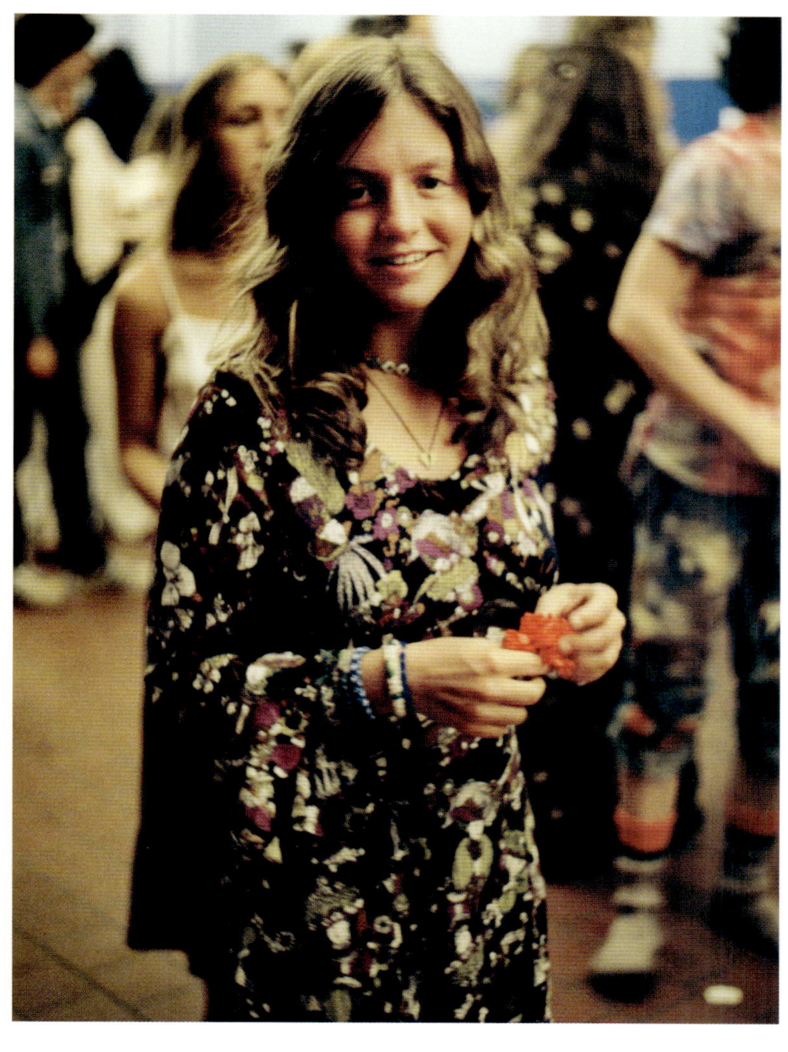
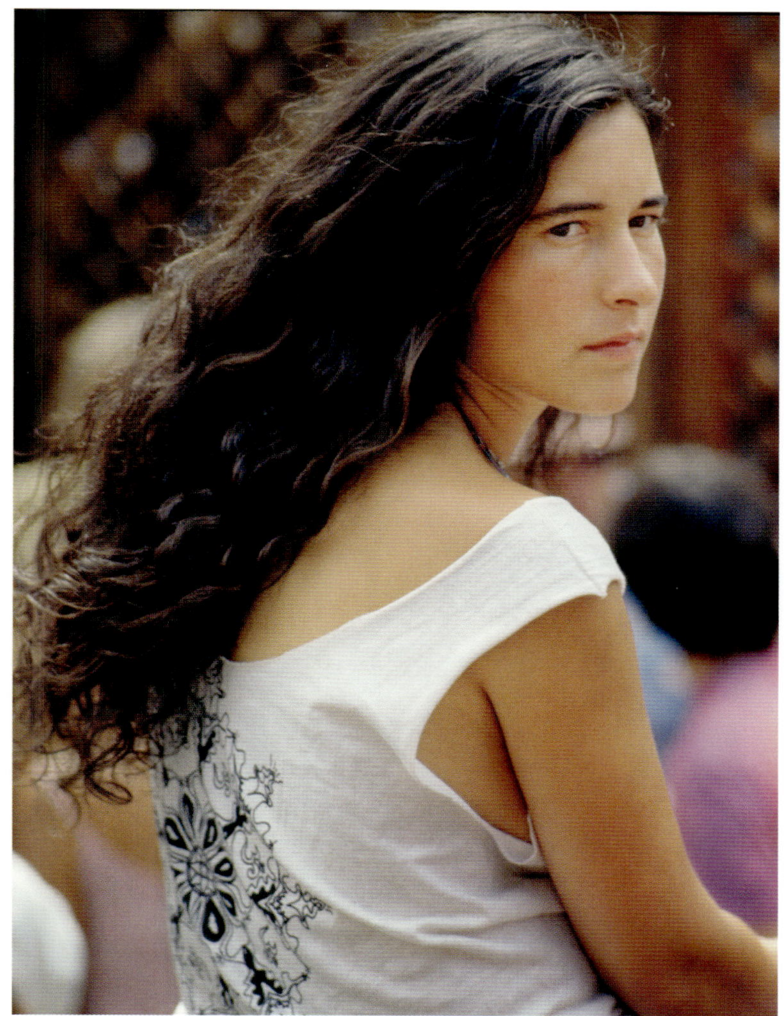
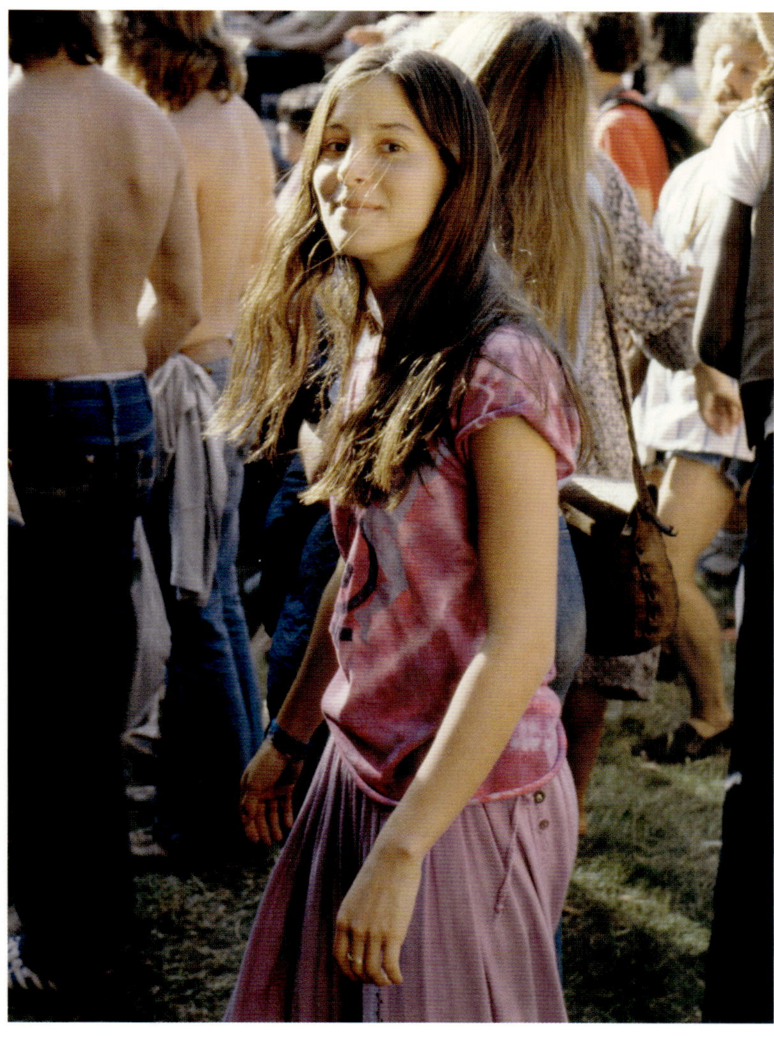
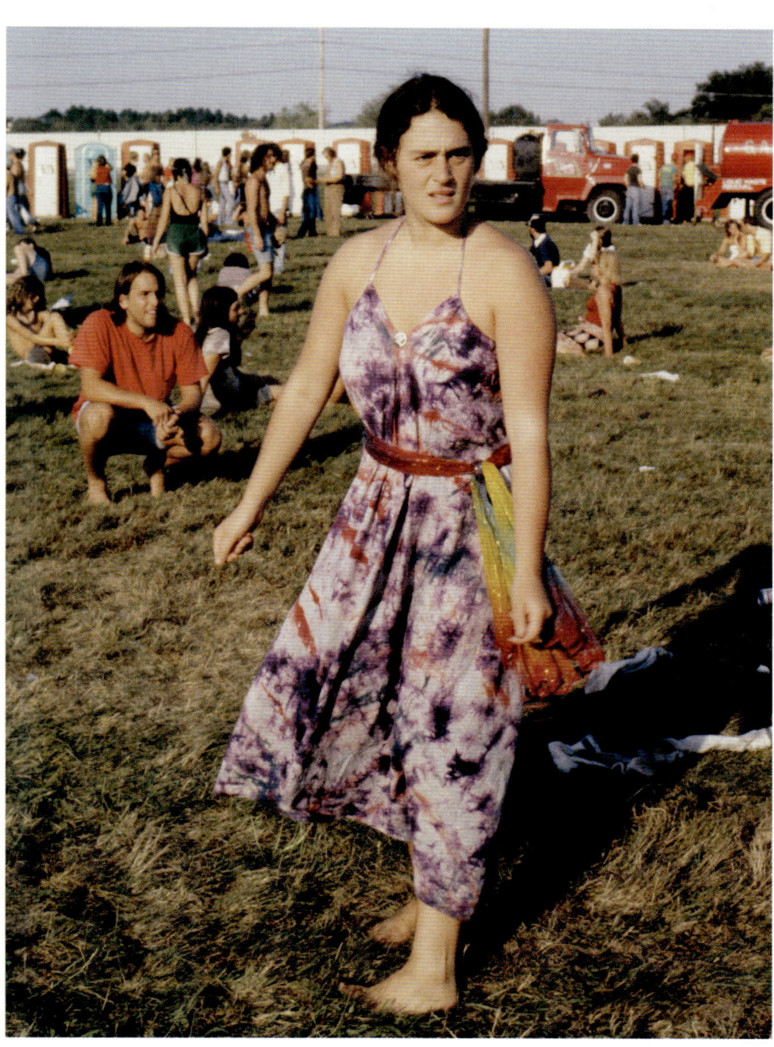

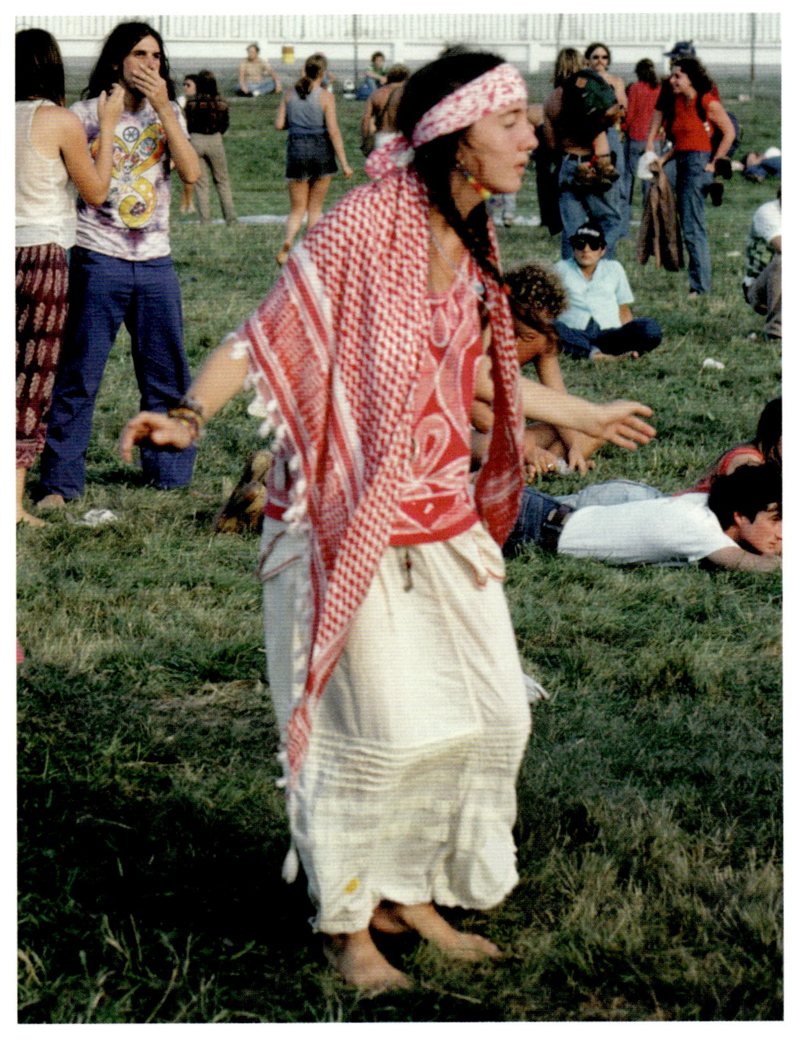
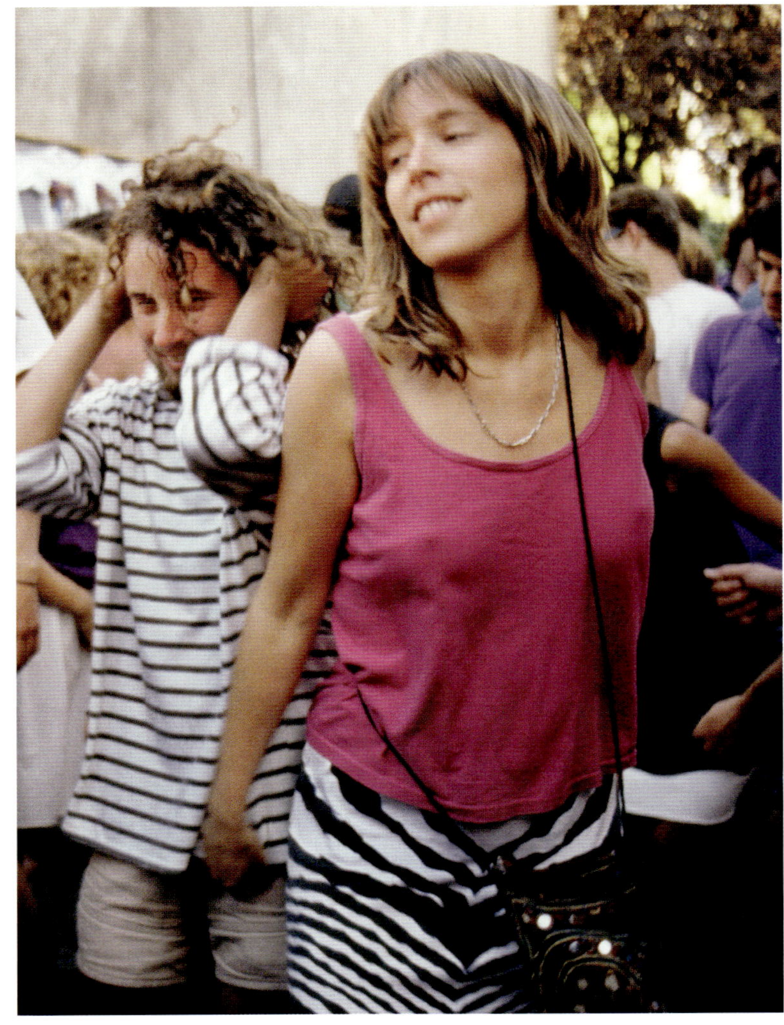
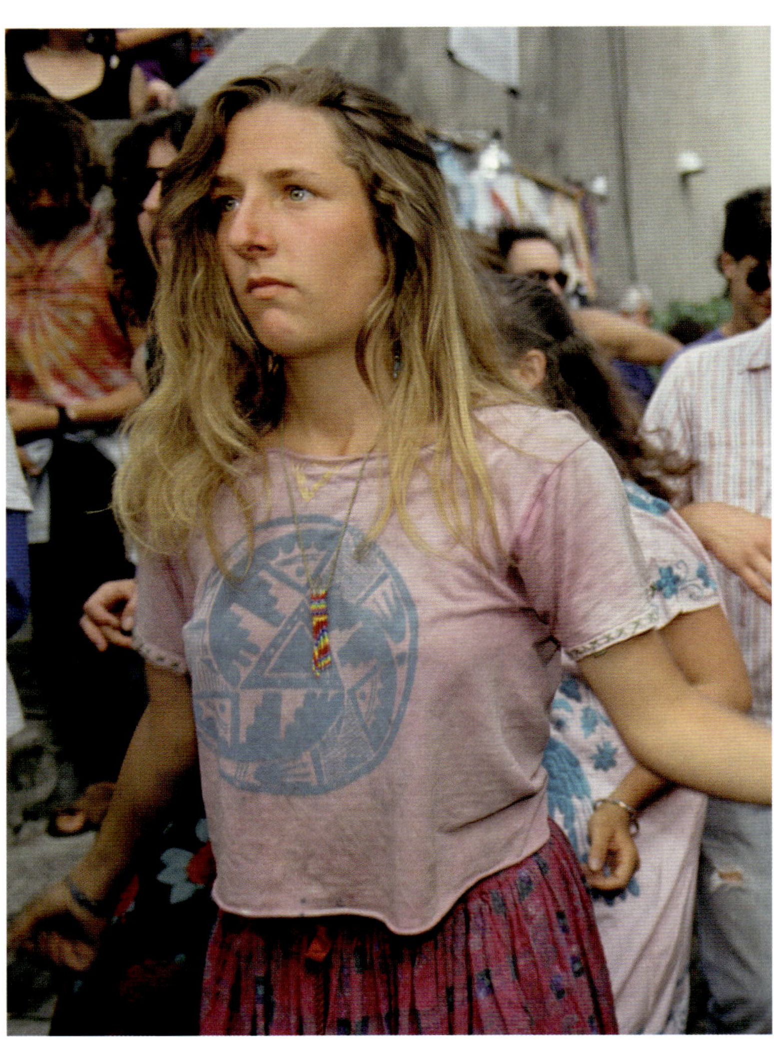
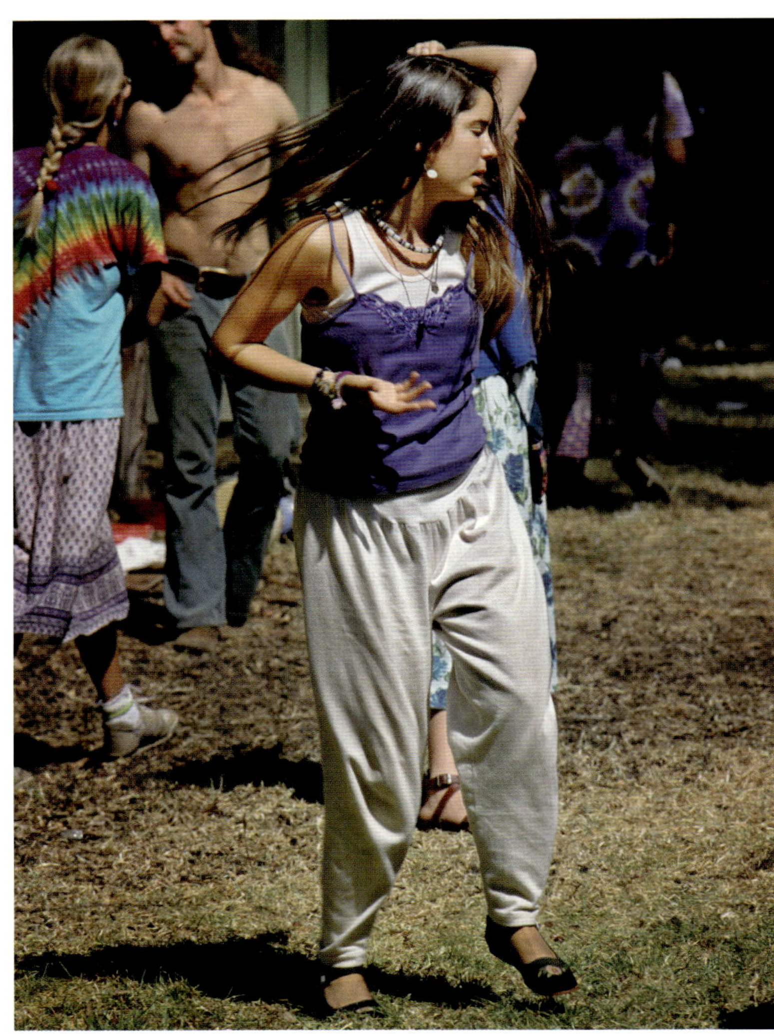

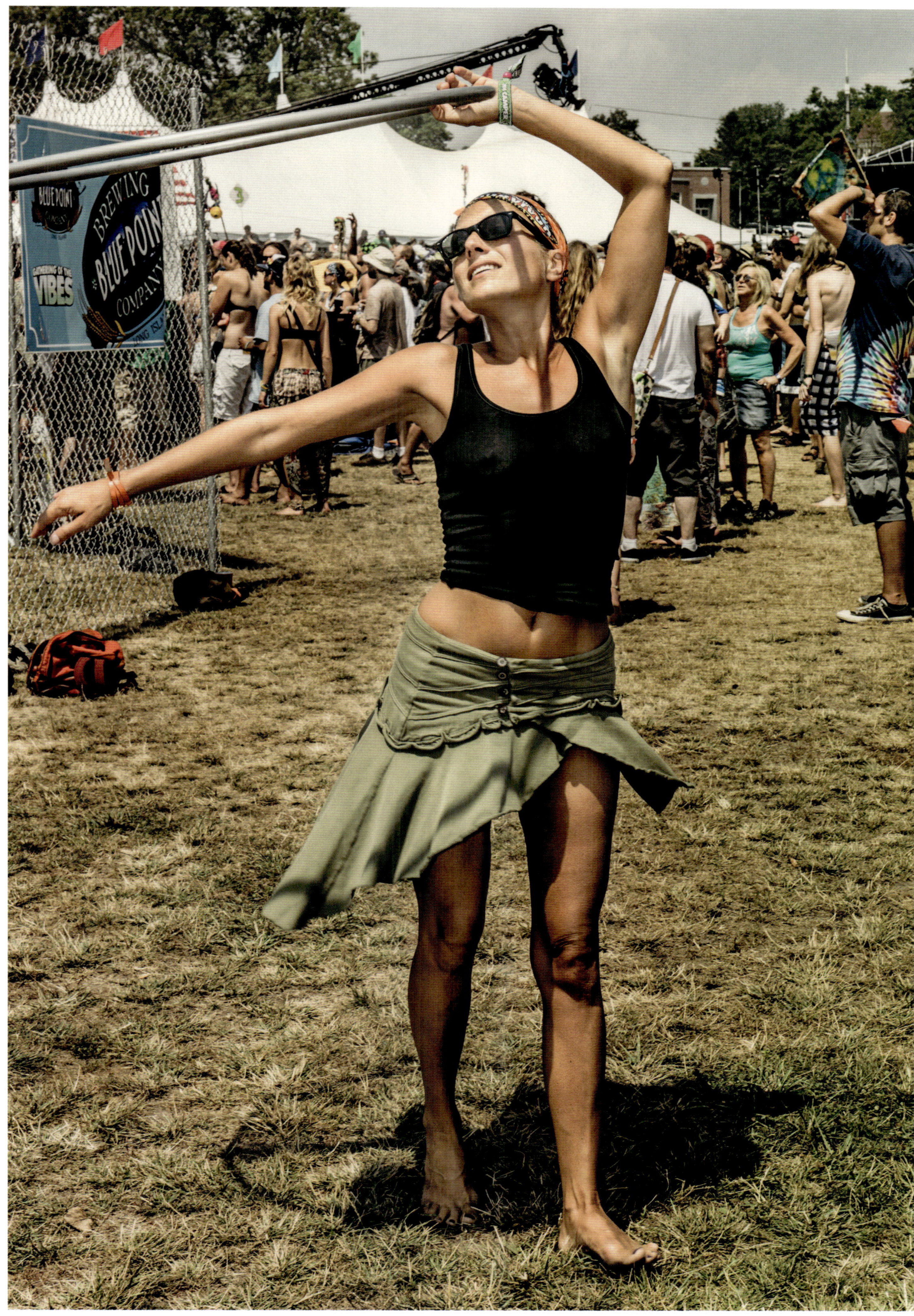
BLUE POINT
BREWING
BLUE POIN
COMPANY
VIBES

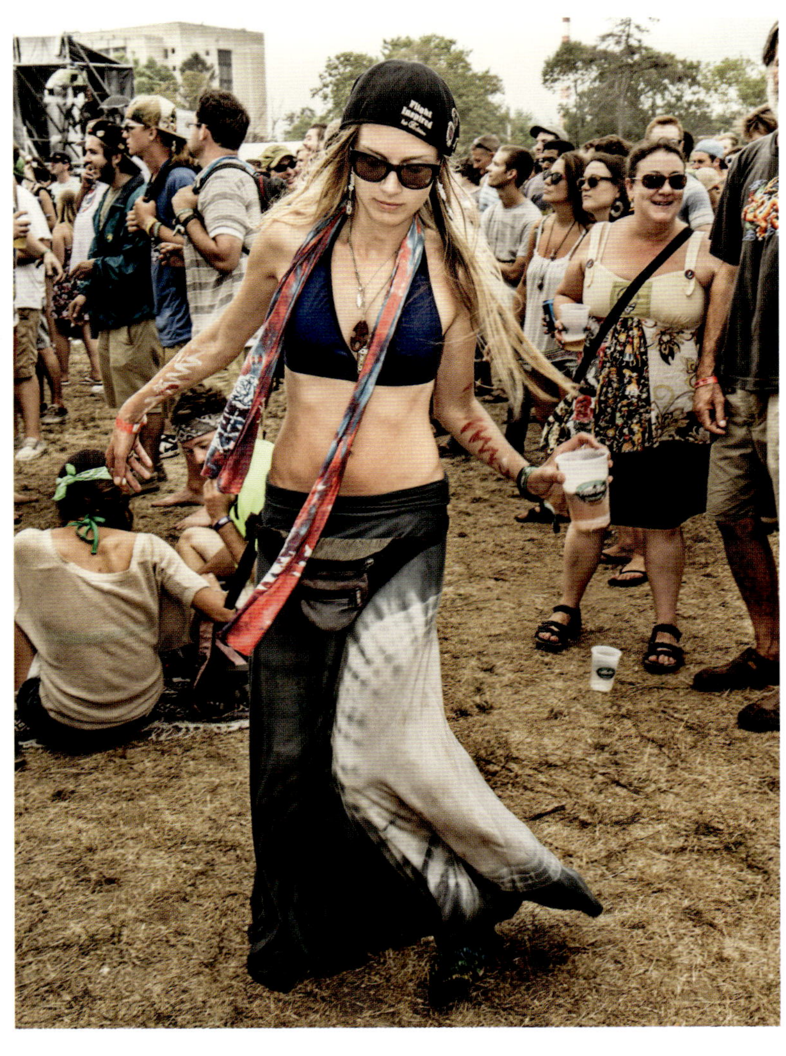
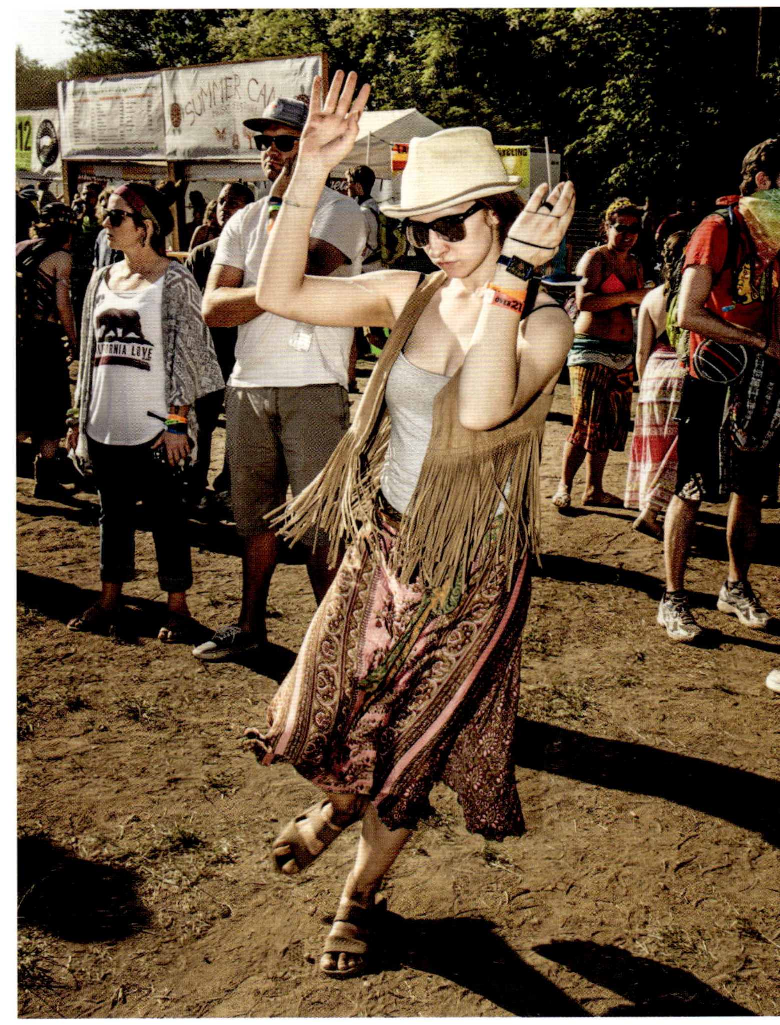
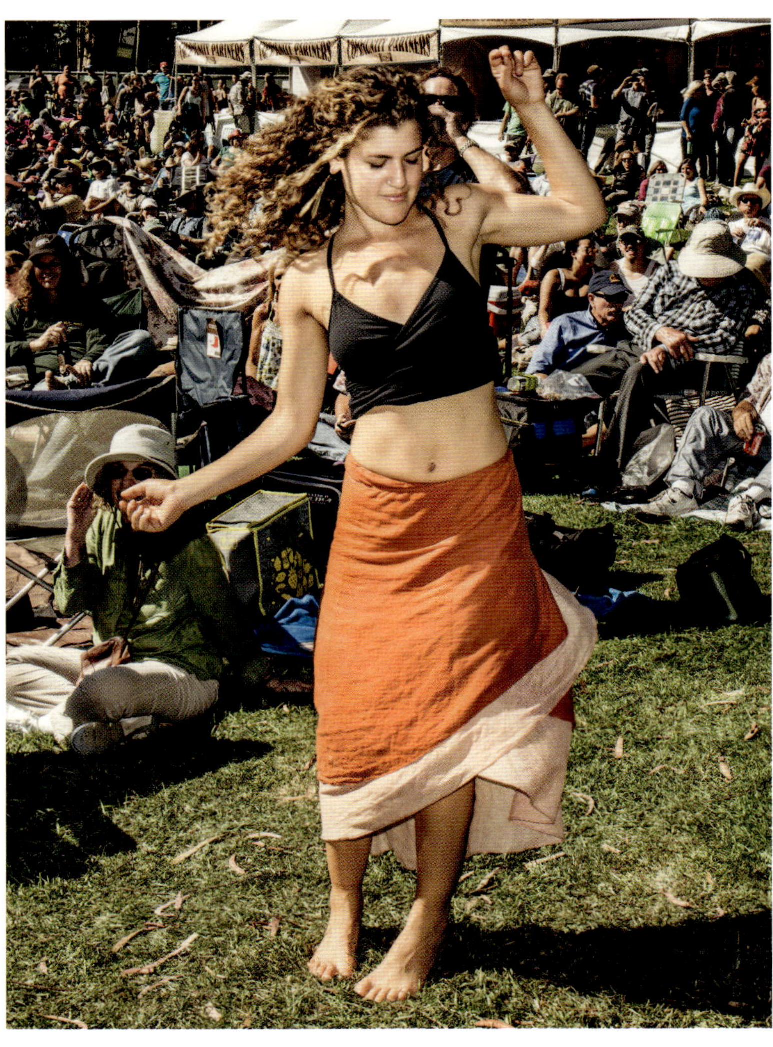
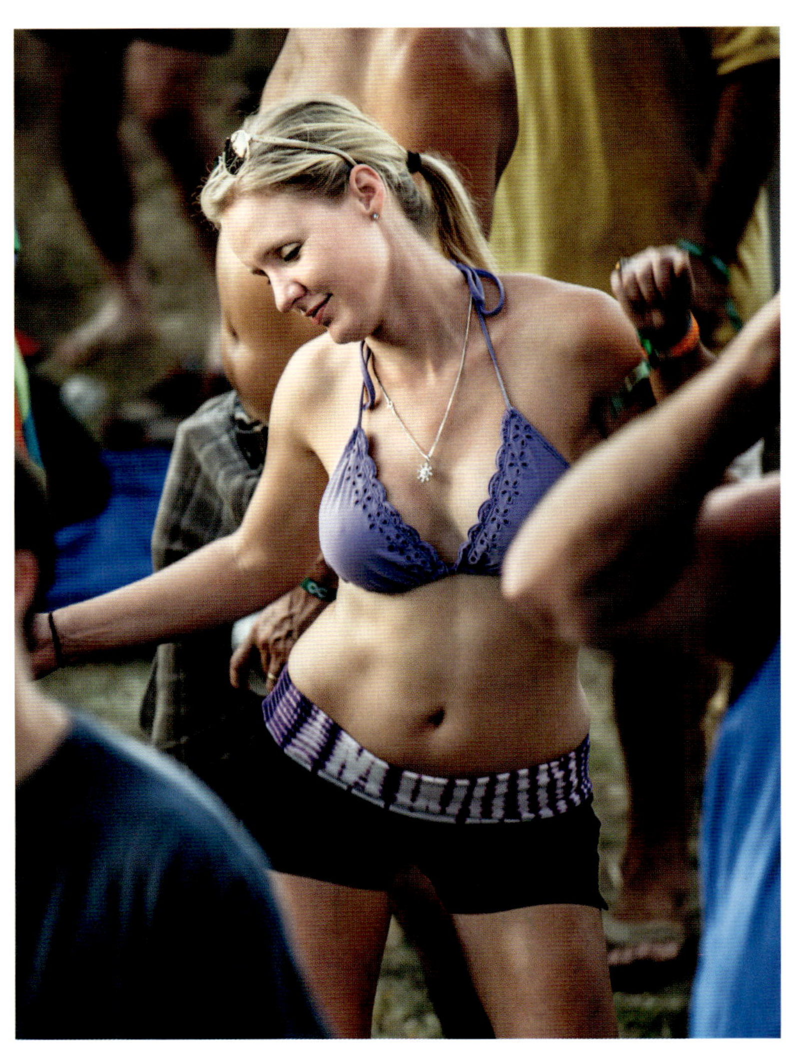

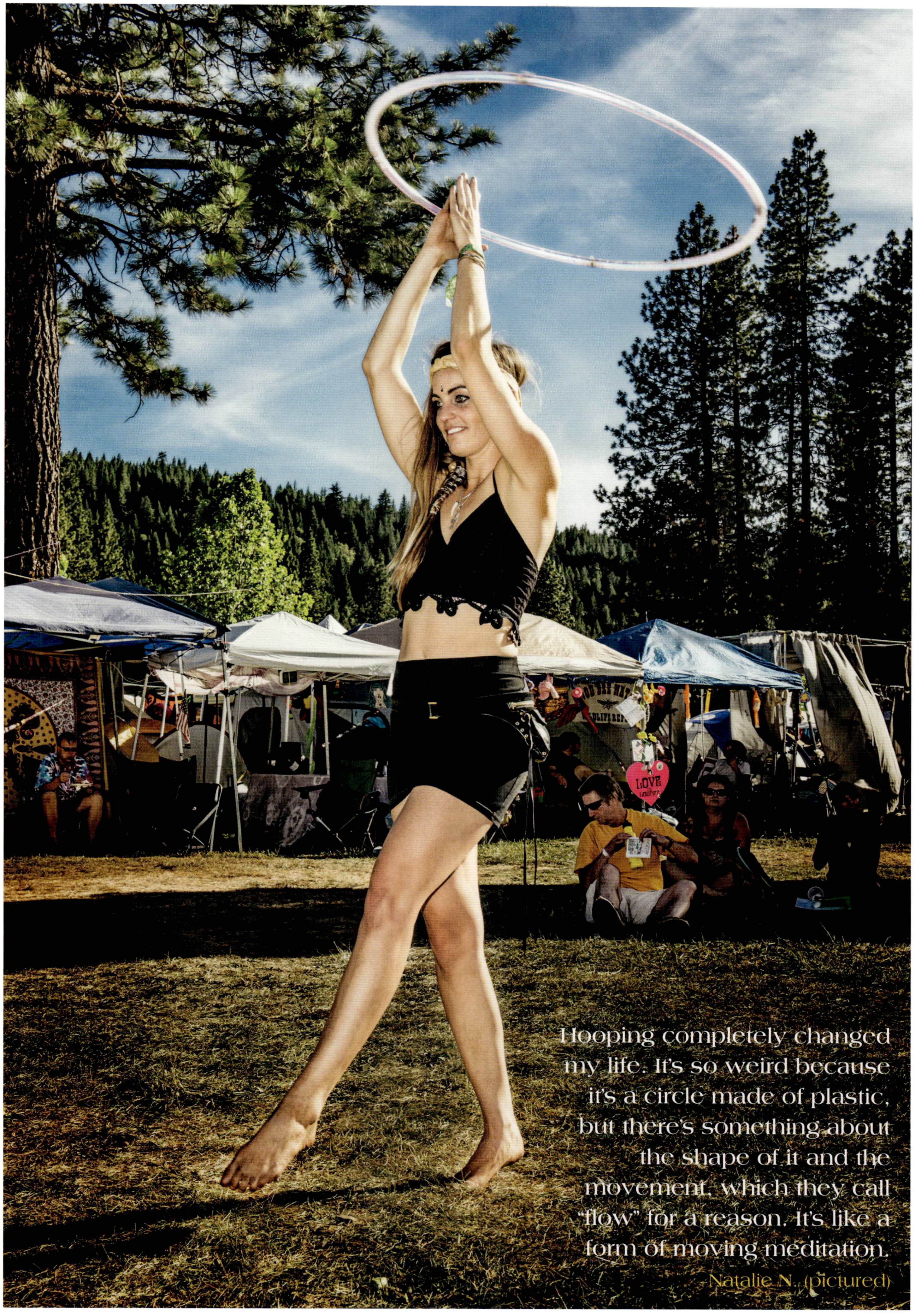

Hooping completely changed my life. It's so weird because it's a circle made of plastic, but there's something about the shape of it and the movement, which they call "flow" for a reason. It's like a form of moving meditation.

Natalie N. (pictured)

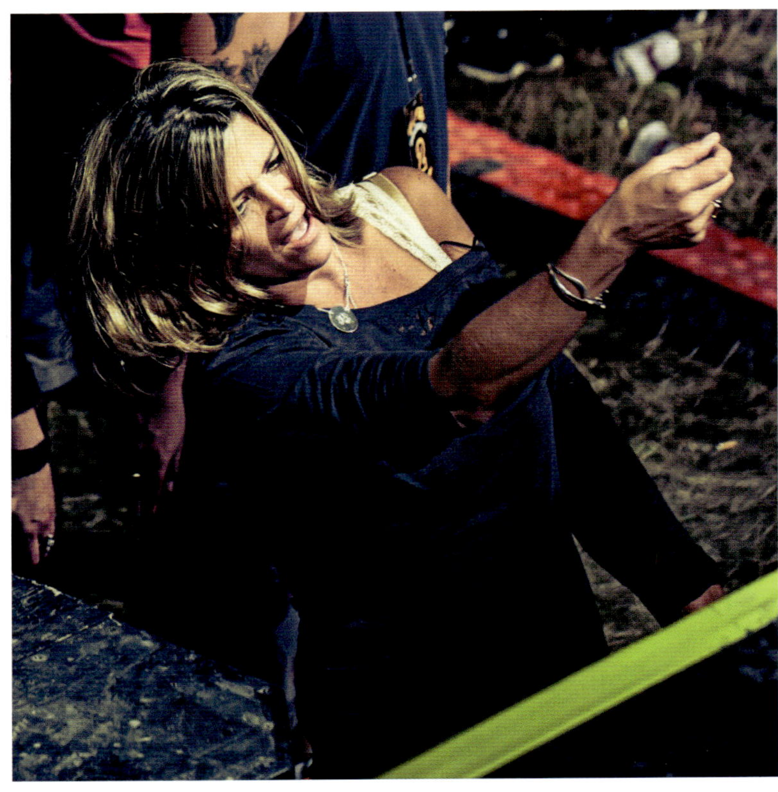

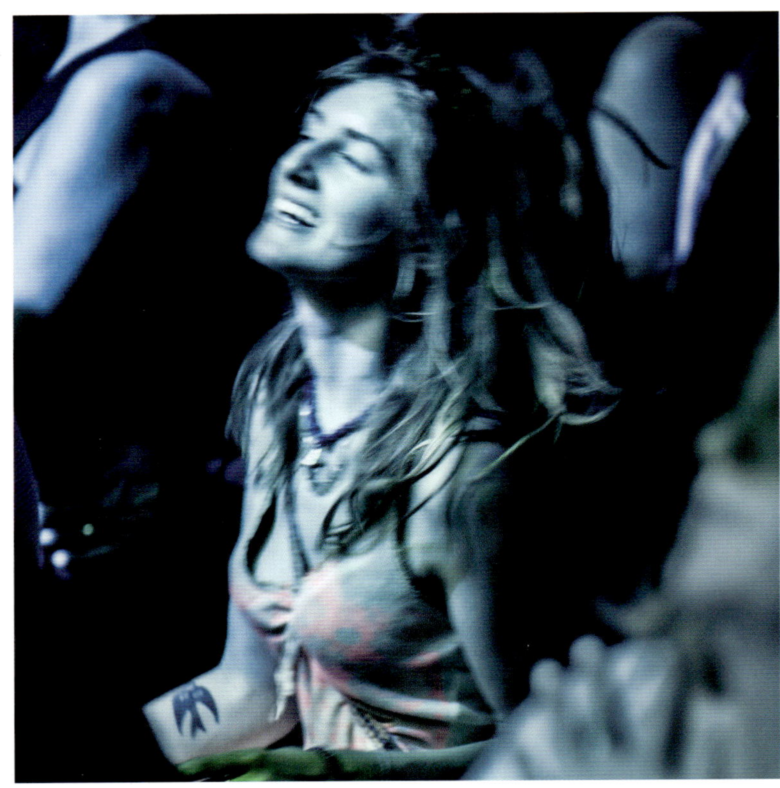

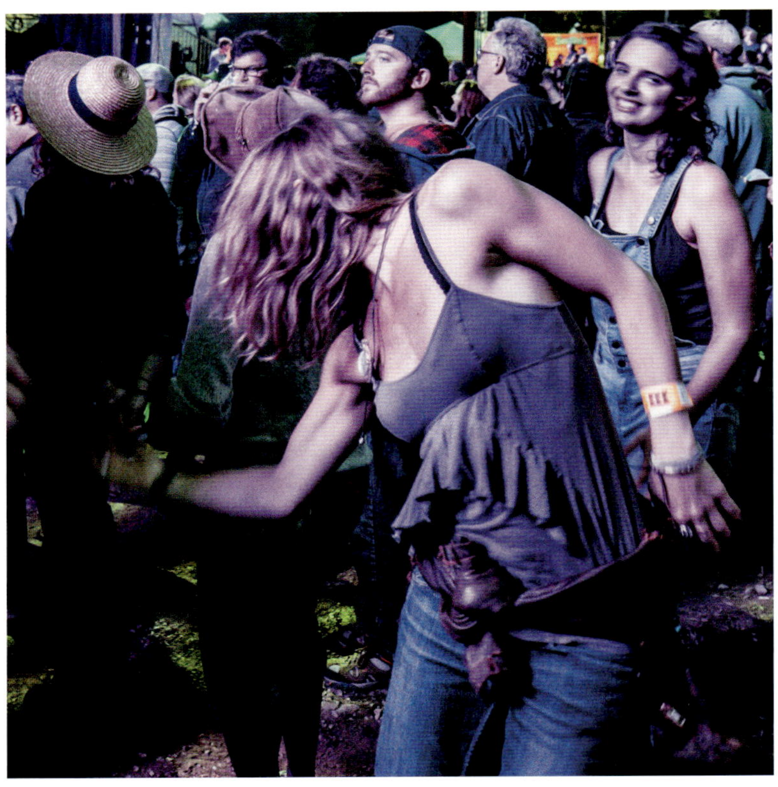

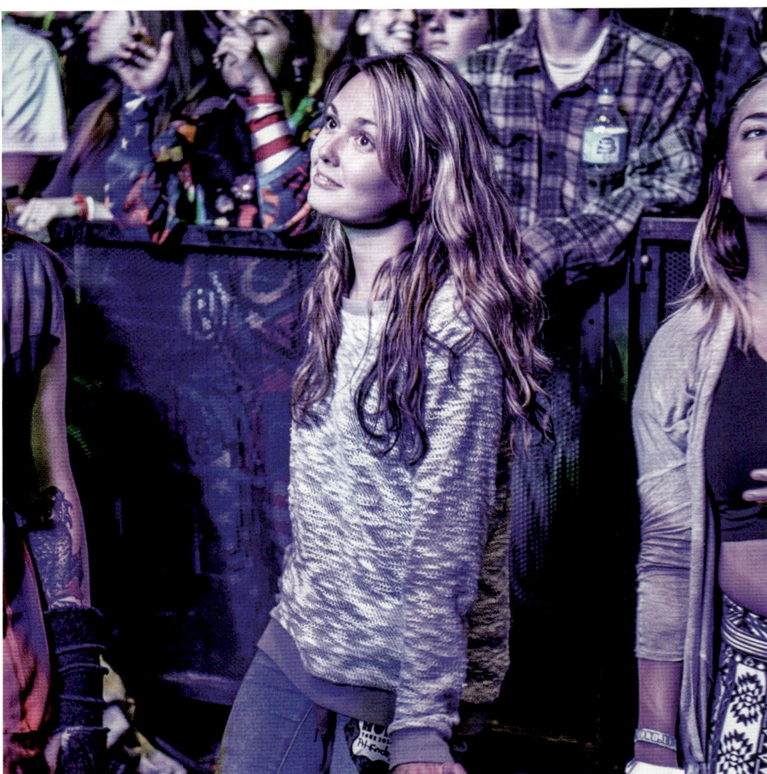

There's something so intimate about being up close and personal with your favorite band. The time I was on the rail, I felt like they were talking to me—listening to me. Kristina M.

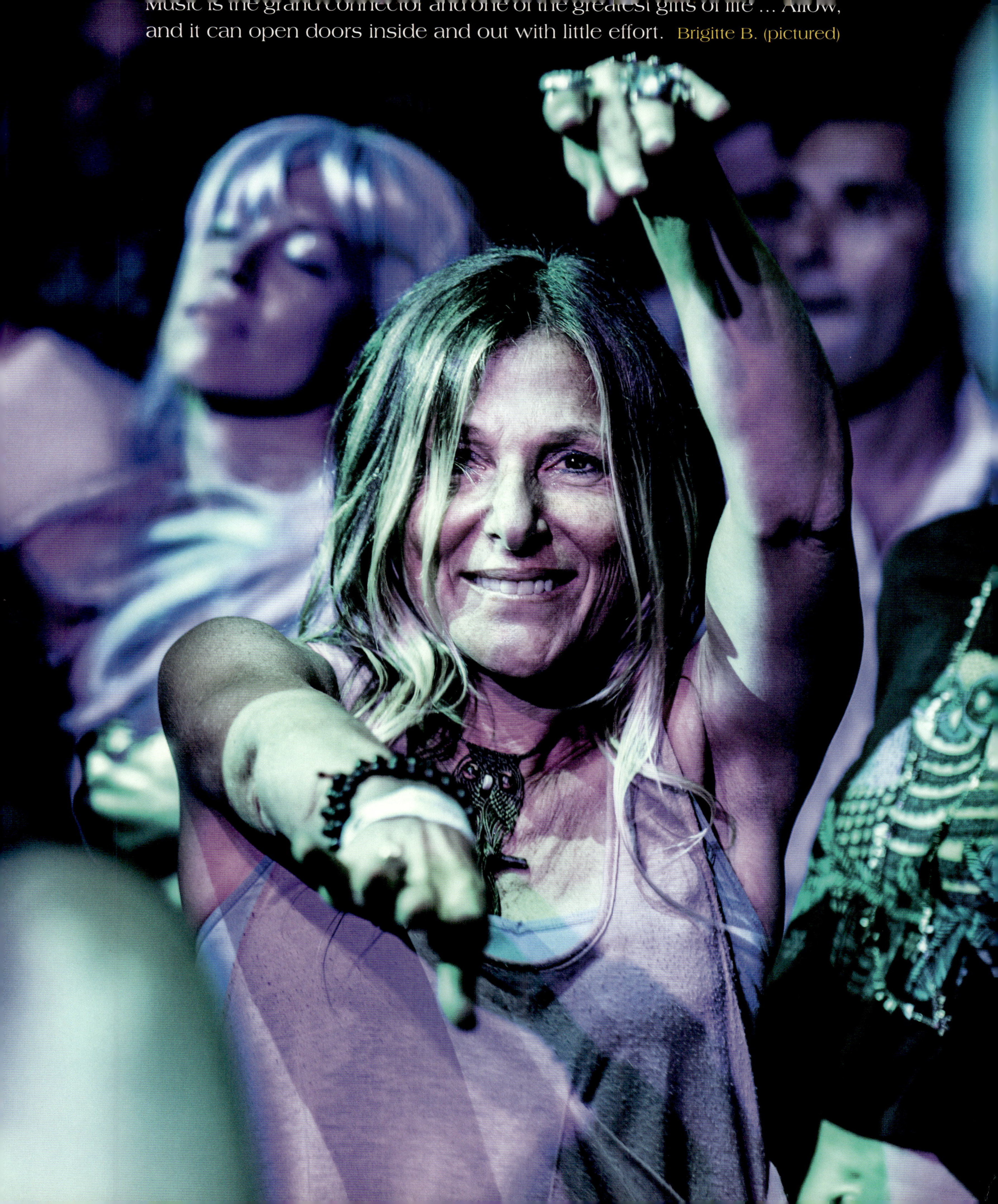

Music is the grand connector and one of the greatest gifts of life ... Allow, and it can open doors inside and out with little effort. Brigitte B. (pictured)

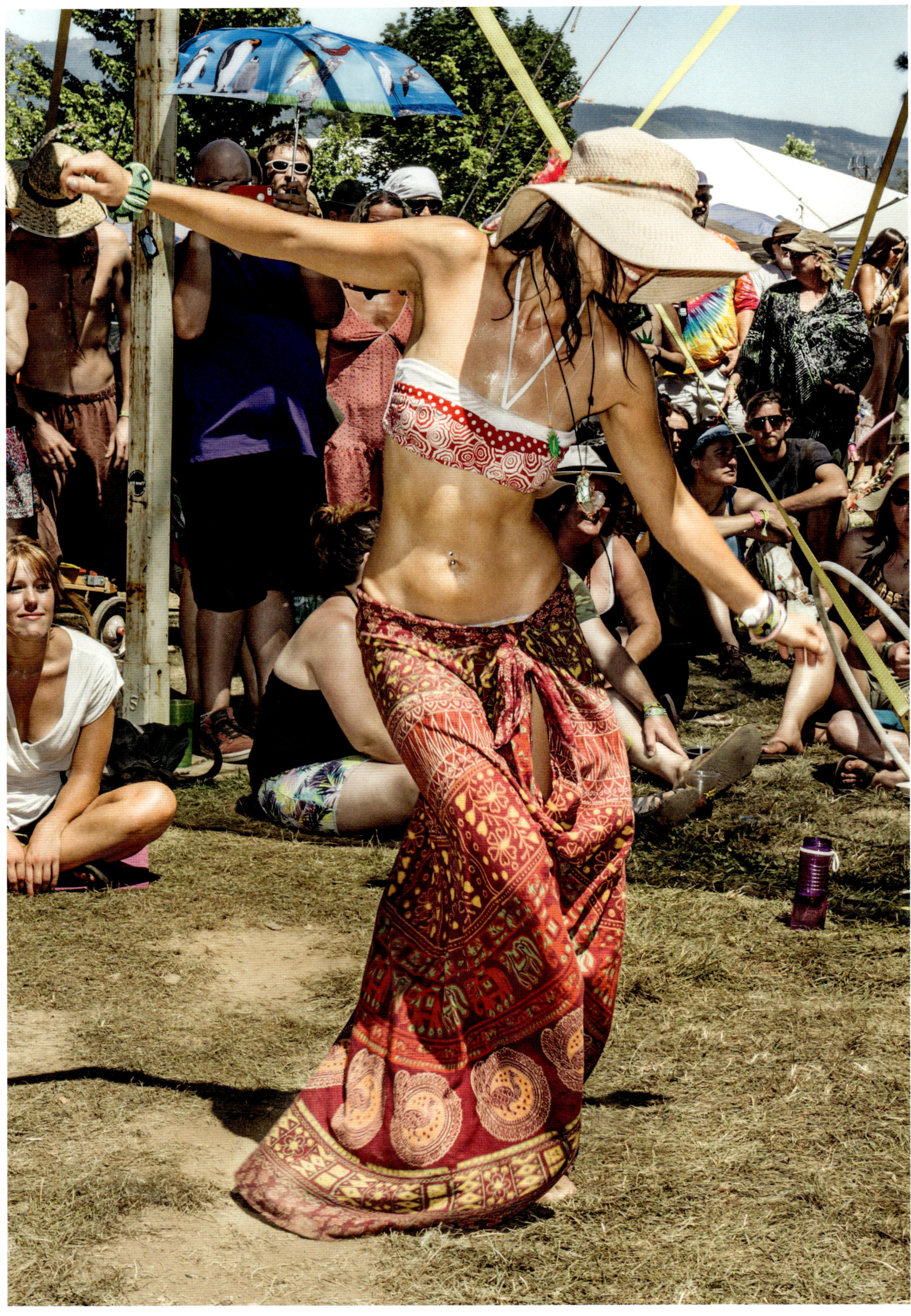

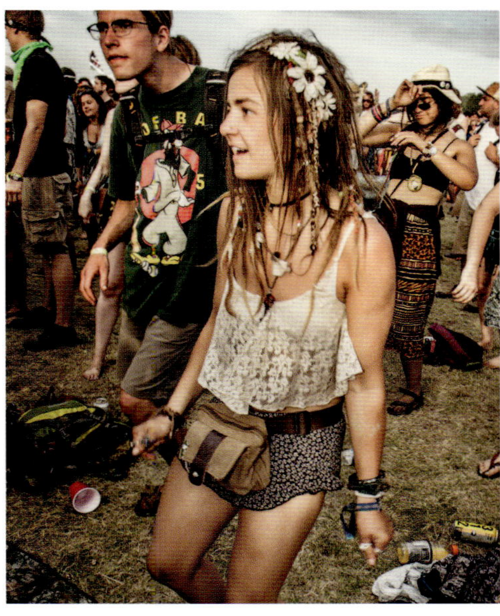

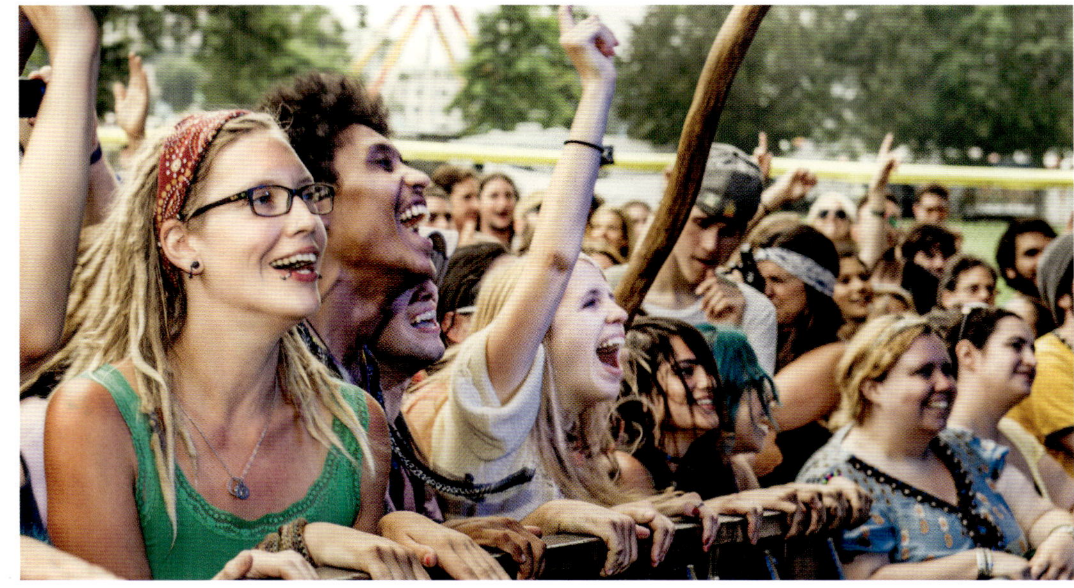

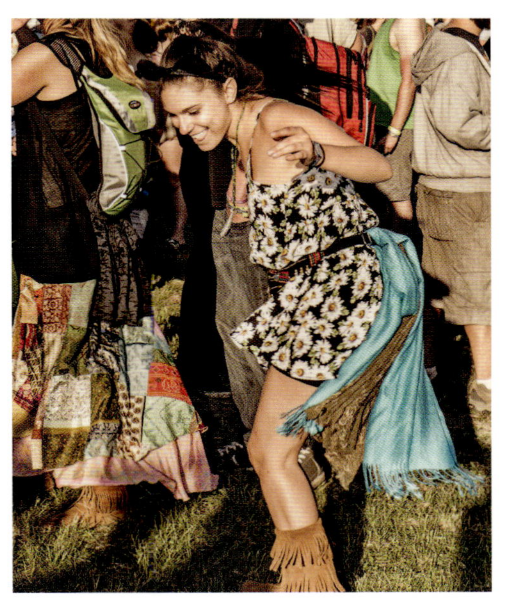

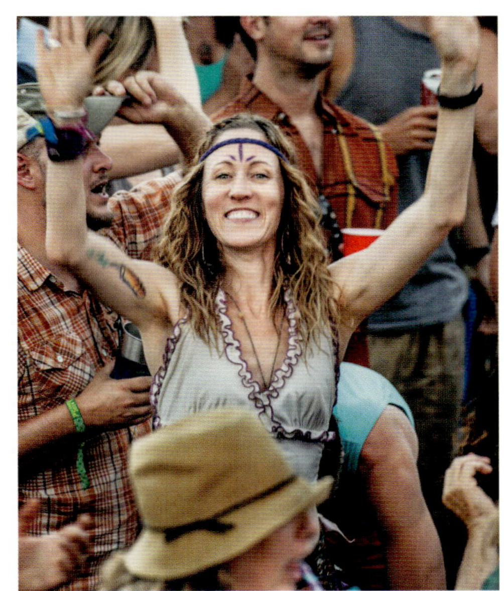

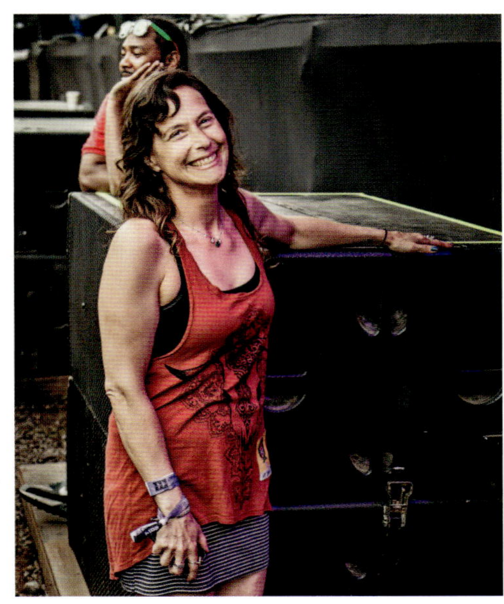

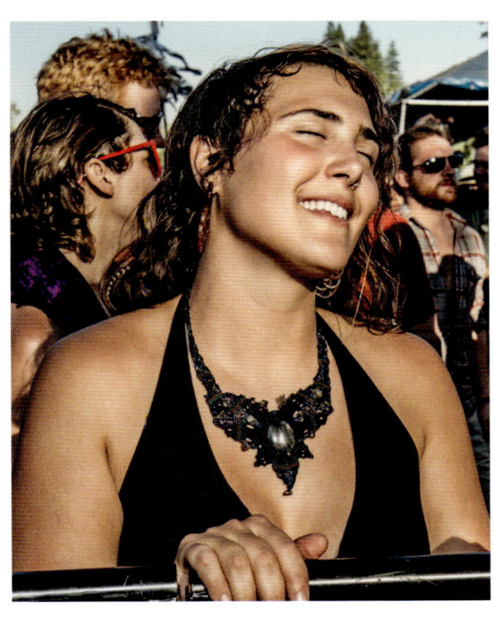

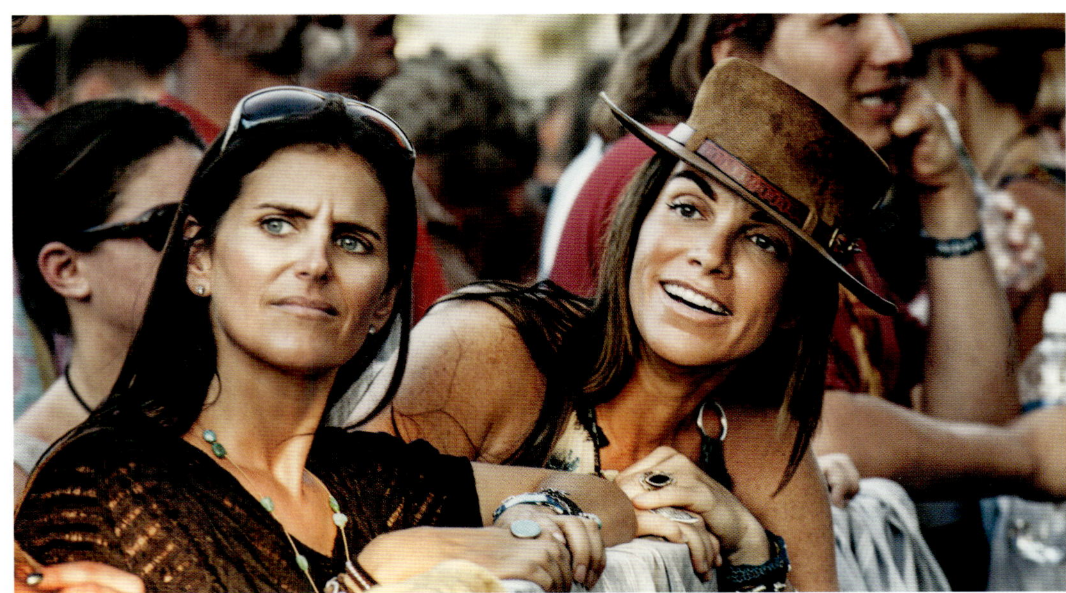

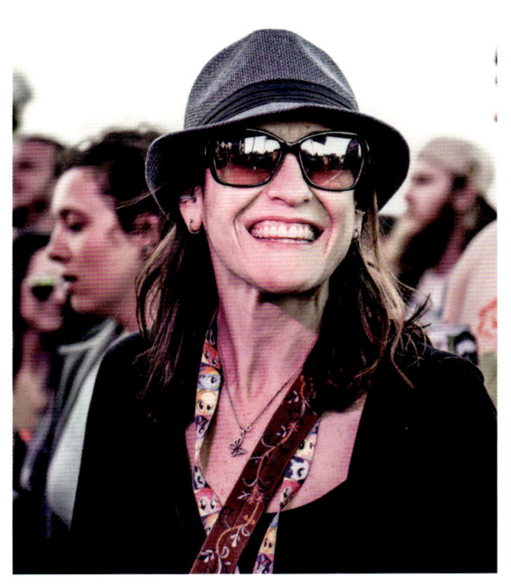

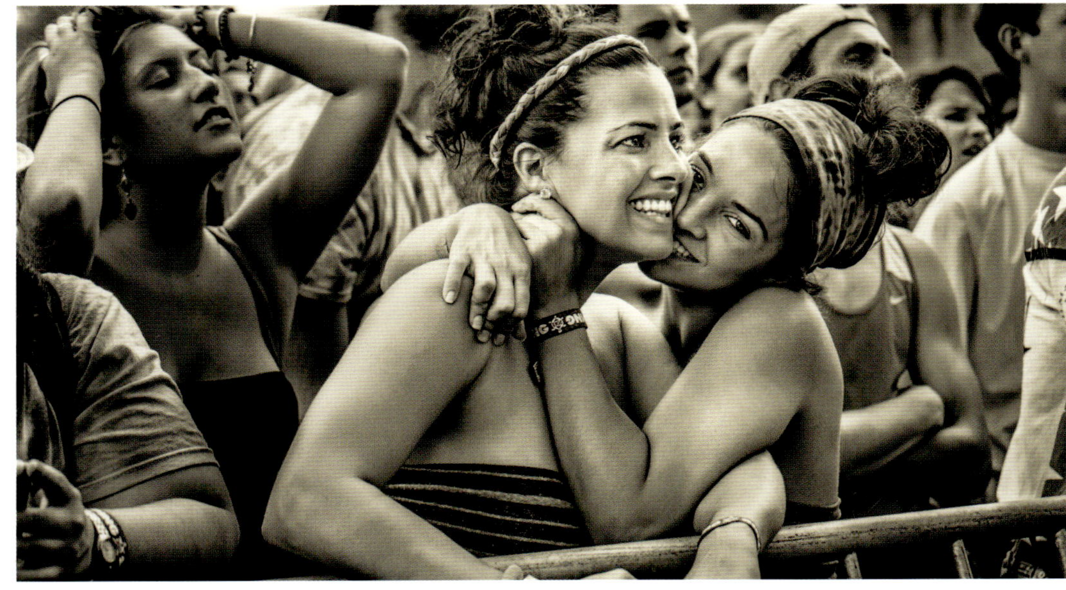

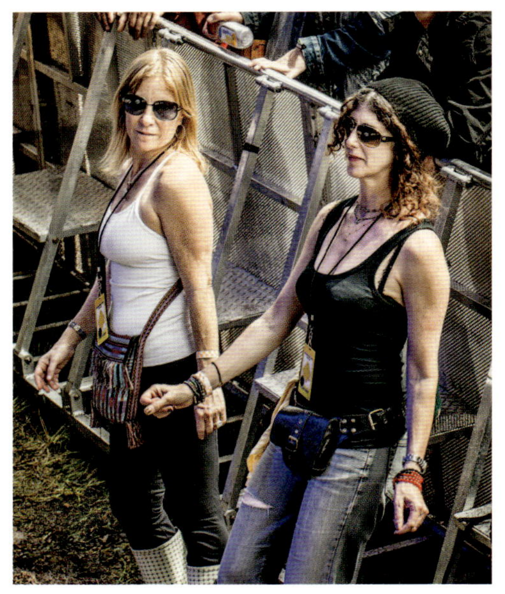

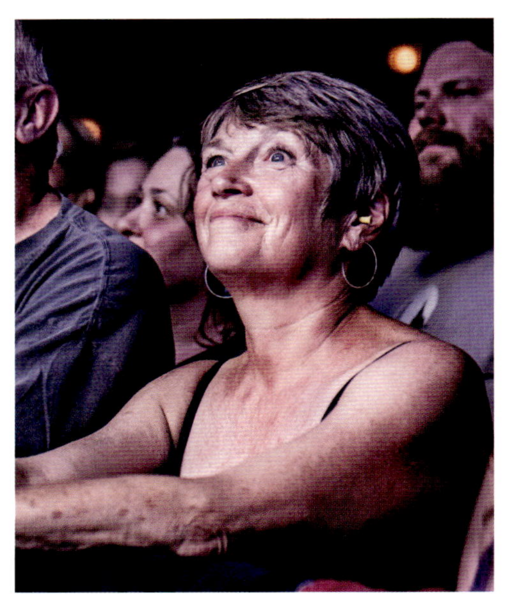

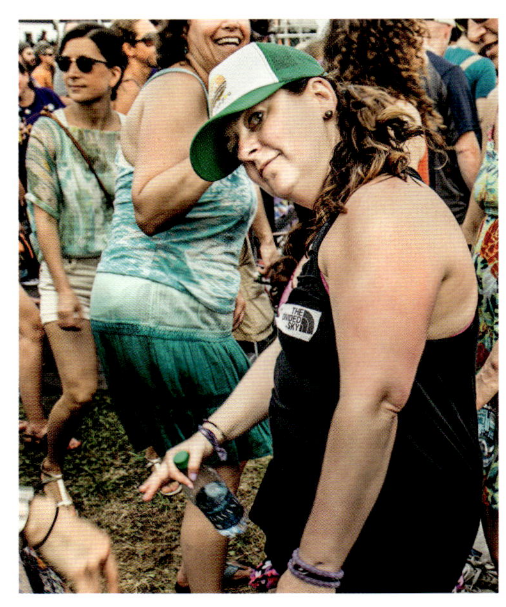

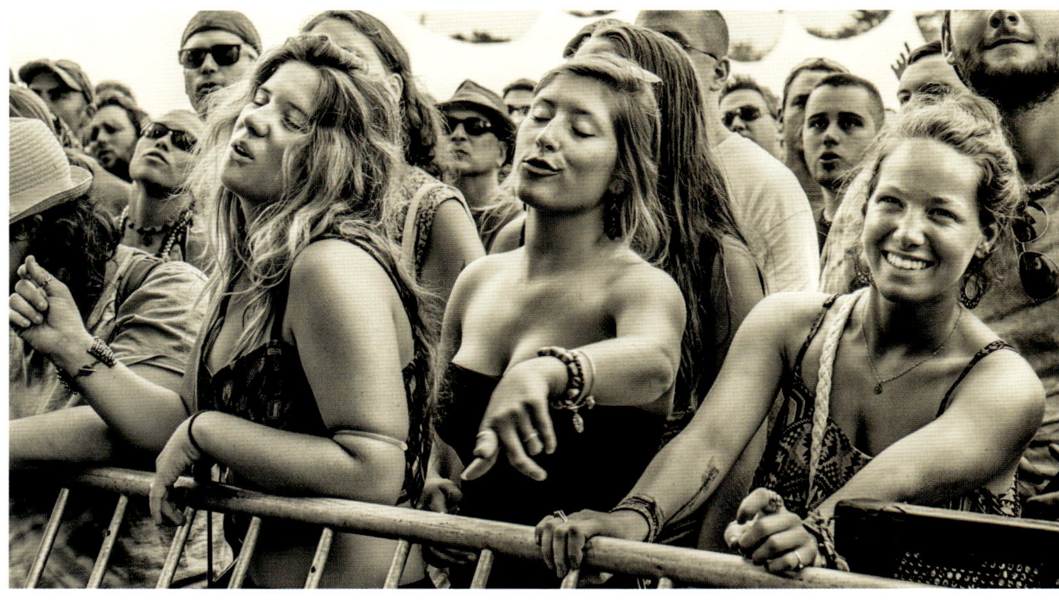

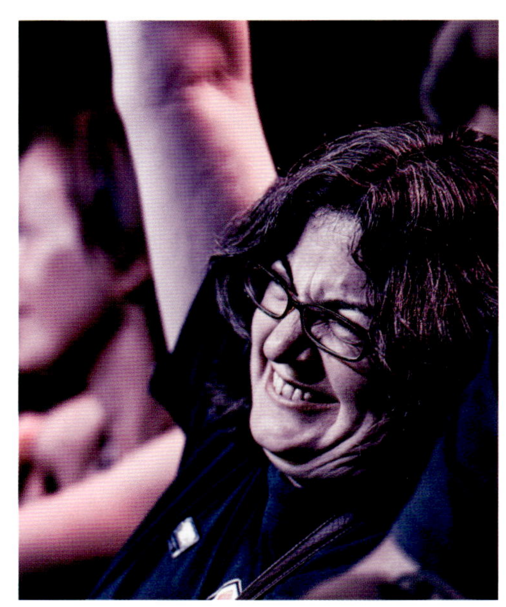

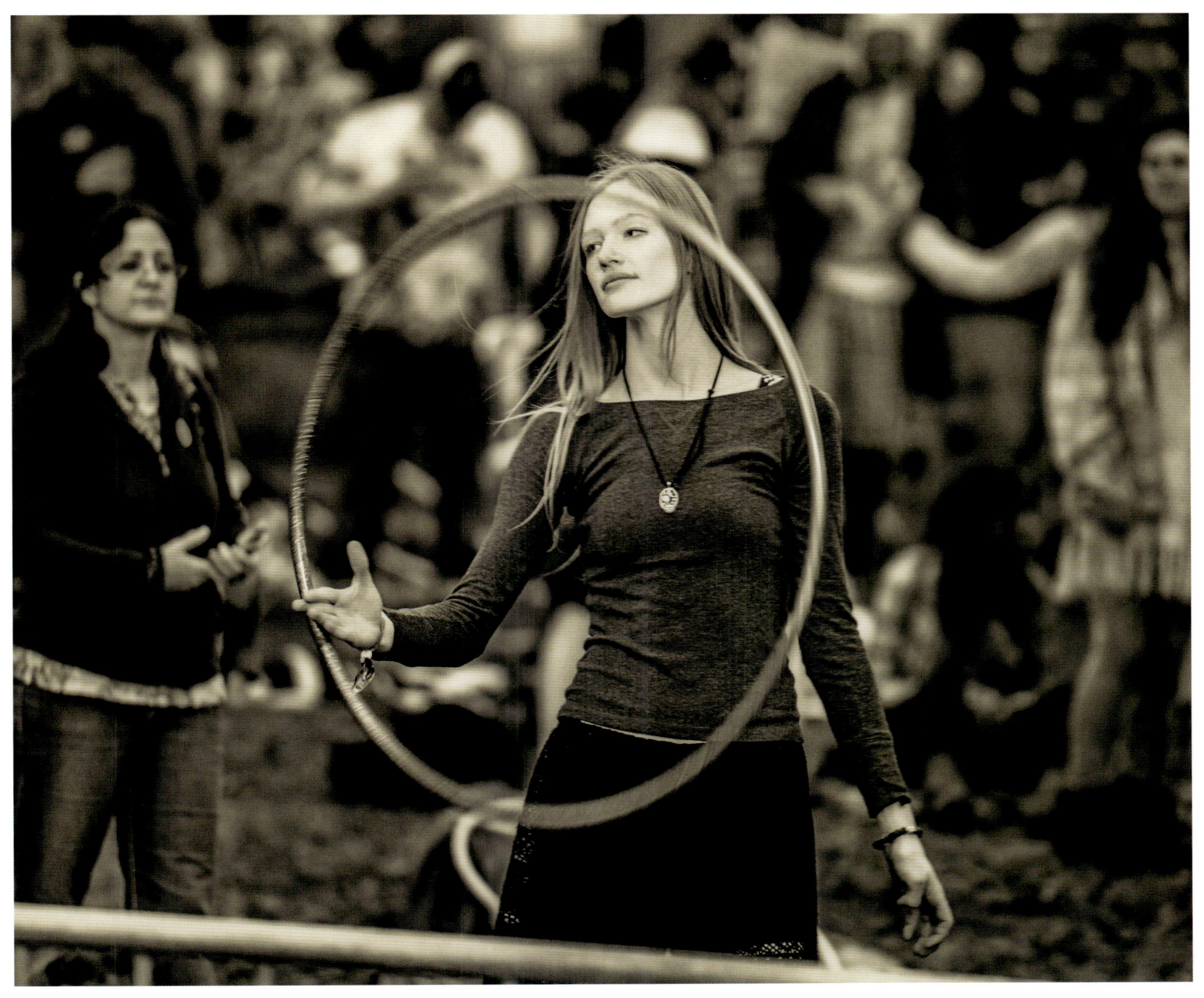

Hooping teaches you the basics again: when to let go, when to hold on, and when to shake it off and start over. The infinite nature of circles and dancing inside them is something magical. Alysa O.

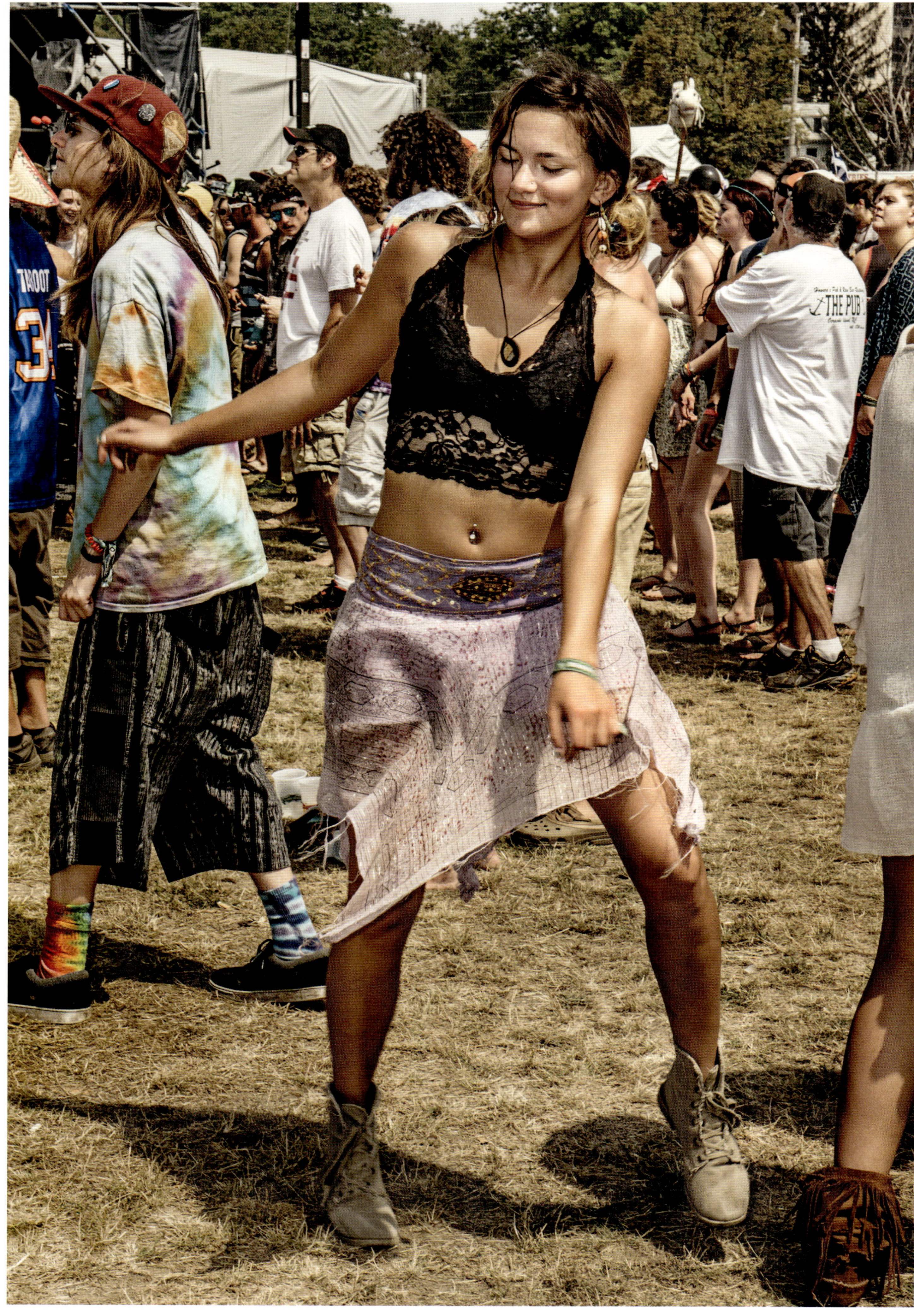
THE PUB

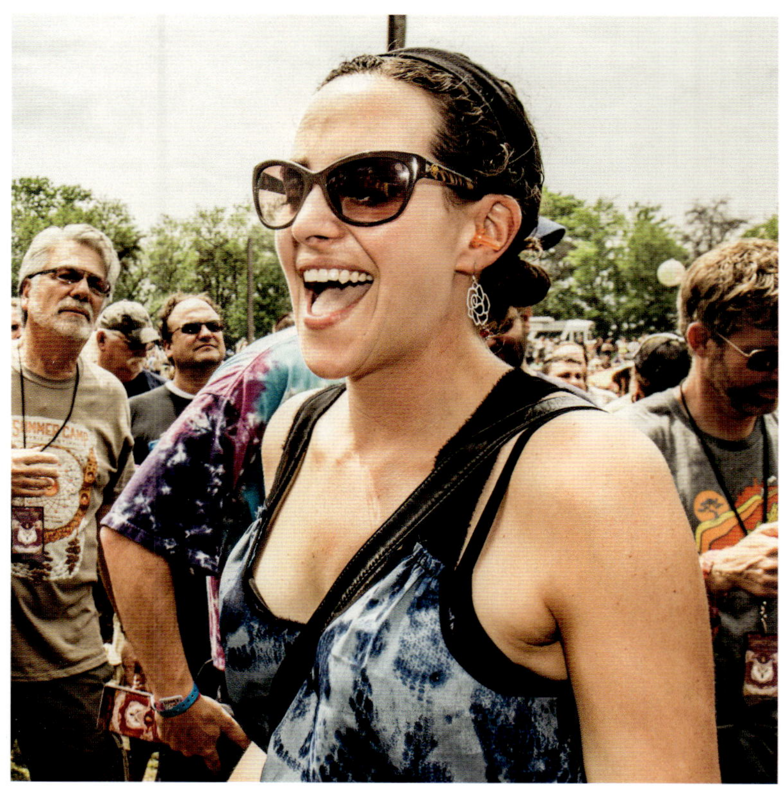

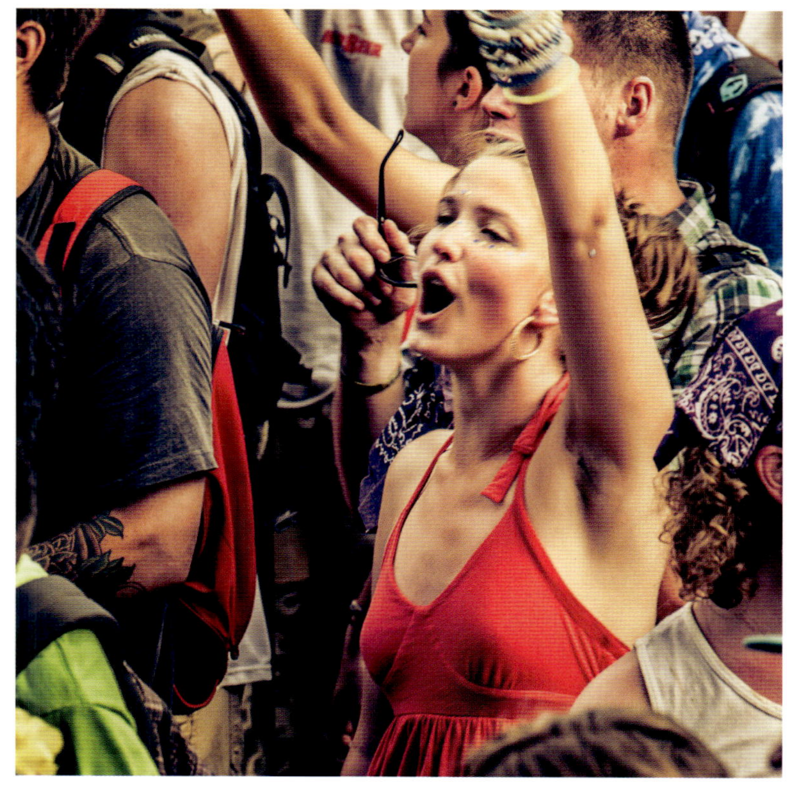

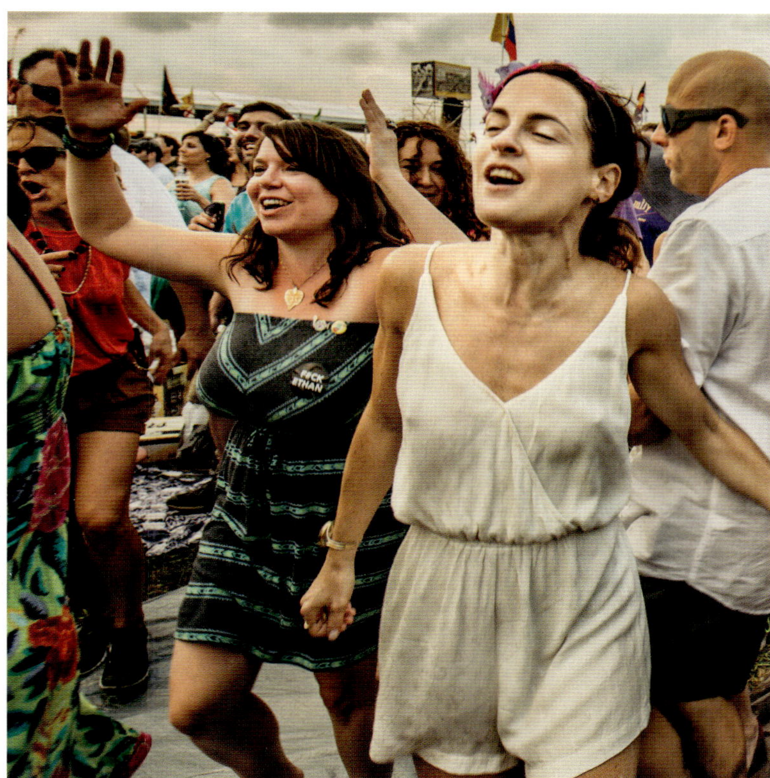

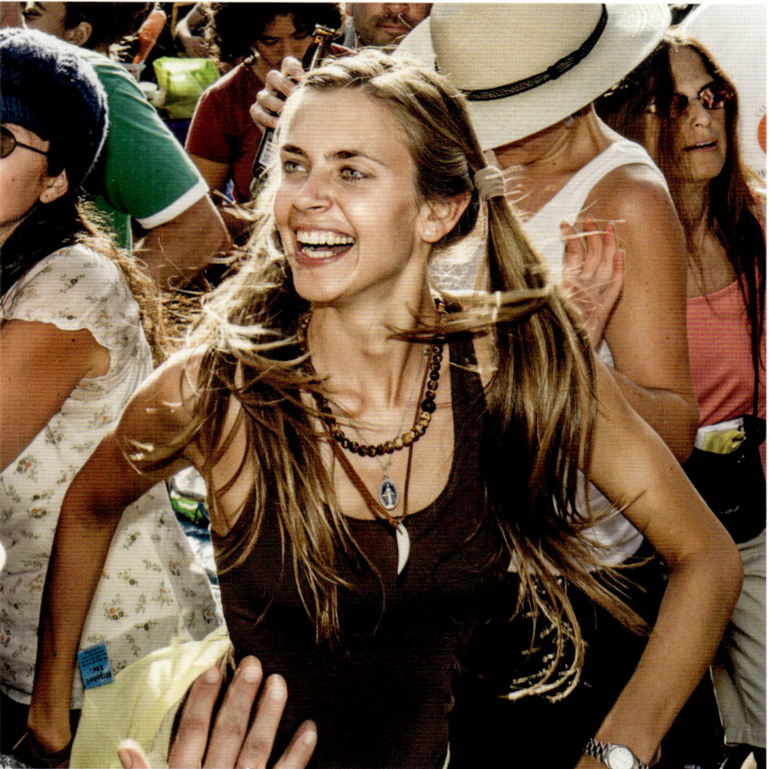

When live music takes hold of your soul, your heart overflowing with happiness, creativity and energy coursing through your body, it is the ultimate high. That feeling has shaped my life more than anything else.

Jessica C. (pictured, top left)

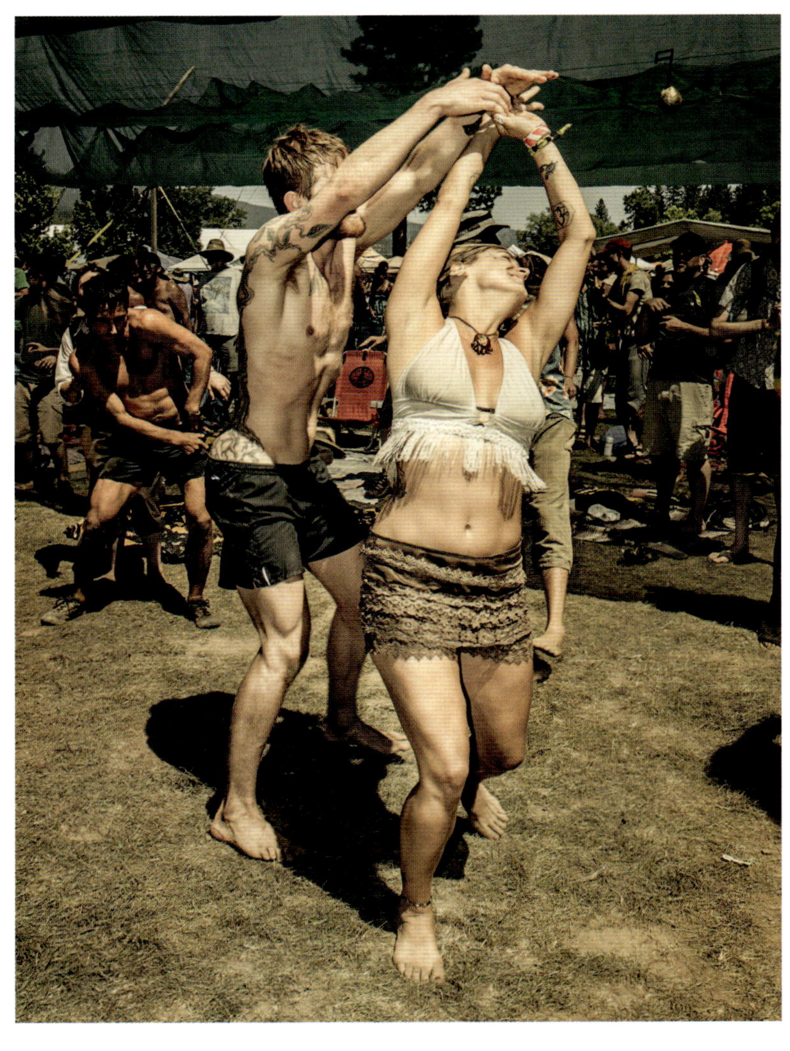

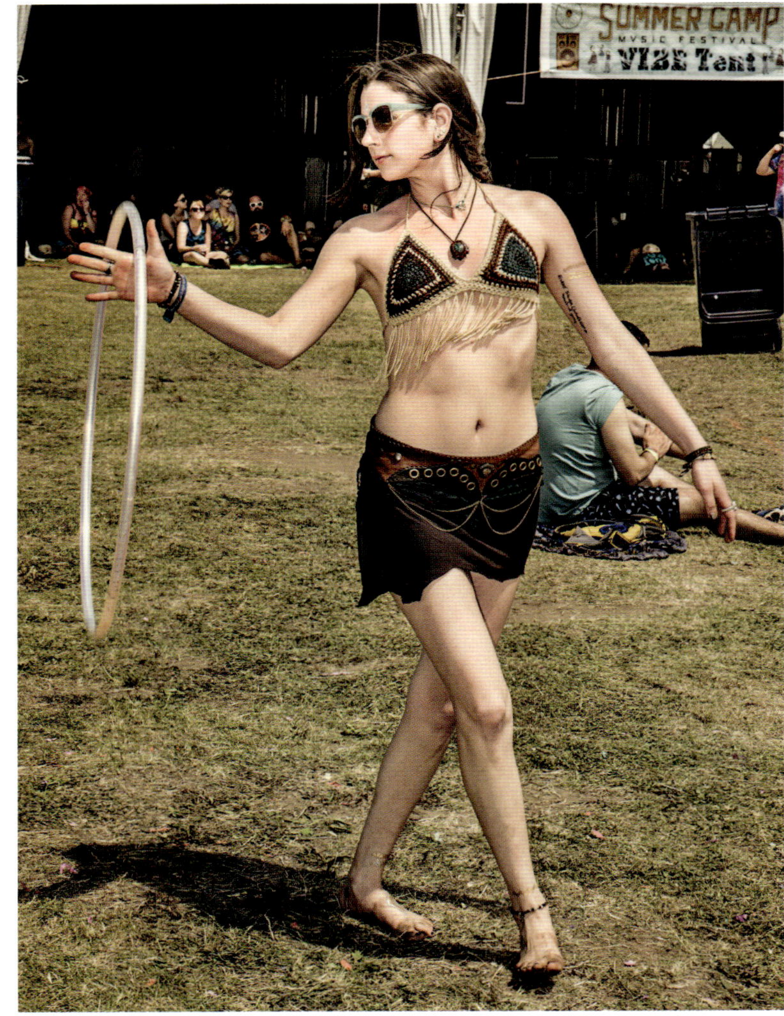

SUMMER CAMP
MUSIC FESTIVAL
VIBE Tent

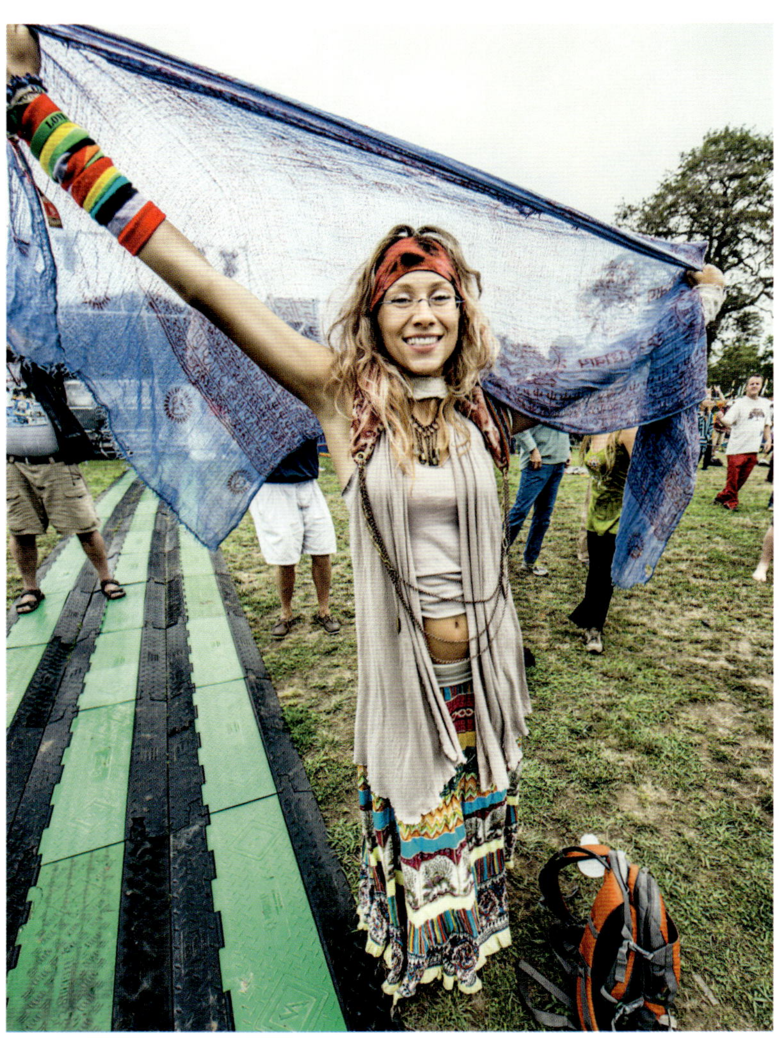

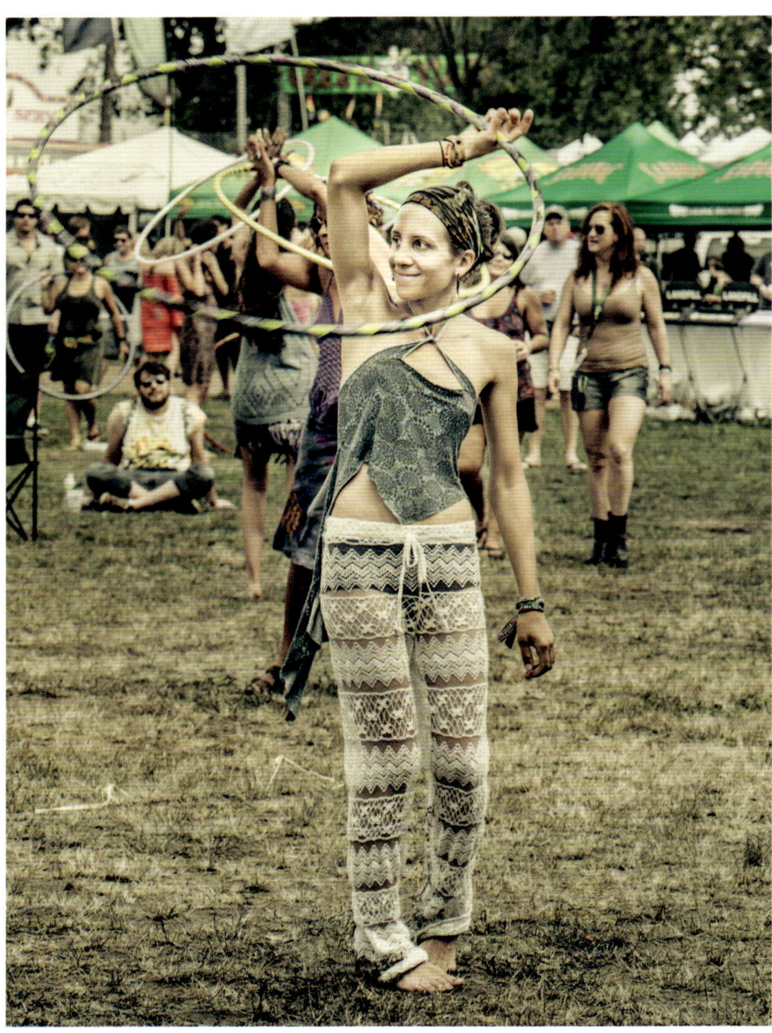

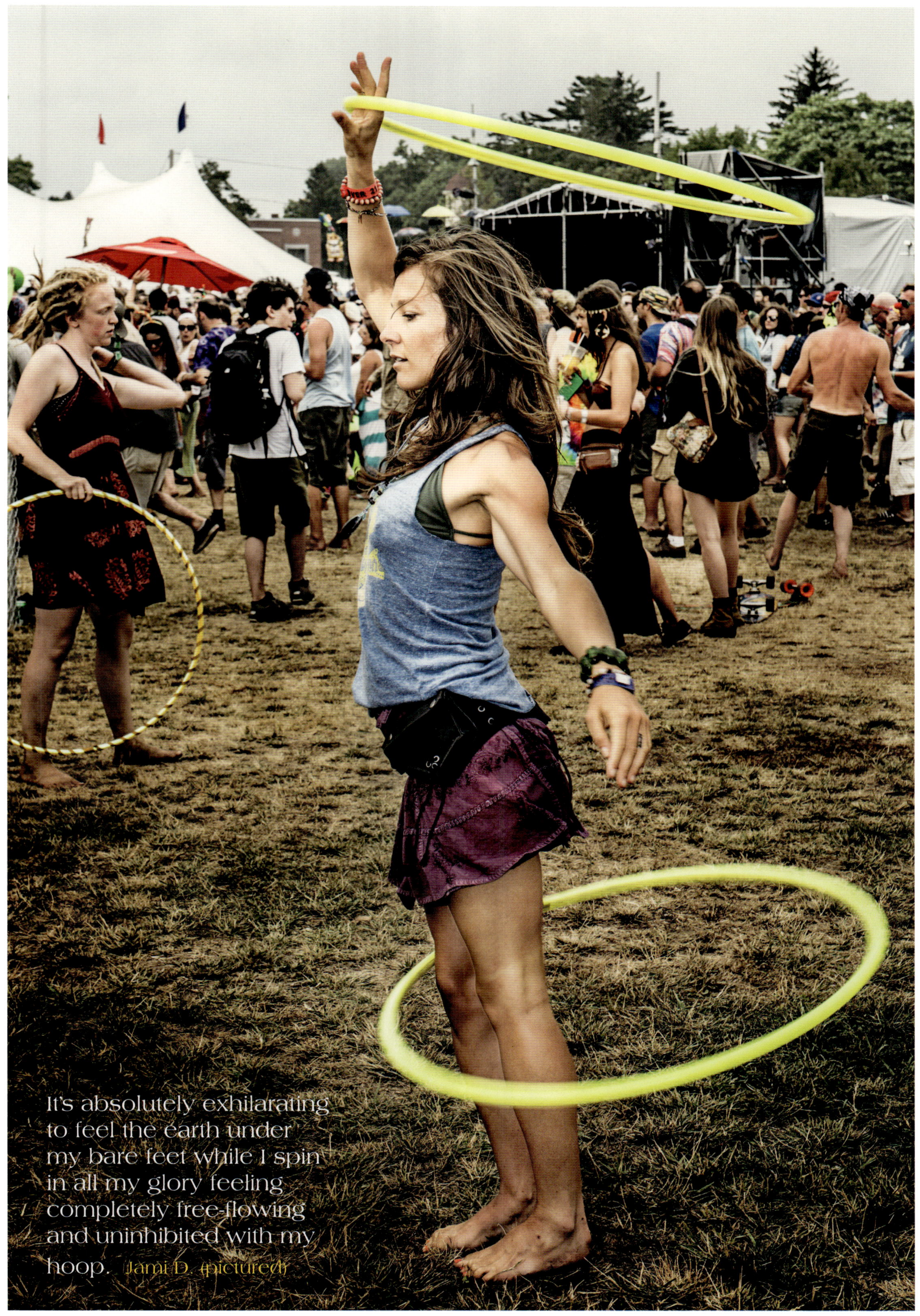

It's absolutely exhilarating to feel the earth under my bare feet while I spin in all my glory feeling completely free-flowing and uninhibited with my hoop. Jami D. (pictured)

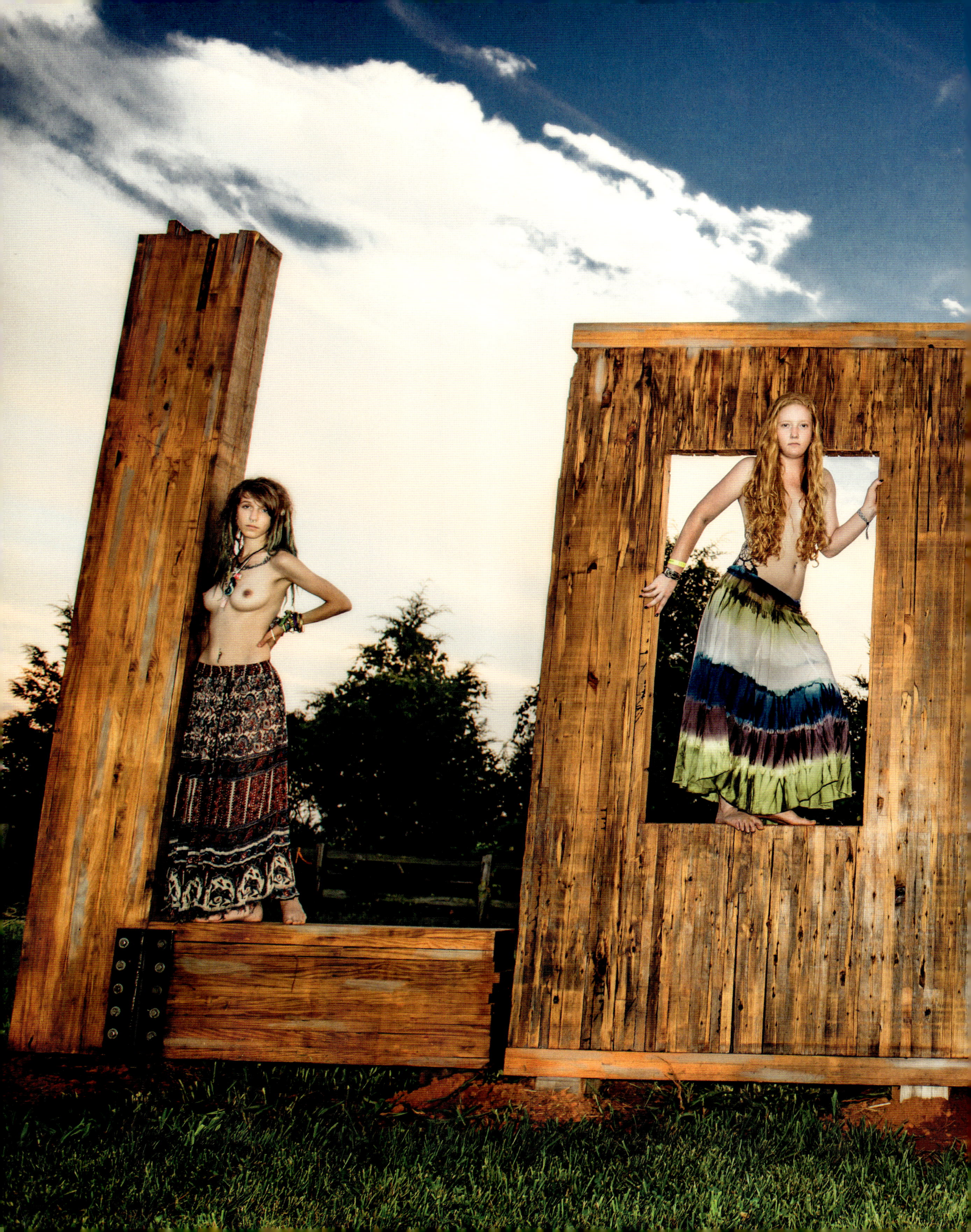

The connection being made between every single person in a crowd is incredible. We're all creating this vibe together. I think that's really powerful. That's the type of thing that can change the world. Keara G. (pictured, far left)

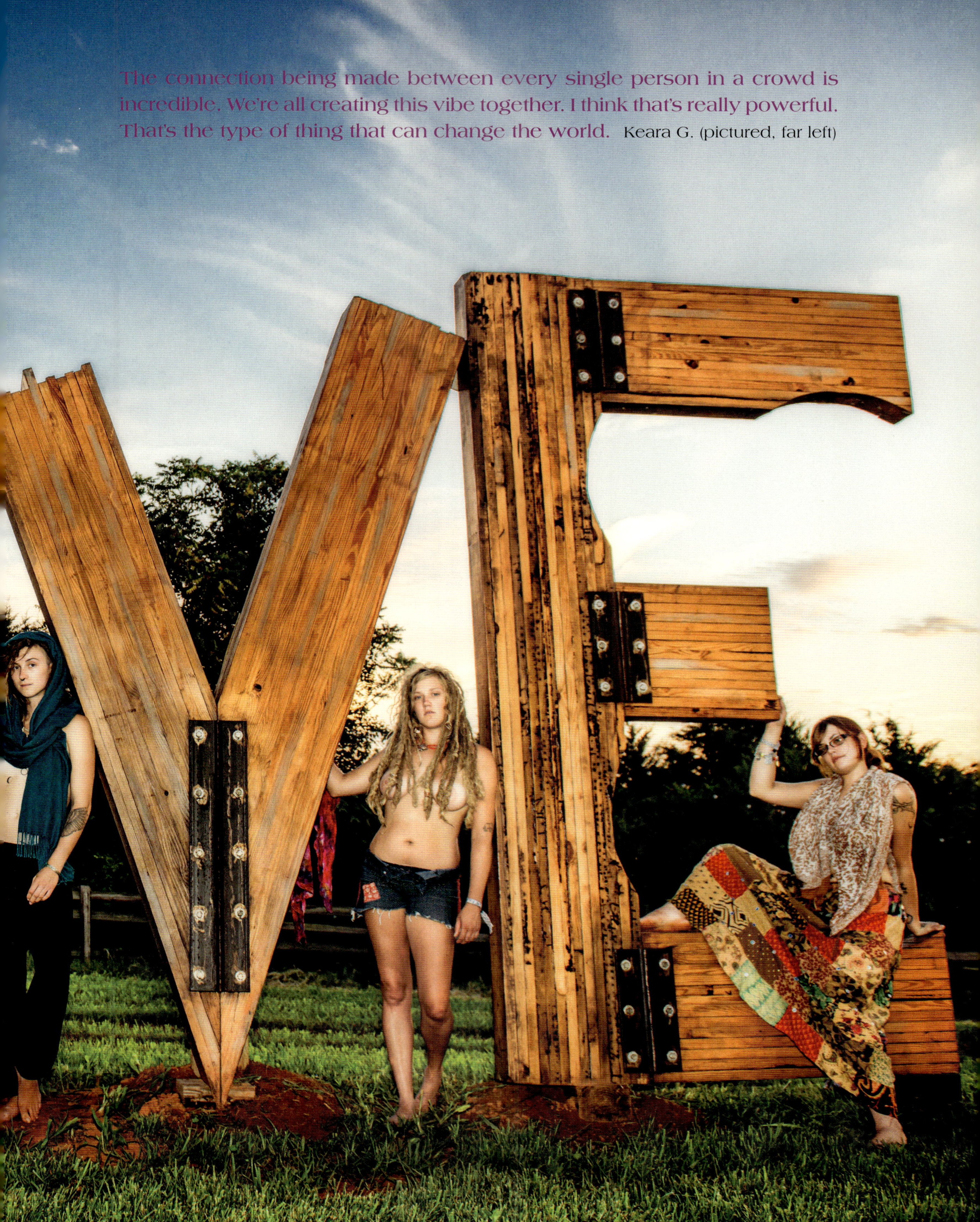

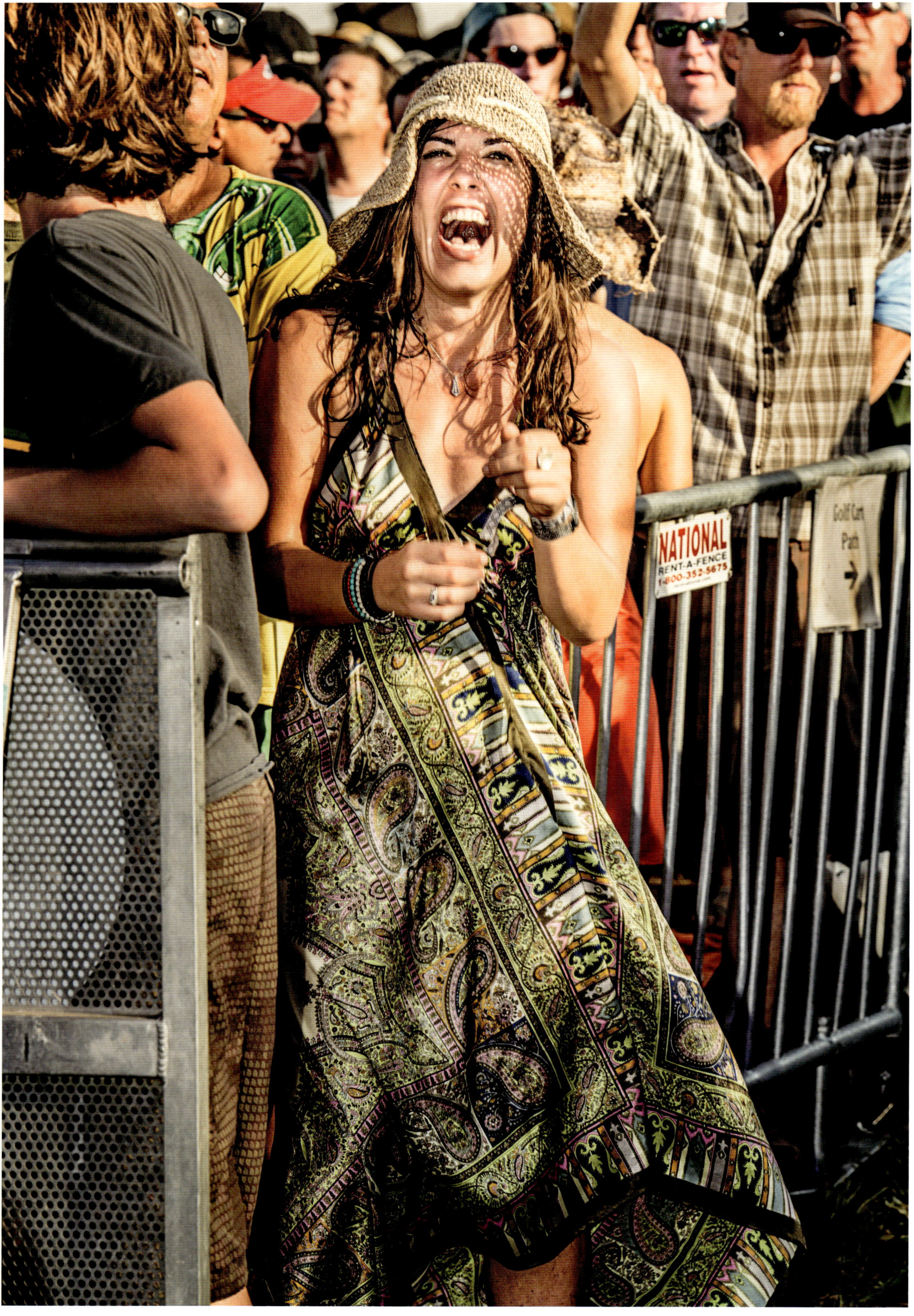
NATIONAL
RENT-A-FENCE
1-800-352-5675
Golf Cart
Path

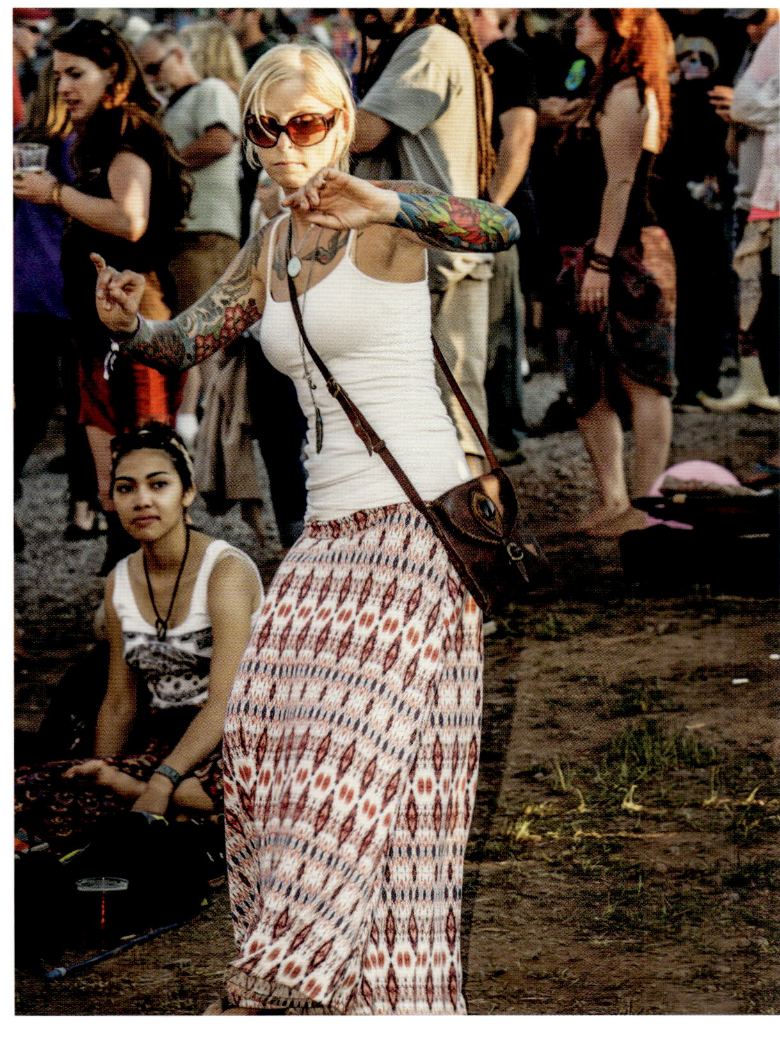
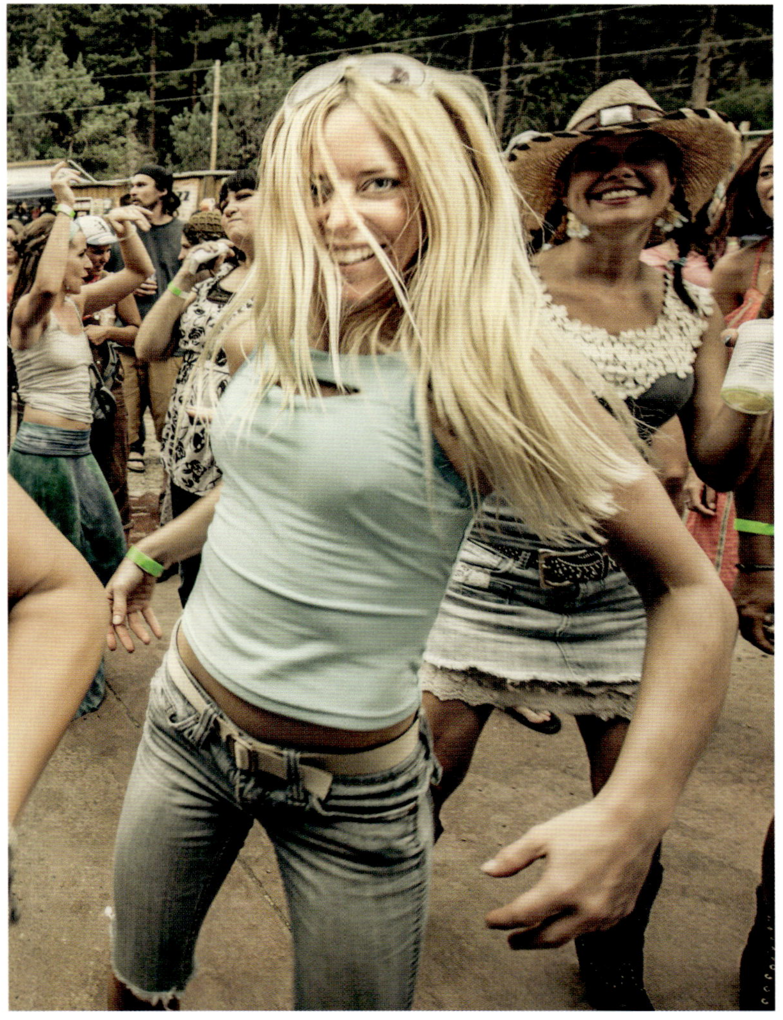
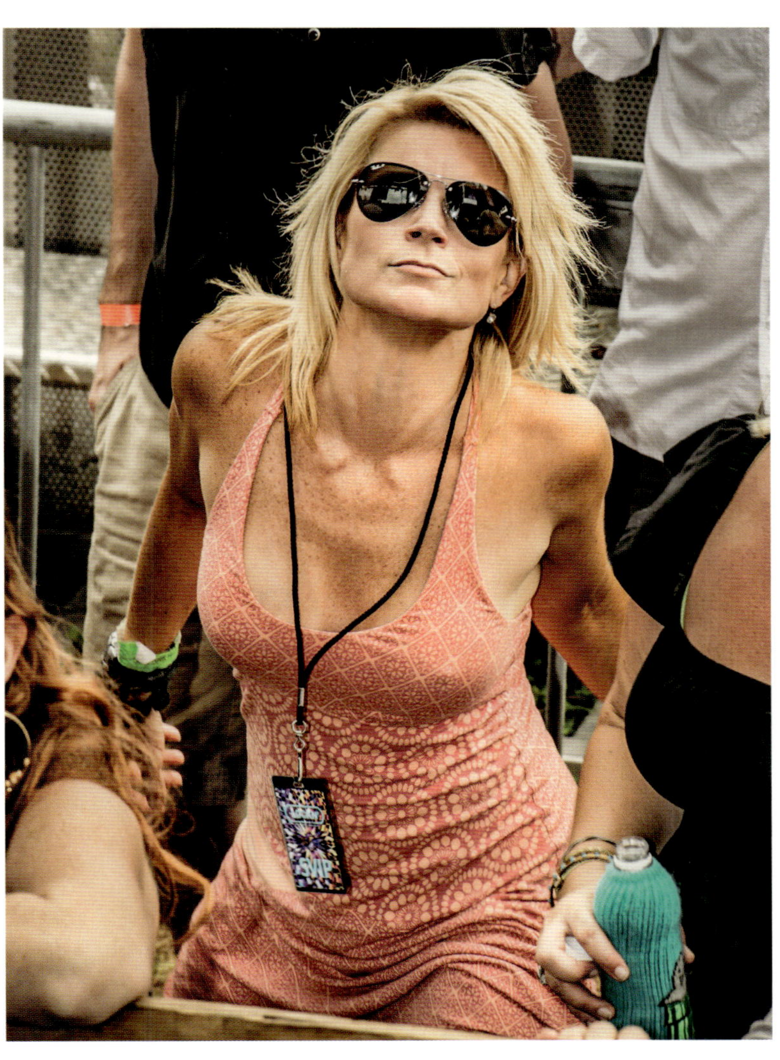
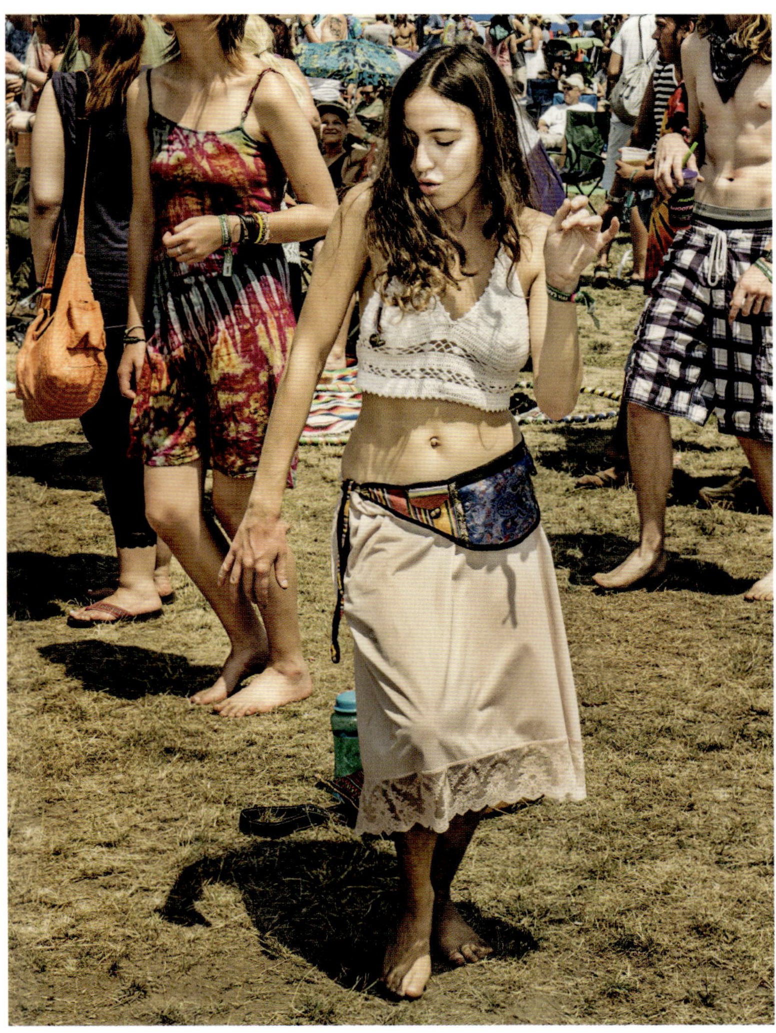

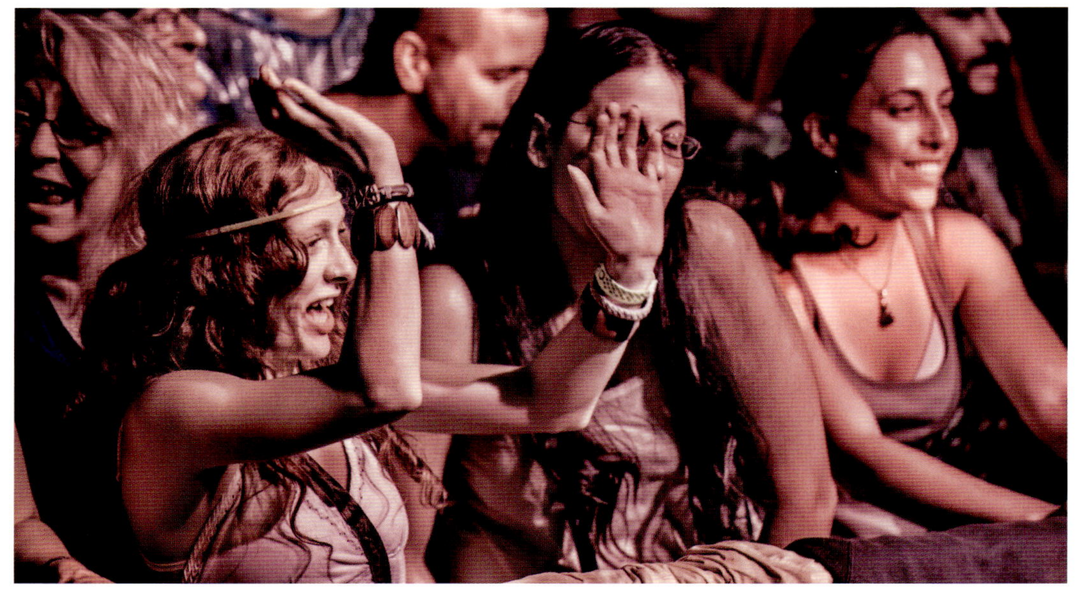
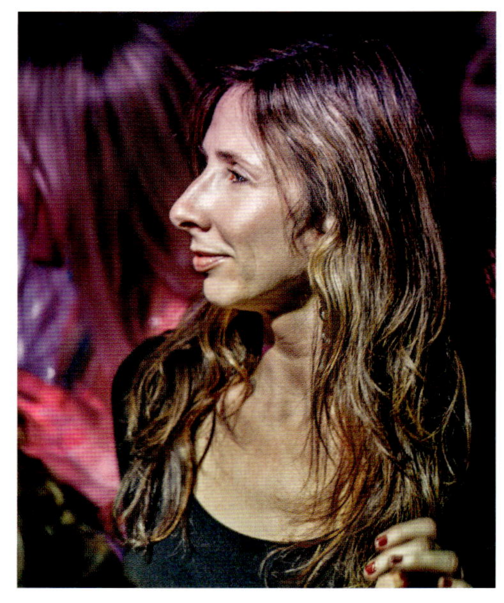
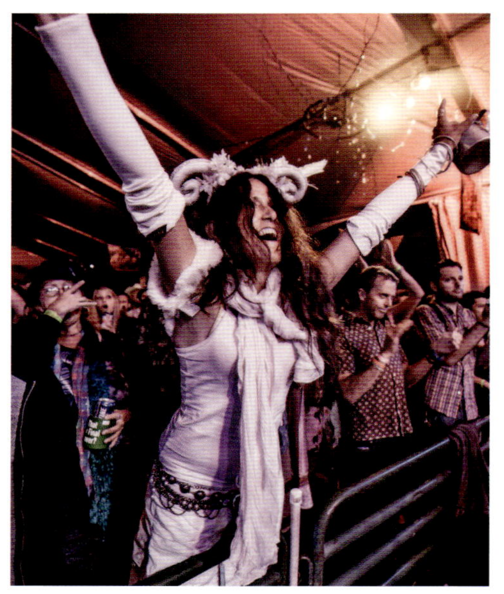
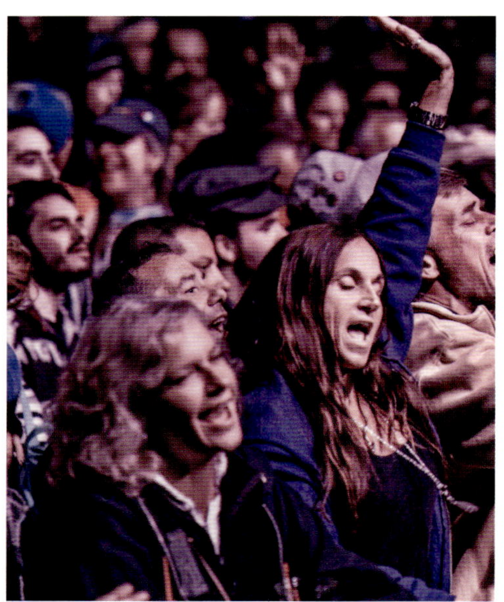
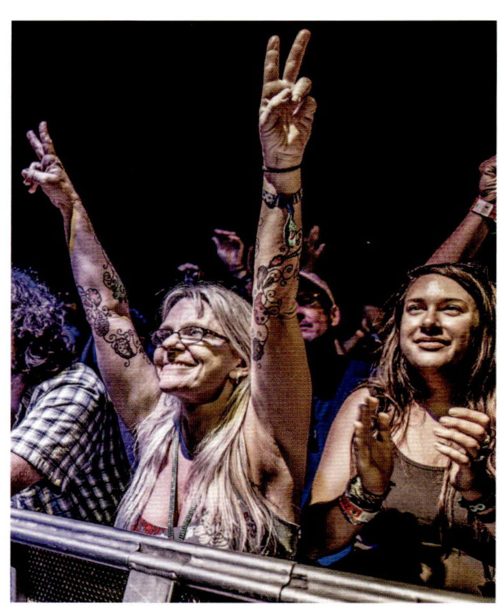
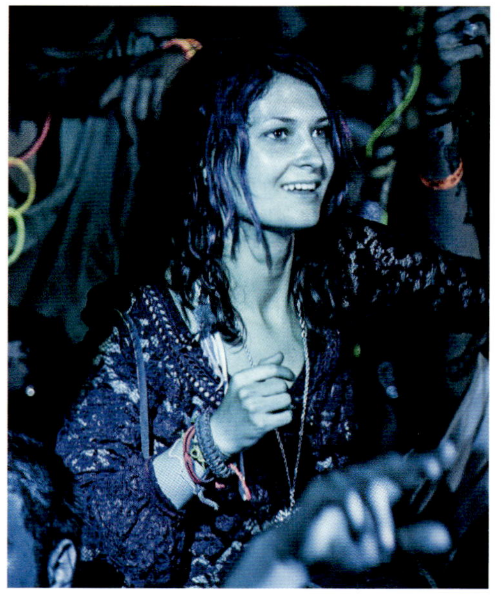
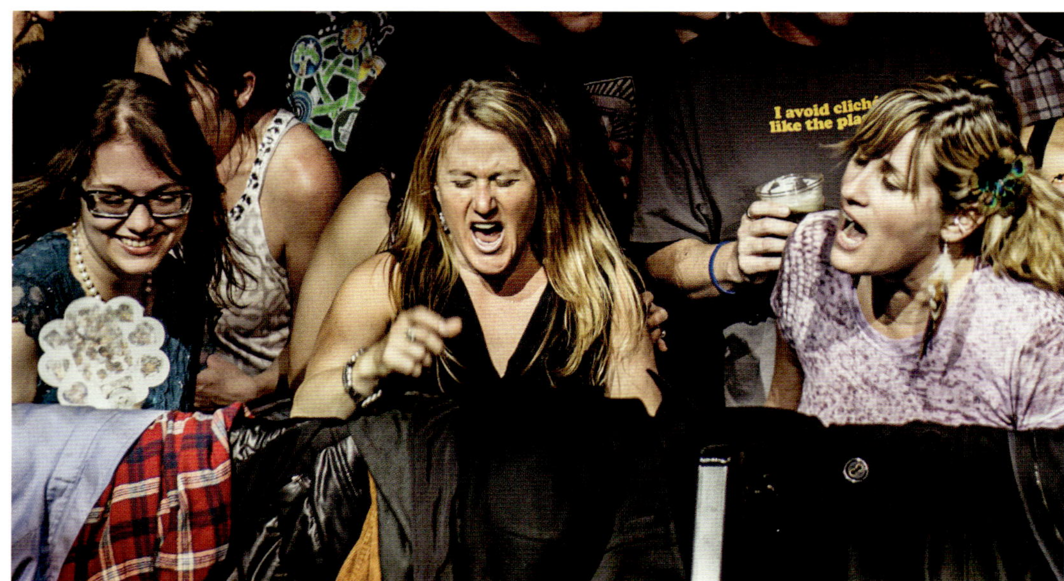
I avoid clich
like the pla

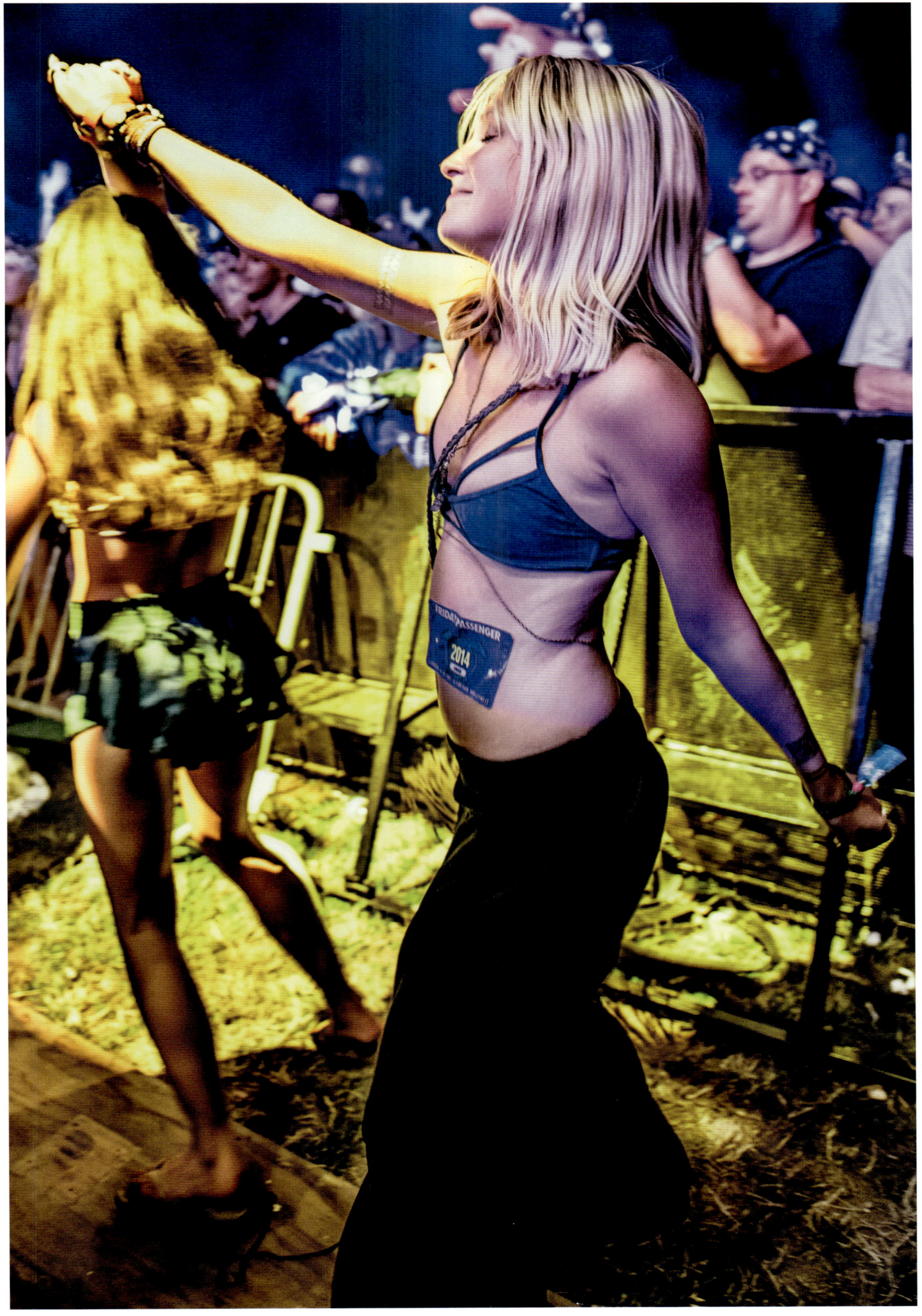
PASSENGER
2014

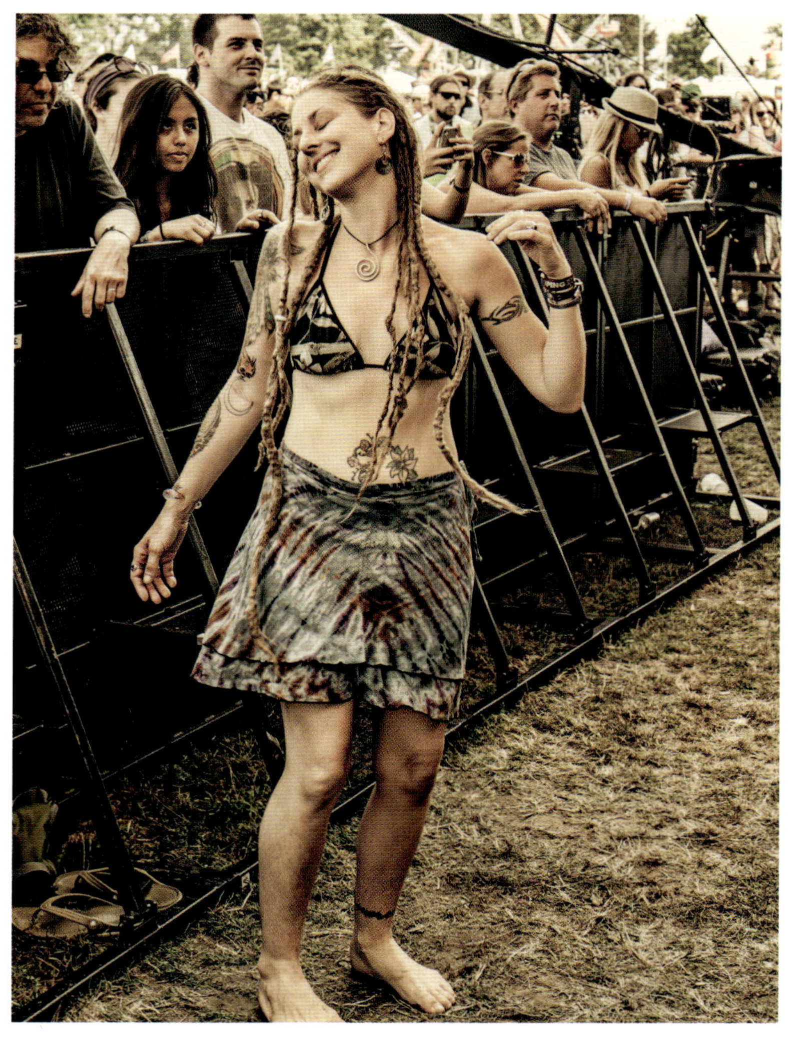
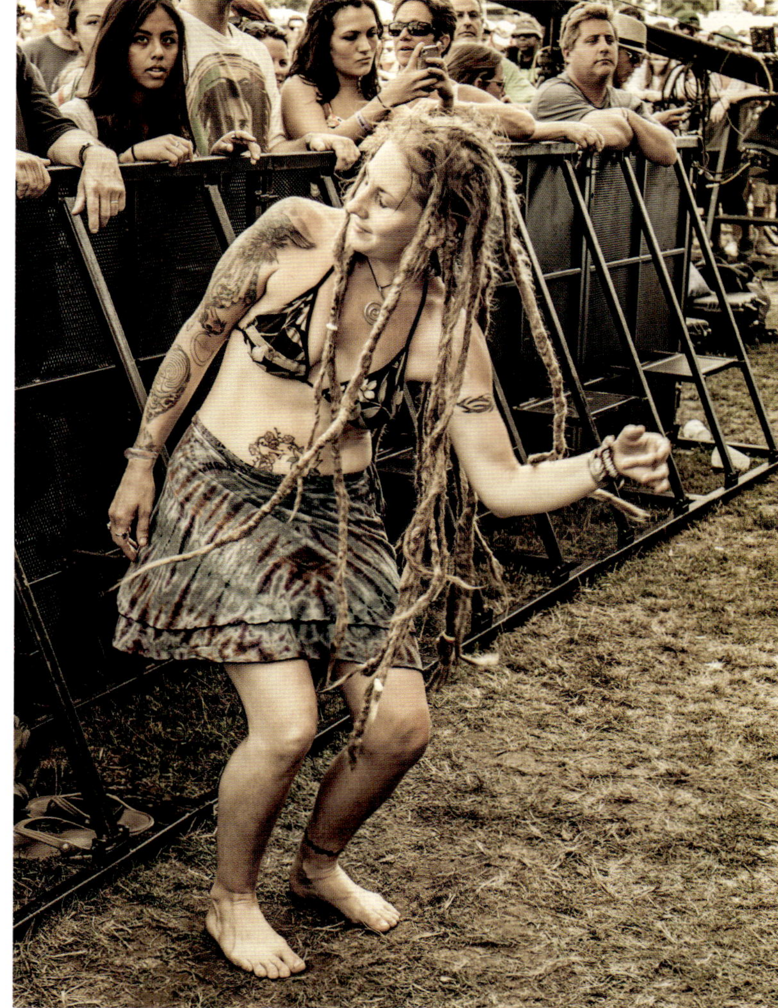
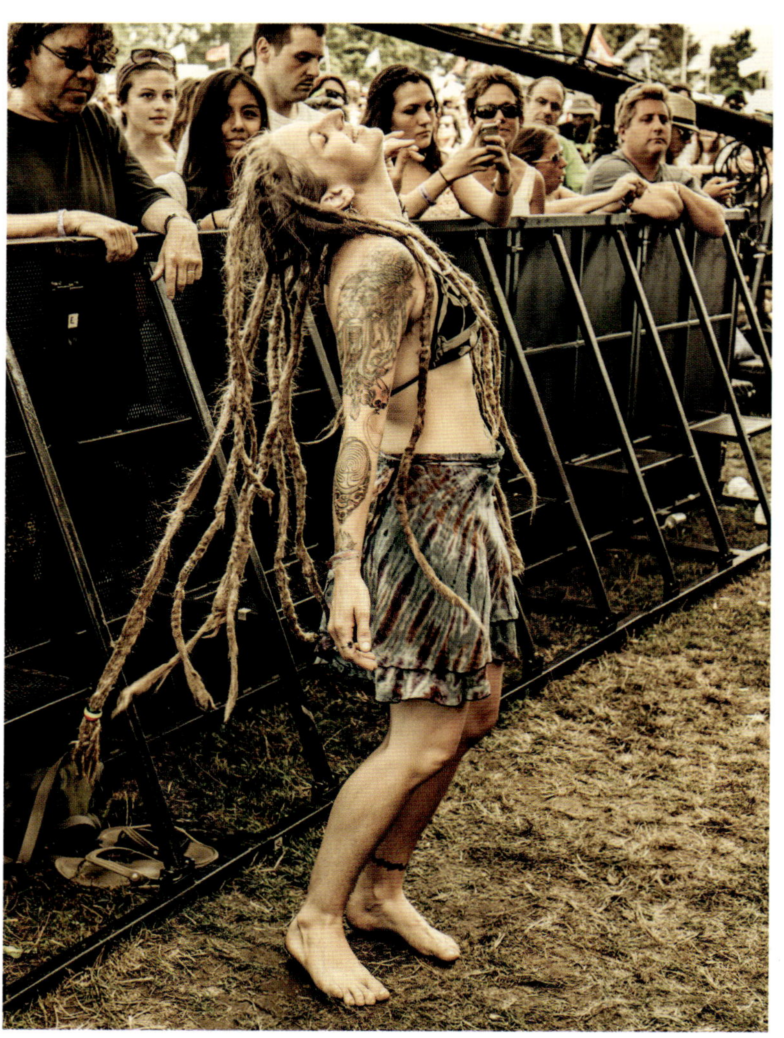
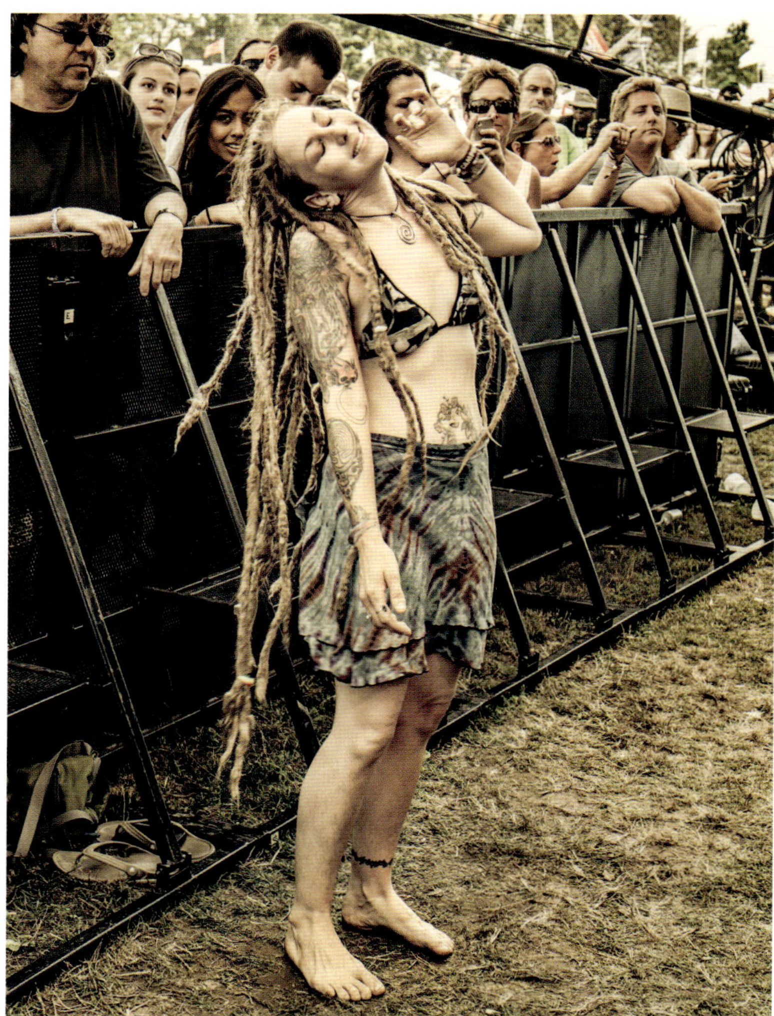

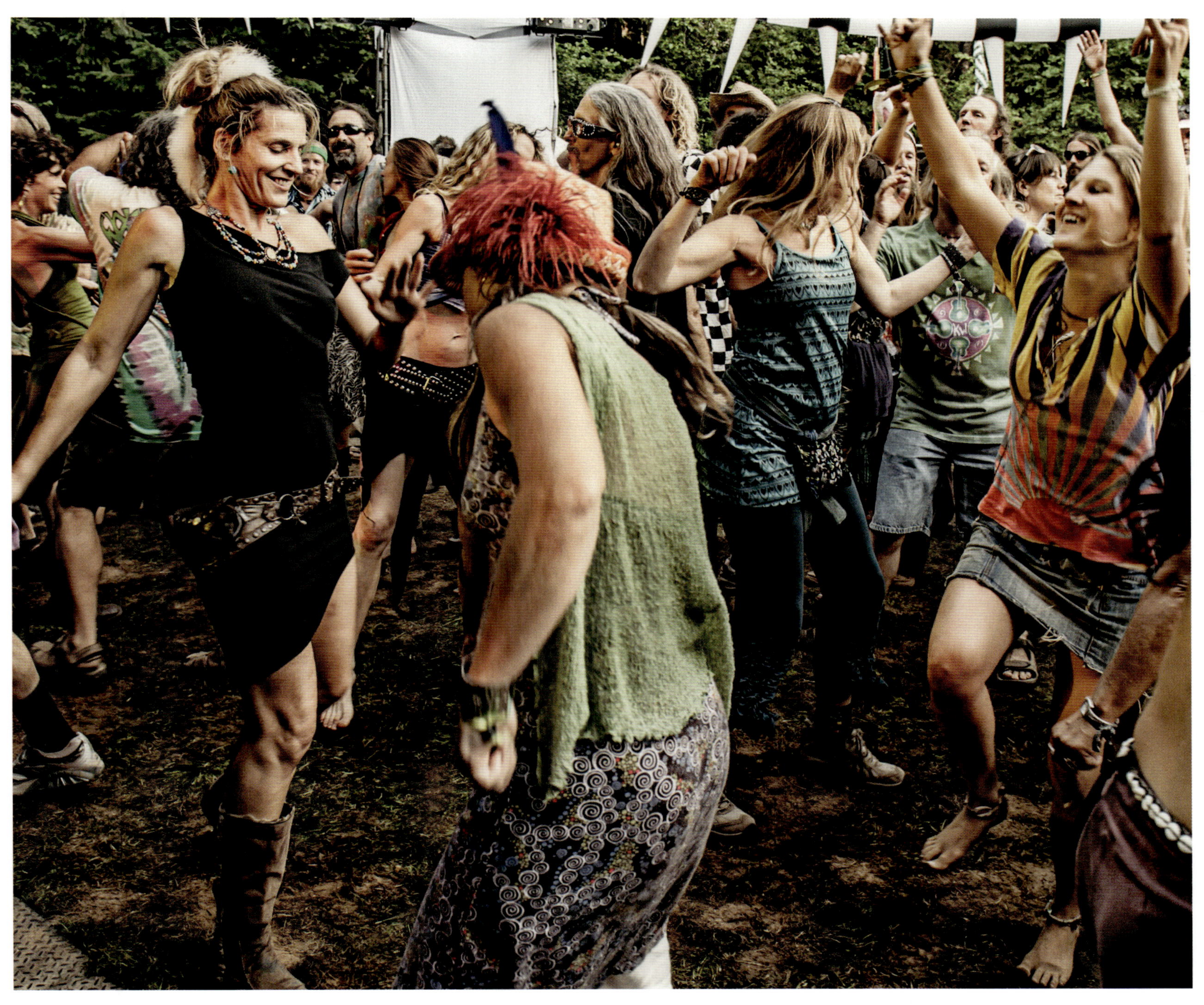

It's the full experience of what I like to call "vibing and tribing." This refers to finding and meeting your festie family, who knows you and loves you immediately, then keeping that tribe until the end of your magical weekend. Or if you're lucky, keeping them for a lifetime. Meredith T.

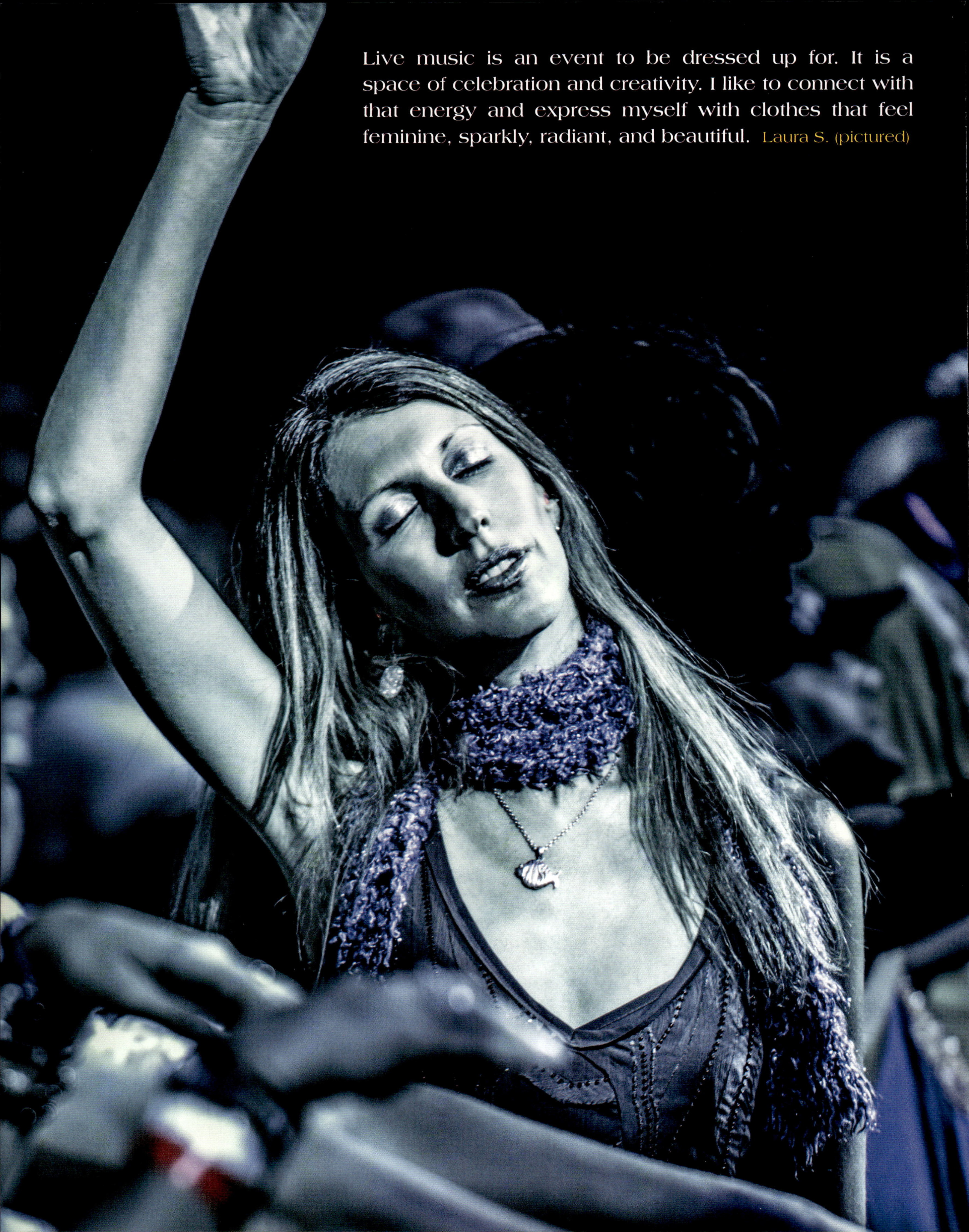

Live music is an event to be dressed up for. It is a space of celebration and creativity. I like to connect with that energy and express myself with clothes that feel feminine, sparkly, radiant, and beautiful. Laura S. (pictured)

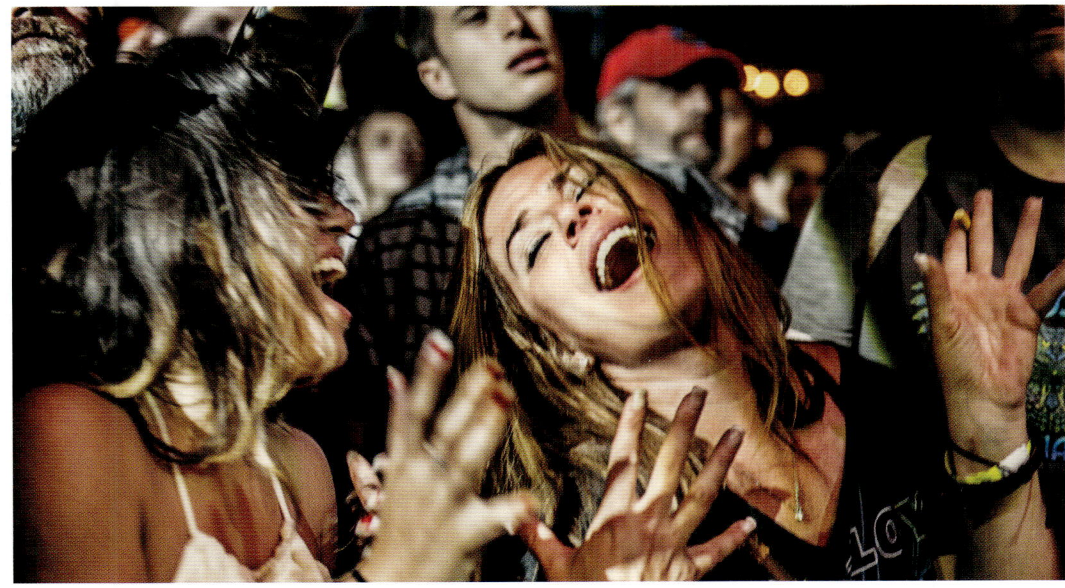
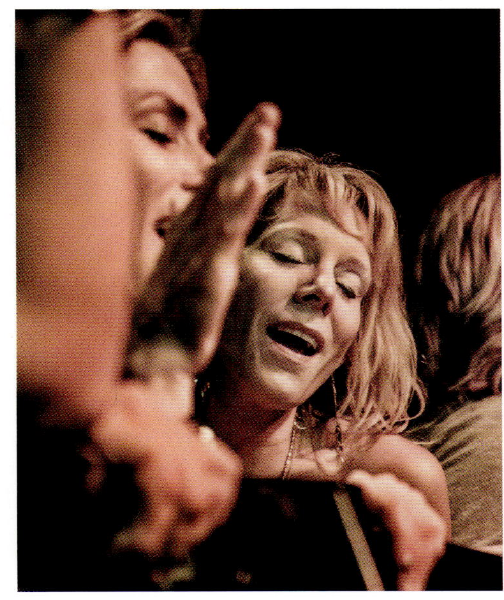
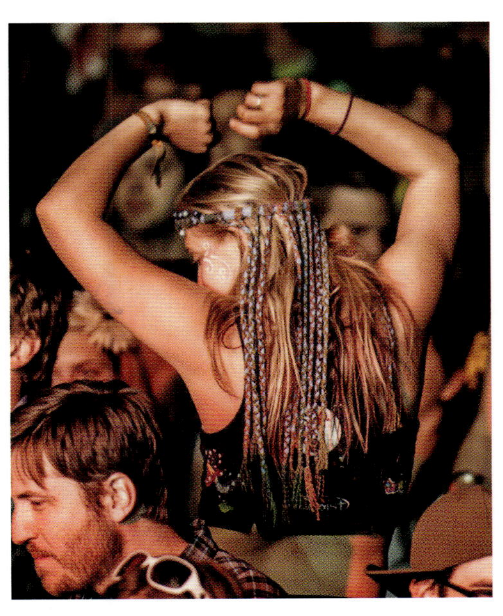
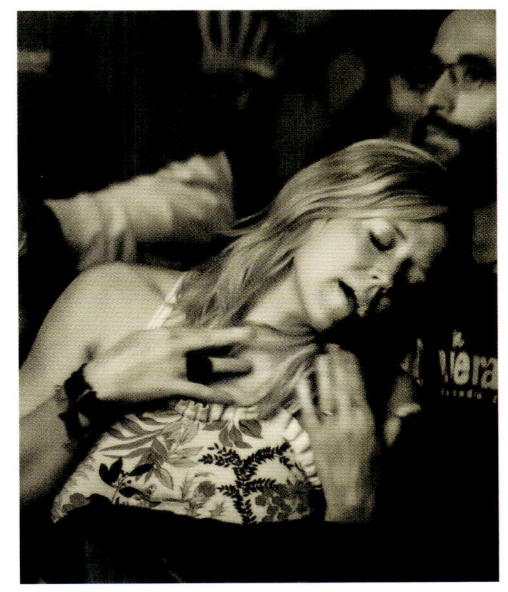
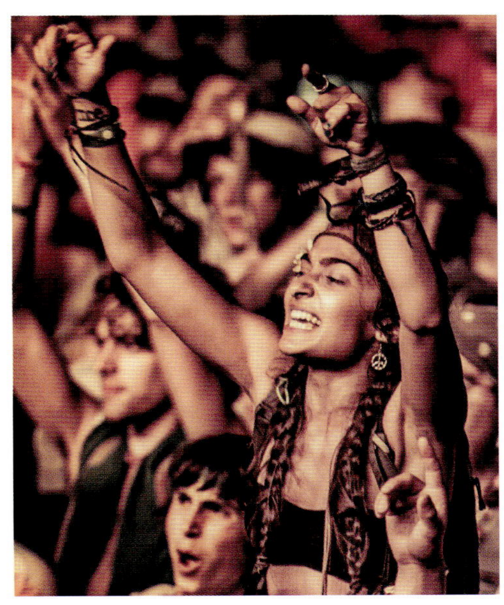
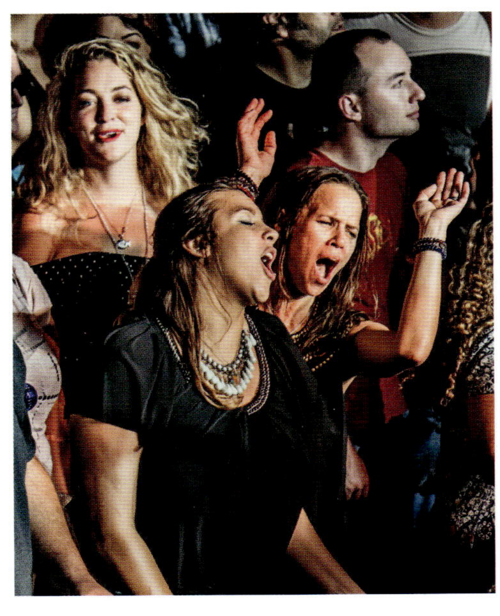
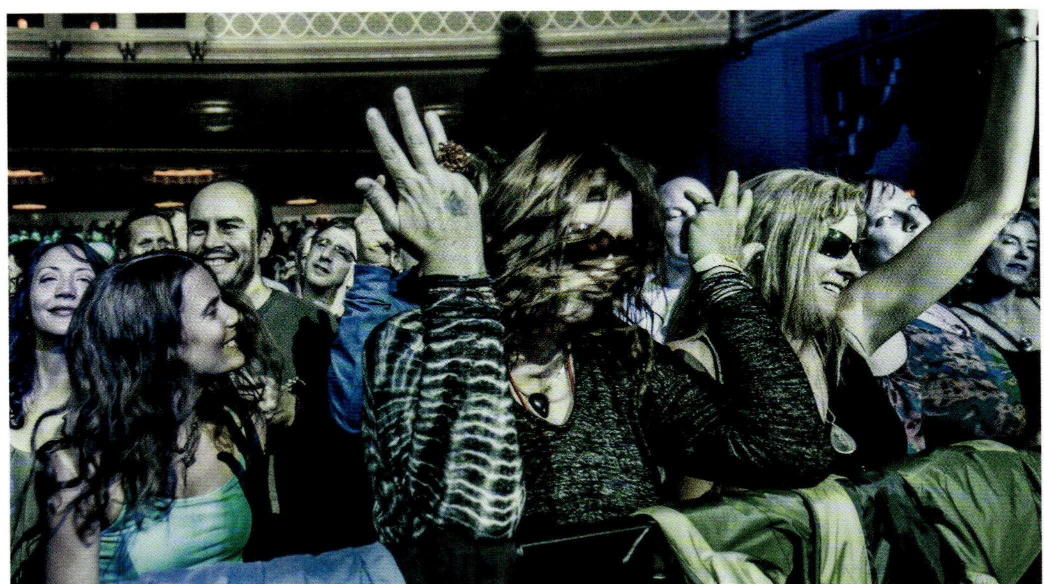

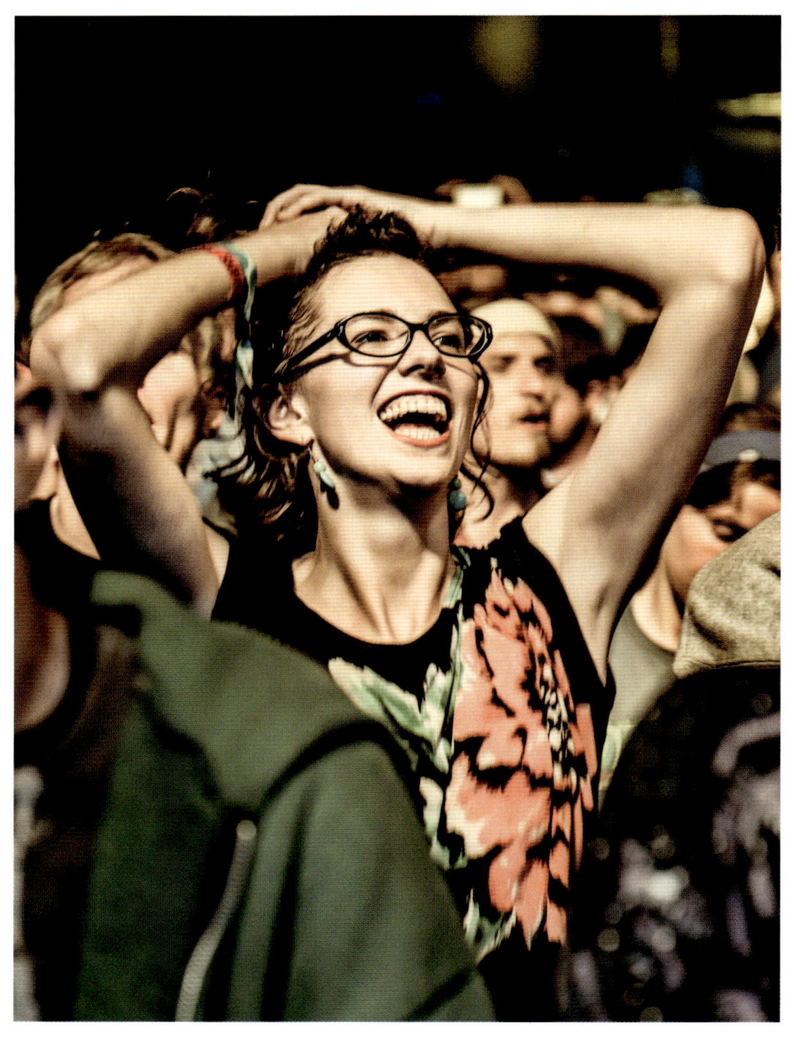
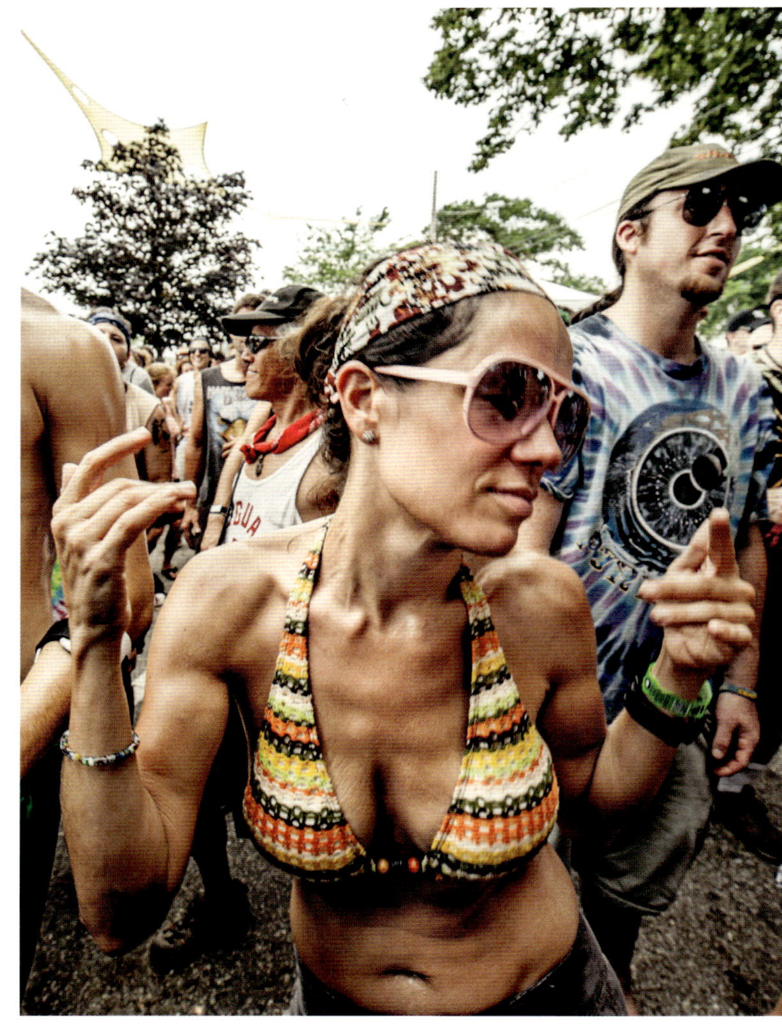
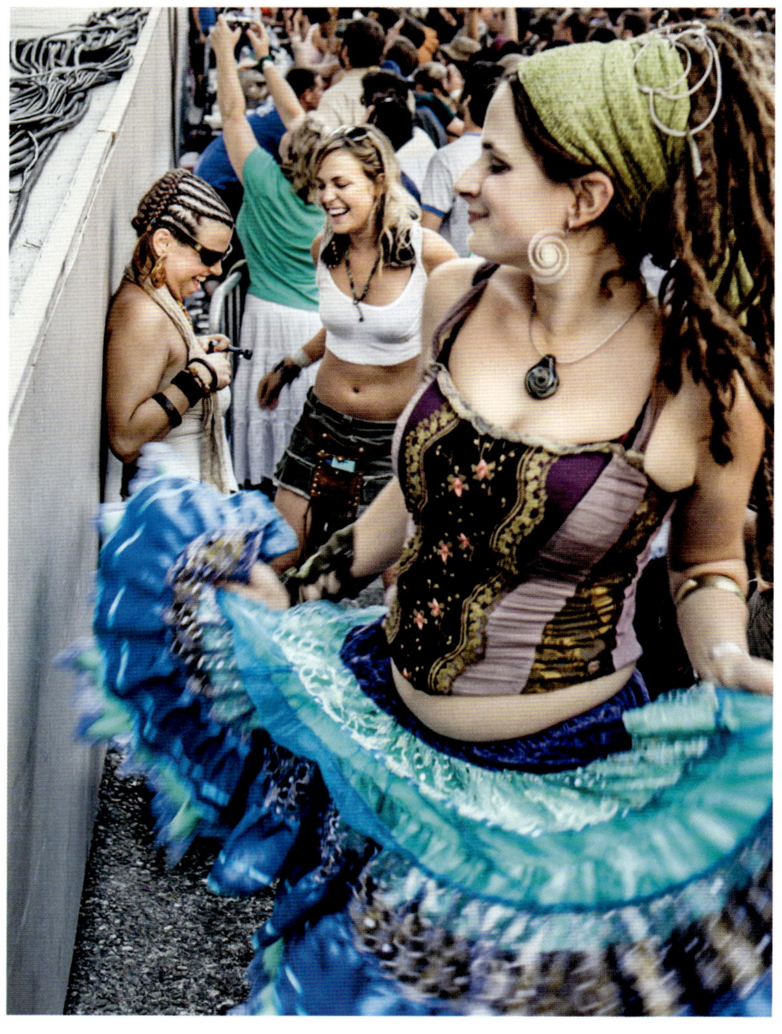
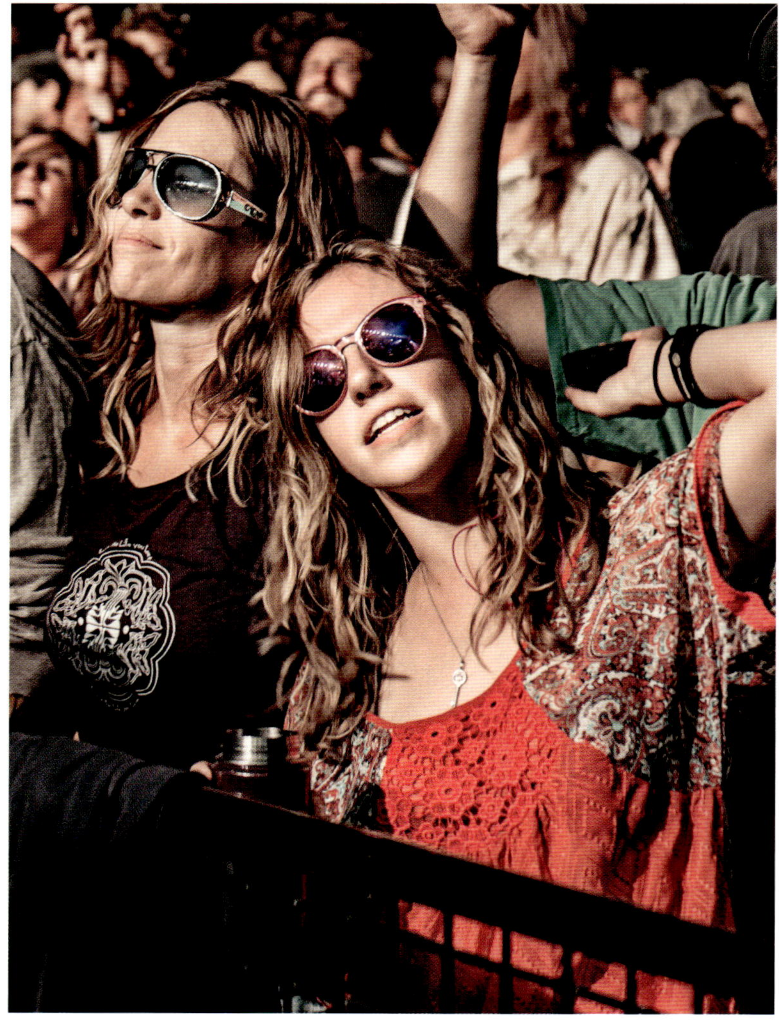

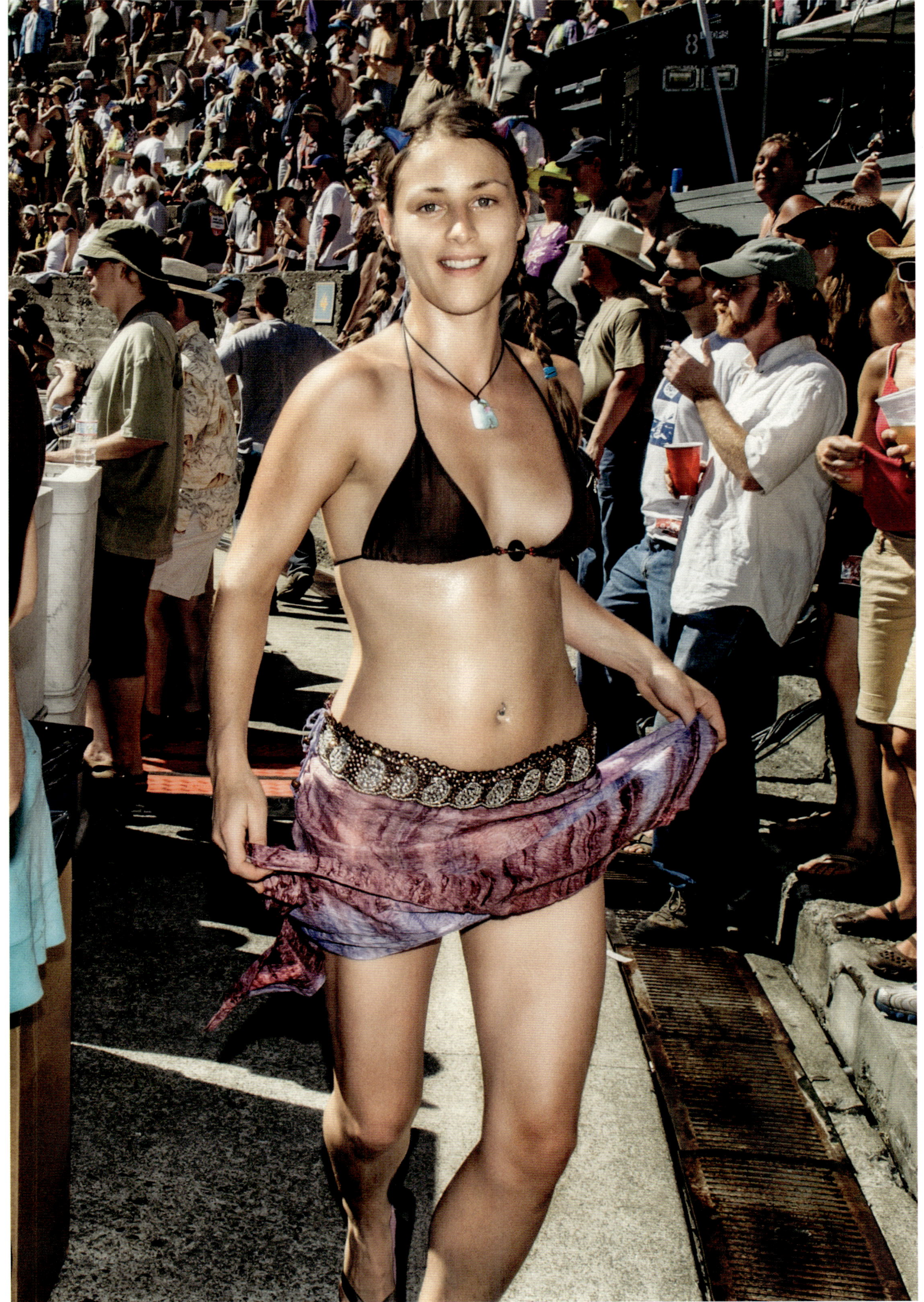

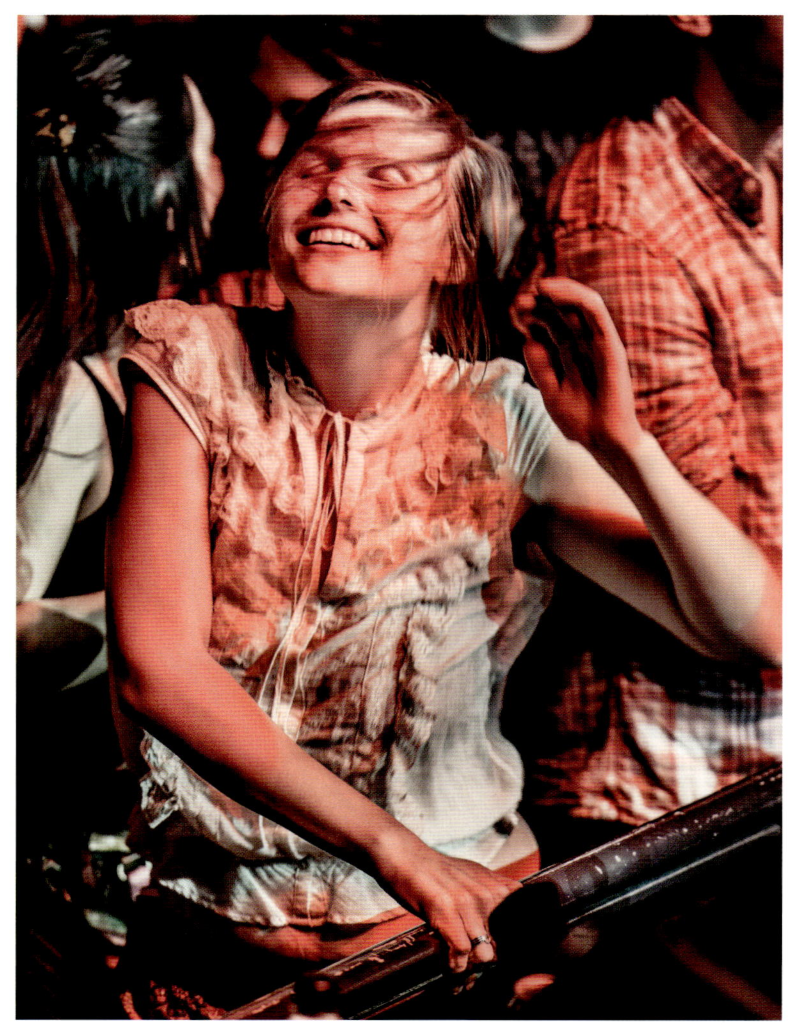

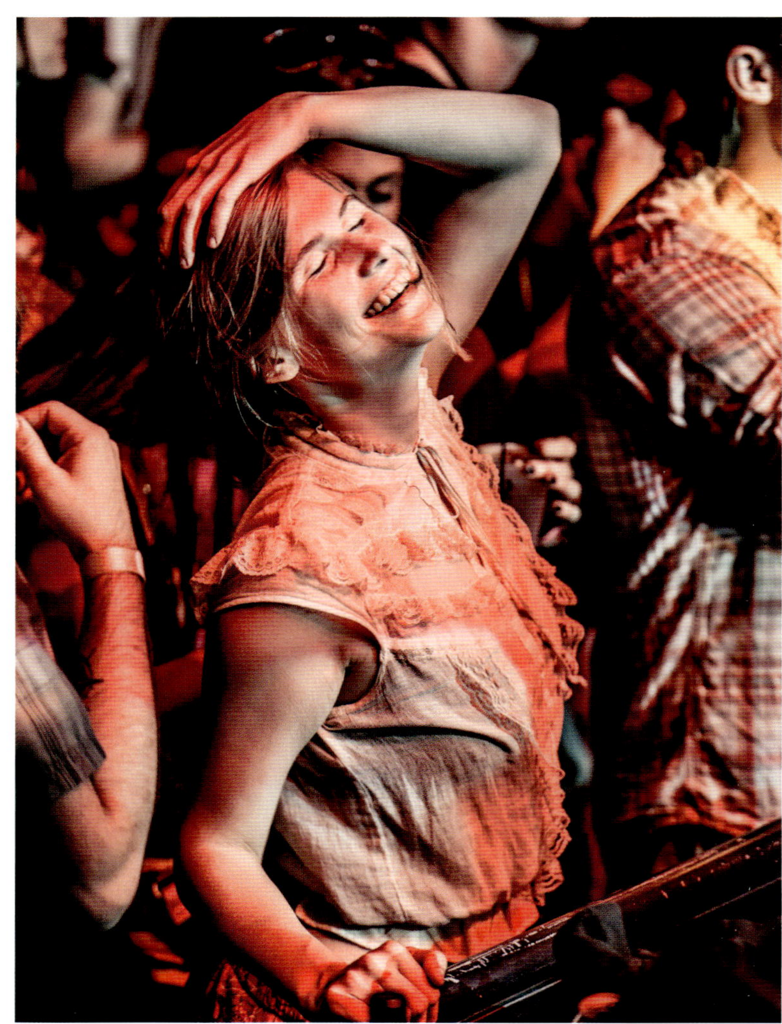

Dancing is like plugging in to who I really am. I'm bigger and brighter while the music plays and it feels incredible. Monica E.

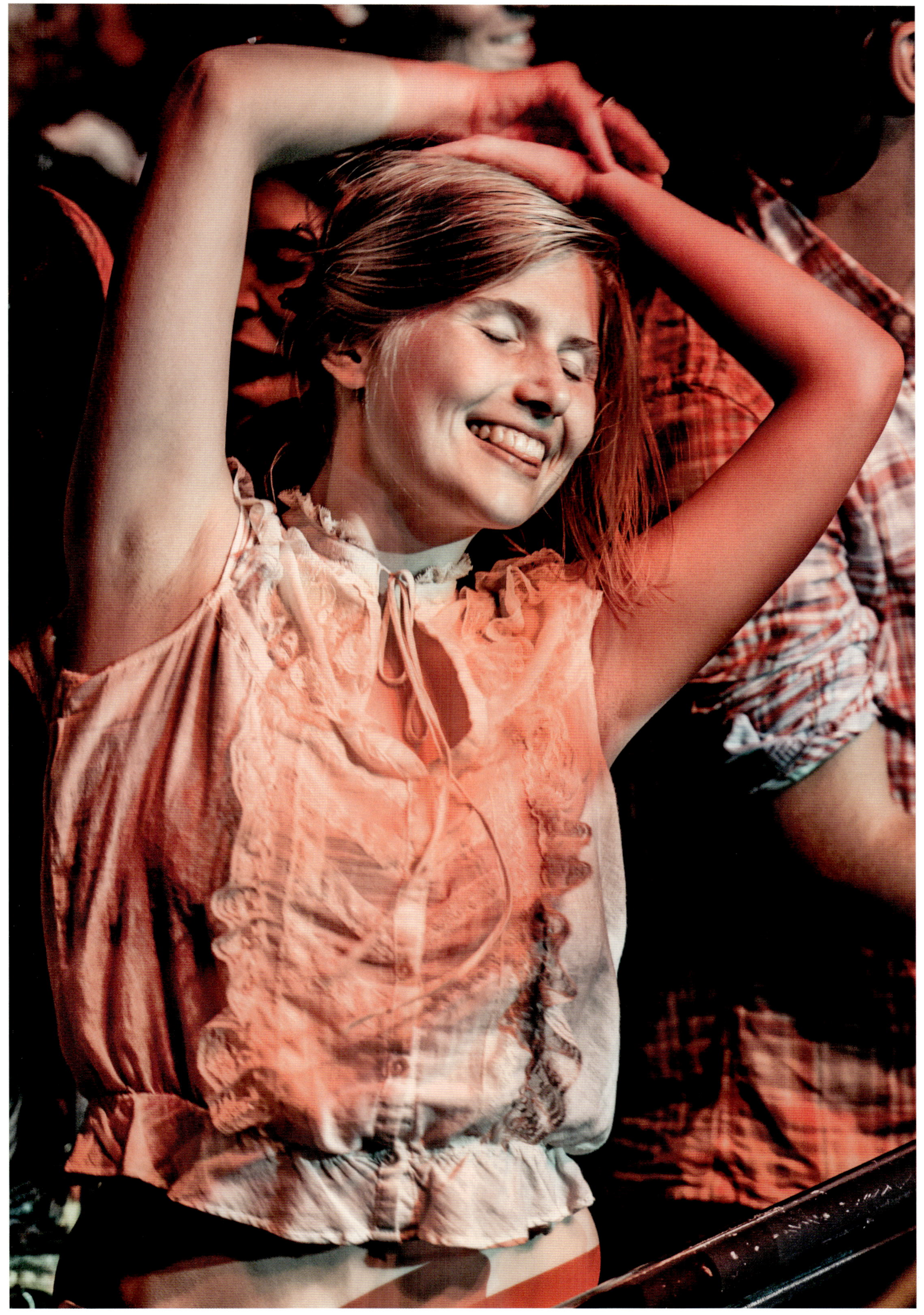

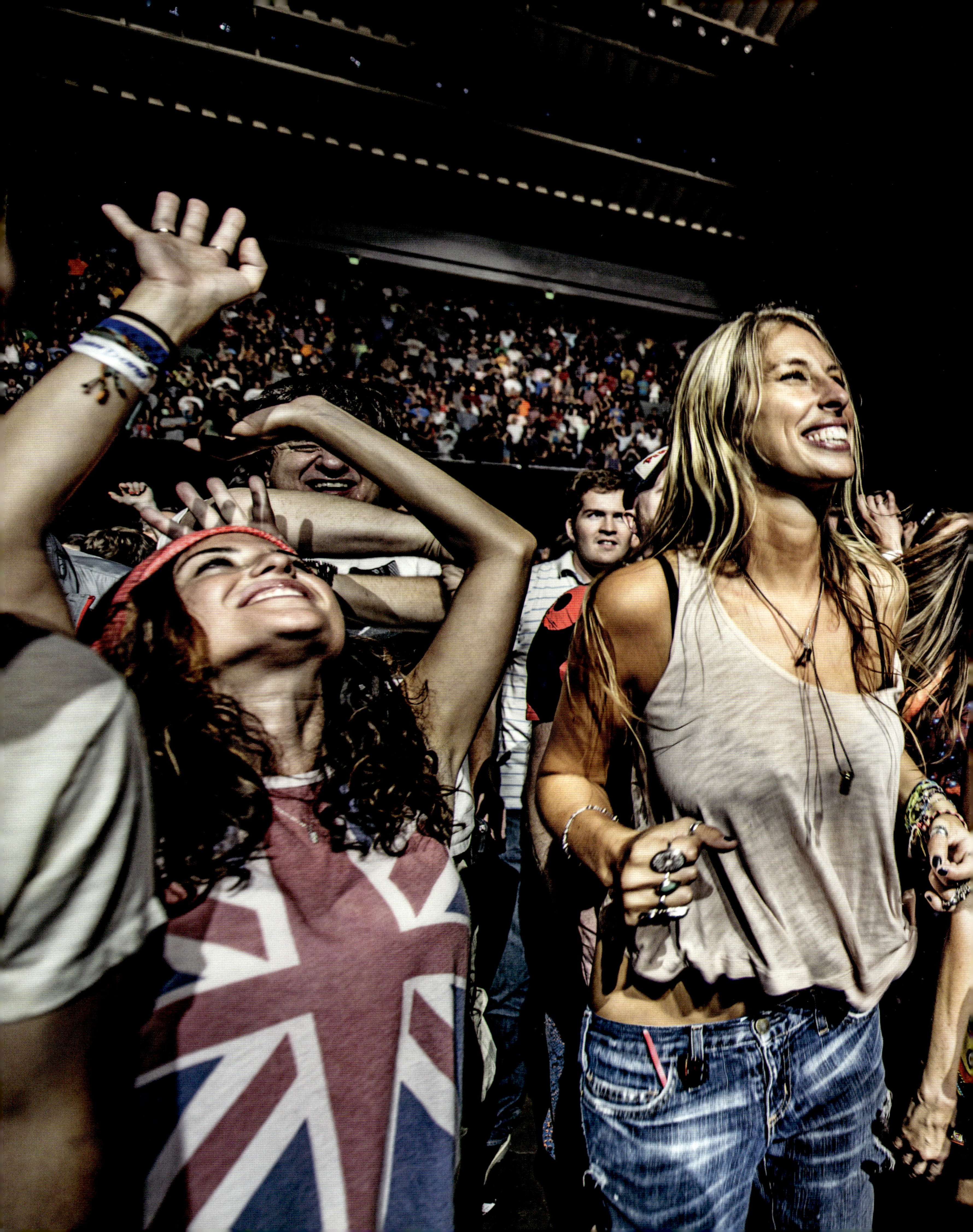

Live music for me has always been a bit of an escape, while also a homecoming. When I was younger, being on the road with nothing but the next show in sight was the epitome of freedom. It still represents that in a lot of ways. Paige C. (pictured, front right)

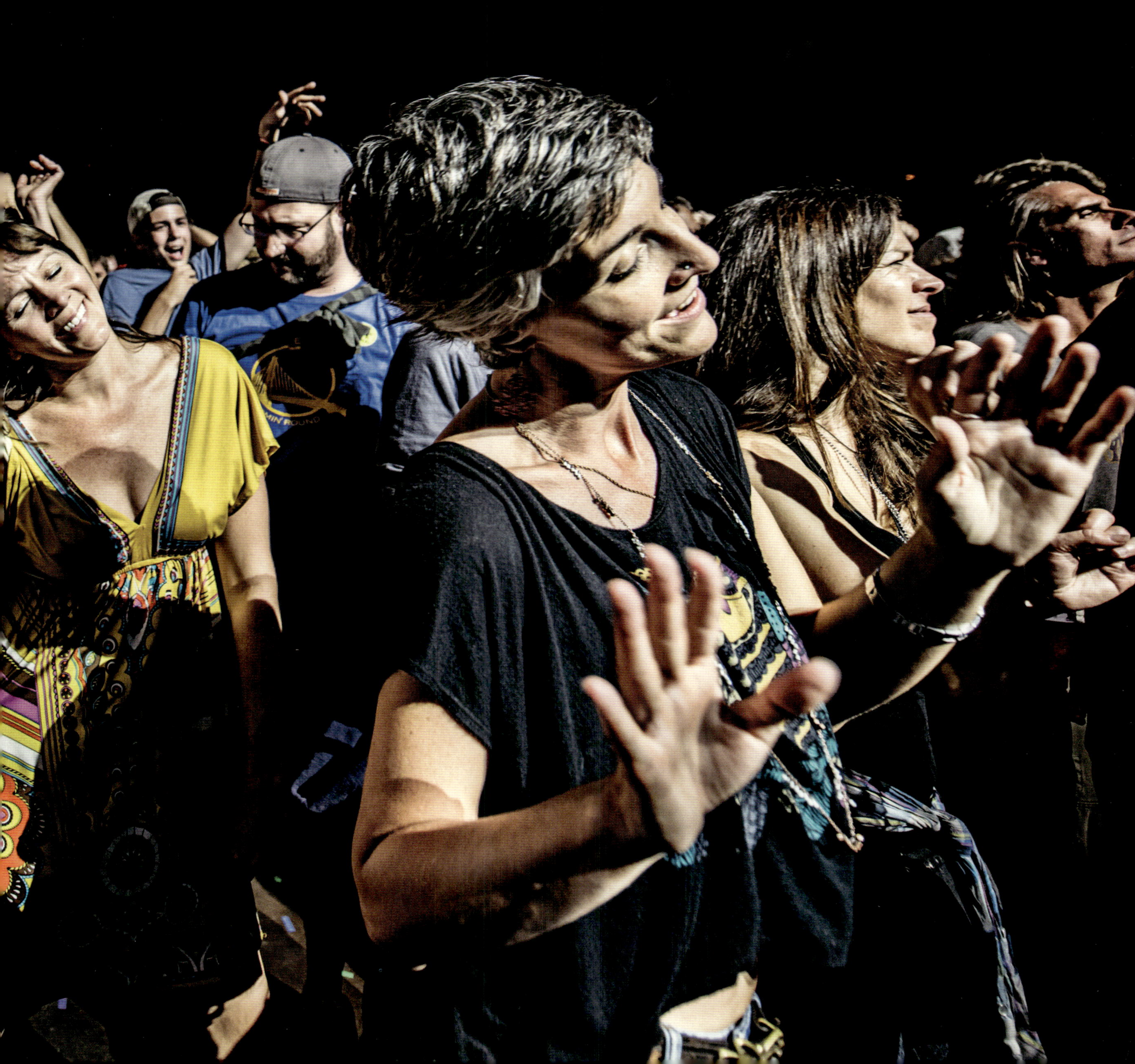

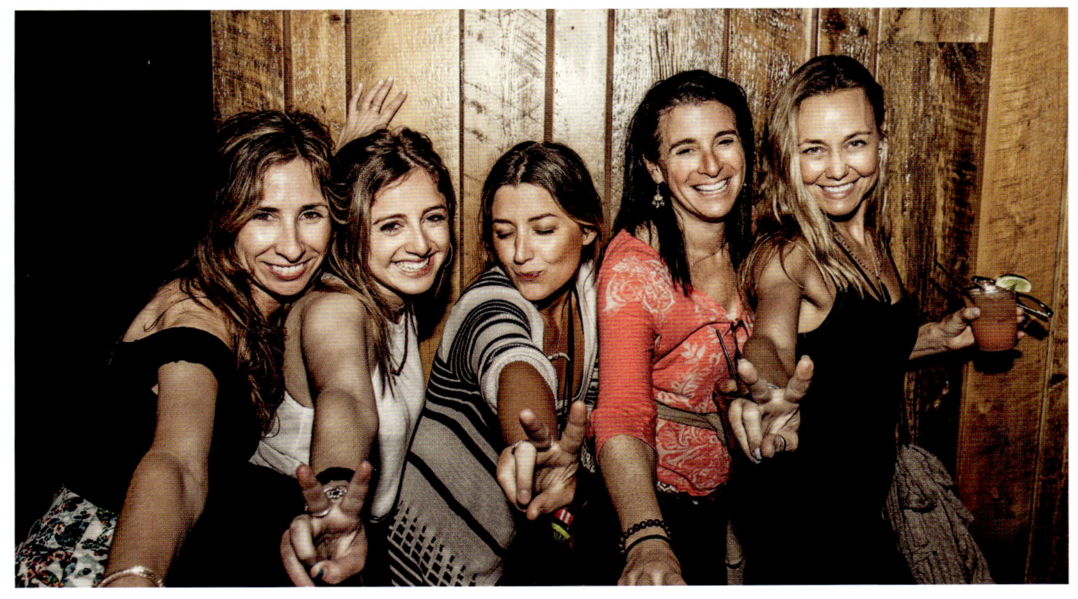

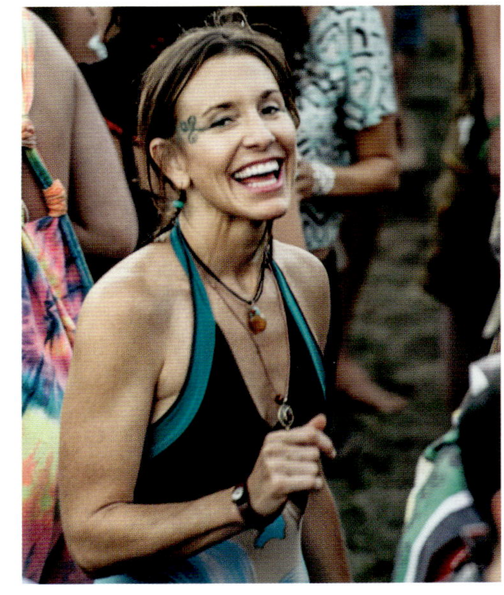

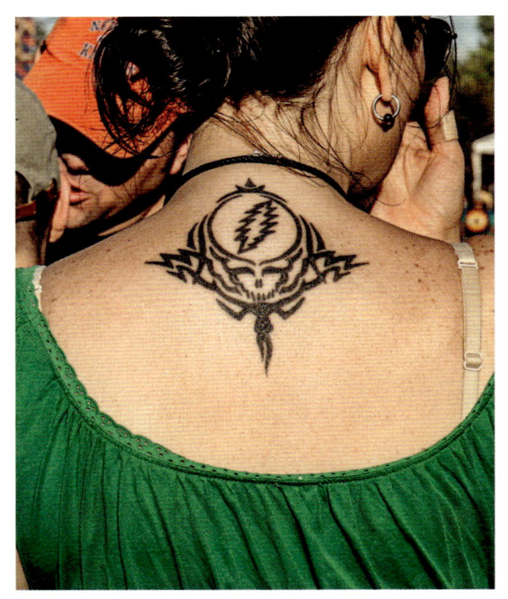

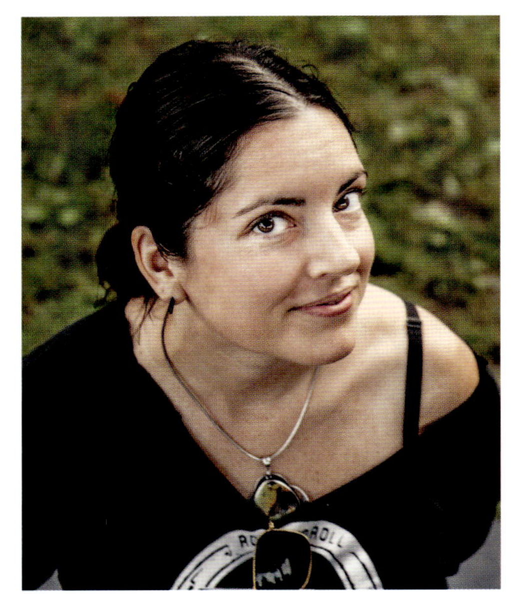

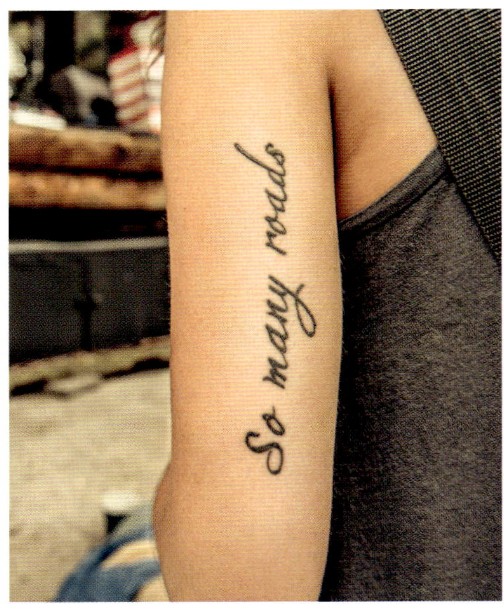
So many roads

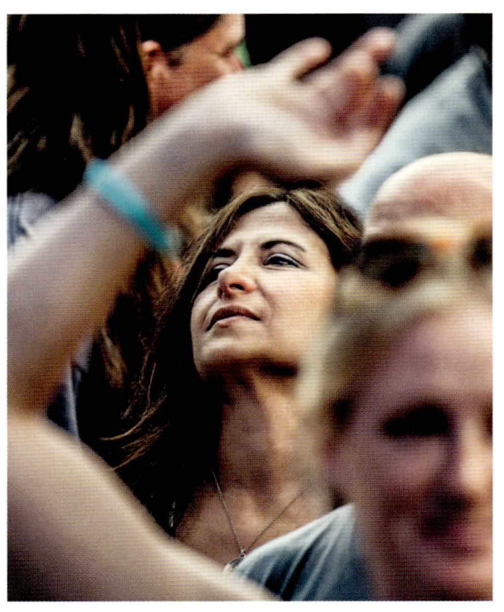

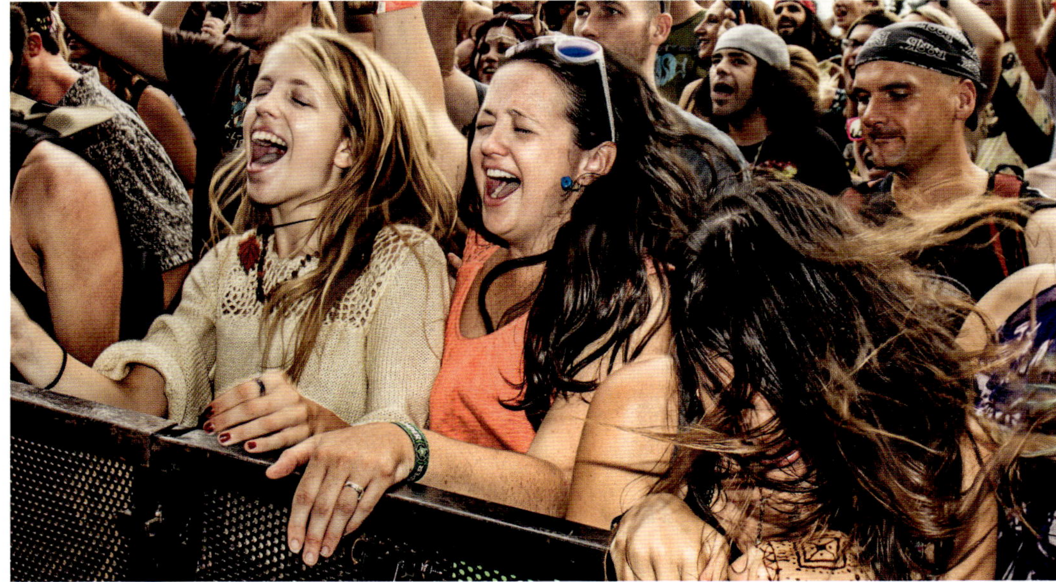

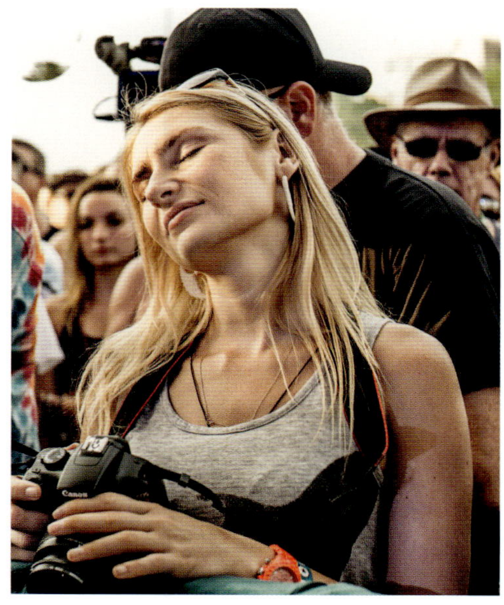

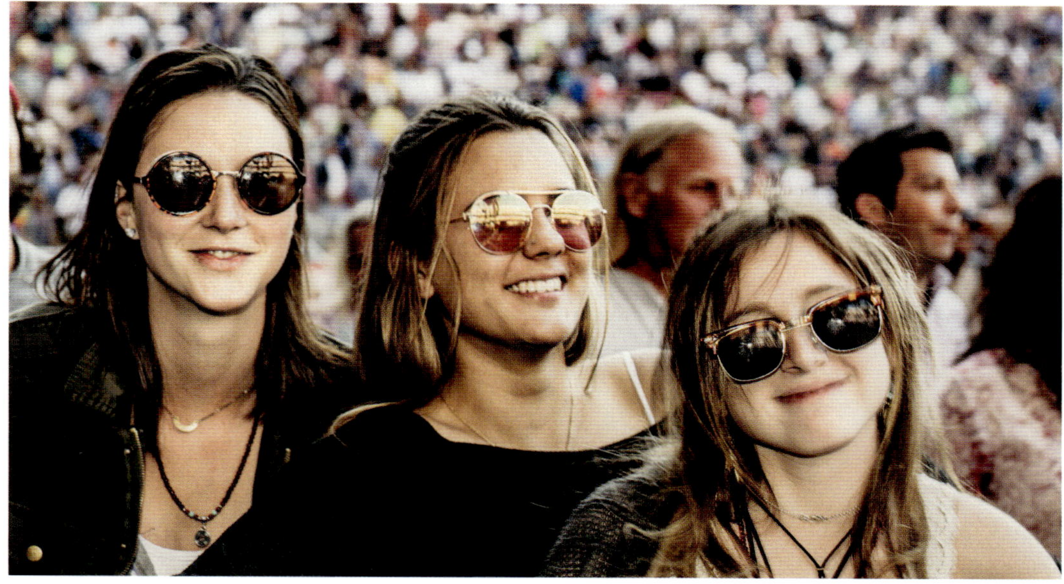

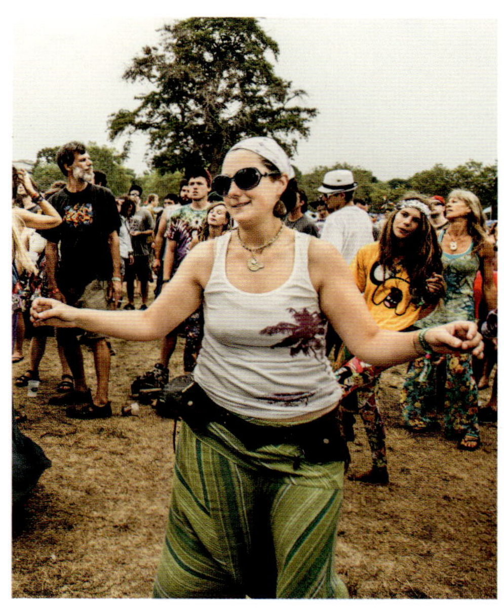

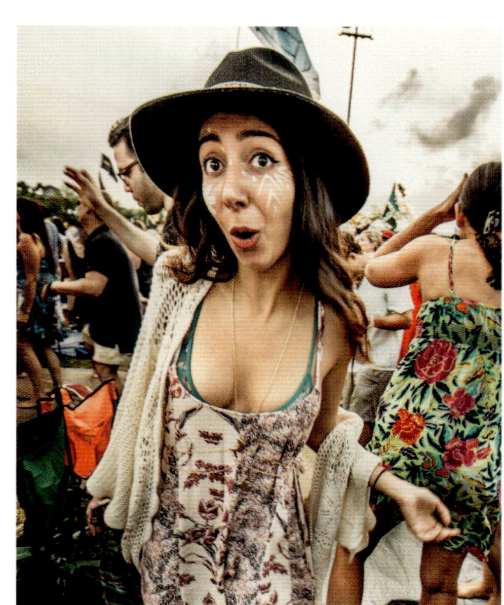

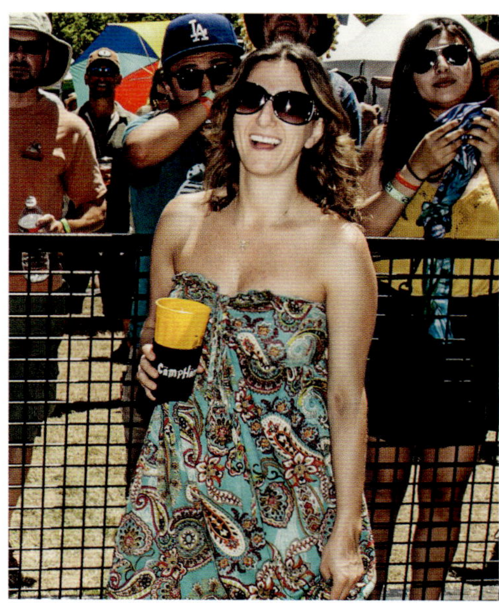

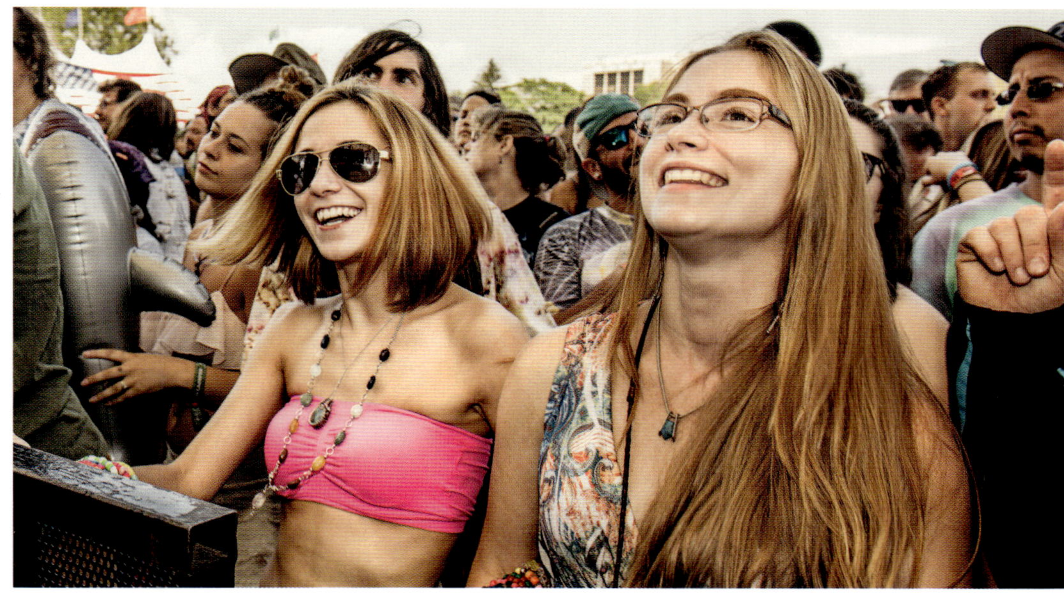

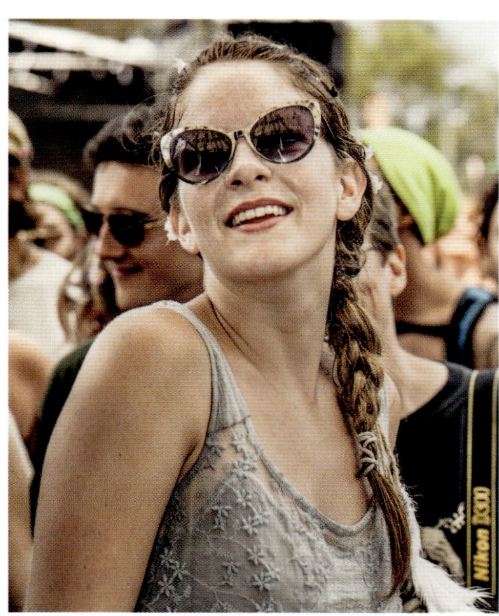
Nikon

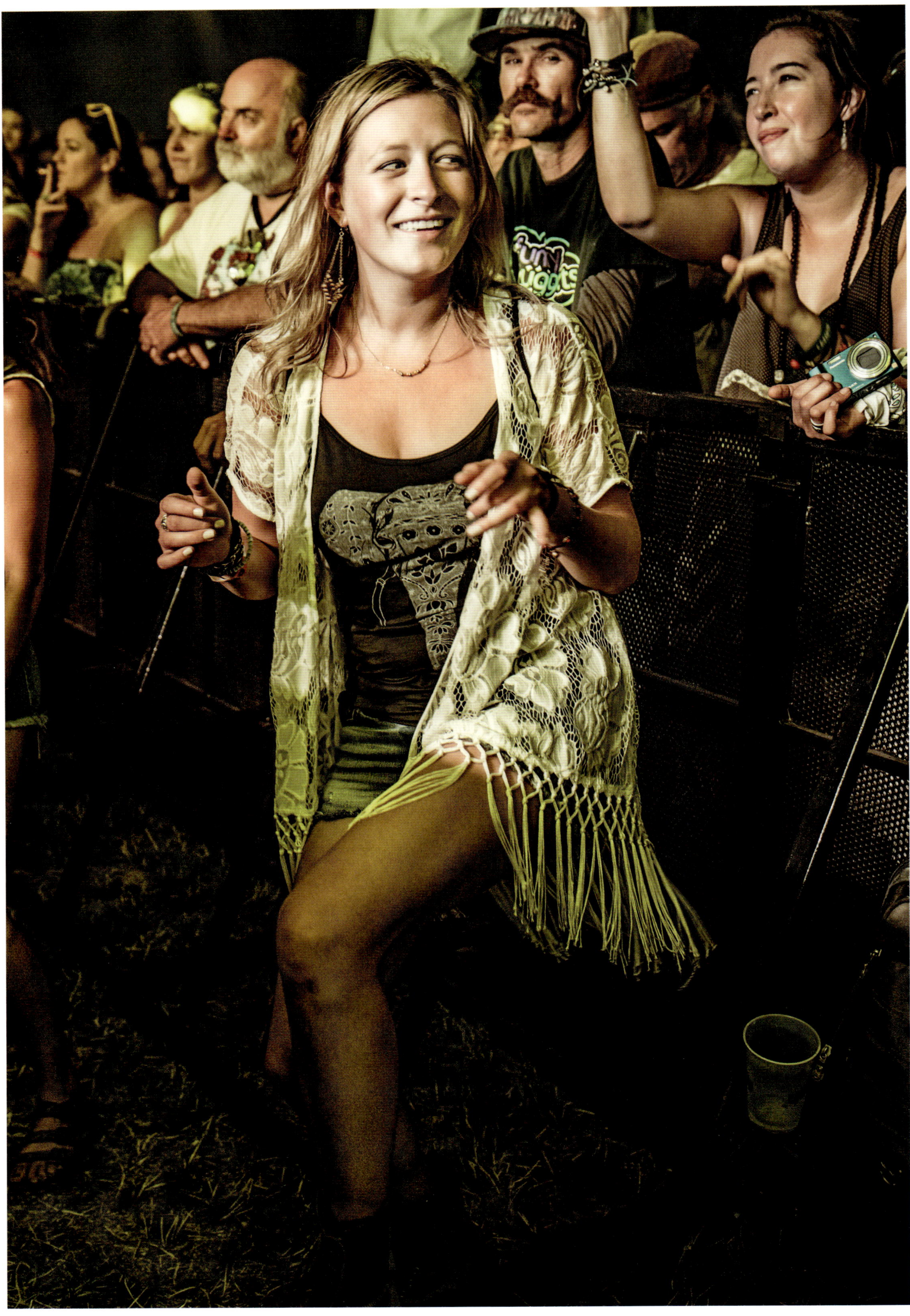

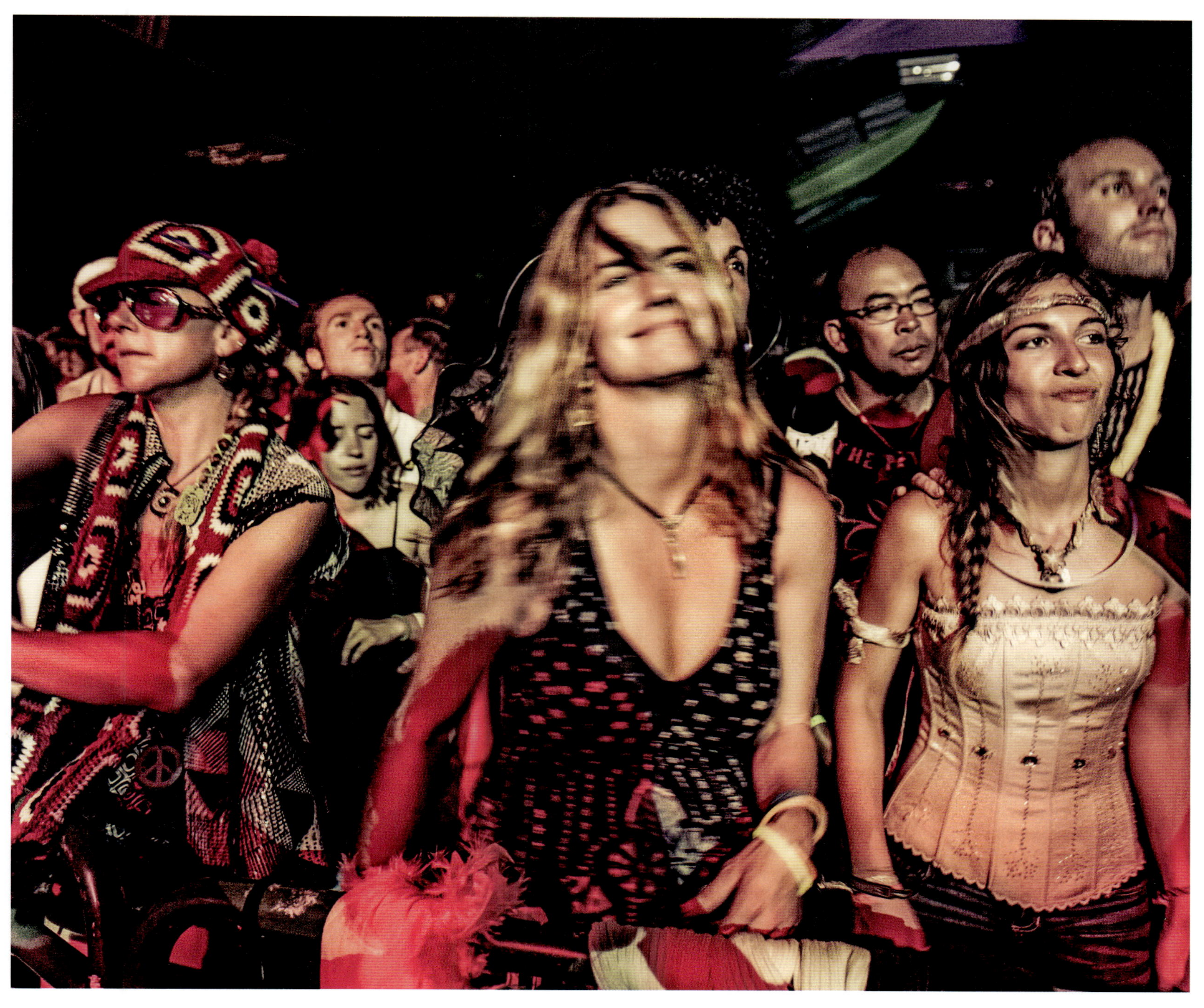

The rail is for the regulars who understand the purpose of a live show. They're there for healing and connectivity. That is their time with their band, face to face, and the crowd melts away. Lindsey H.

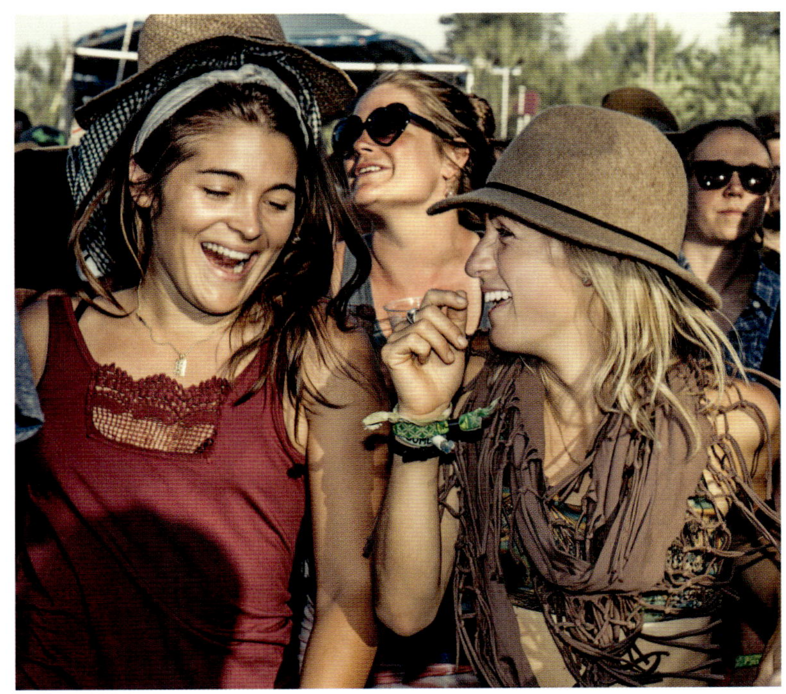

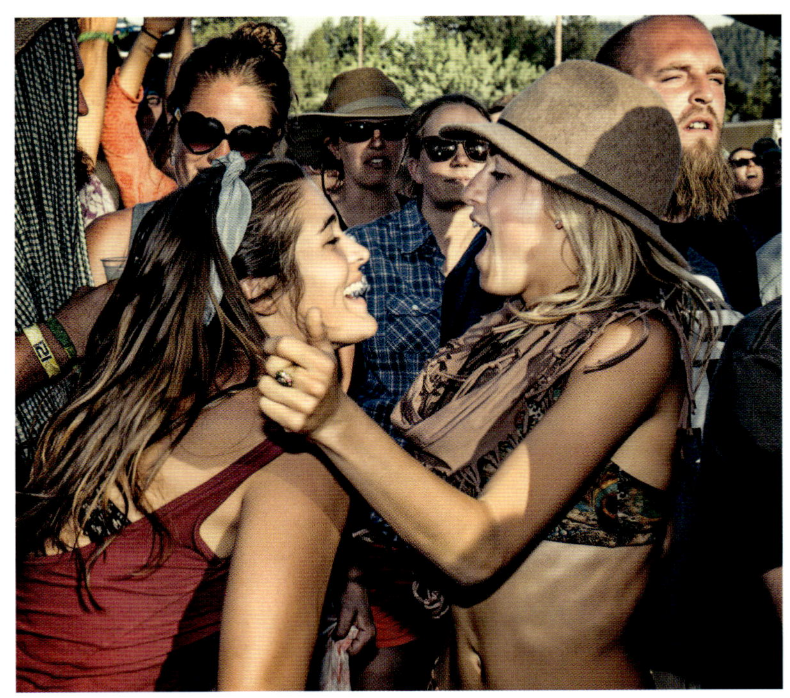

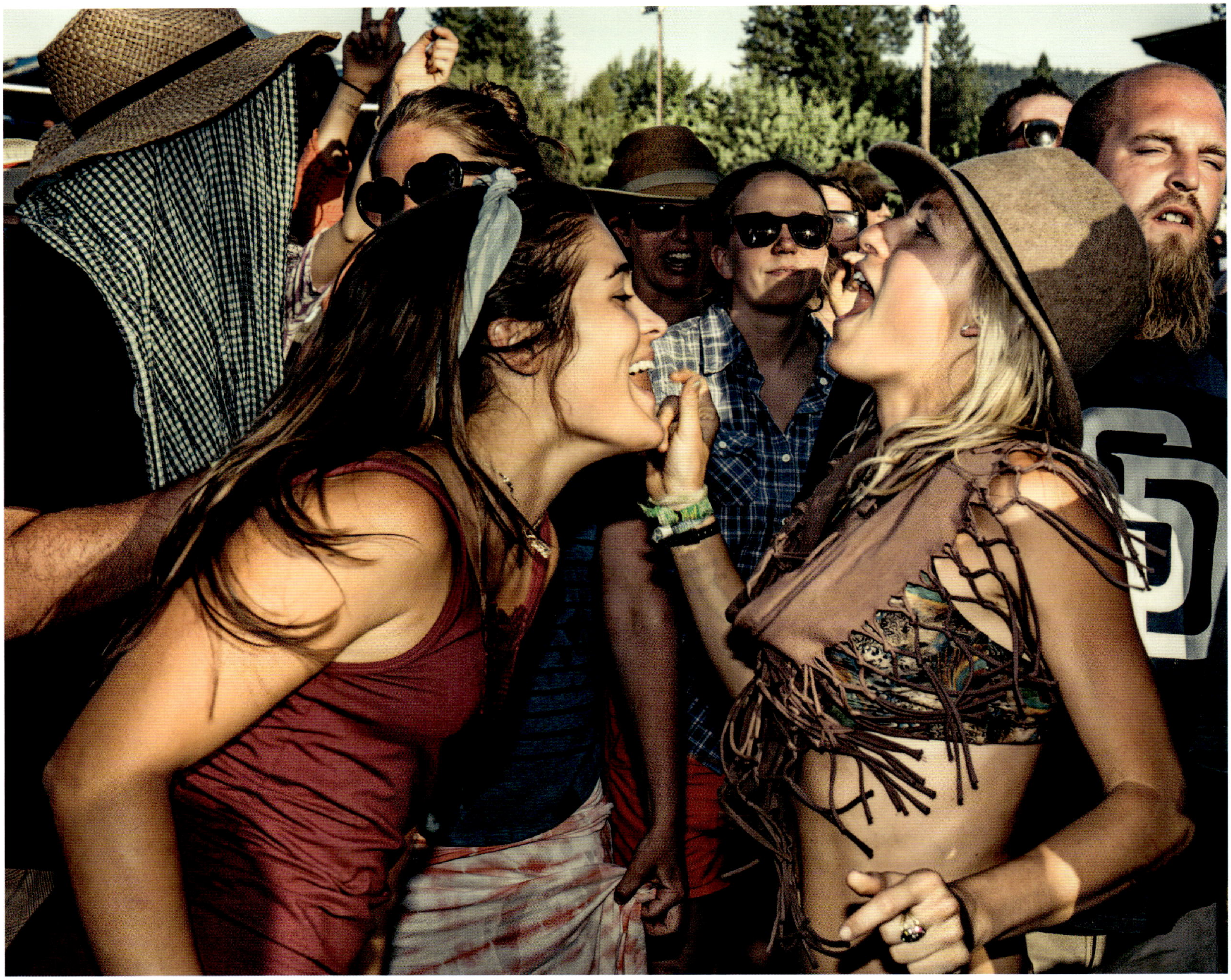

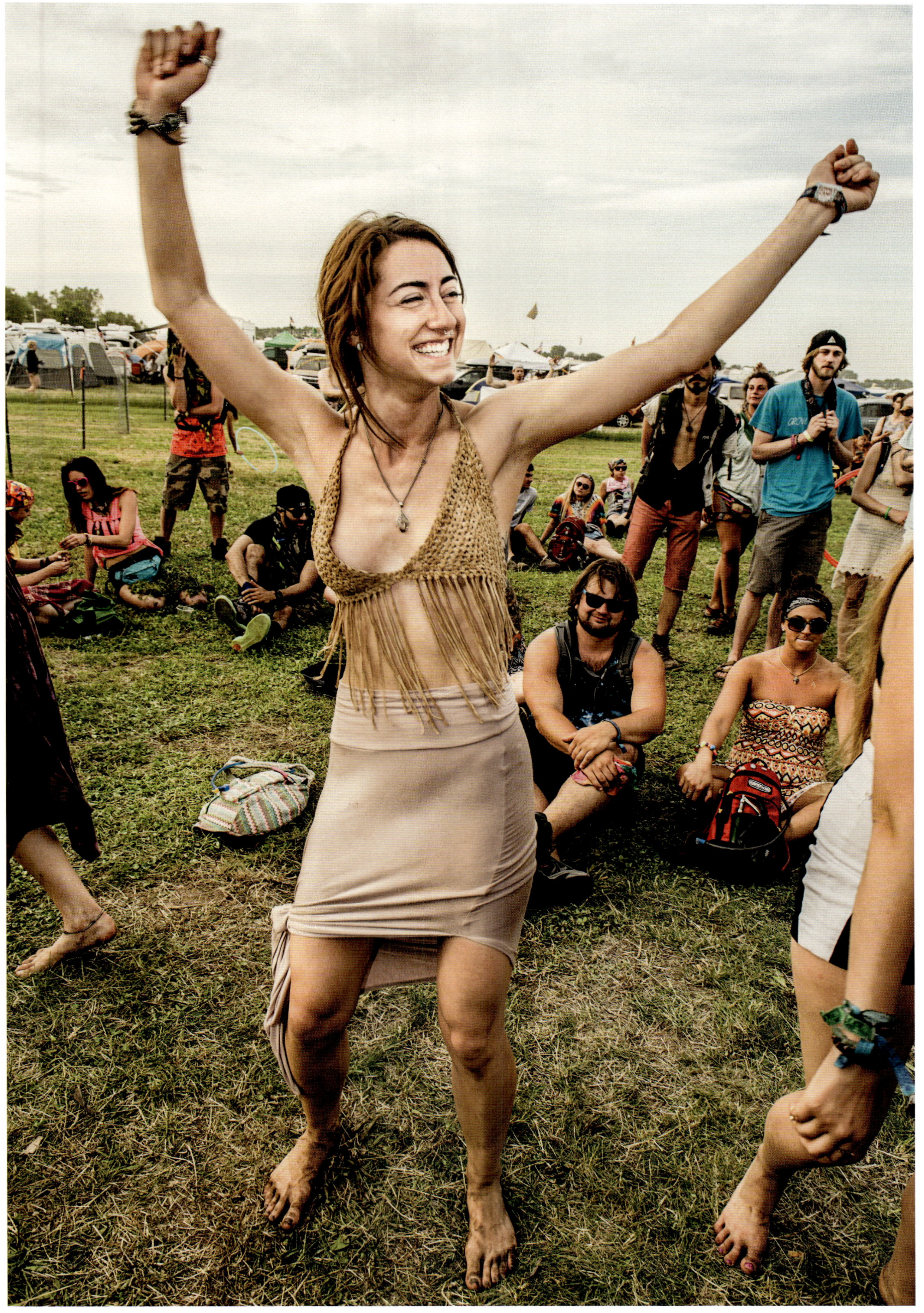

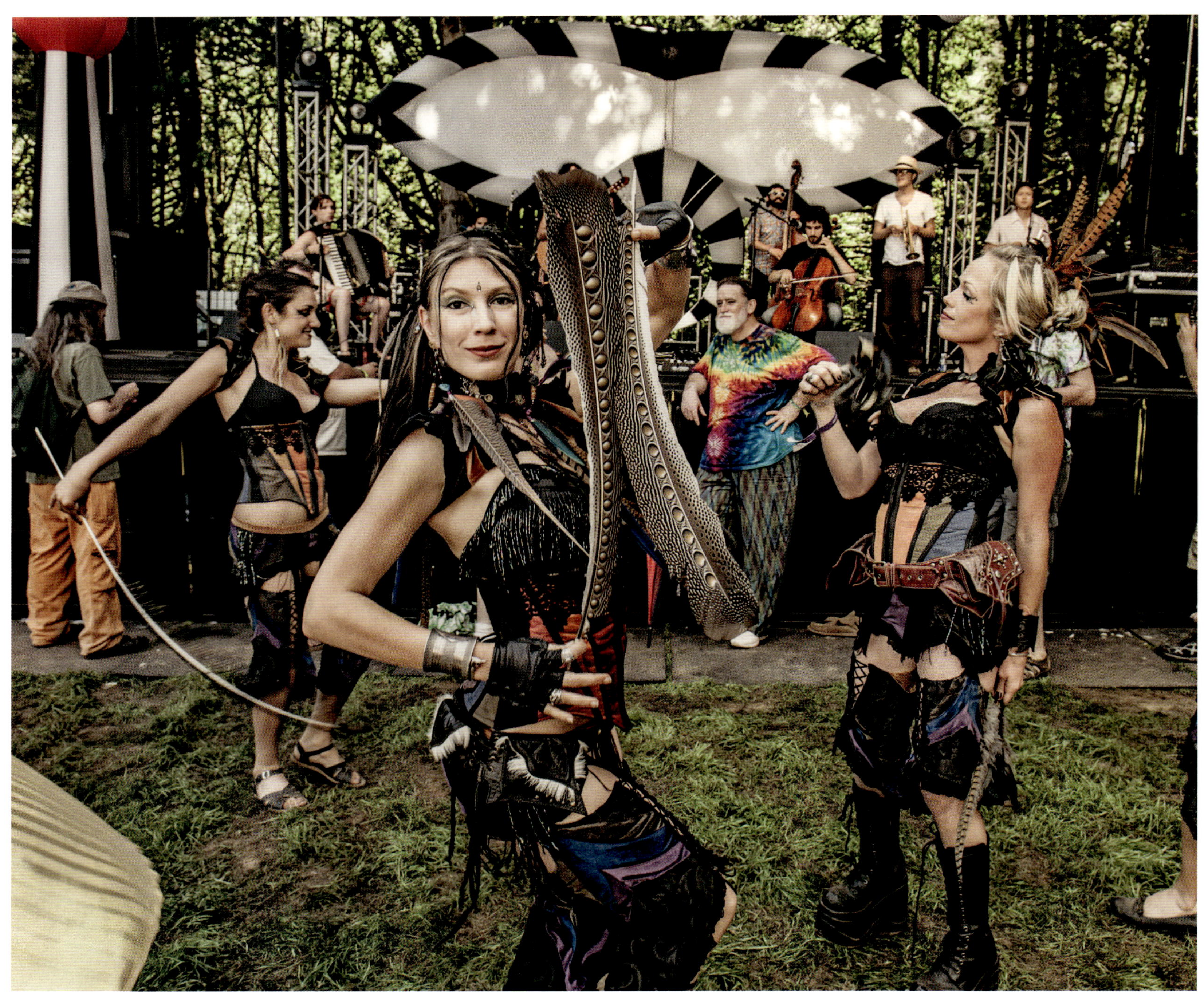

Fashion is one of the greatest ways to express yourself. I always love to get wild and weird with my outfit choices! Sydney C.

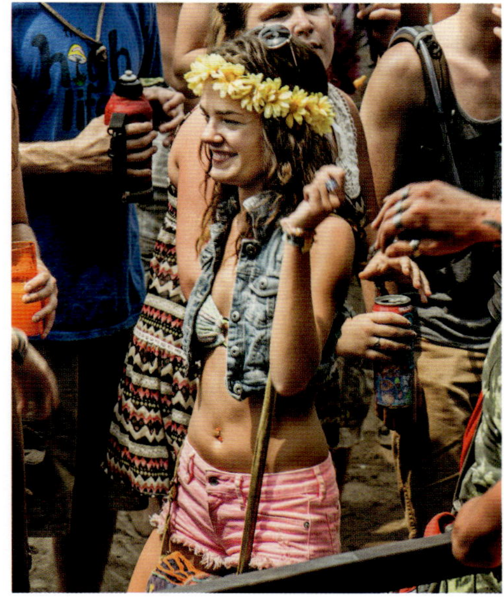

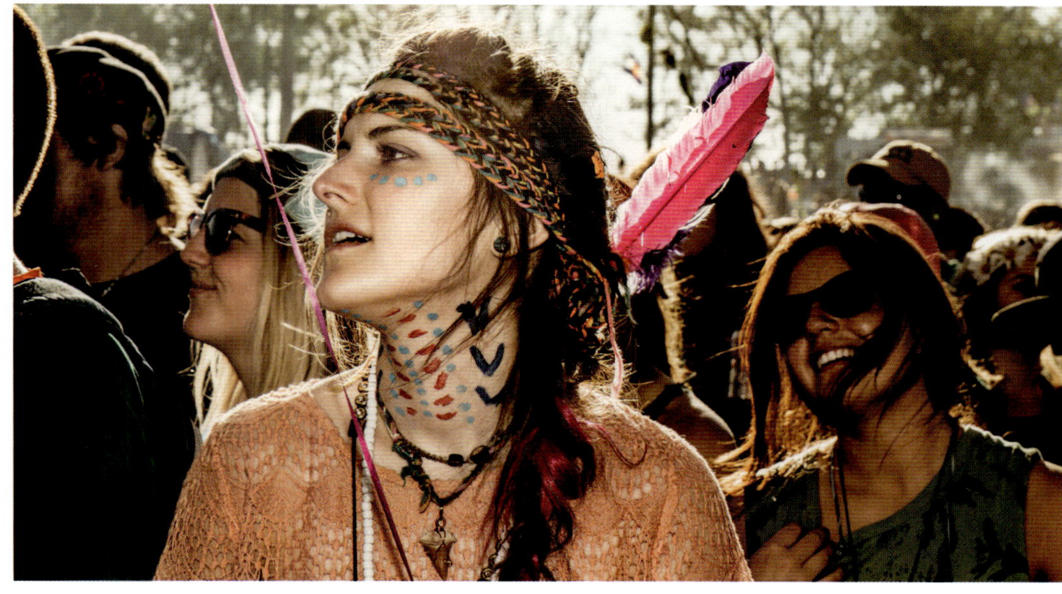

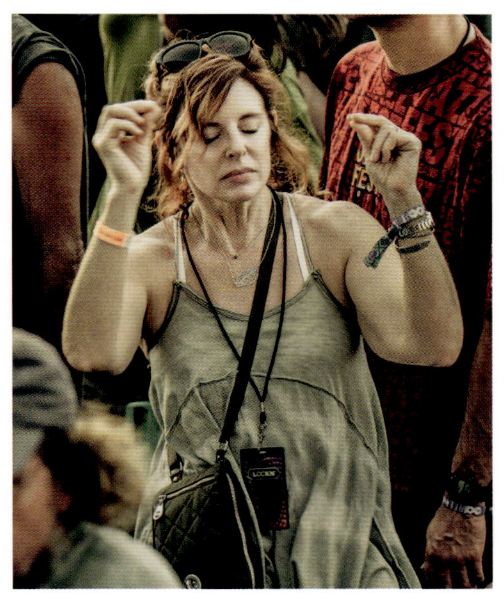

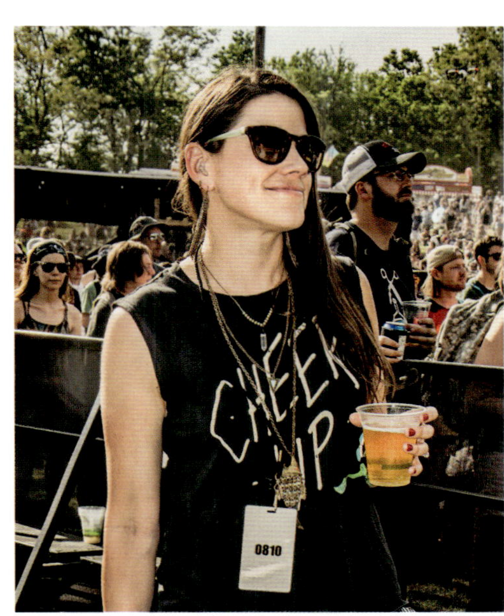
0810

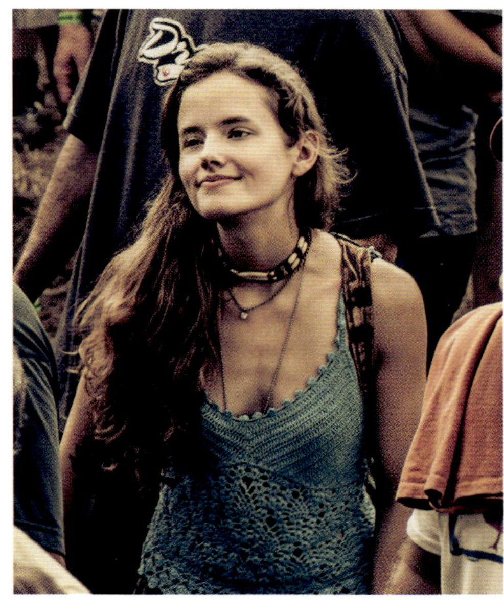

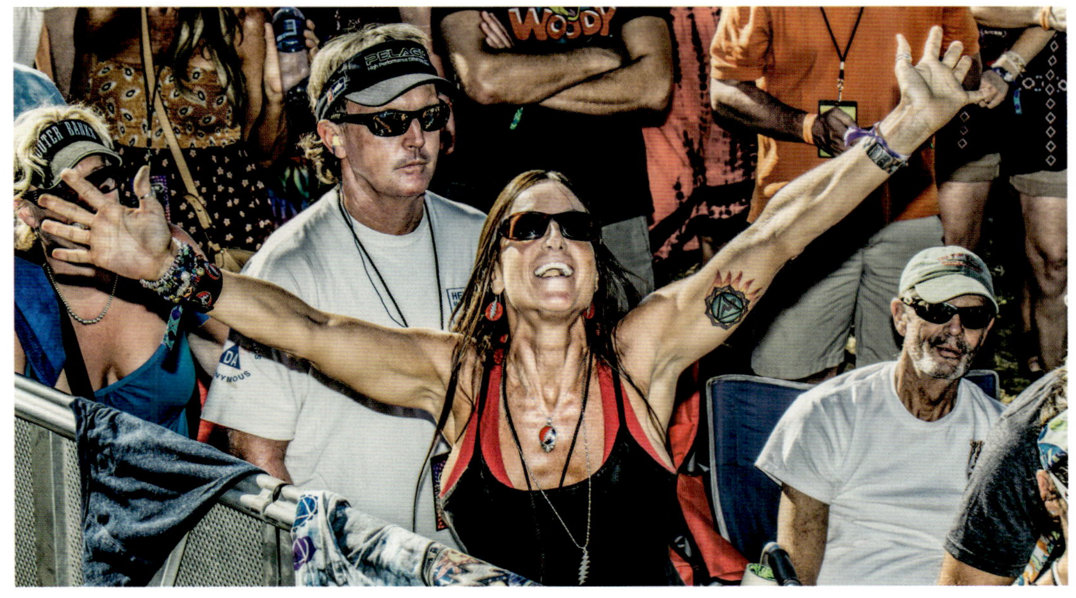

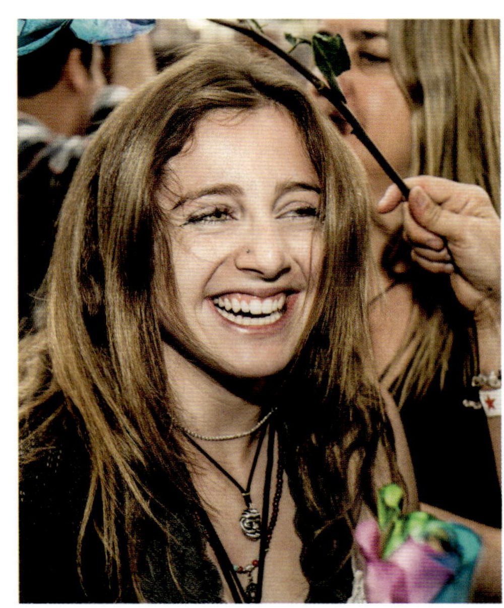

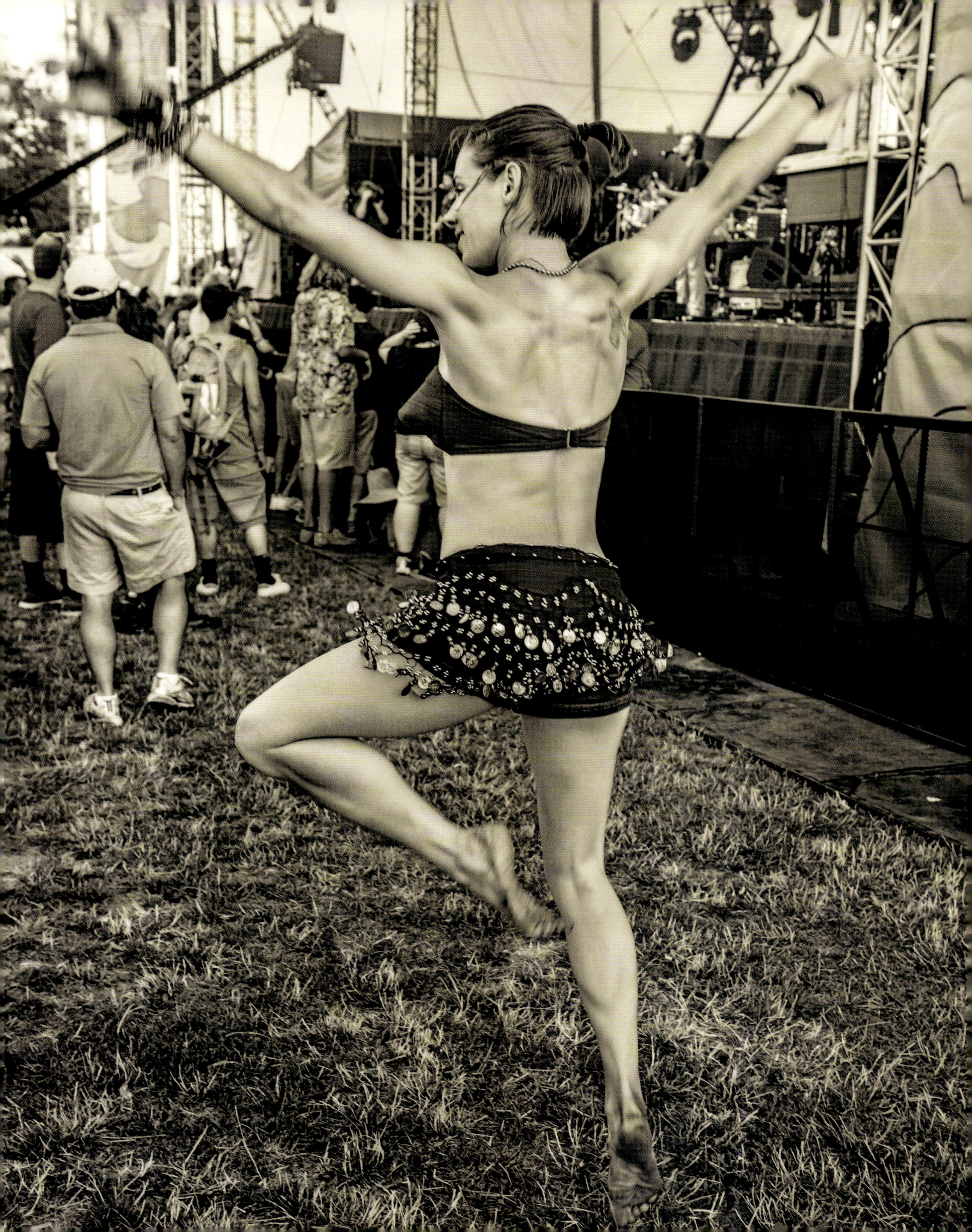

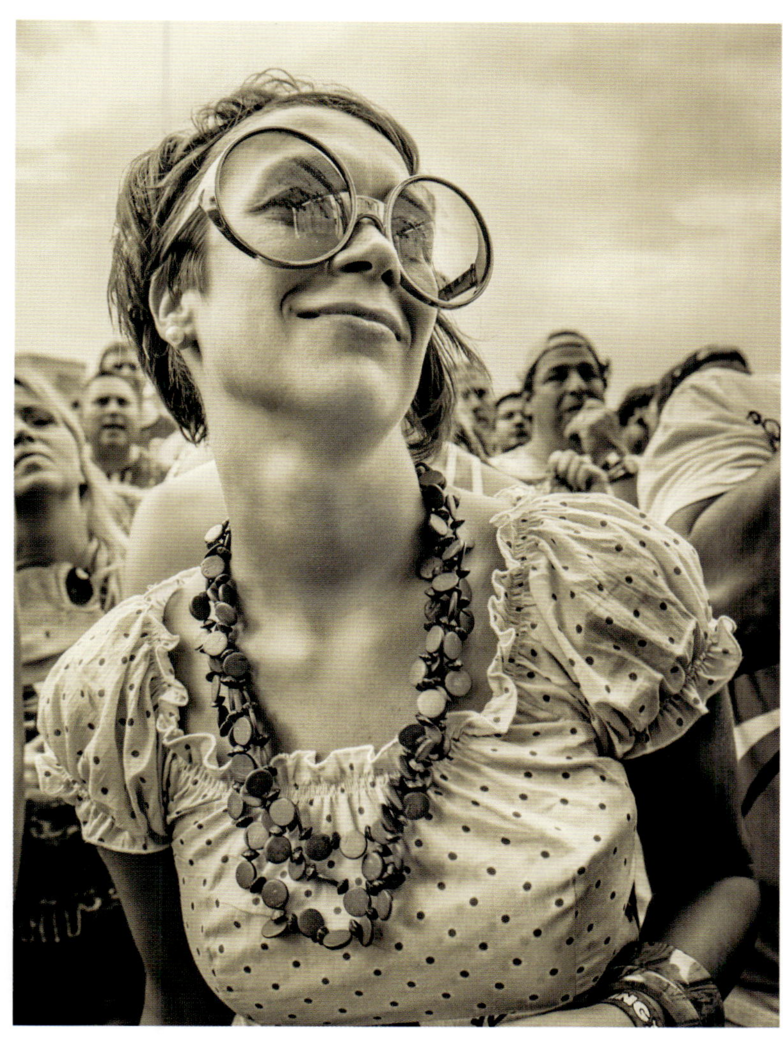

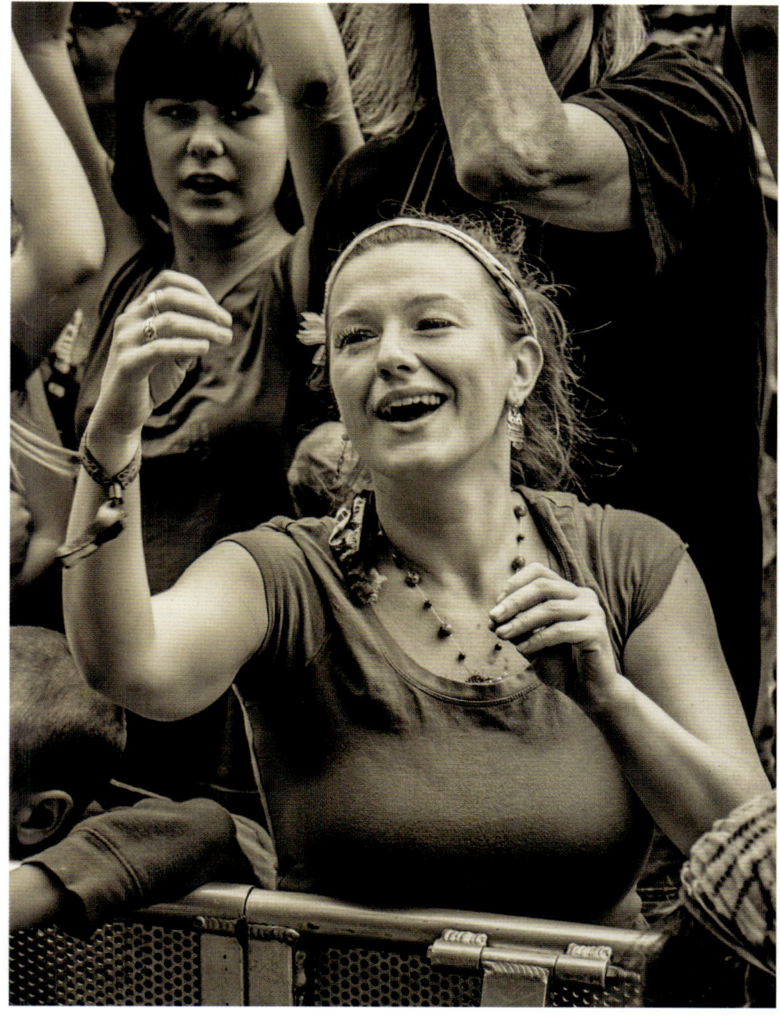

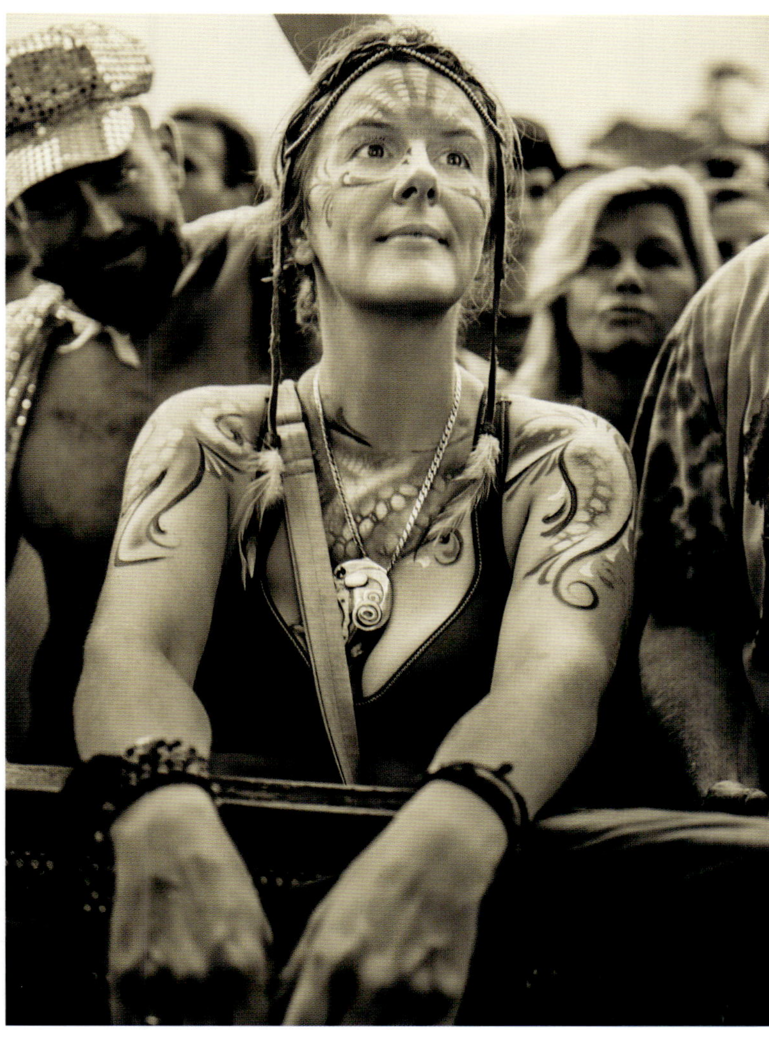

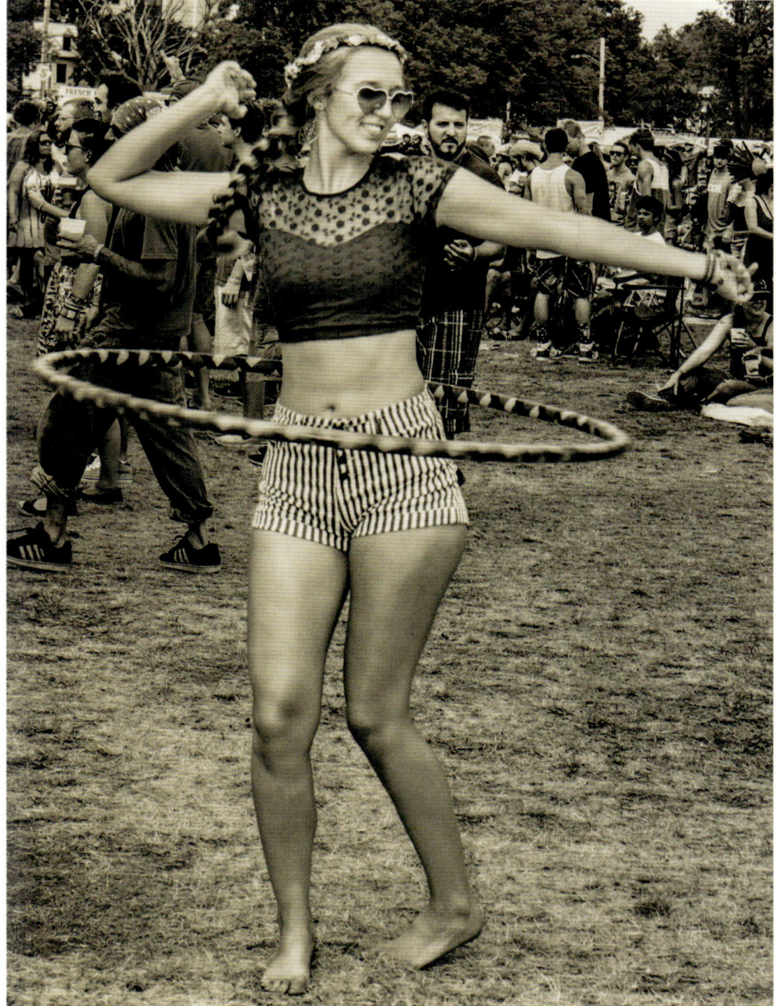

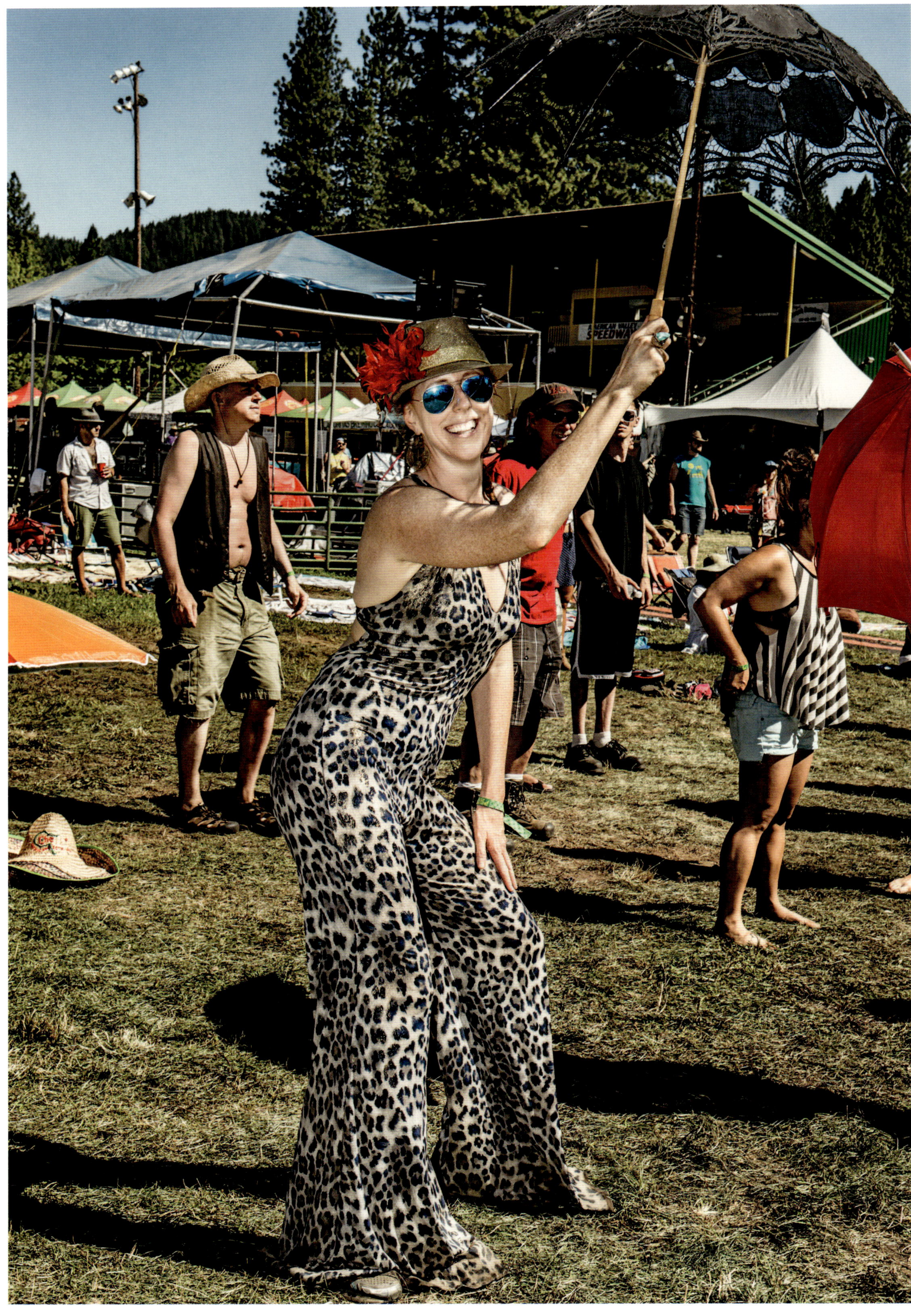

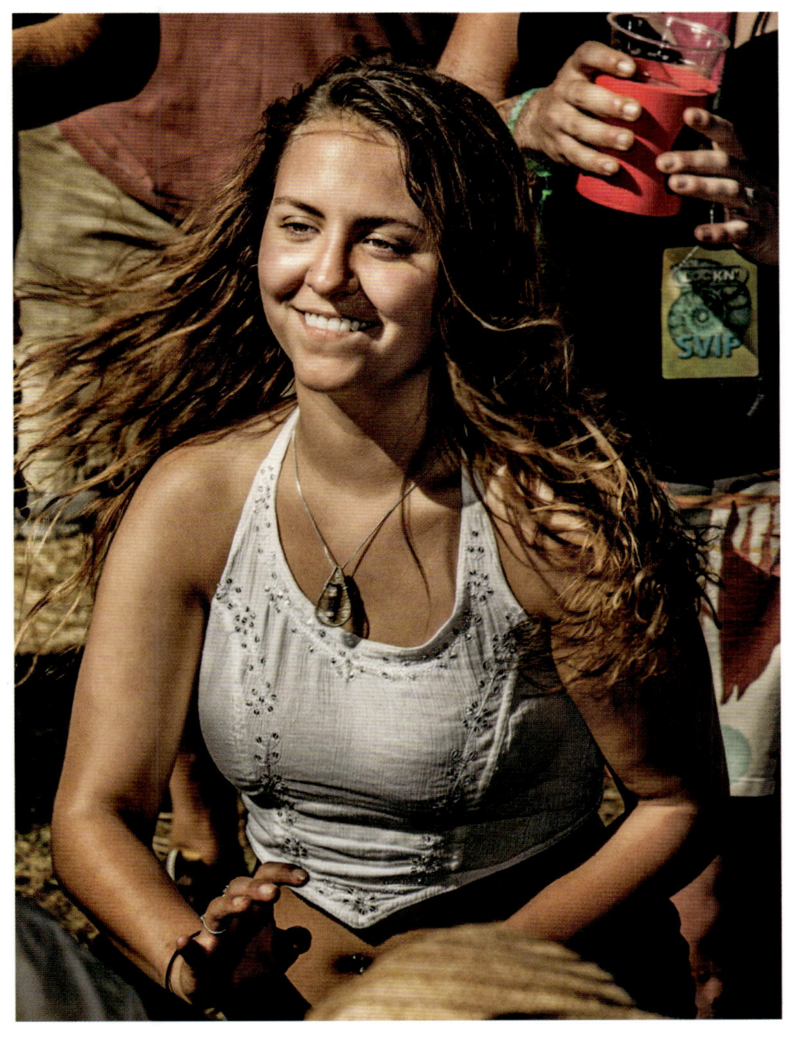

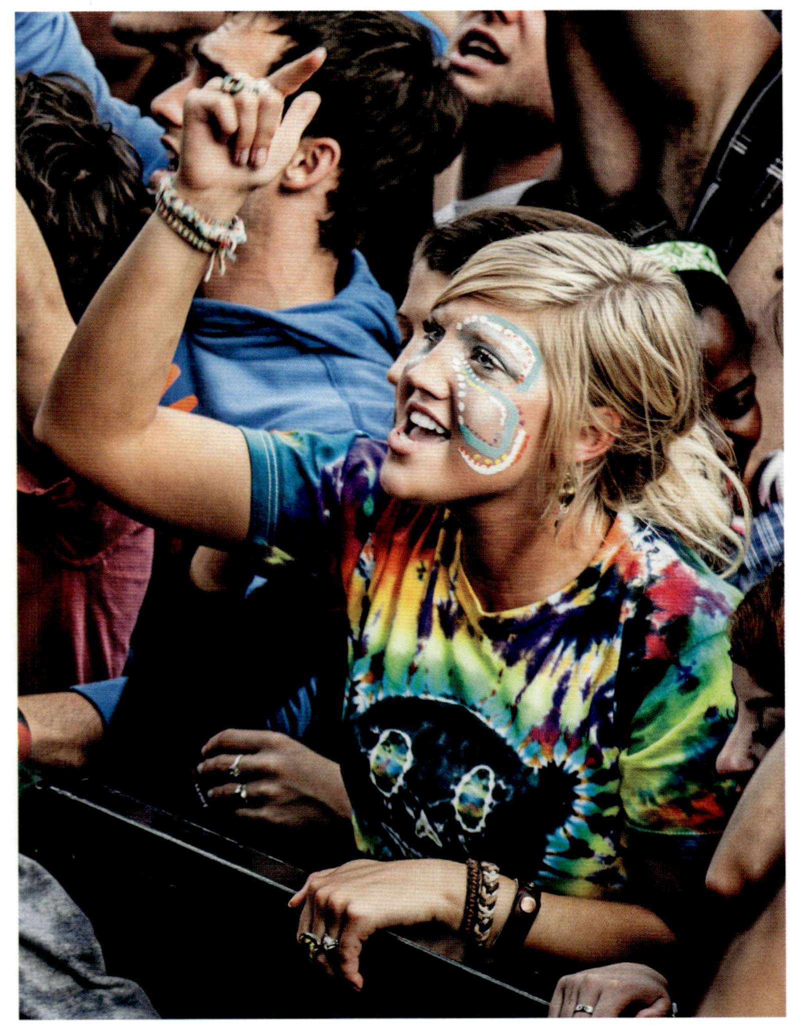

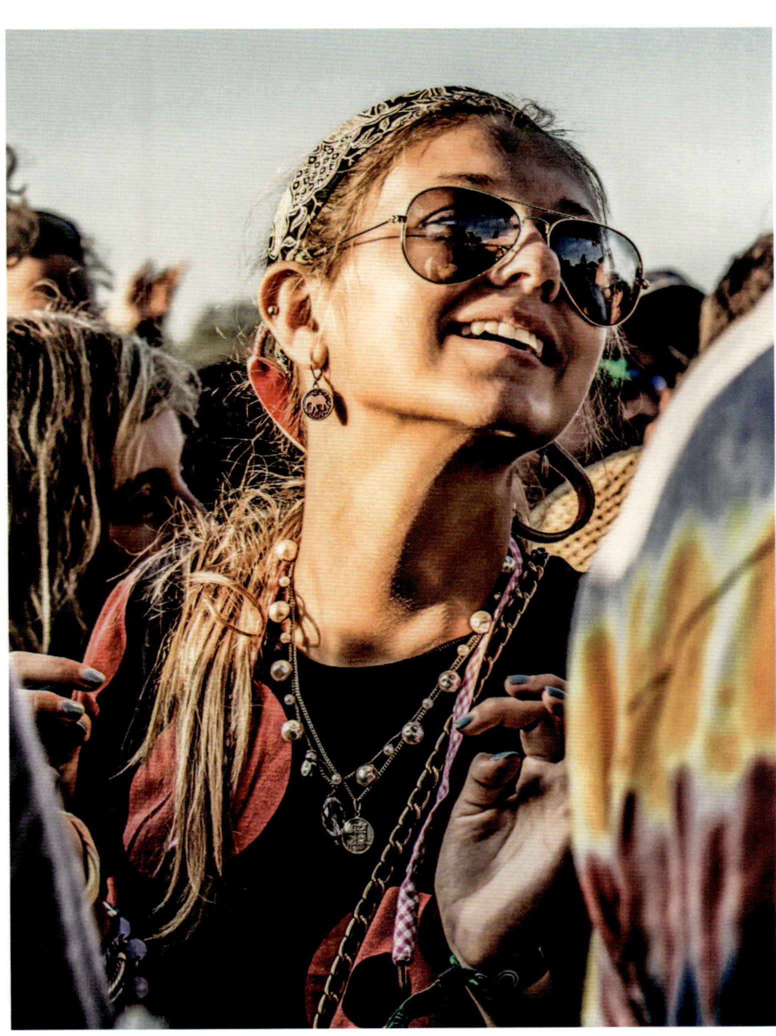

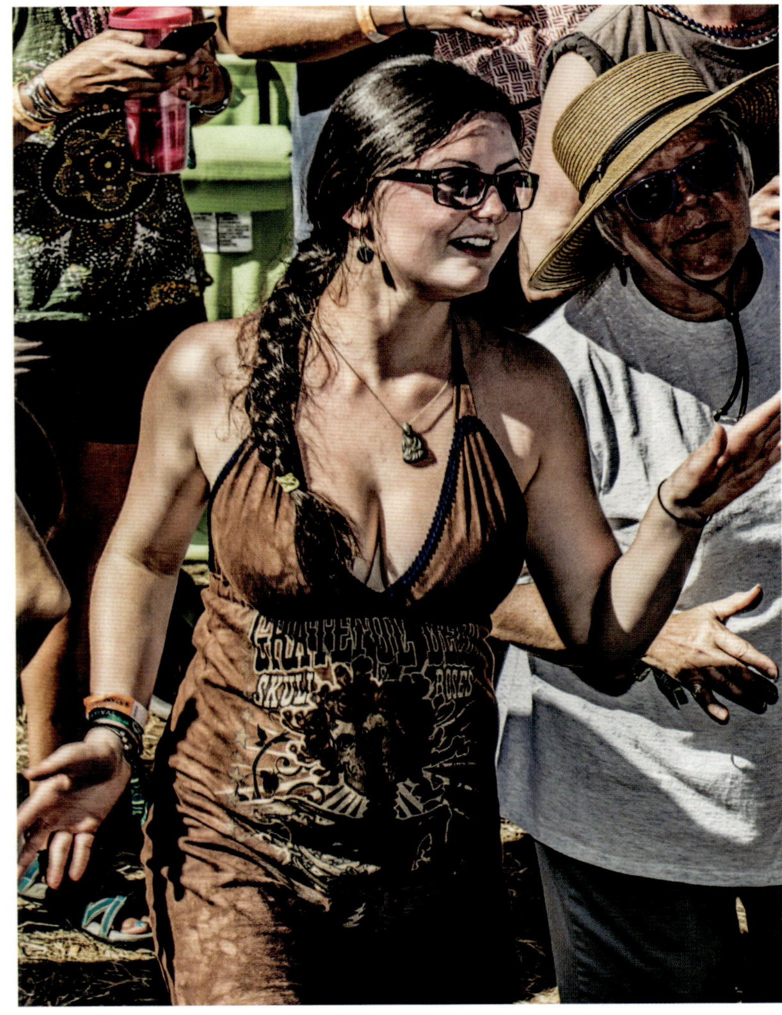

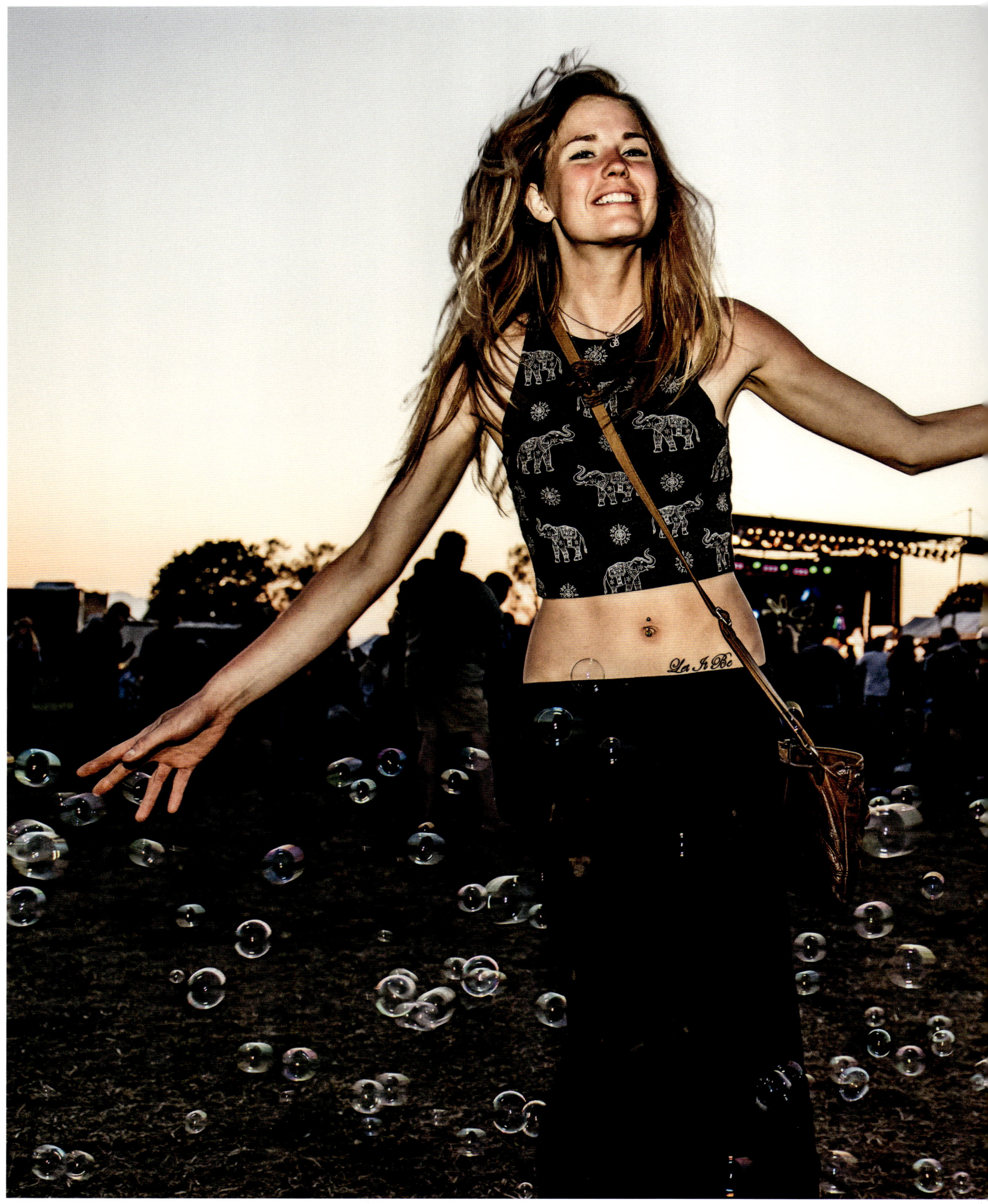

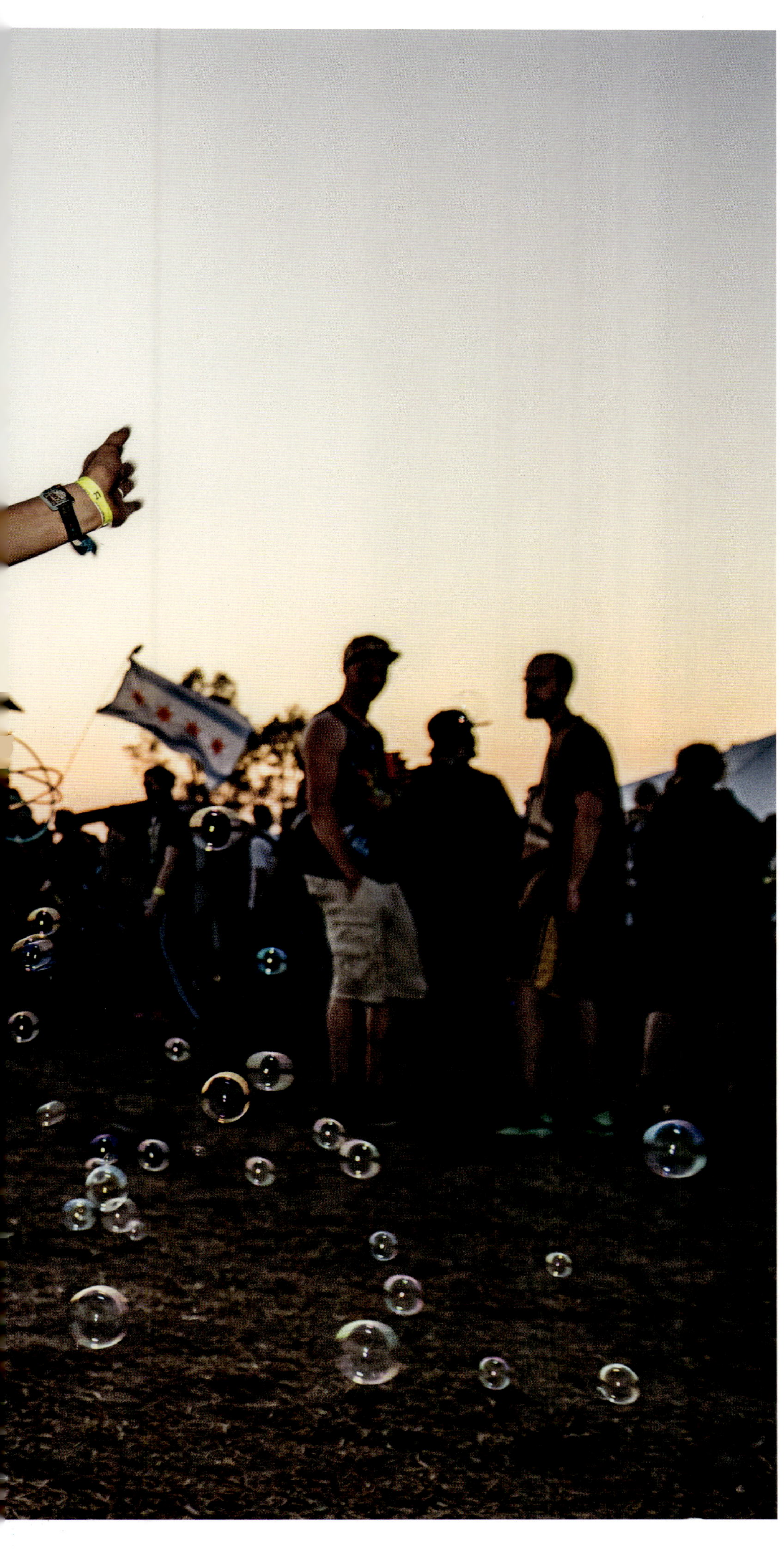

Travel light. Be the light. The world is especially beautiful when we trust and do exactly what we feel. Victoria W.

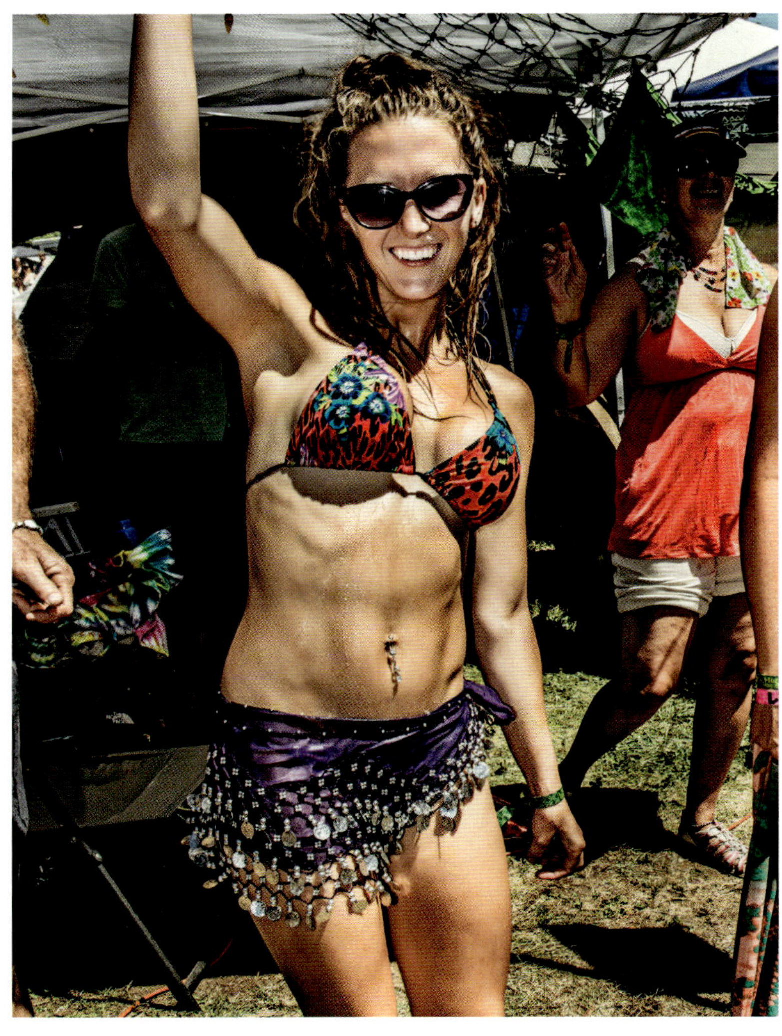

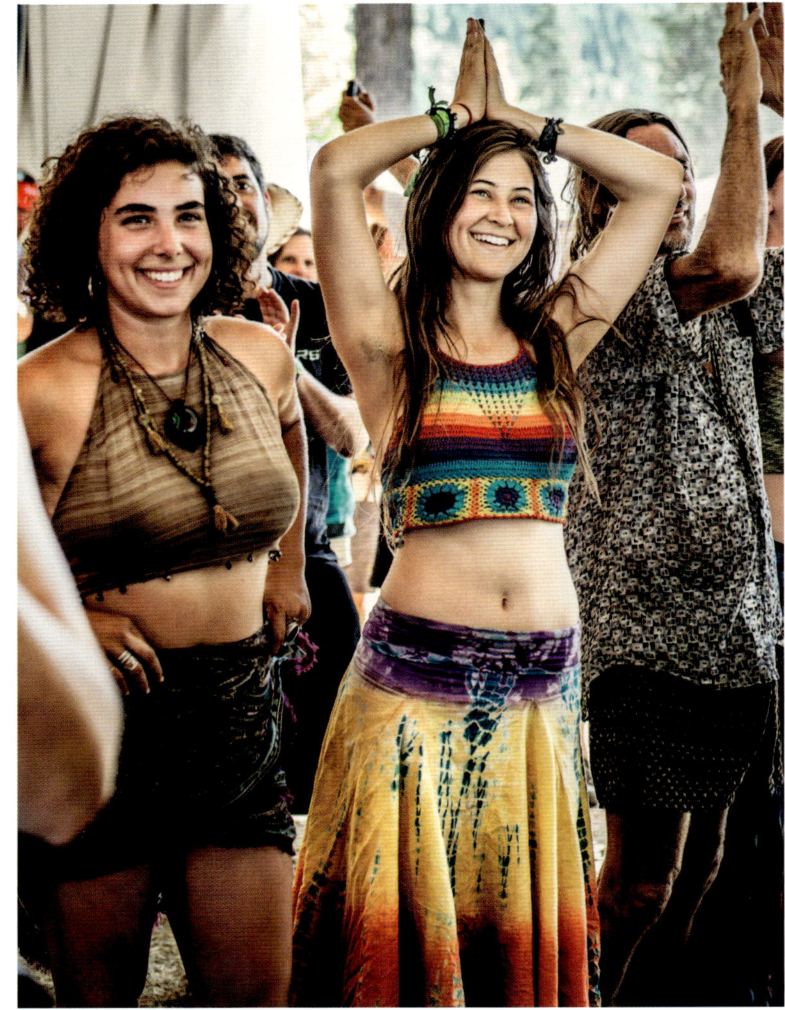

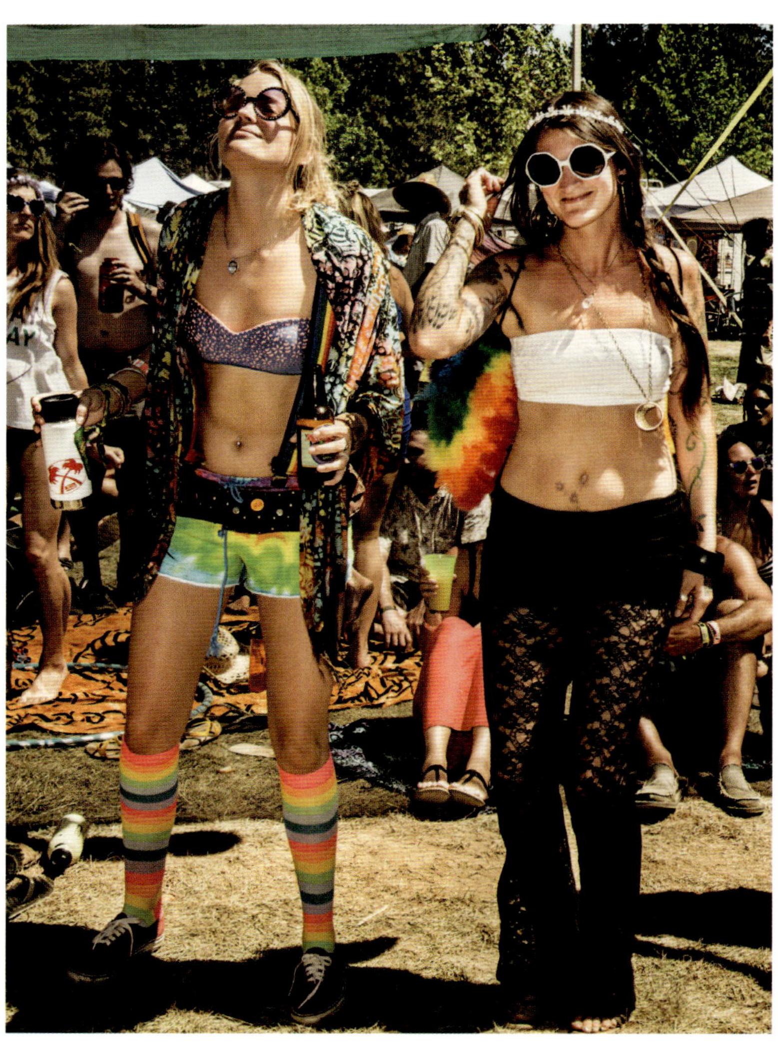

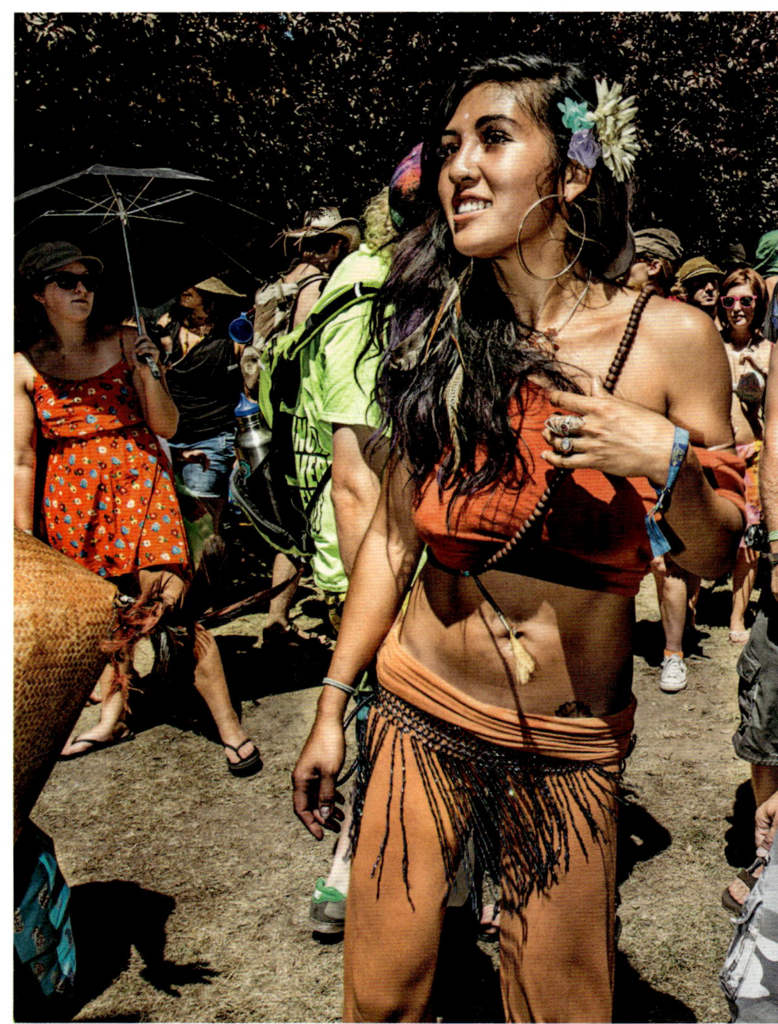

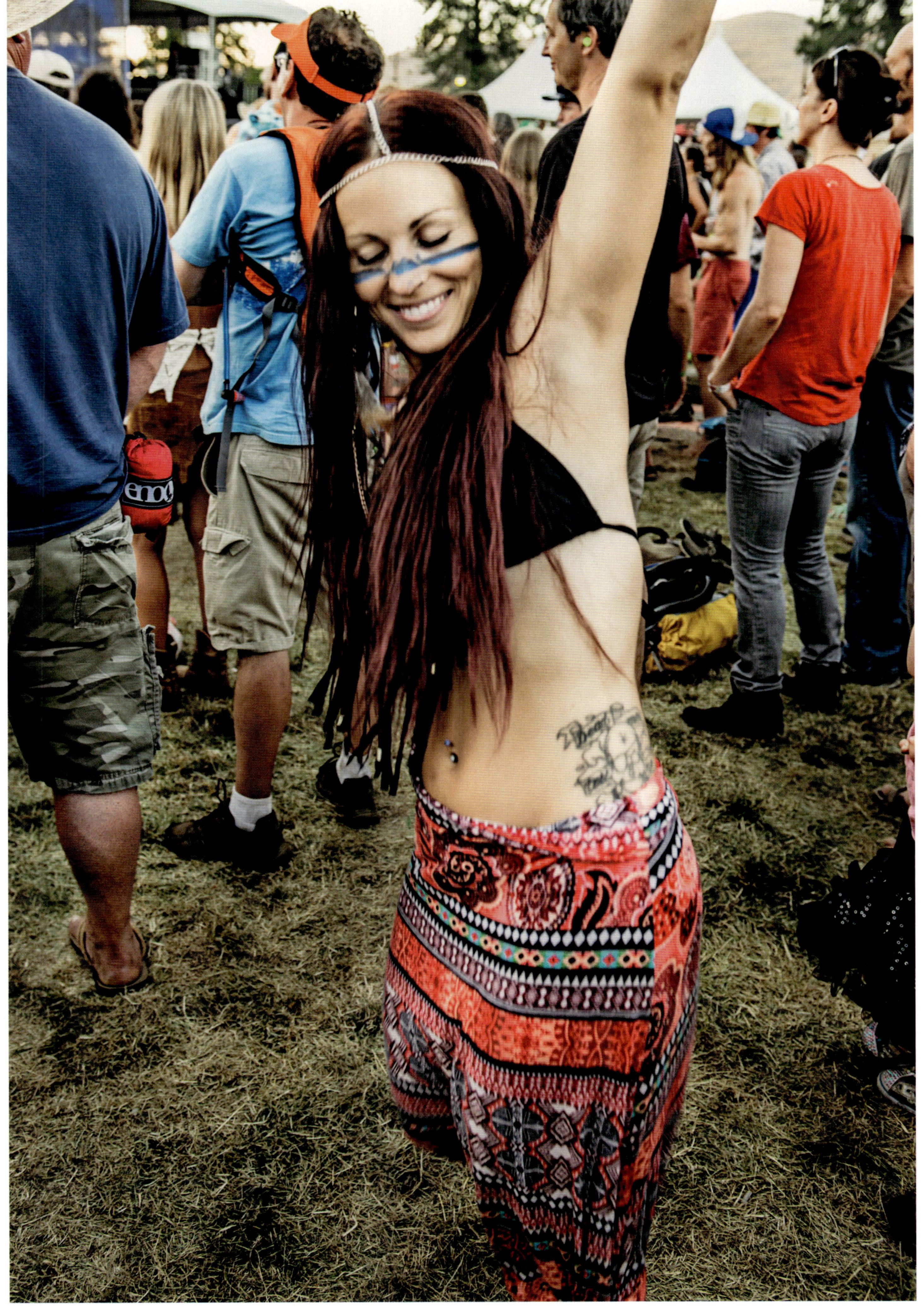

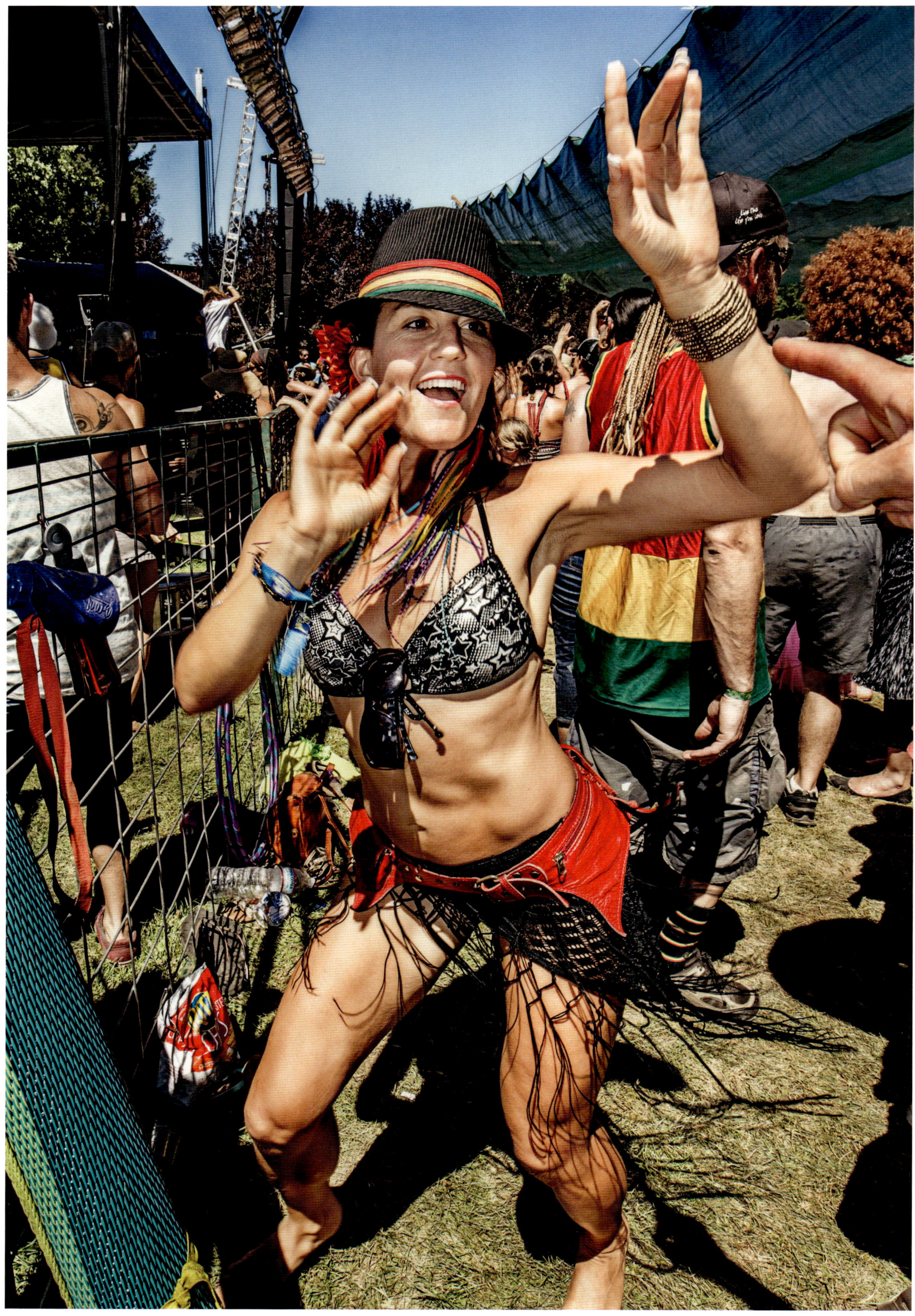

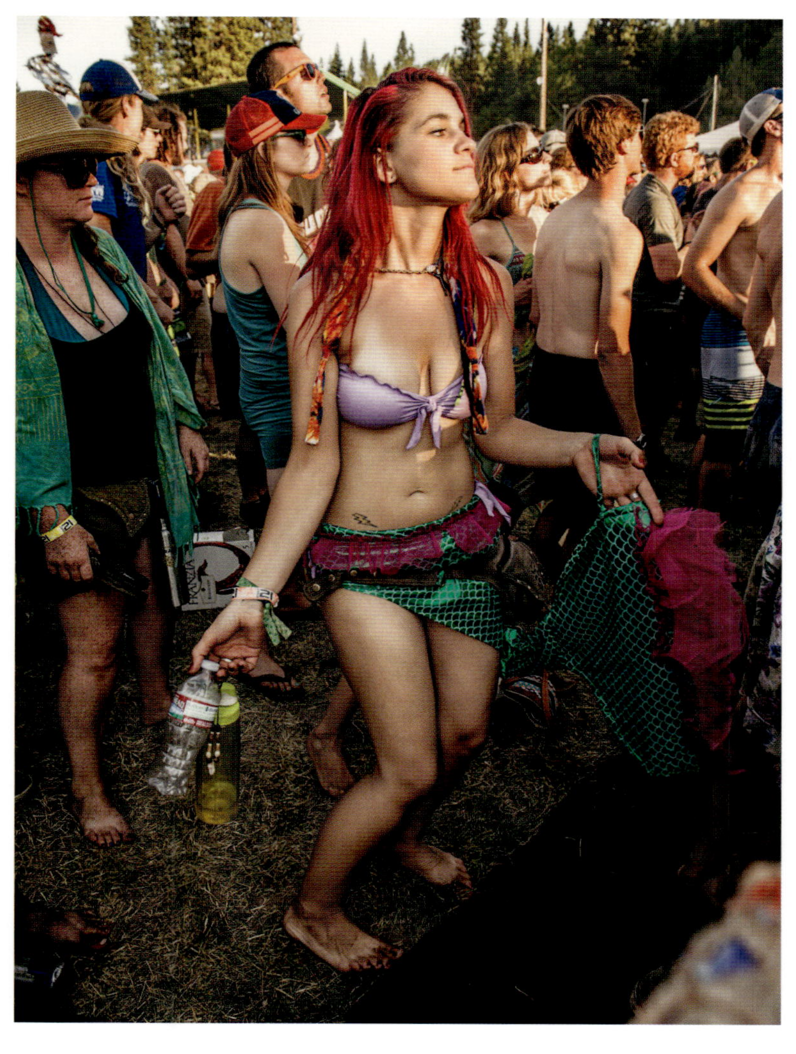

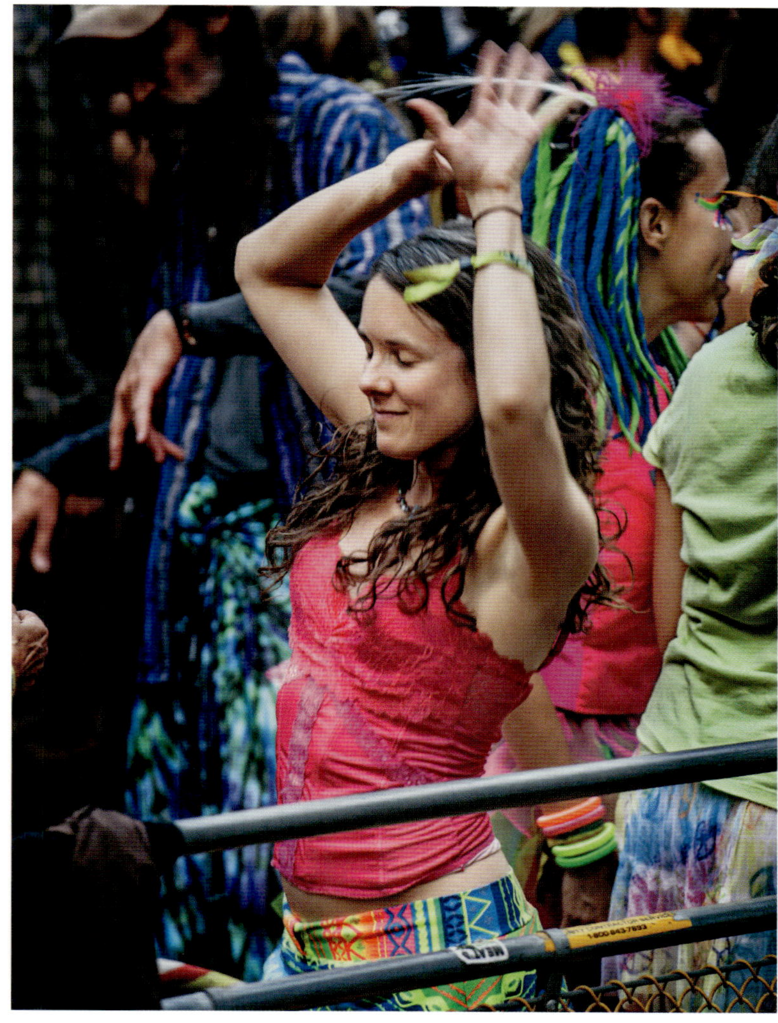

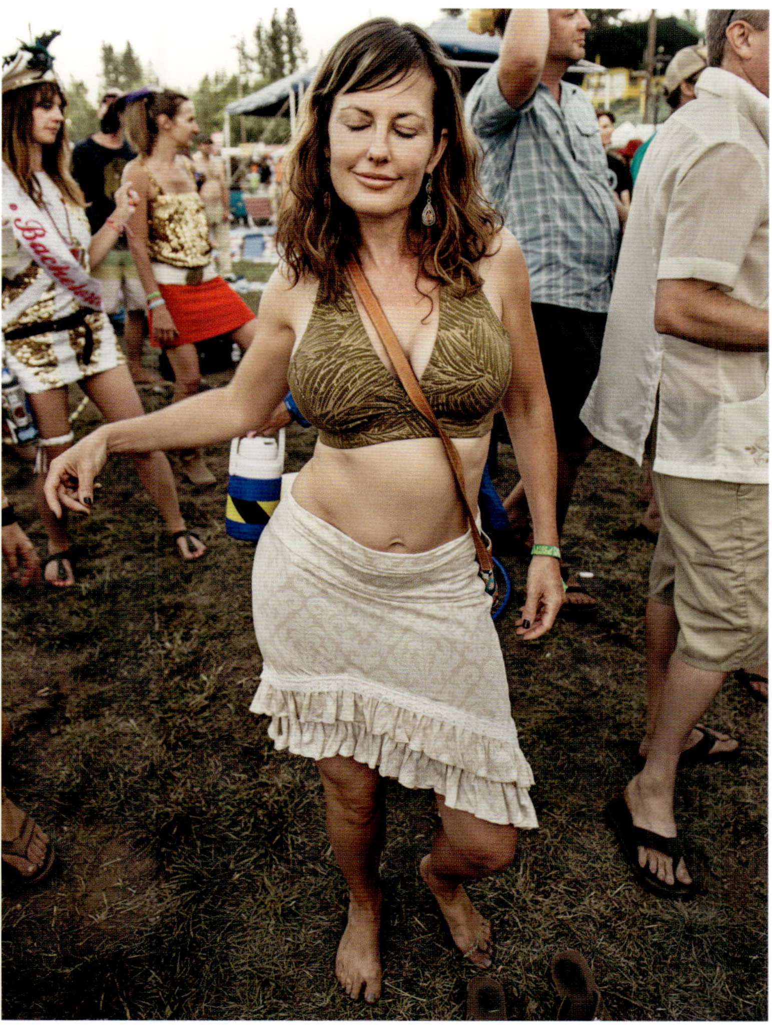

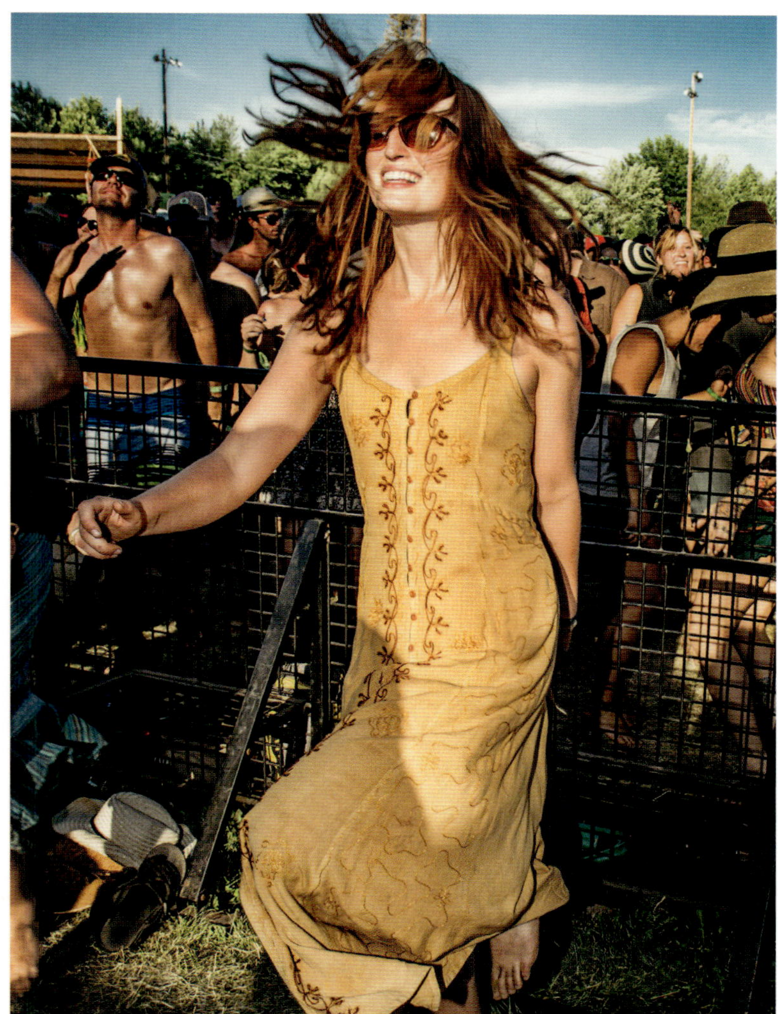

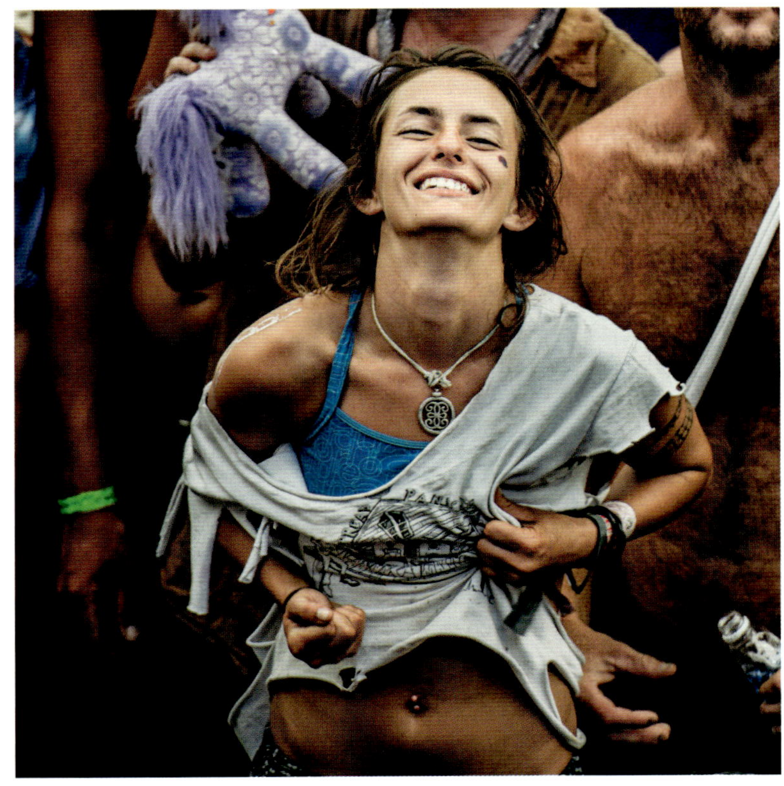

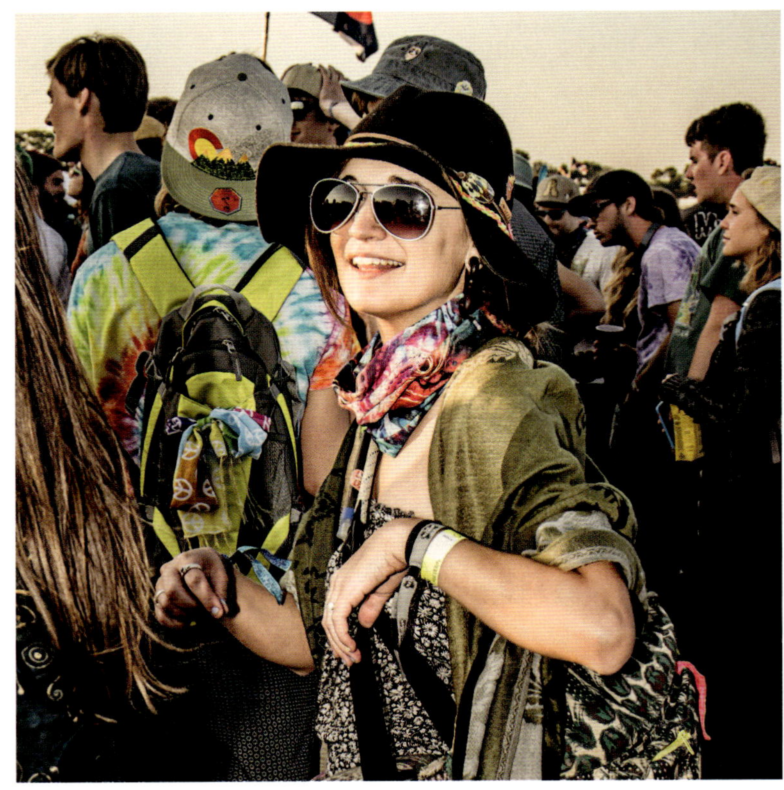

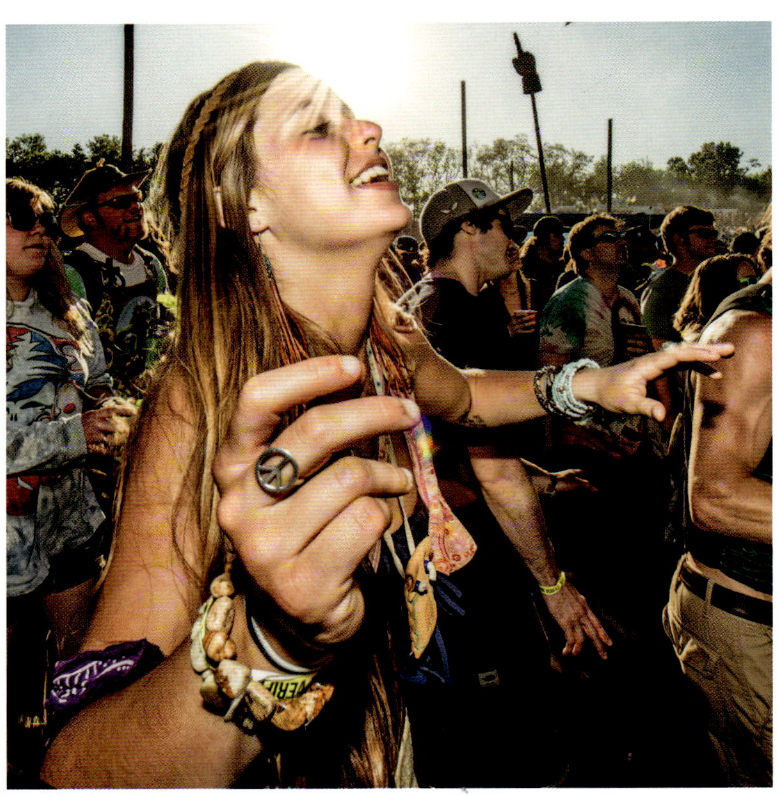

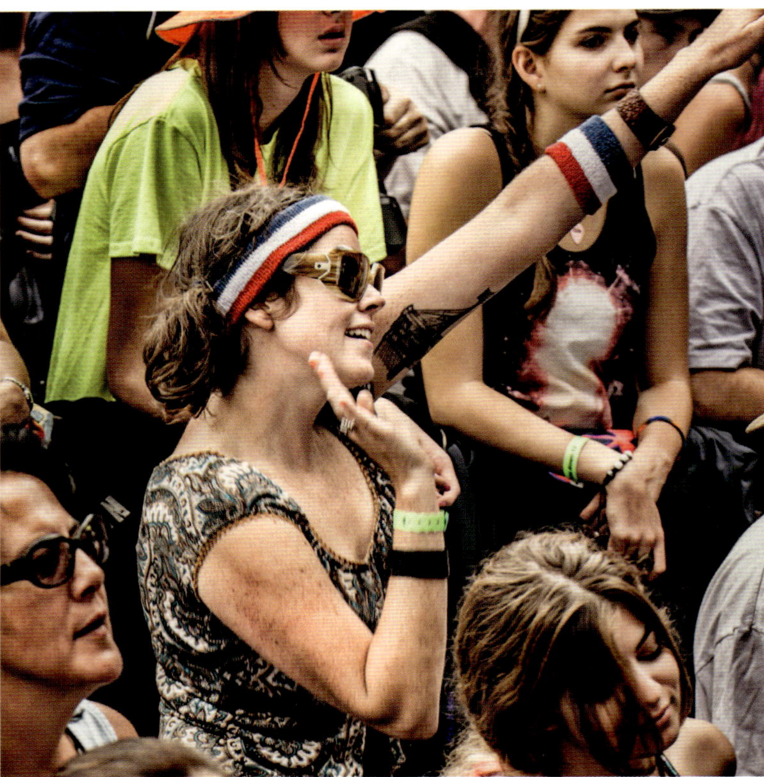

The first song kicks in and I throw myself into a blissed out dance party. For the next few hours of my existence, that is all that matters.

Karen T. (pictured, bottom right)

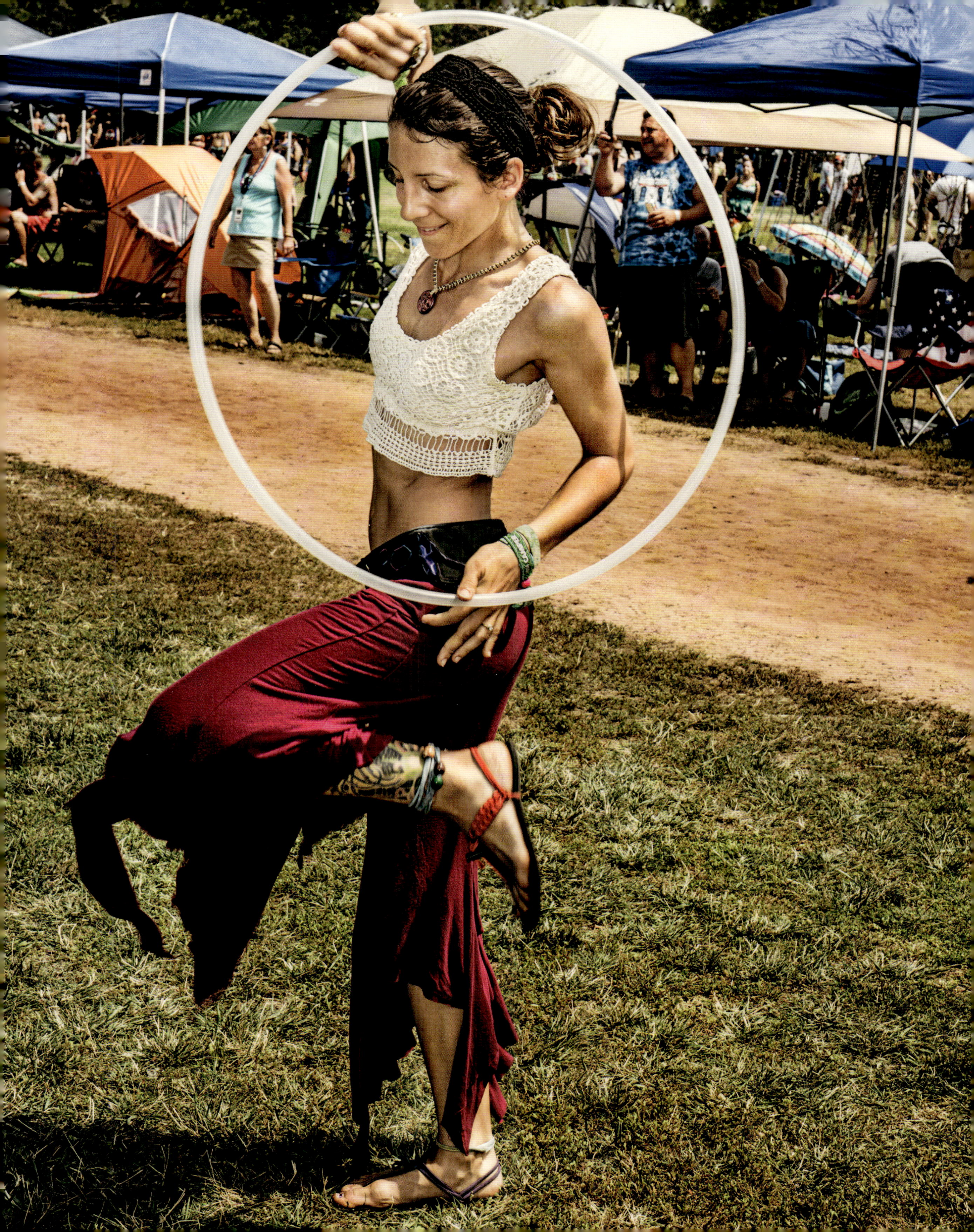

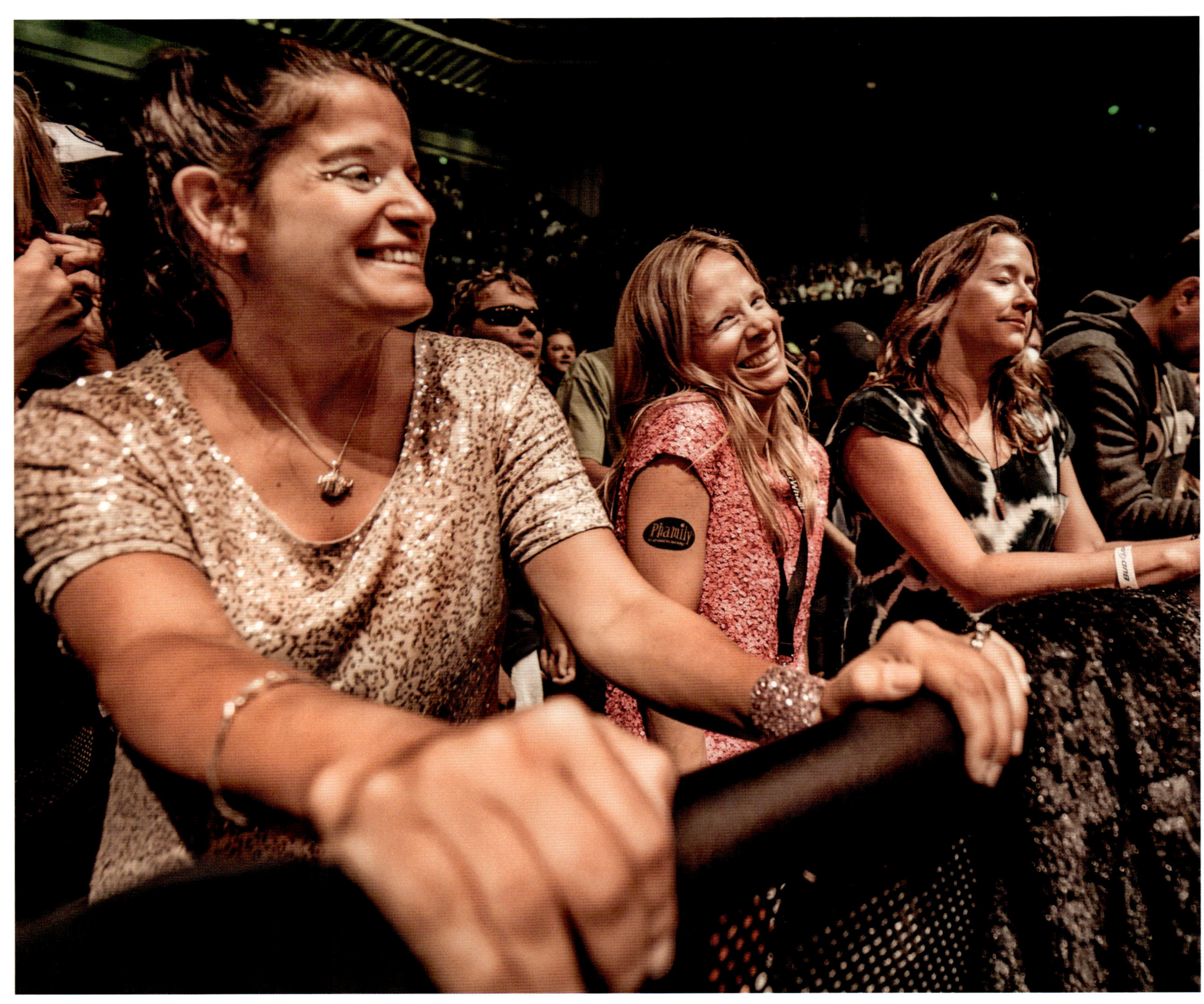

I think the three things that make a show are the ability to feel connected to the music, enough space to physically interpret my connection, and the blessing of being with friends. Blythe M. (pictured, center)

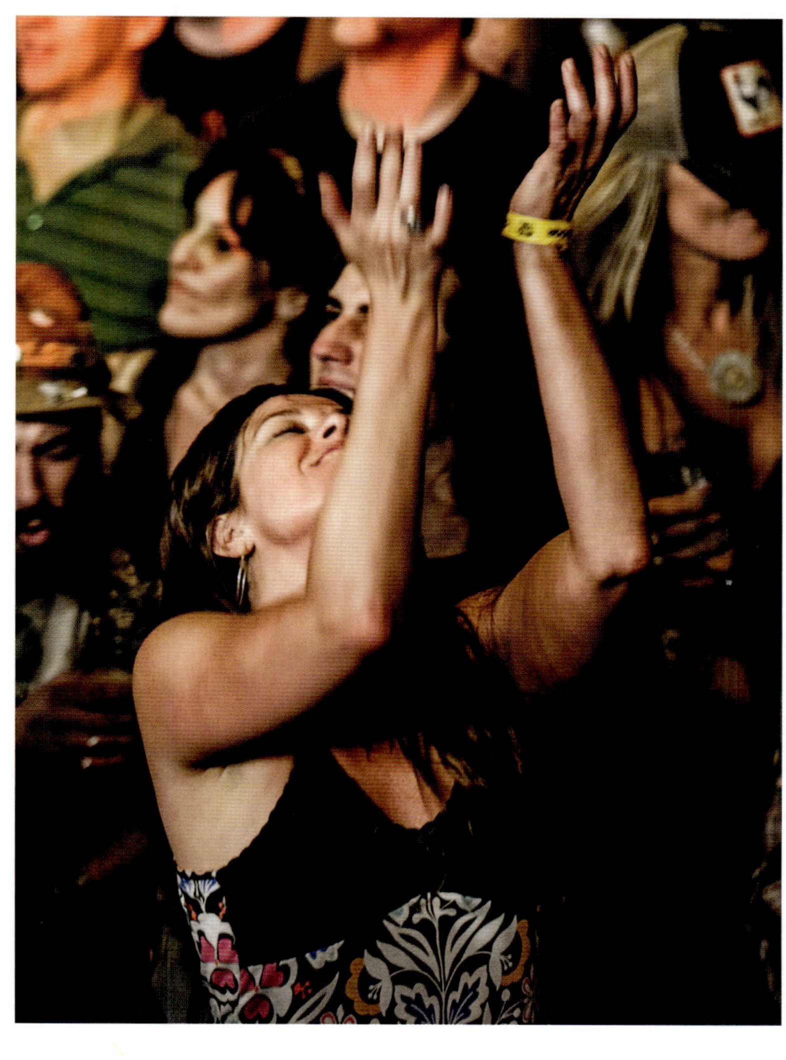
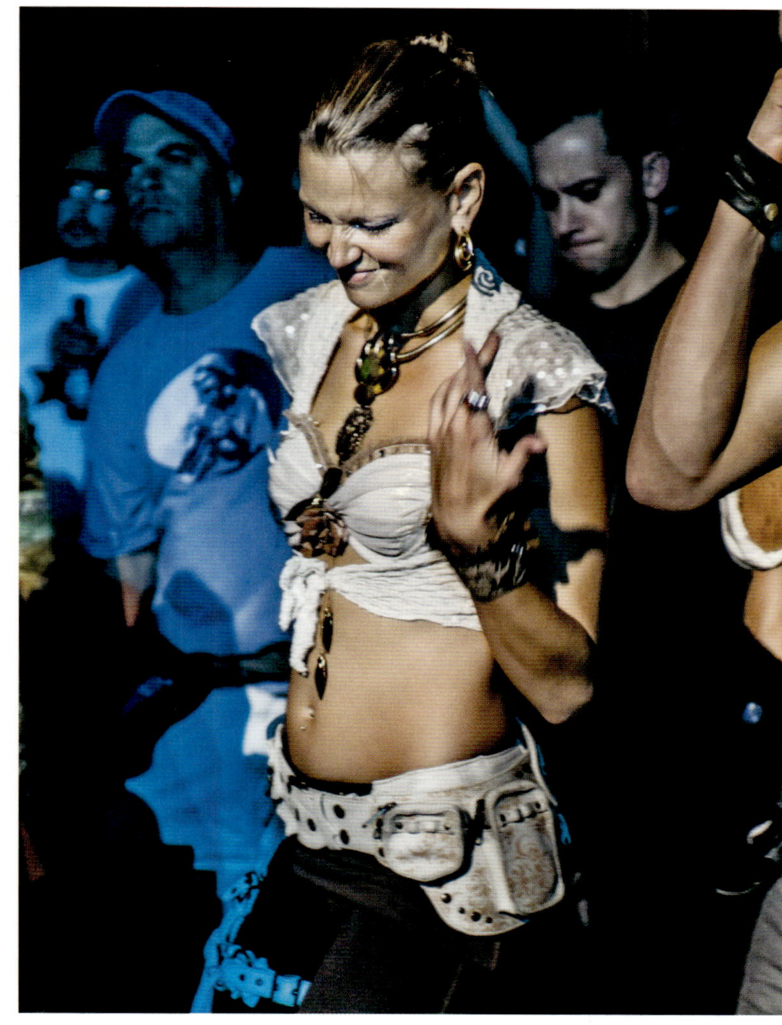
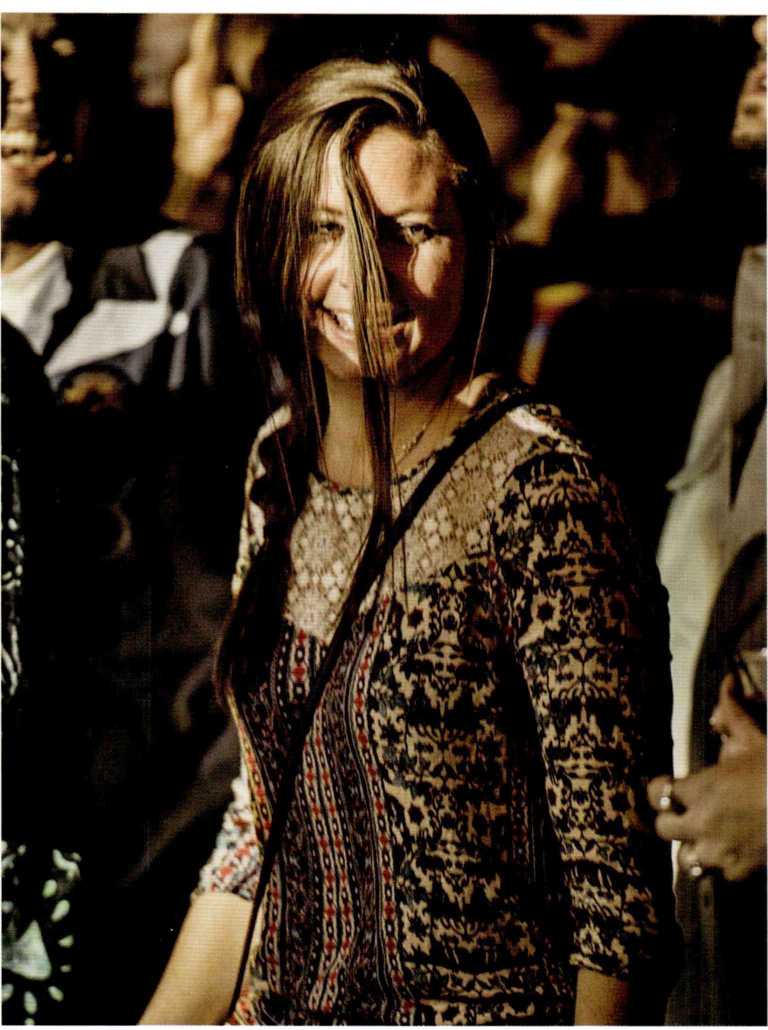
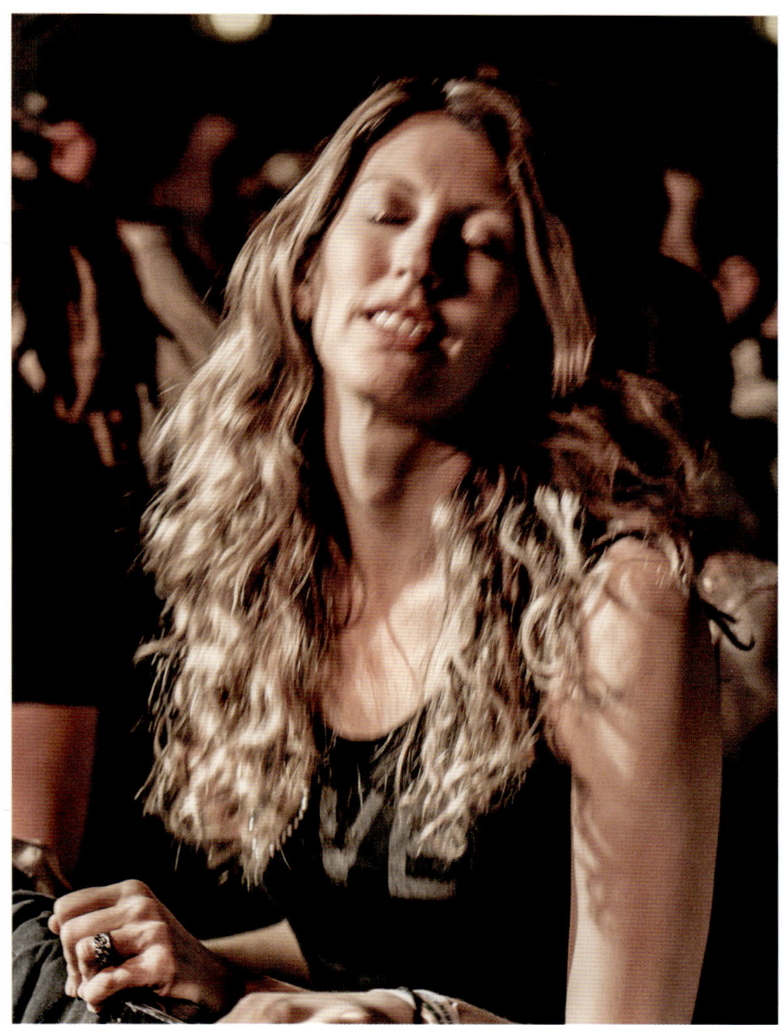

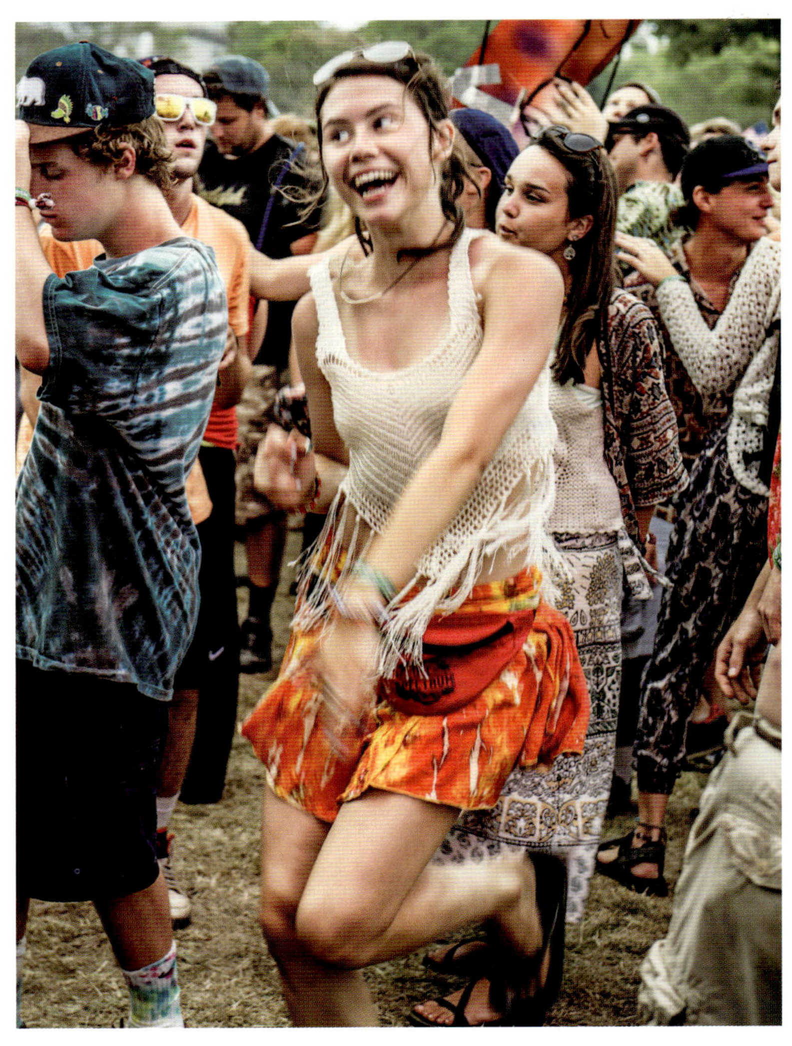

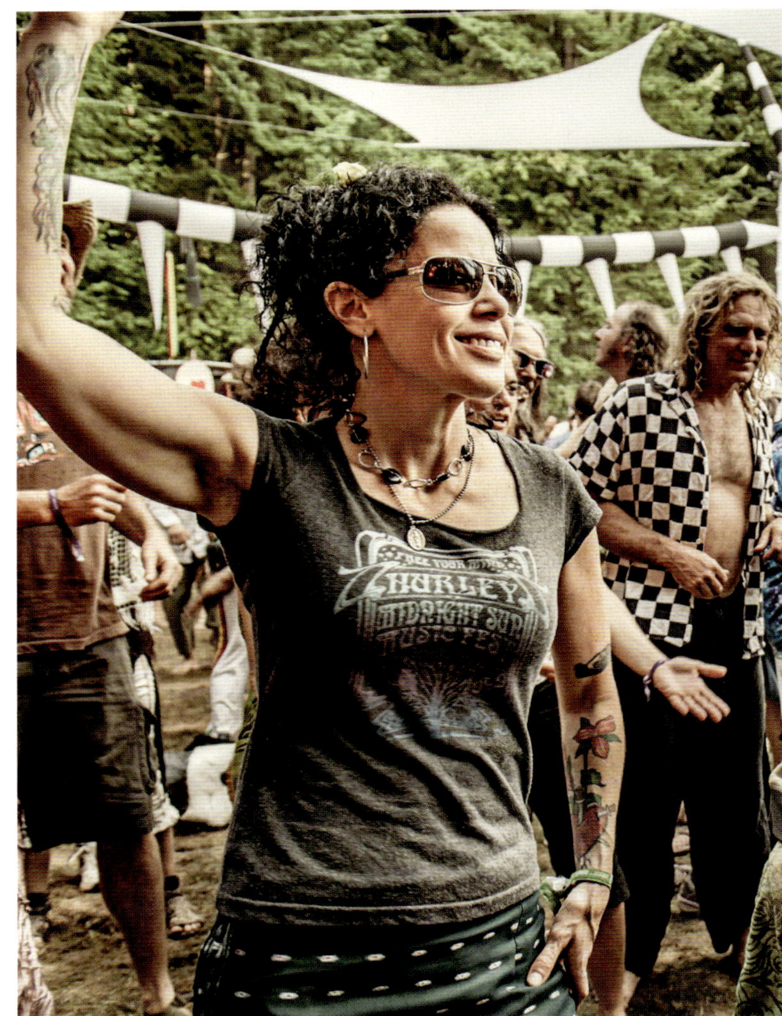
HURLEY

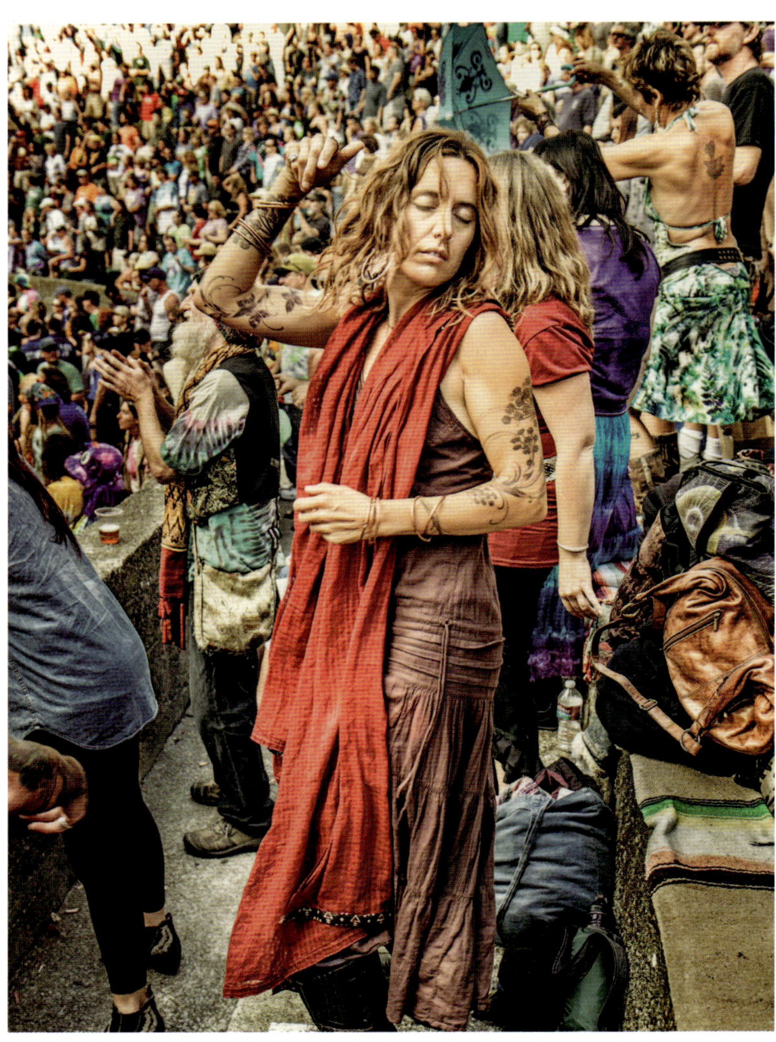

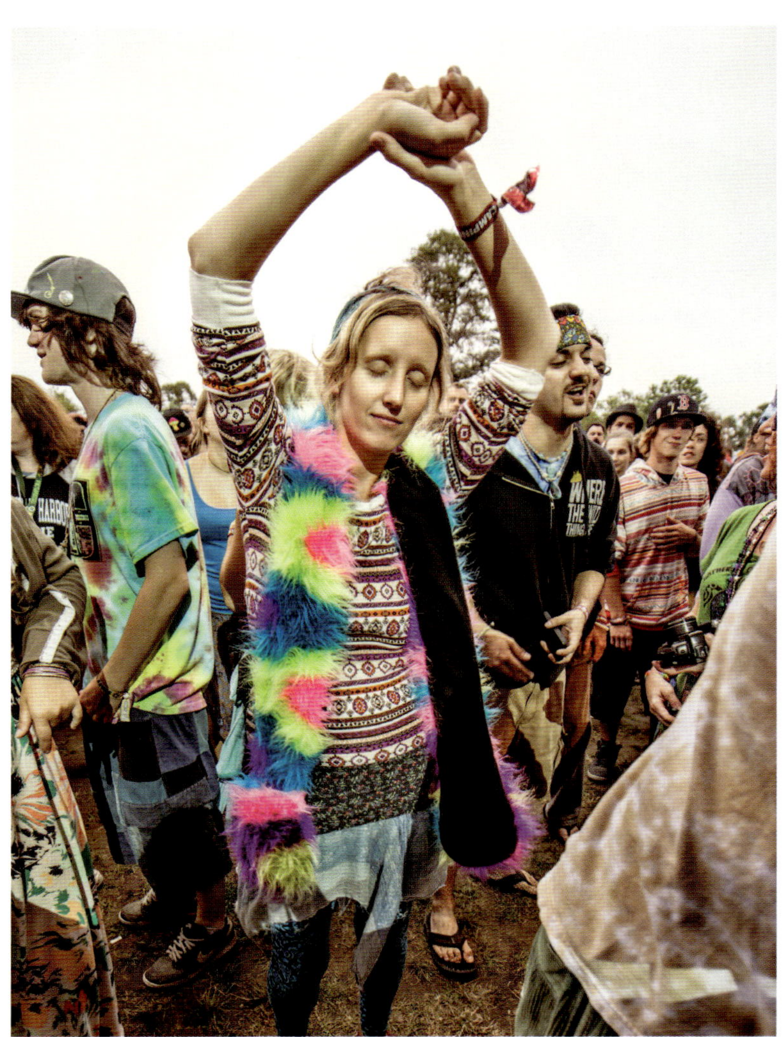

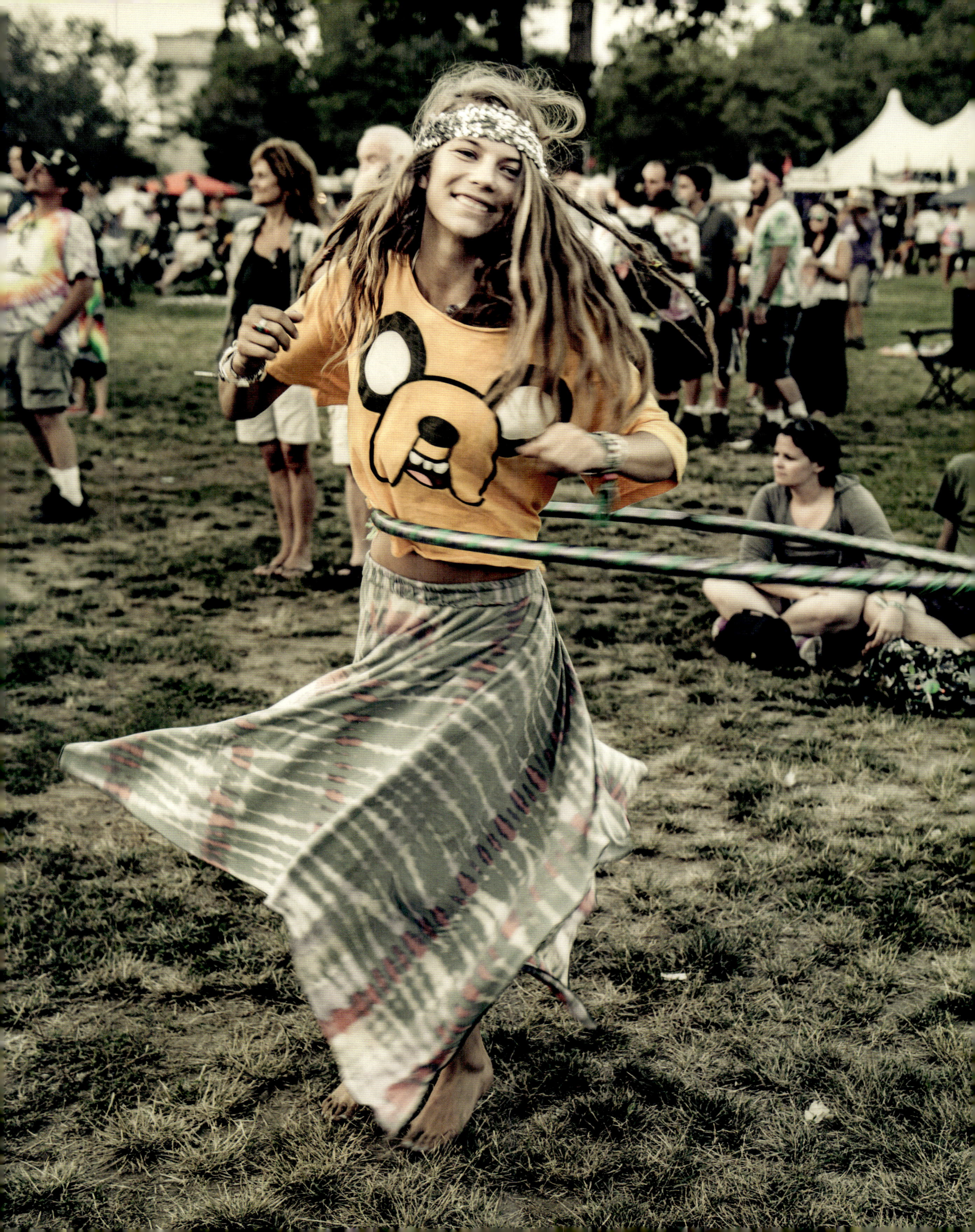

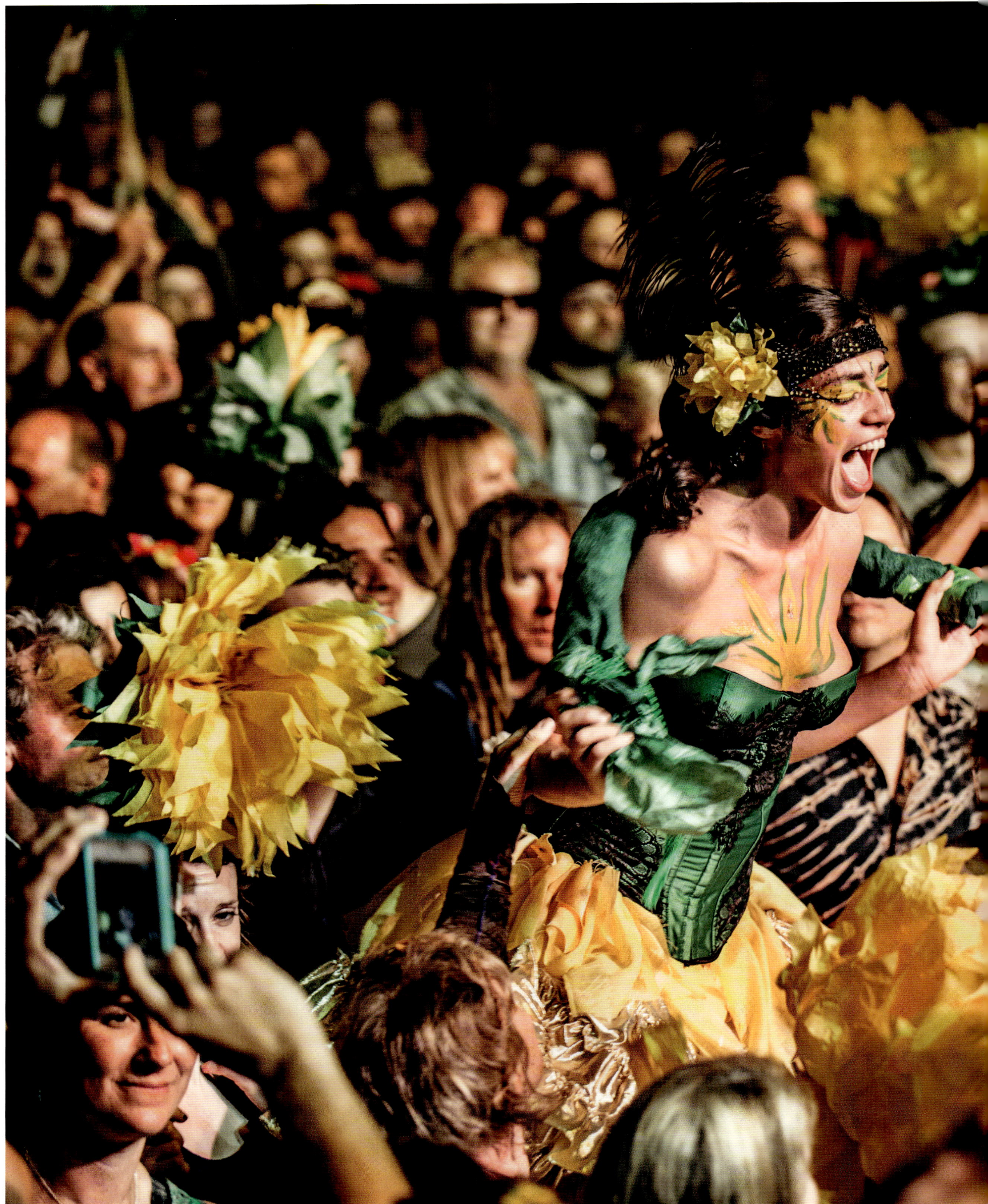

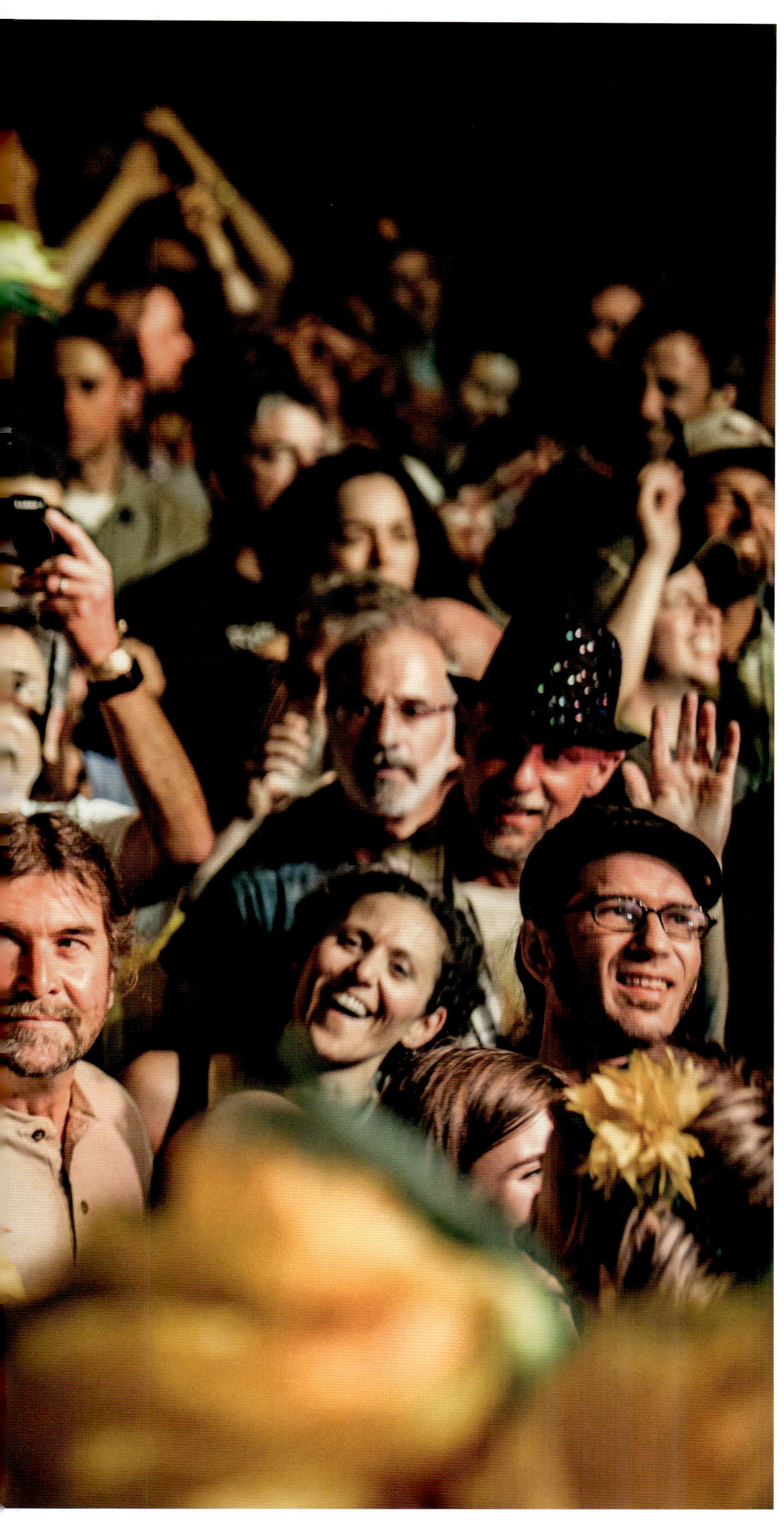

I want to be in that transfer of energy, receiving it from the band and sending it back to them in a surge of thousands!
Phyllis K.

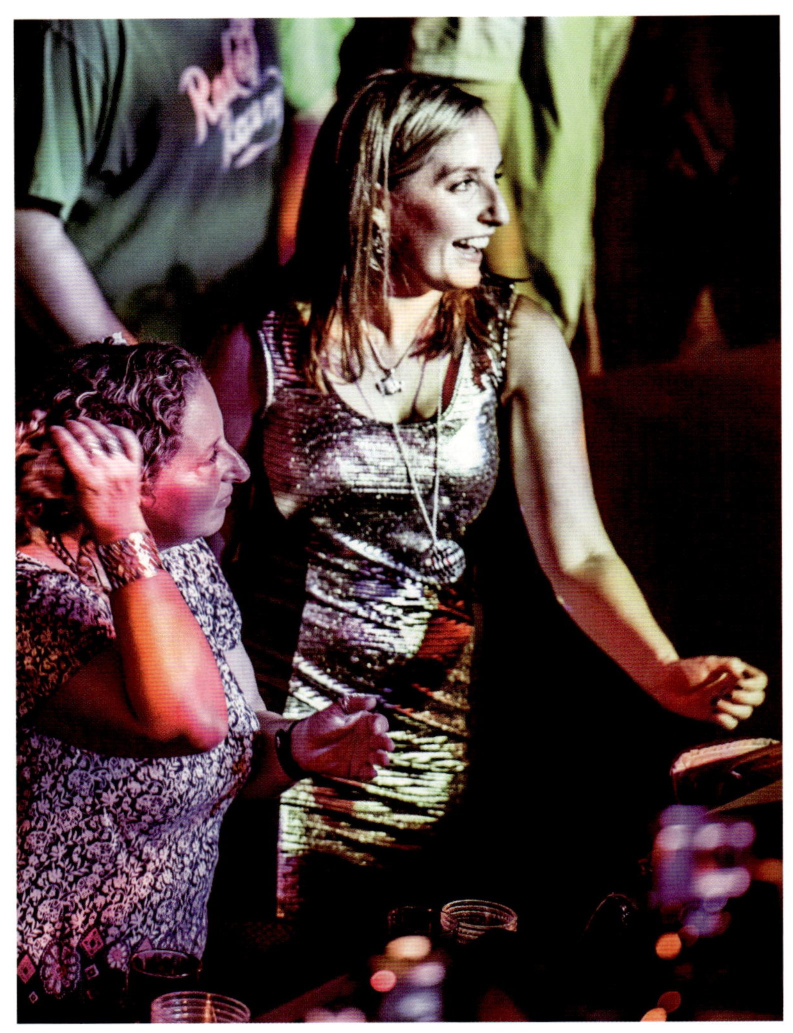

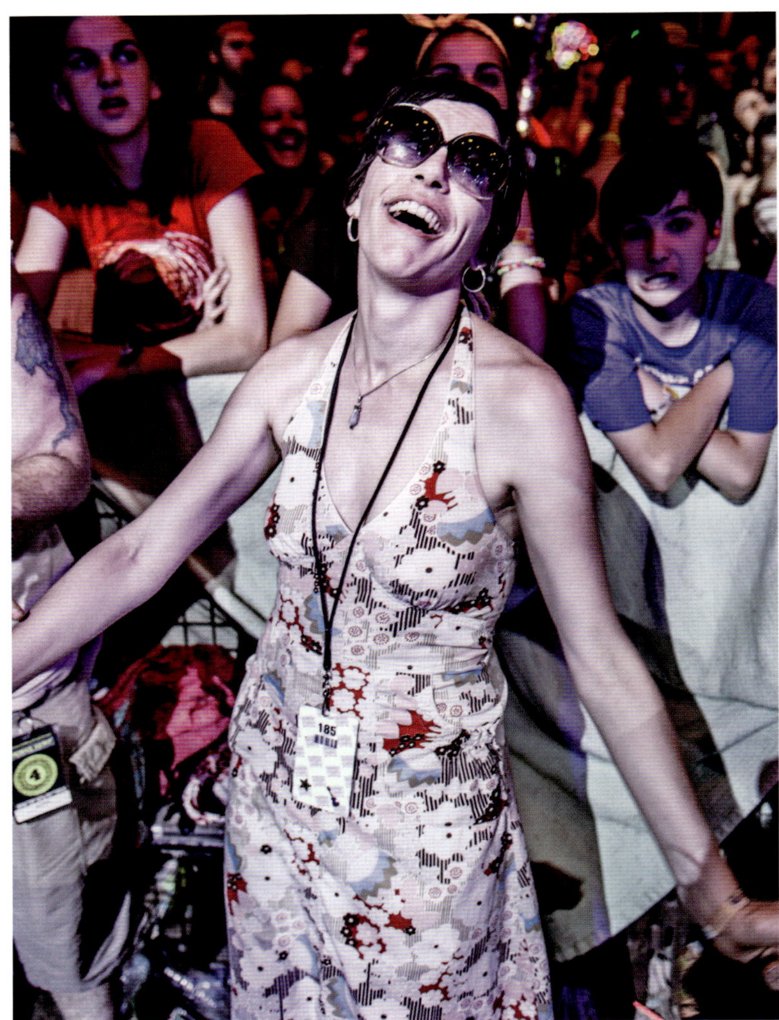

Live music is all about escapism. Leaving my troubles behind and diving into the sense of free. Jen B. (pictured, left)

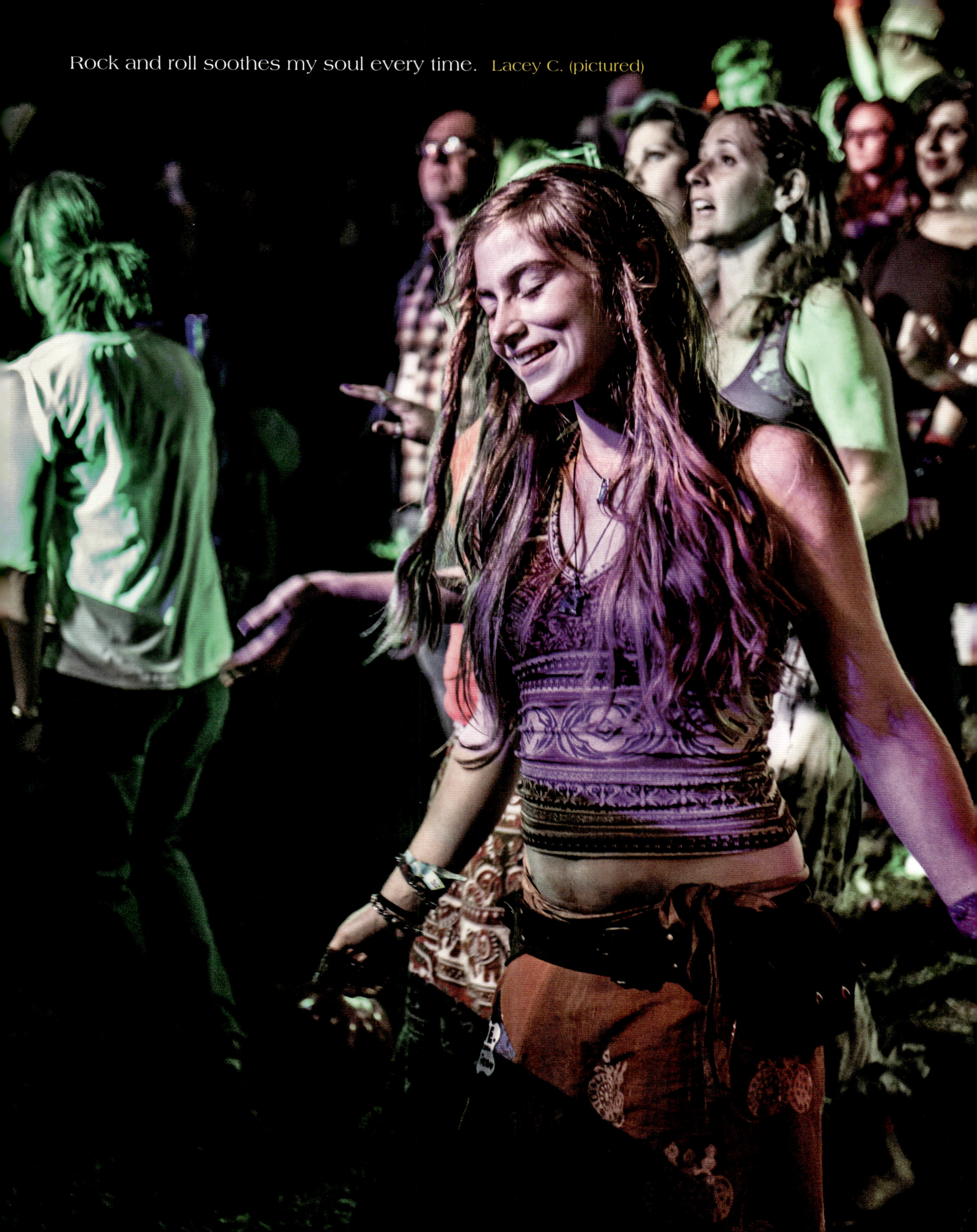

Rock and roll soothes my soul every time. Lacey C. (pictured)

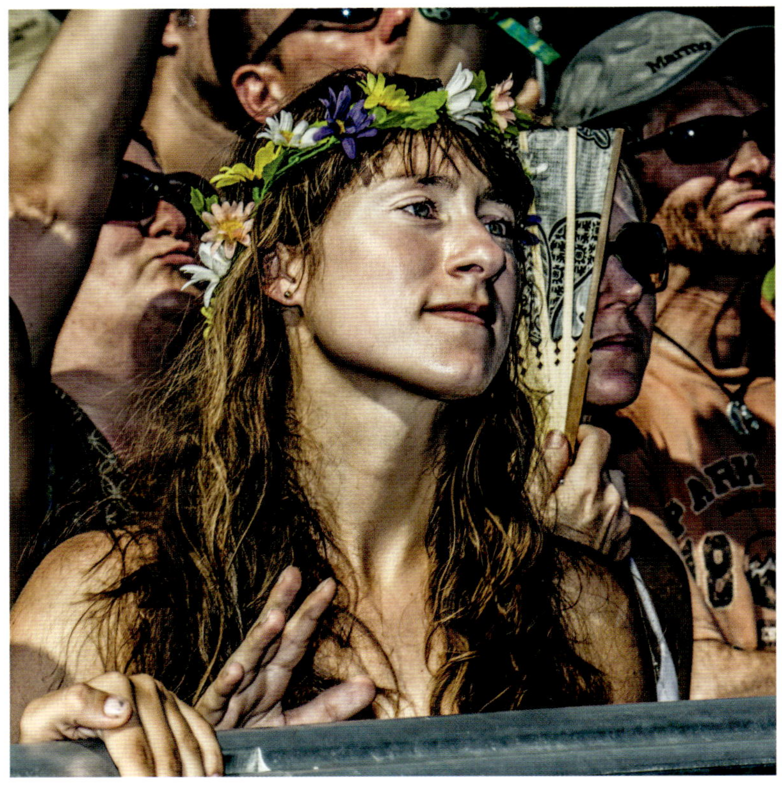

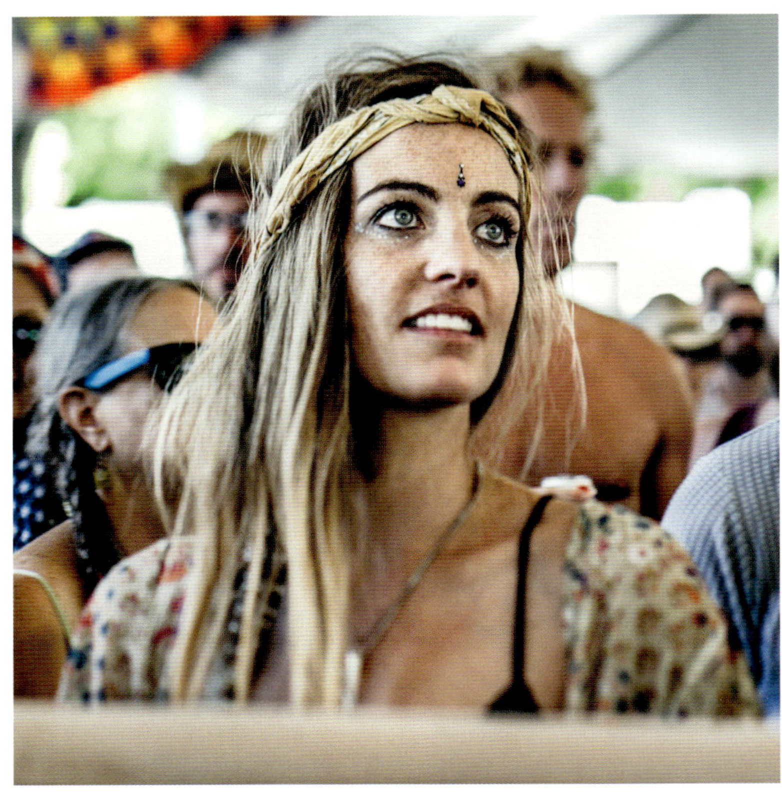

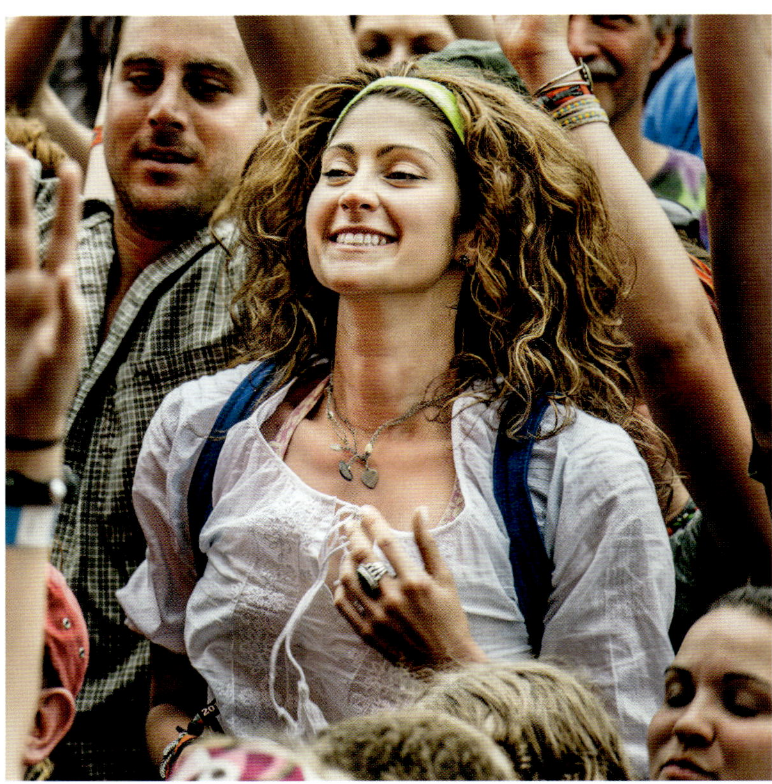

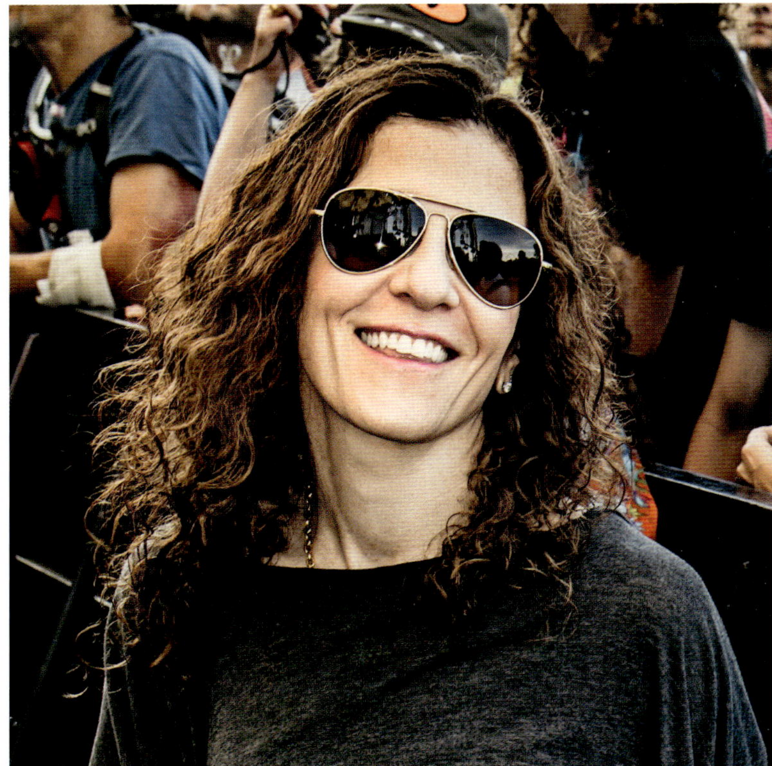

The music moves my soul and inspires me to dress the way I do. My festival fashion helps me flow to the music. Kathia B. (pictured, facing page)

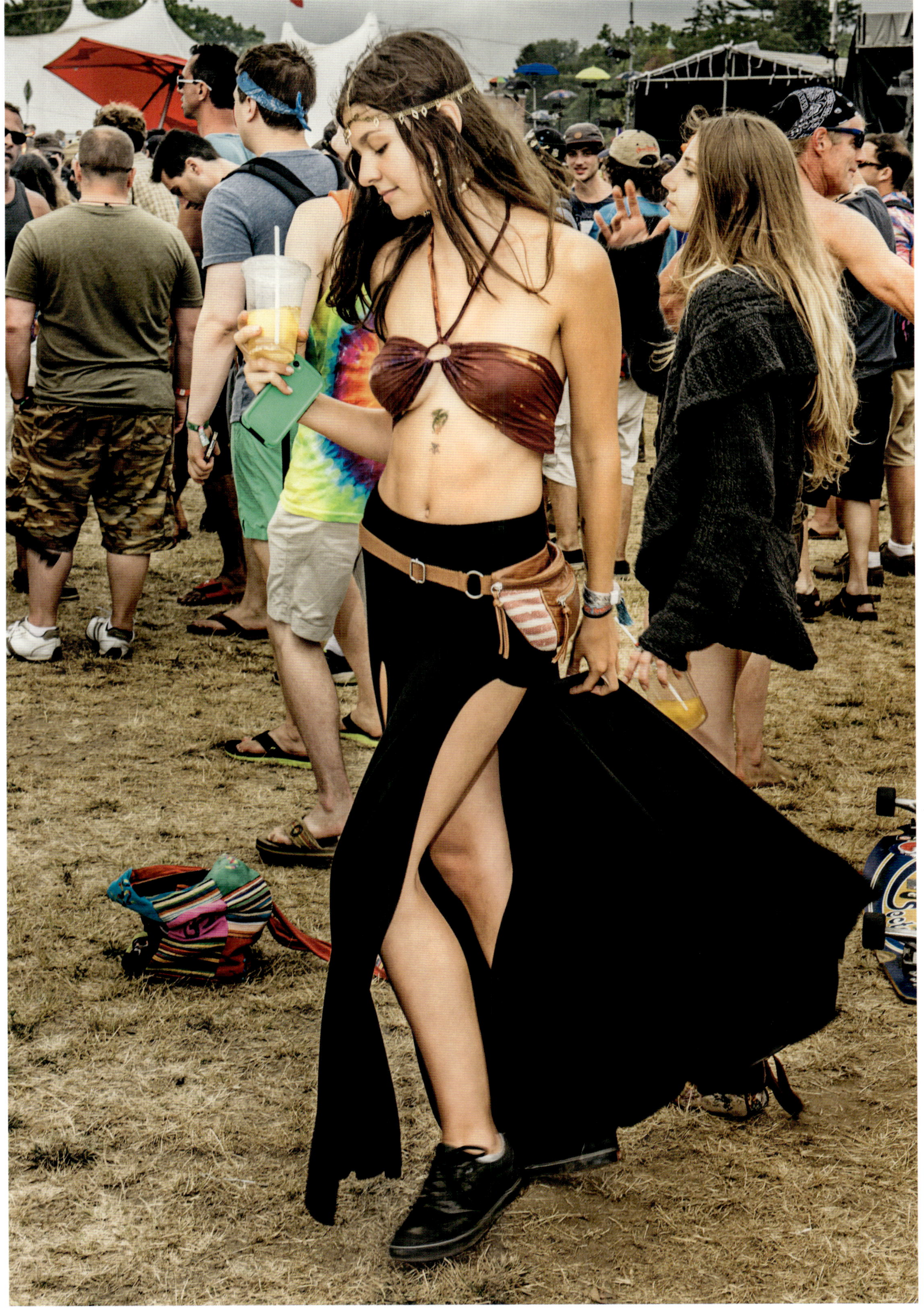

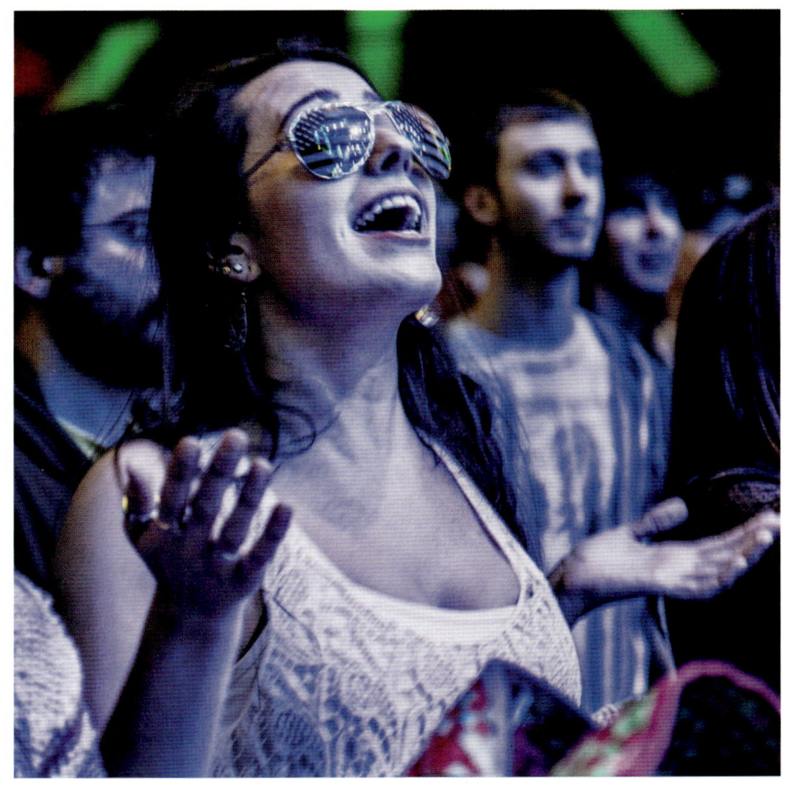

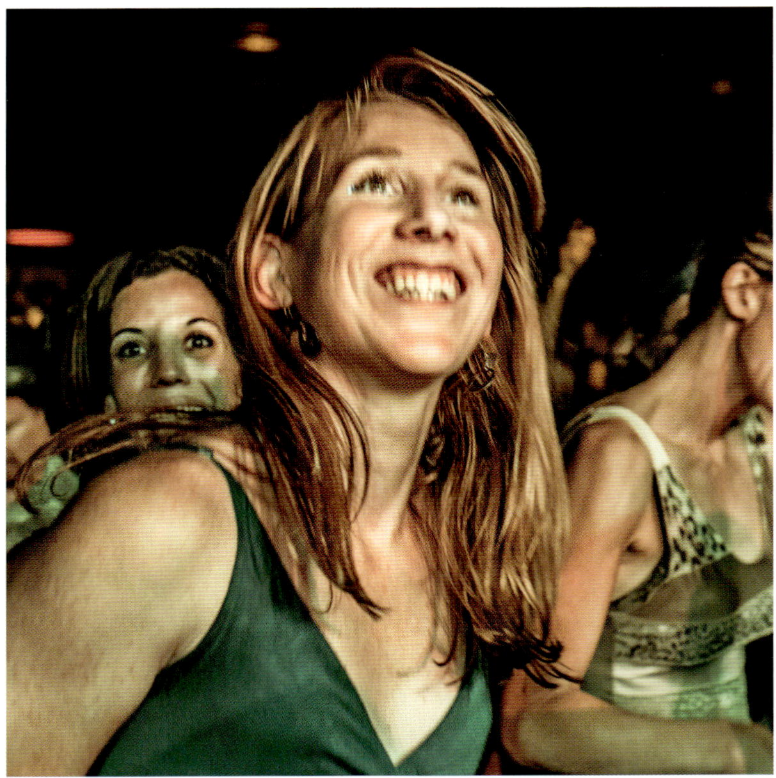

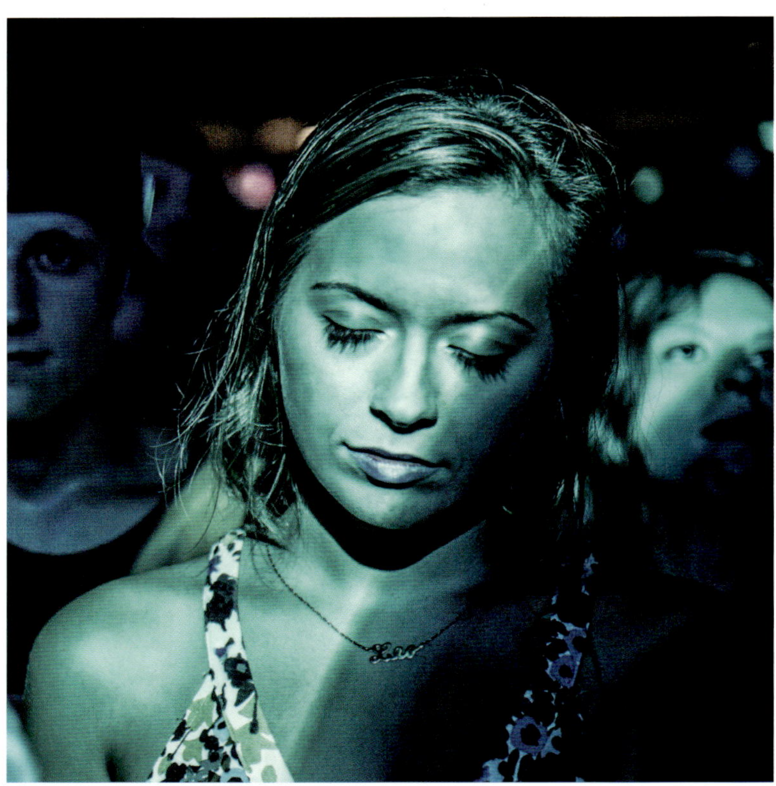

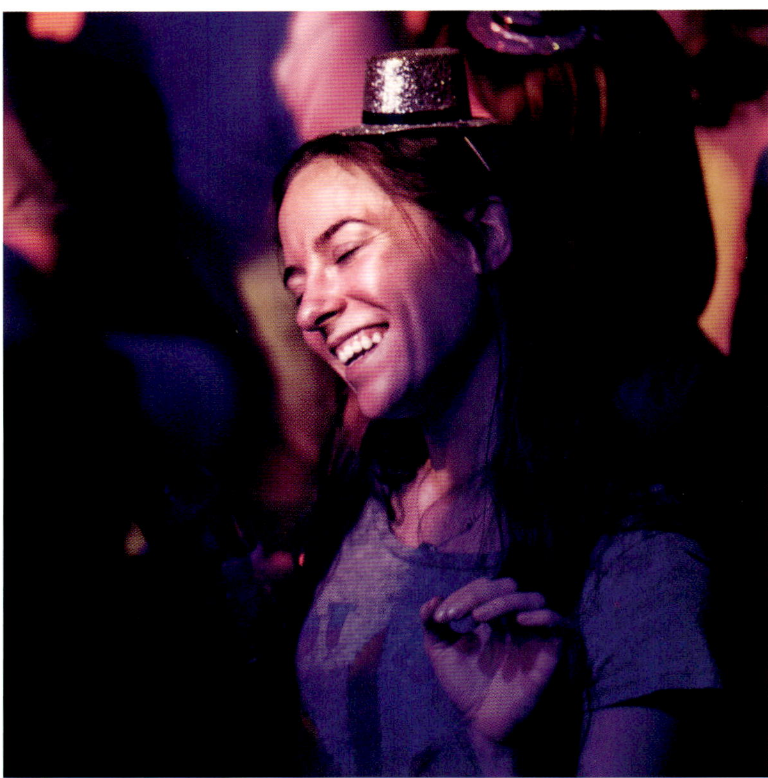

Music is my priority. No matter how many times, how many nights on the road, or where the venue is, it's never enough. Mary S.

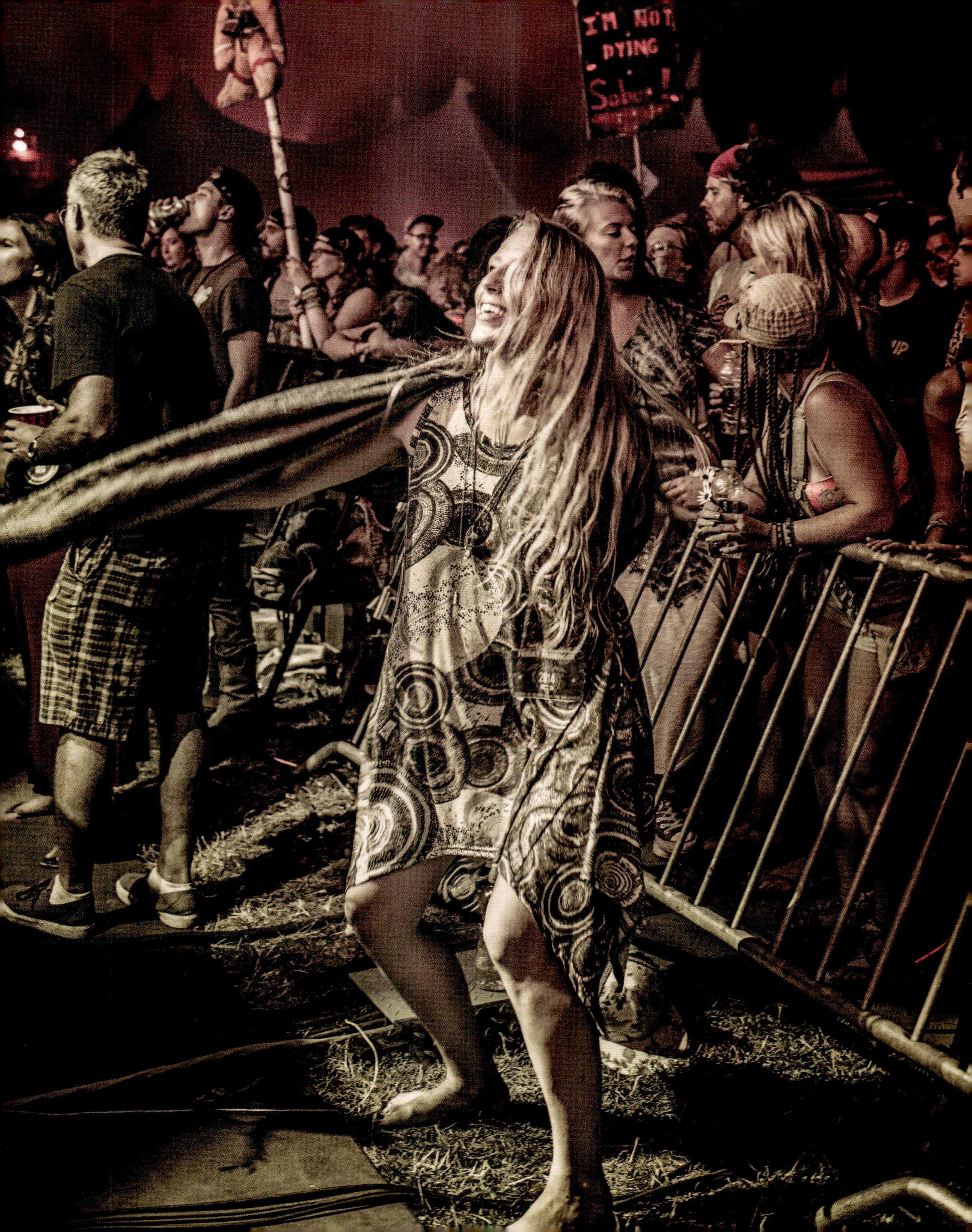
I'M NOT
DYING

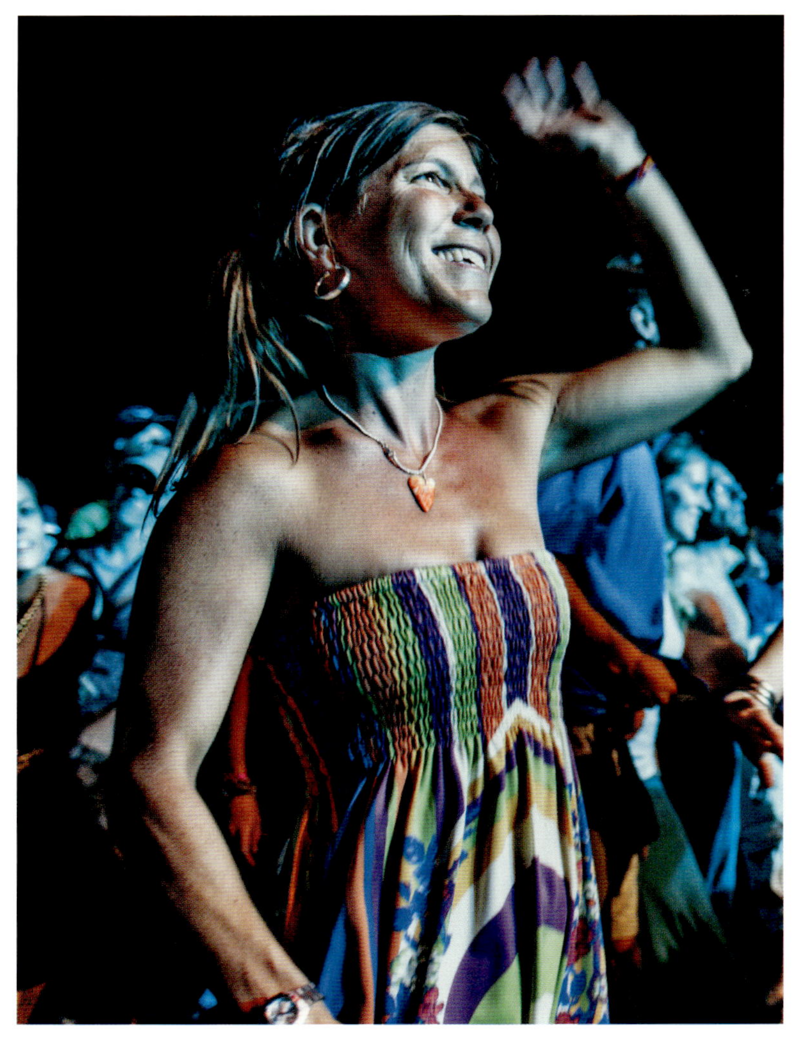

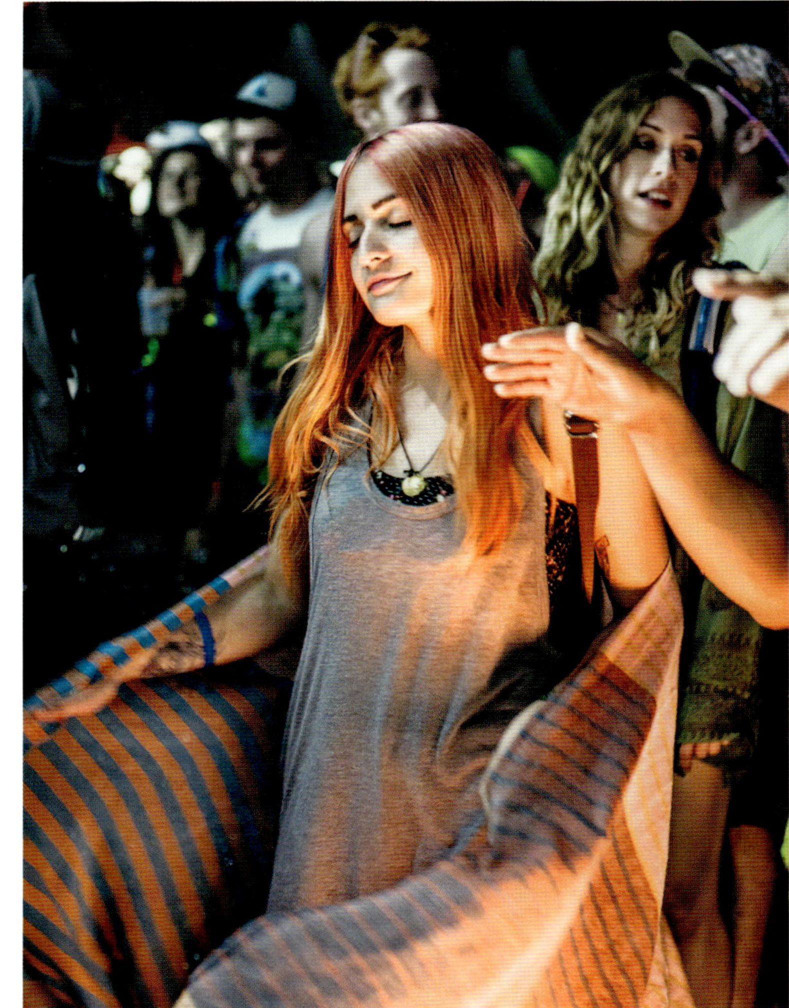

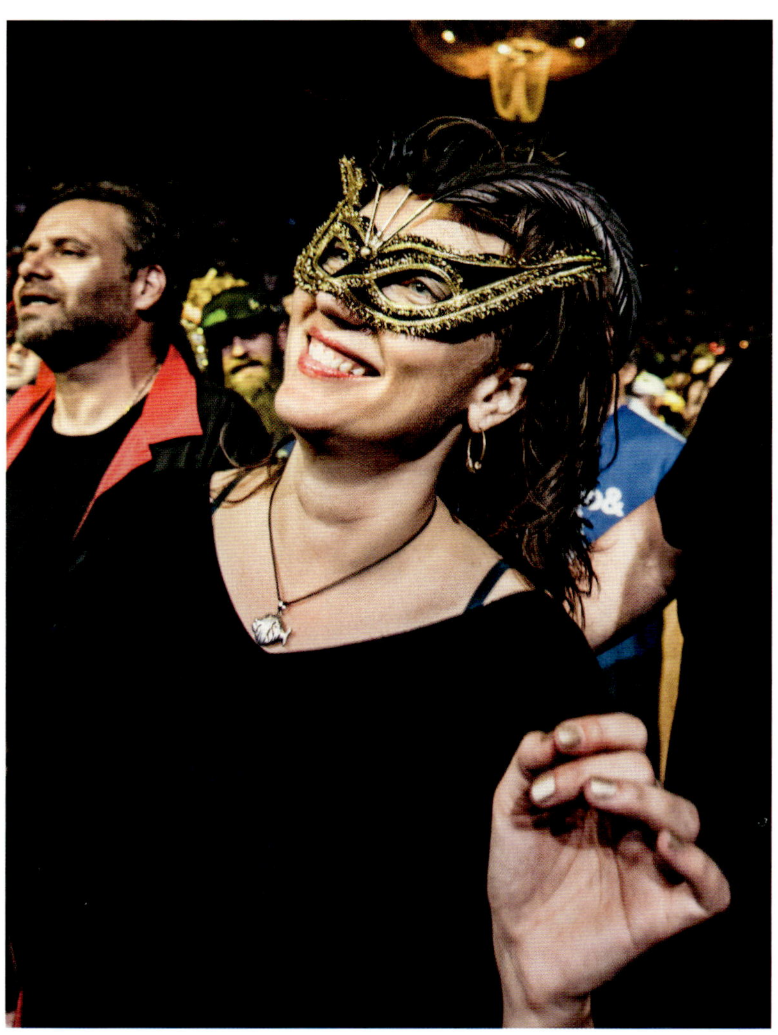

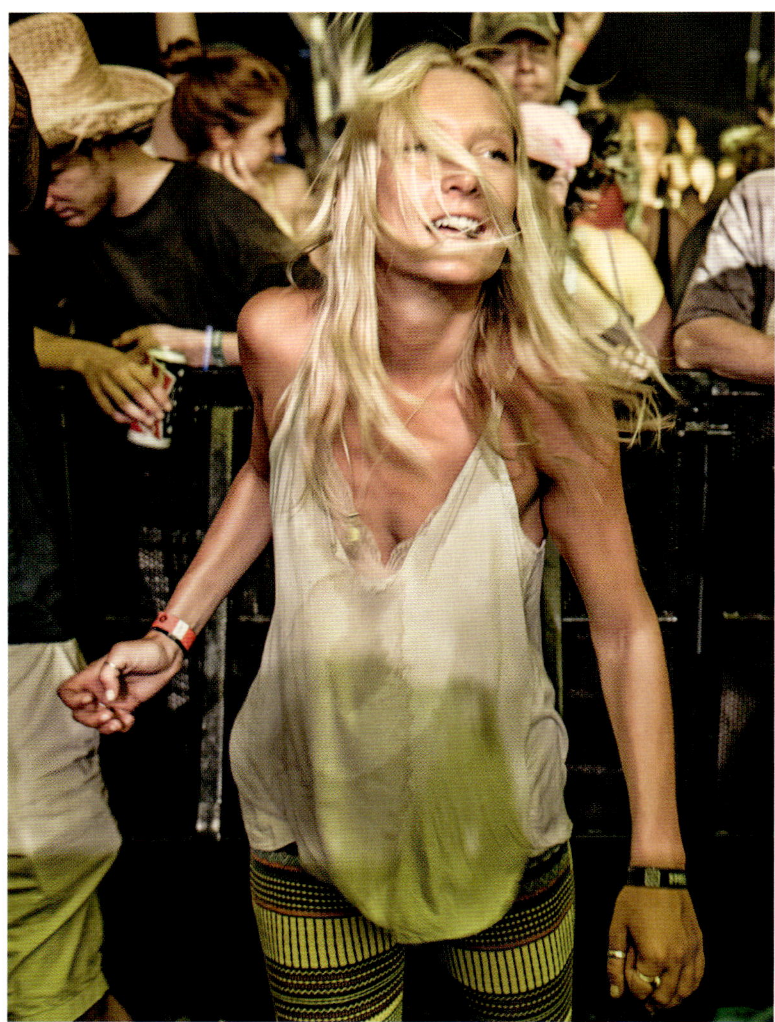

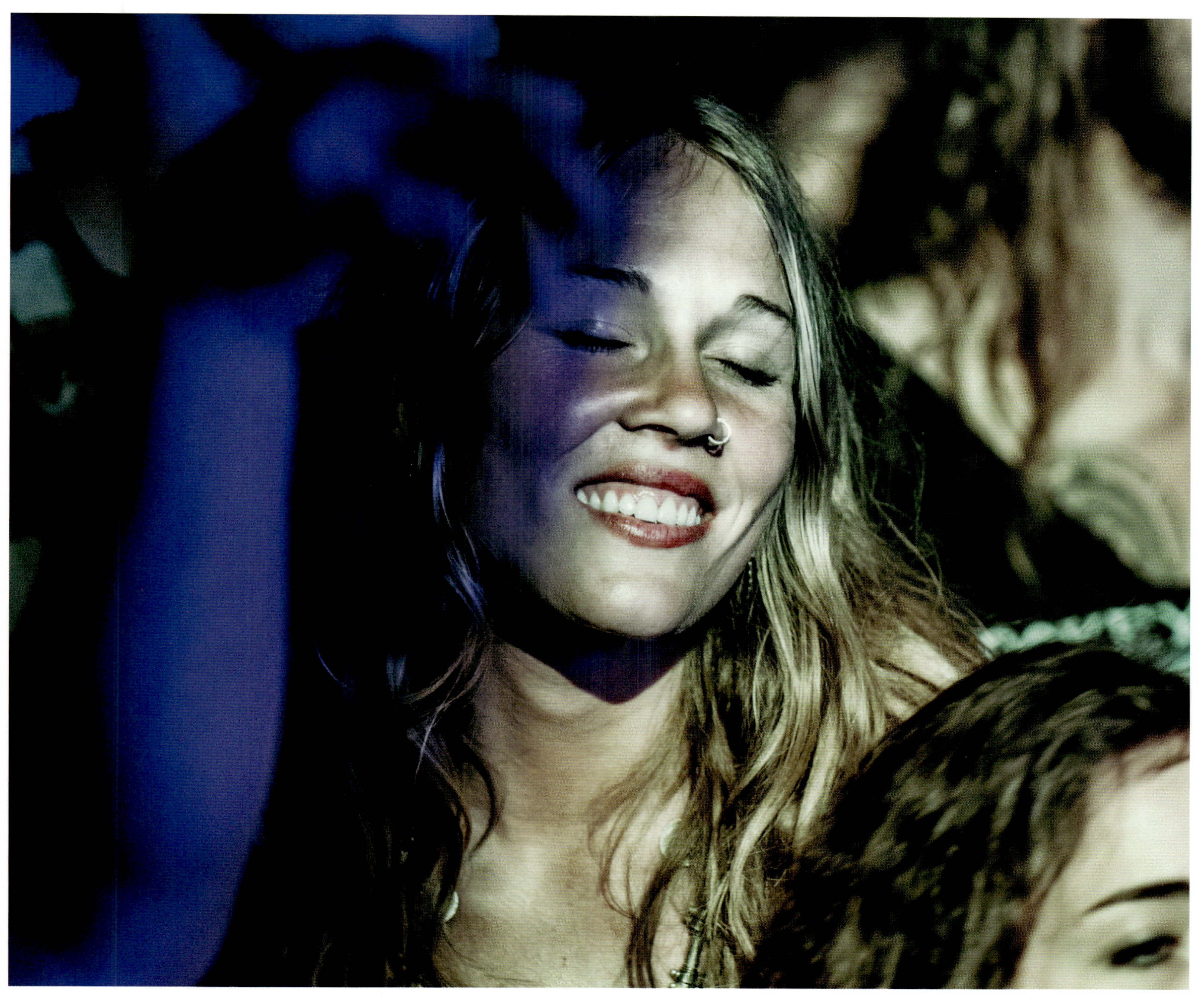

Live music gives me the opportunity to check in with myself. Batya N.

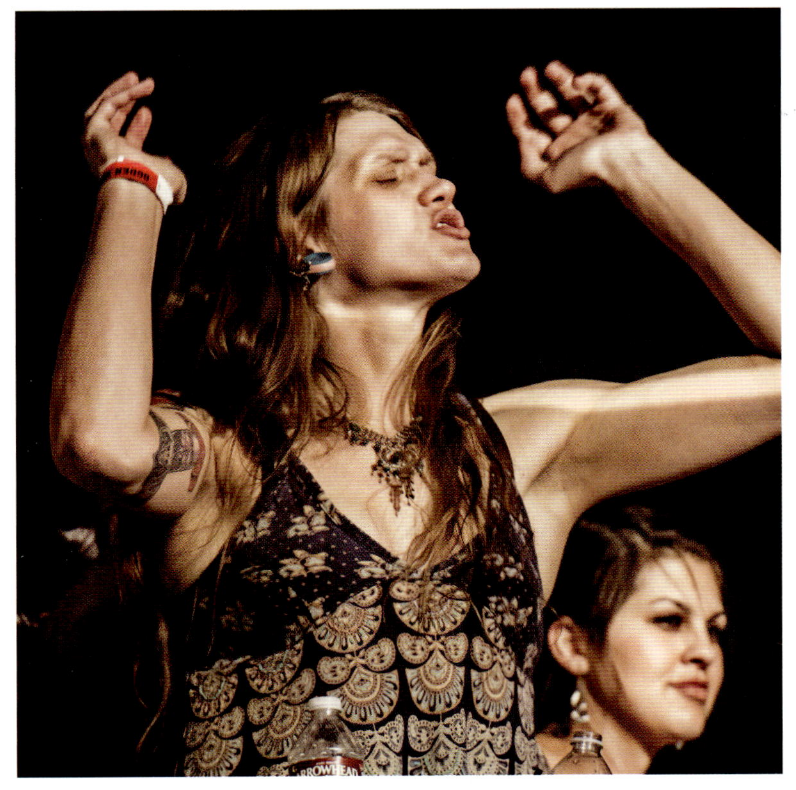

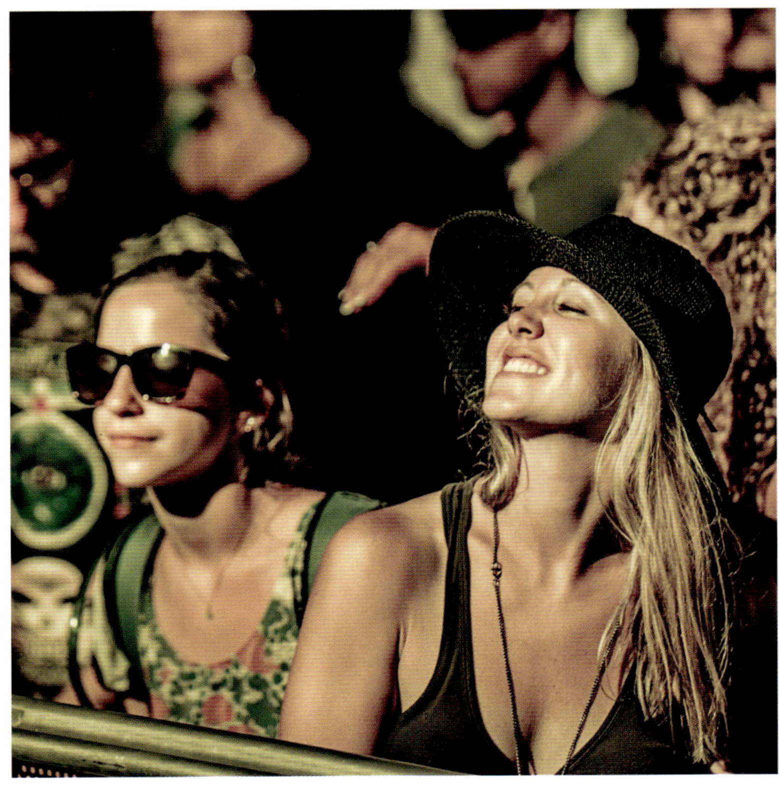

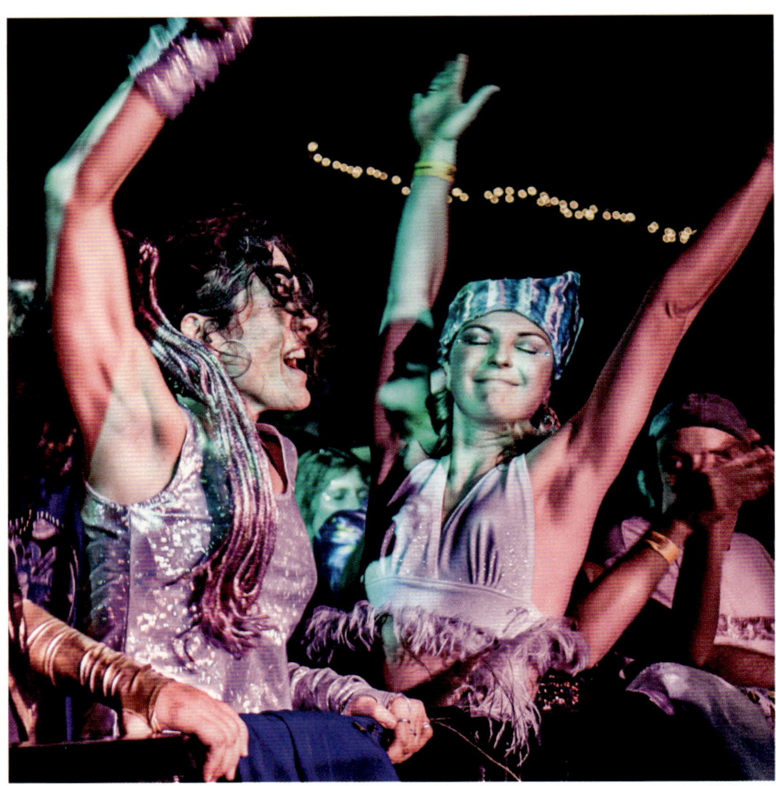

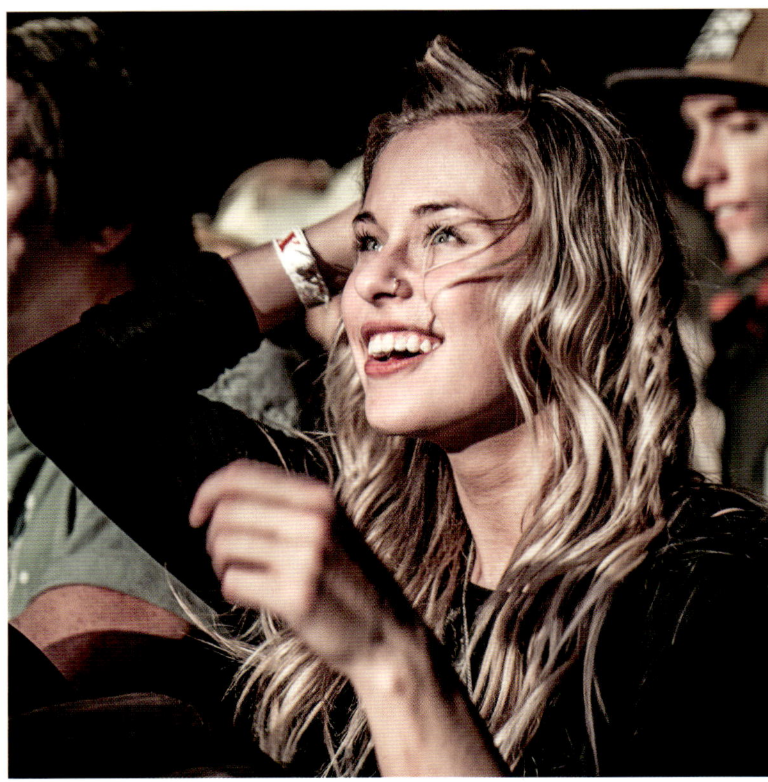

When you're not on the rail, you're just at the show. But when you're on the rail, you're IN IT with the band. It's a completely different experience.

Jenny D.

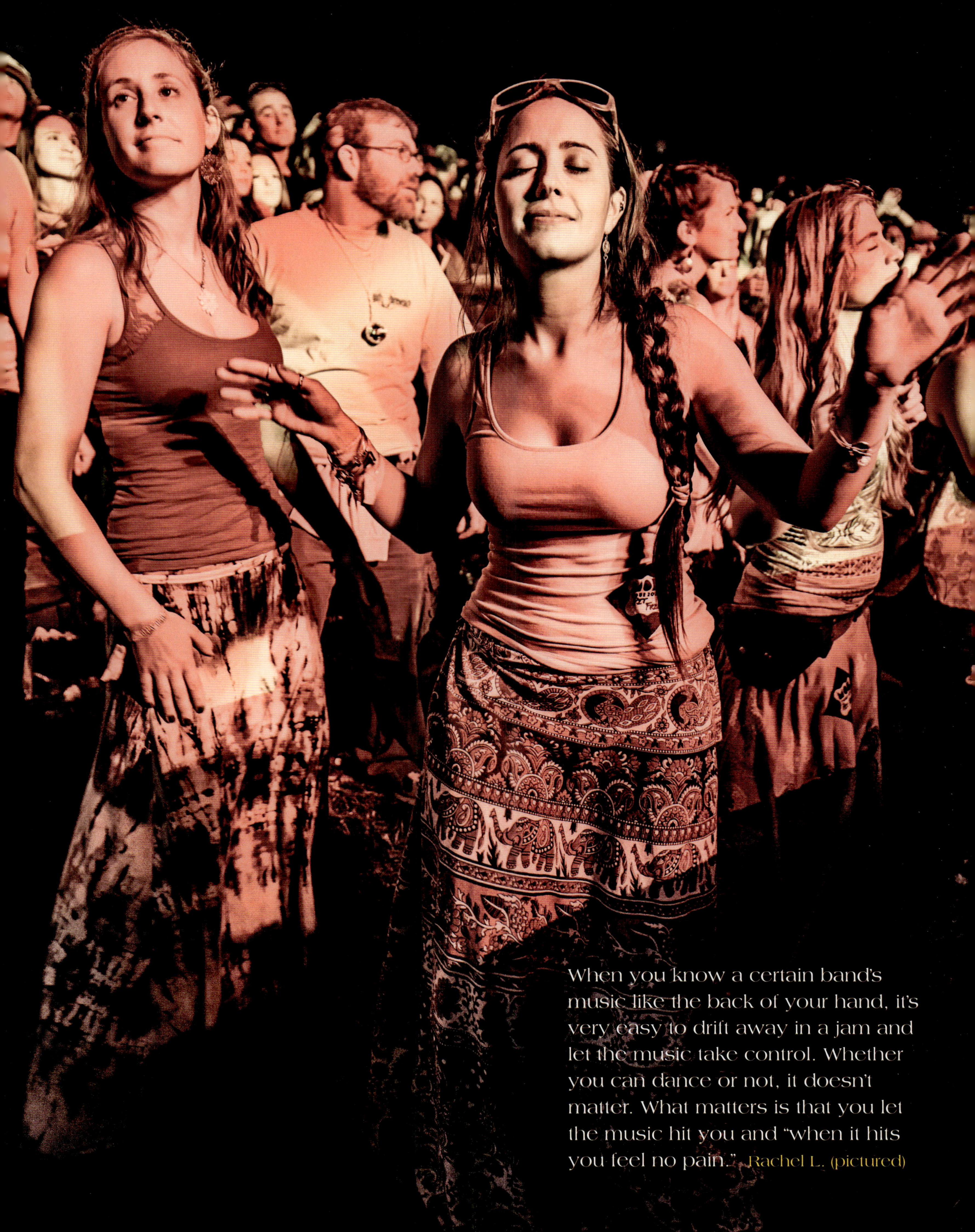

When you know a certain band's music like the back of your hand, it's very easy to drift away in a jam and let the music take control. Whether you can dance or not, it doesn't matter. What matters is that you let the music hit you and "when it hits you feel no pain." Rachel L. (pictured)

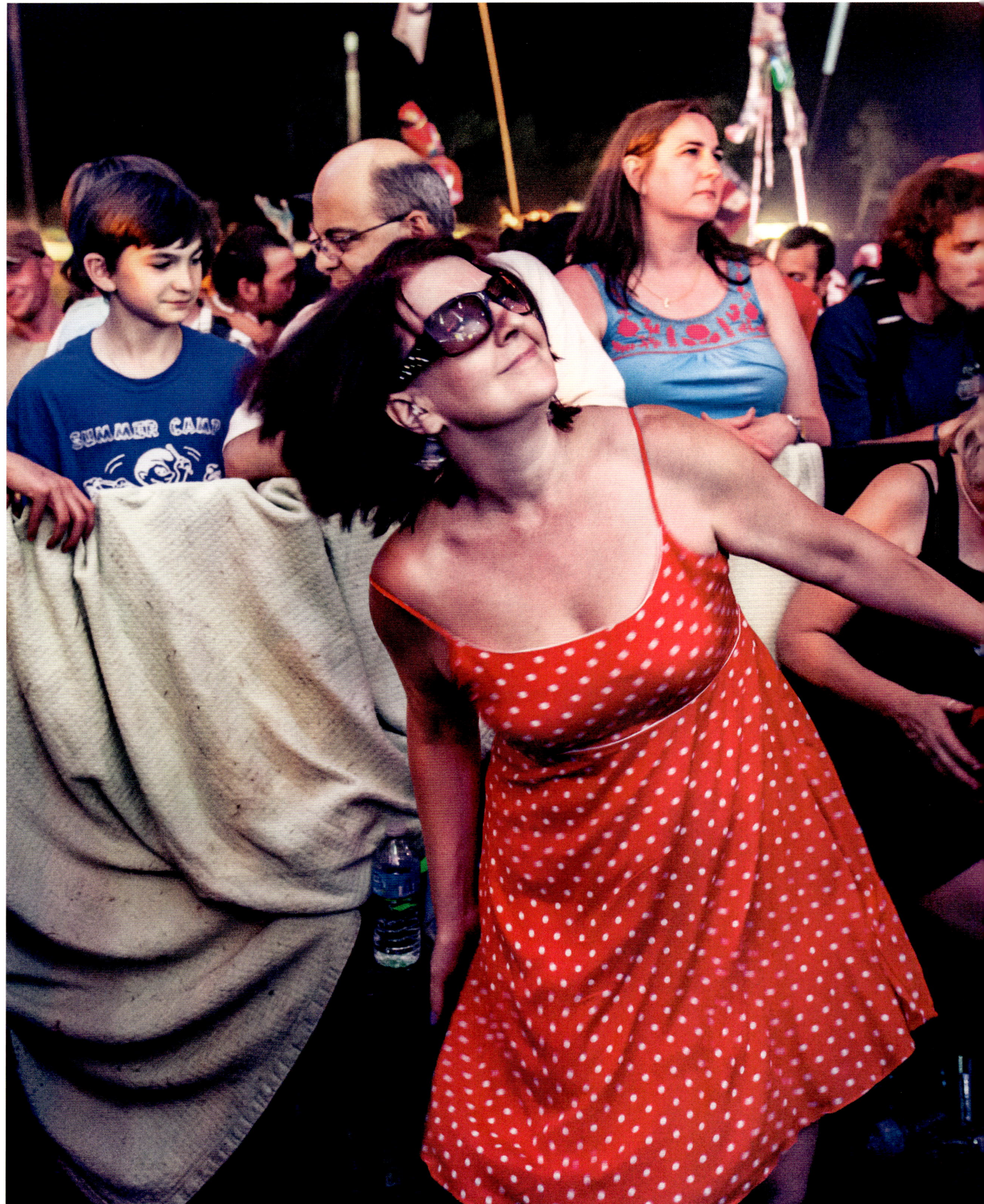
SUMMER CAMP

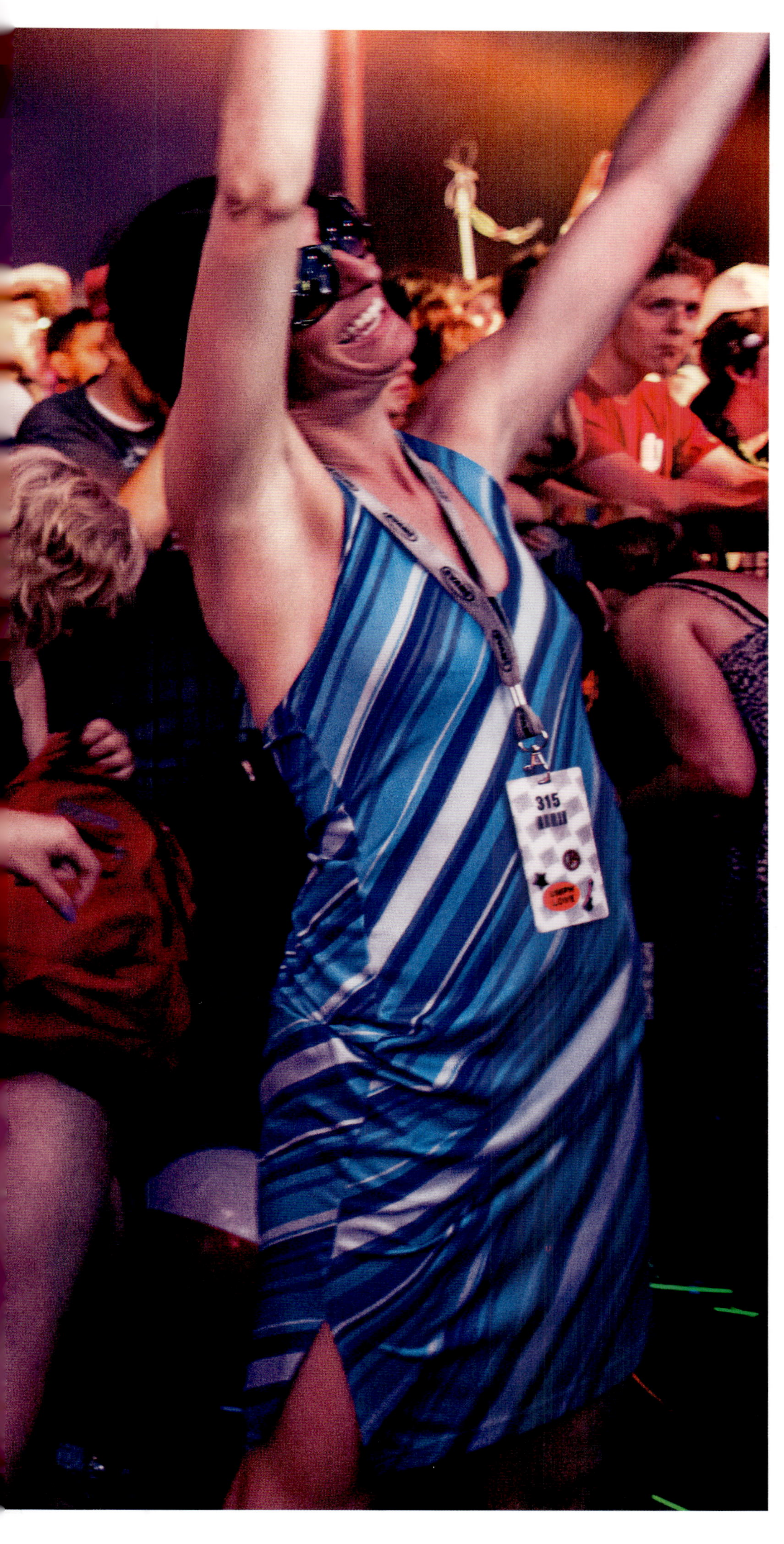

We are all there in the moment, lifting the energy of the space, encouraging the musicians to push the envelope, to give more, to play harder, to shred relentlessly. And they do. I've witnessed it and it's healed me. It heals us all. Jenn R. (pictured, left)

Devotion

This is the wonder of devotion—I see the torch we all must hold.

Led Zeppelin, "The Rain Song"

In the religion of rock and roll, ours is the path of DEVOTION. Whether we are born into it or born again, we offer ourselves humbly to the sound. Music is our gospel, the venue is our shrine, and the show is our Mecca. To those of us who truly believe, no distance is too great, no pilgrimage too arduous, to worship in joyful communion with our soul family. It's a homecoming. It's our lineage and destiny. Tour becomes our teacher and the endless road beckons us to gather the tribe.

For those who heed its call, the journey can lead to unexpected places. A single show, or even a song lyric, can forever transform us. A new tune suddenly becomes our North Star, a melody our mantra. We pledge allegiance to certain bands and identify with specific instruments. The thrill of the keys, the thump of the bass—whatever ignites us, we choose our spot in the crowd accordingly and return over and over to stoke the flames. Traditions develop and evolve with each mile traveled. Rituals reaffirm our commitment. The more we repeat them, the closer we get, and the more it feels like we've been there before.

Live music can lift the veil of illusion, offering us a view into our deepest, inner reality; an invisible world, previously unknown but immediately recognized. It's spiritual déjà vu. We hear our lives in the lyrics. We feel at home with the songs. We search for answers and find things we didn't even know we were looking for. Set list order becomes significant; synchronicities emerge. When we ask, we receive, because we create the meaning that sustains us. We move beyond faith and into knowledge. We feel connected to each other, to the music, and to life, as we fall further down the rabbit hole of realization.

Immersing ourselves in the scene, we let daily concerns dissolve. We are cleansed by the sights and sounds, and bathed in unconditional love. Our first show is a rite of passage. We come as we are and the music accepts us, providing sweet sanctuary for those seeking refuge. Where we are in life, how we feel at any given moment, animates our relationship to what we hear. Magic happens, miracles occur, and the music heals us. Initiated and embraced, we are blanketed by the tribal bond. We belong. We are part of it and feel loyal to it. The music nourishes us and we long to give back.

We express our gratitude through devotional acts. We follow; we attend; we offer up our energy. We support the community and bring others into the flock. We collect objects of worship to consecrate our beliefs—we buy merch, save ticket stubs, and trade recordings. We lovingly preserve the material culture of our favorite bands. We frame show posters and wear tour t-shirts threadbare. We make sacrifices to be closer to the source. We arrive early and wait patiently to secure a spot up front, on the mystical vortex of the rail.

Our hearts, bodies, and minds give the music resonance. Movement becomes an act of meditation, bringing us into sacred alignment. We connect to collective consciousness, flowing along a shared, supernatural rhythm, in complete harmony with the earth and each other—grooving. We become the notes. We are the instruments. Losing ourselves wholly in waves of sound, we peak, flooded with bliss. We are transcendent. We are grateful devotees, goddesses at the temple.

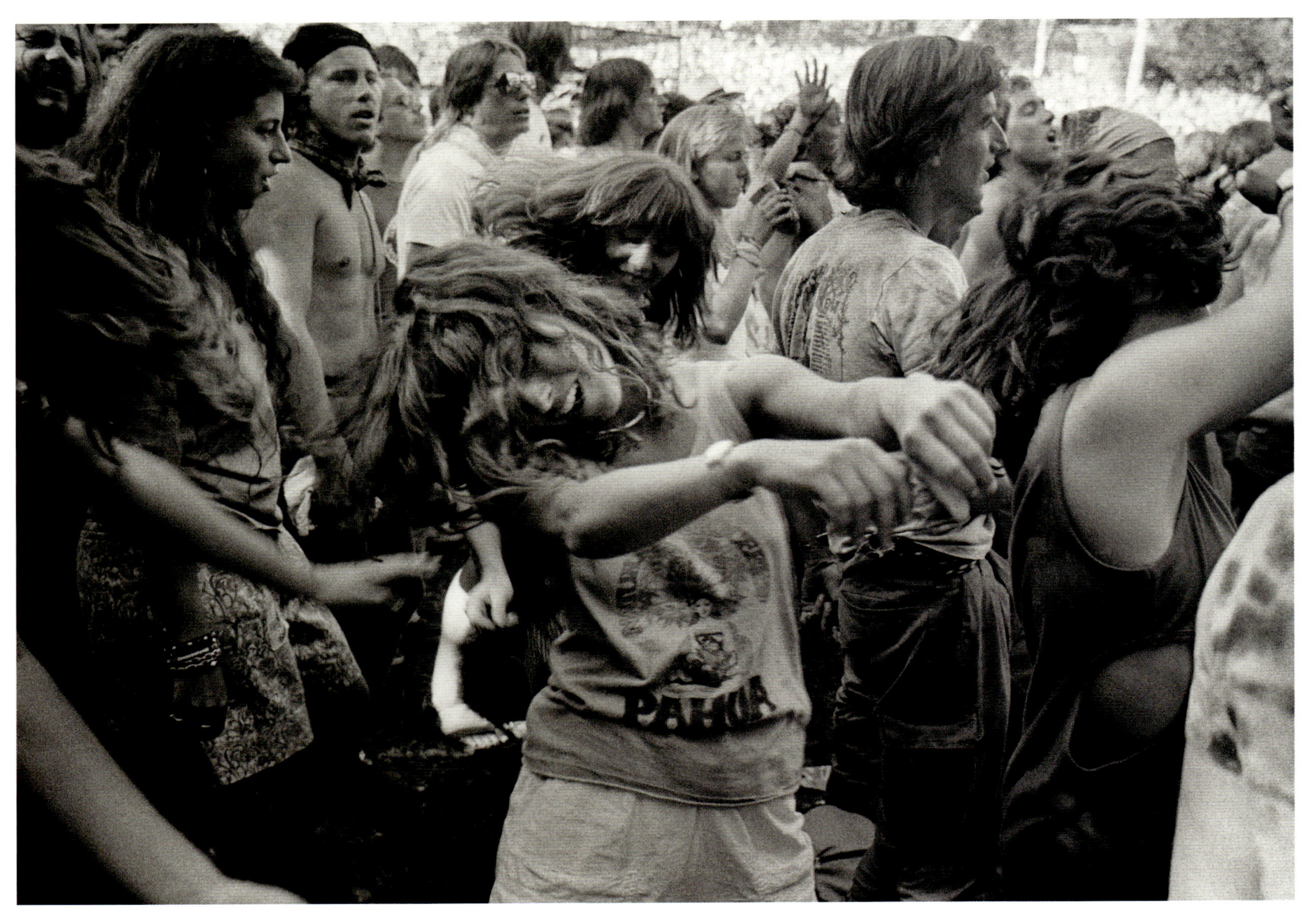

Music lights up my soul. It's a transcendental experience. That feeling of overwhelming emotion where you can feel your very essence bursting with so much love you can't get the smile off your face and you feel oh so very alive—that's the best part. Erica B.

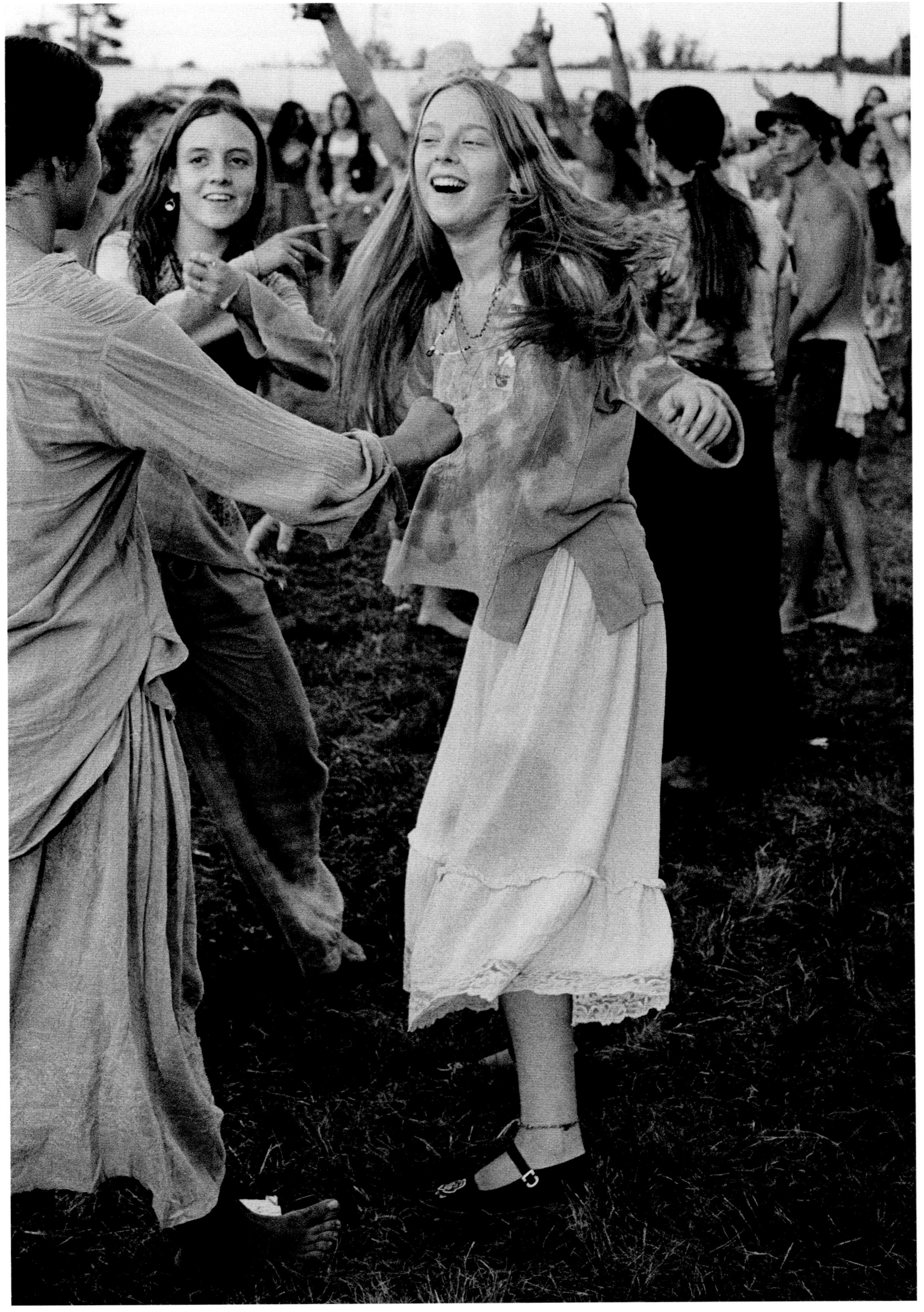

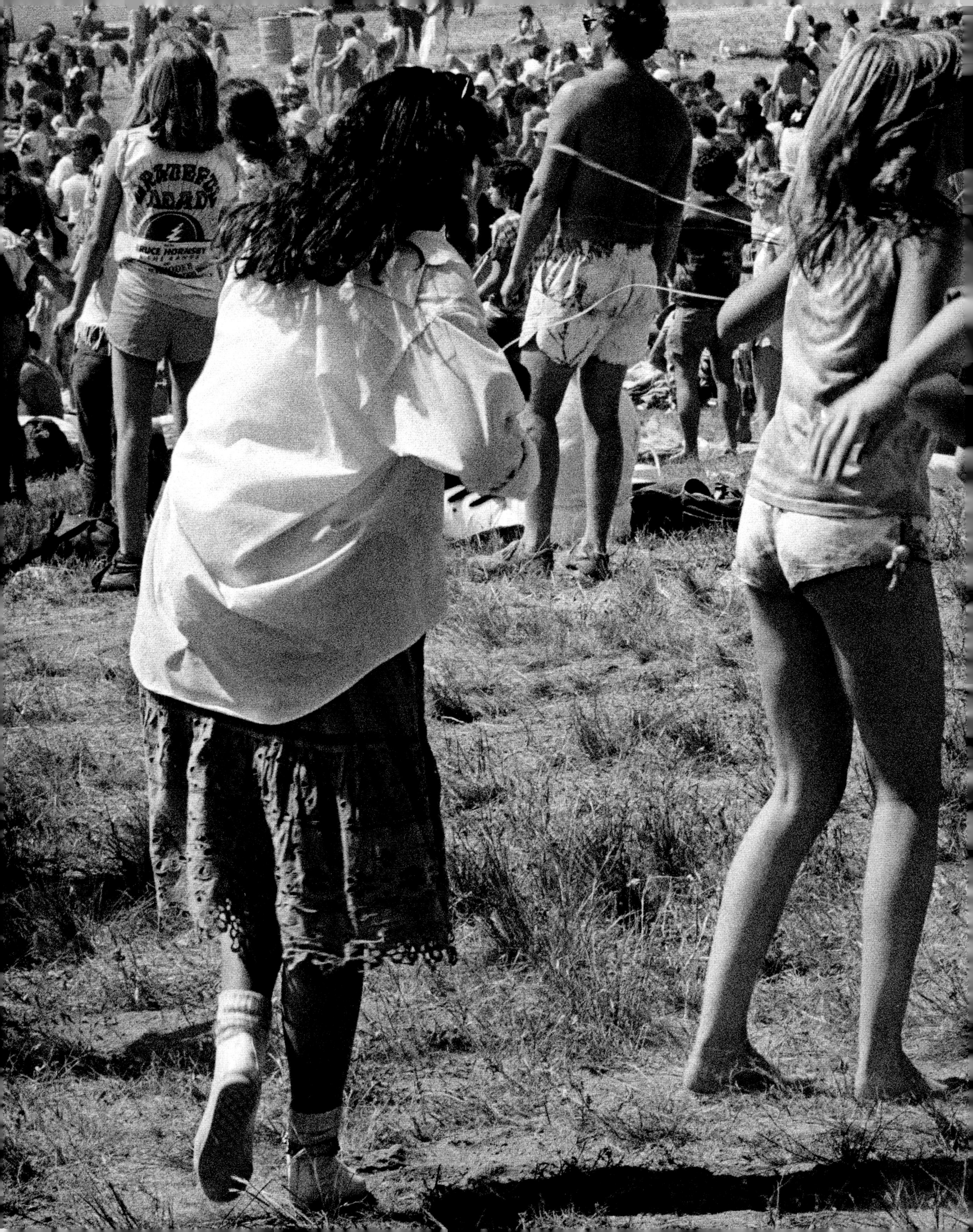

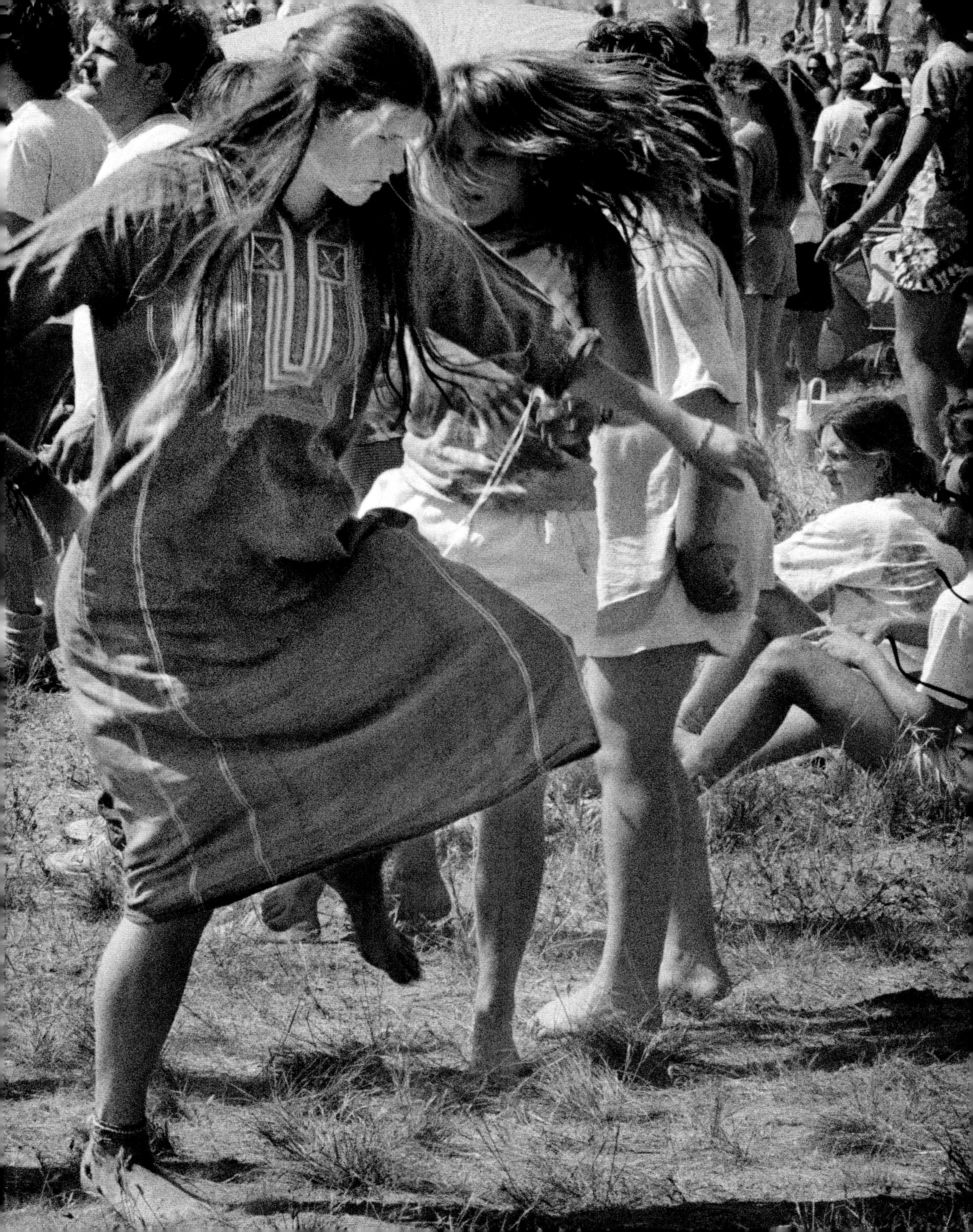

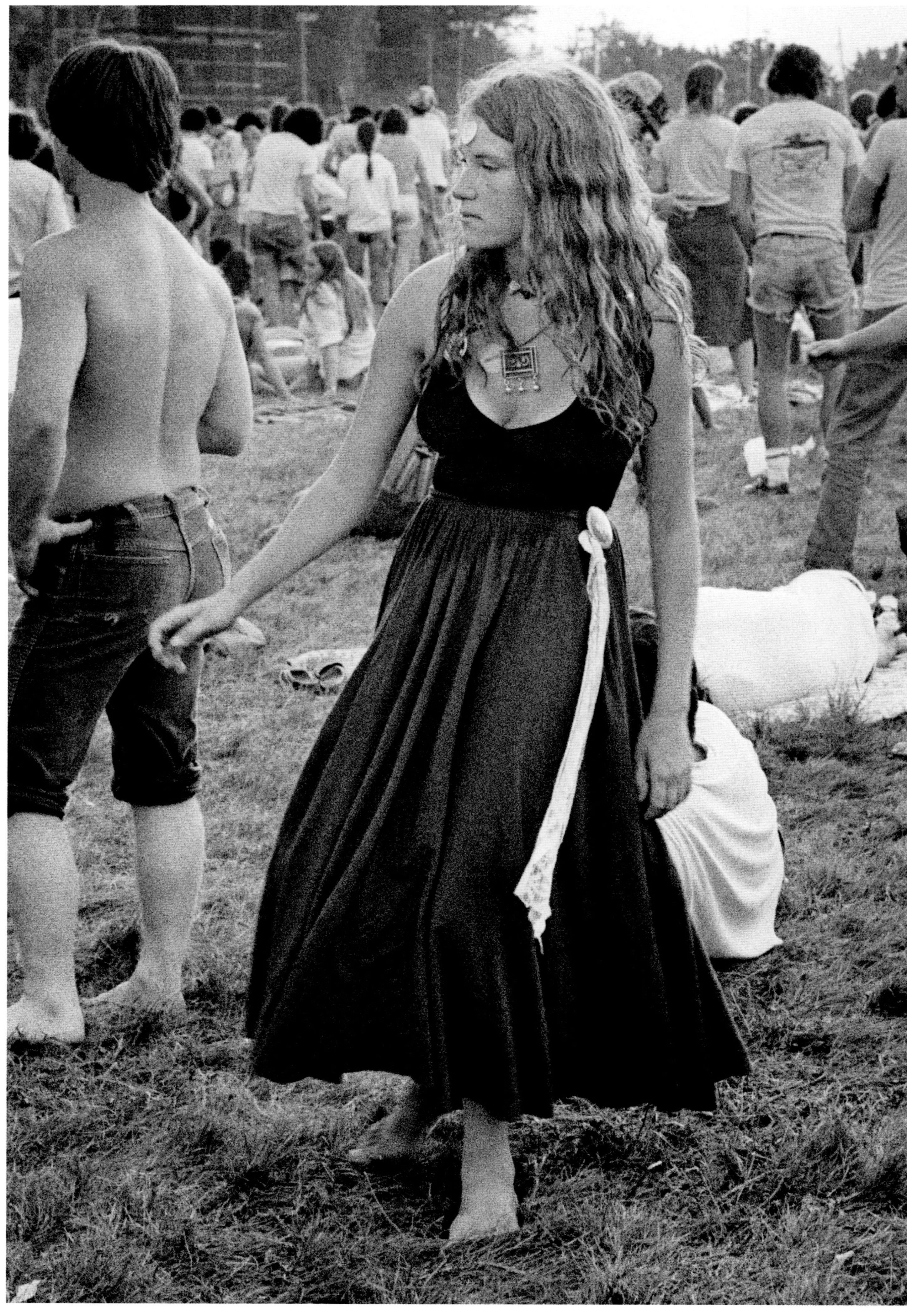

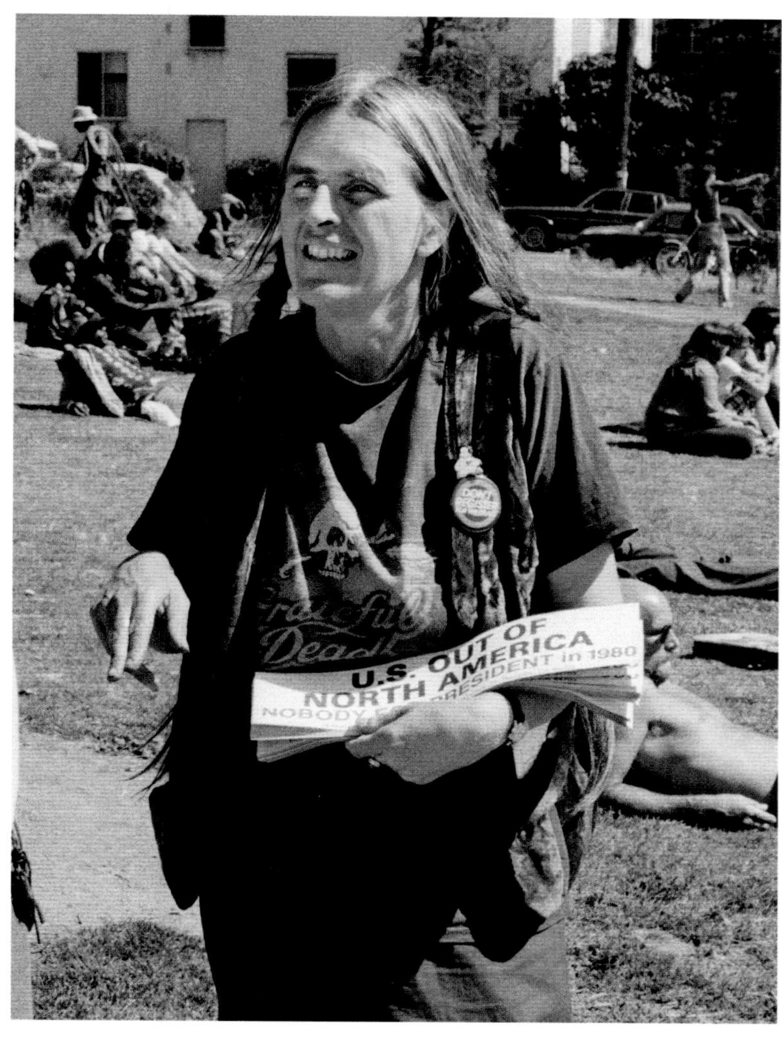
U.S. OUT OF
NORTH AMERICA
PRESIDENT in 1980

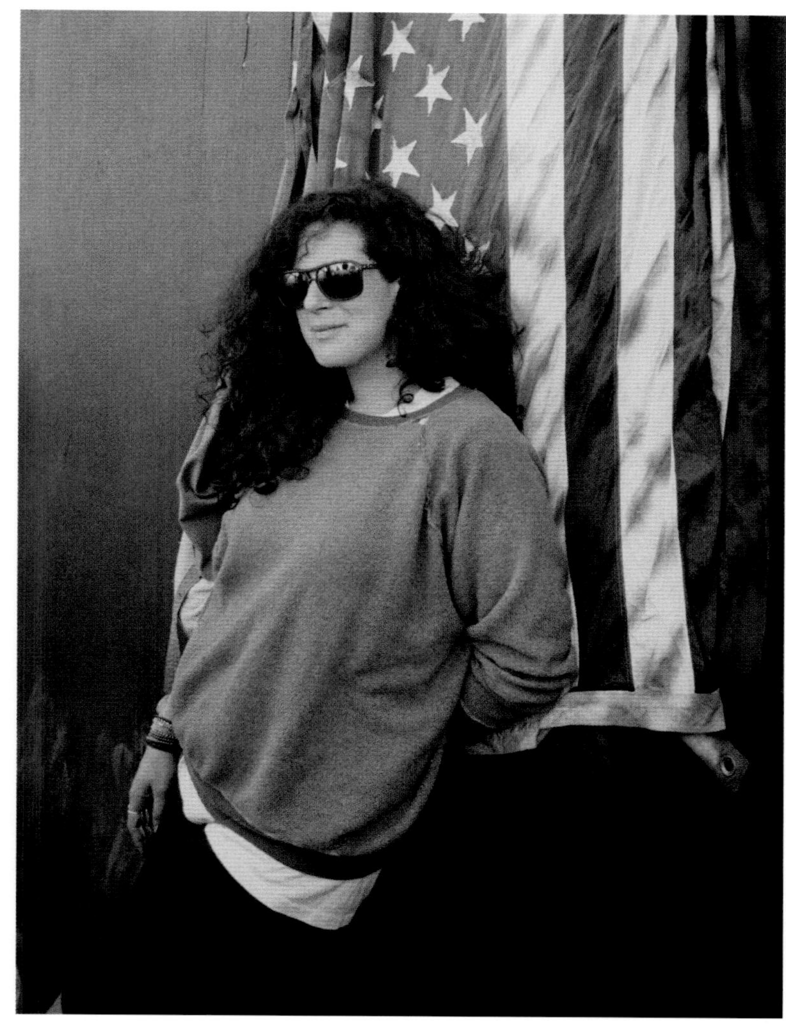

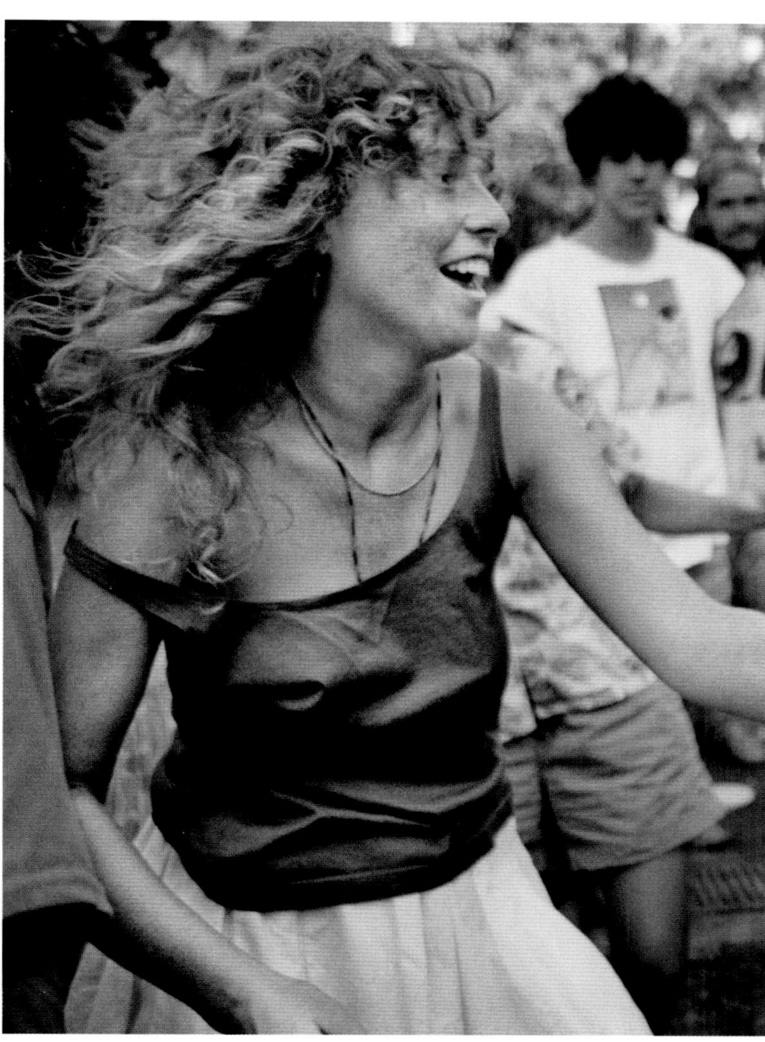

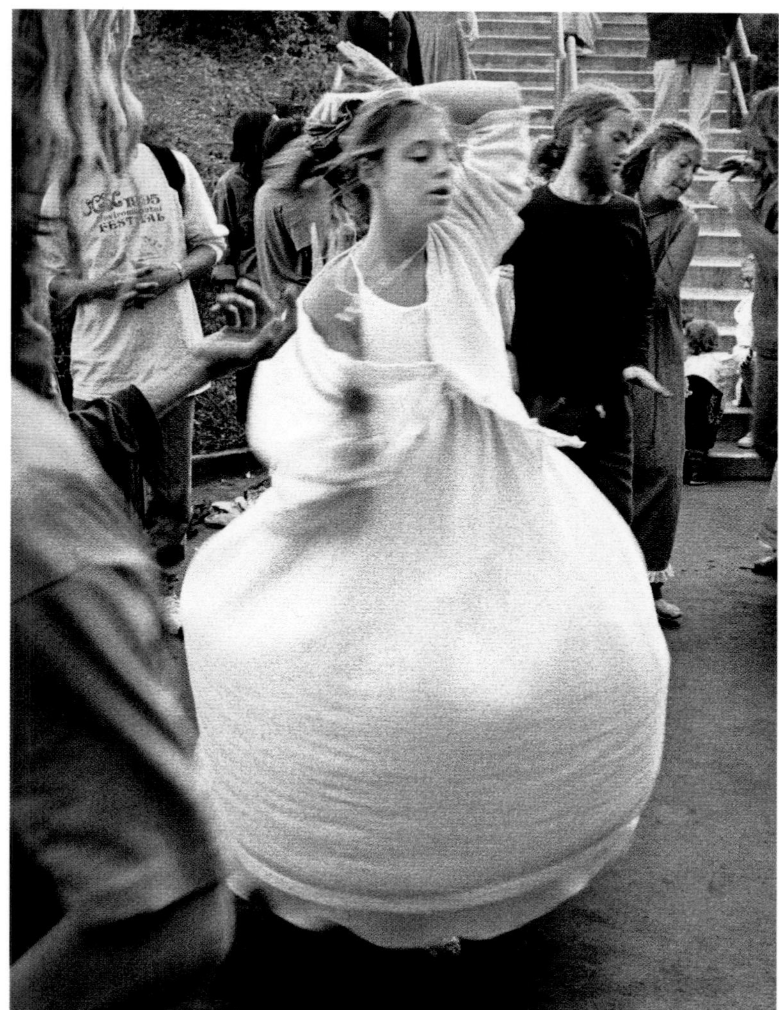

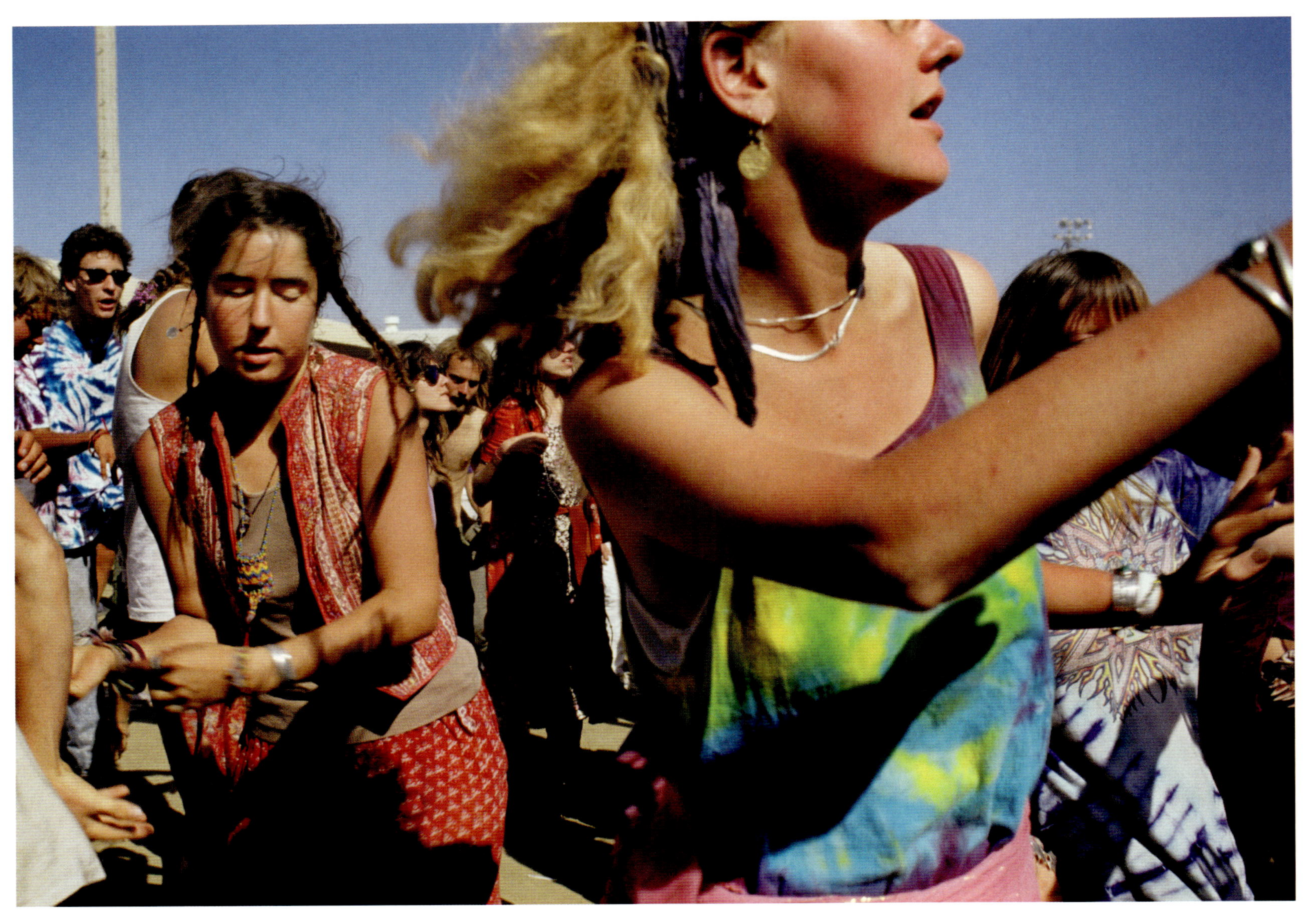

Eyes closed, hips pulsing, I'm catching the funky grooves in my heart and moving in rhythm. There is nothing better. Stefanie R.

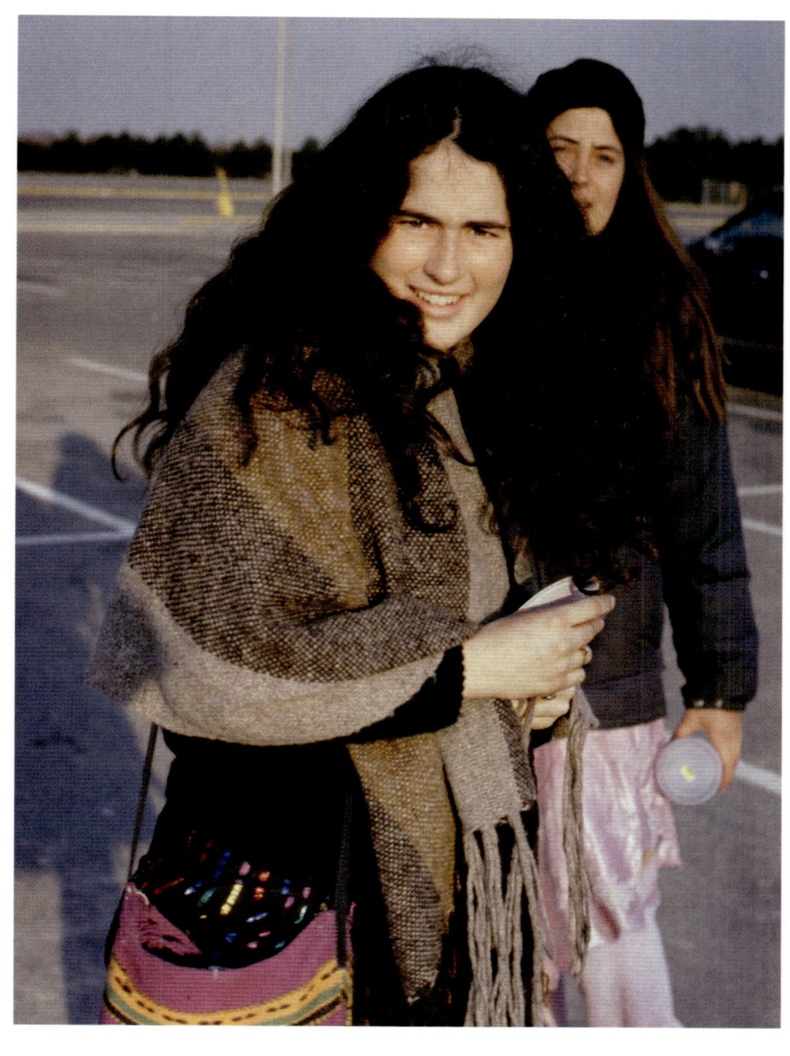

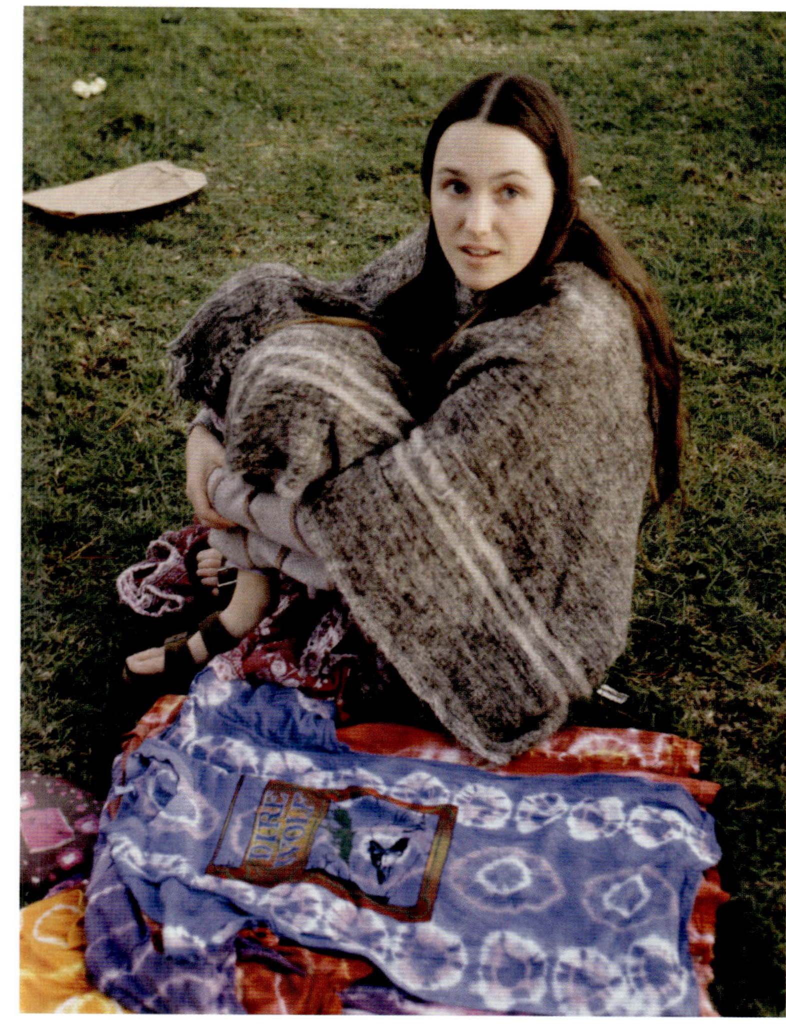

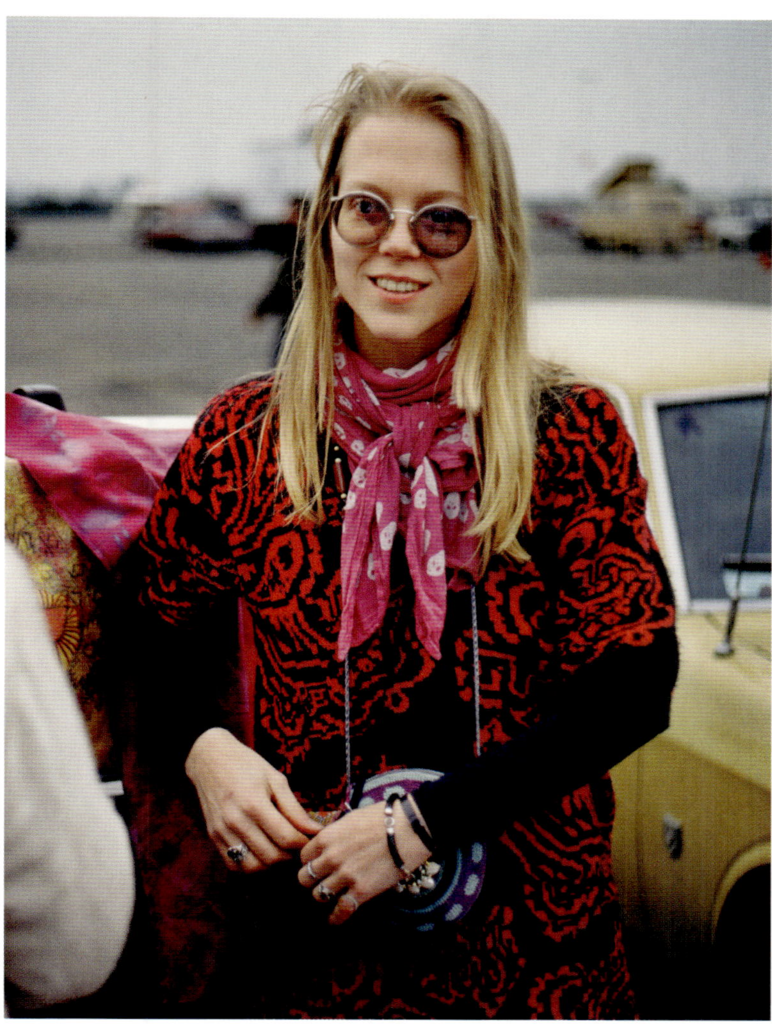

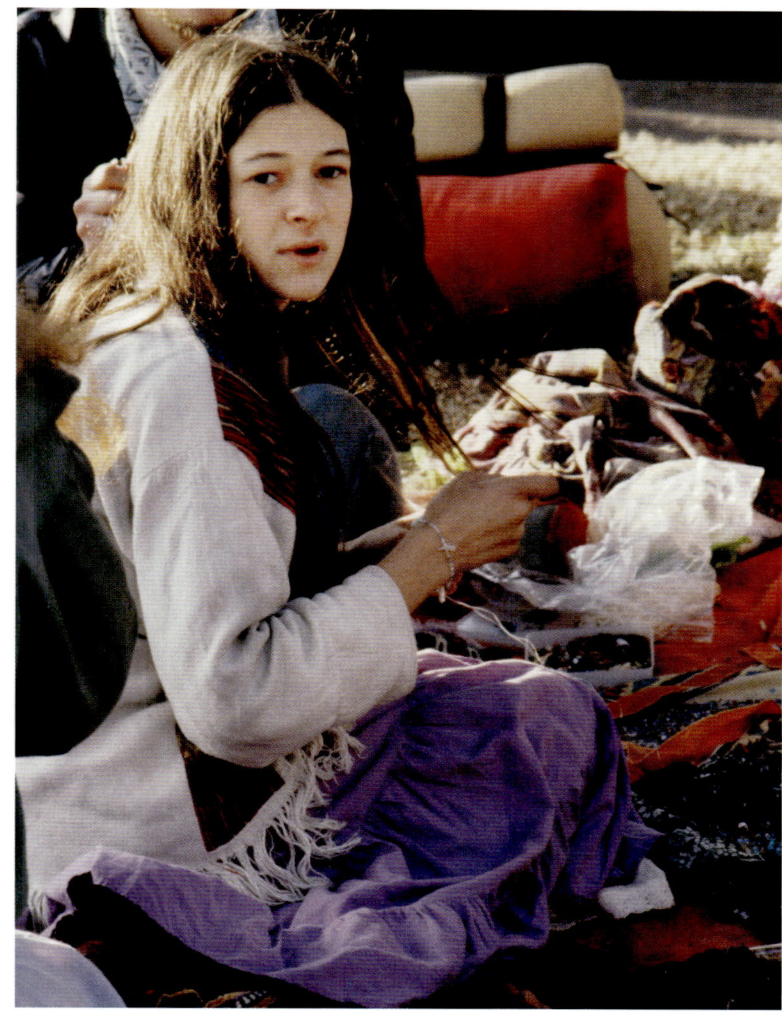

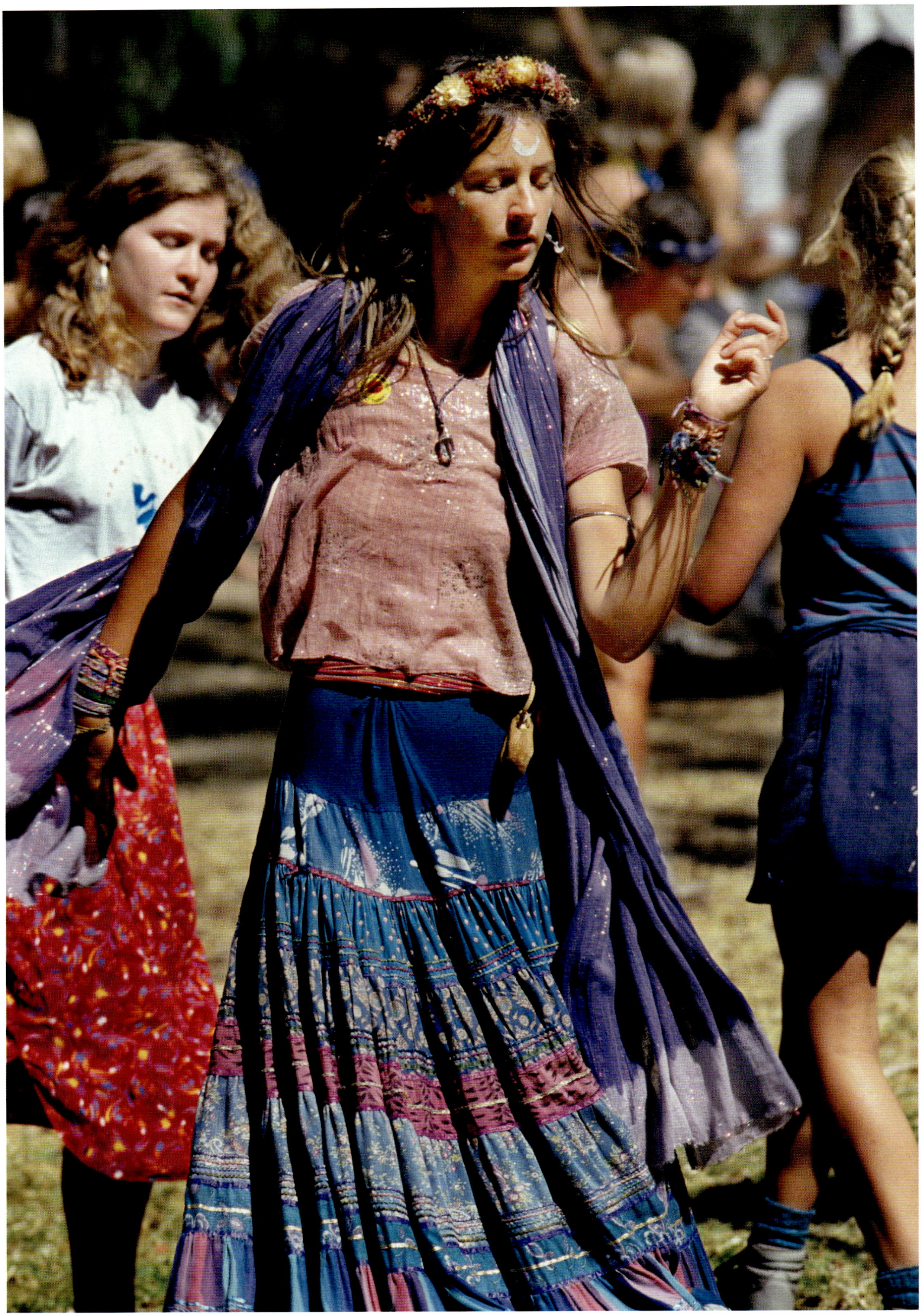

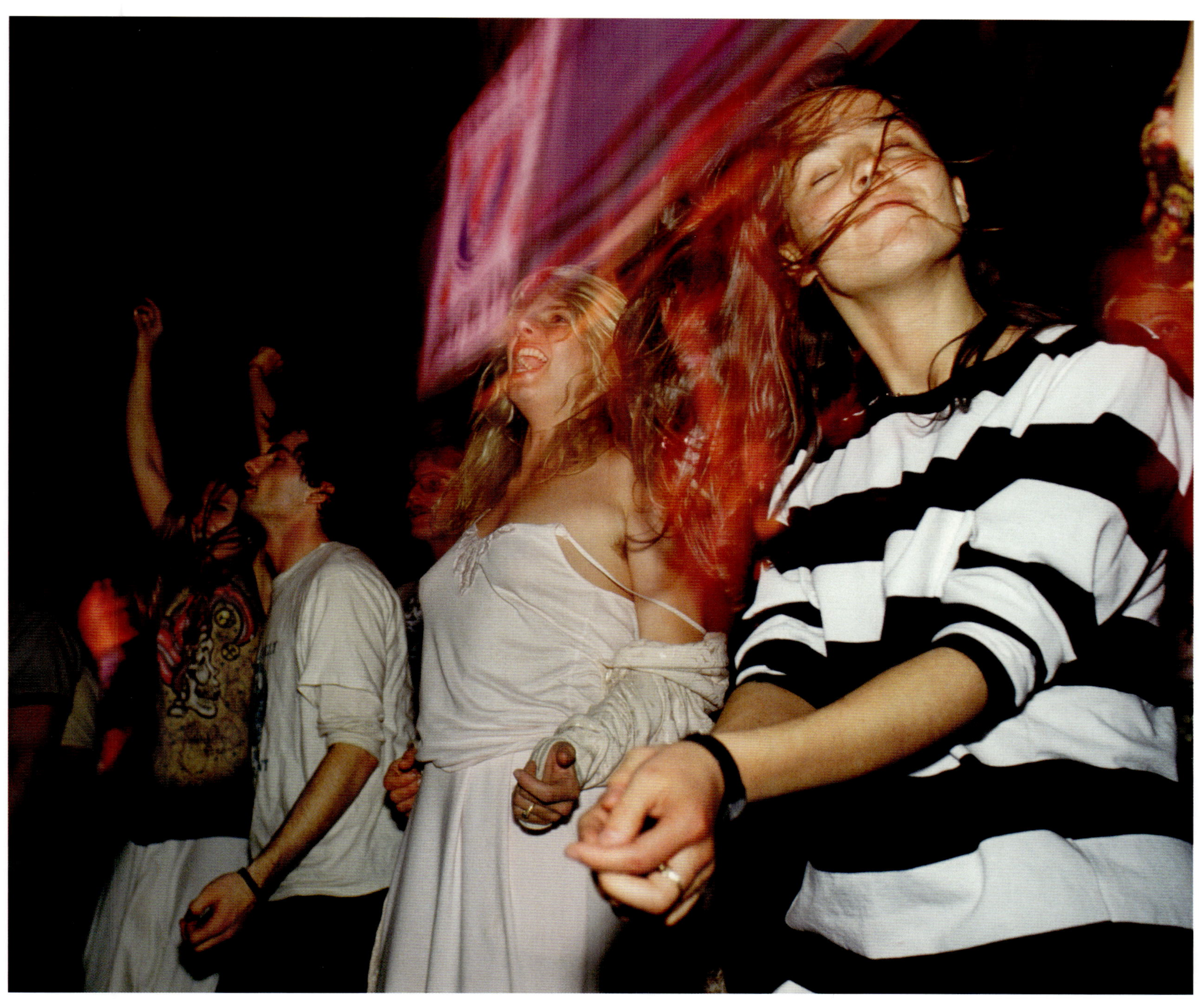

When I am lucky enough to be right at the stage, I feel like my heart just might burst and my cheeks shatter from the constant smile on my face. Michele K.

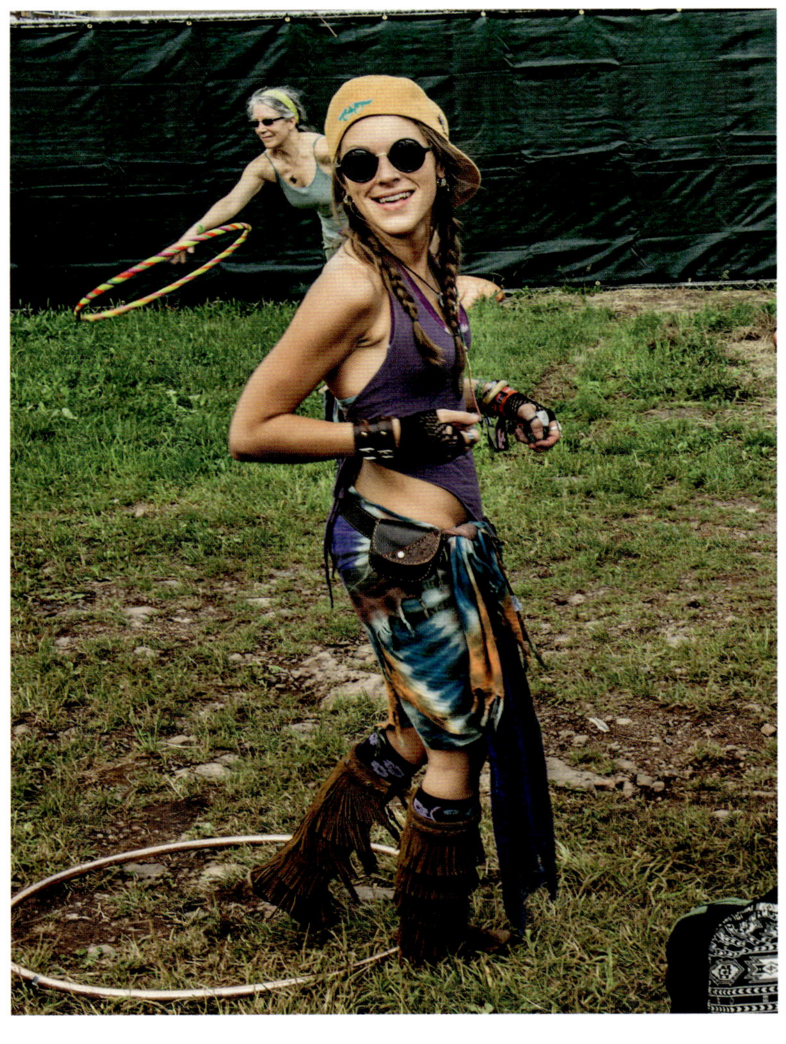
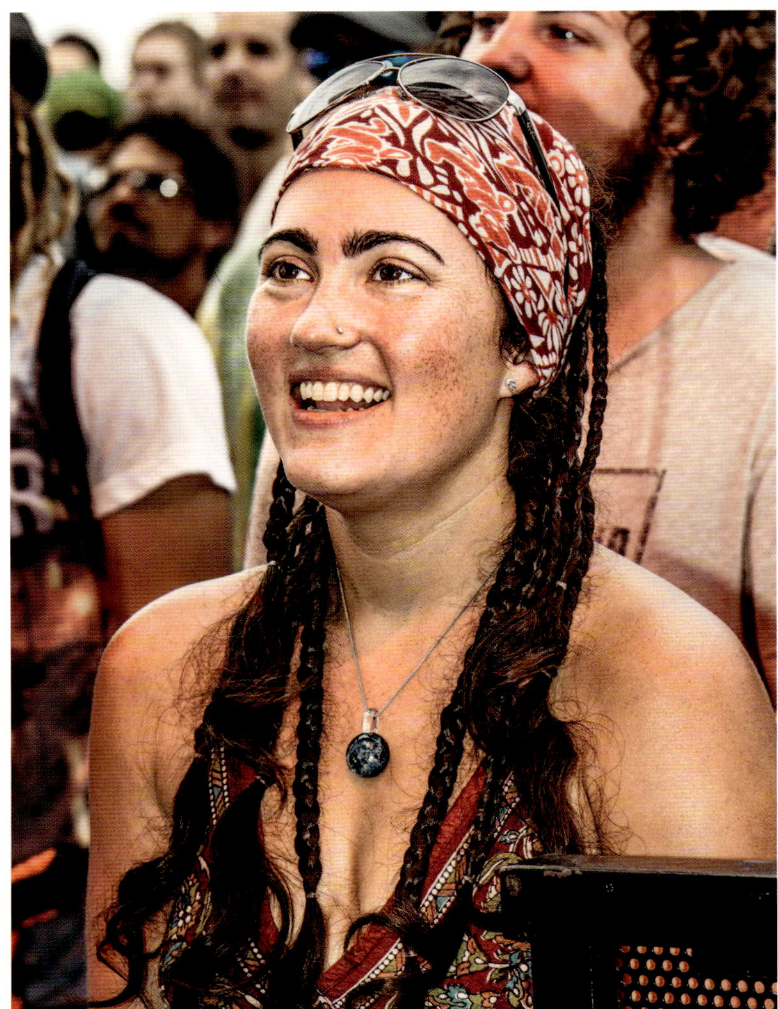
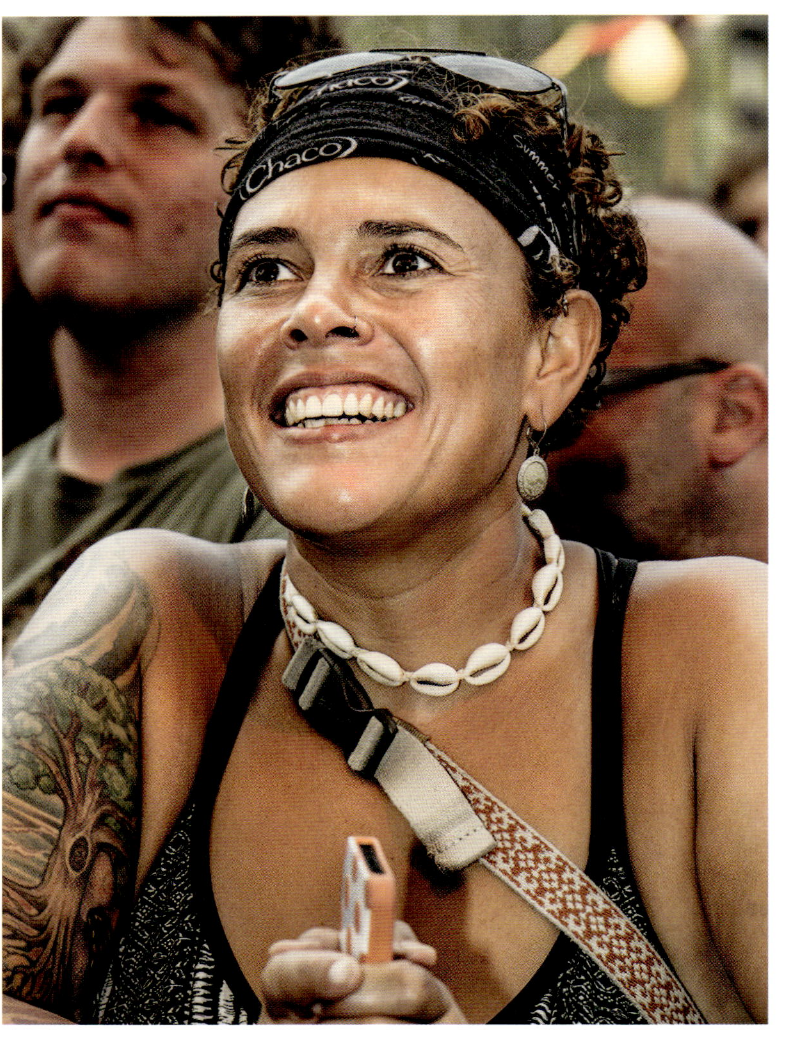
Chaco
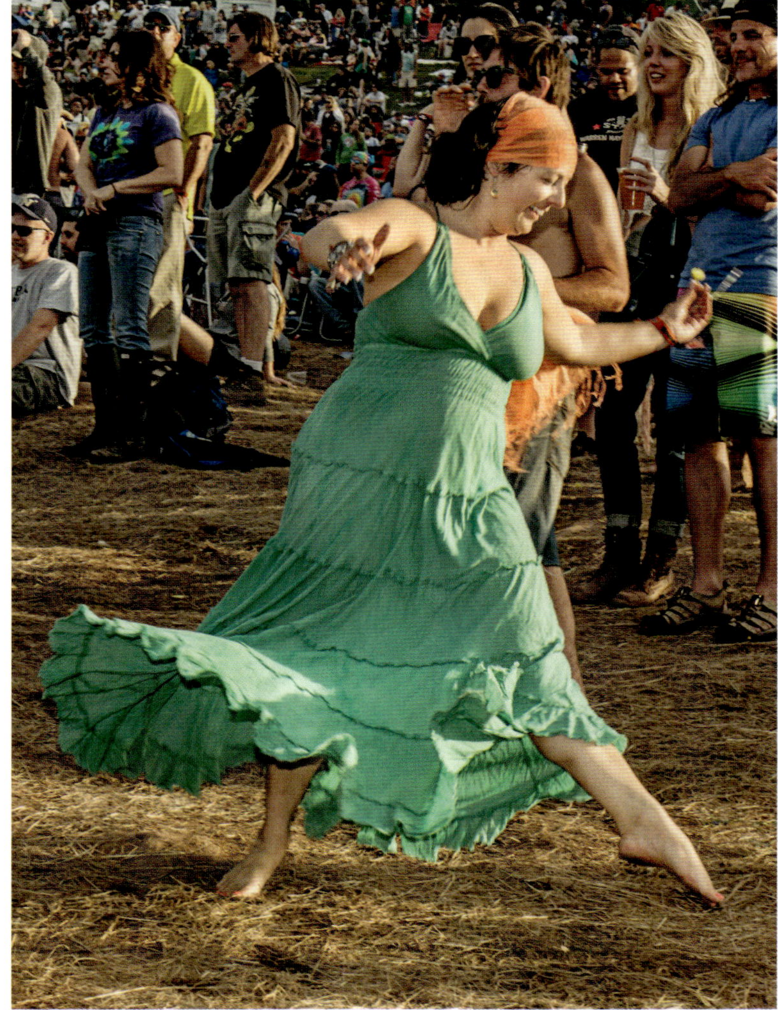

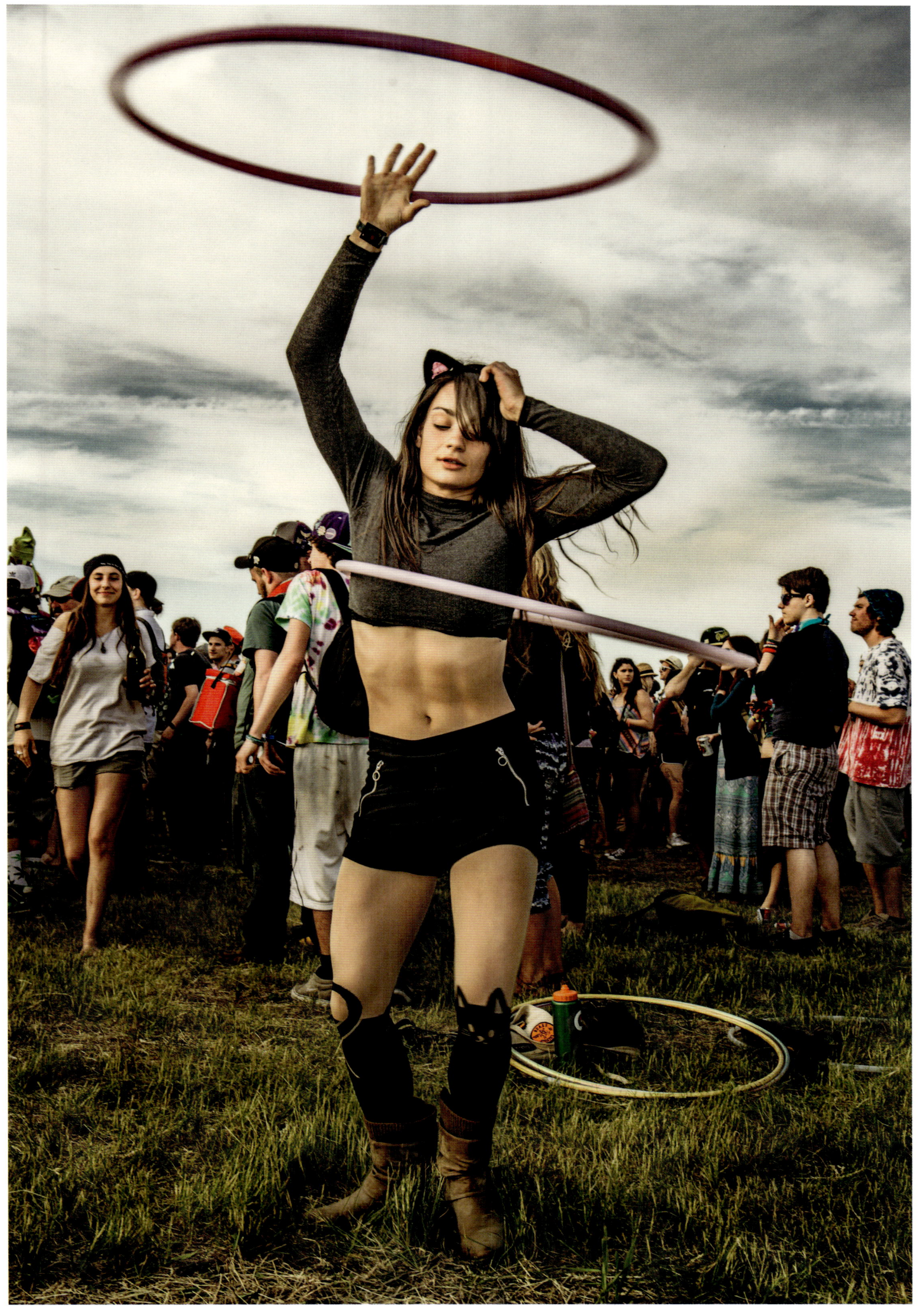

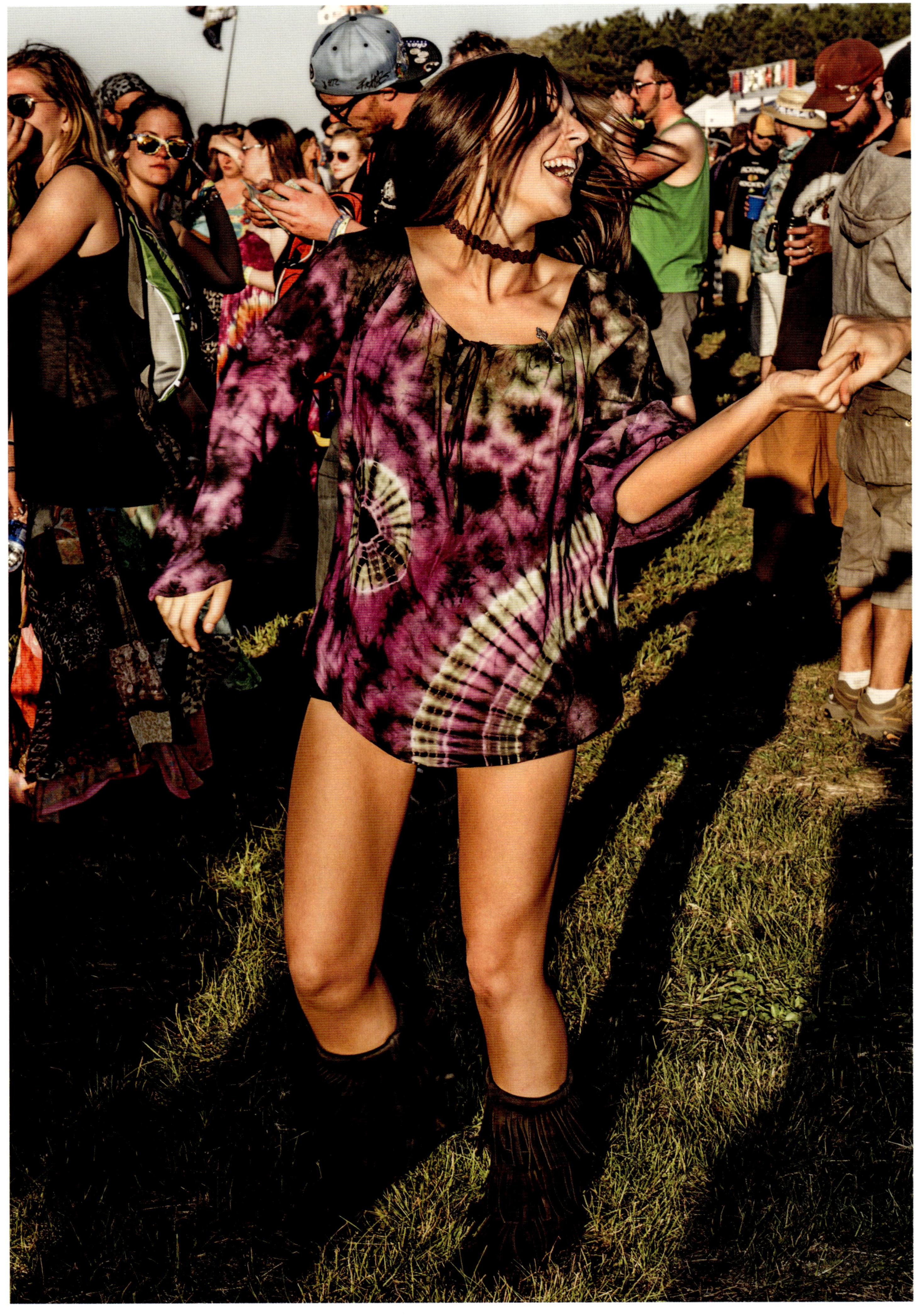

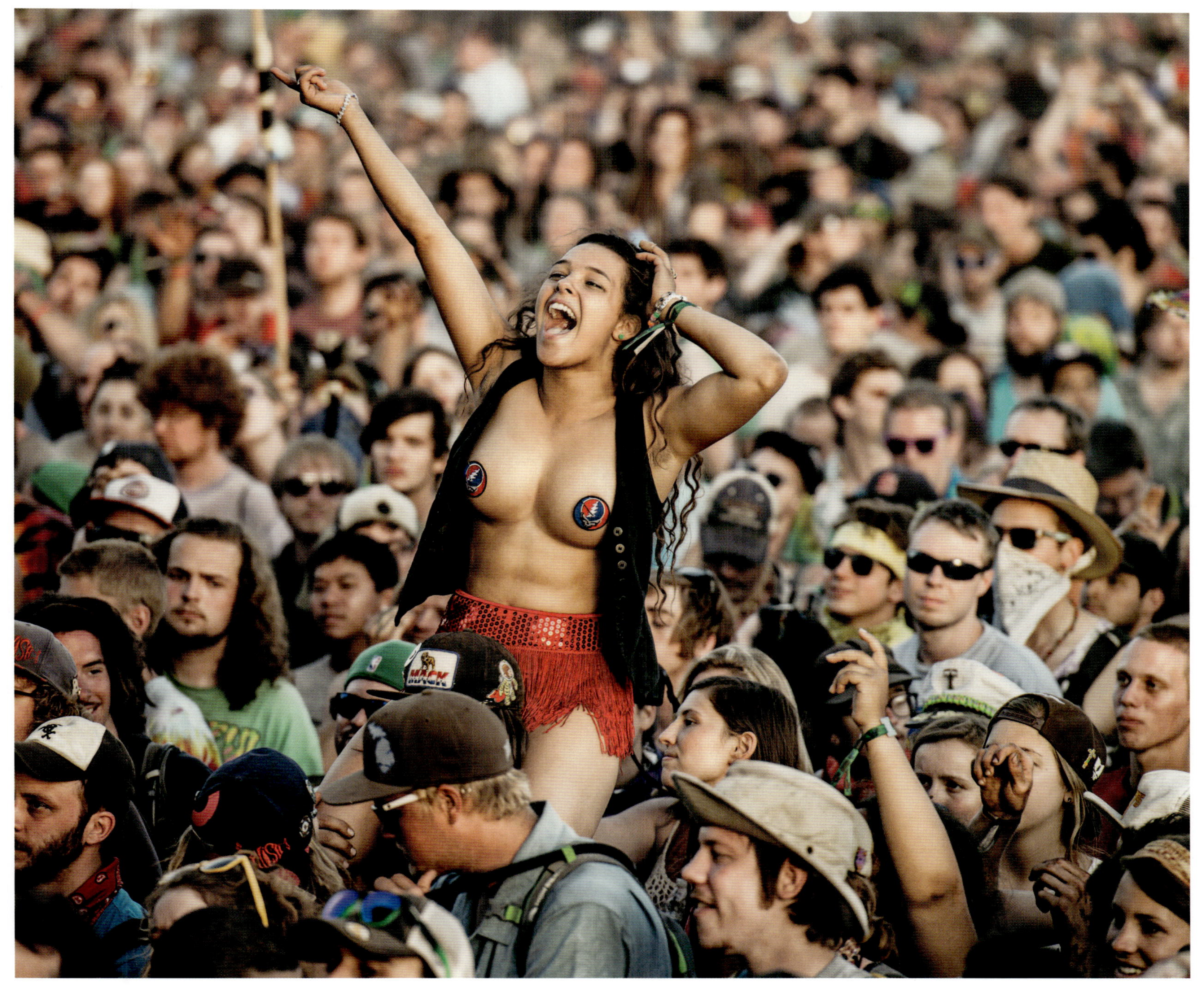

Being able to see the music and make eye contact with the musicians themselves gives me the biggest rush ever. The more I love the band, the closer I want to be. Ashley J. (pictured)

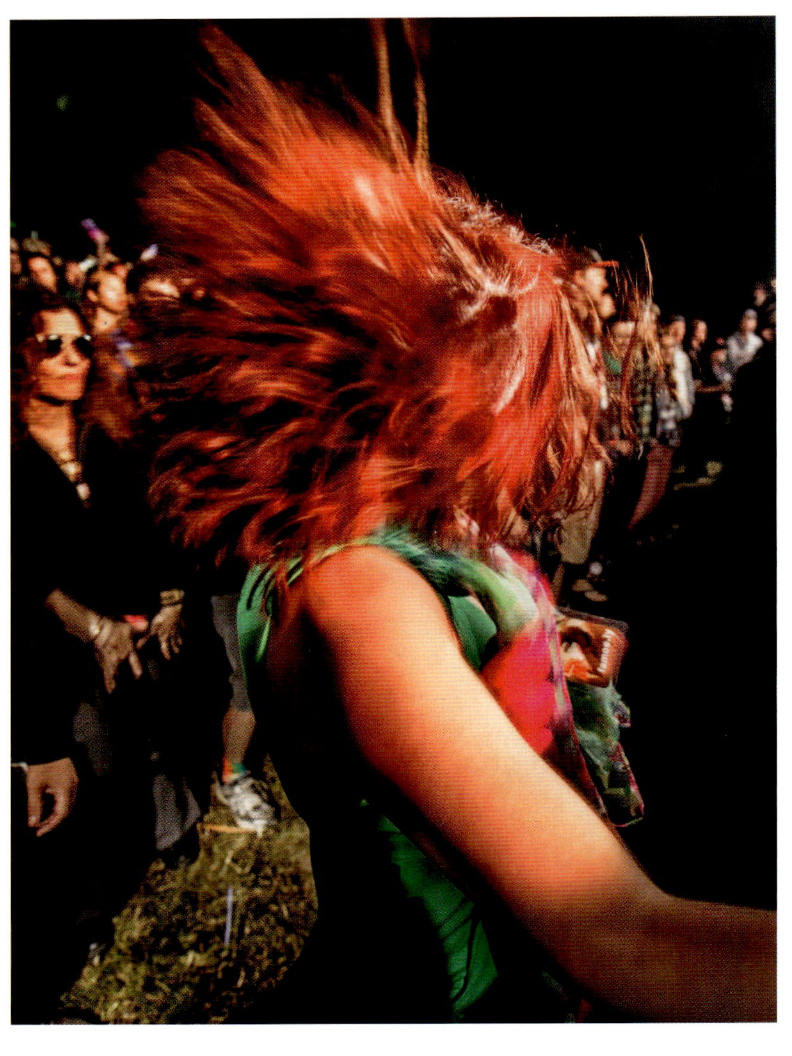

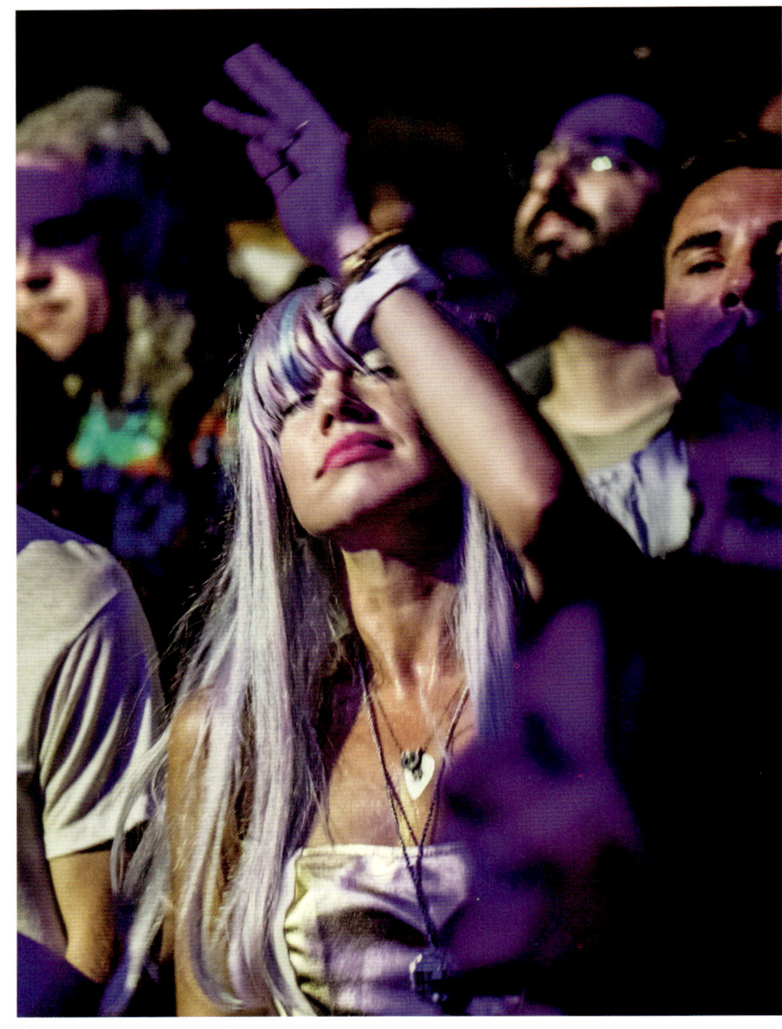

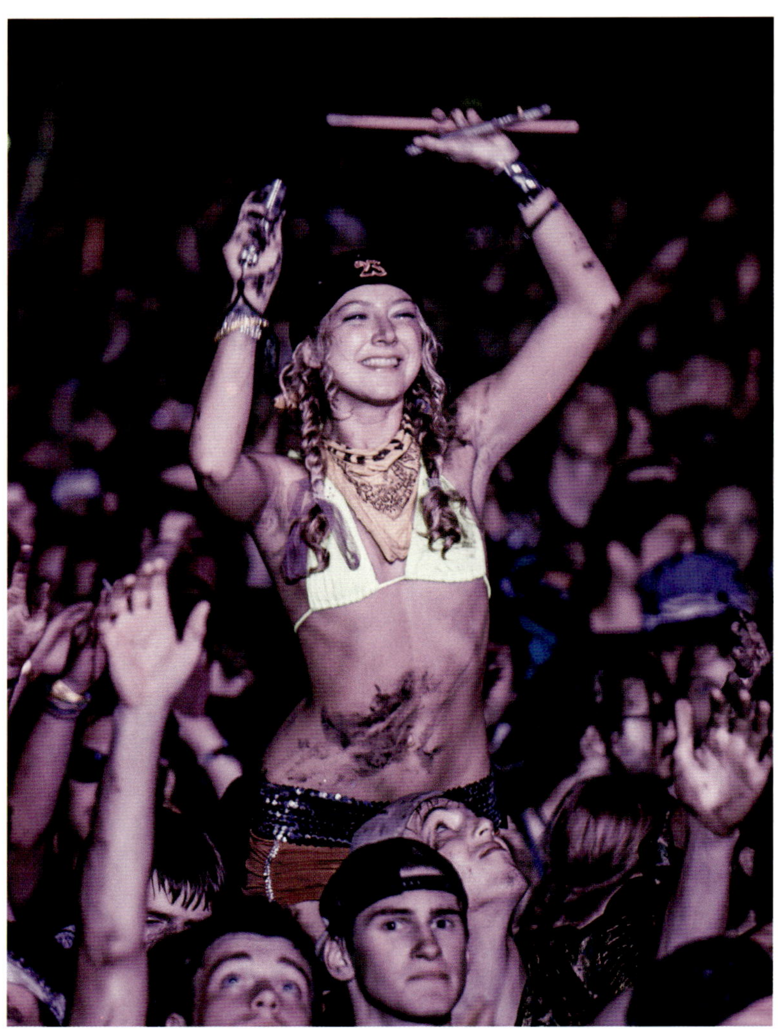

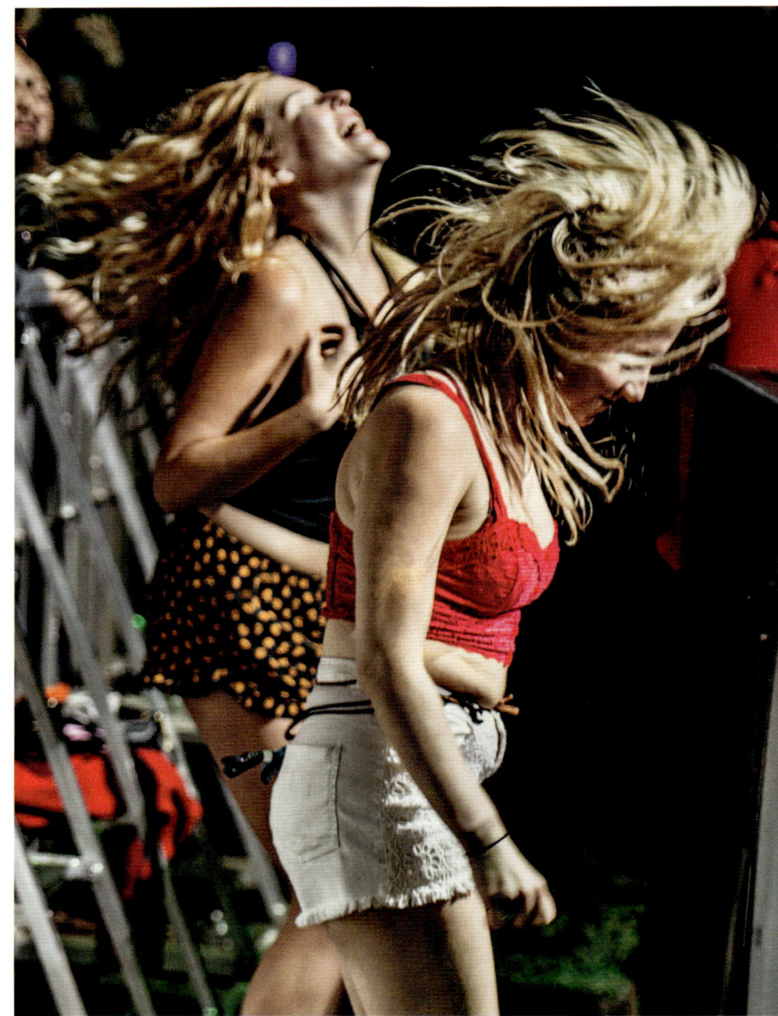

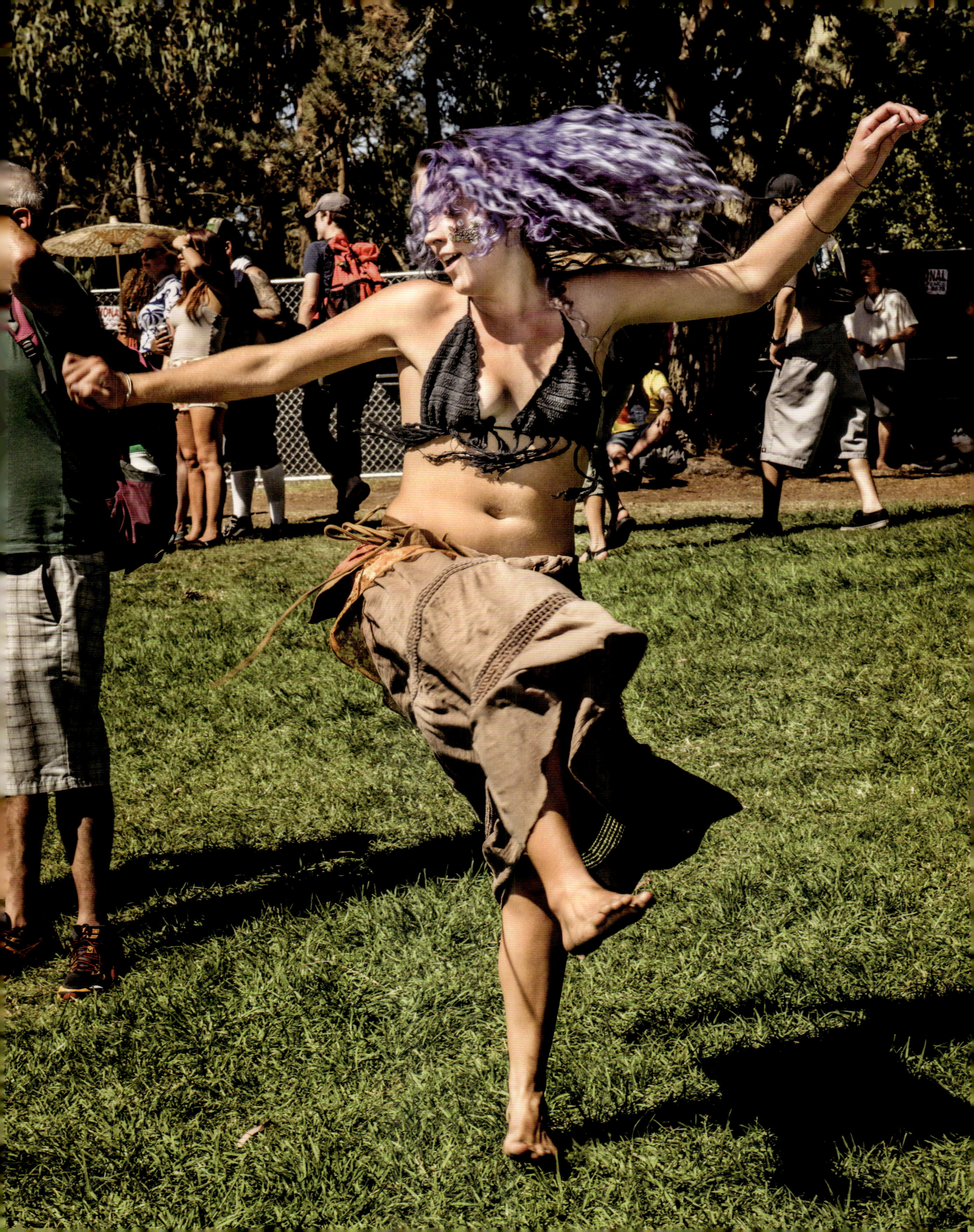

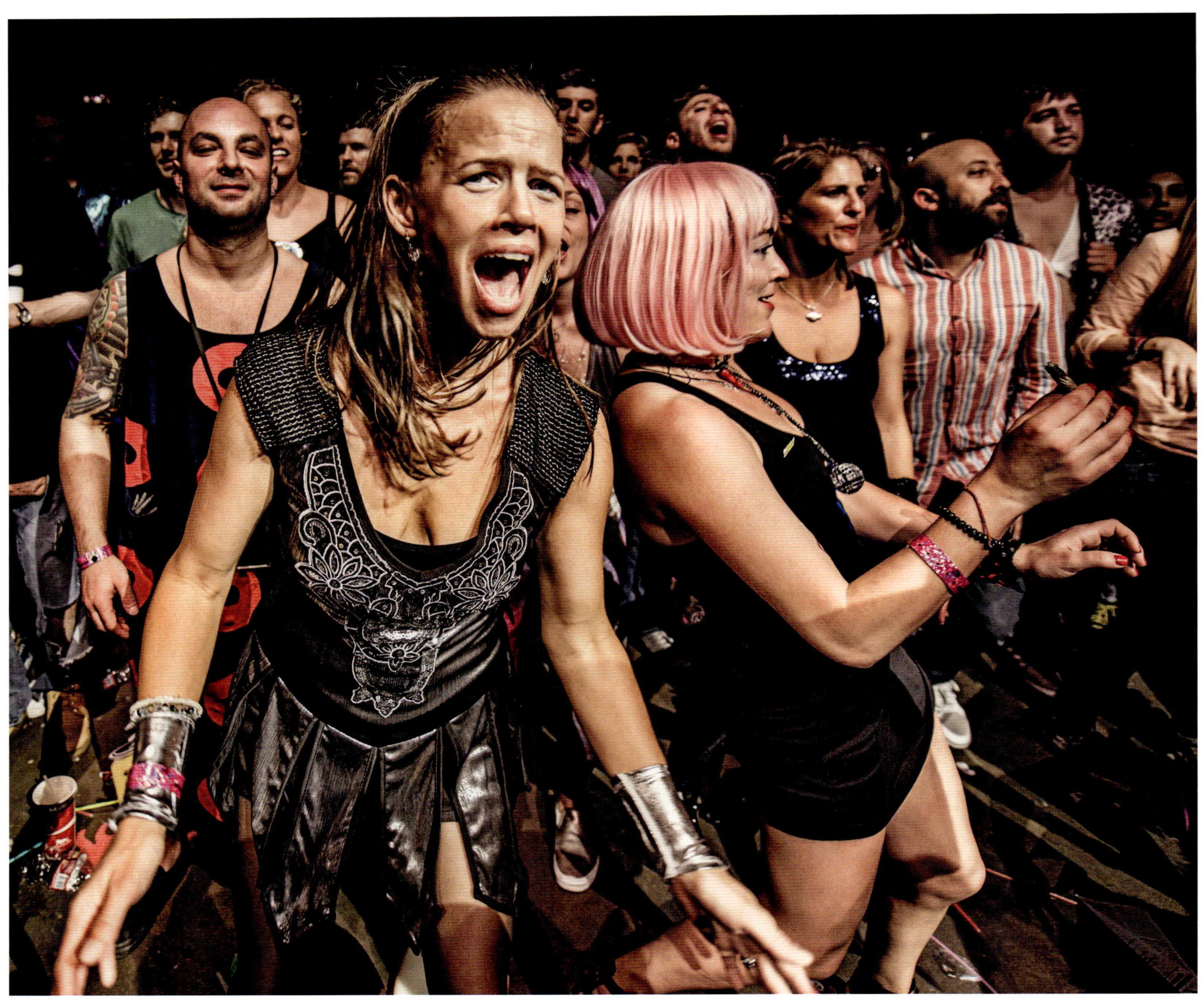

Dancing at a show is where I feel most alive. Nothing to worry about in the past, nothing to think about for the future, just there to listen and enjoy and move with music as it's happening in real time. Olivia M. (pictured, front right)

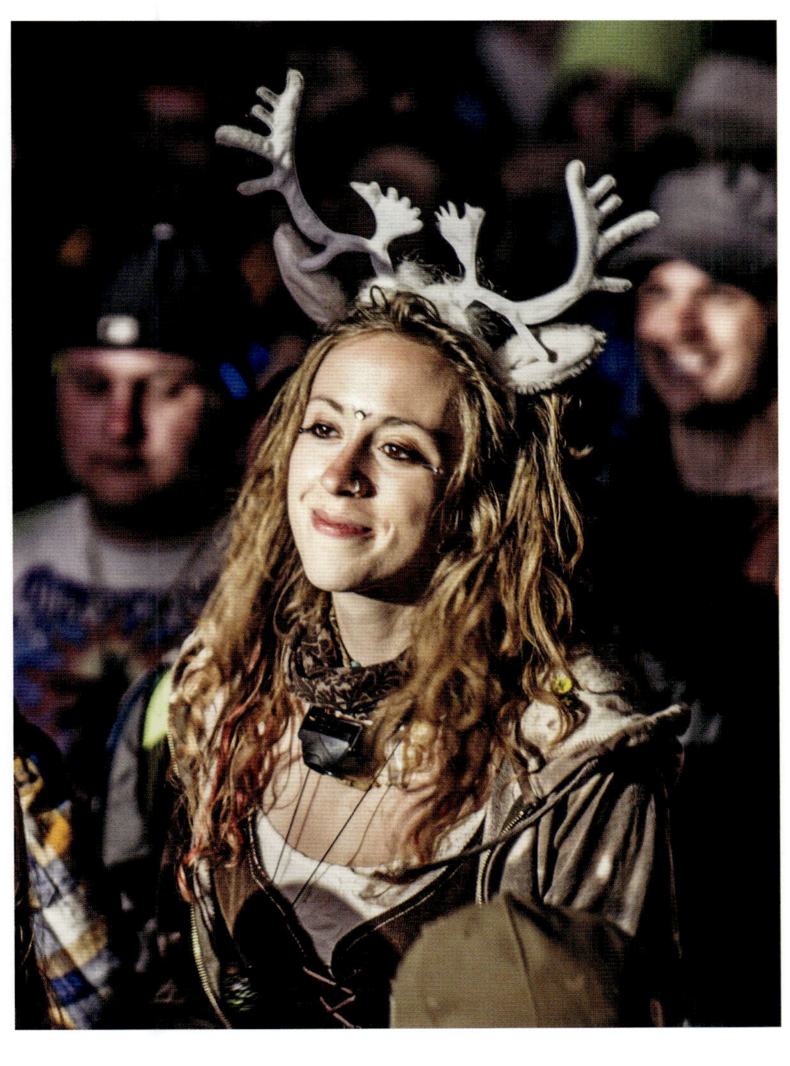
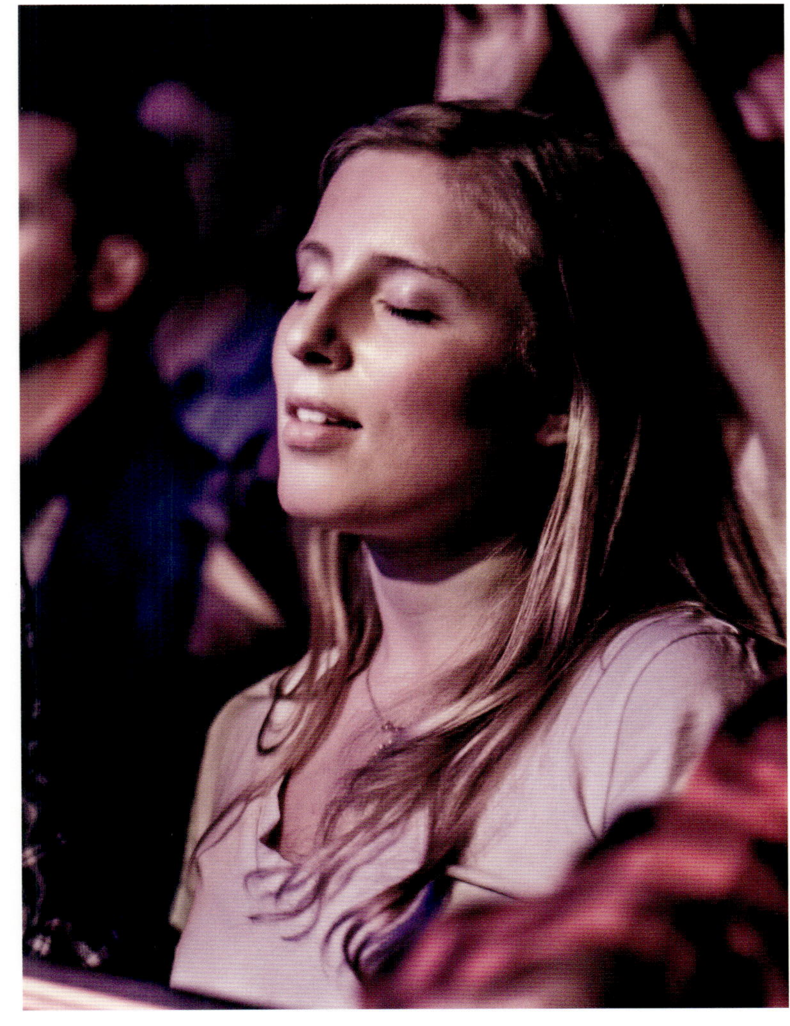
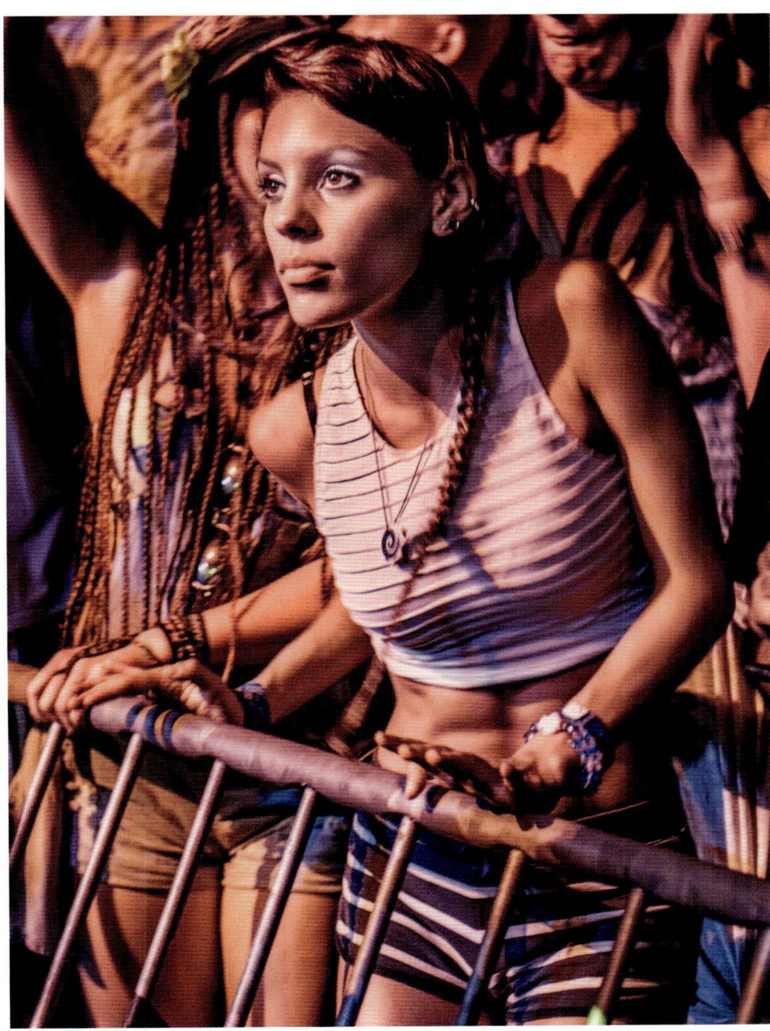
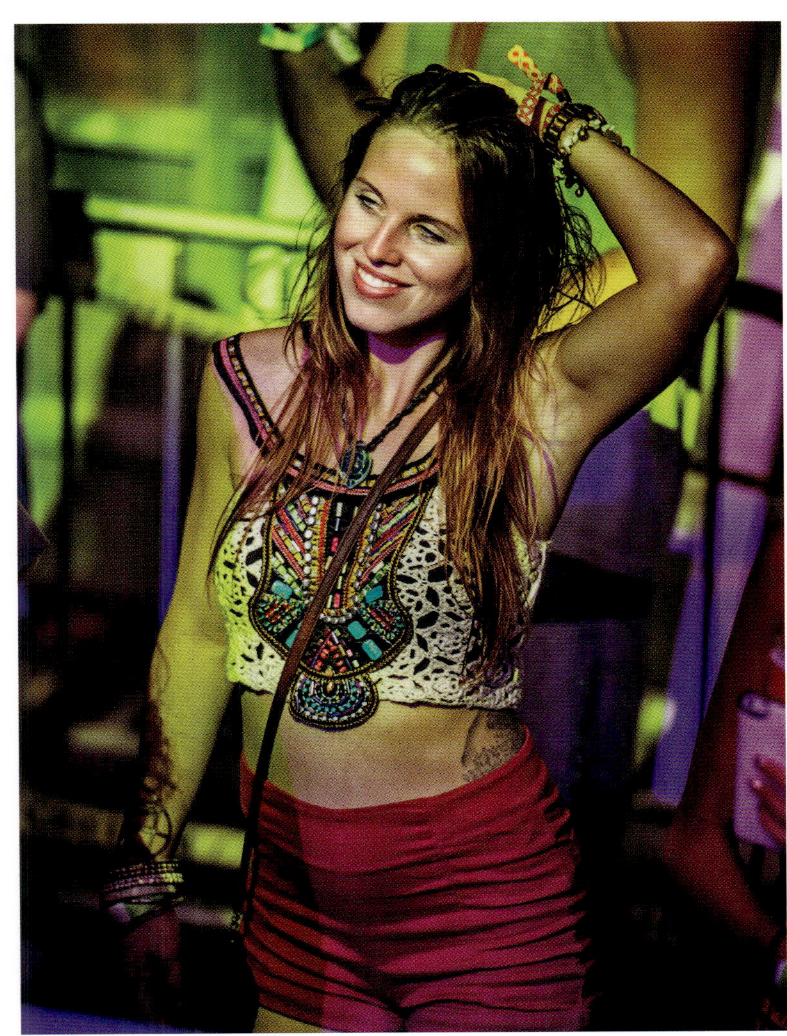

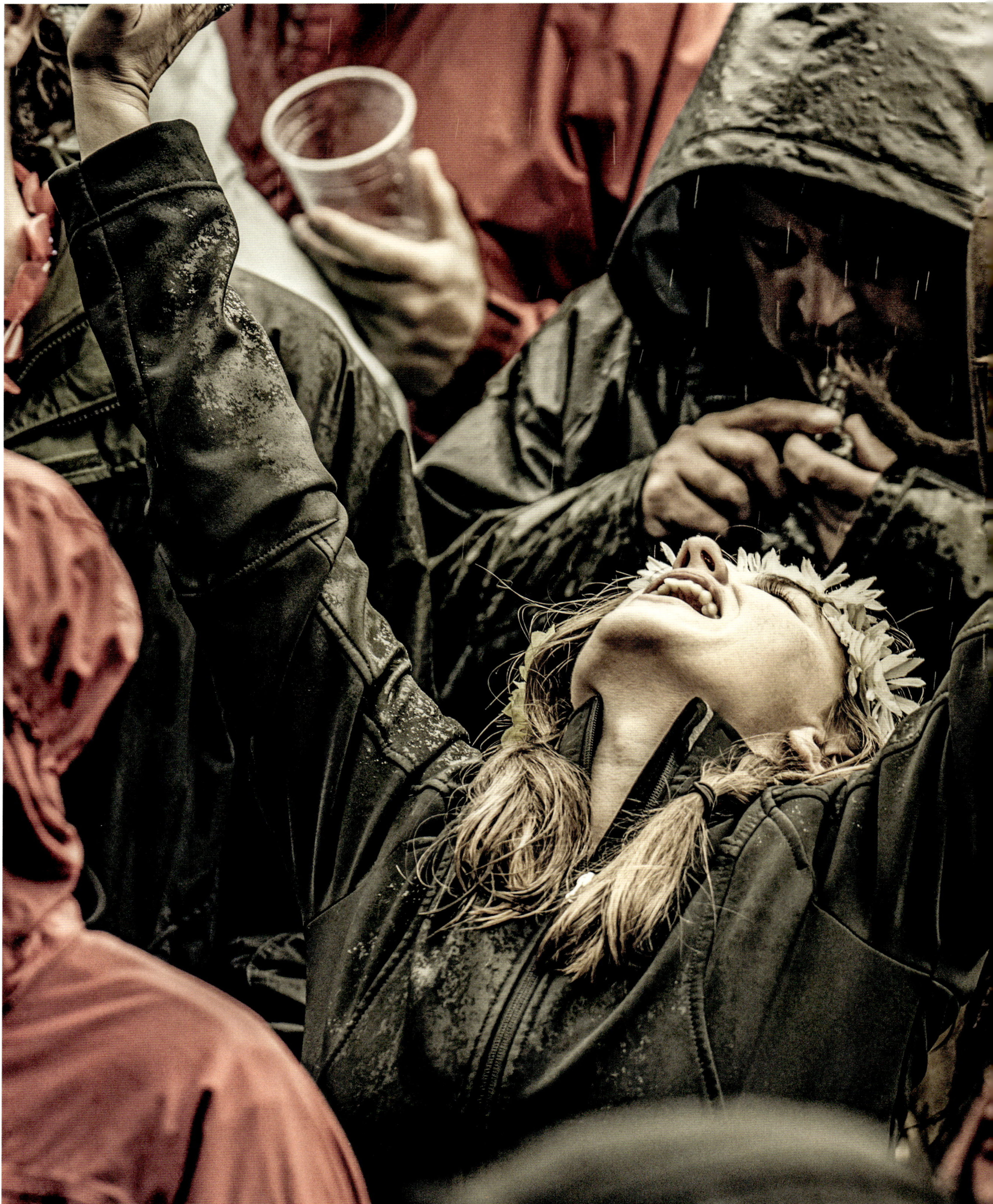

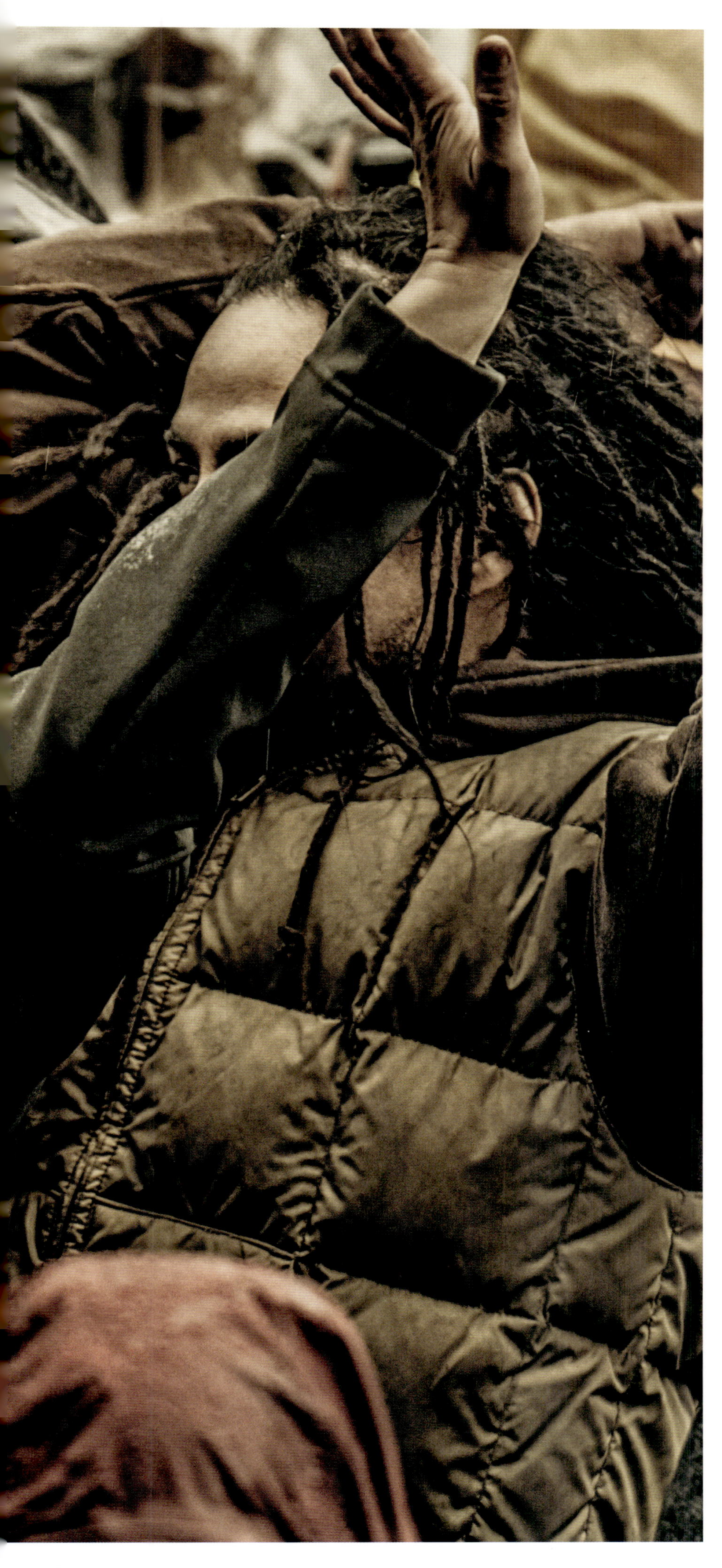

I live for the feeling of true connection I experience and witness at shows. Eye contact can feel like a hug. Hugs tend to feel more genuine, even if given by a stranger. The internal freedom I receive from this environment, and the freedom-flow I witness in others, elates me.

Marinda S.R. (pictured)

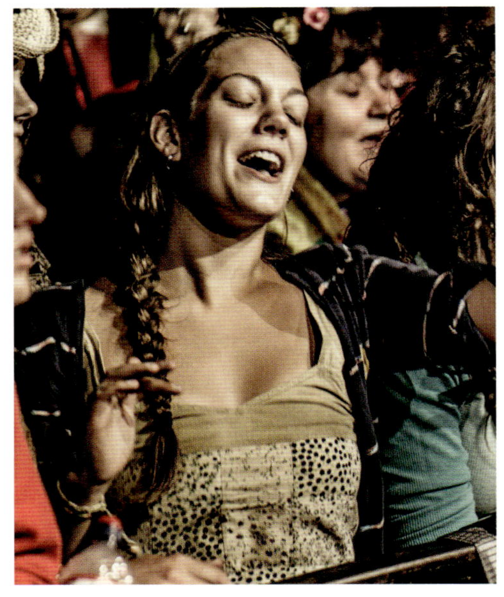
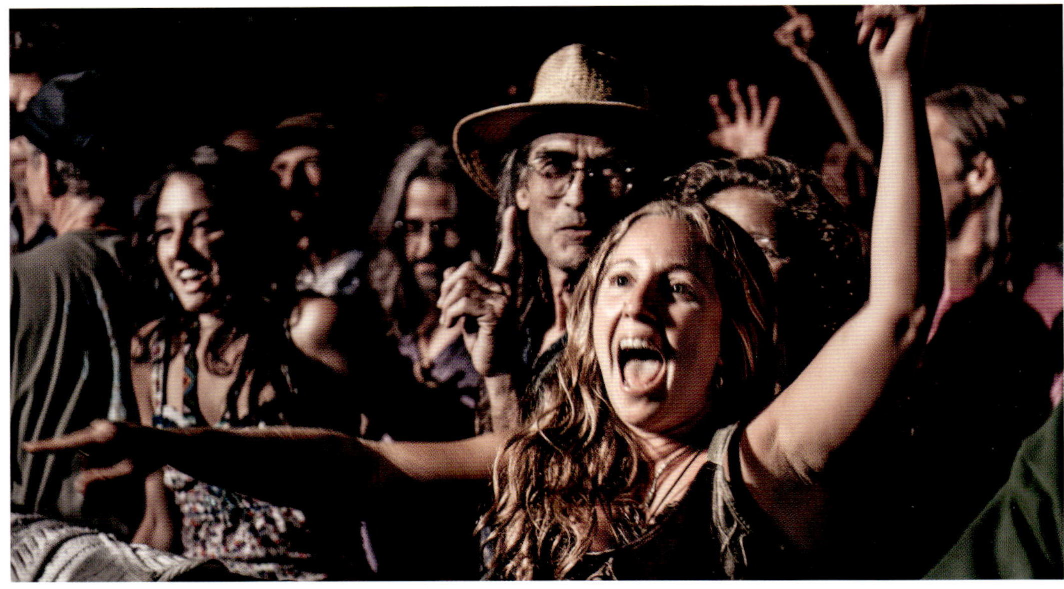
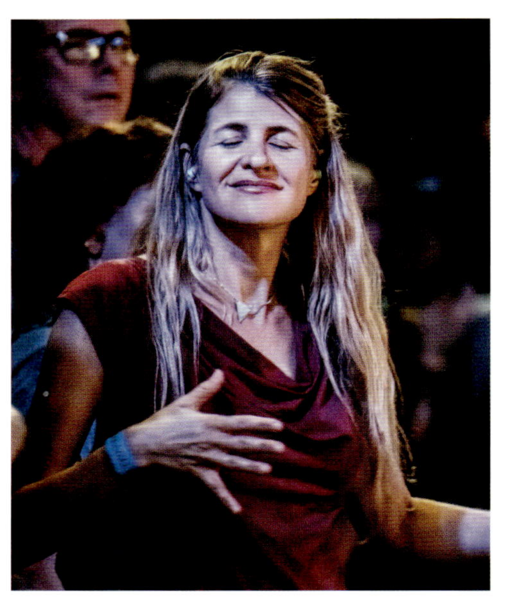
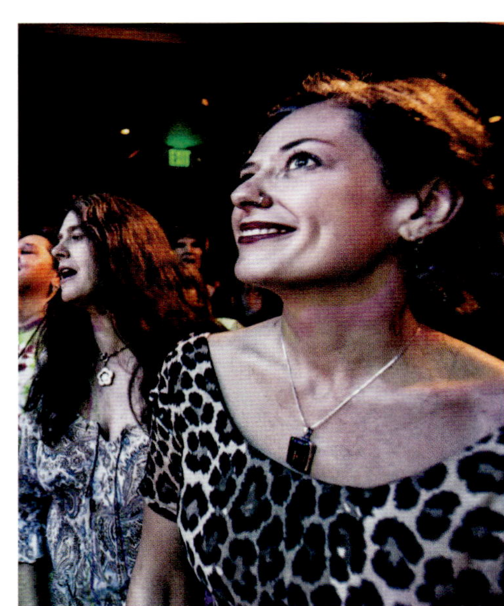
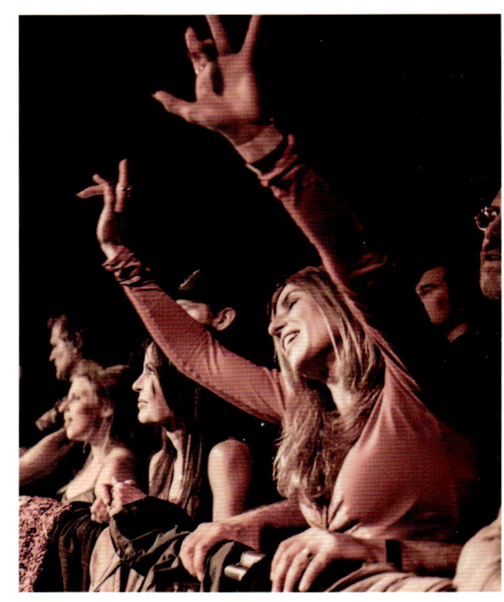
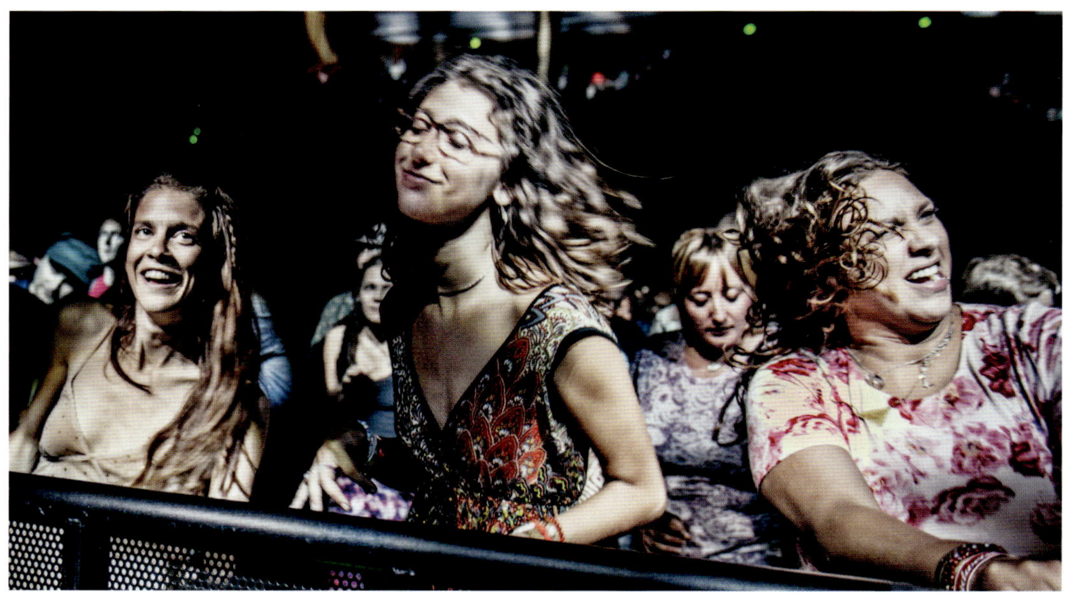
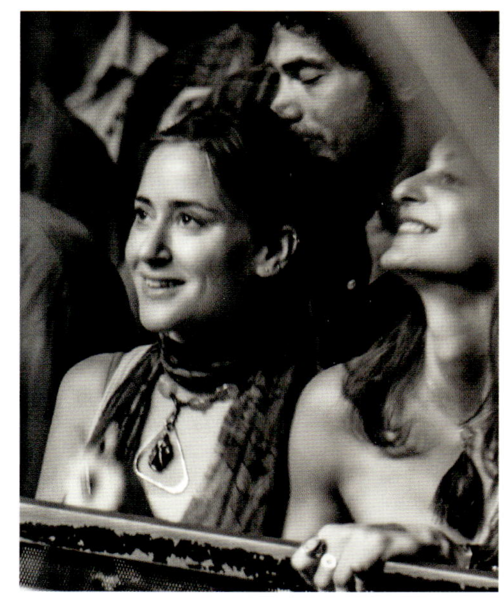

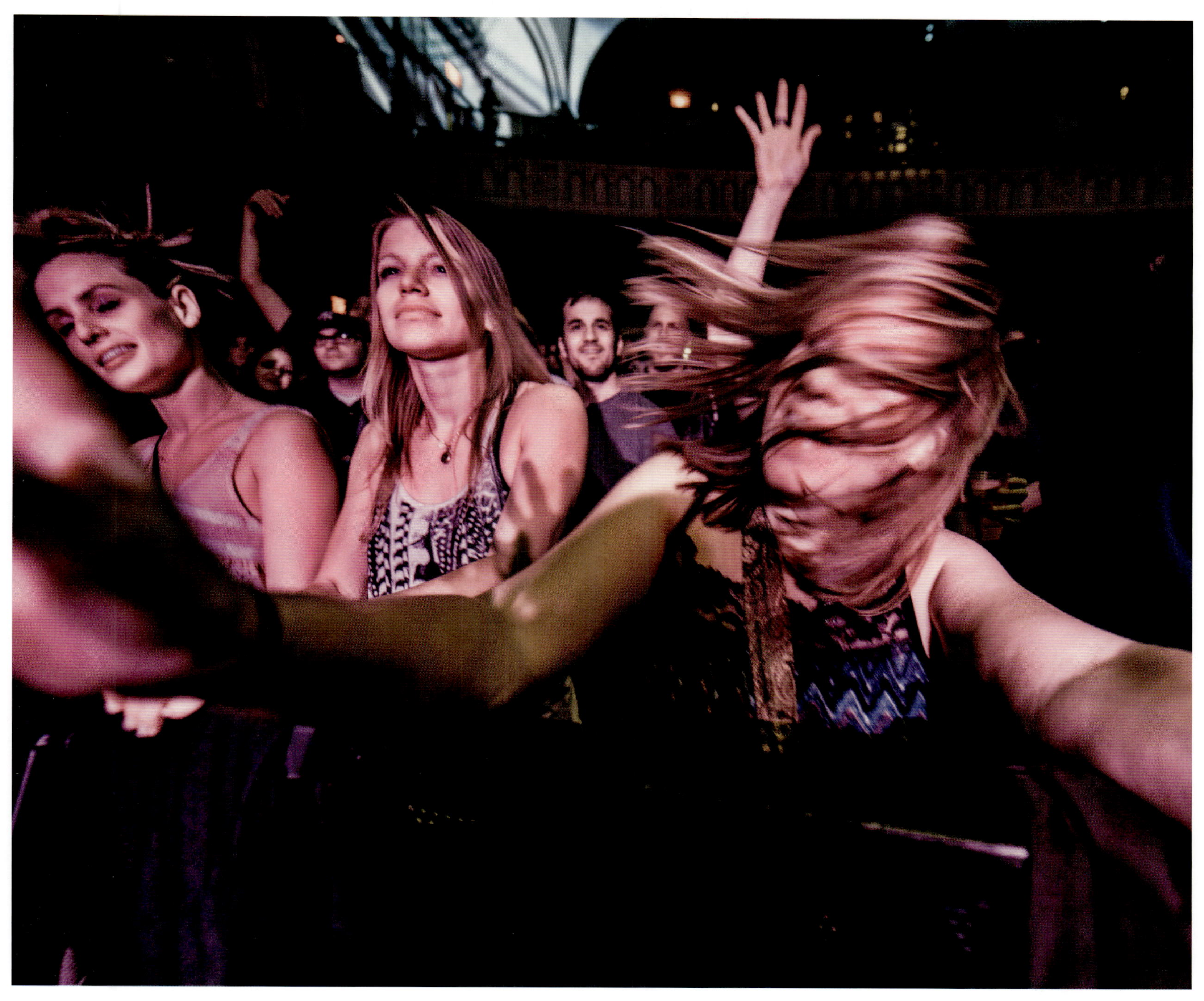

I am a rail rider. I love being up front because you can connect with the band better and tune the rest of the world out while getting down. I get in line early to secure my spot up front, but waiting in line is a beautiful way to meet new fans and connect with friends before the show. Bonus: soundchecks! Lacy B.

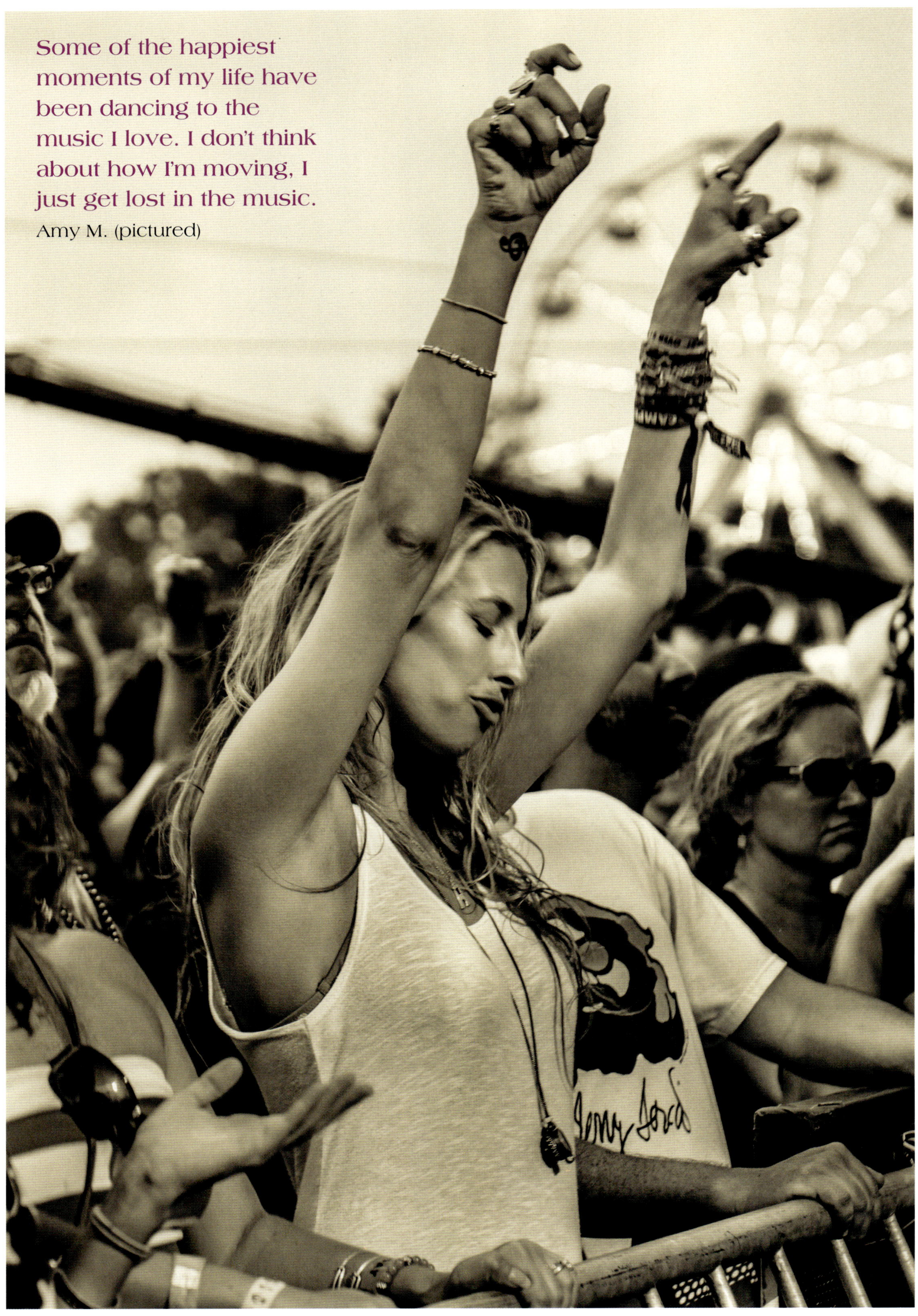

Some of the happiest moments of my life have been dancing to the music I love. I don't think about how I'm moving, I just get lost in the music.

Amy M. (pictured)

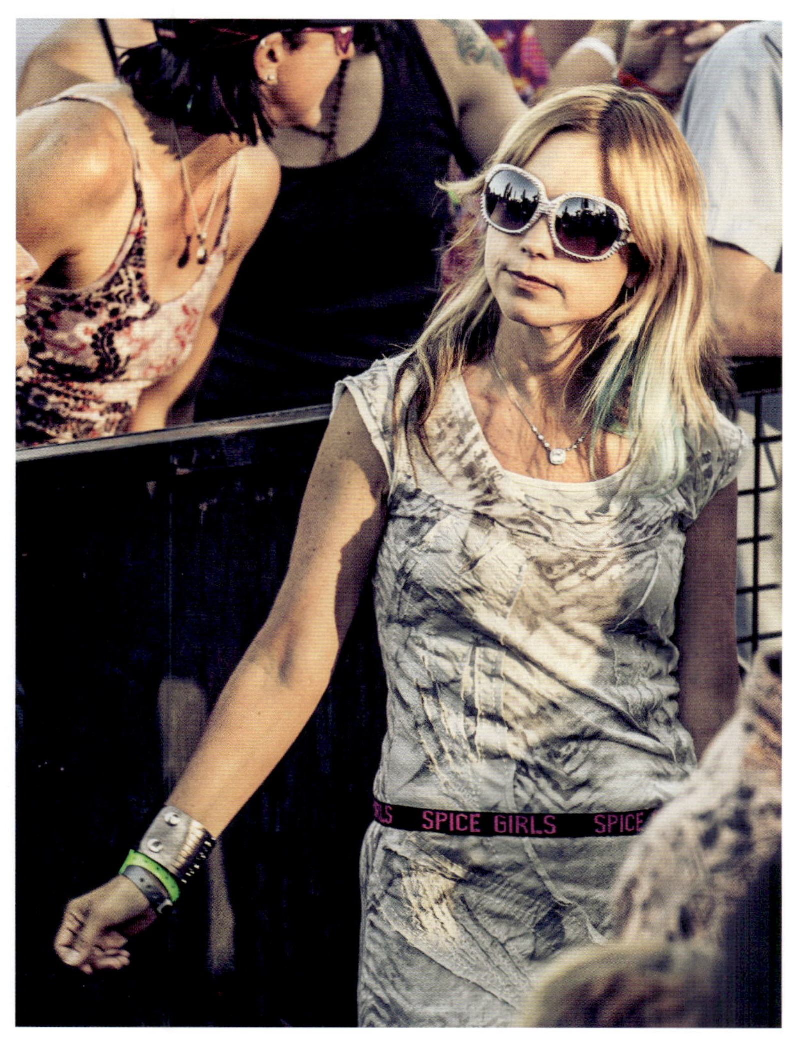
SPICE GIRLS

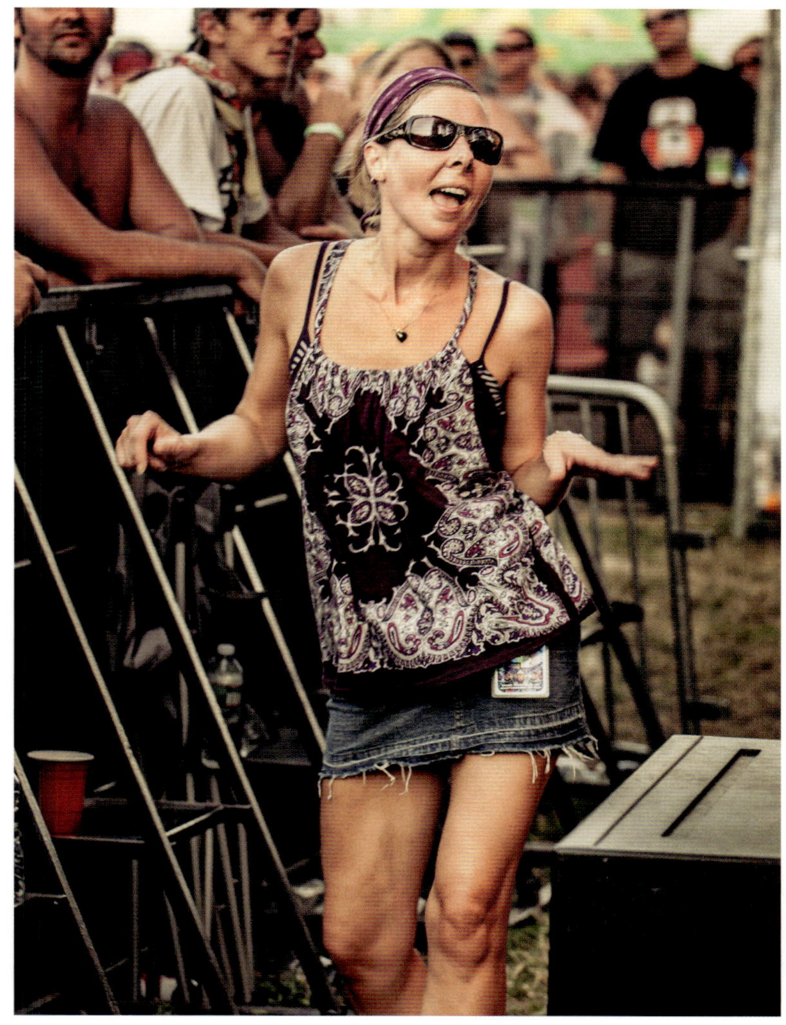

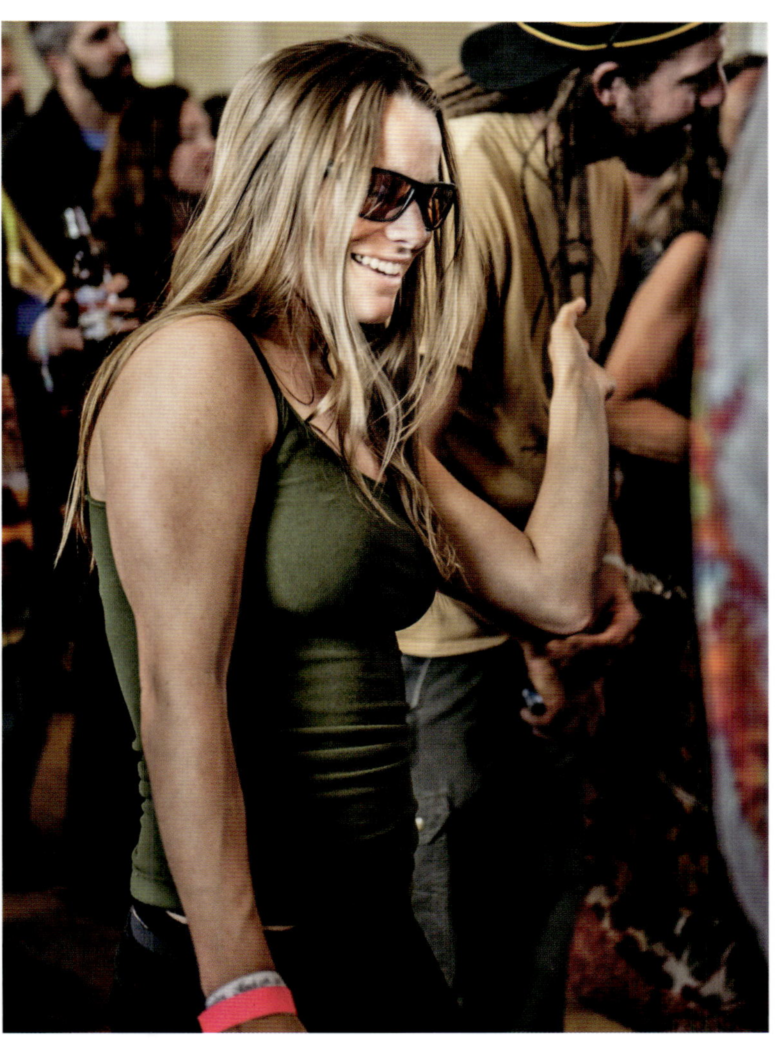

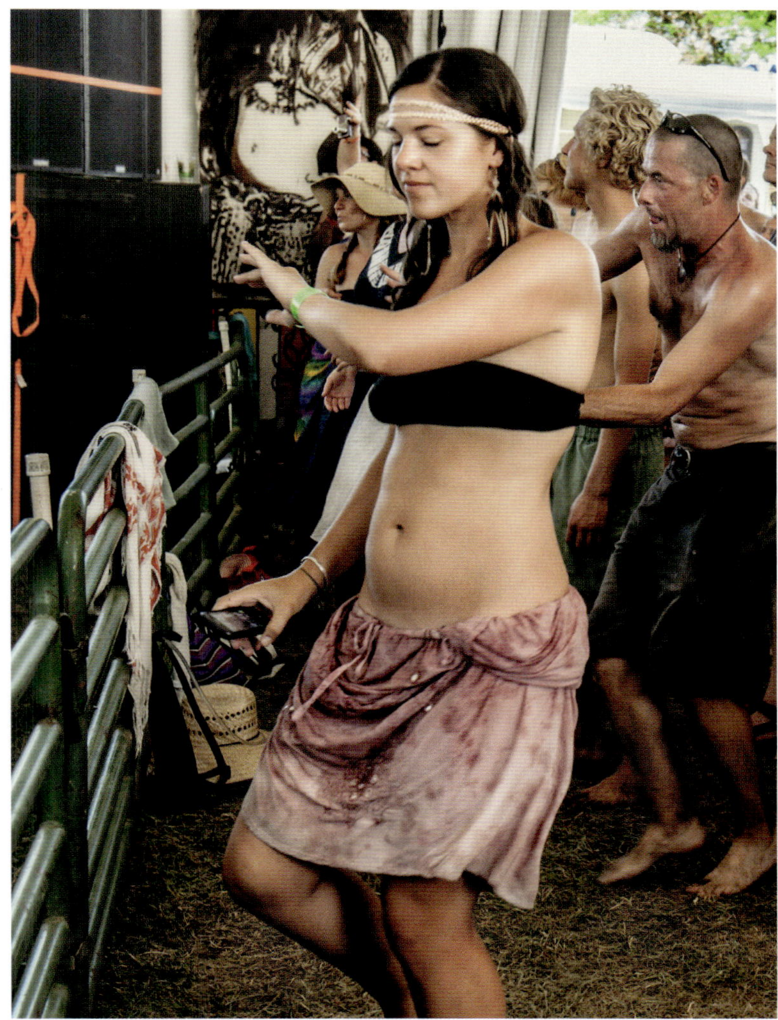

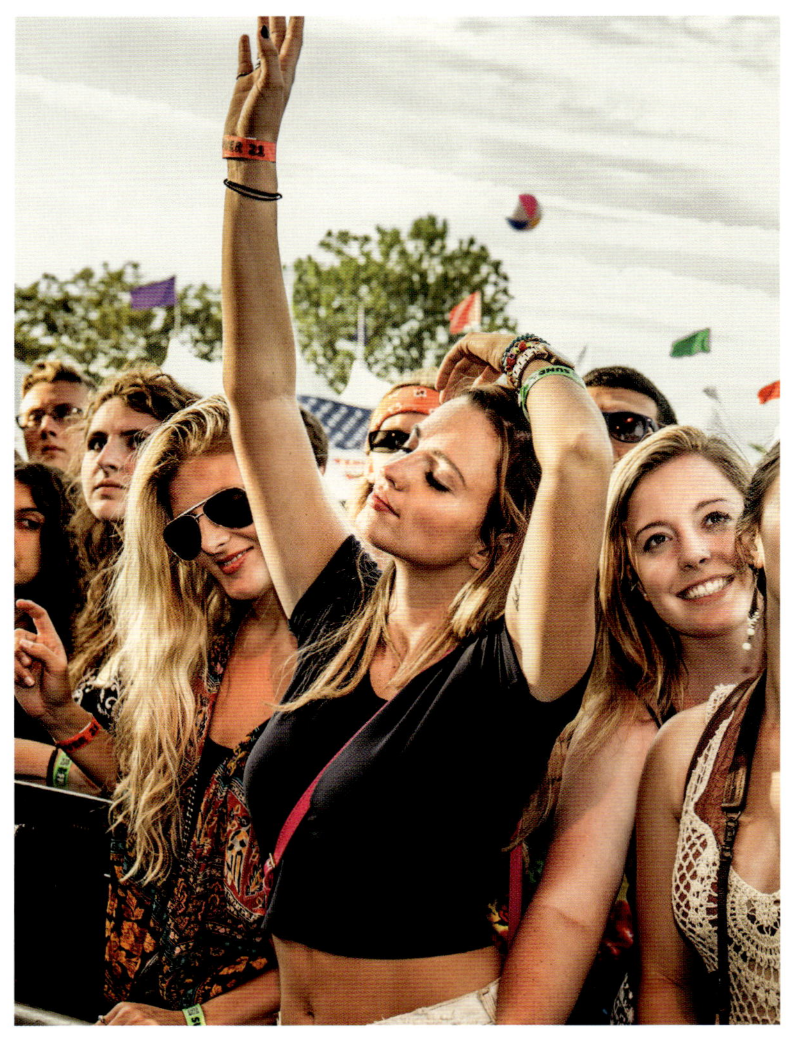

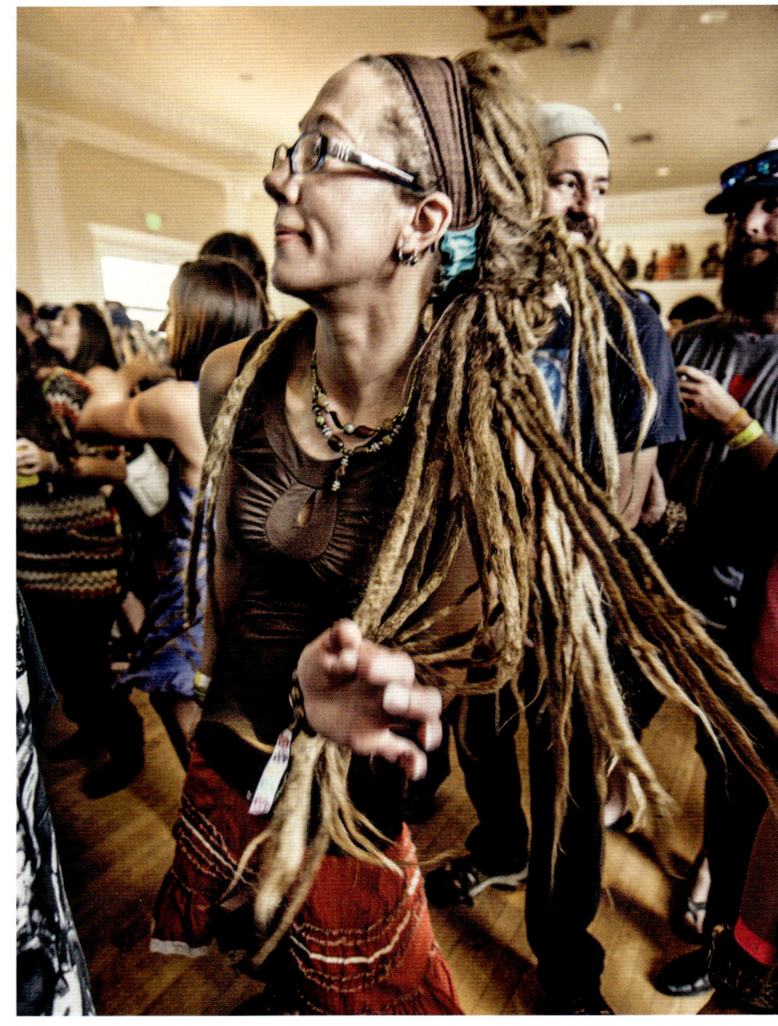

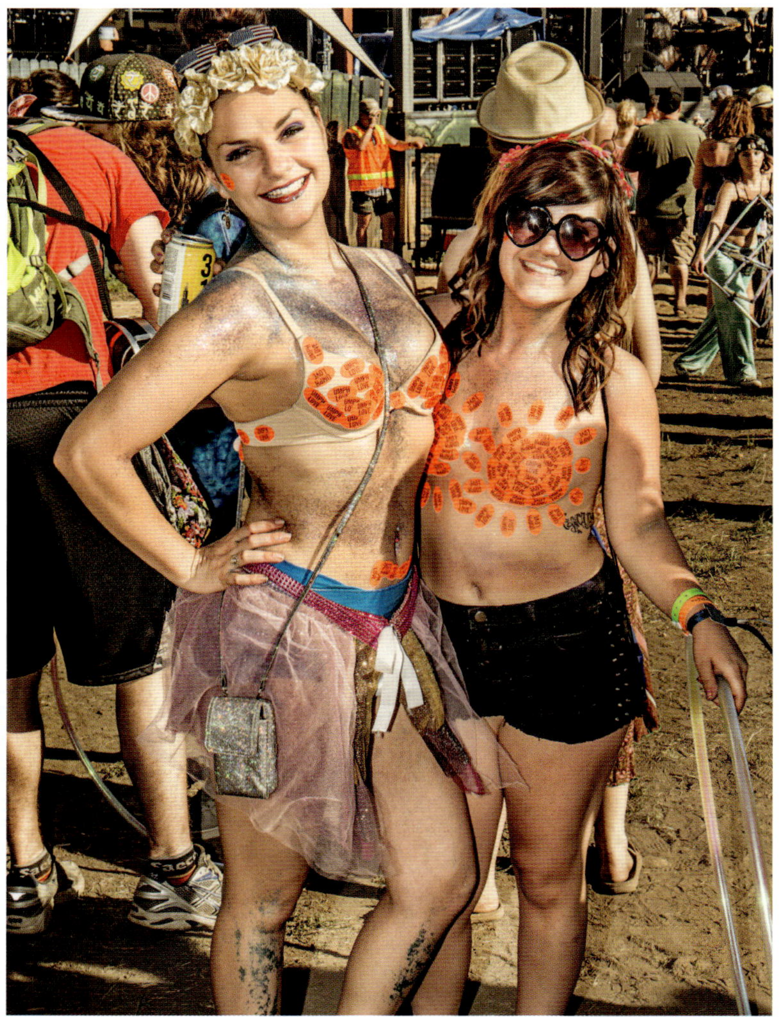

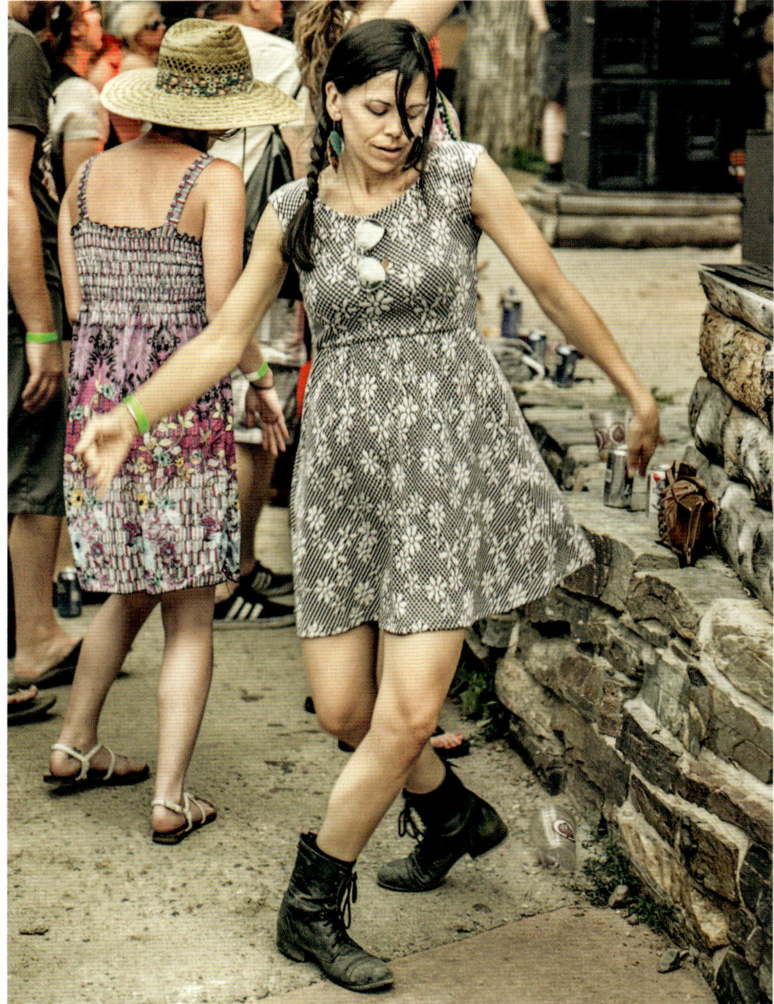

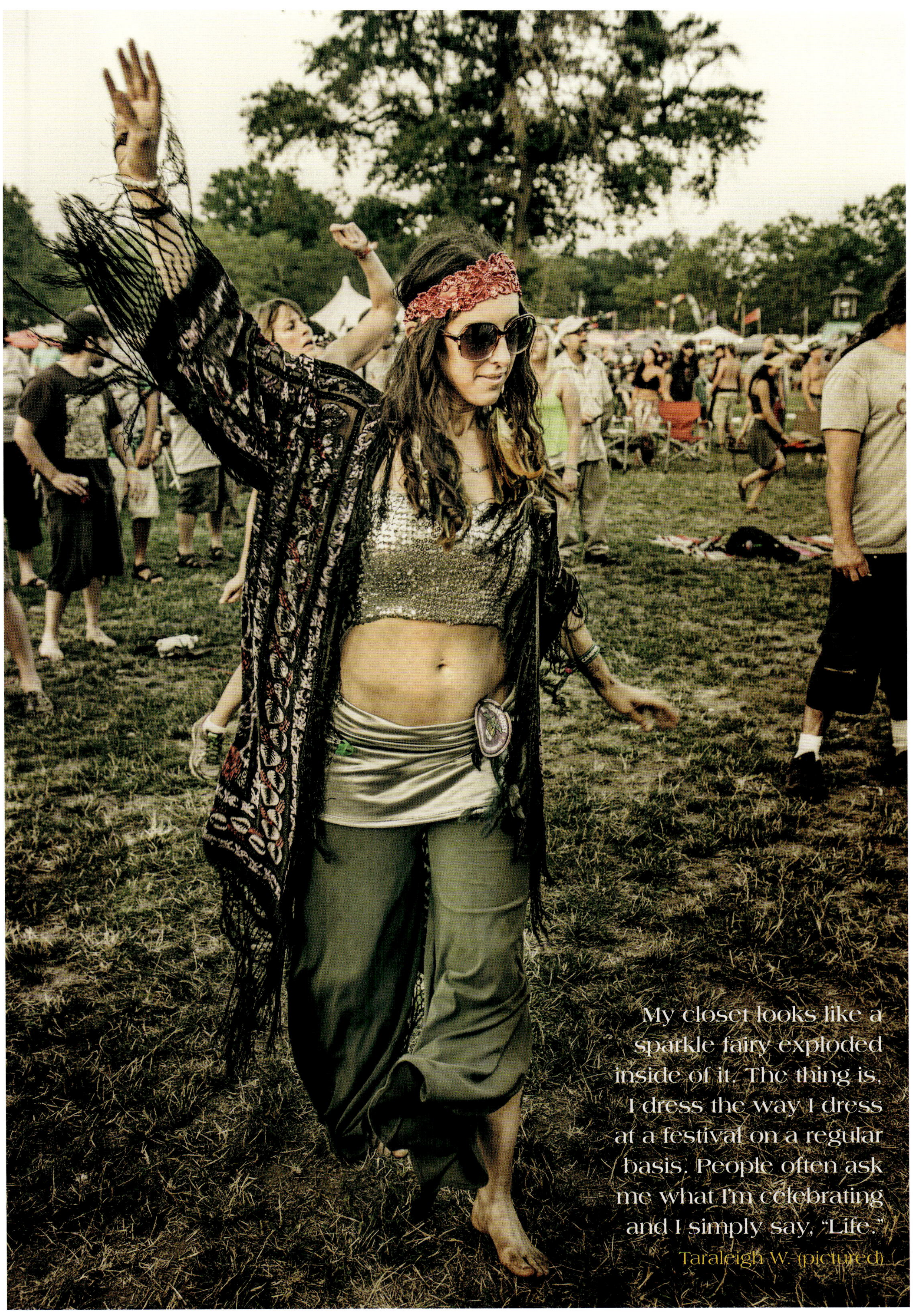

My closet looks like a sparkle fairy exploded inside of it. The thing is, I dress the way I dress at a festival on a regular basis. People often ask me what I'm celebrating and I simply say, "Life."

Taraleigh W. (pictured)

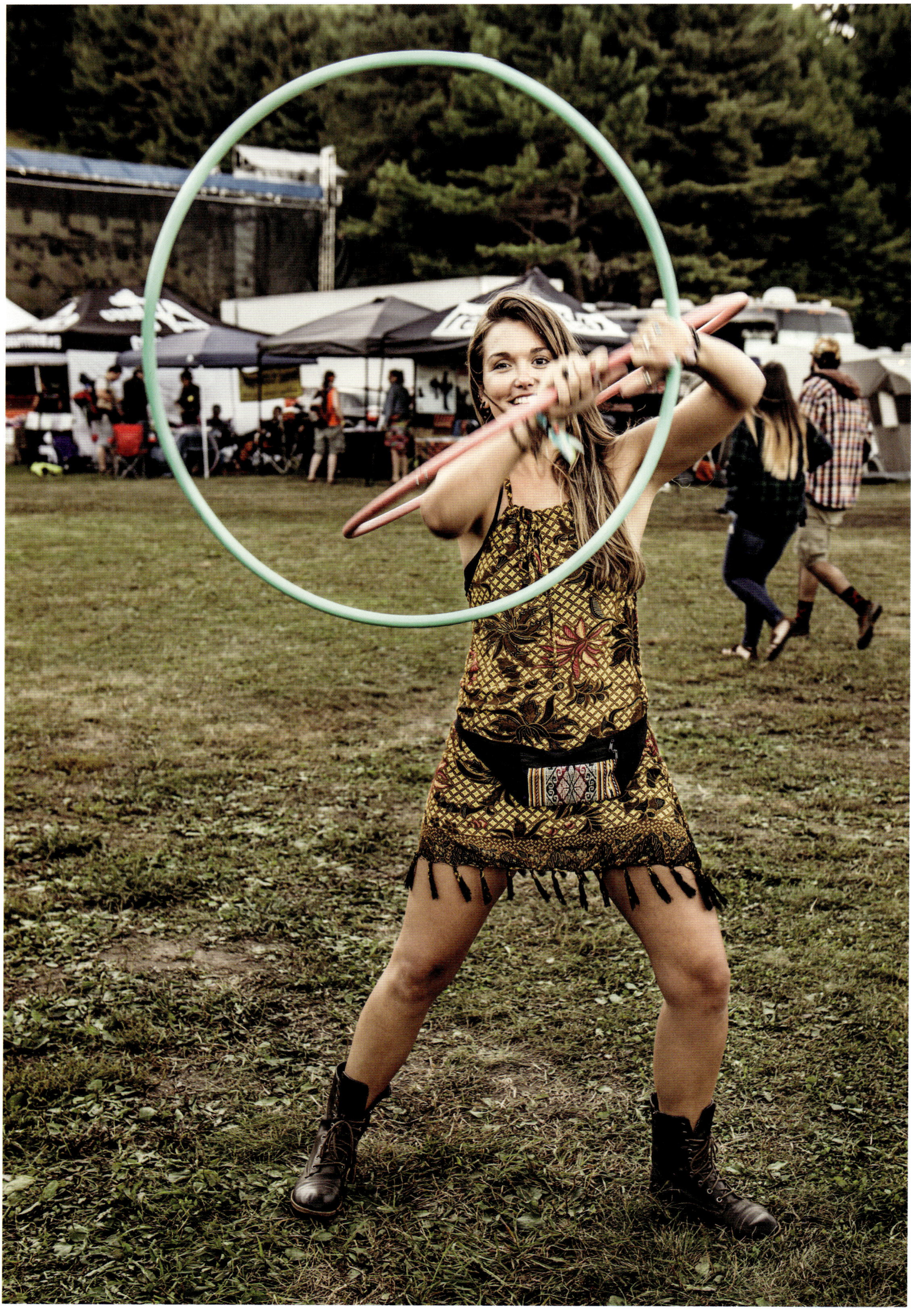

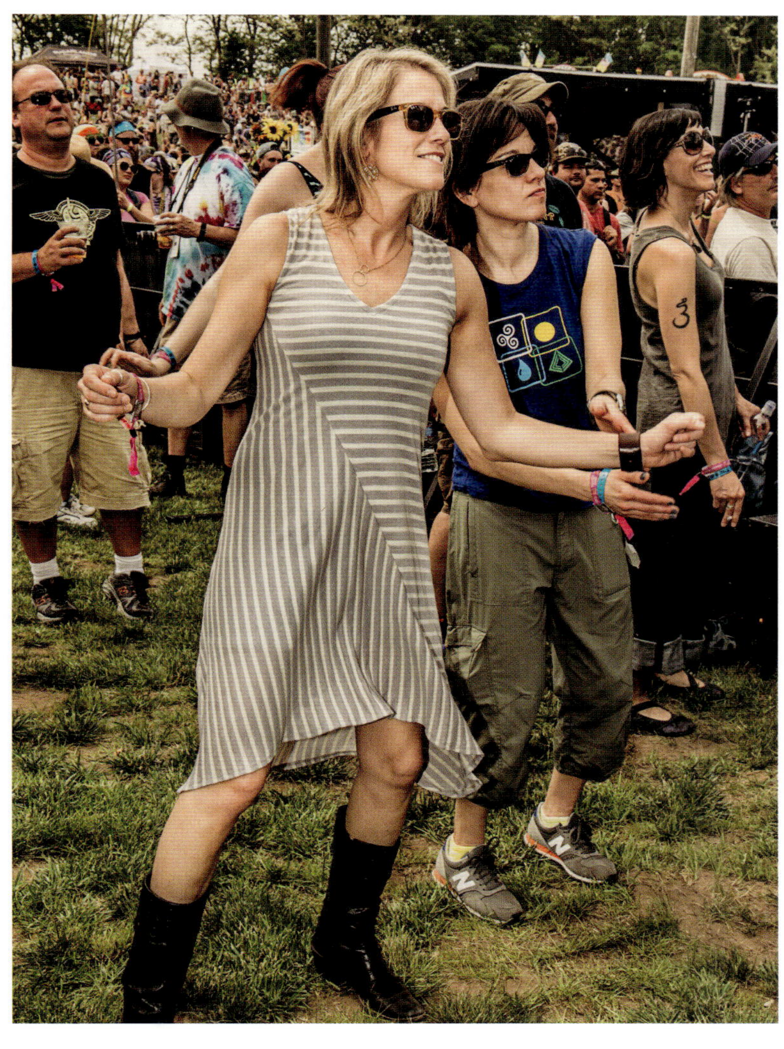

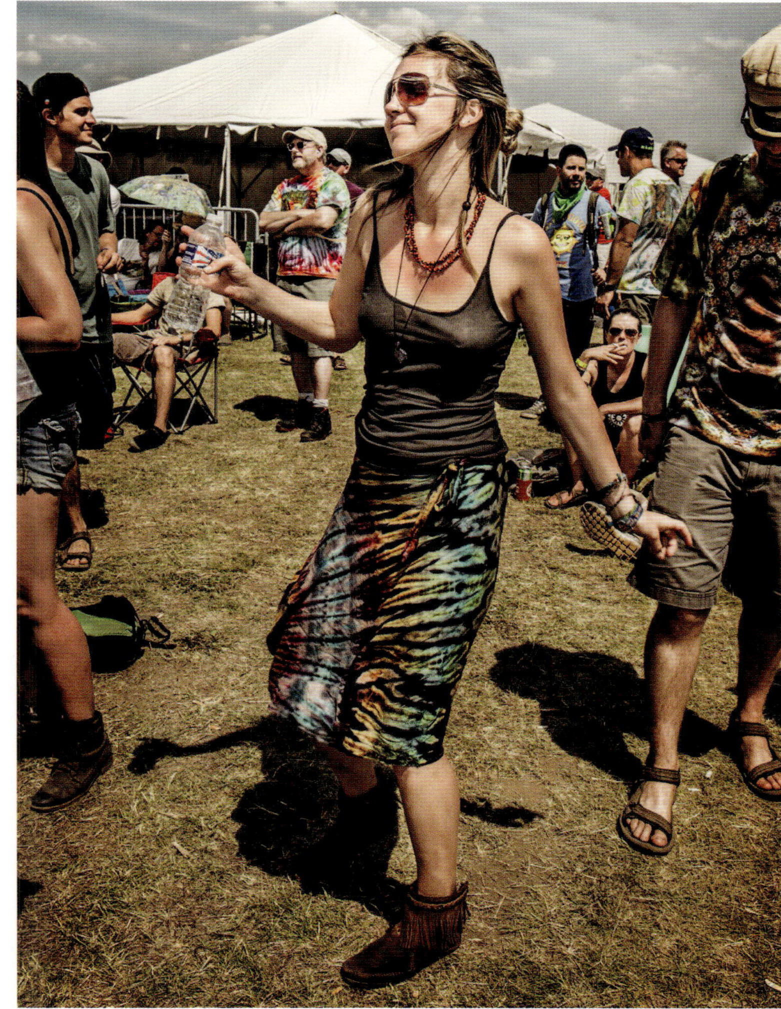

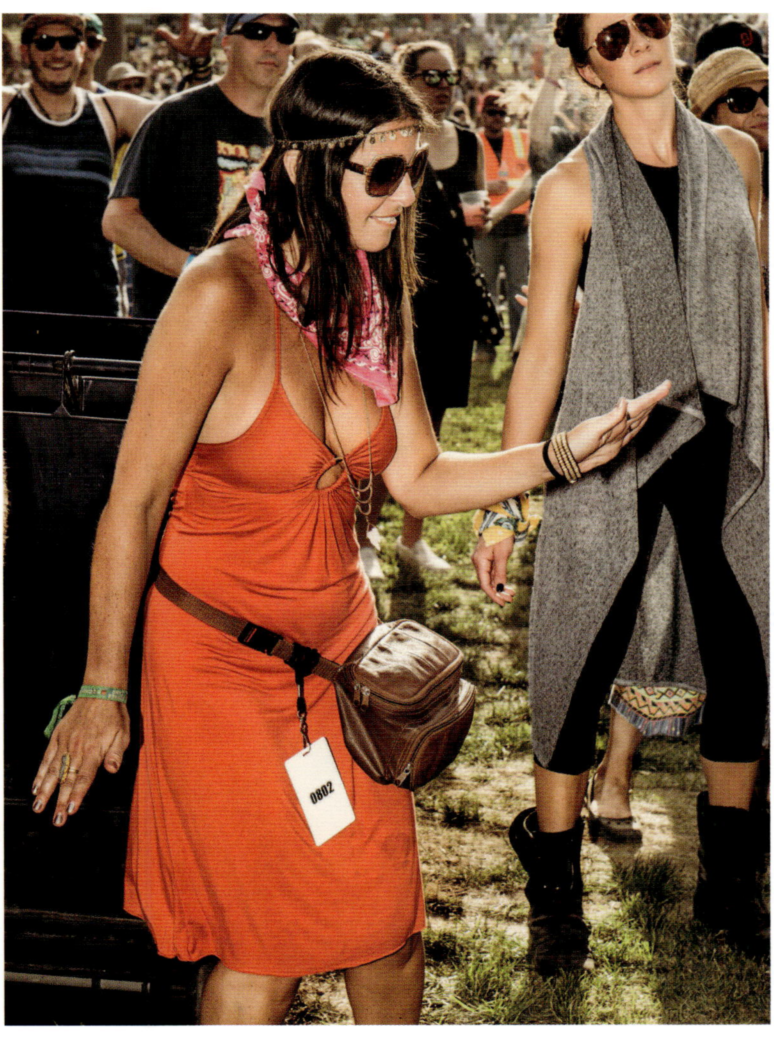
0802

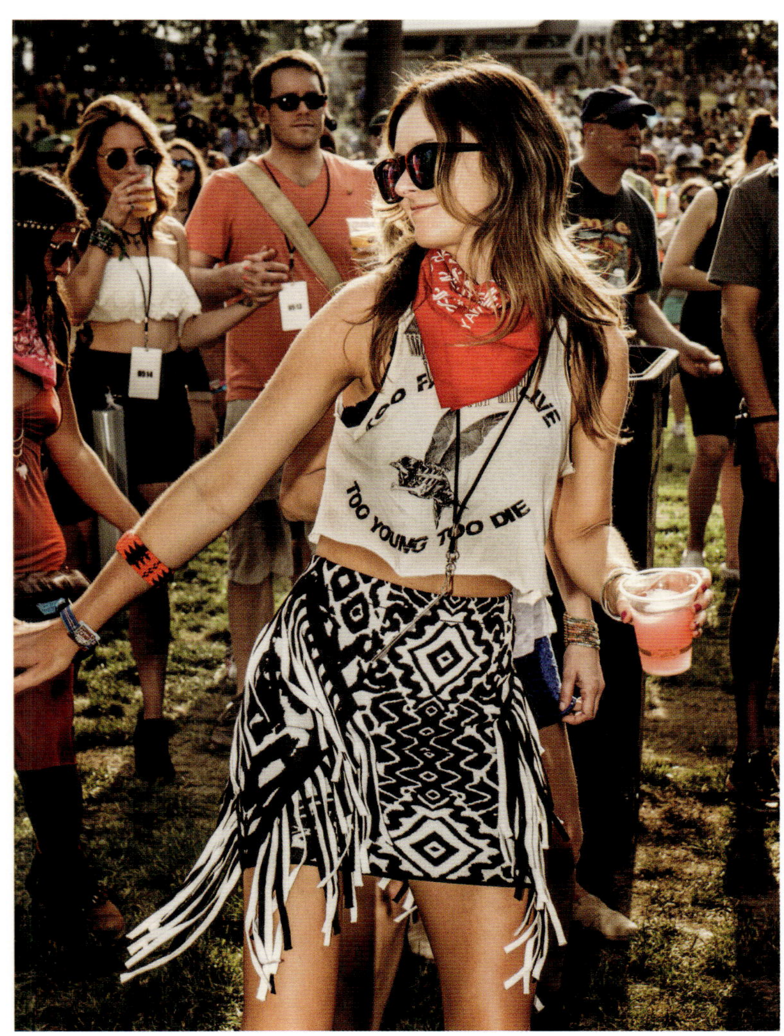
TOO YOUNG TOO DIE

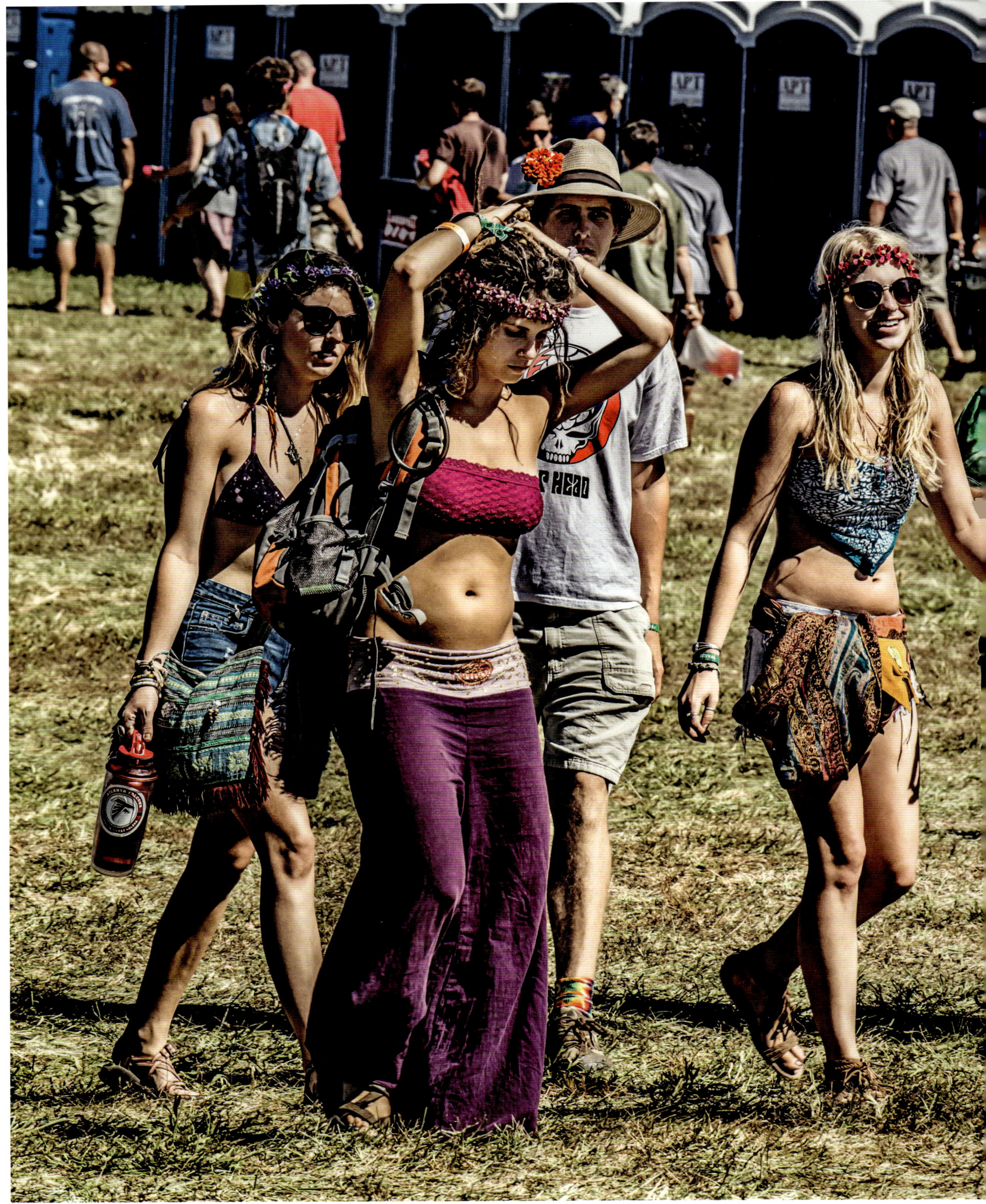
APT

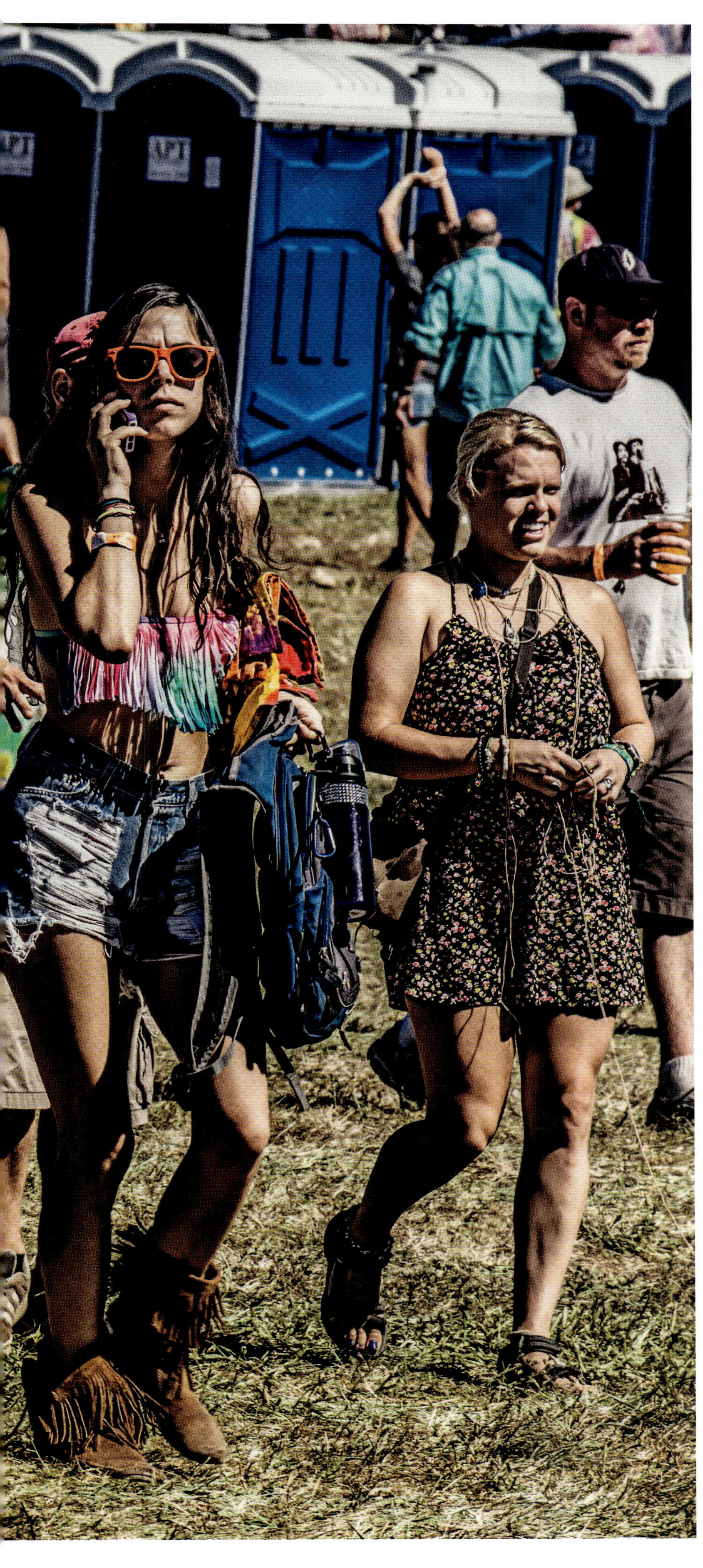

Festivals create a canvas where participants have a chance to add their own splash of color to the scene. Everyone acting together to create this temporary utopia. Michelle S.

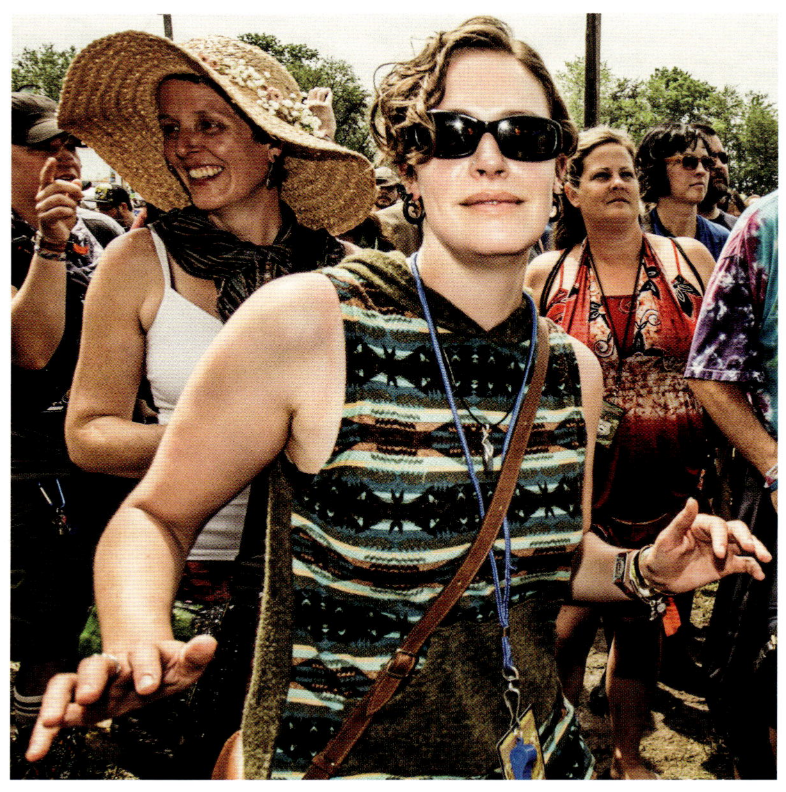

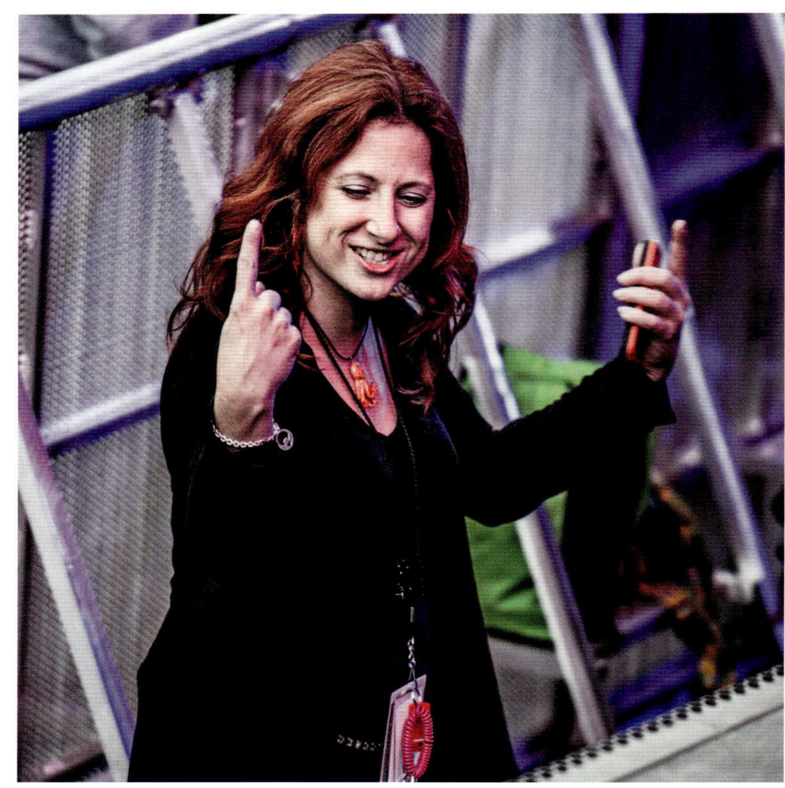

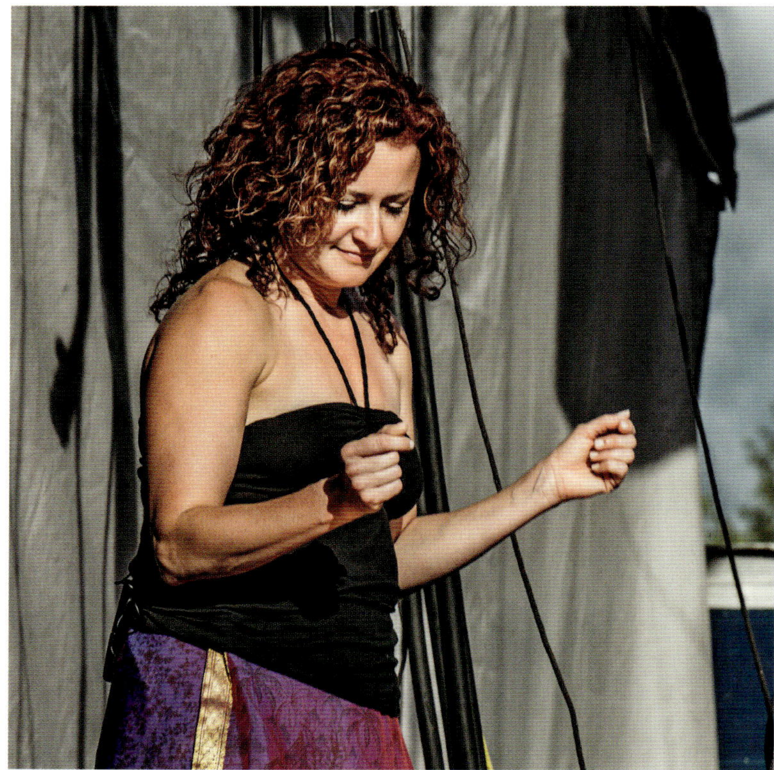

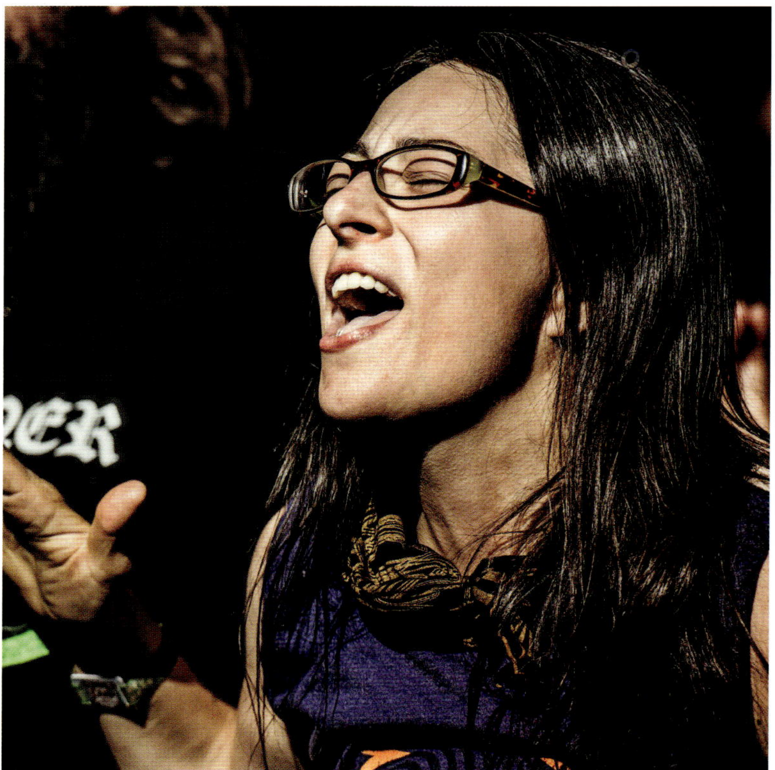

A live show is the perfect place to center myself and fuel my soul. I absolutely love the energy. It's my church. Lauren N.

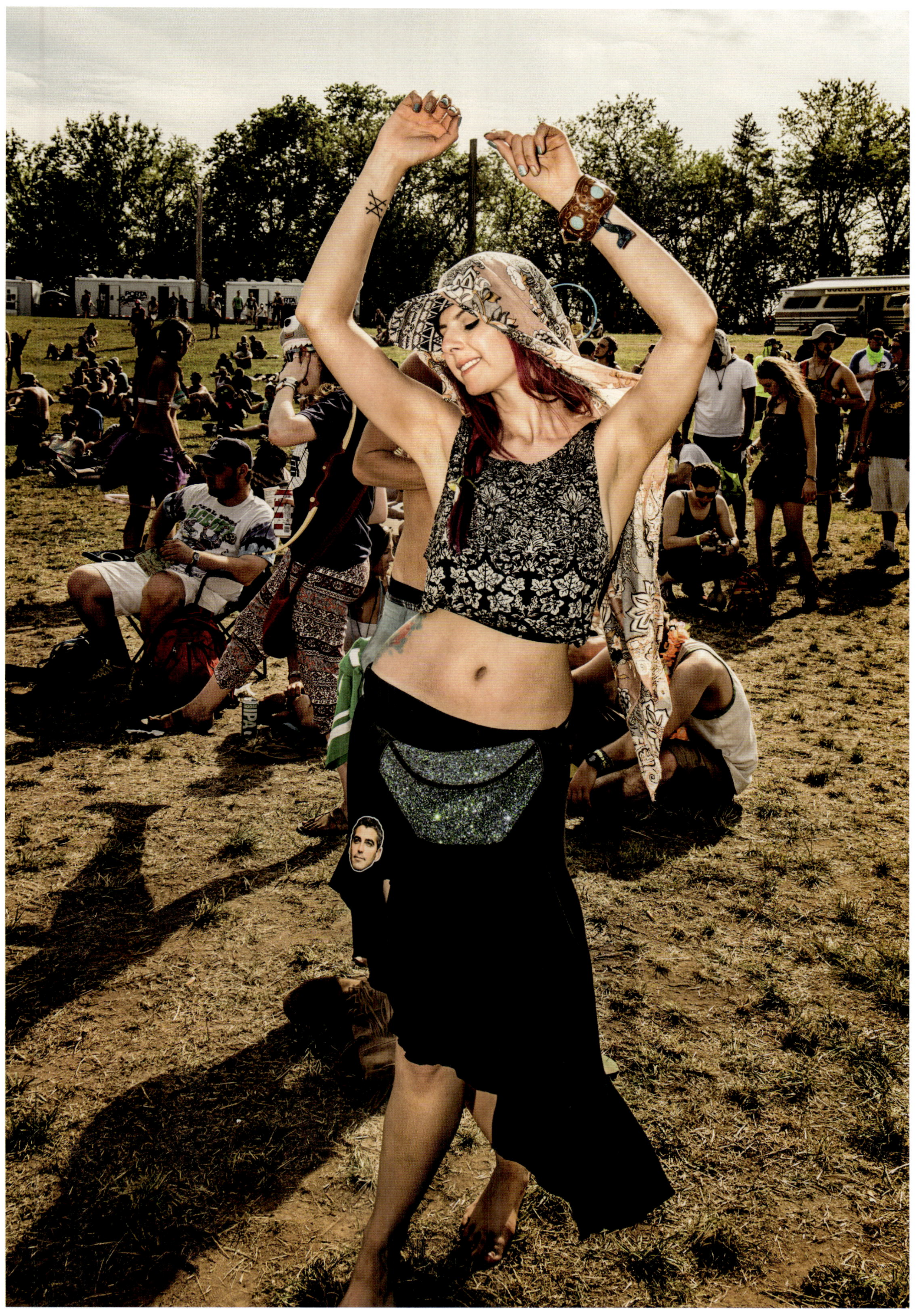

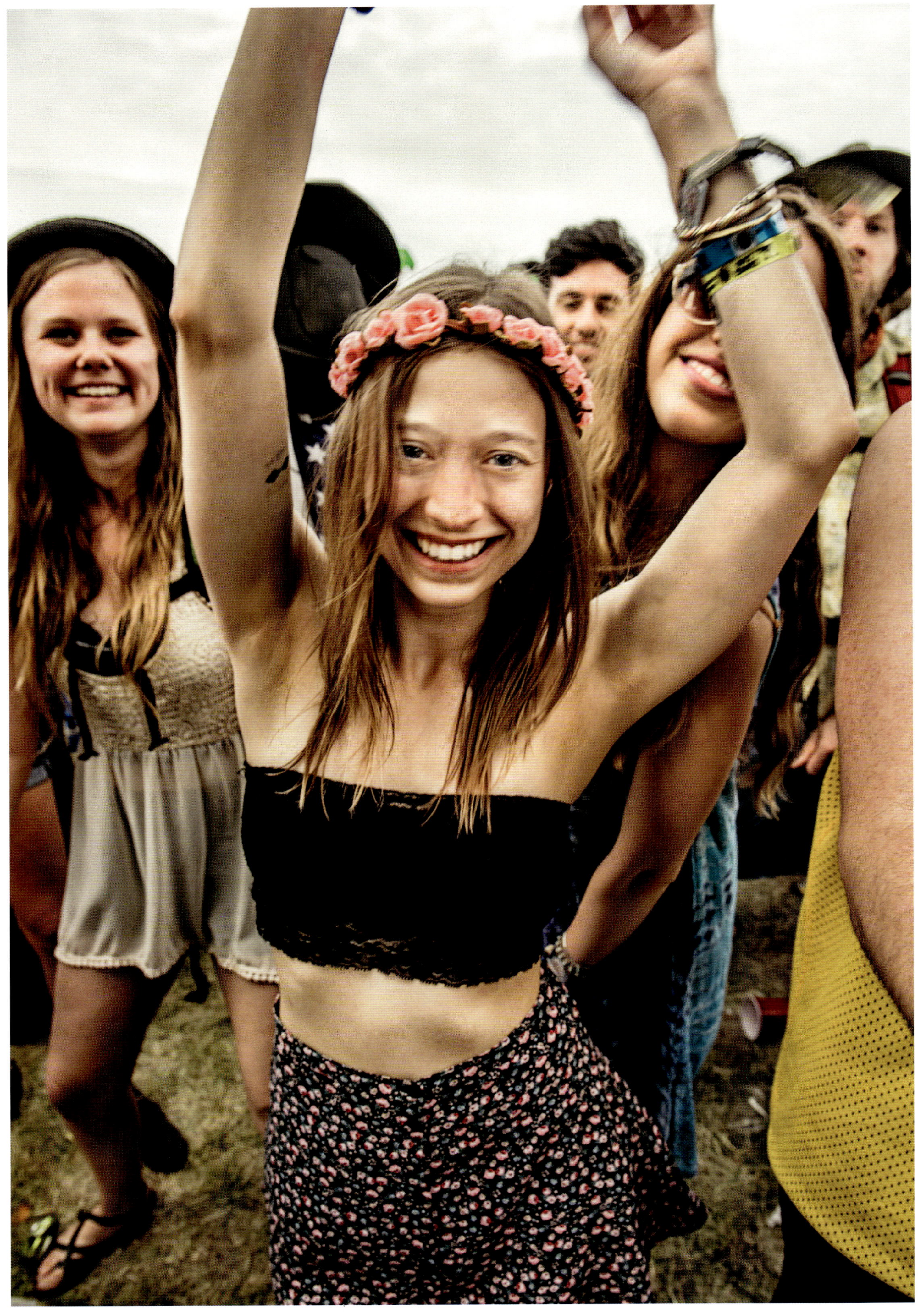

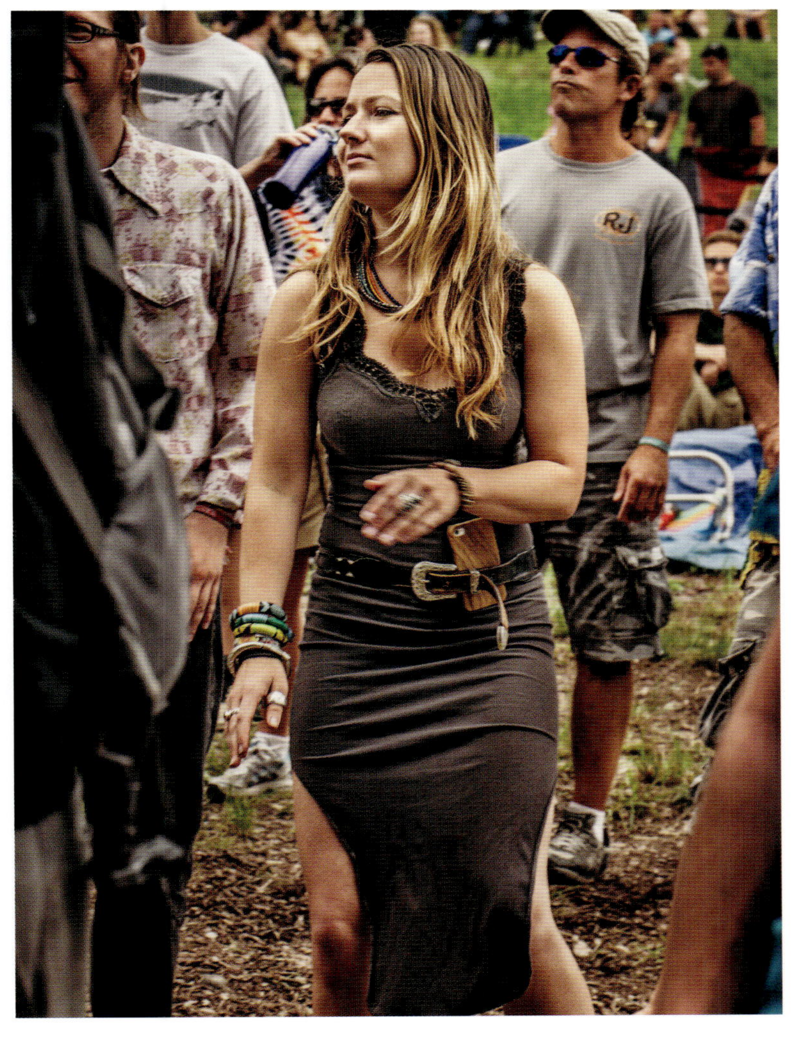

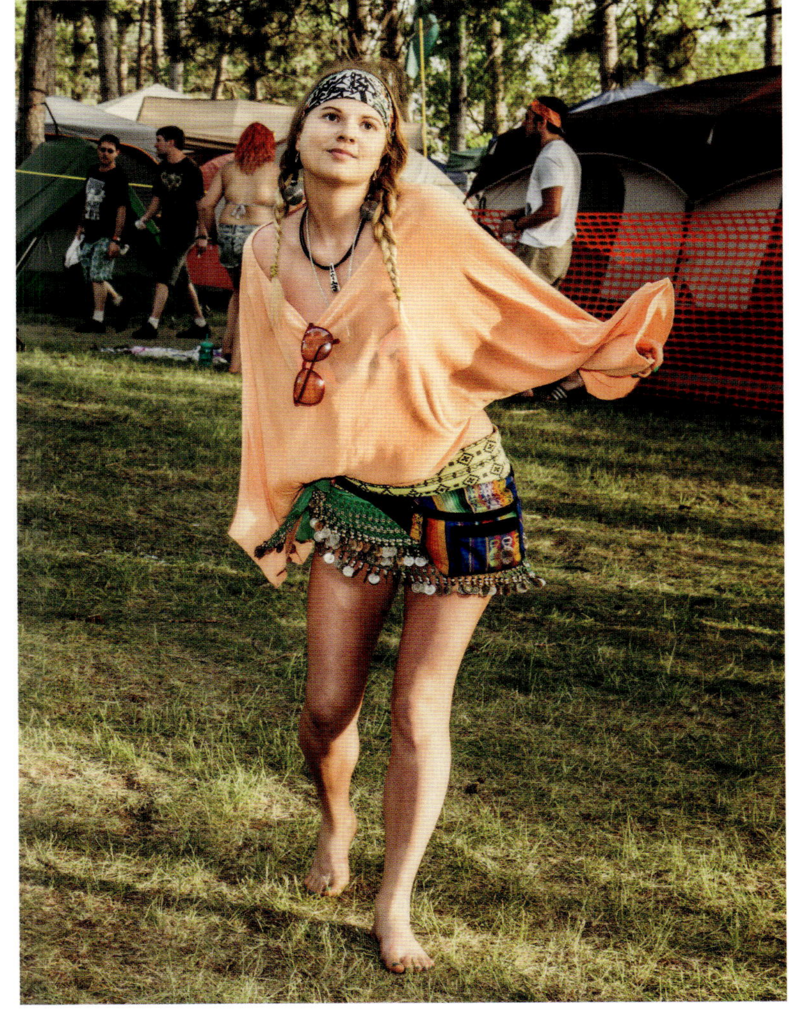

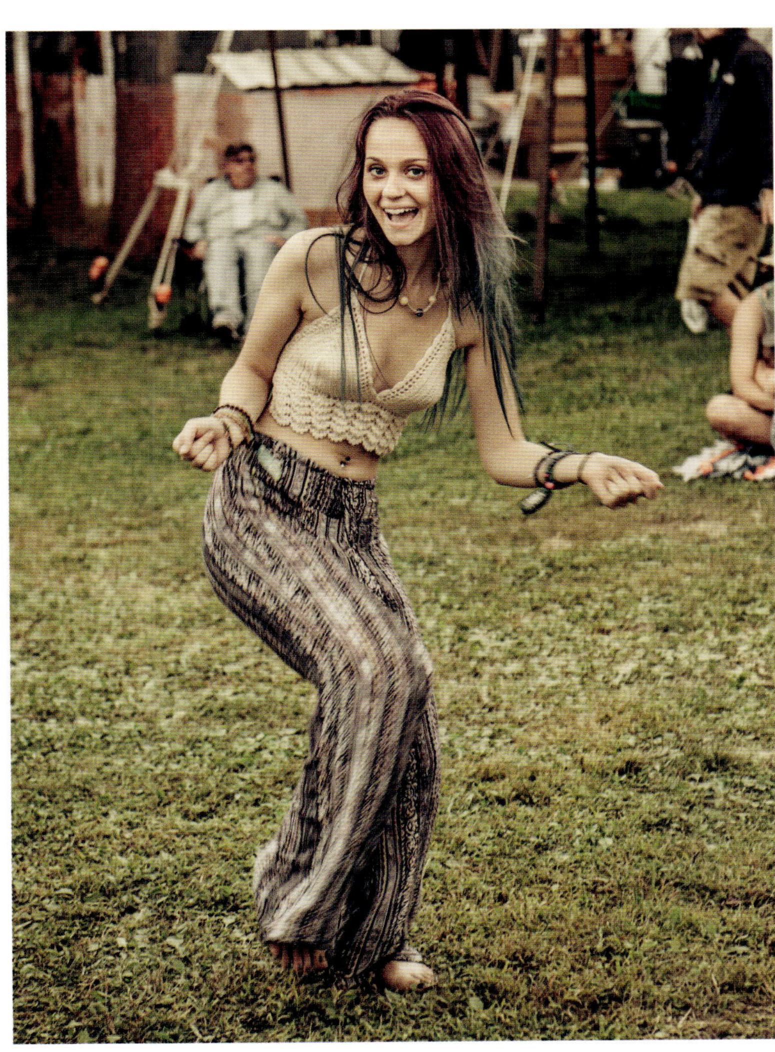

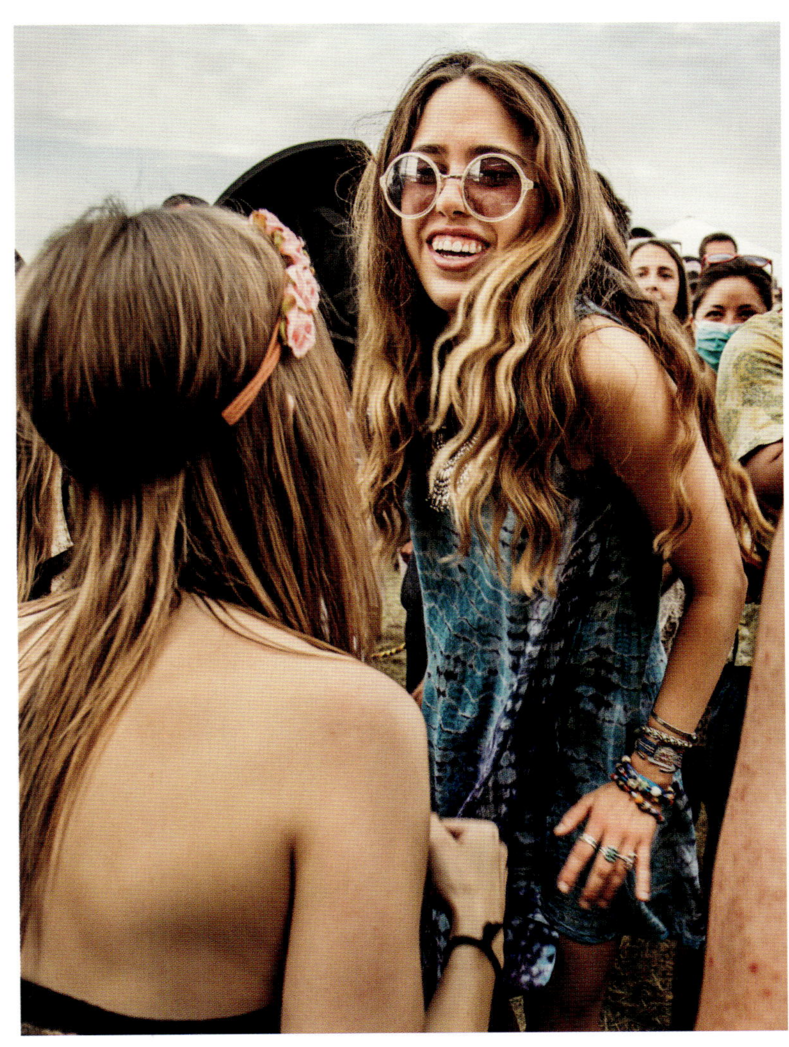

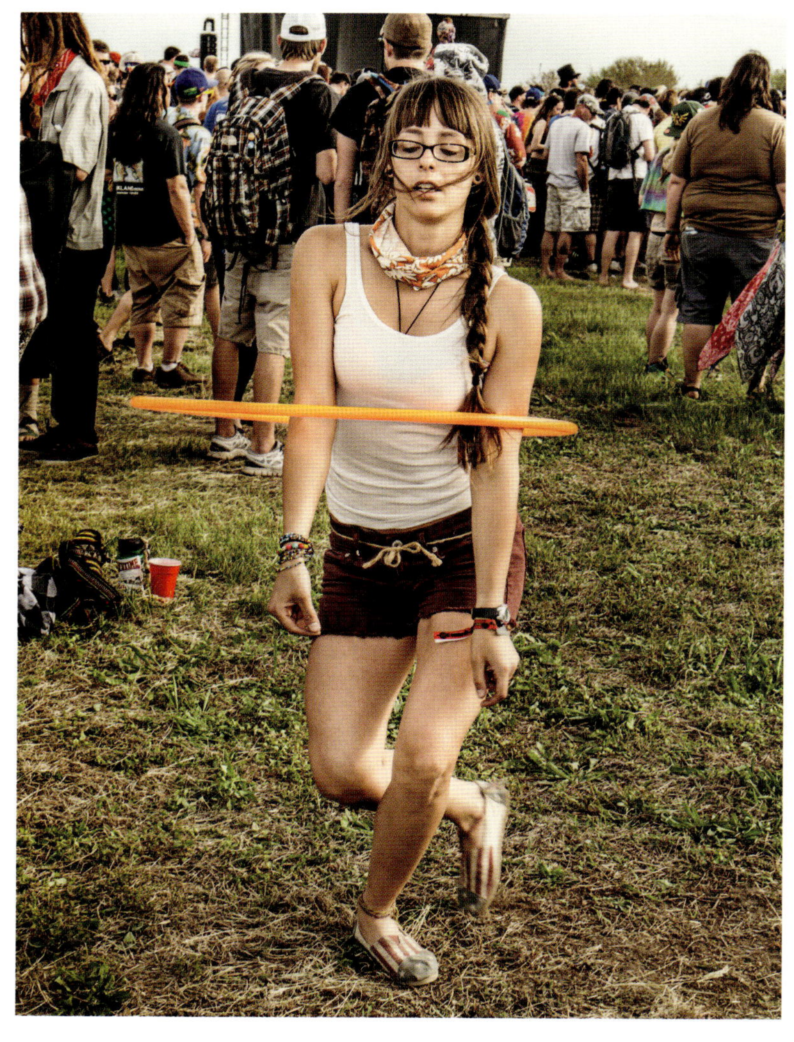

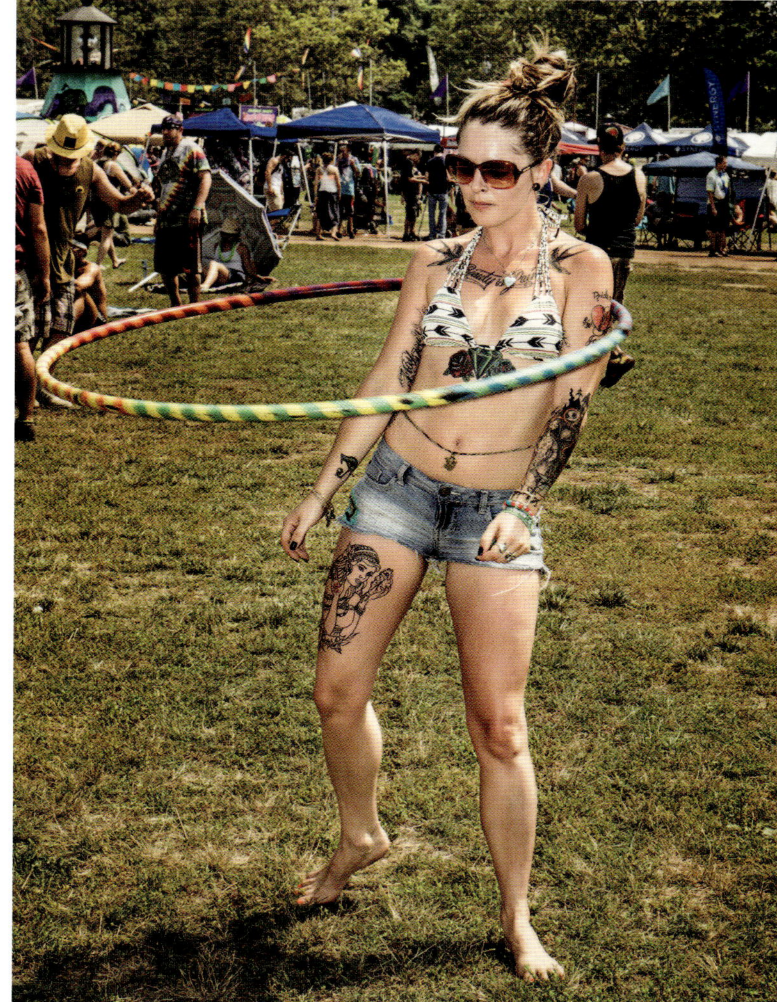

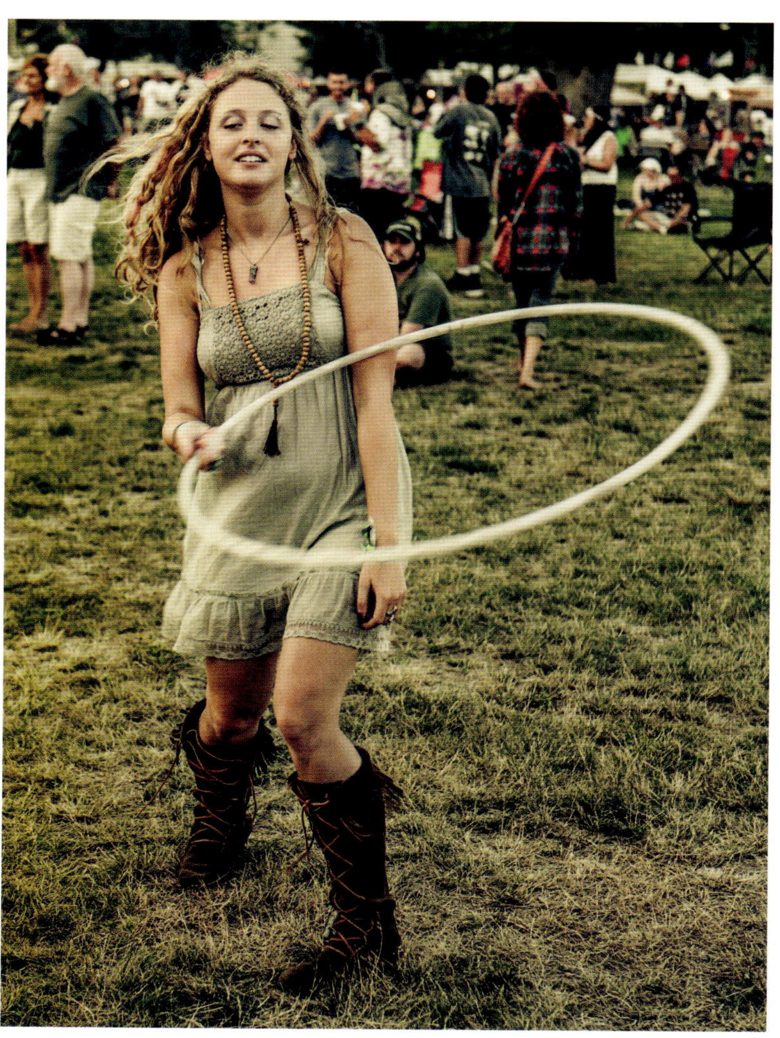

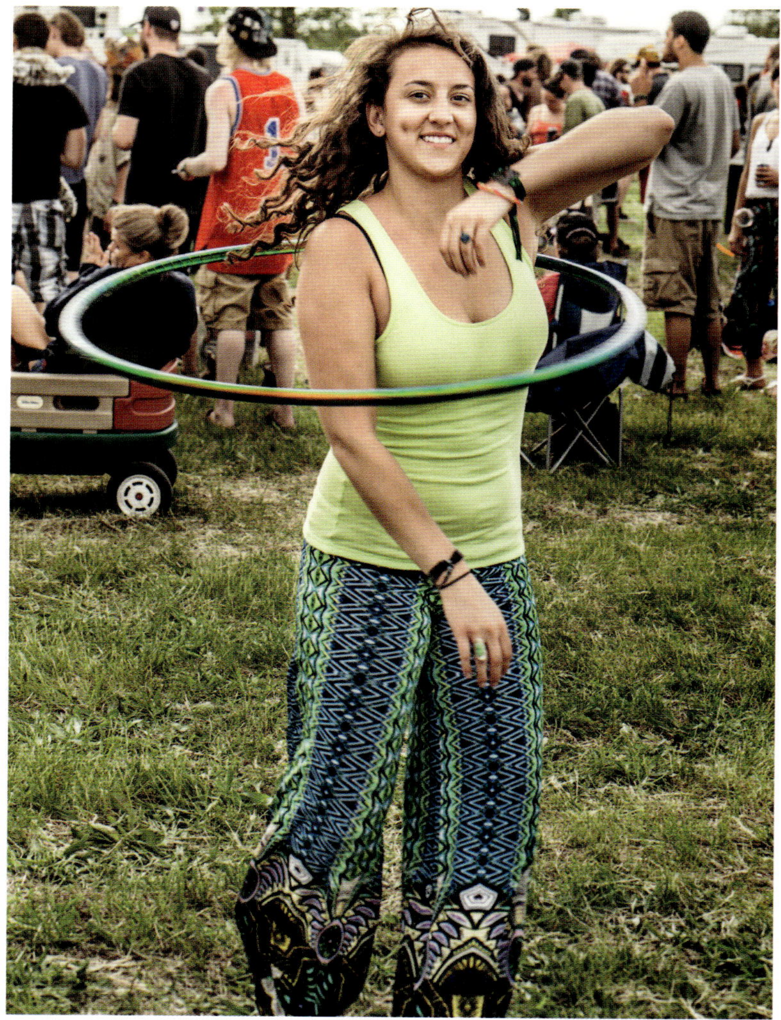

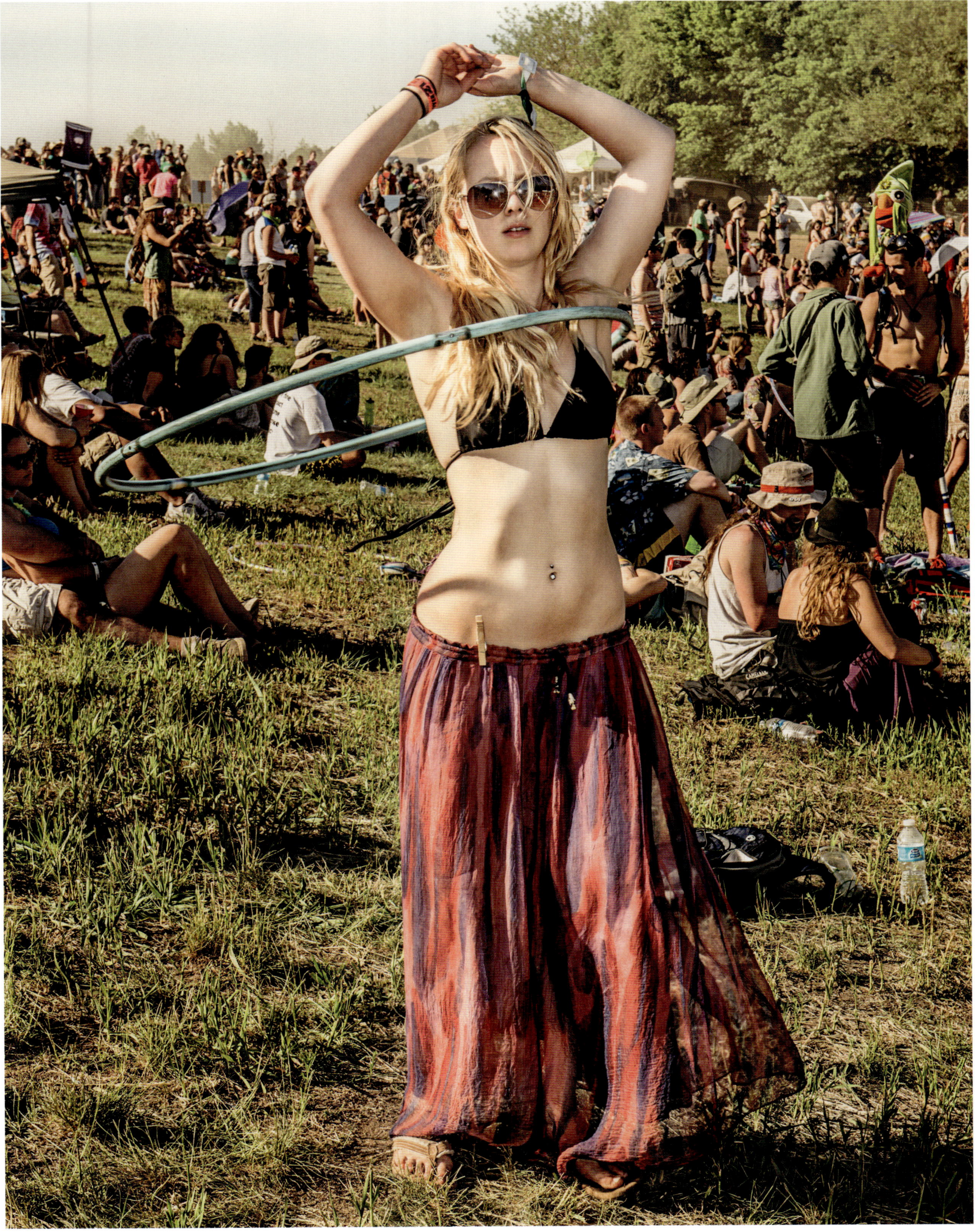

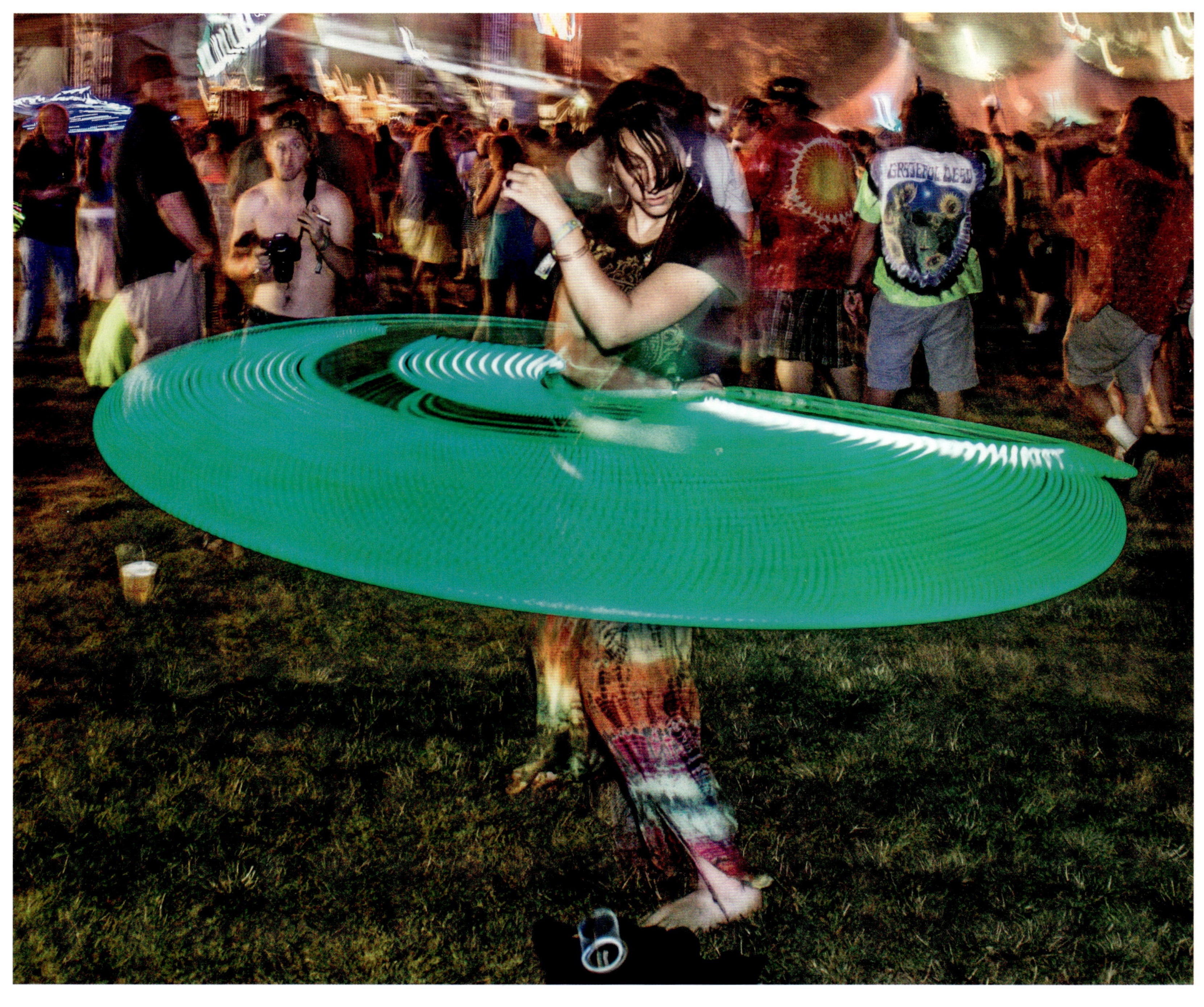

Color, sparkles, tutus, hula hoops, glitter, costume boxes, wings, wardrobe tent—these are a few of my favorite things! Pamela G.

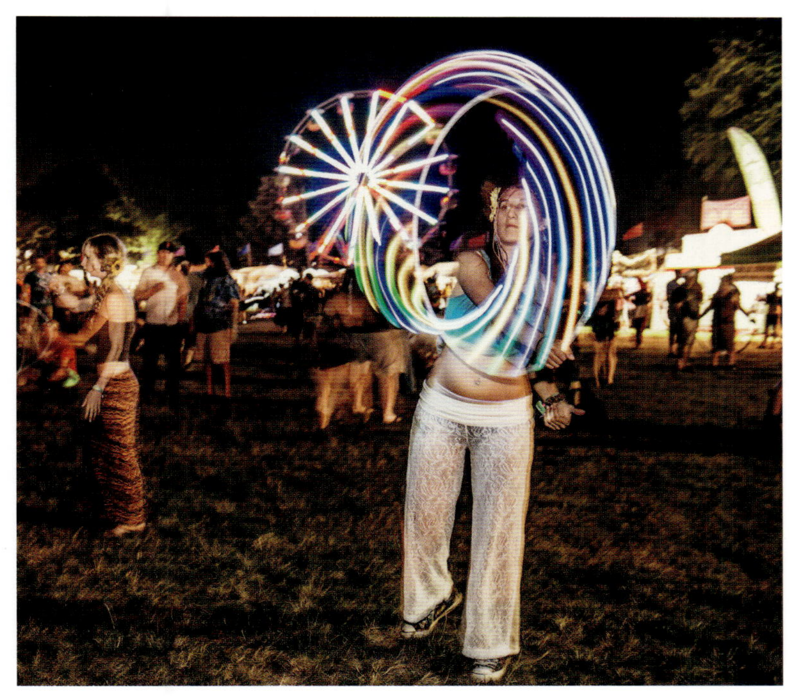

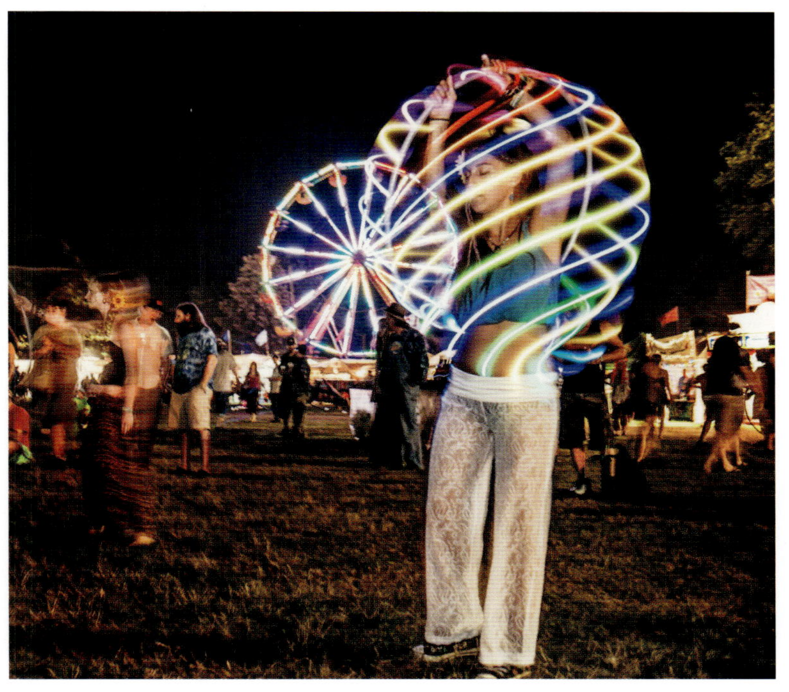

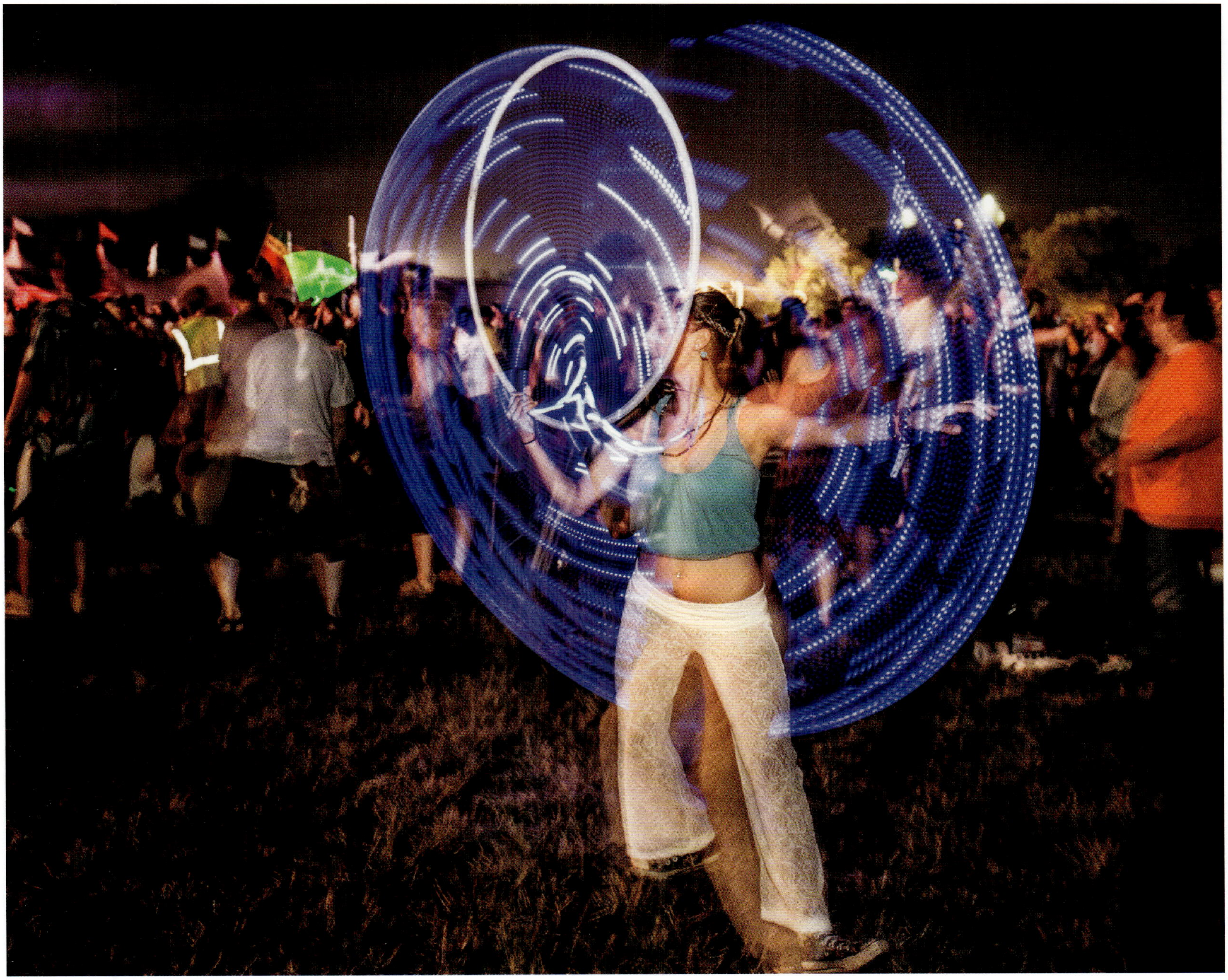

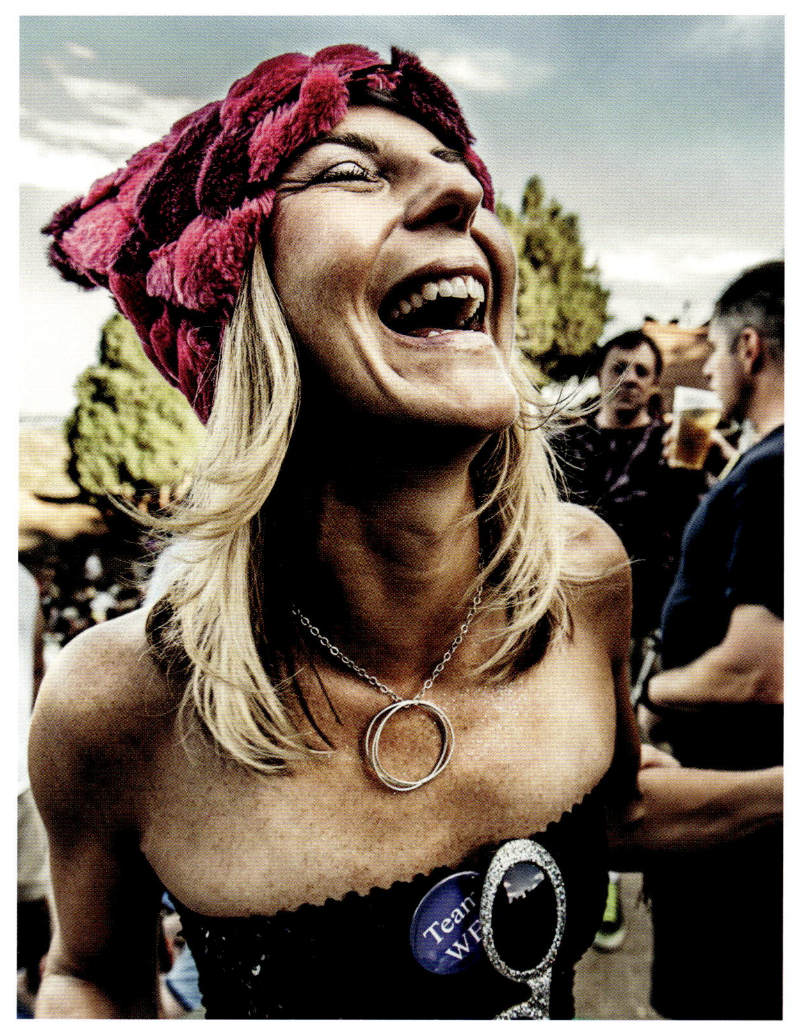

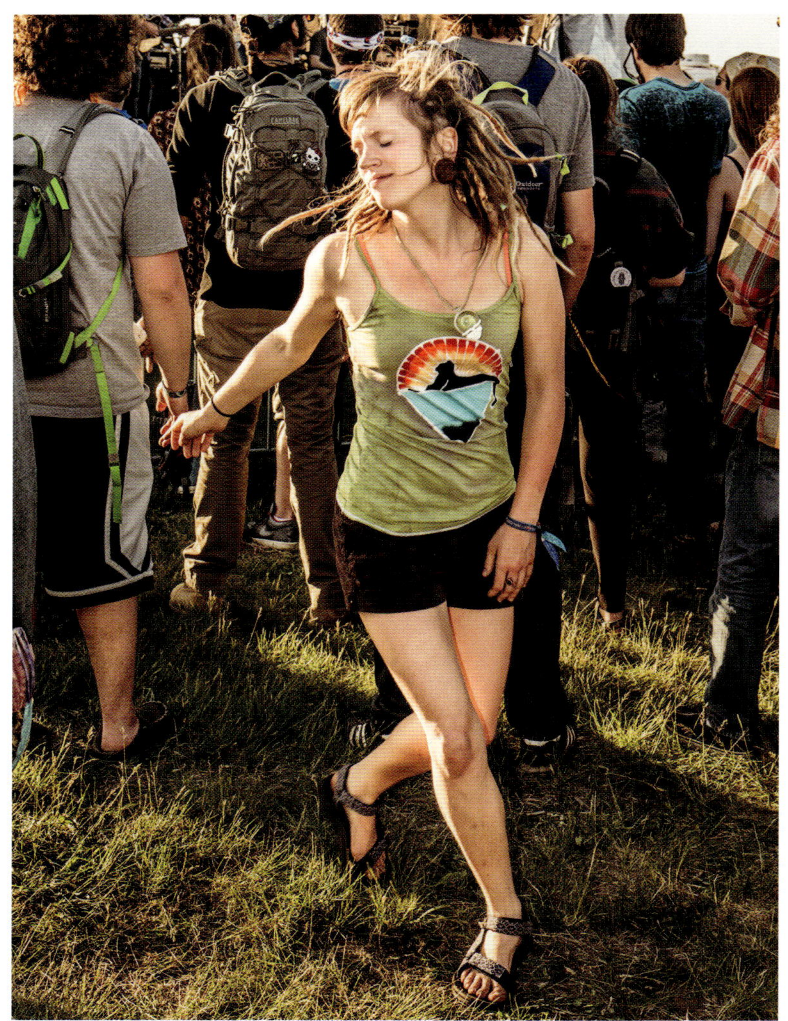

The best thing about live music, for me, is the ability to escape thoughts. When you close your eyes and tune in to the music, it allows you to go to a different place. It connects your heart to your soul and lets you be free.

Kim W. (pictured, left)

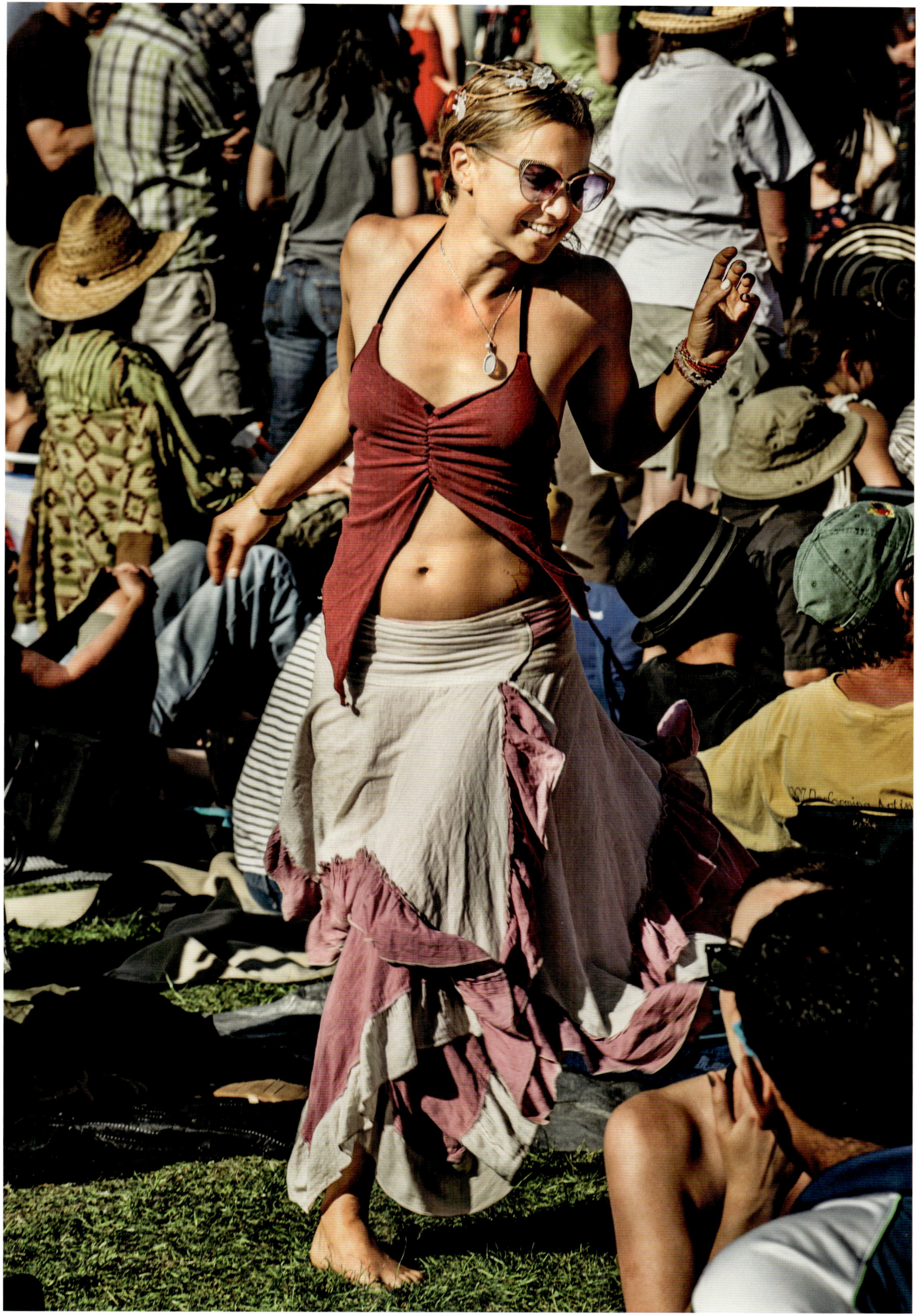

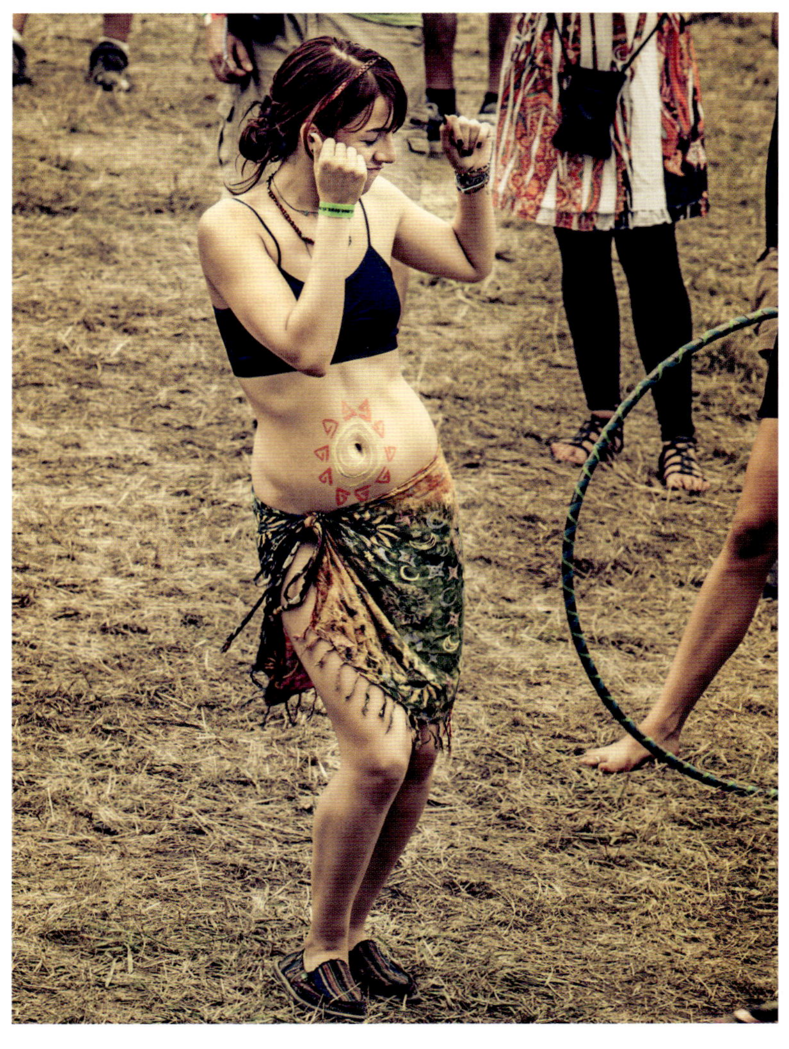

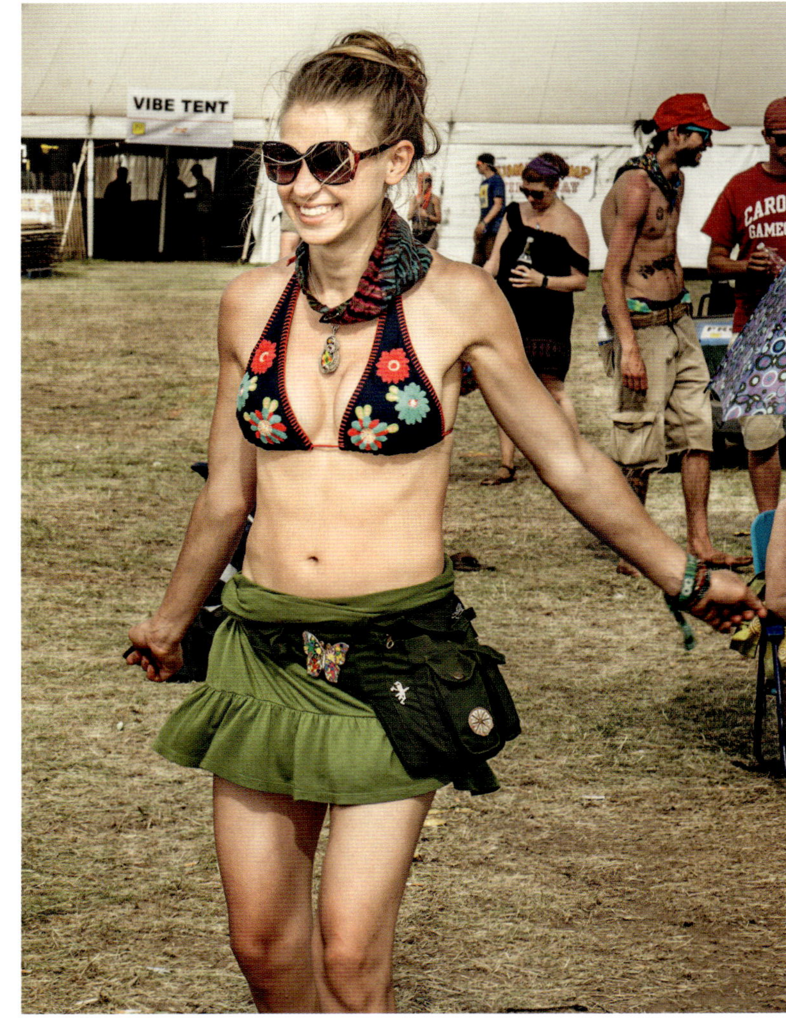
VIBE TENT

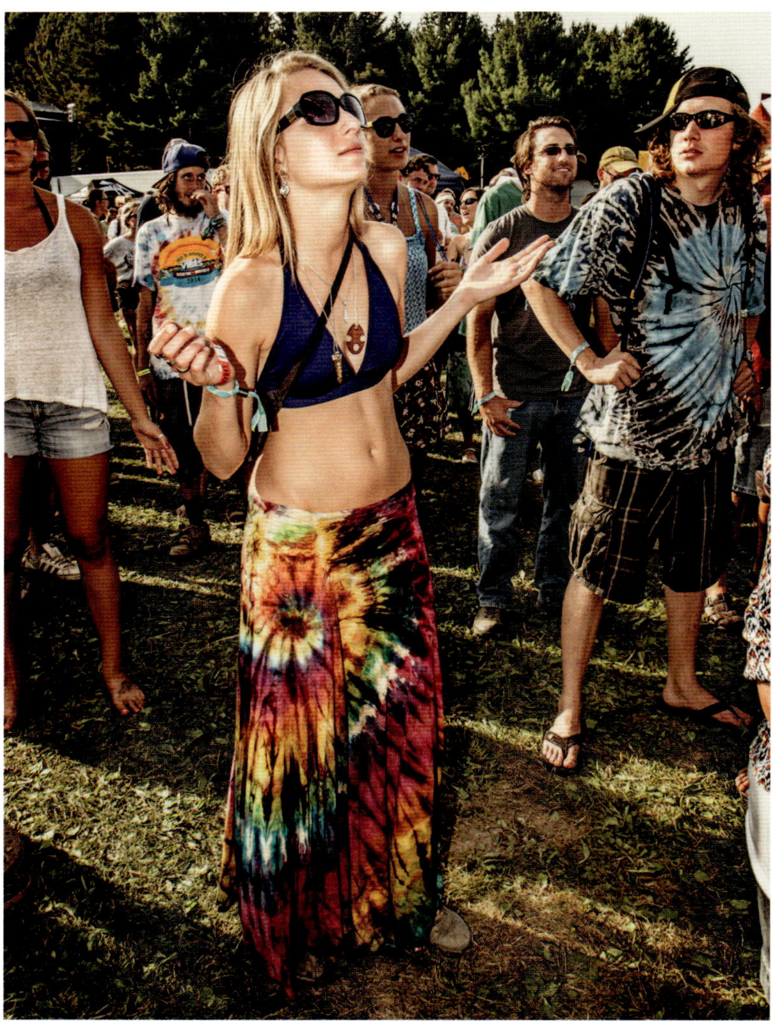

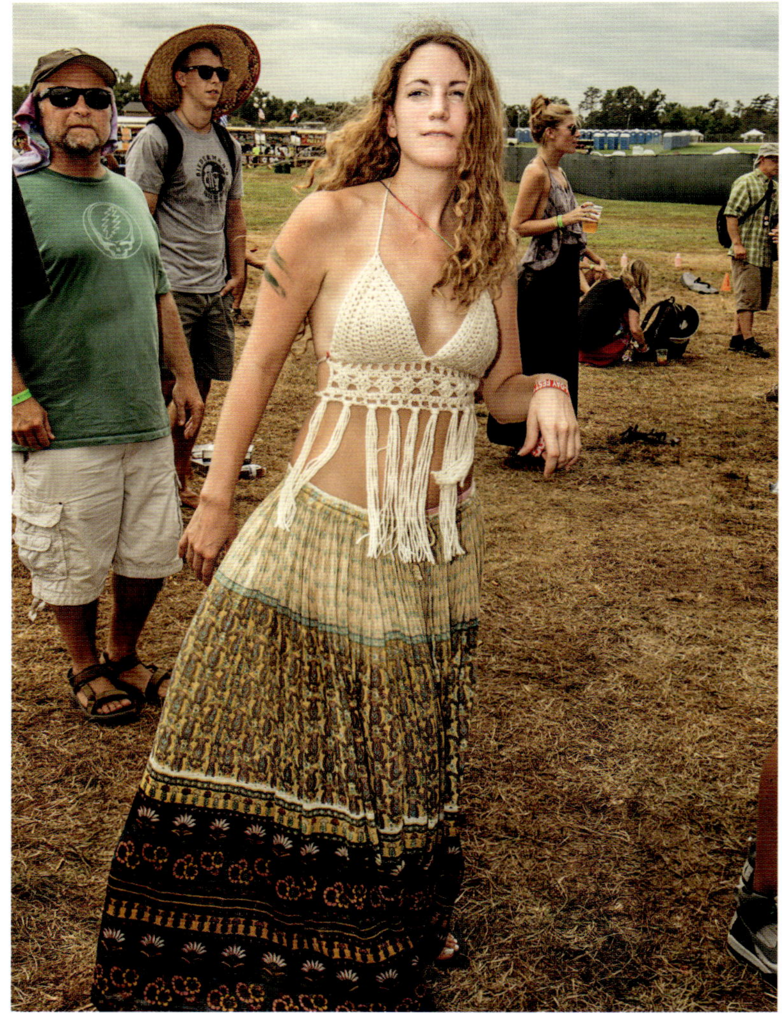

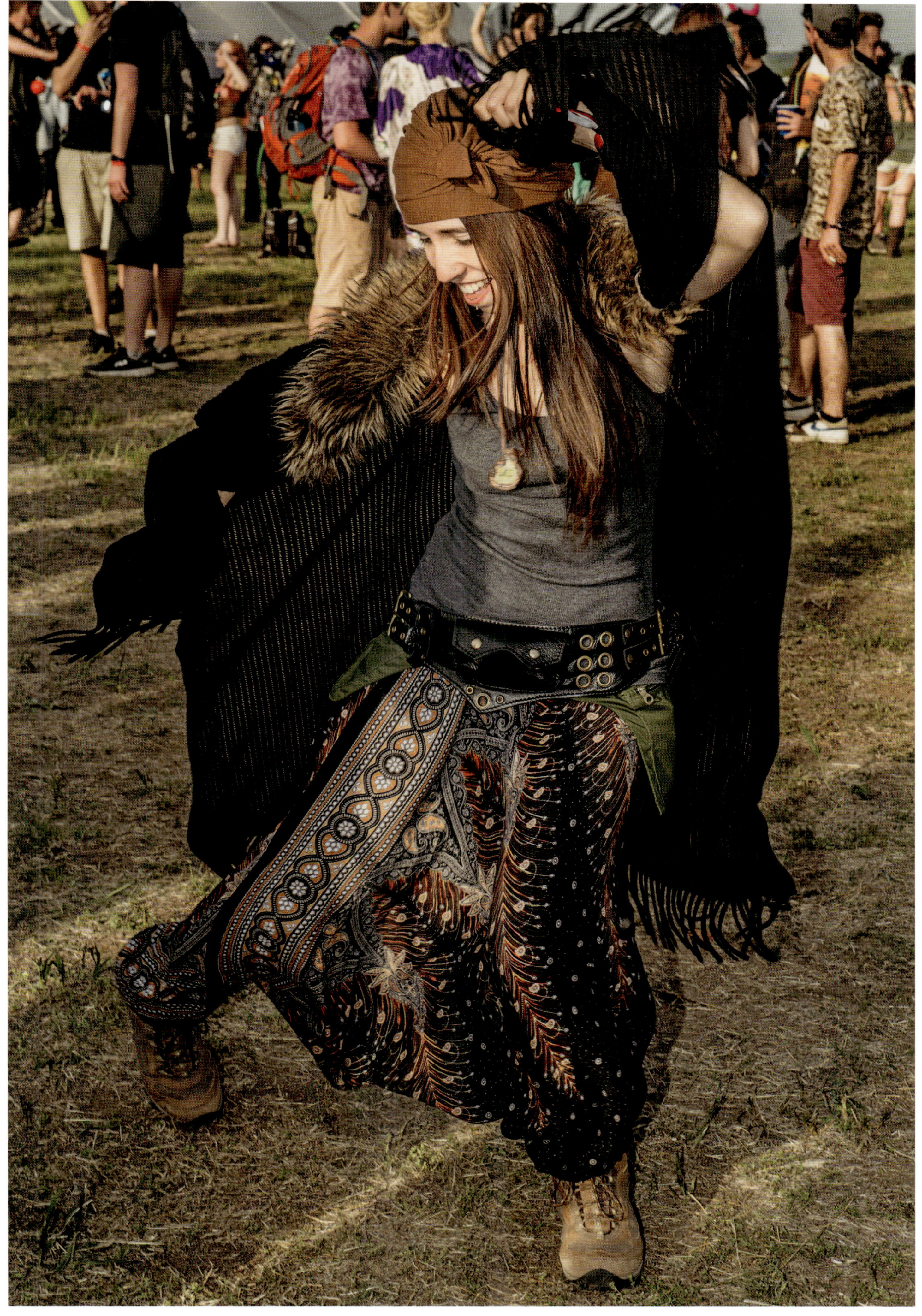

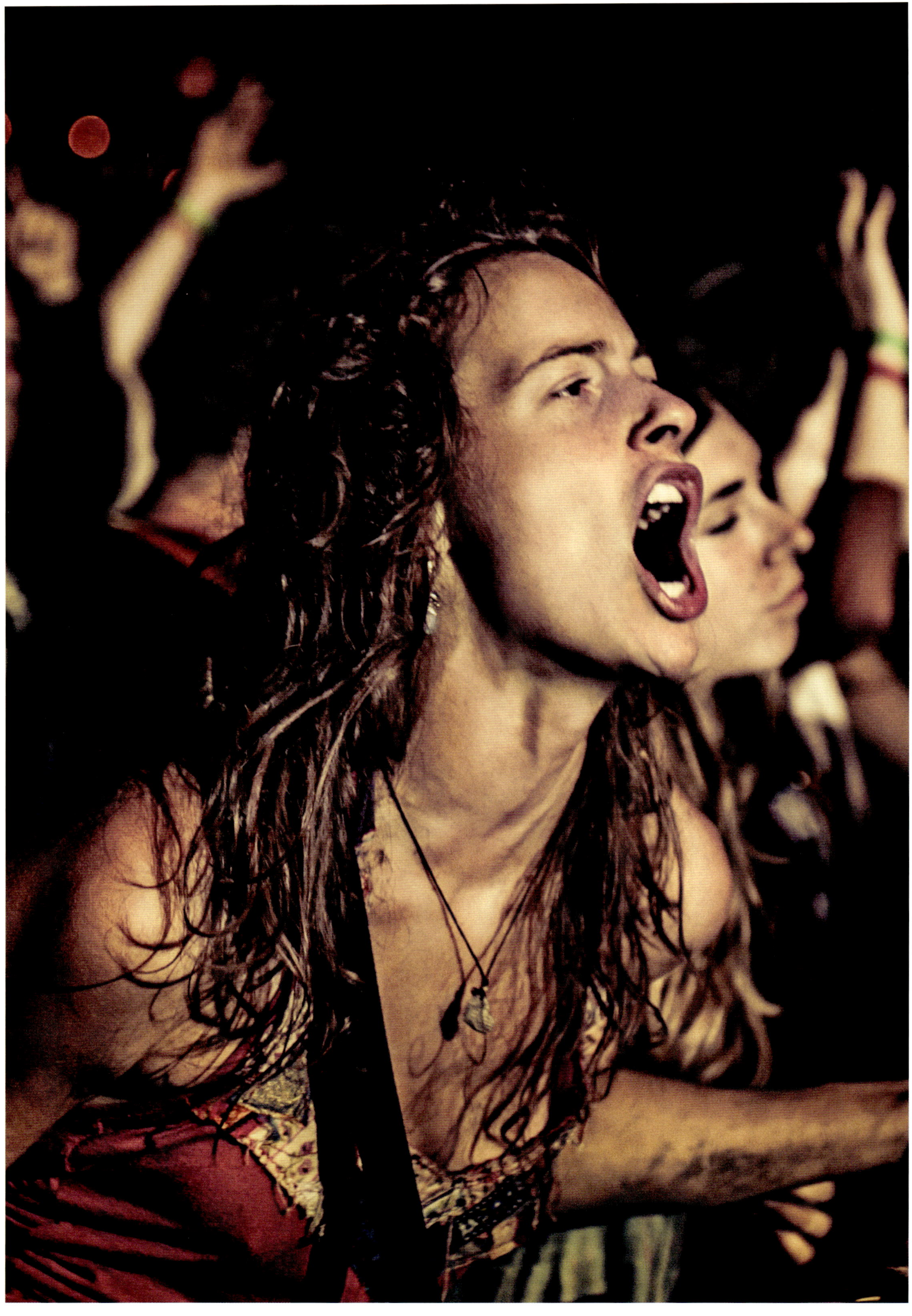

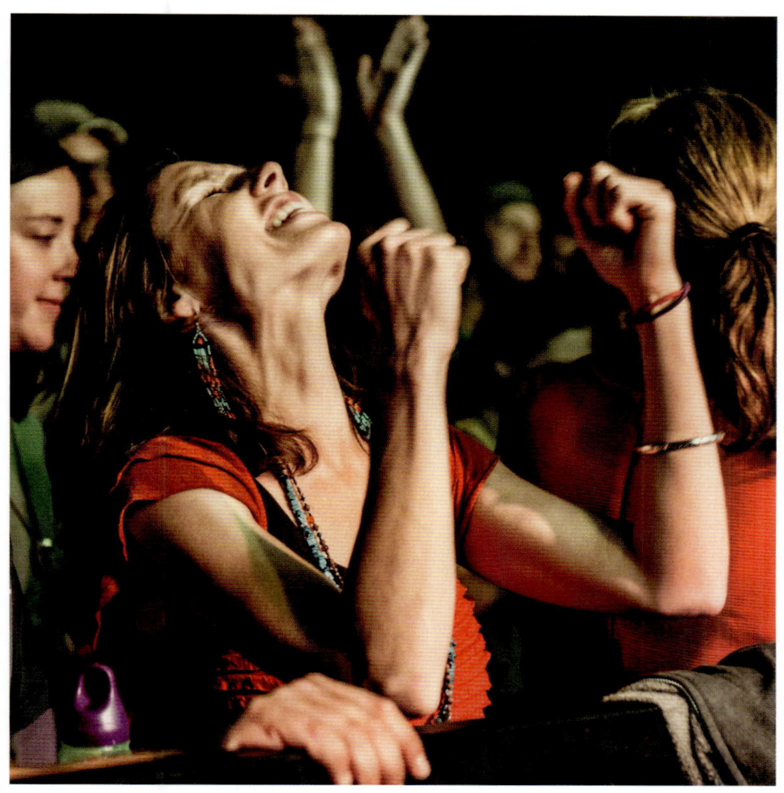

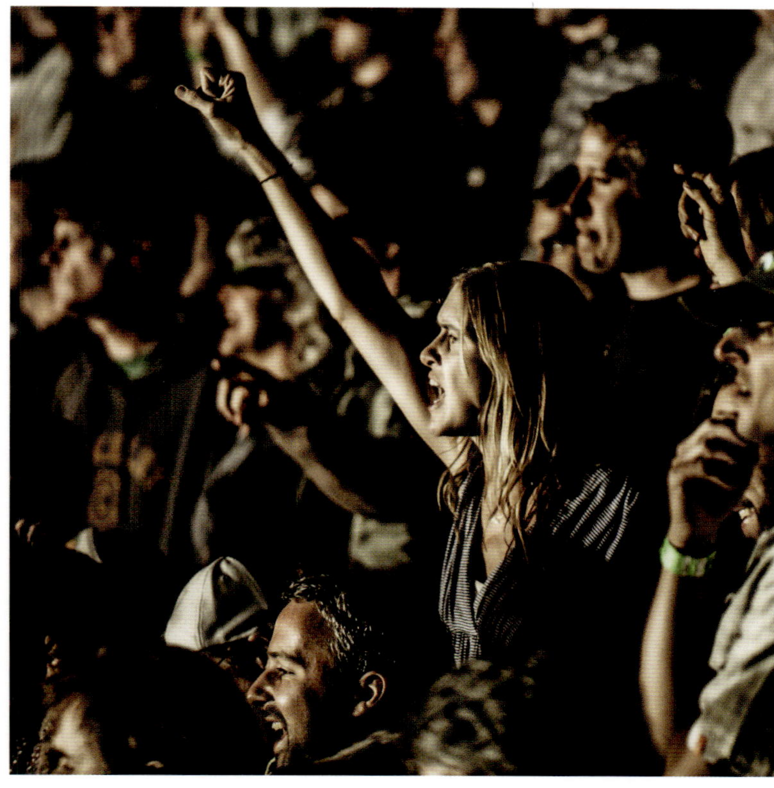

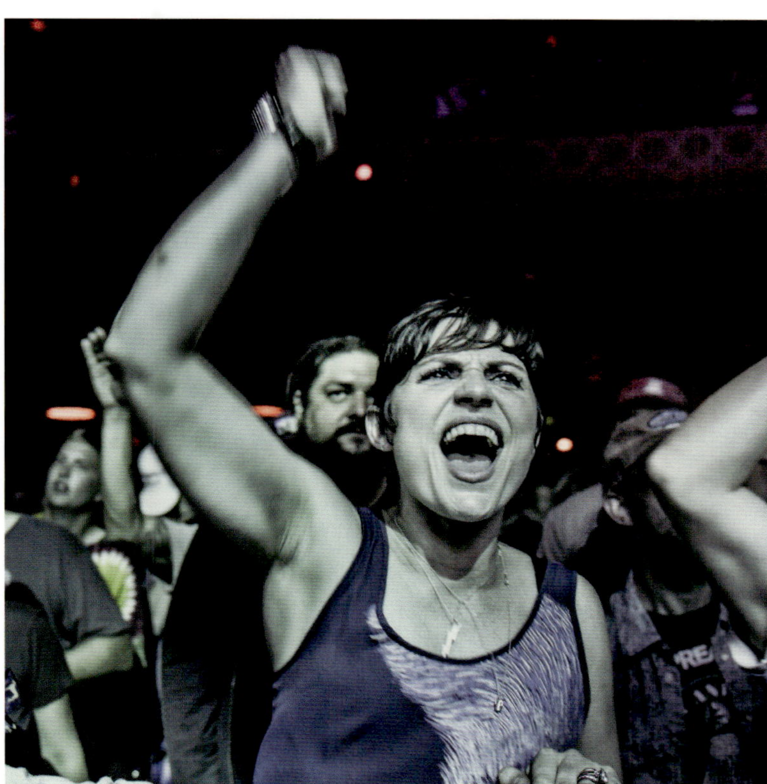

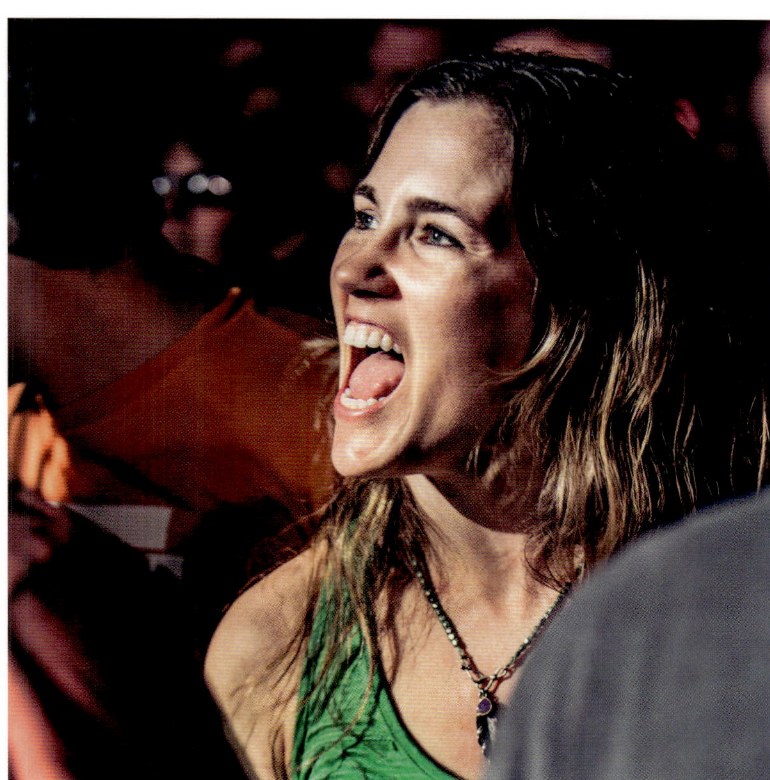

I'm a fucking fierce love warrior. I'm on this ride and I'm not getting off. Millie M.

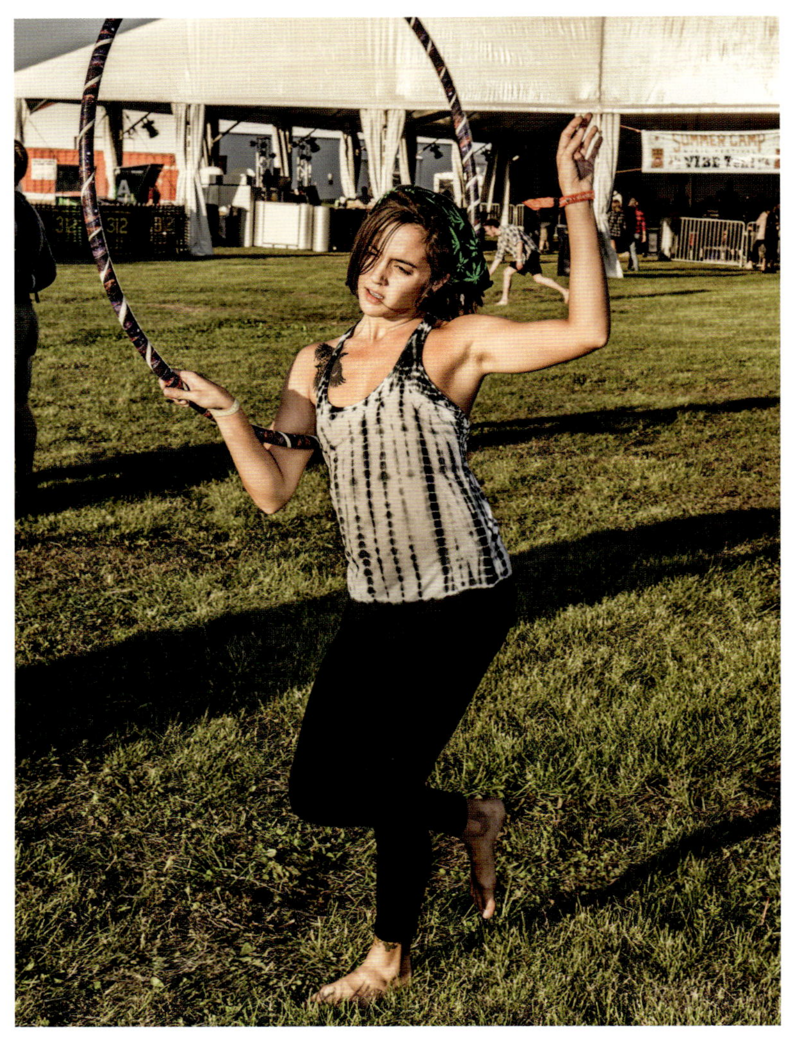

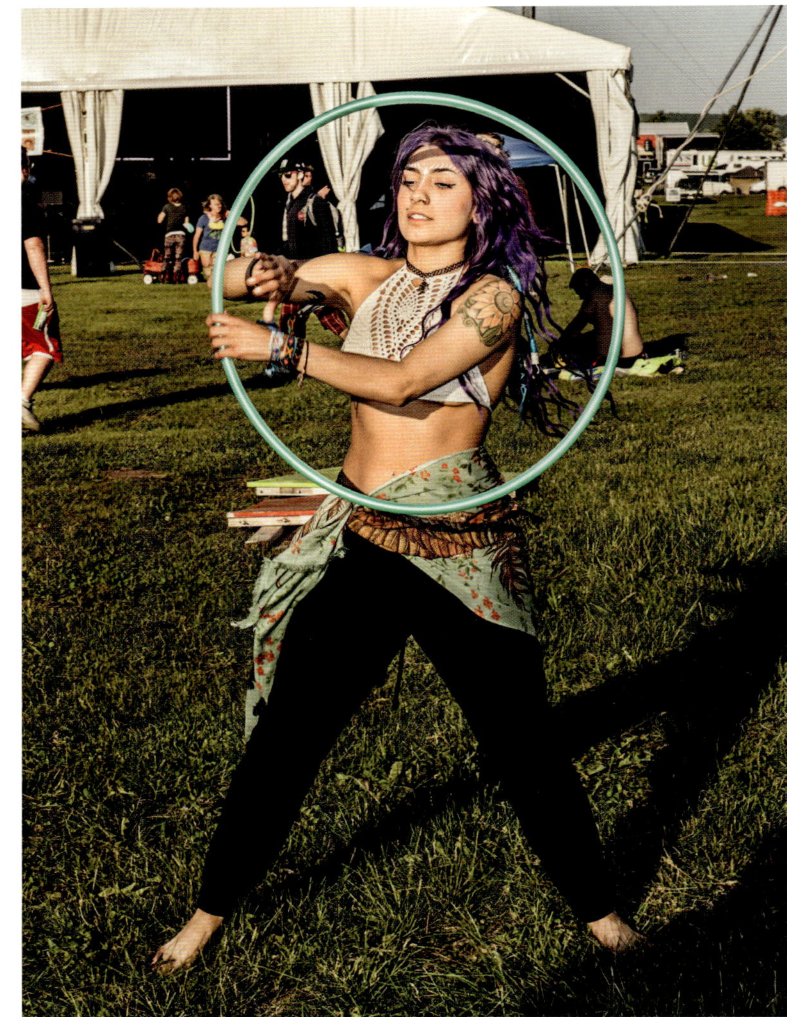

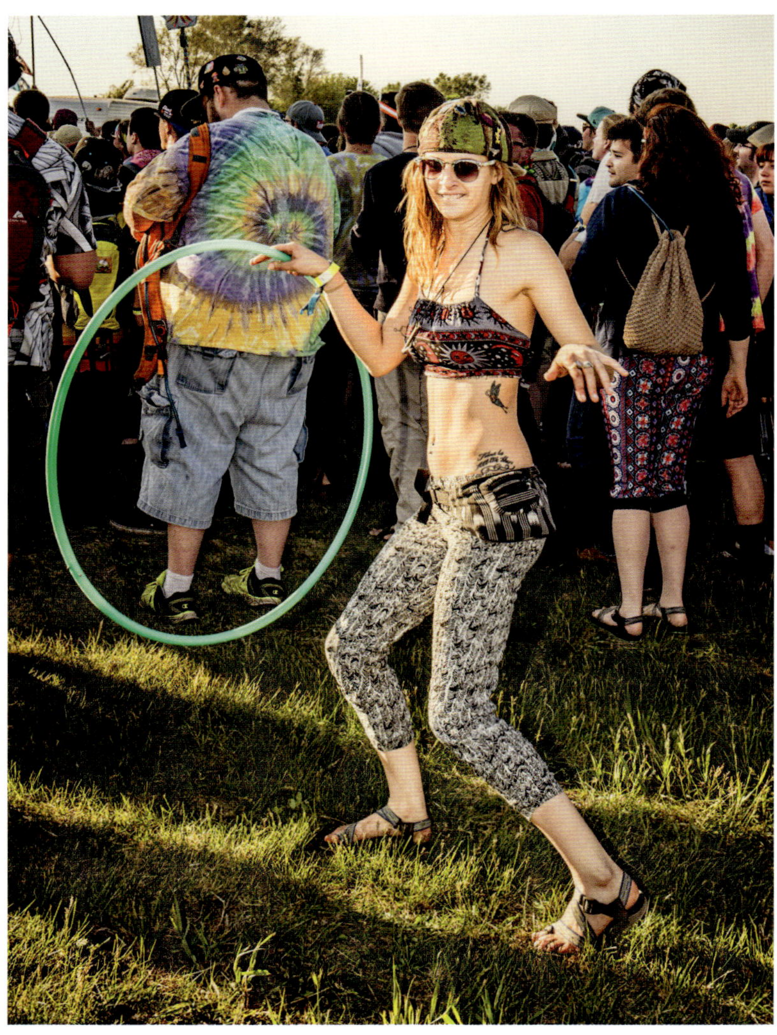

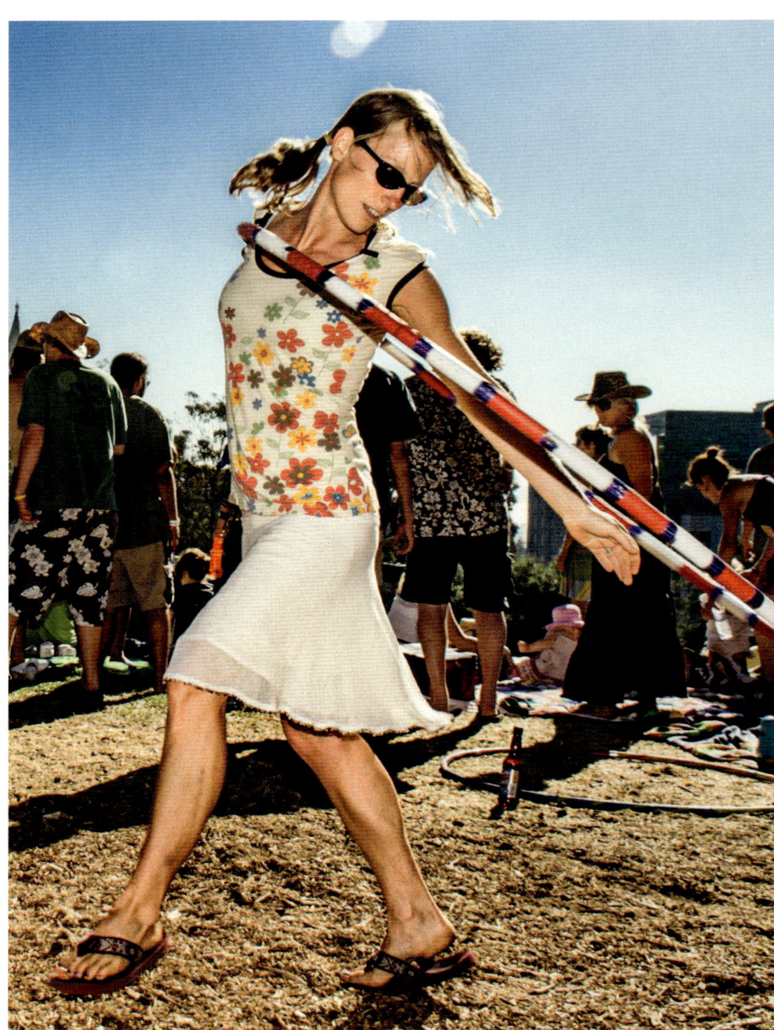

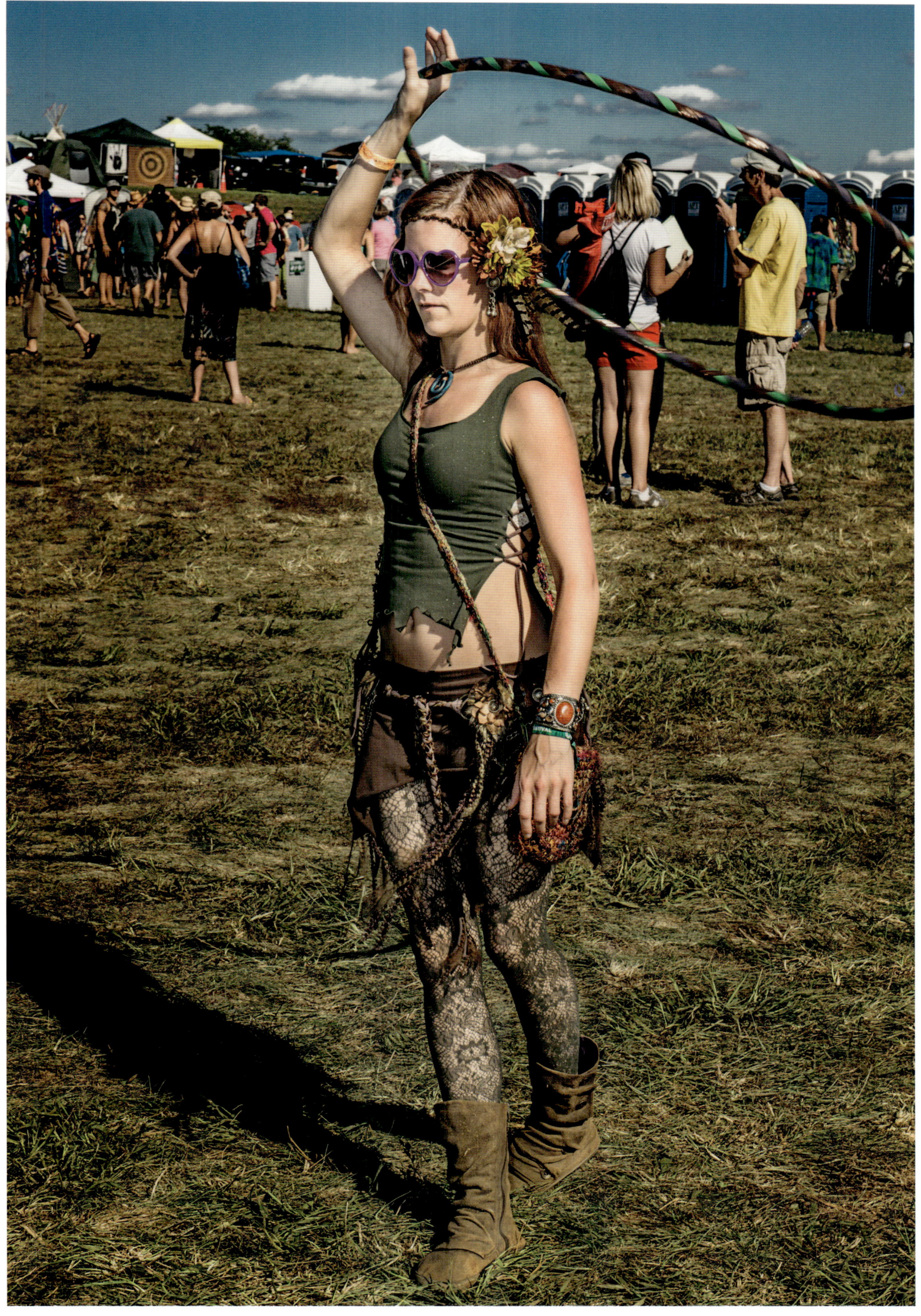

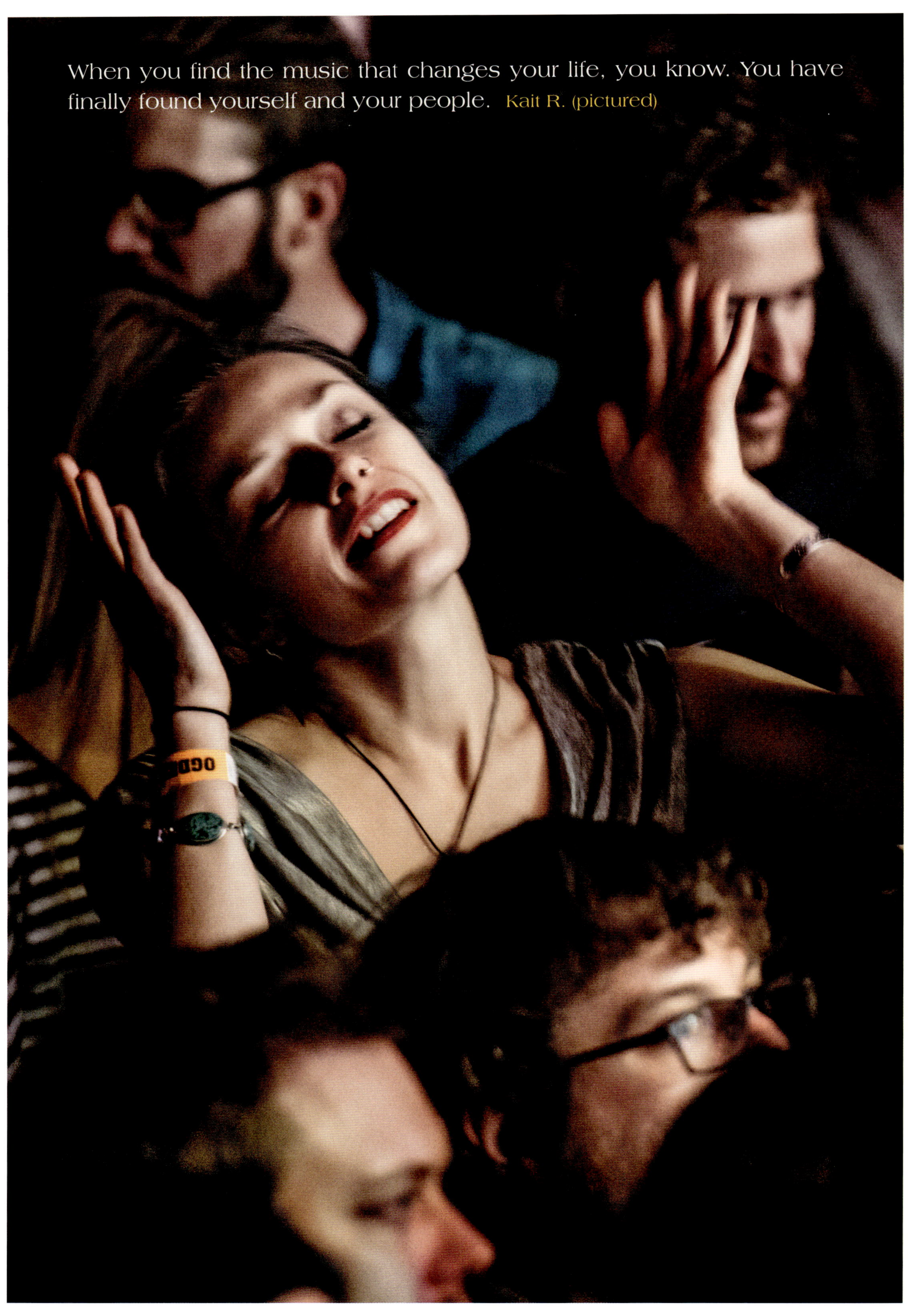

When you find the music that changes your life, you know. You have finally found yourself and your people. Kait R. (pictured)

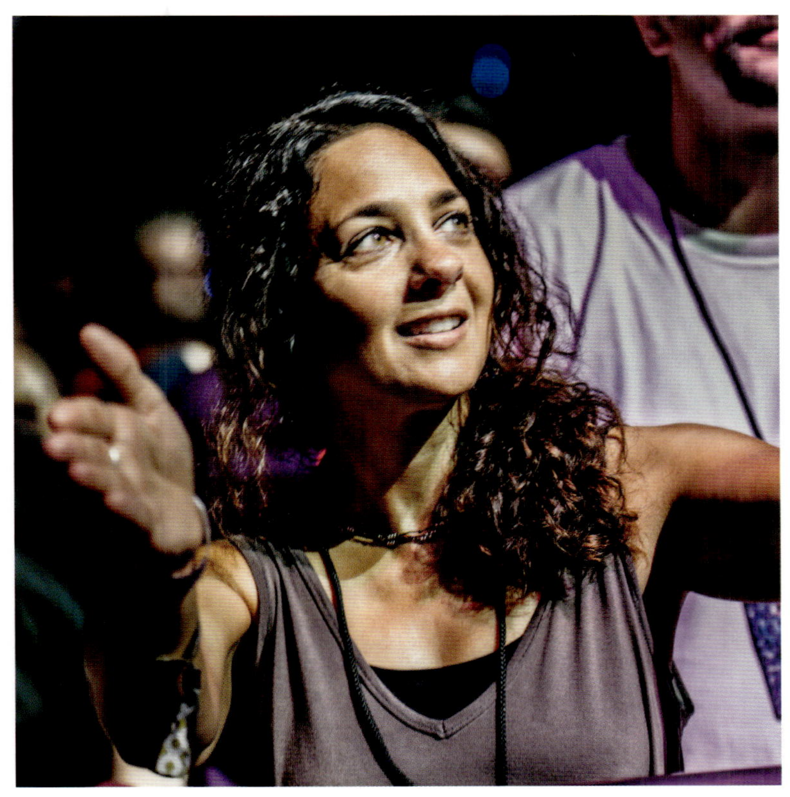

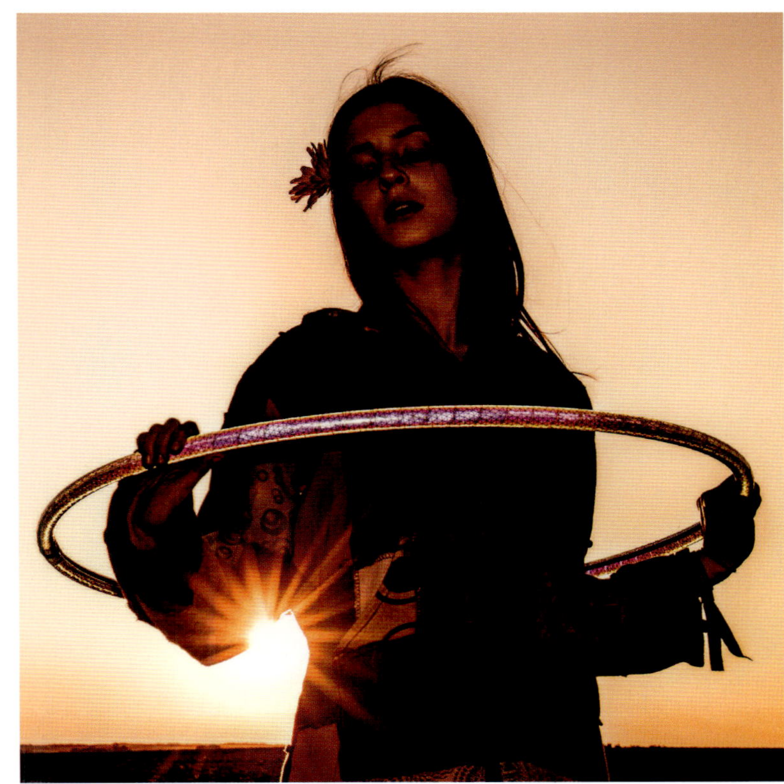

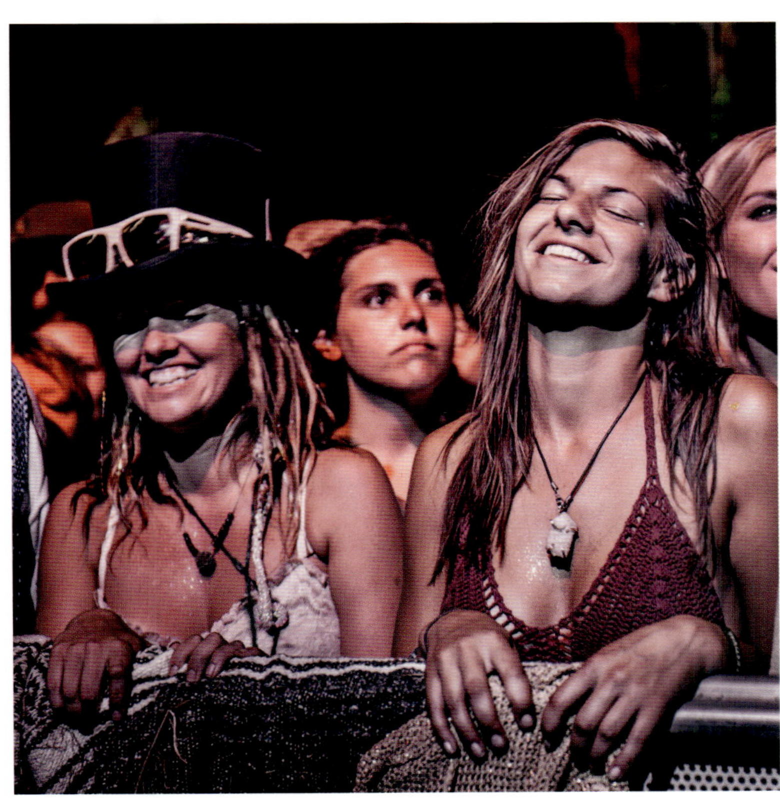

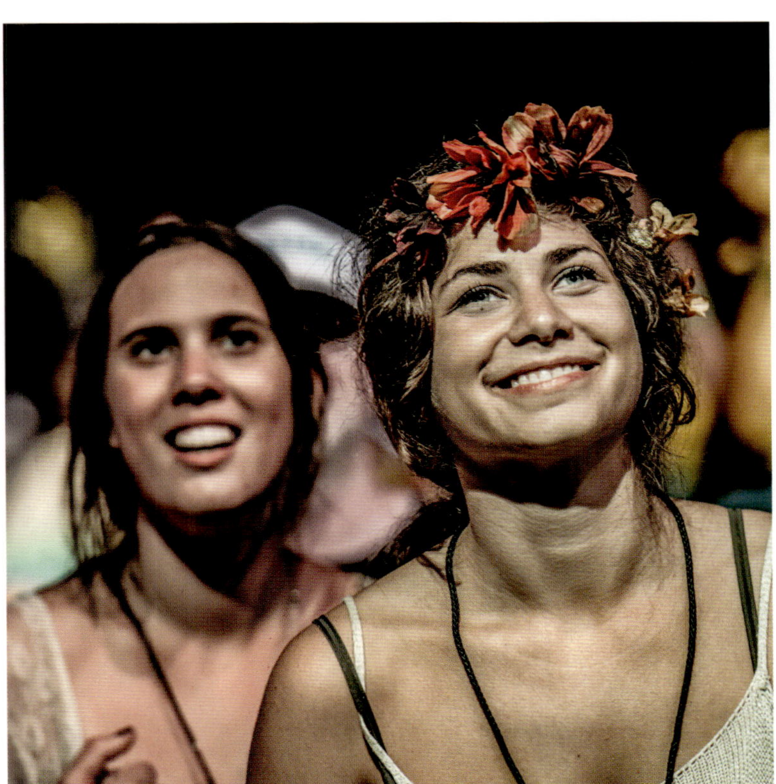

Live music feeds my soul. Christein A.

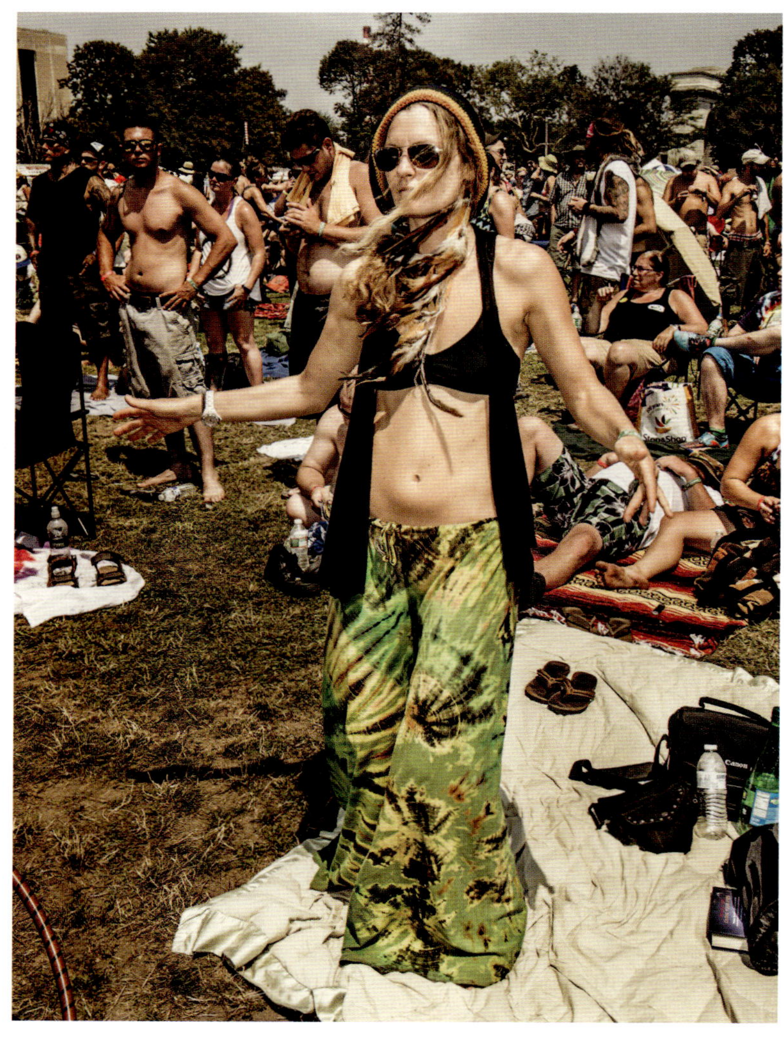

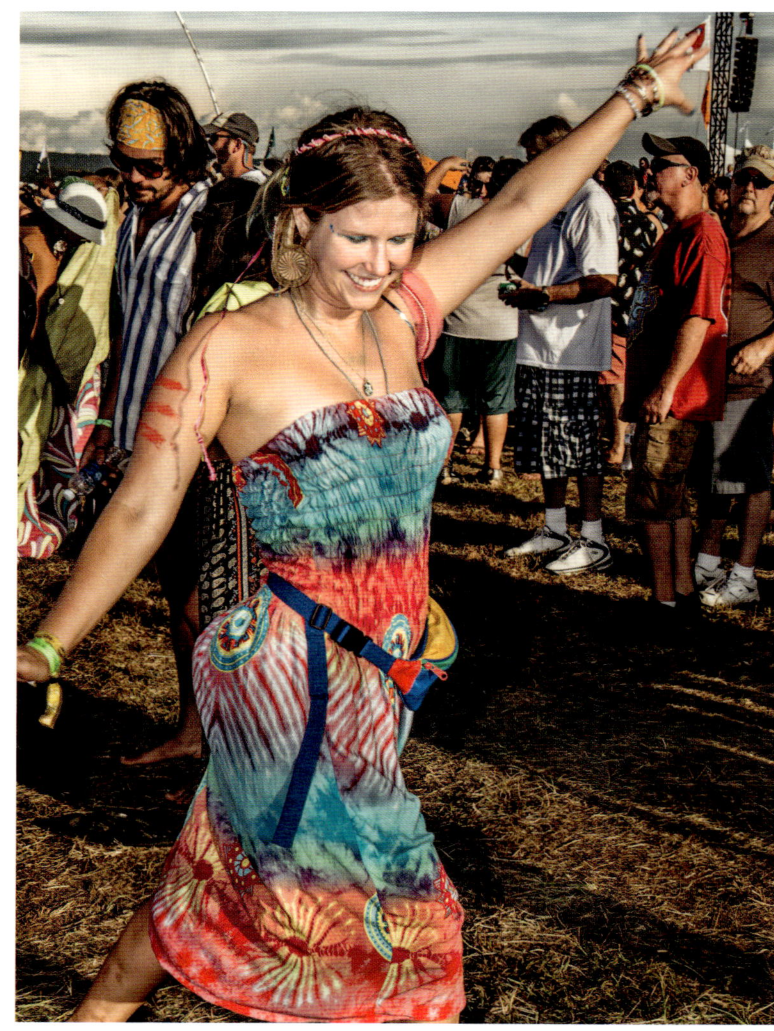

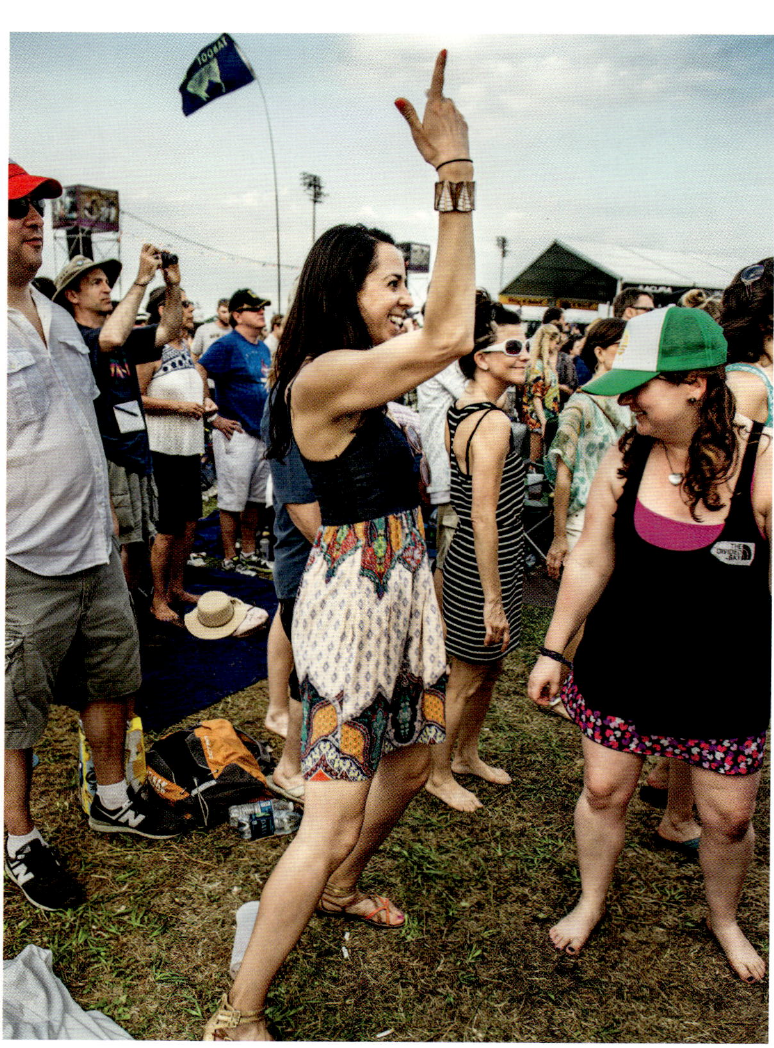

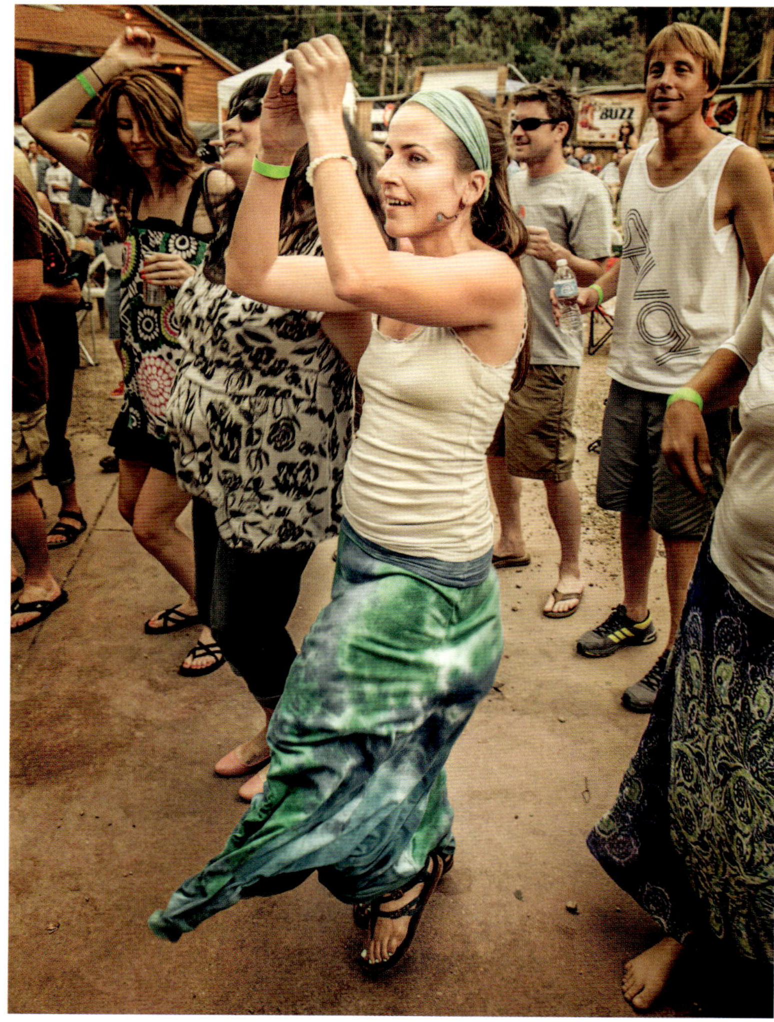

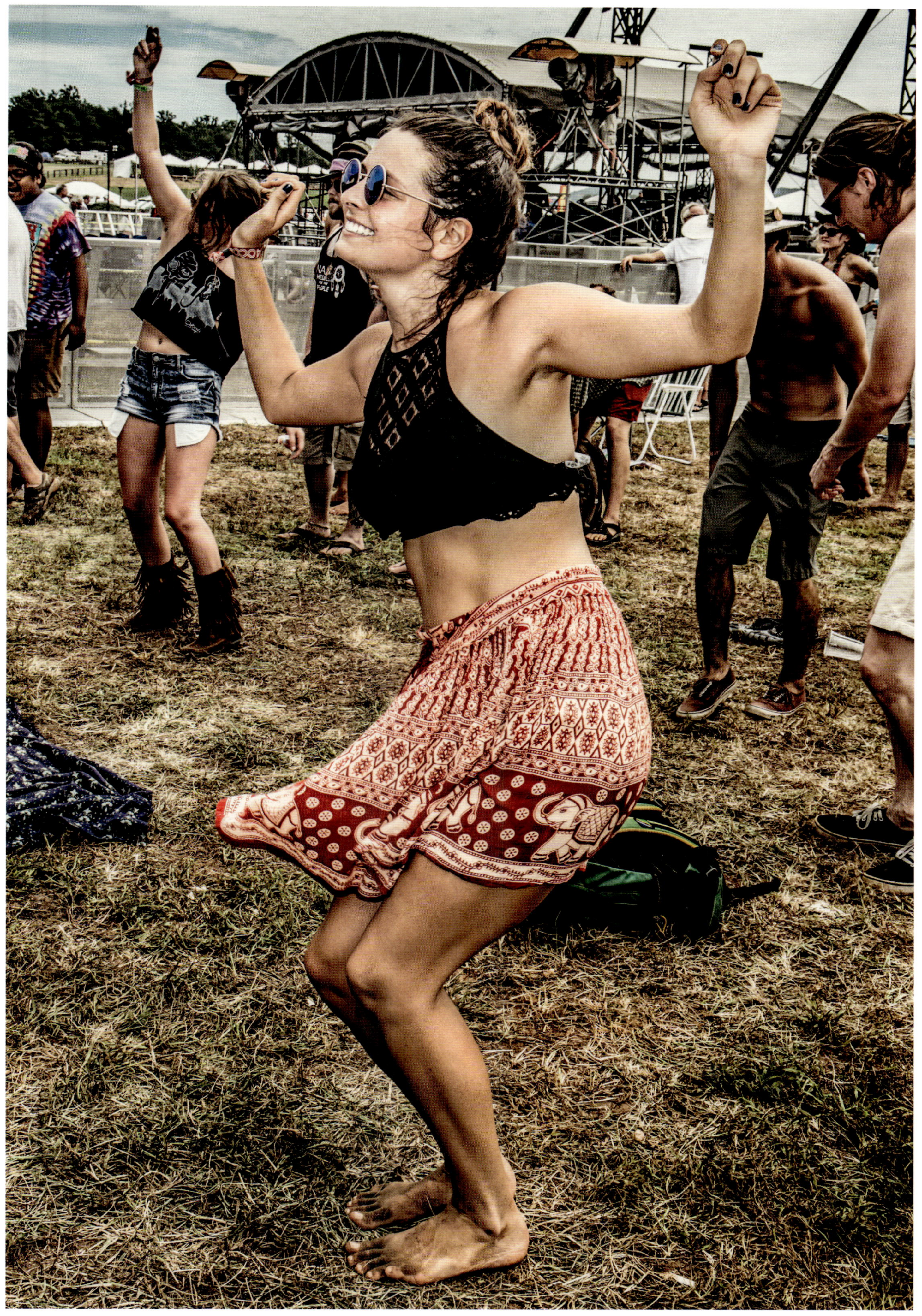

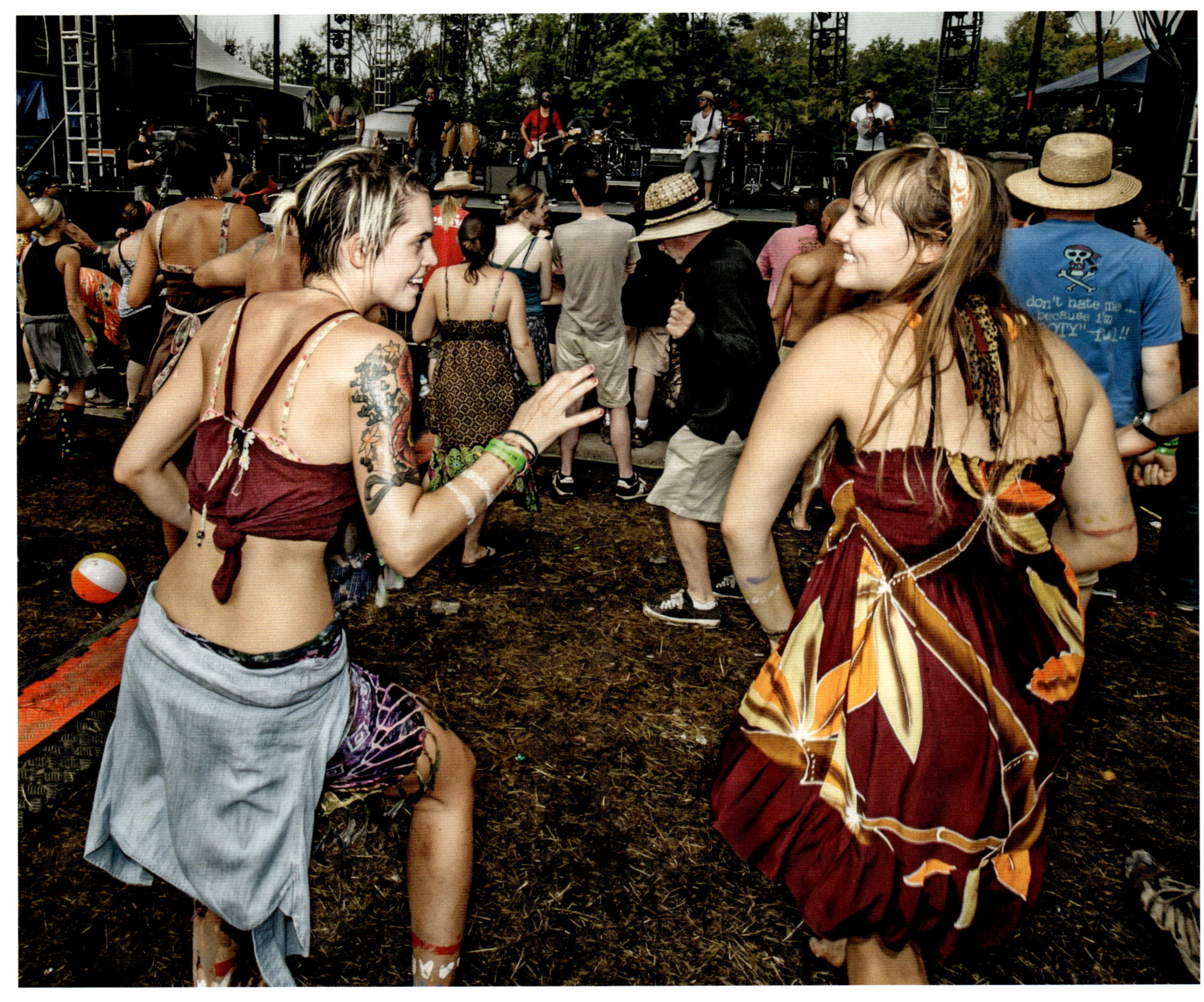

I love the self-reliance aspect of festivals the most. By trusting your gut, you always end up in the right place—those moments your soul craves, or the ones you're blindsided by that you live to tell everyone about afterward. Sami P.

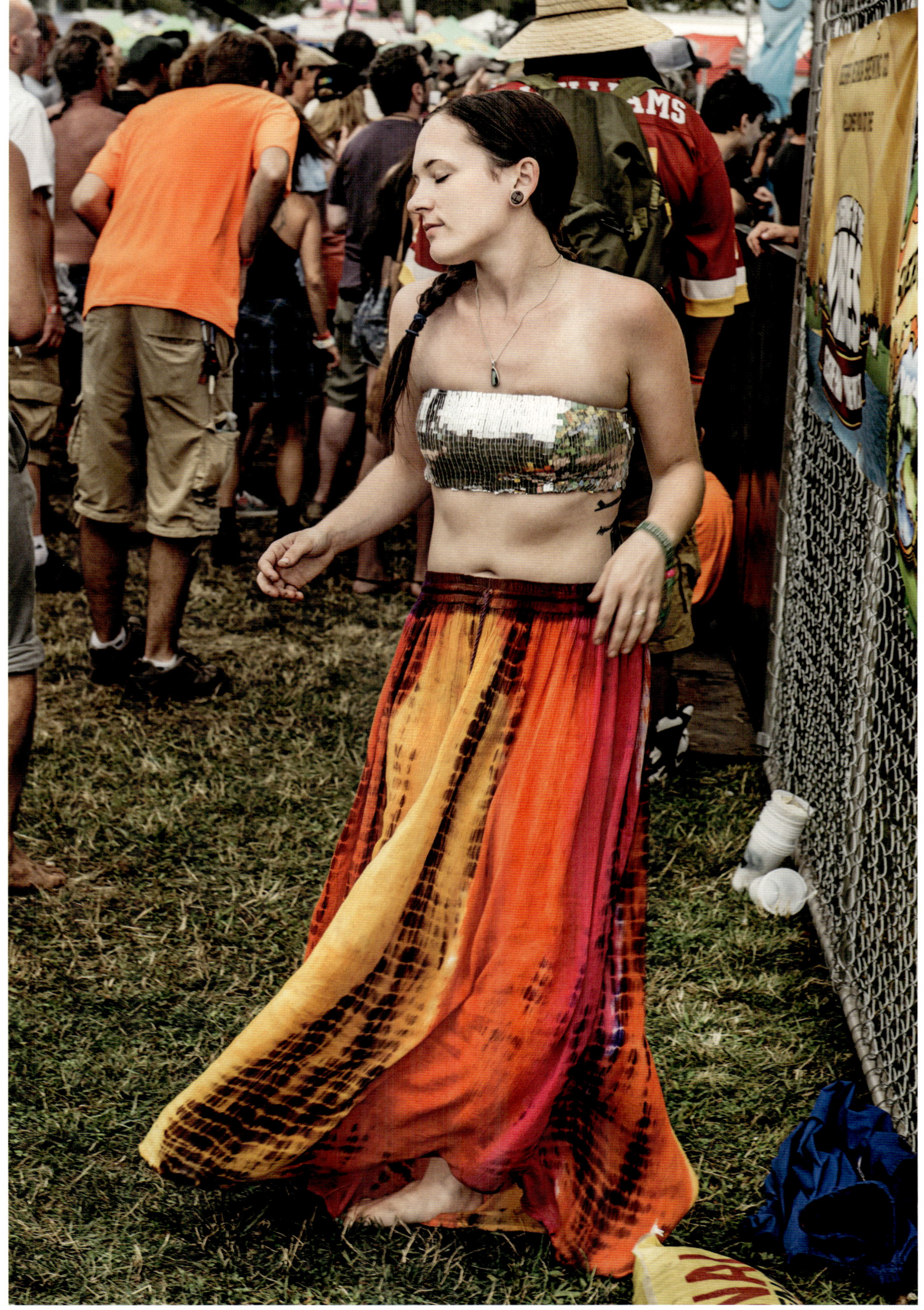

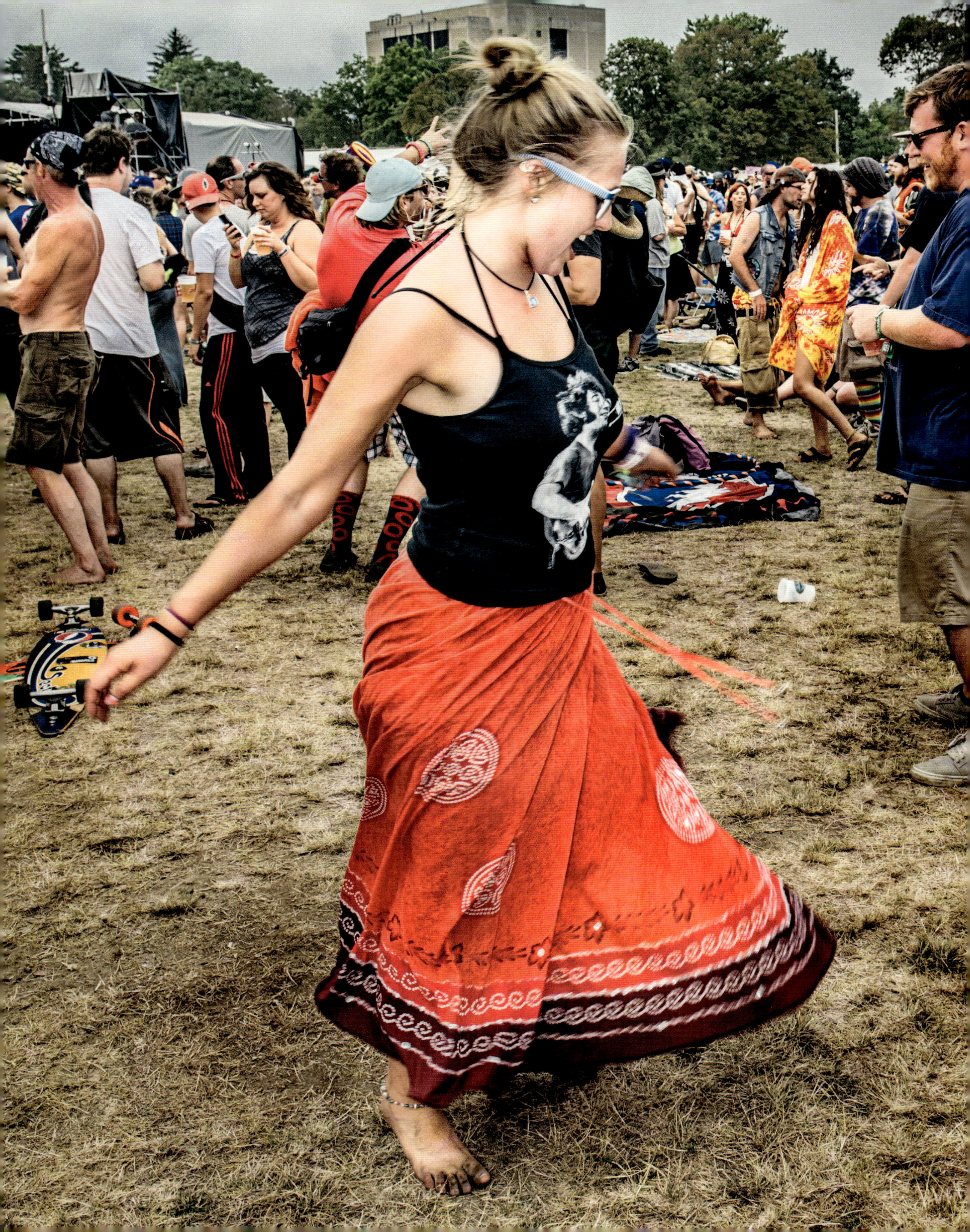

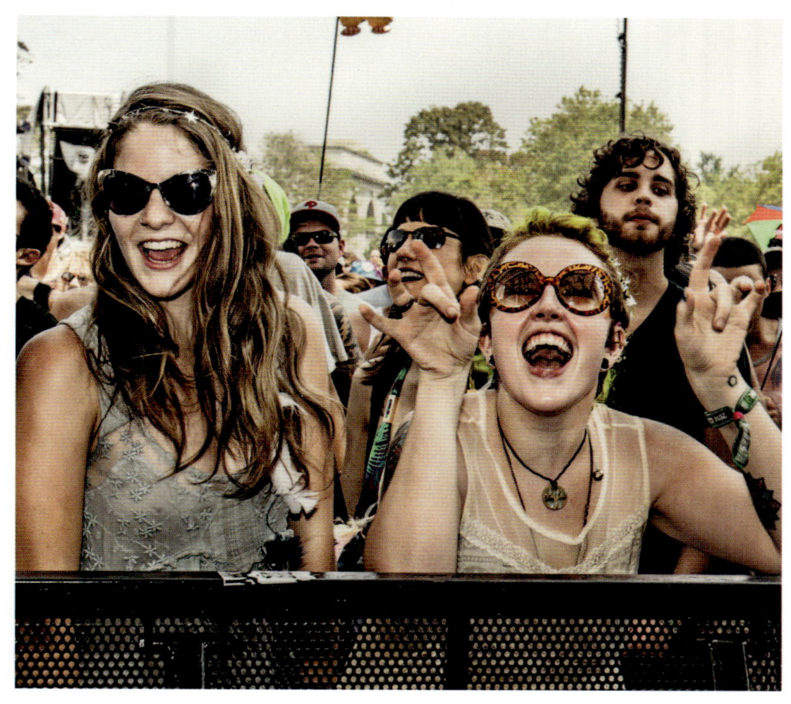

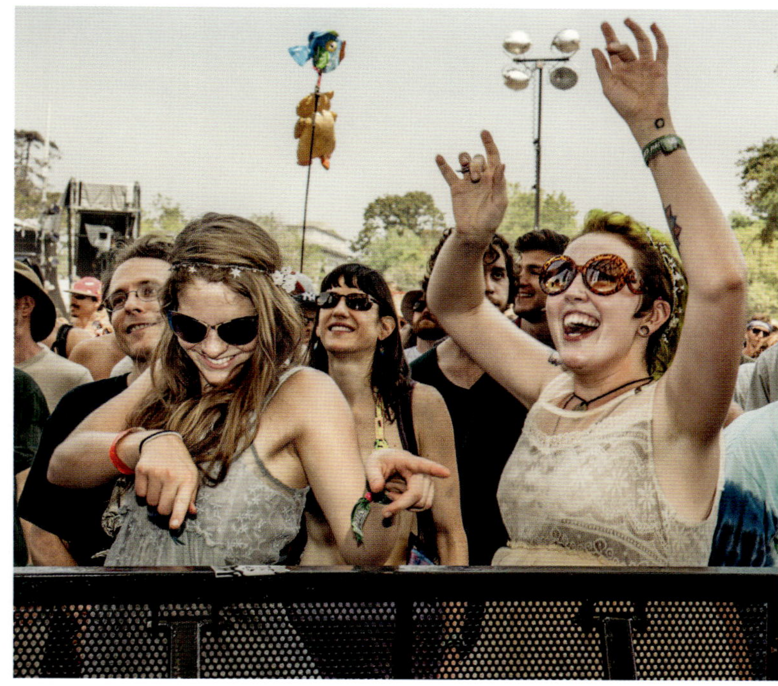

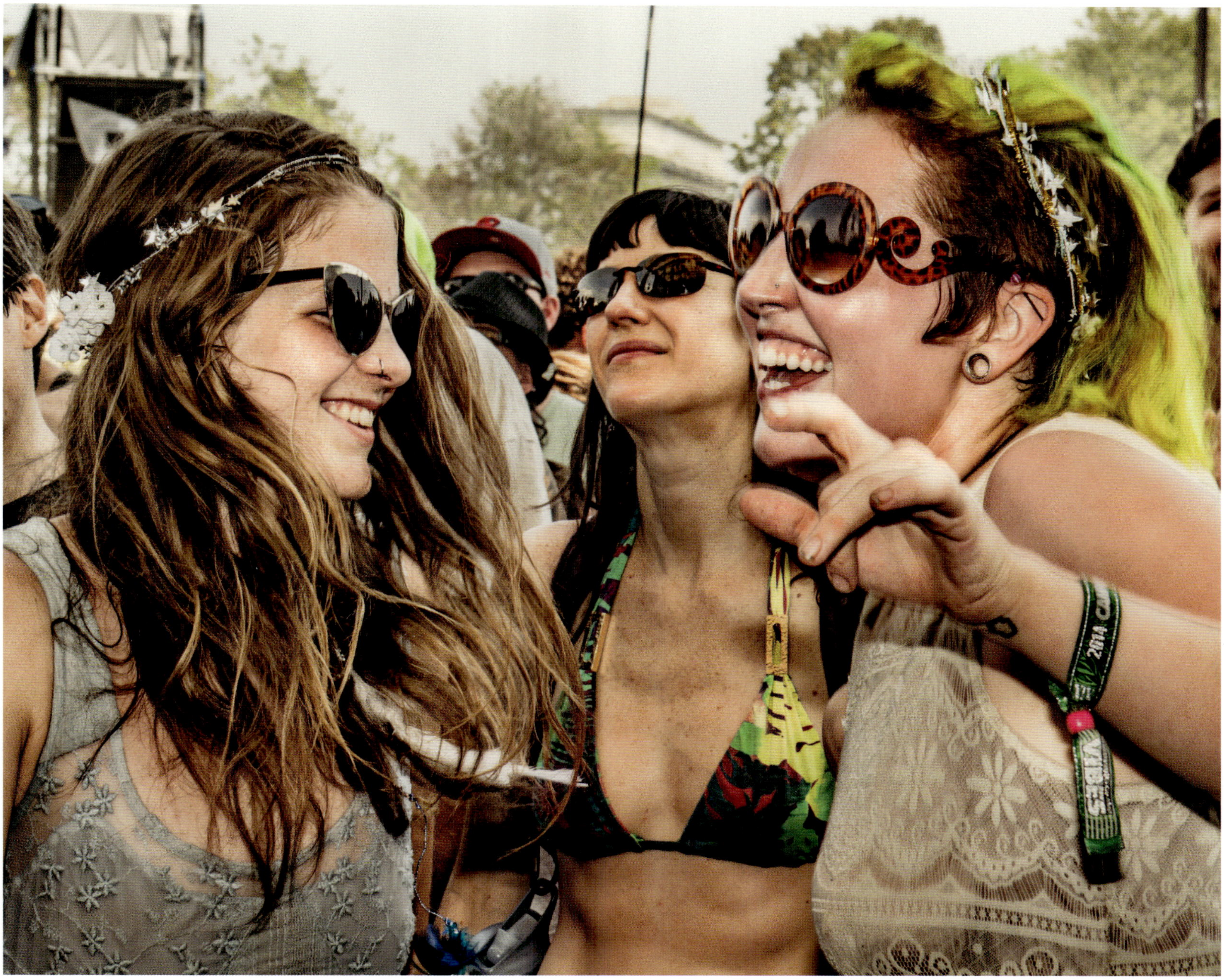

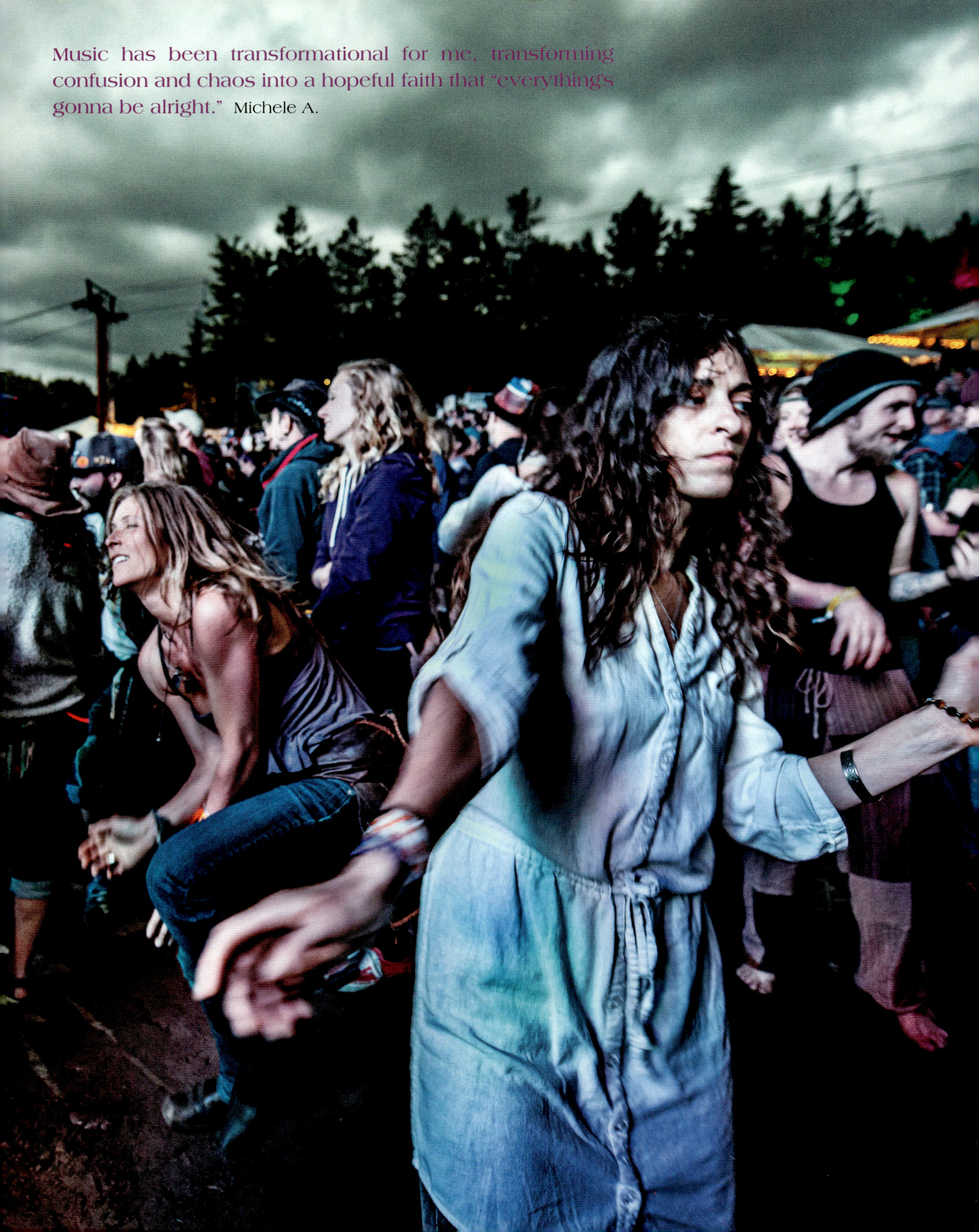

Music has been transformational for me, transforming confusion and chaos into a hopeful faith that "everything's gonna be alright." Michele A.

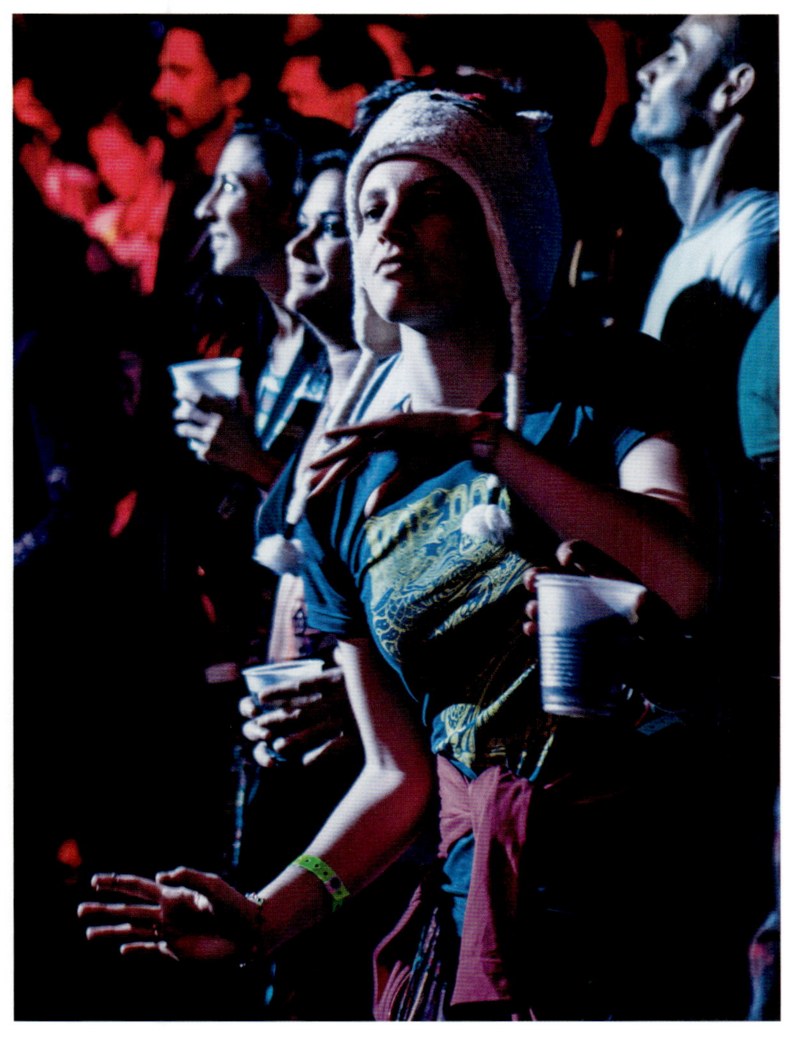

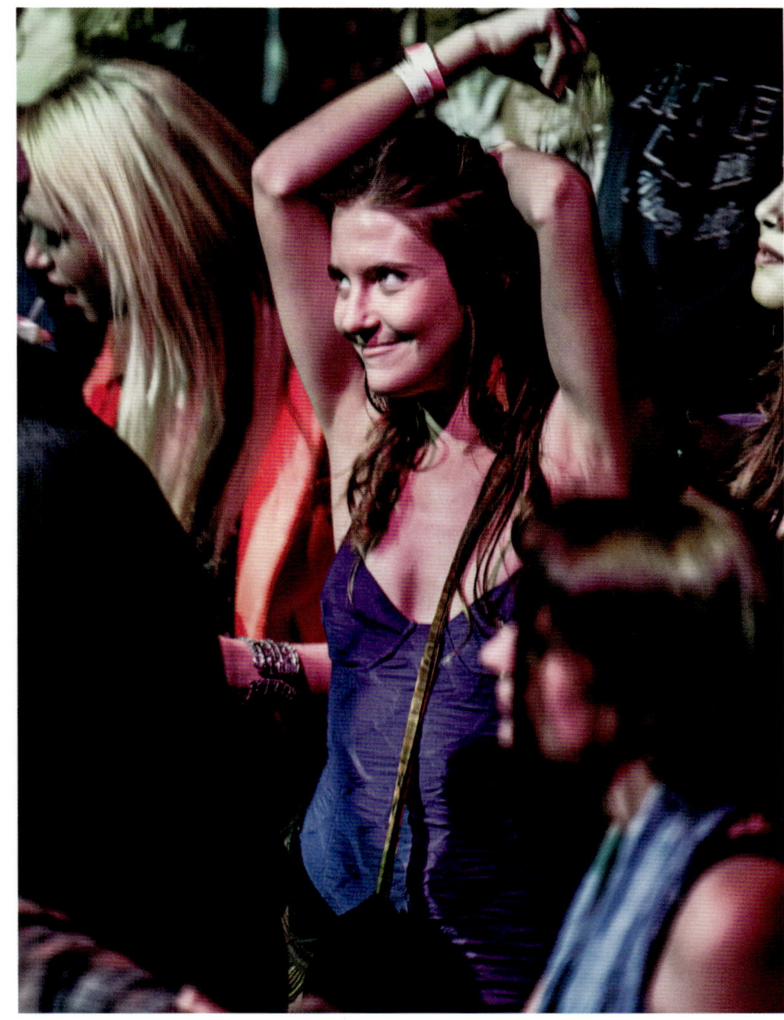

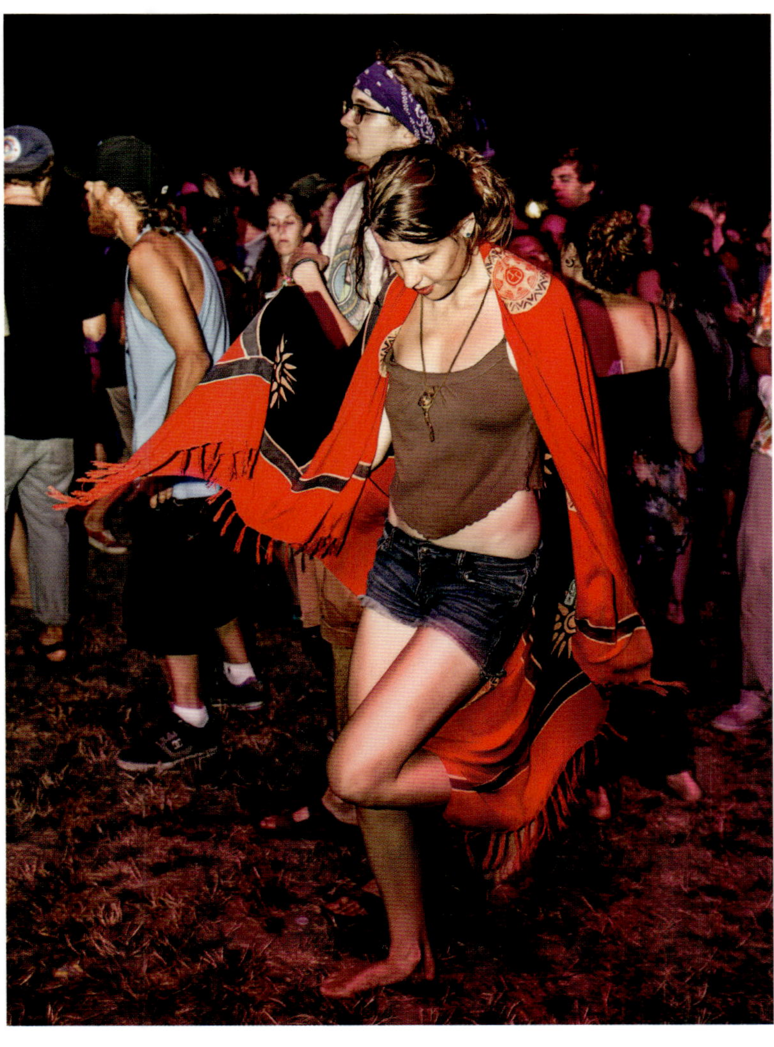

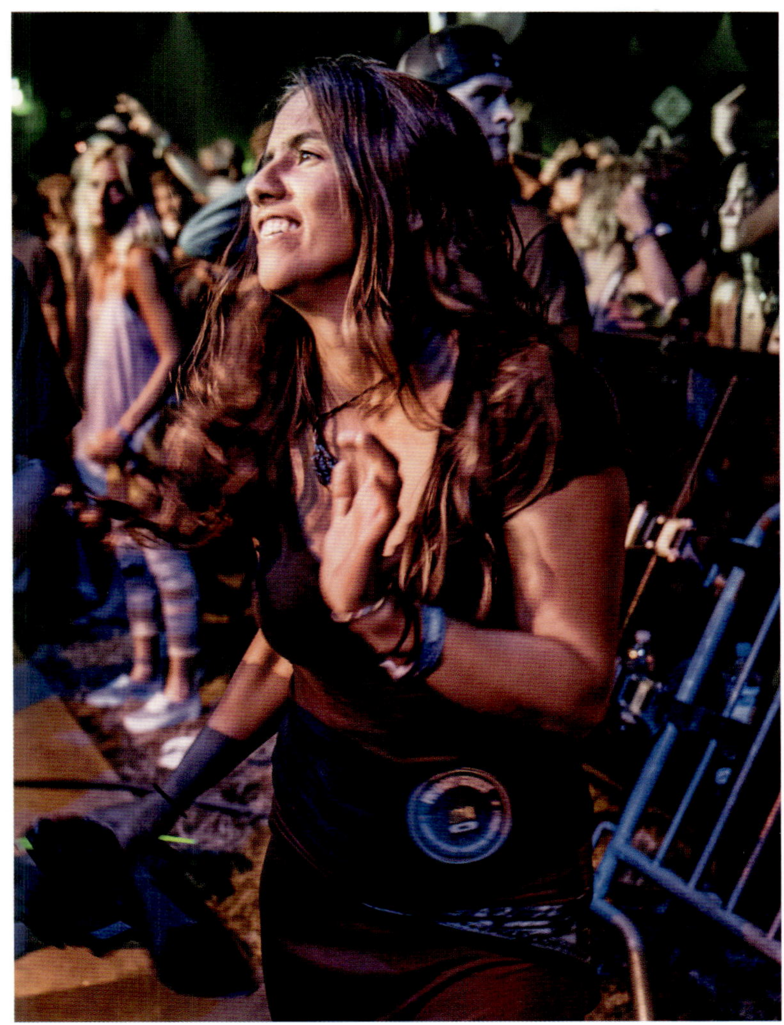

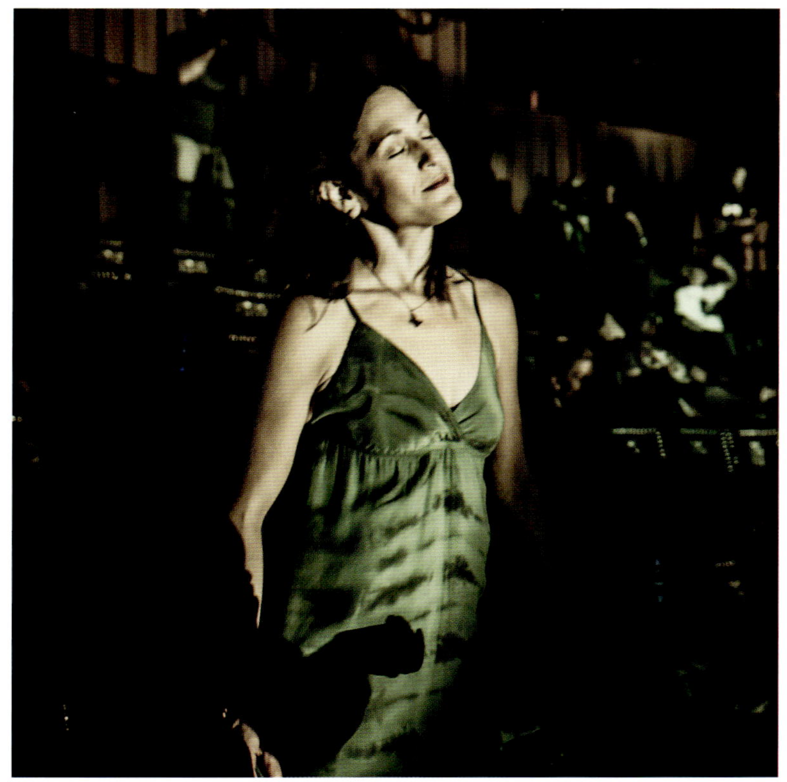

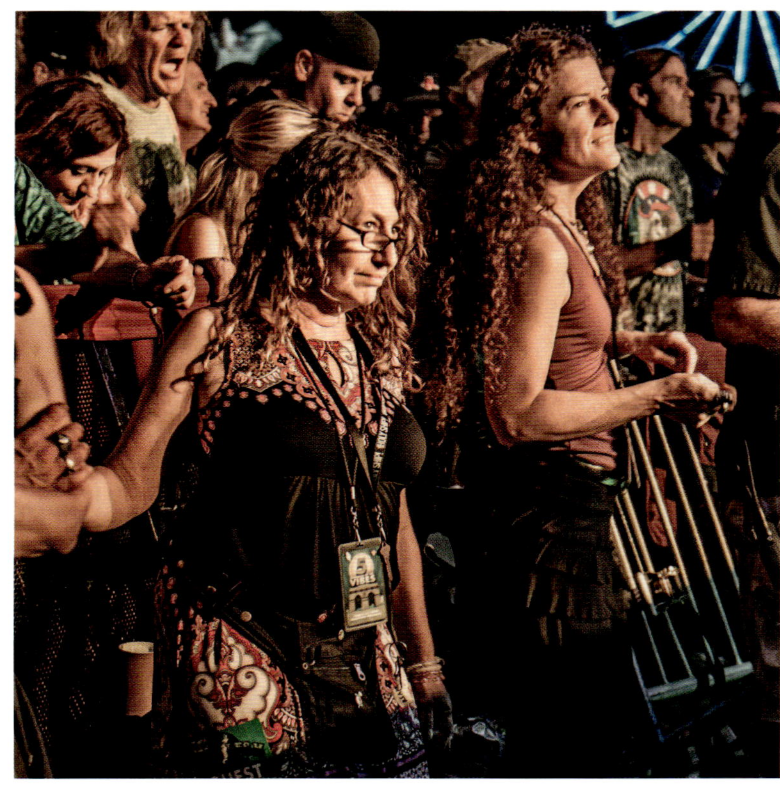

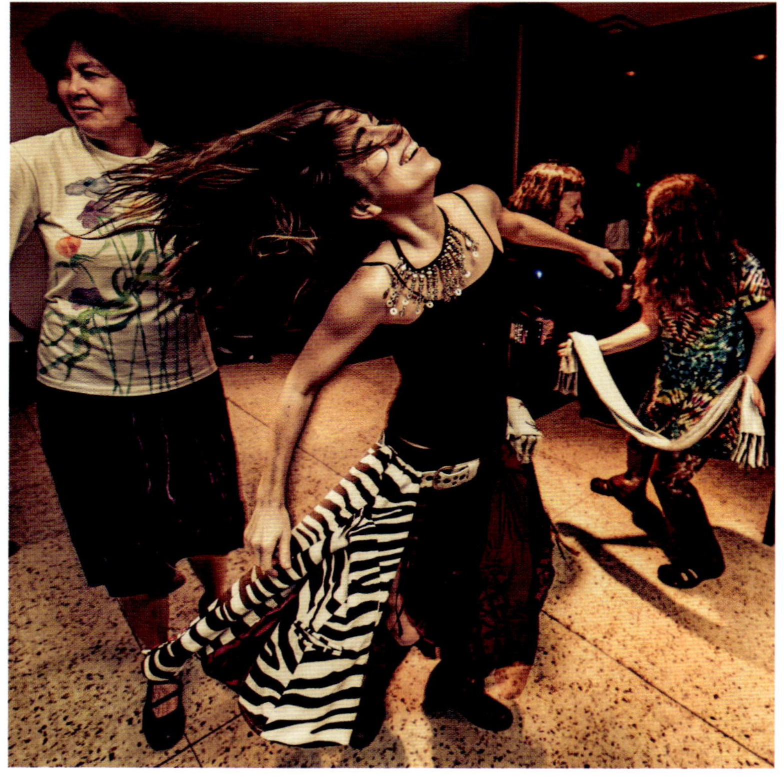

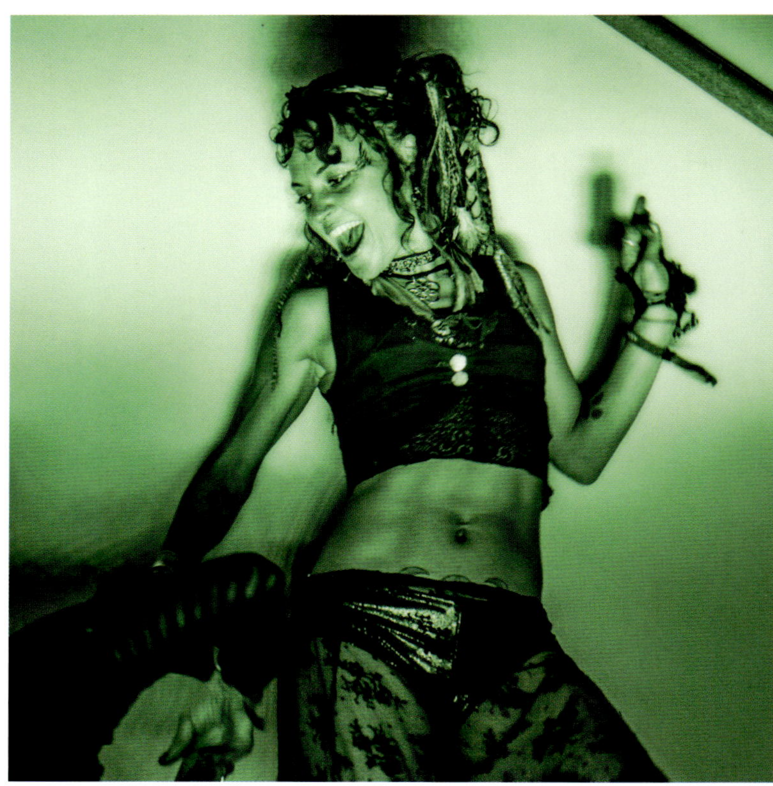

I love turning off my mind and seeing what shapes the music pulls my body into. Lauren B.

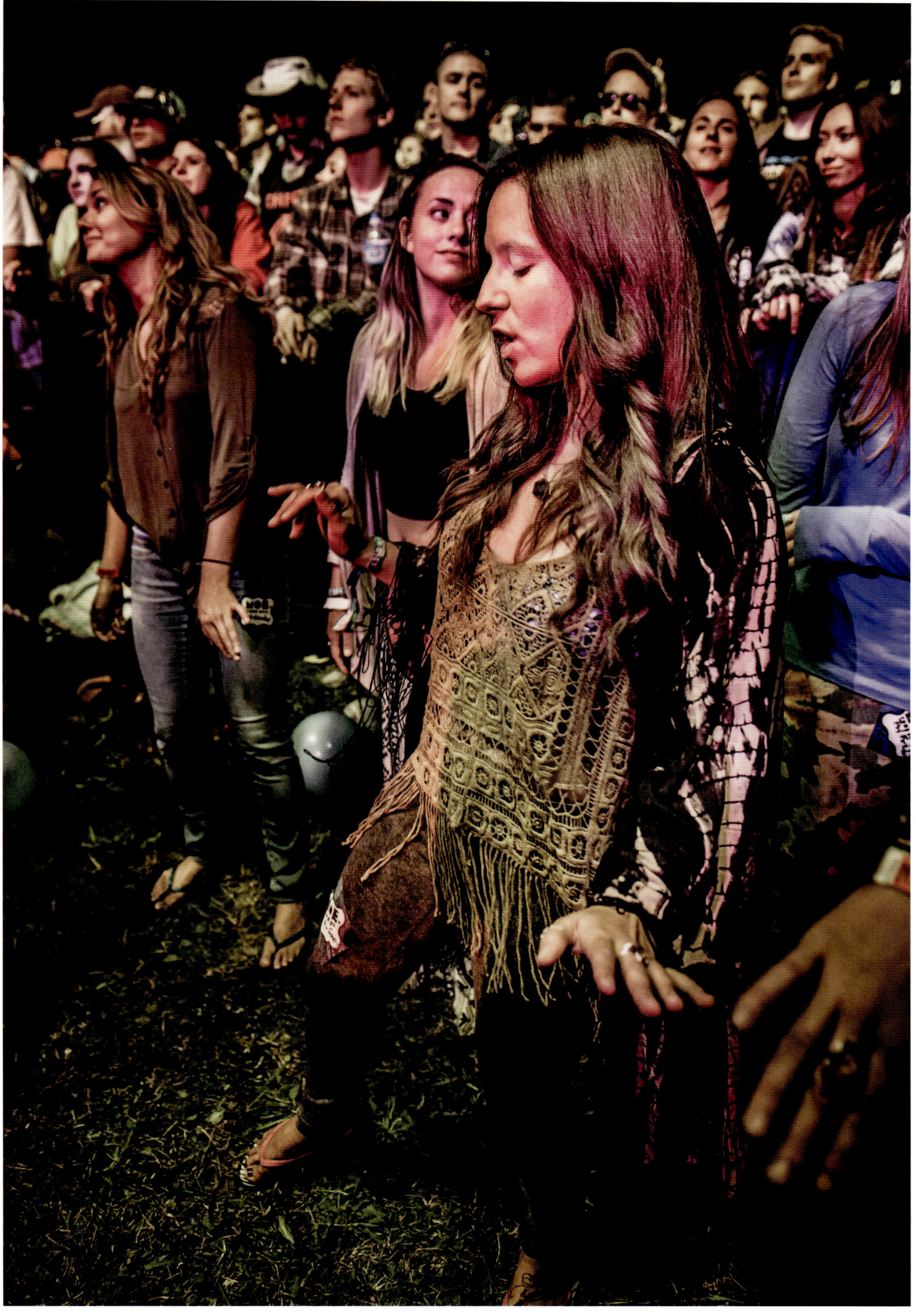

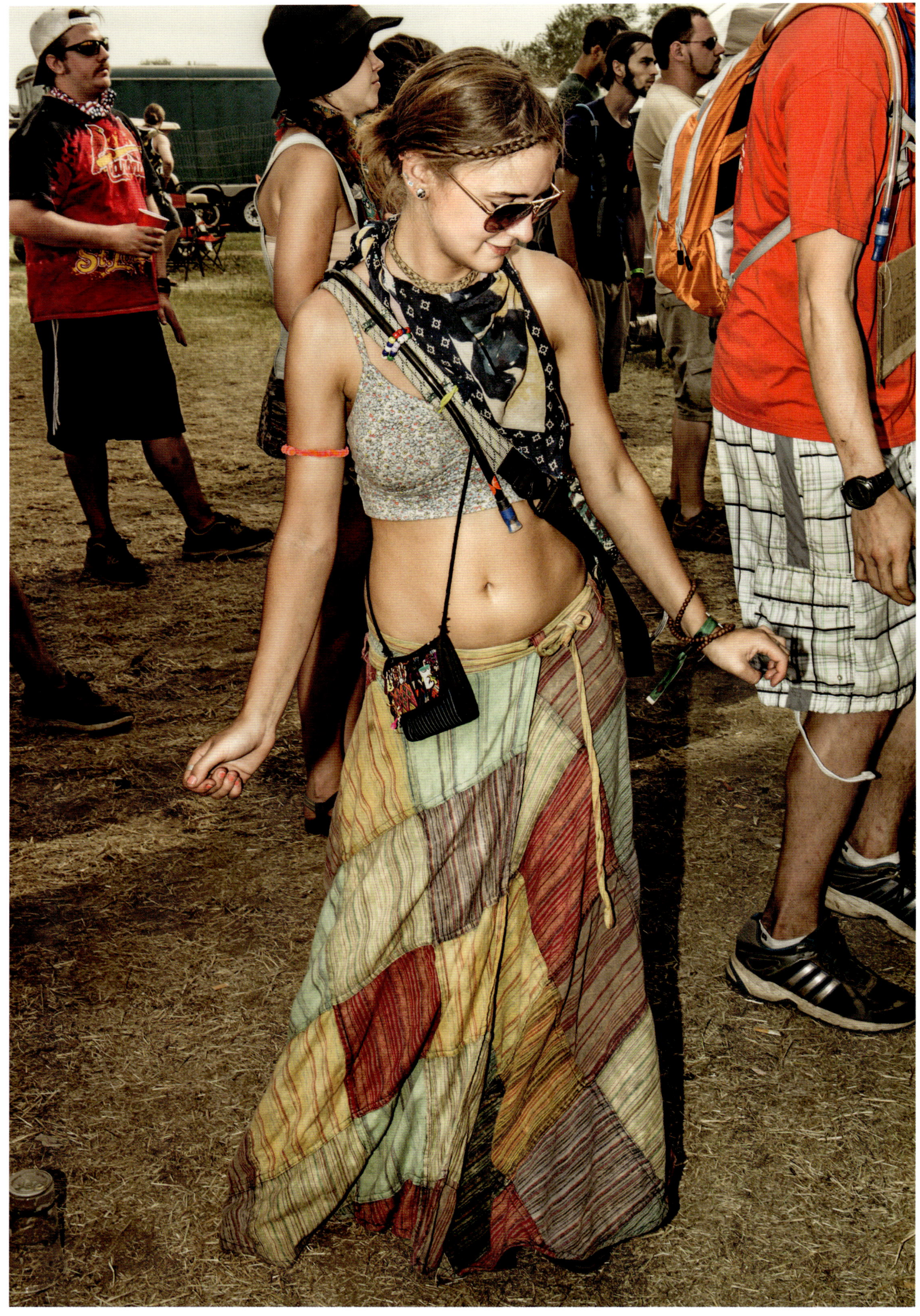

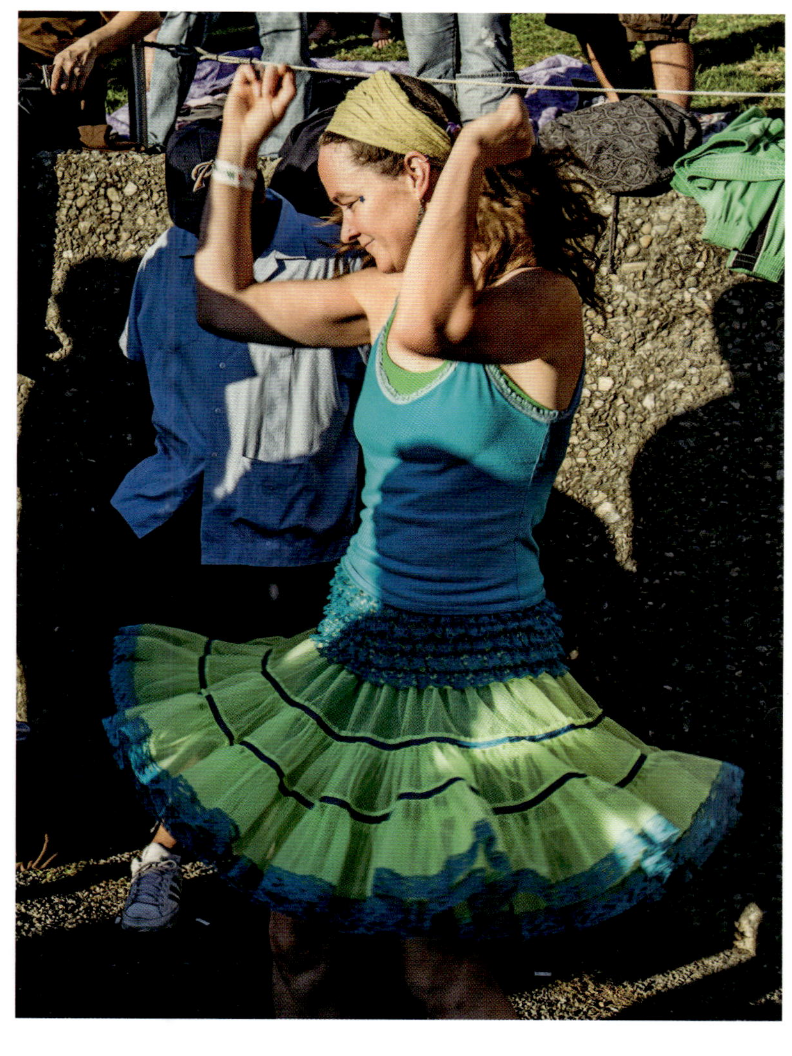

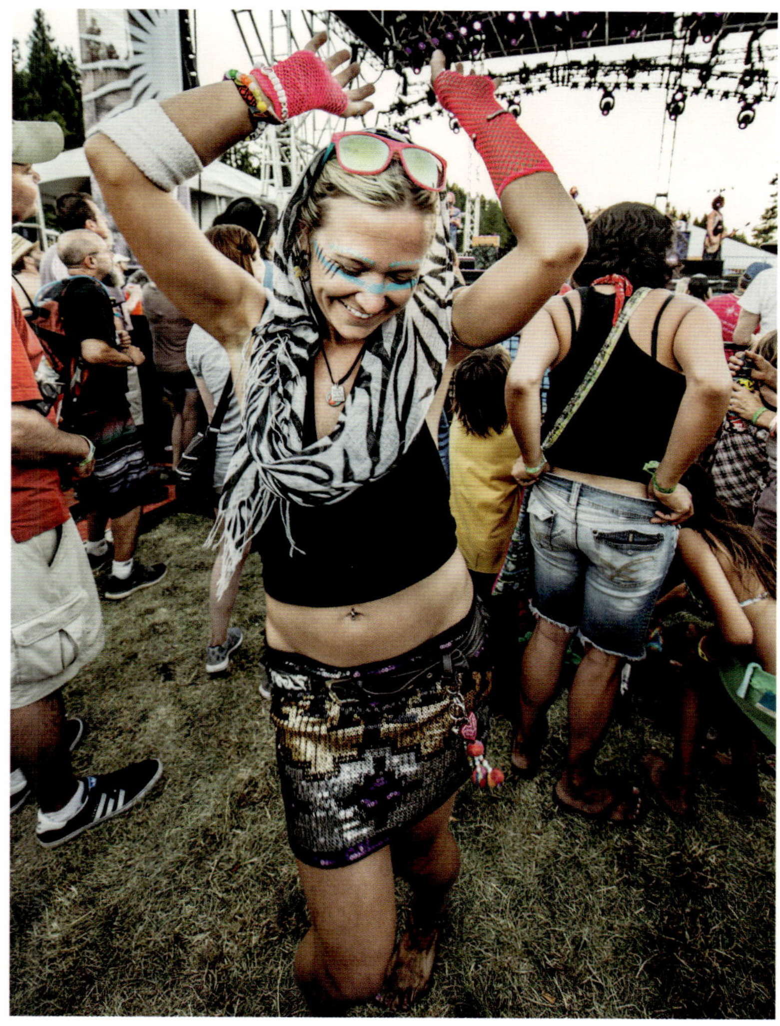

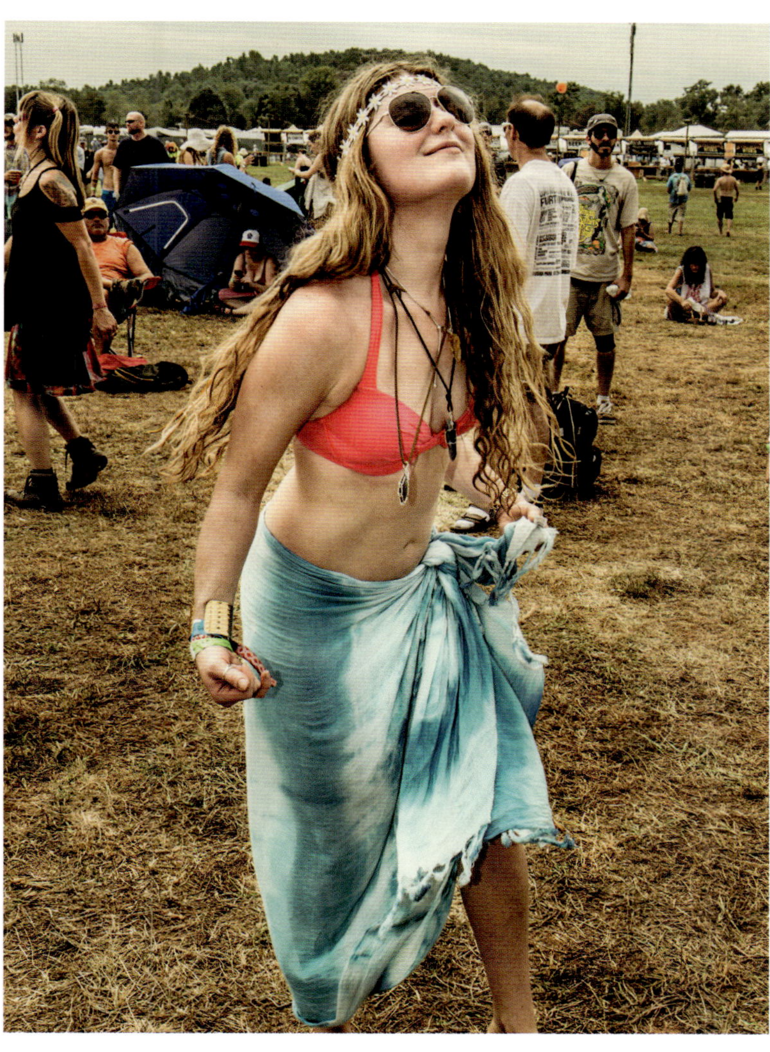

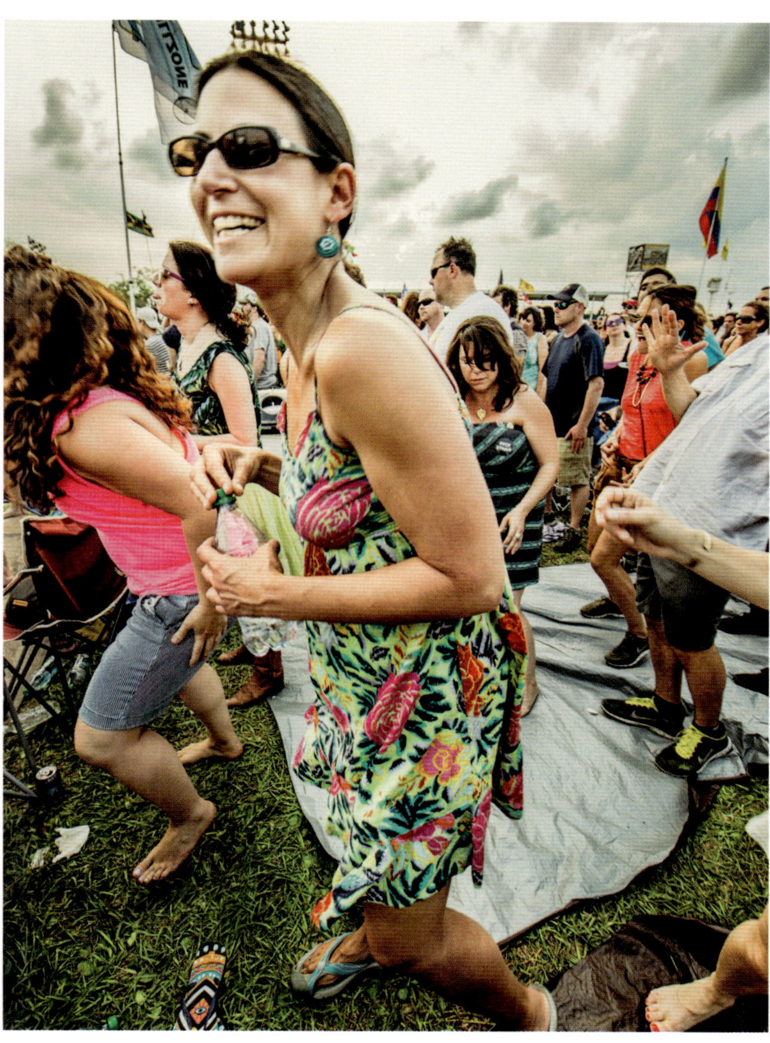

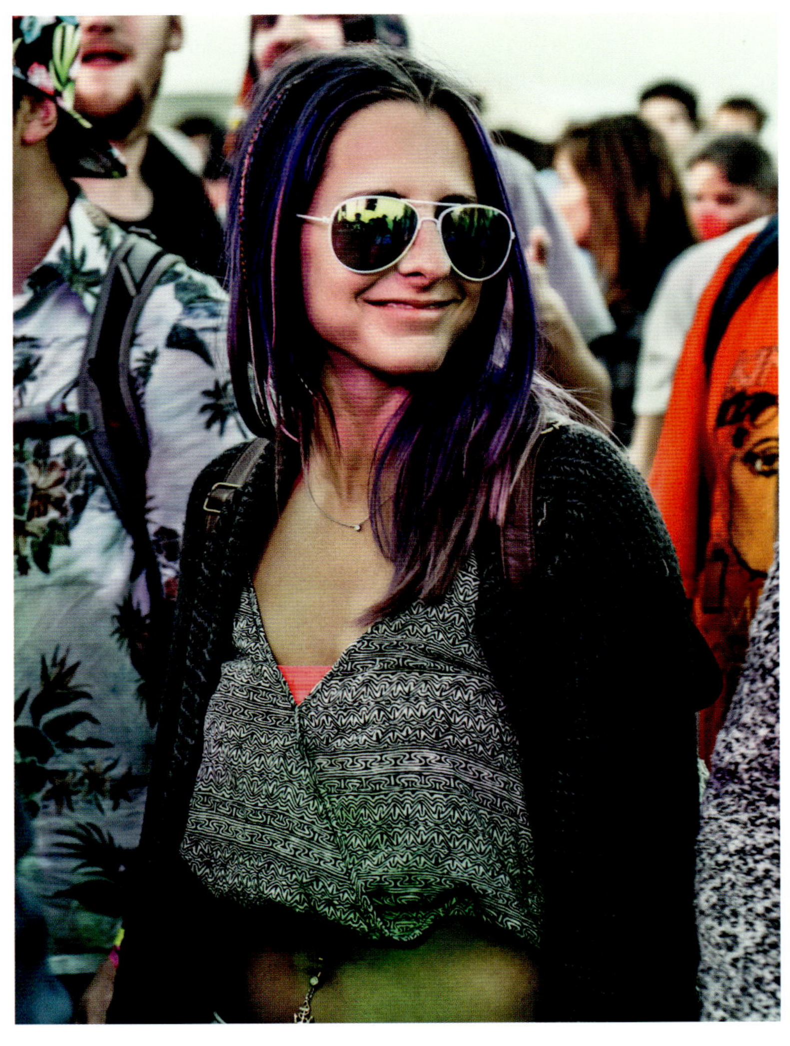

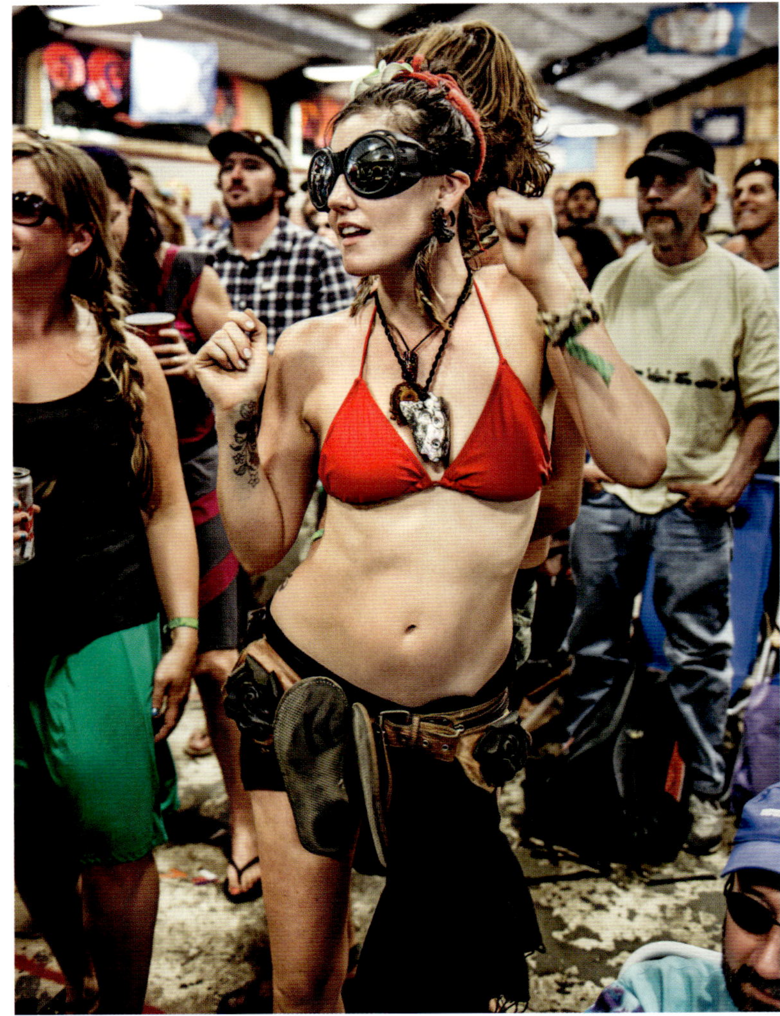

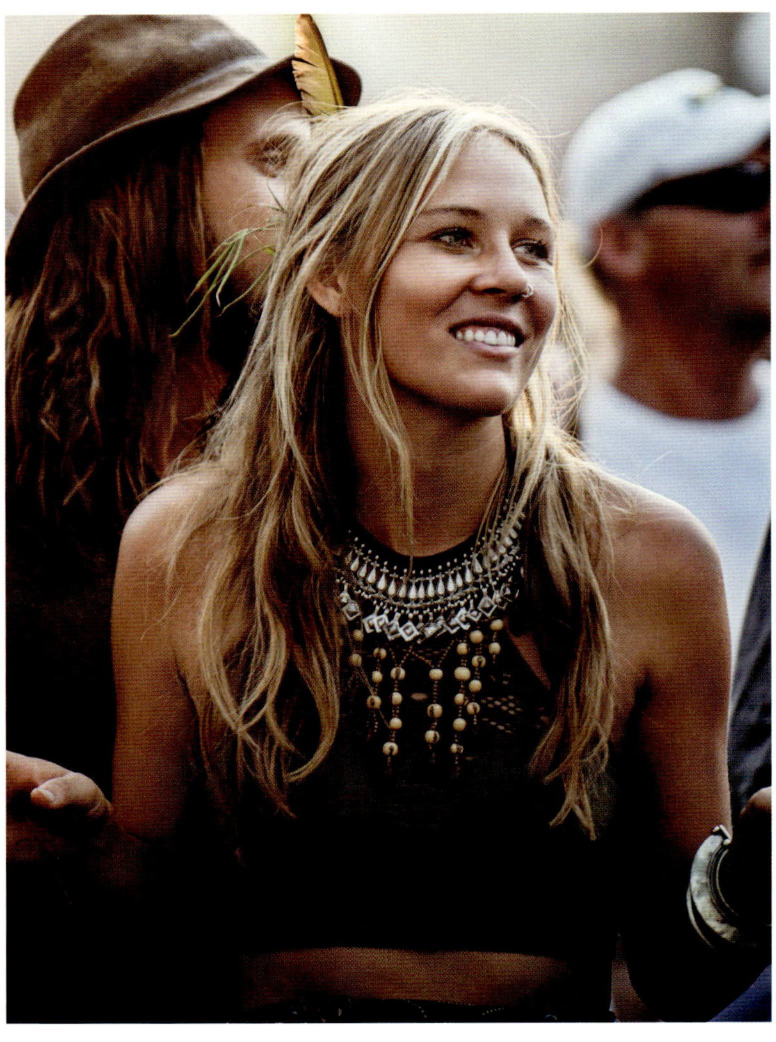

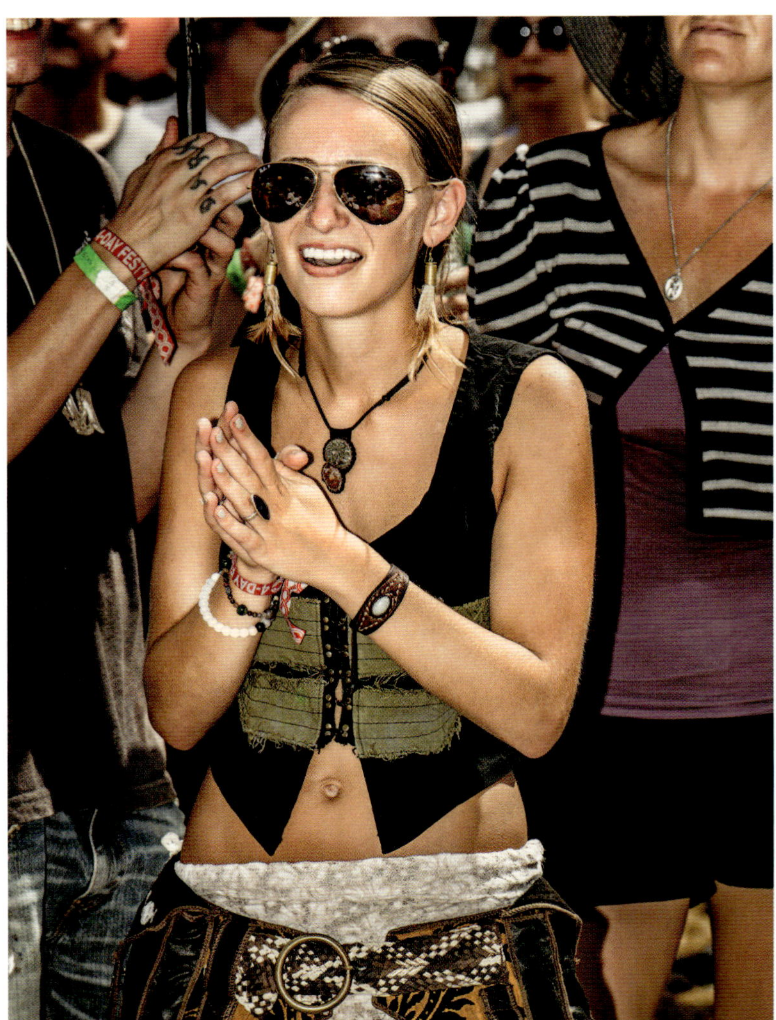

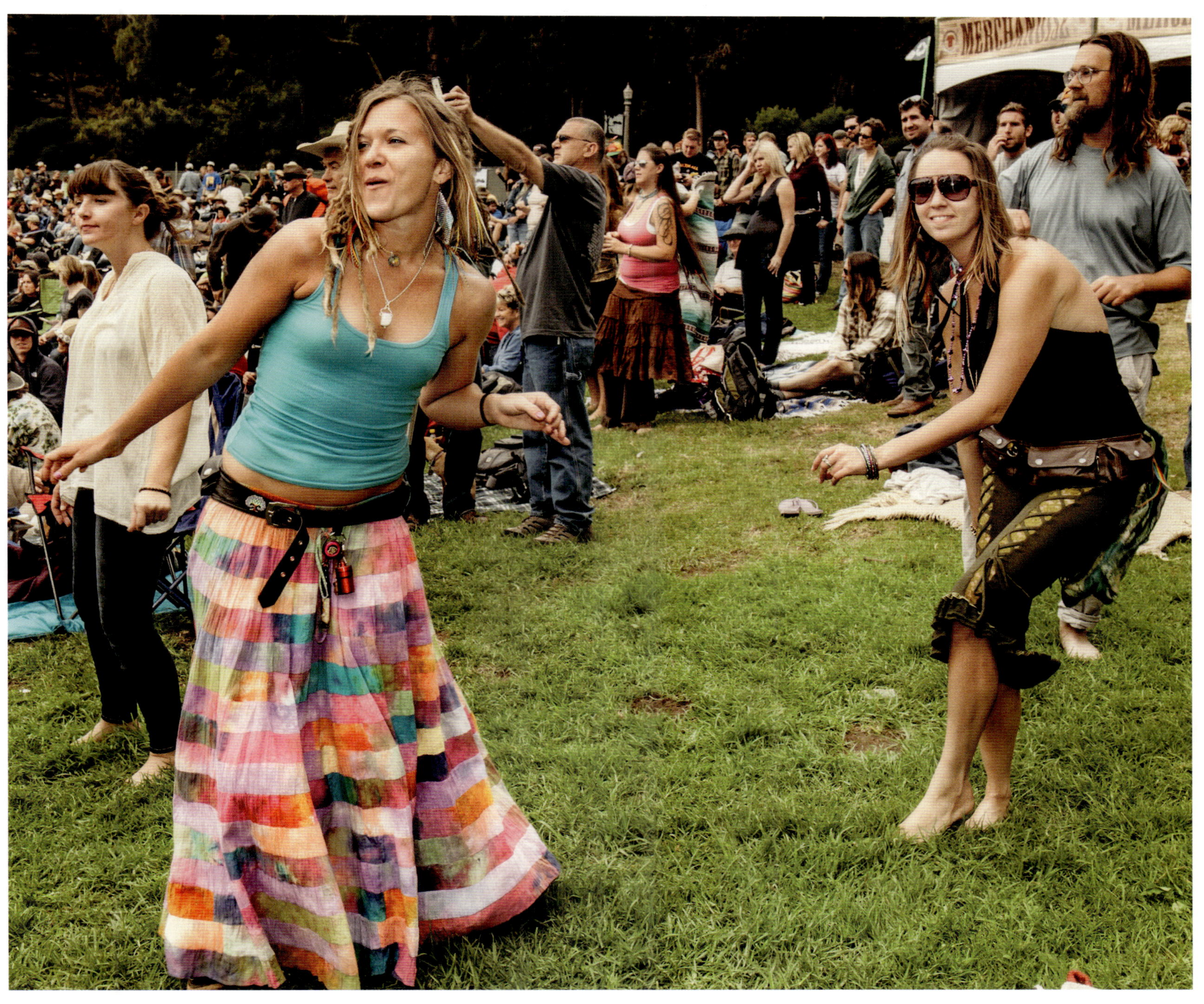

I feel my role at a festival is one of discovery. I'm there to discover new music. I'm there to find the artist that I'd never heard of before that breaks my heart three songs into his set. I'm there to watch the sunset to my favorite songs. I'm there to watch the sunrise from the Ferris wheel. I'm there for cold peanut noodles and porta potties. Rachel S.

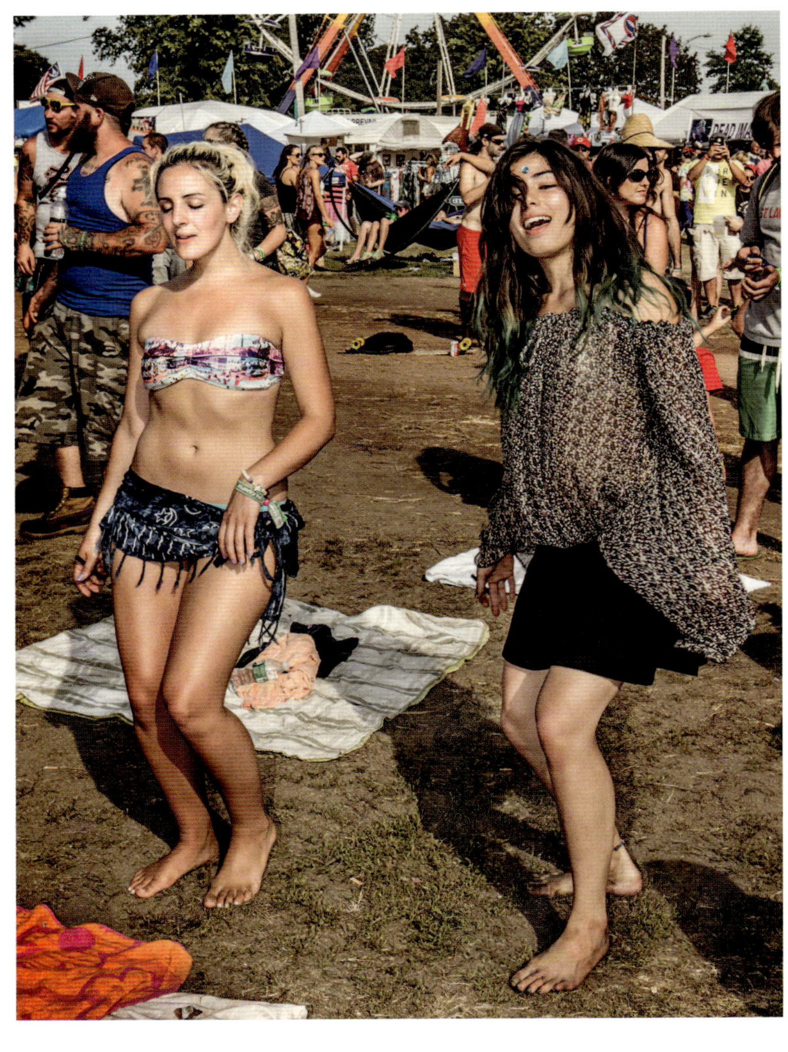

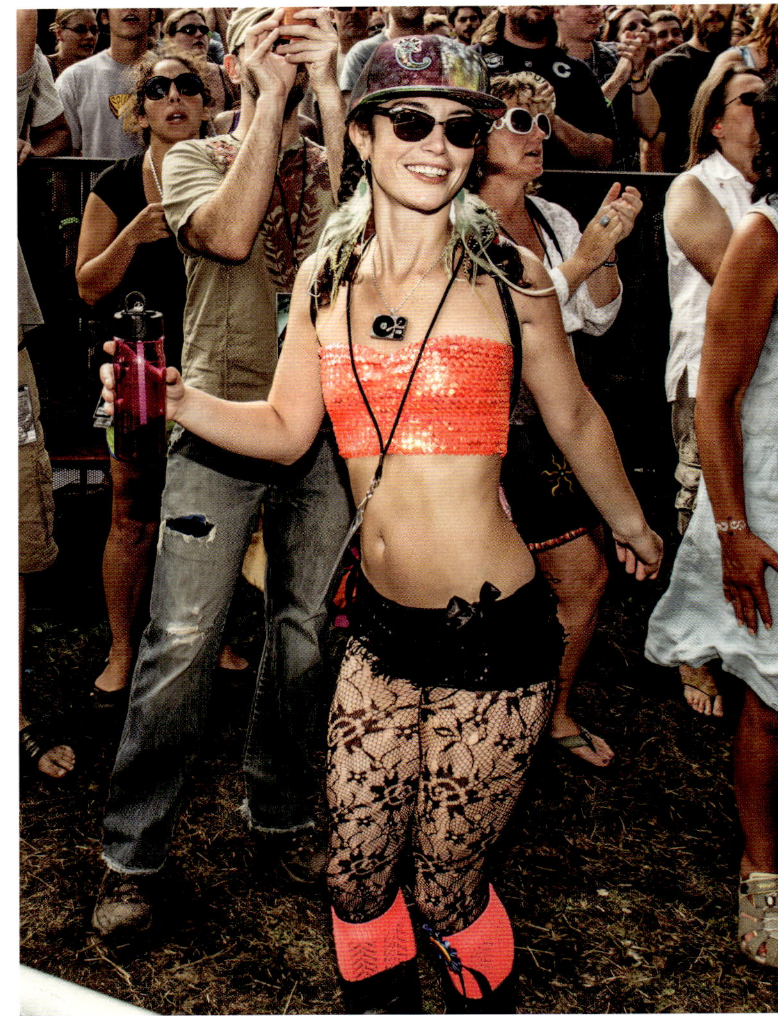

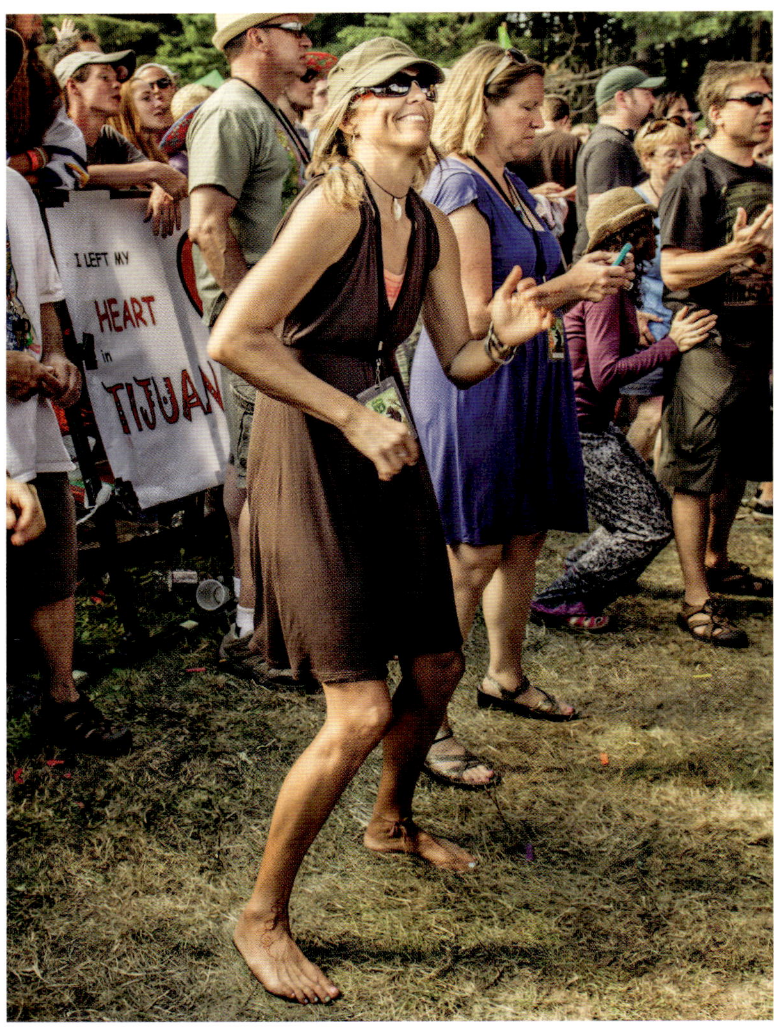
I LEFT MY
HEART
in
TIJUAN

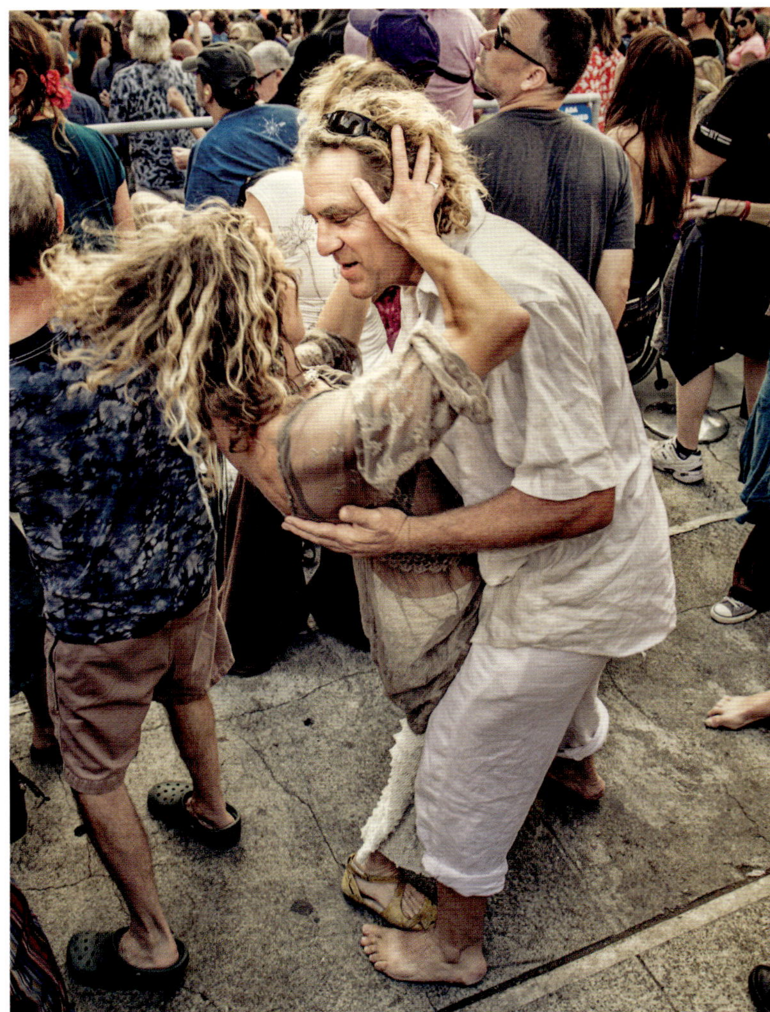

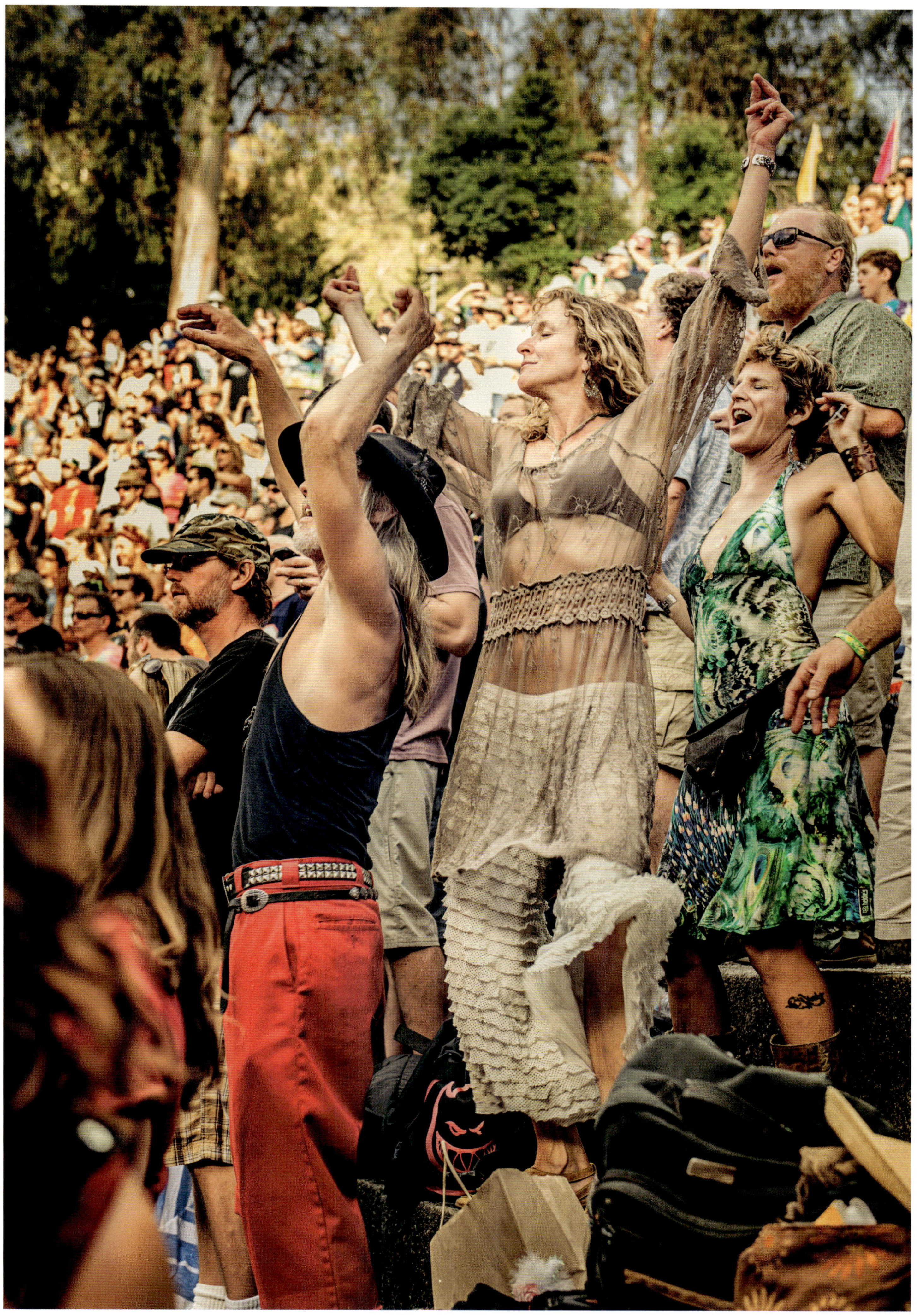

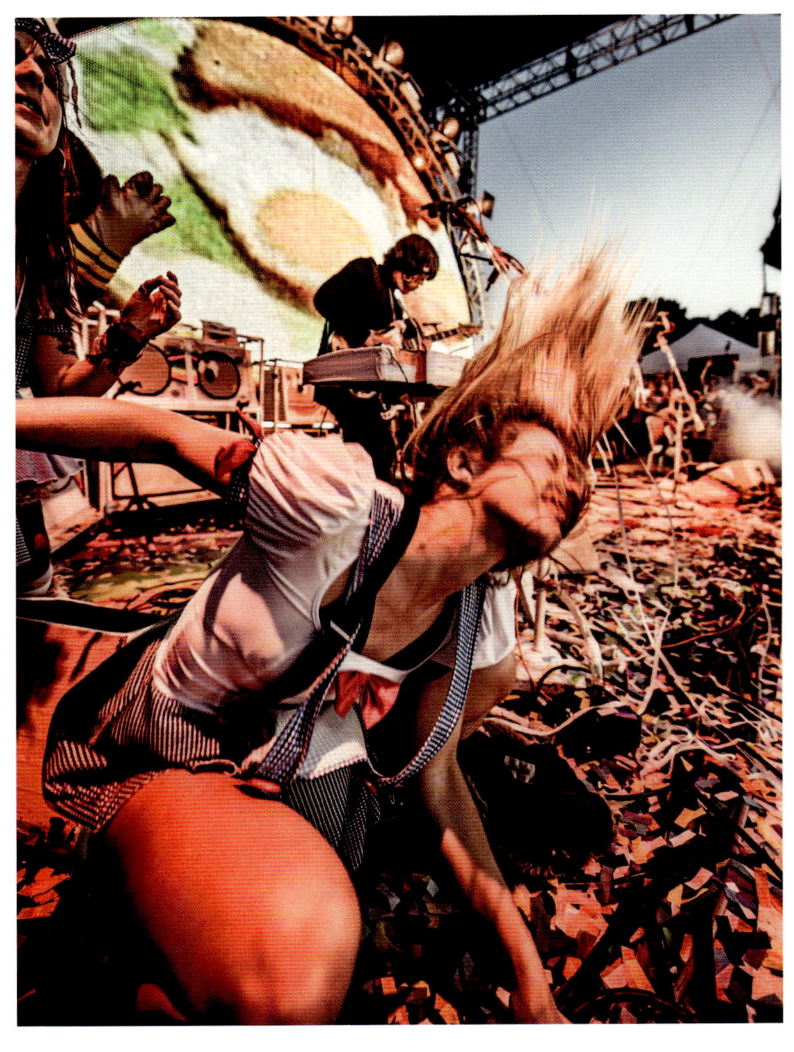
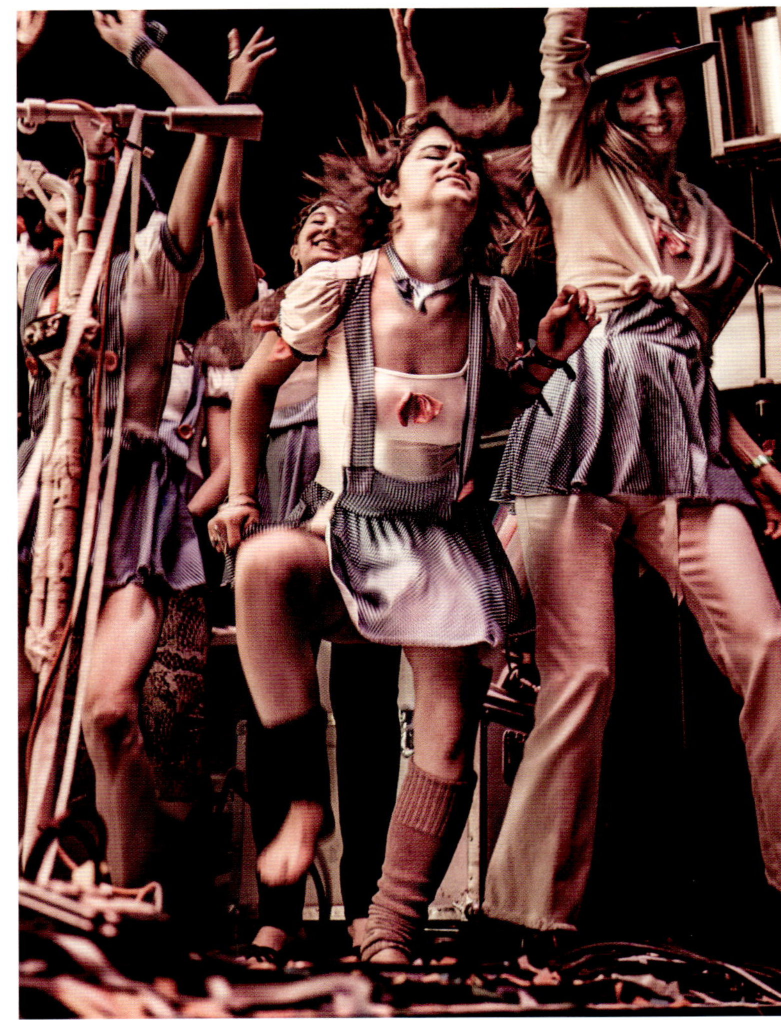
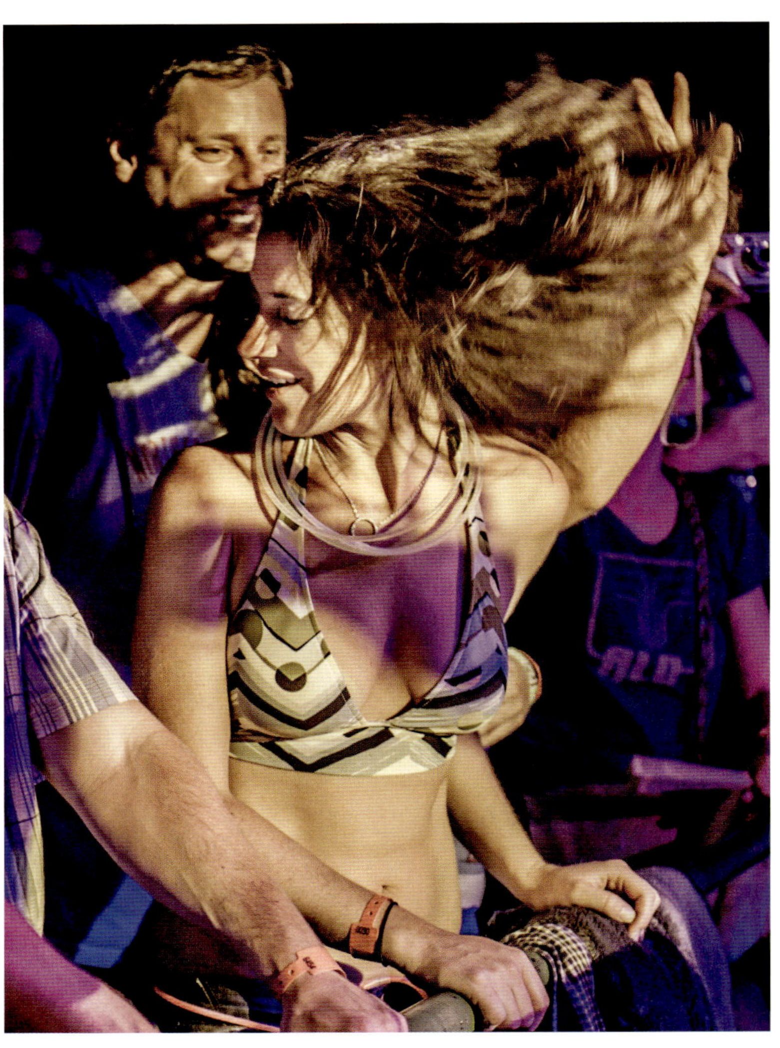
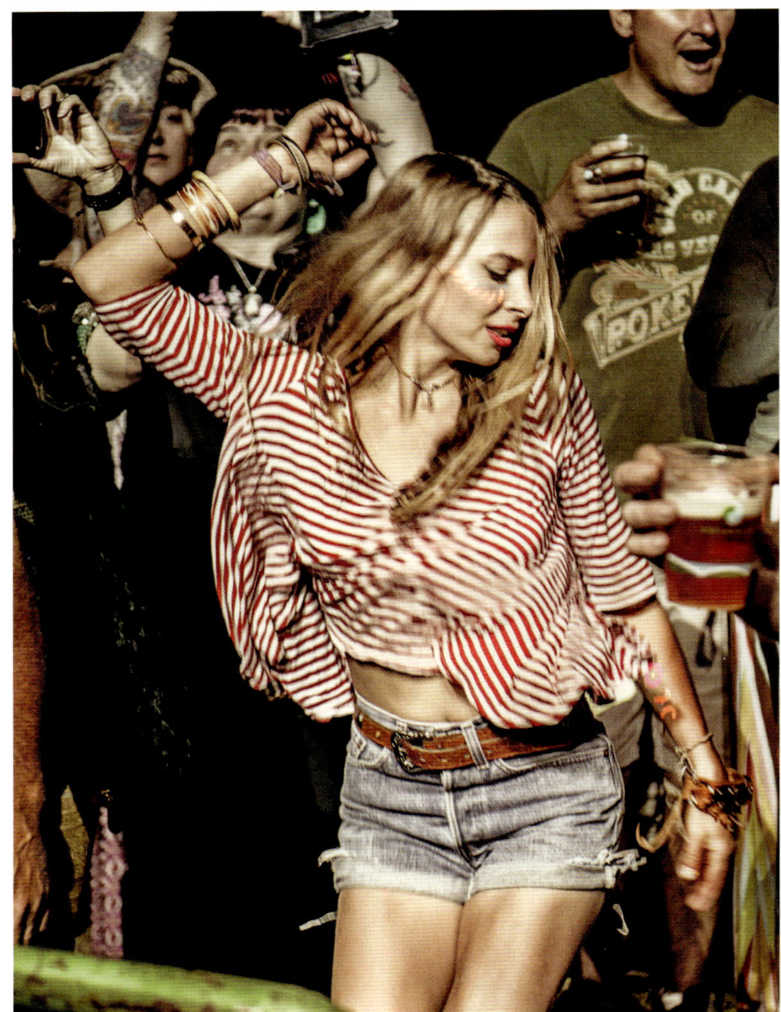

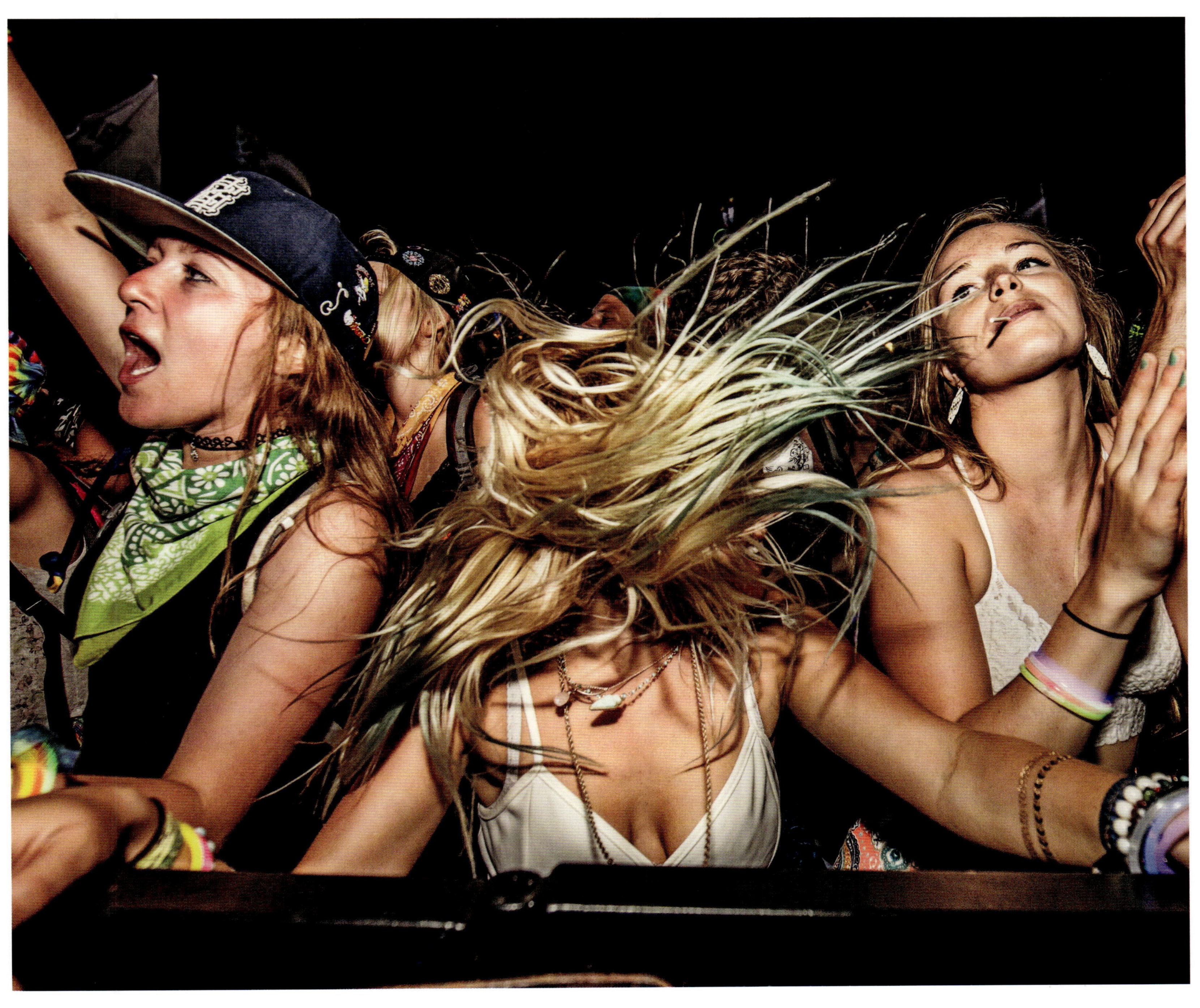

Music makes me feel alive. Letting my hair down and dancing in a crowd is where I feel like I belong, where judgment is absent. It's a spiritual experience.

Shannon

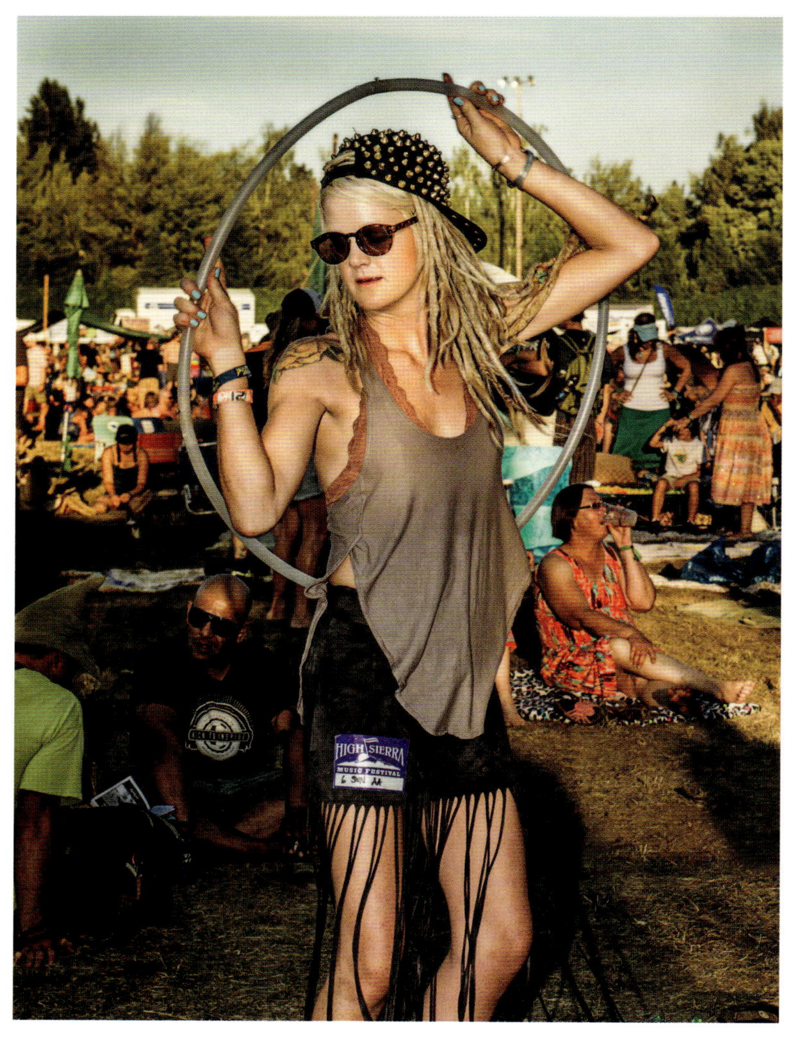
HIGH SIERRA

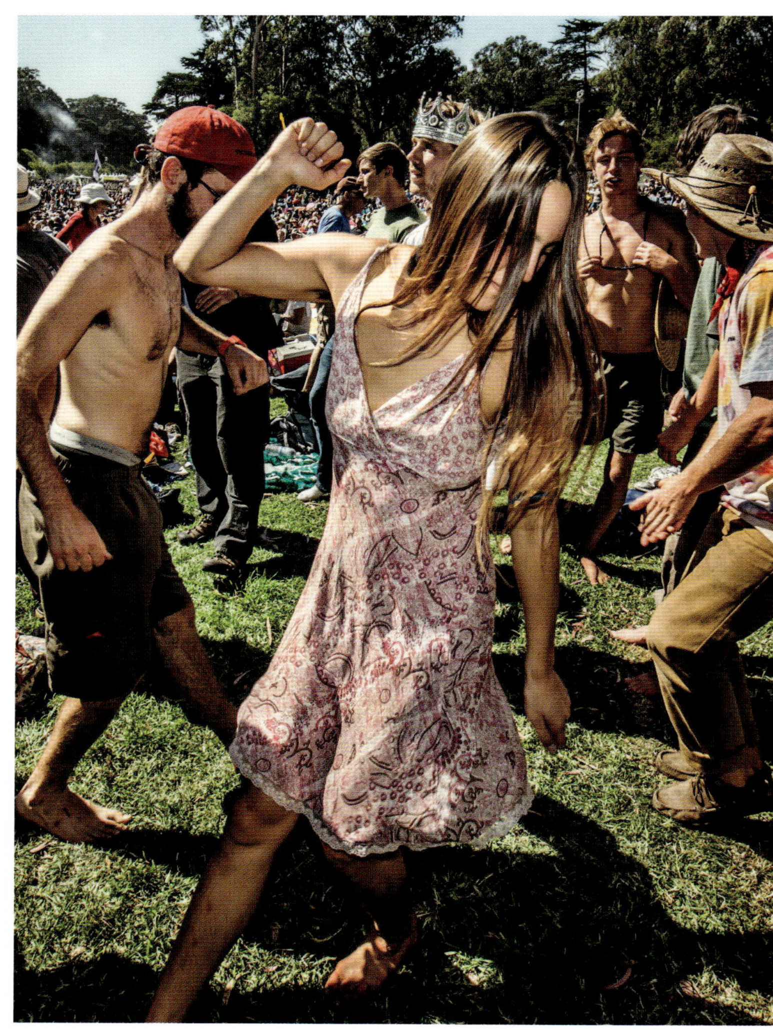

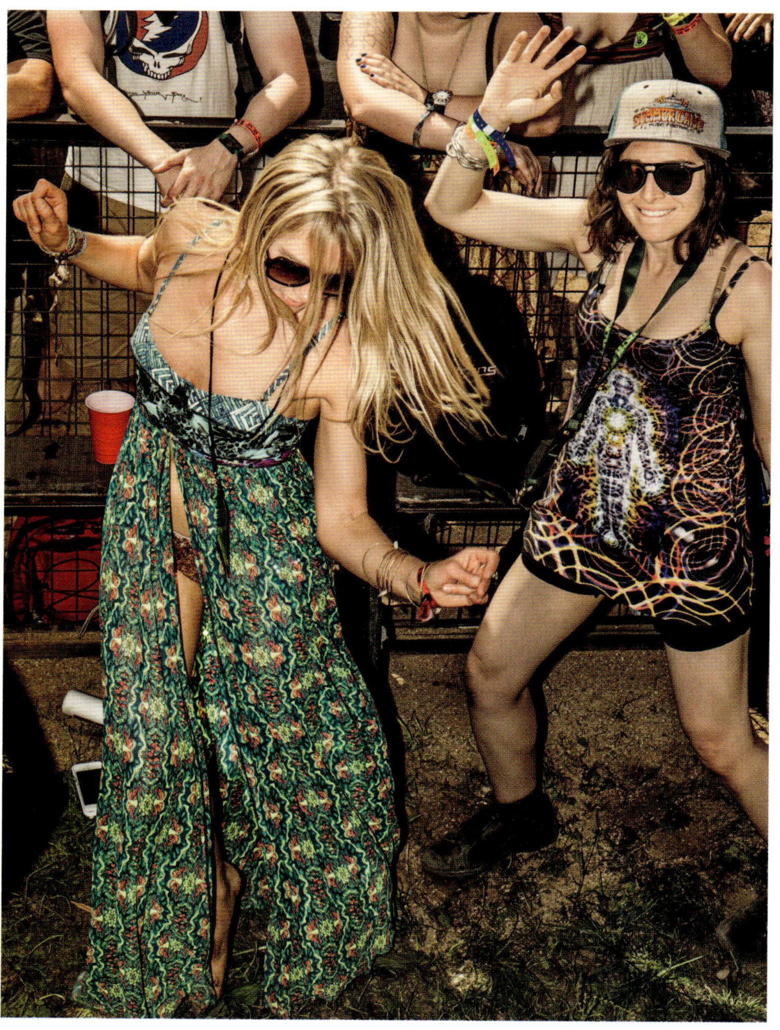

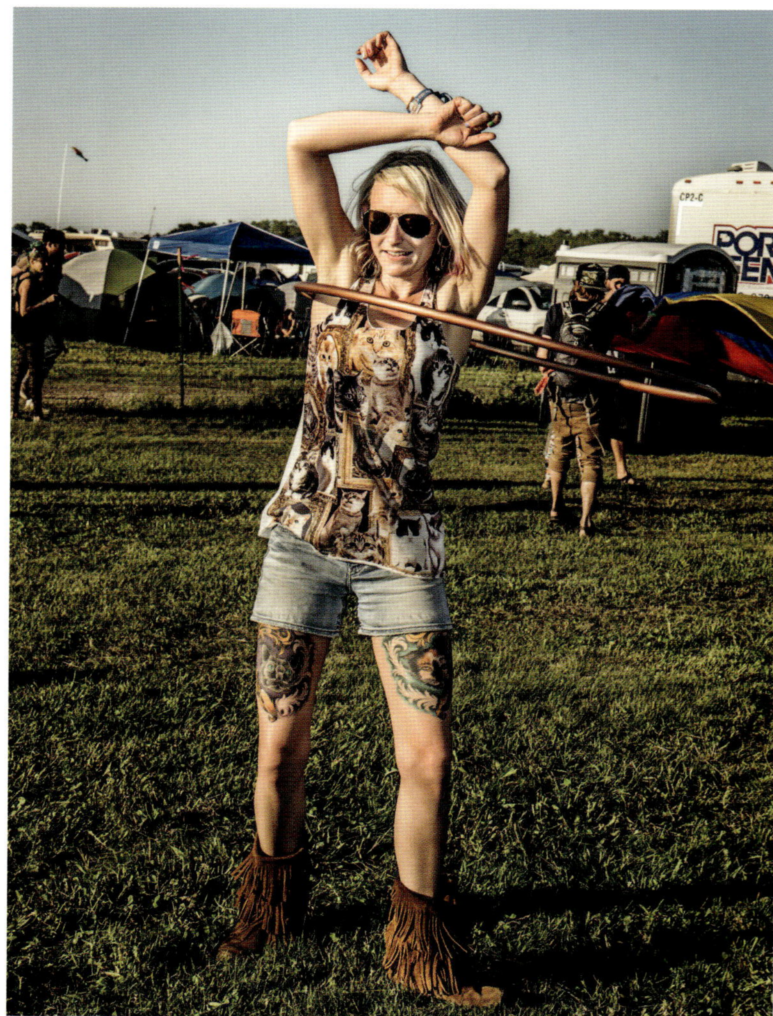

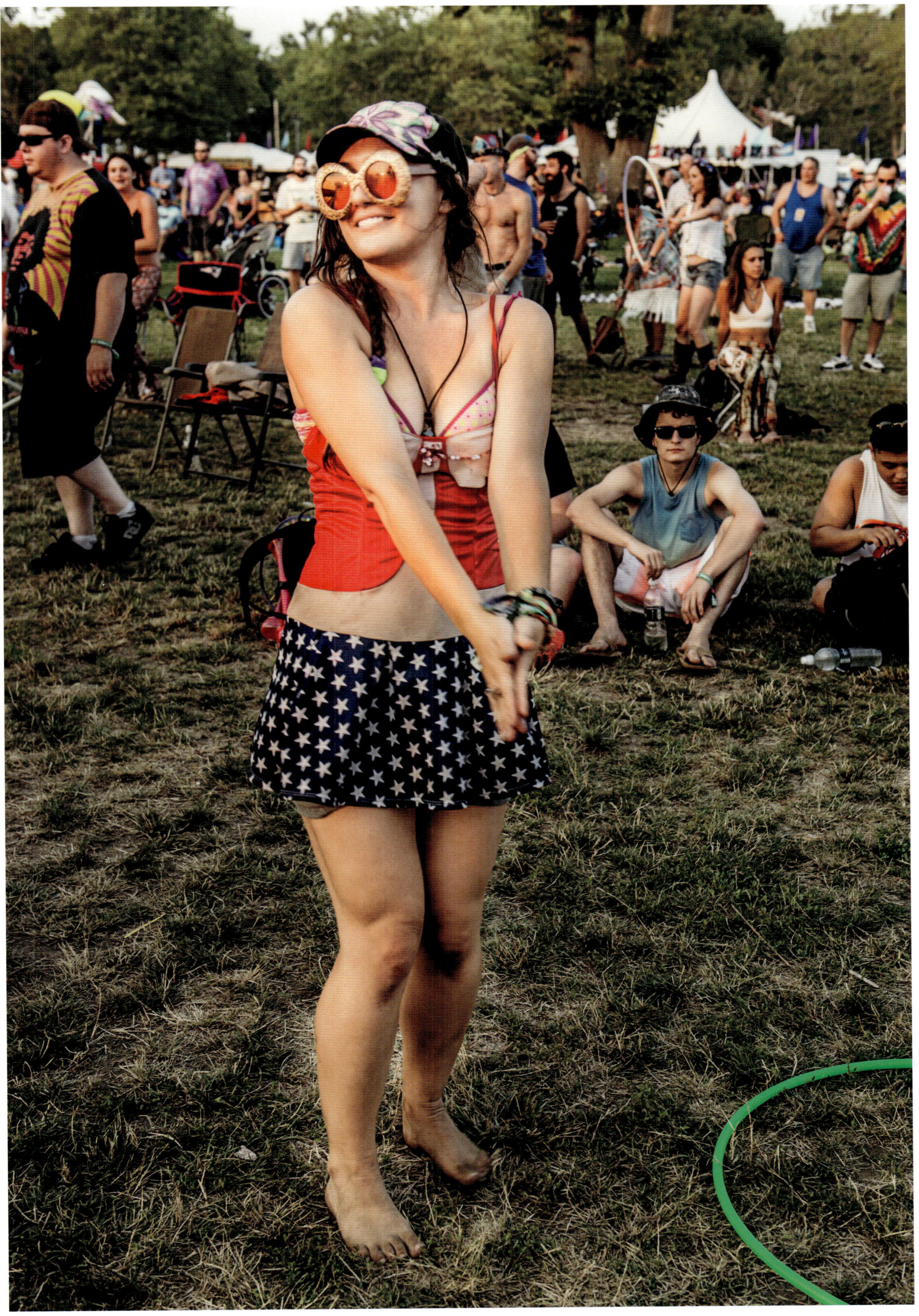

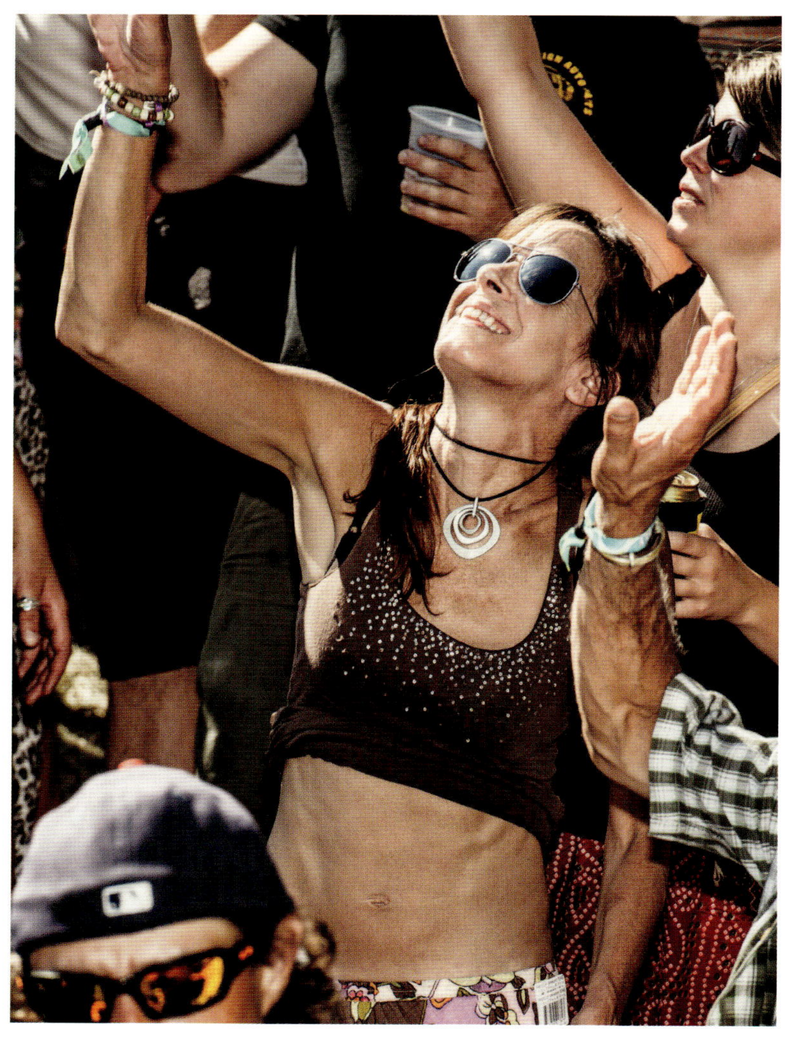

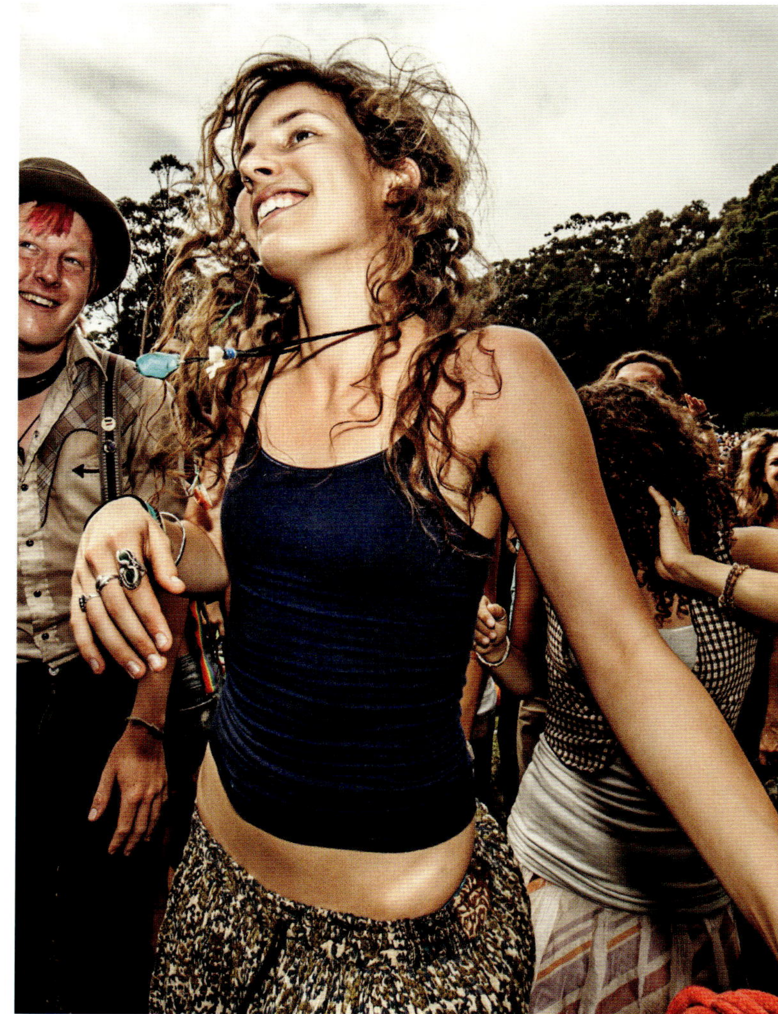

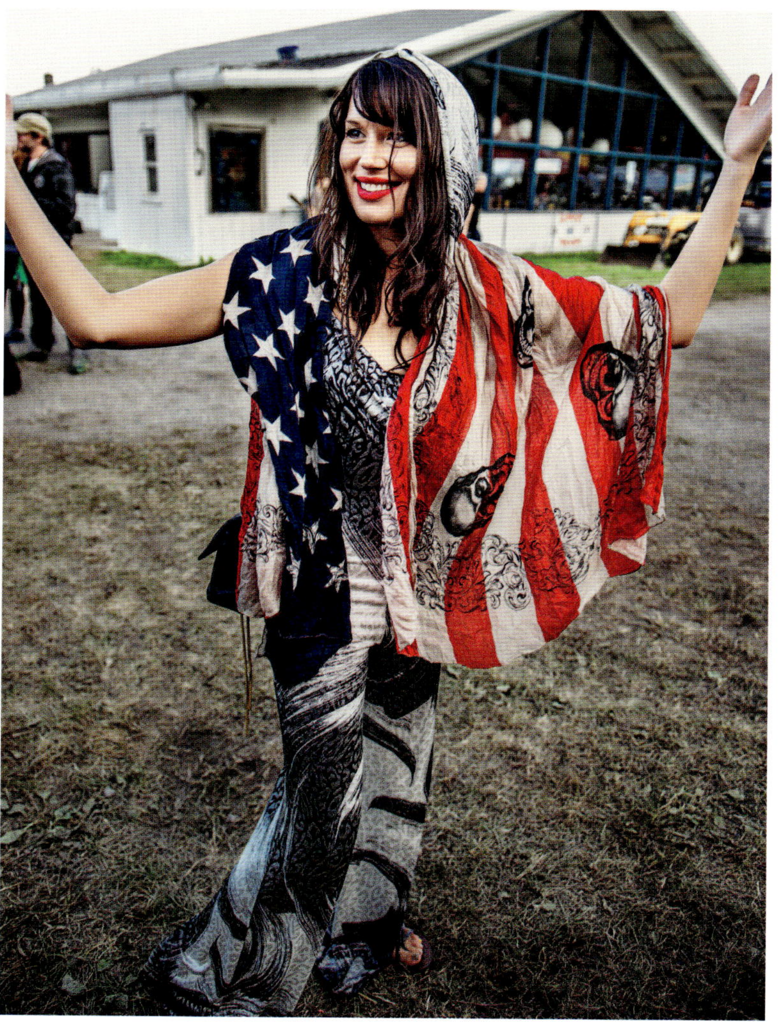

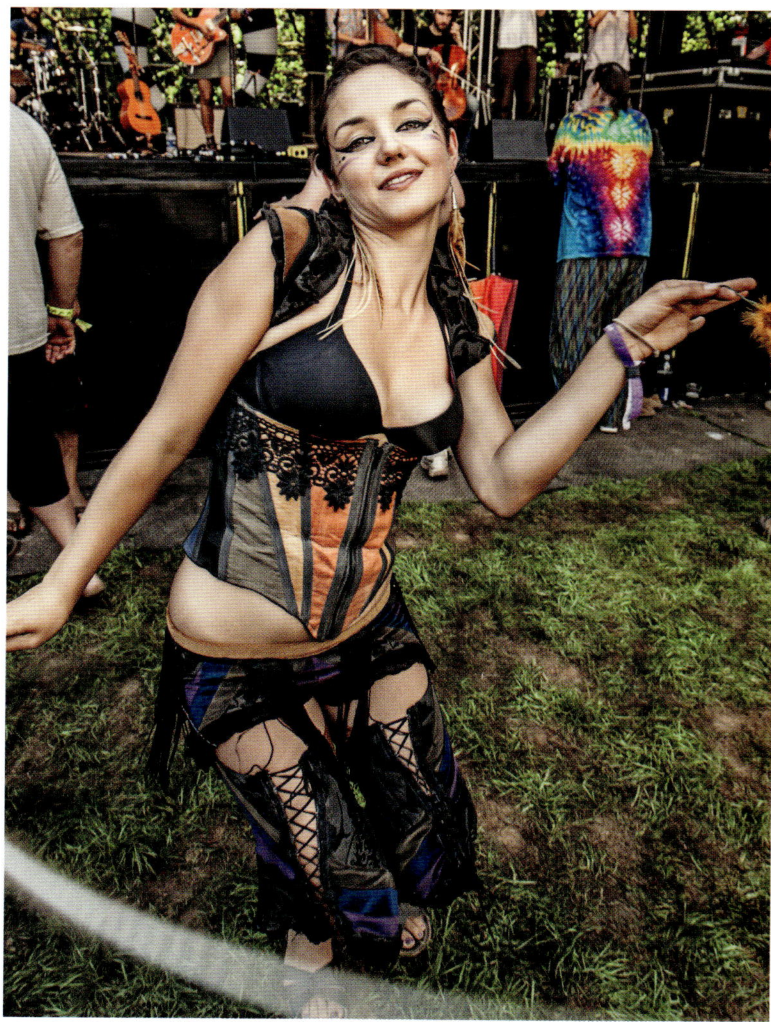

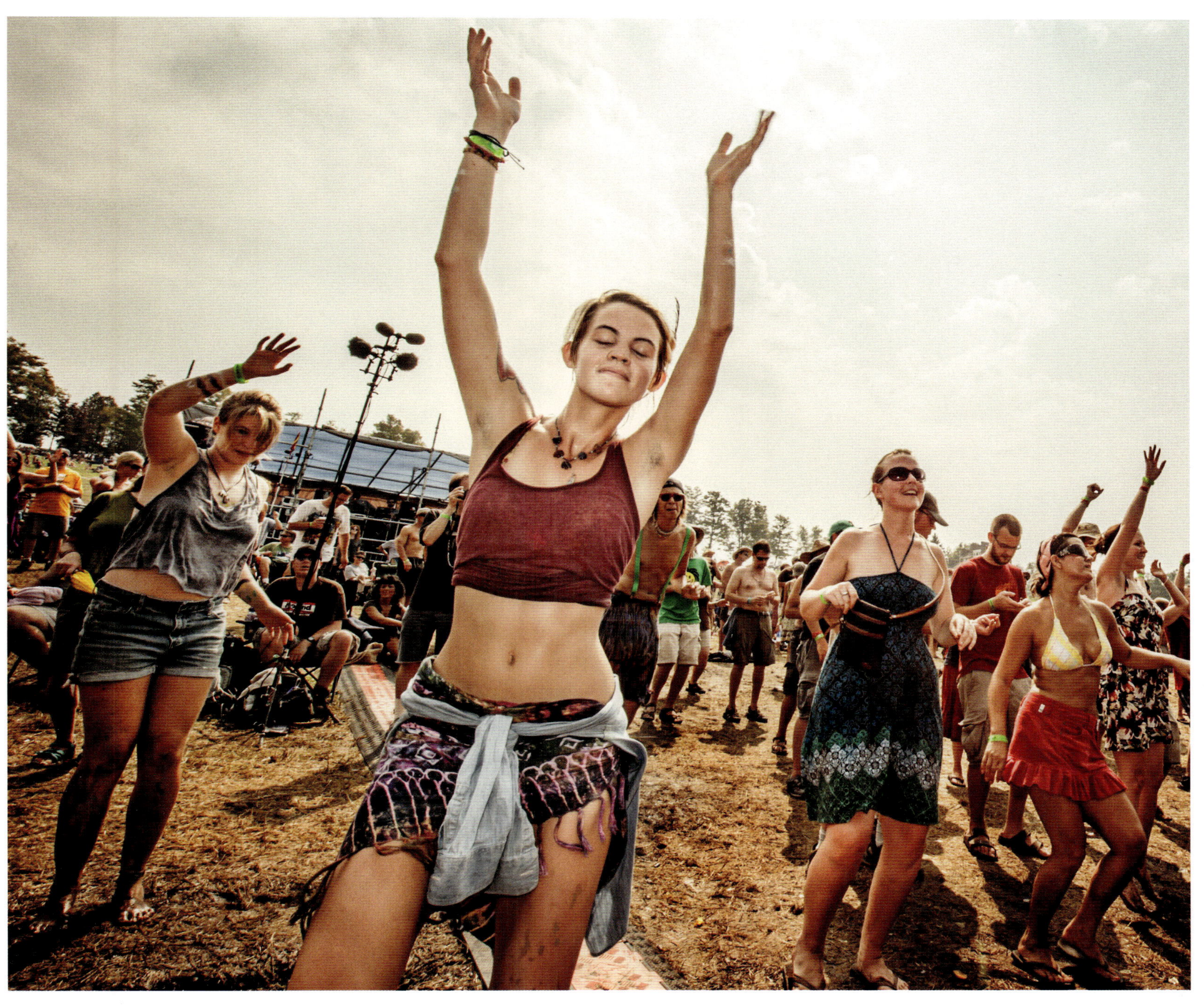

My fashion is determined by the mood of my morning, the rags in my bags, and the weather God gives. Kendall D.

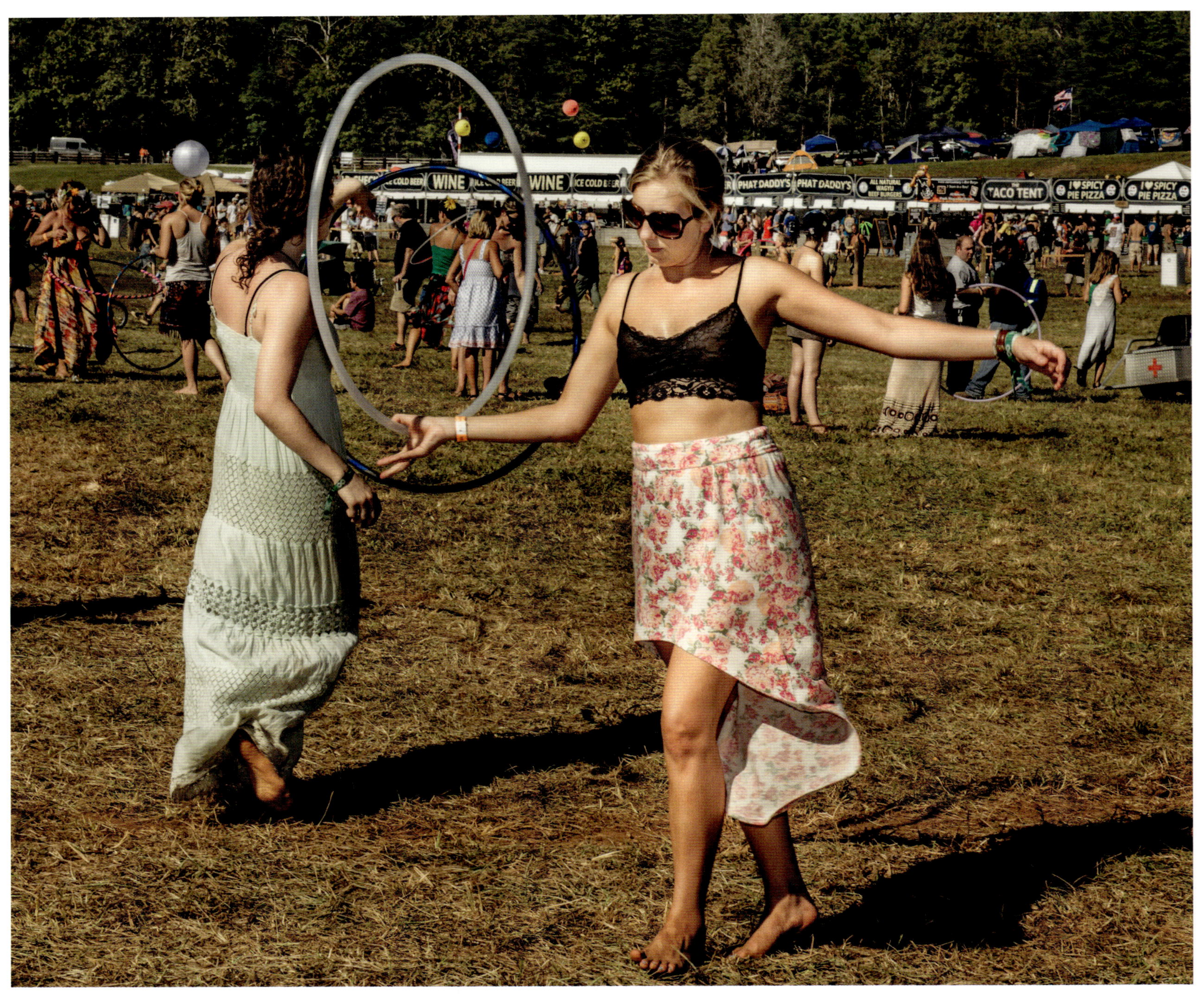

Hooping and dancing, feeling the flow, being the flow ... I feel like I'm a planet and the hoop is my orbit, and I can do anything I want inside of that orbit, as long as I follow the music. Jessica L.

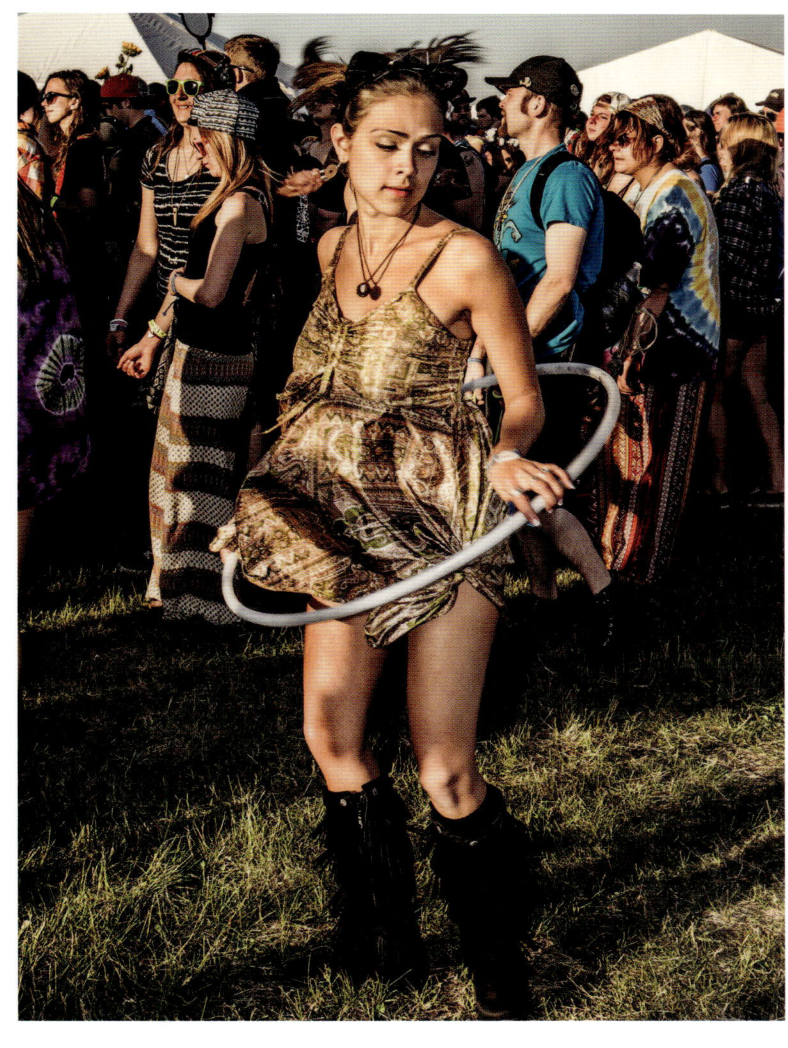

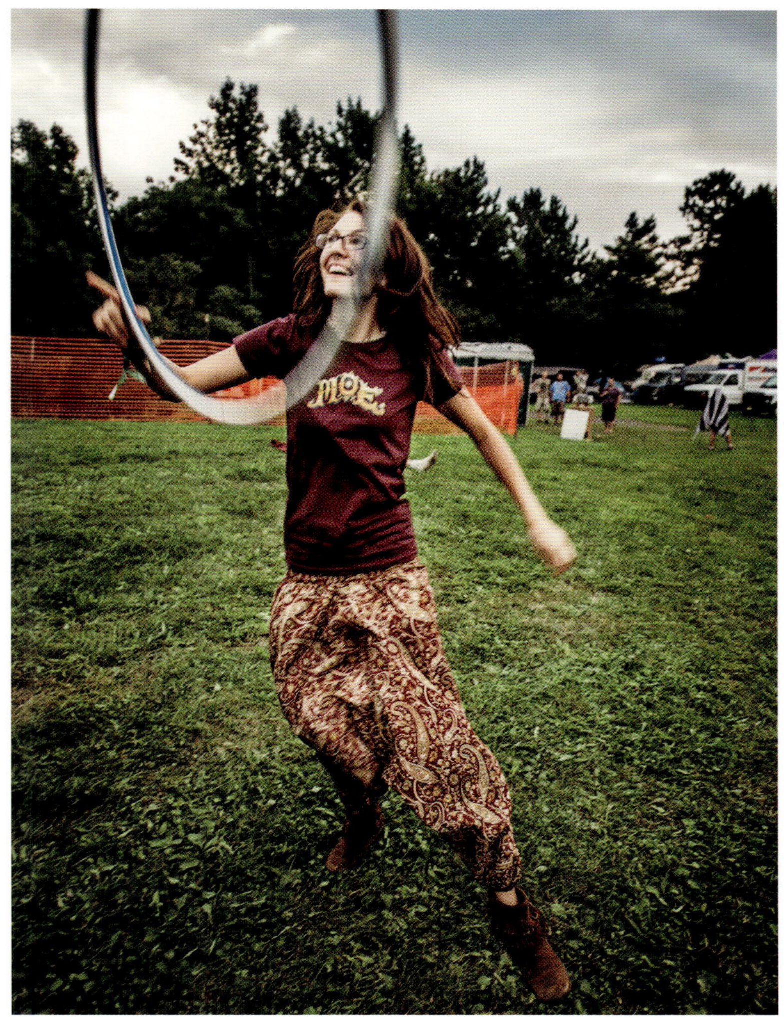

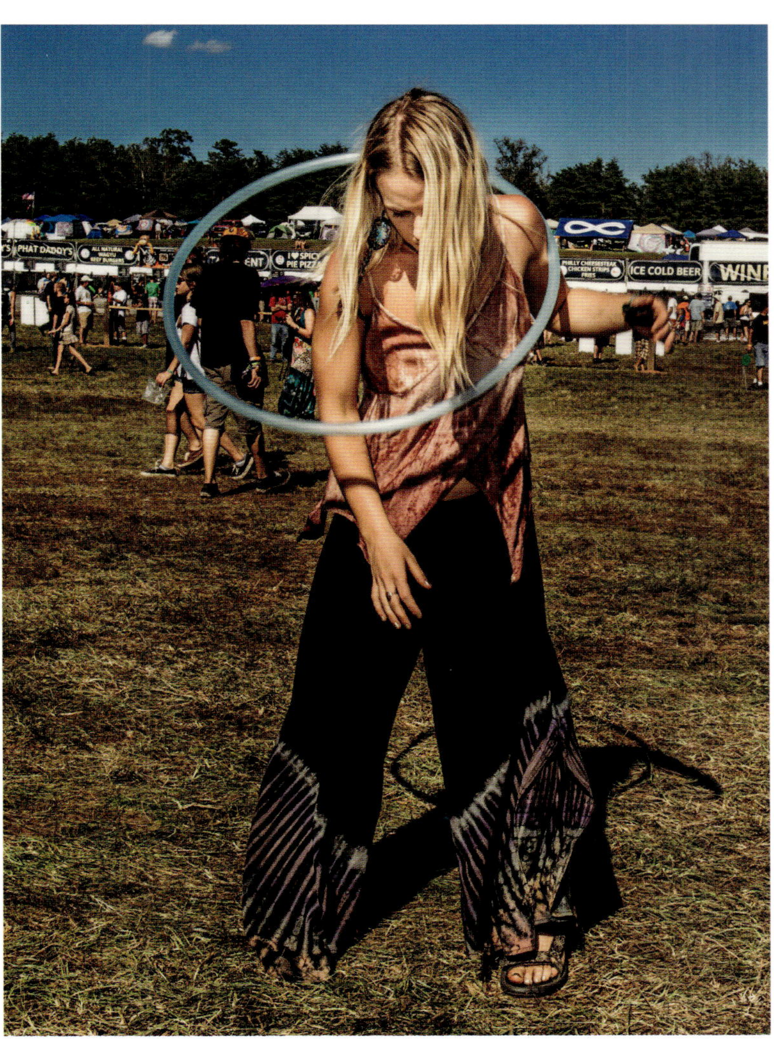
PHAT DADDY'S
ICE COLD BEER

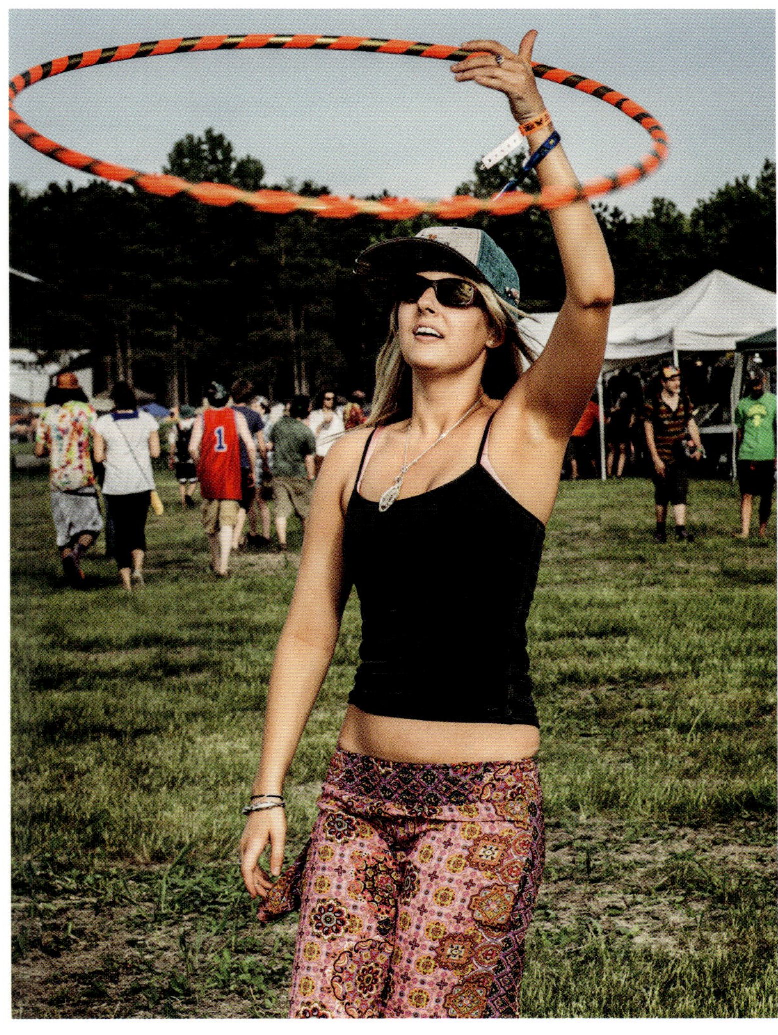

Surrender

Lay down all thoughts, surrender to the void—it is shining ...

The Beatles, "Tomorrow Never Knows"

The key to unlocking the full splendor of a live music experience is SURRENDER. Not giving up, but giving in. Participation unbound. Drifting out of the mind, we float into pure presence. We turn it all over to the music, emptying everything, expecting nothing, and making room to be rocked. The sound fills us. It takes us and teaches us. Each show is an opportunity to step out of time and into the flow; to release the wheel and let it ride. Eyes closed, hands to the sky, we relinquish control and dance into the unknown.

We dance wildly, awkwardly, badly or beautifully, but most importantly, freely and without fear. We let our hair down. We let it all hang out. We shed our inhibitions, our insecurities, and even our clothing. We return to our natural state led by feeling, not thinking; emotions, not intellect. It's not about doing, just being. We listen to the music and let the spirit move us. We are available and receptive, untamed and infinite. We cast off the mask of personality and let our freak flags fly. And we let them fly high.

Freedom comes from letting go; freedom to go way the hell out and come back with ease. Lose our minds. Lose our way. Get lost and get found. This is where the muse resides, ready to guide us from the smallness of our ego selves into limitless divine oneness. We are stardust, after all, tiny shimmering pieces of a brilliant cosmic puzzle. By abandoning attachment to our individual personalities, we integrate into the vastness of experience. What emancipates us is realizing that the enigma of existence is best understood through interacting with others. Live music makes that happen.

Music unites us and we begin to see the exquisite interconnectedness of it all. Through this lens of awareness, we resonate and relate. We enjoy the thrill of self-expression knowing that when we liberate our brightest, most authentic selves, we are supporting the creative potential of the whole. Surrendering to our long-buried instinct to share rather than hoard—our time, our resources, our love, our music—we drop everything and join together with the band. We dive into fantasy and delight in uncertainty, prepared to discover whatever awaits.

Flowers in our hair, glitter on our skin, bells around our ankles ... We don't need a reason to do what feels right. Responding to the song of our hearts' desires, we are enraptured by the rhythm of the right now. We give ourselves over completely, pouring the contents of our souls into the stream of energy at a show. We leave it all on the rail, the floor, the field, and the stands, ascending to ethereal dimensions. We are content to know by either faith or experience that we will soon be lifted again. The rock and roll gods always provide.

We treat each show like our first and last. We are grateful for each note and fully present. We take it as it comes knowing this exact show can never be replicated. Our adaptability allows an appreciation of the unpredictable. From midsummer hailstorms to canceled headliners, from golden lottery tickets to impromptu super jams, we are ready for anything. We dance in the rain and slide in the mud. We know a higher power exists in lyrics, riffs, and performances. We sing and shout and get silent. We live the music. We yield to the mystery and it spoils us in its riches. It makes us who we are. We give all we have, and the music forever gives more.

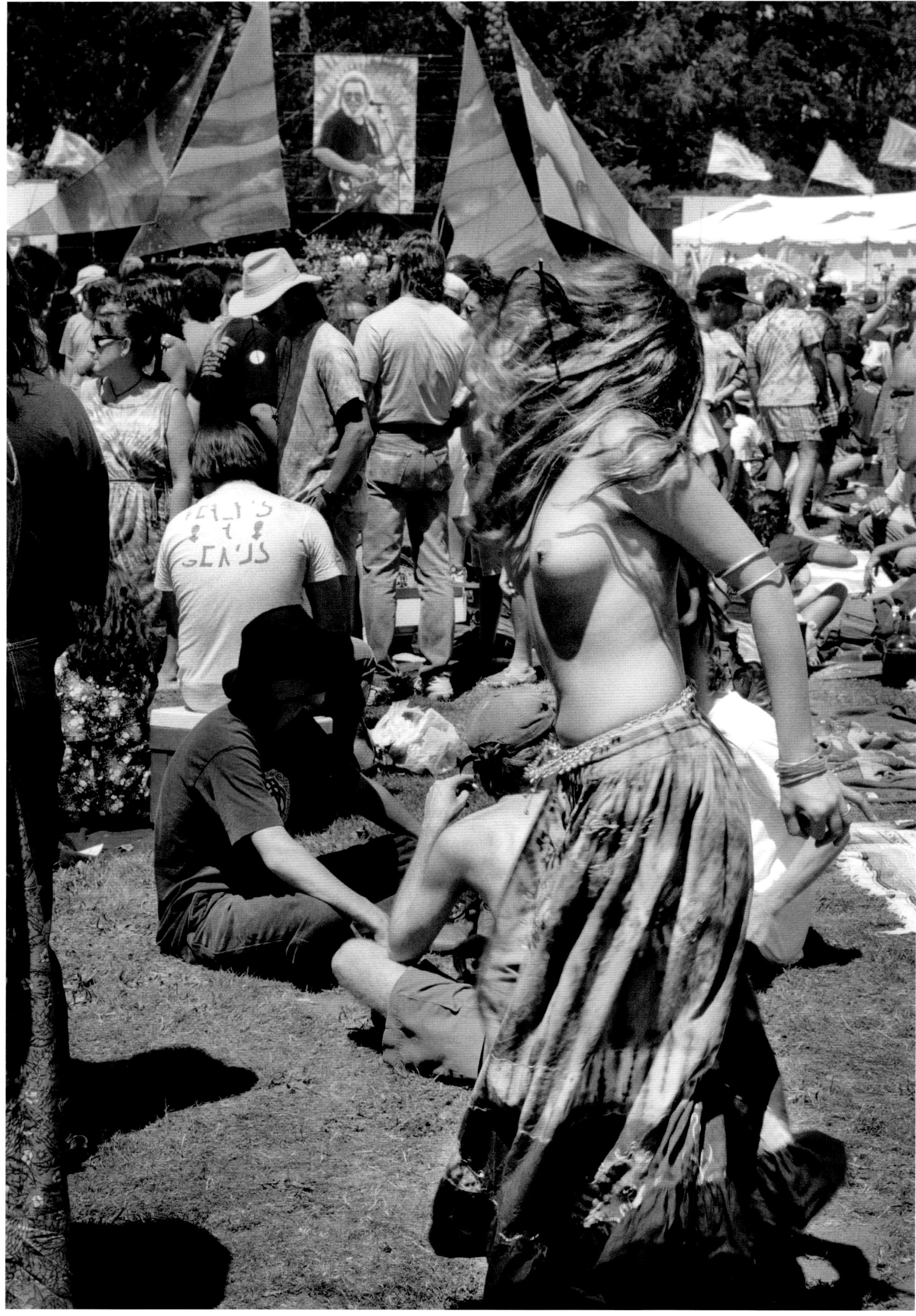

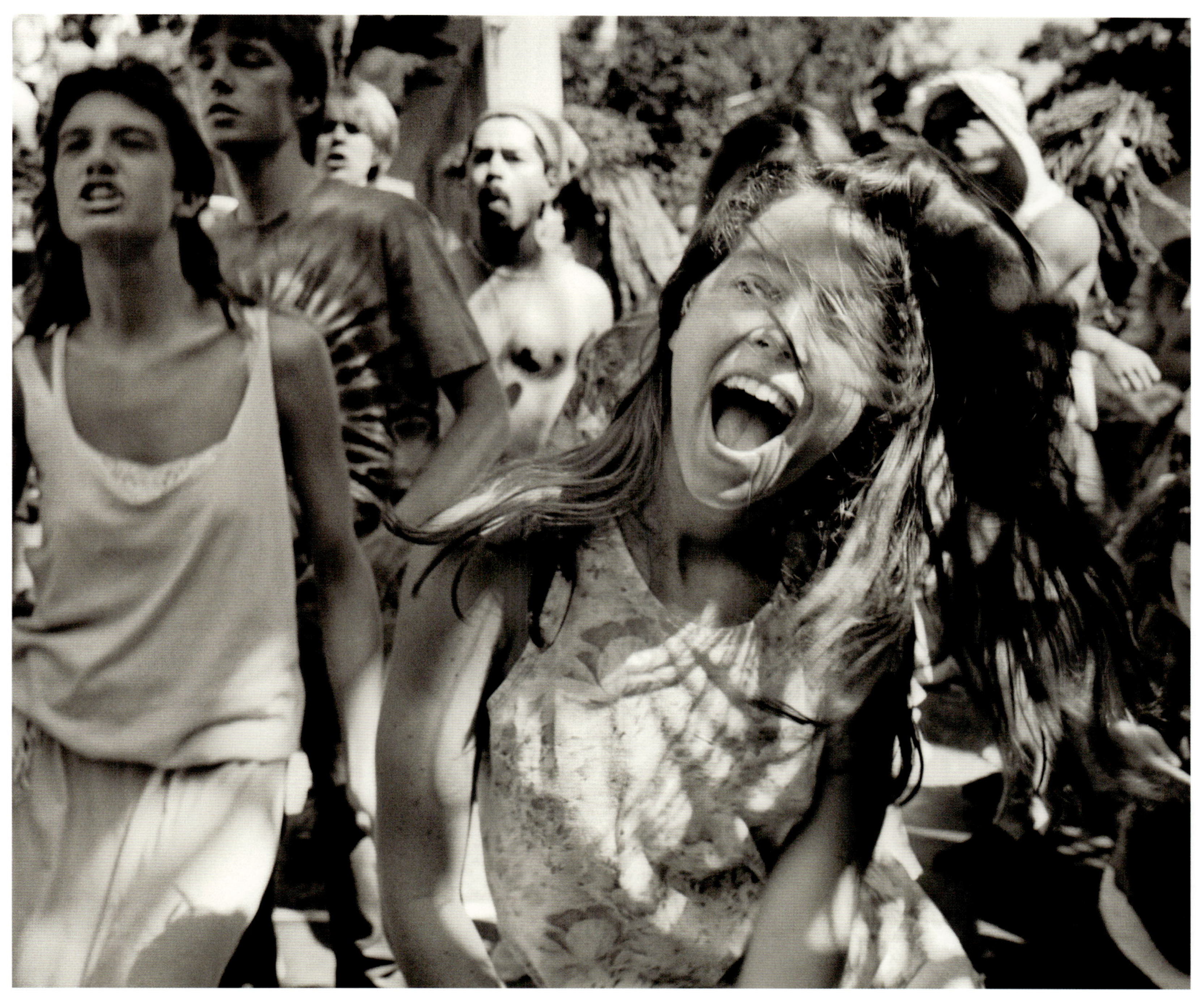

I love how you can be a kid again and wear sparkles on your face, and I don't have to worry if I have dirt all over my white skirt by Sunday. Ariel B.

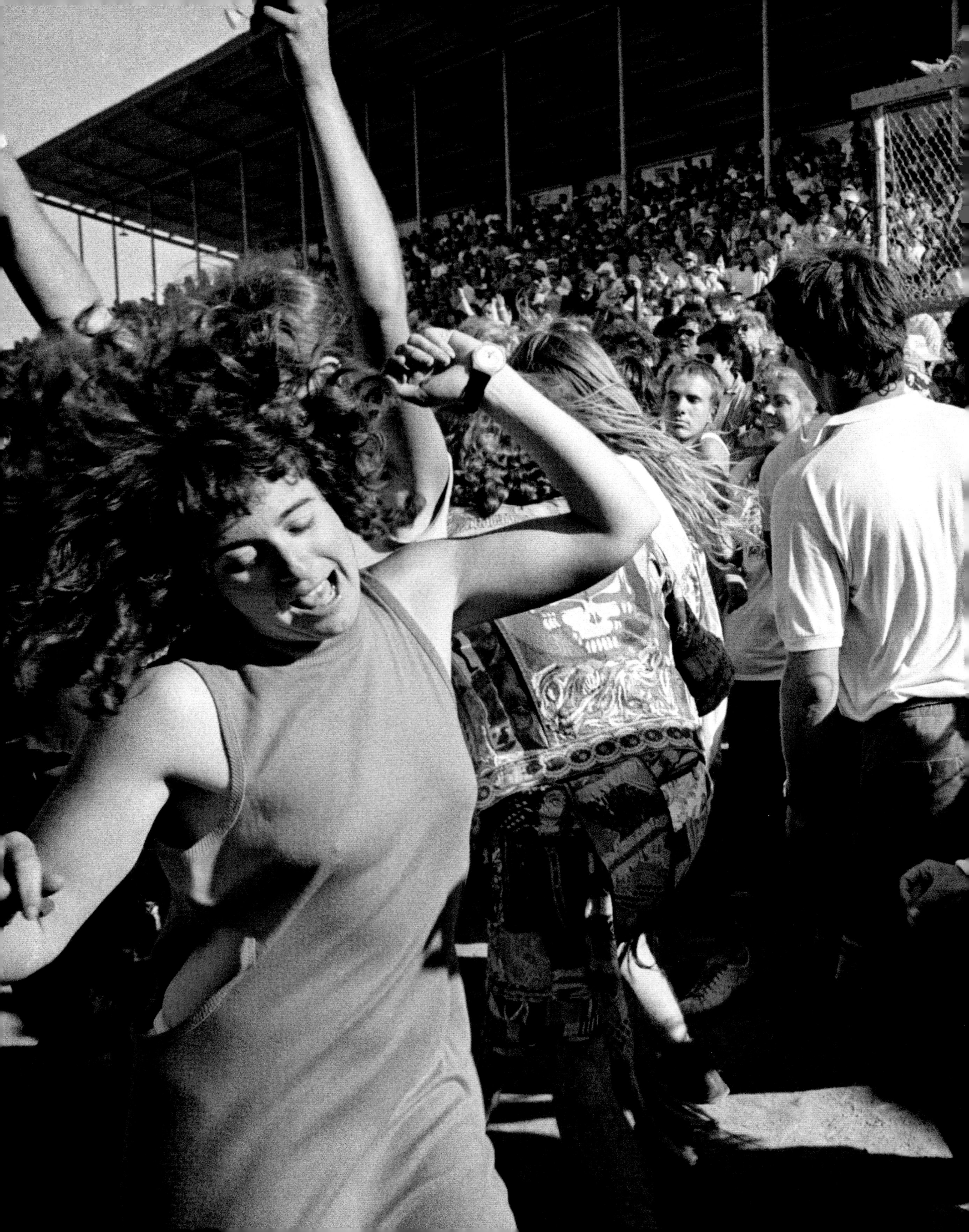

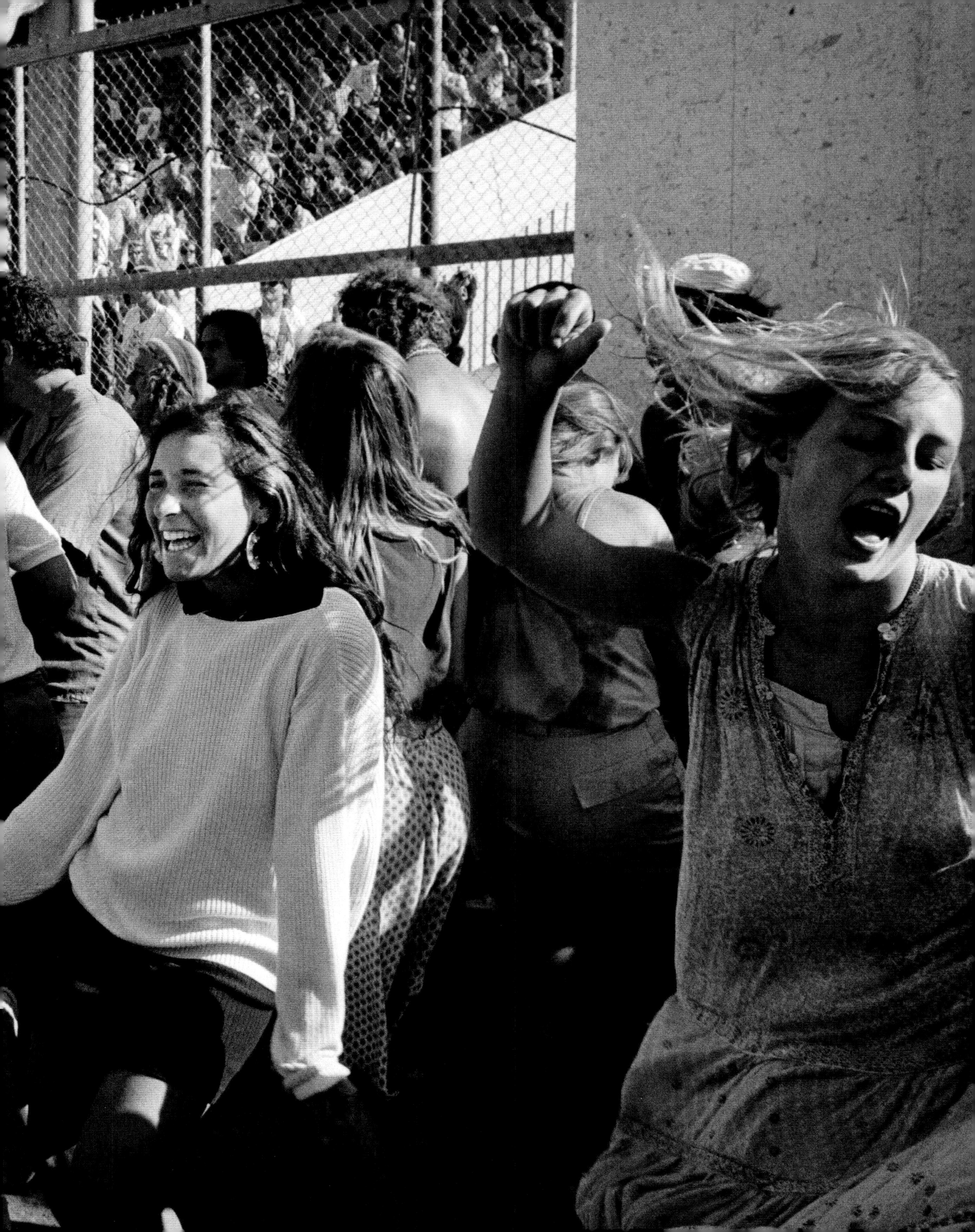

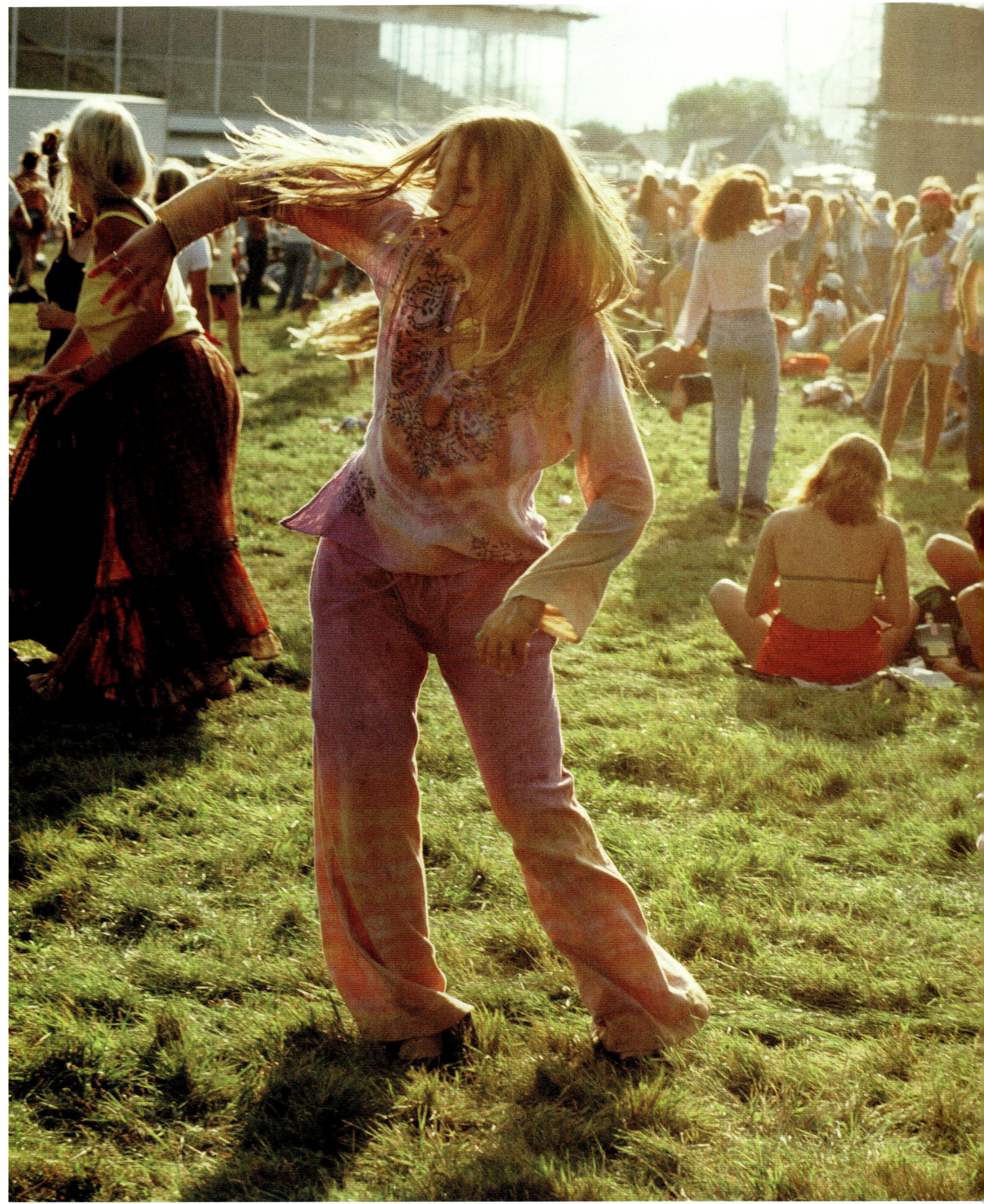

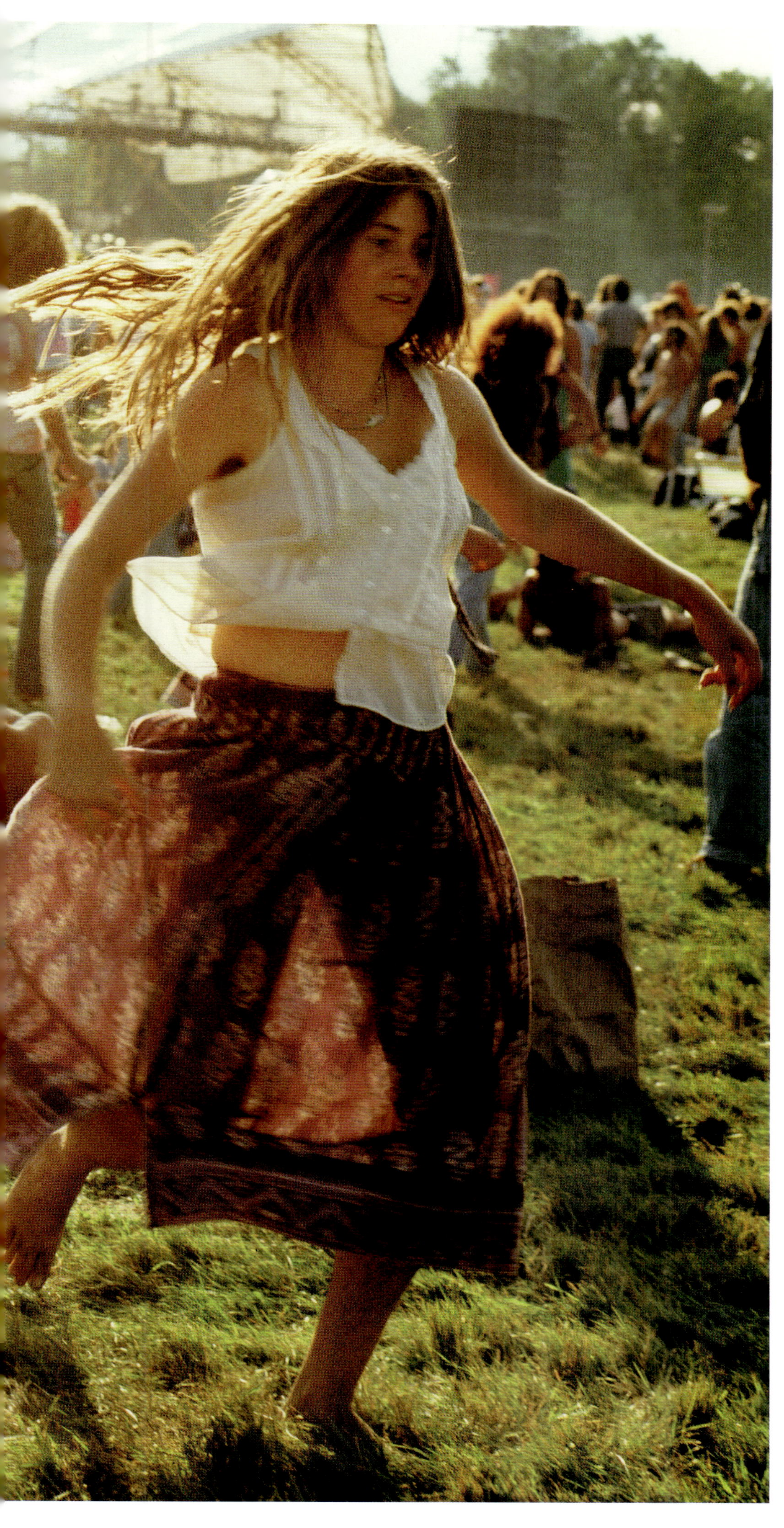

My walk turned into a jog that turned into a dance until I got as close as I could to the stage. It was as if the music had just taken over my body and I had no control. Brittany F.

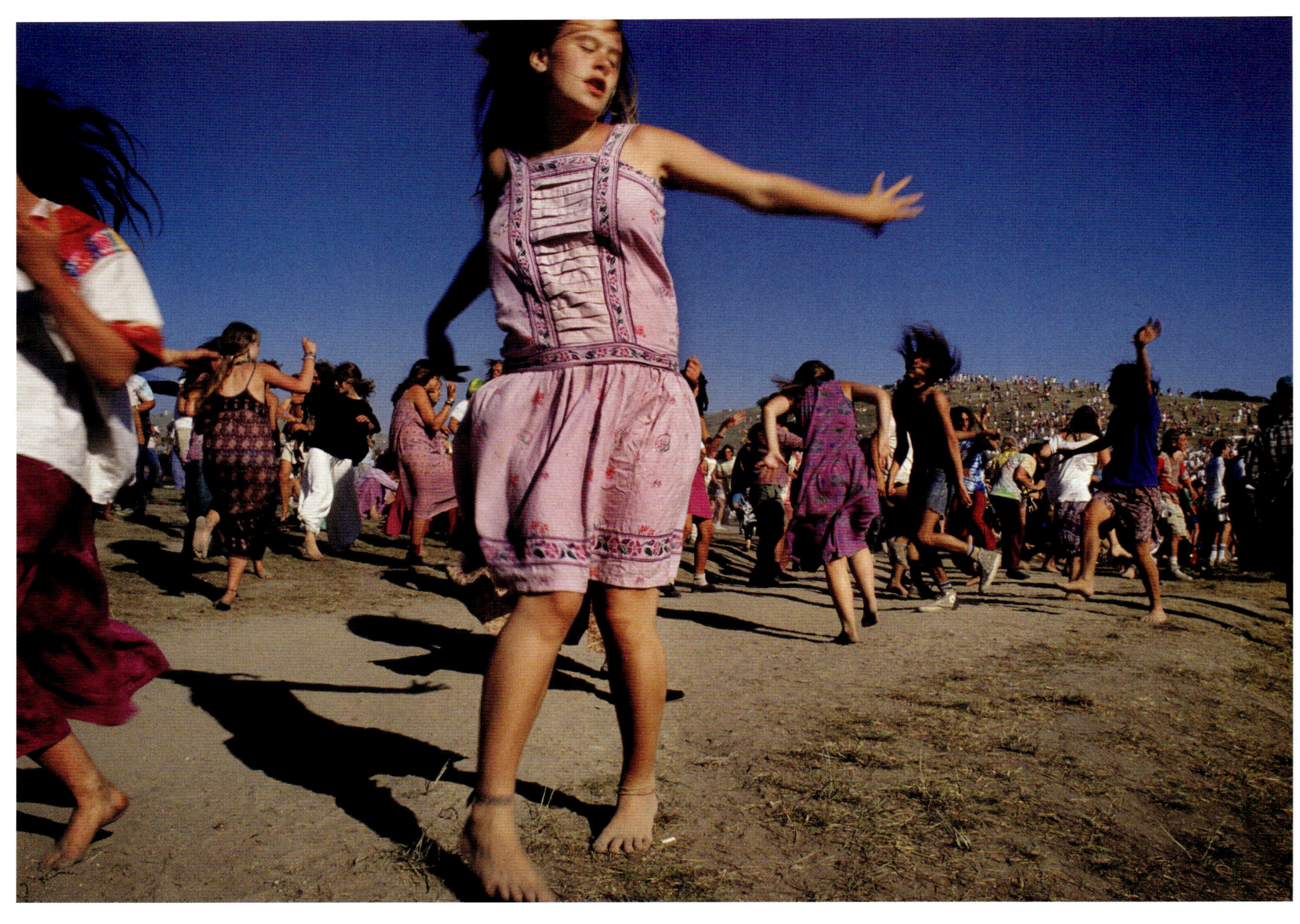

When the music is playing, my body is moving. It just happens and there's no stopping it. Joyce L.

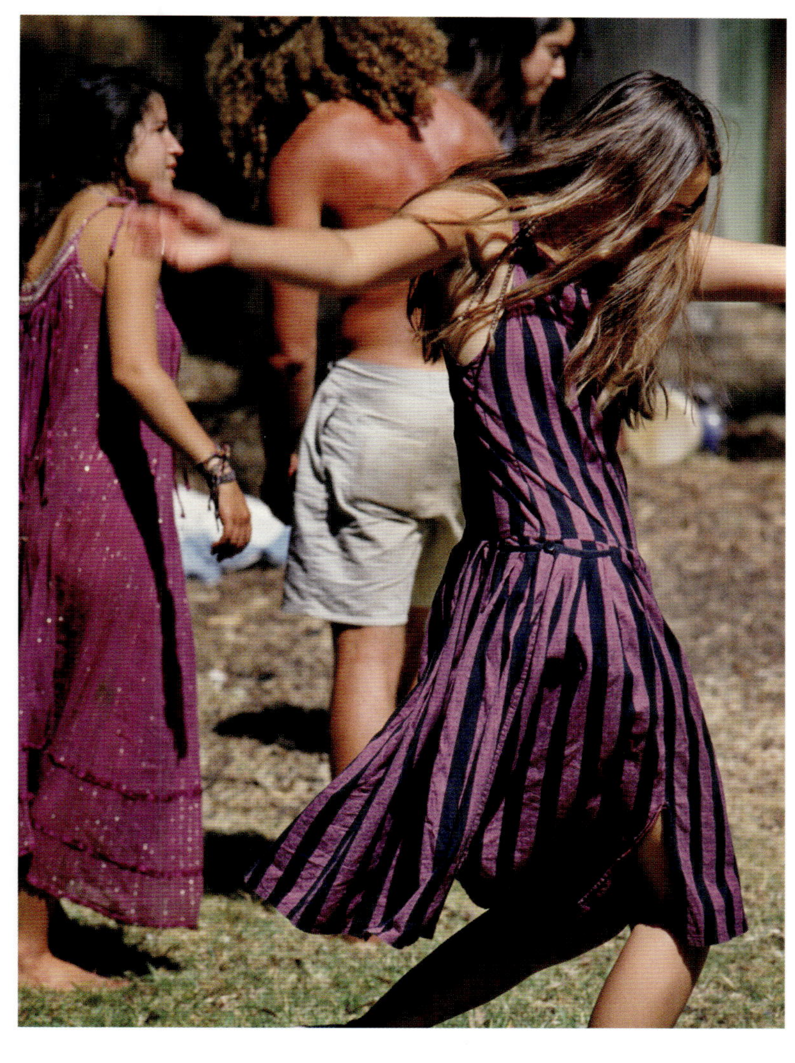

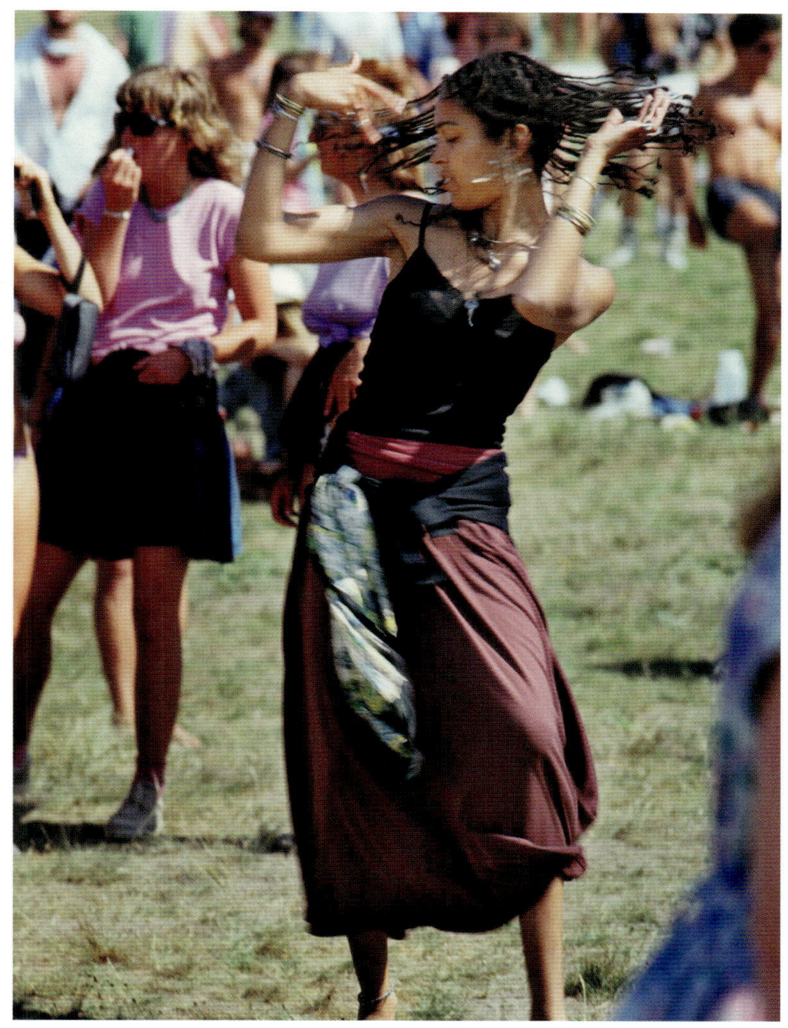

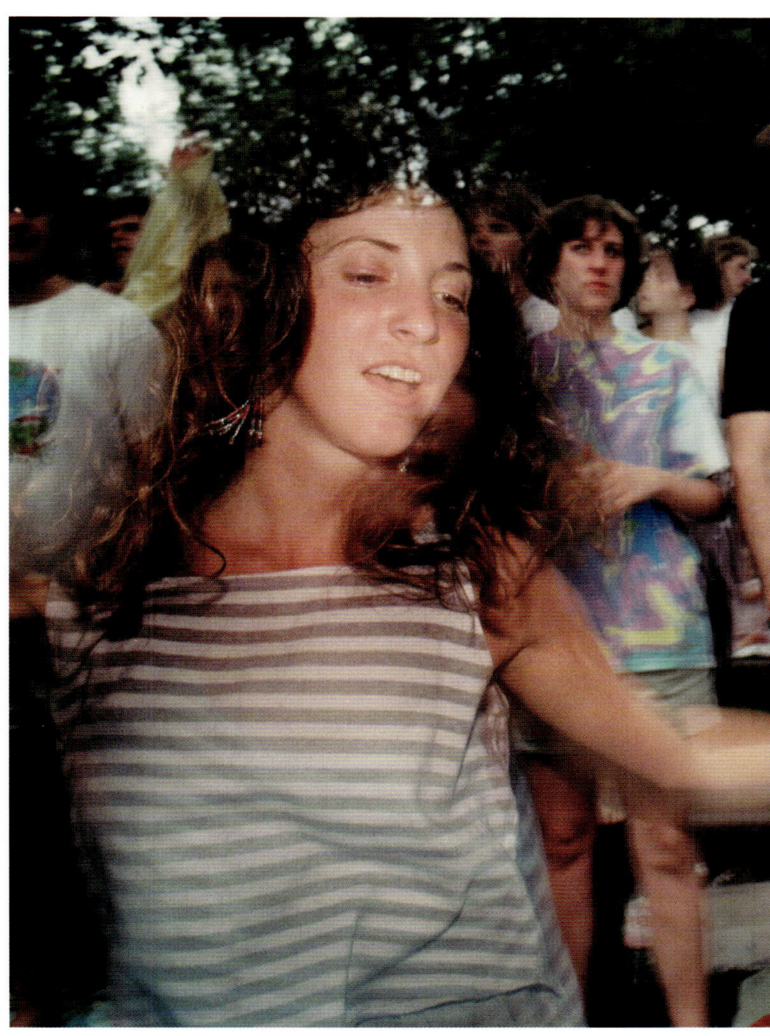

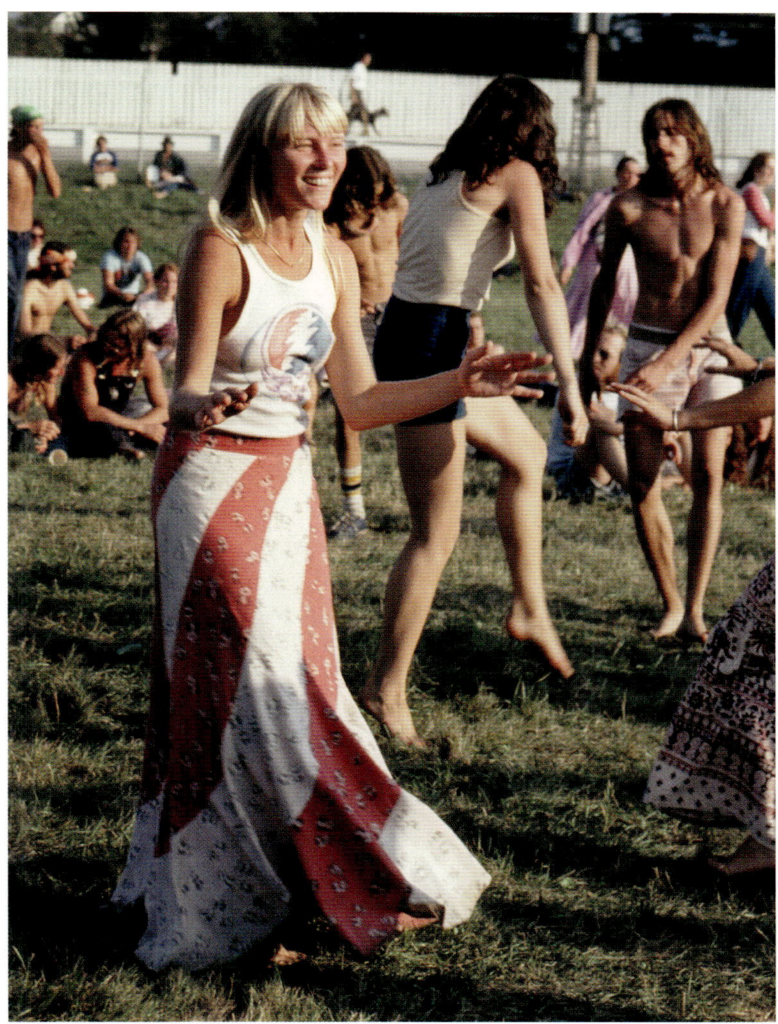

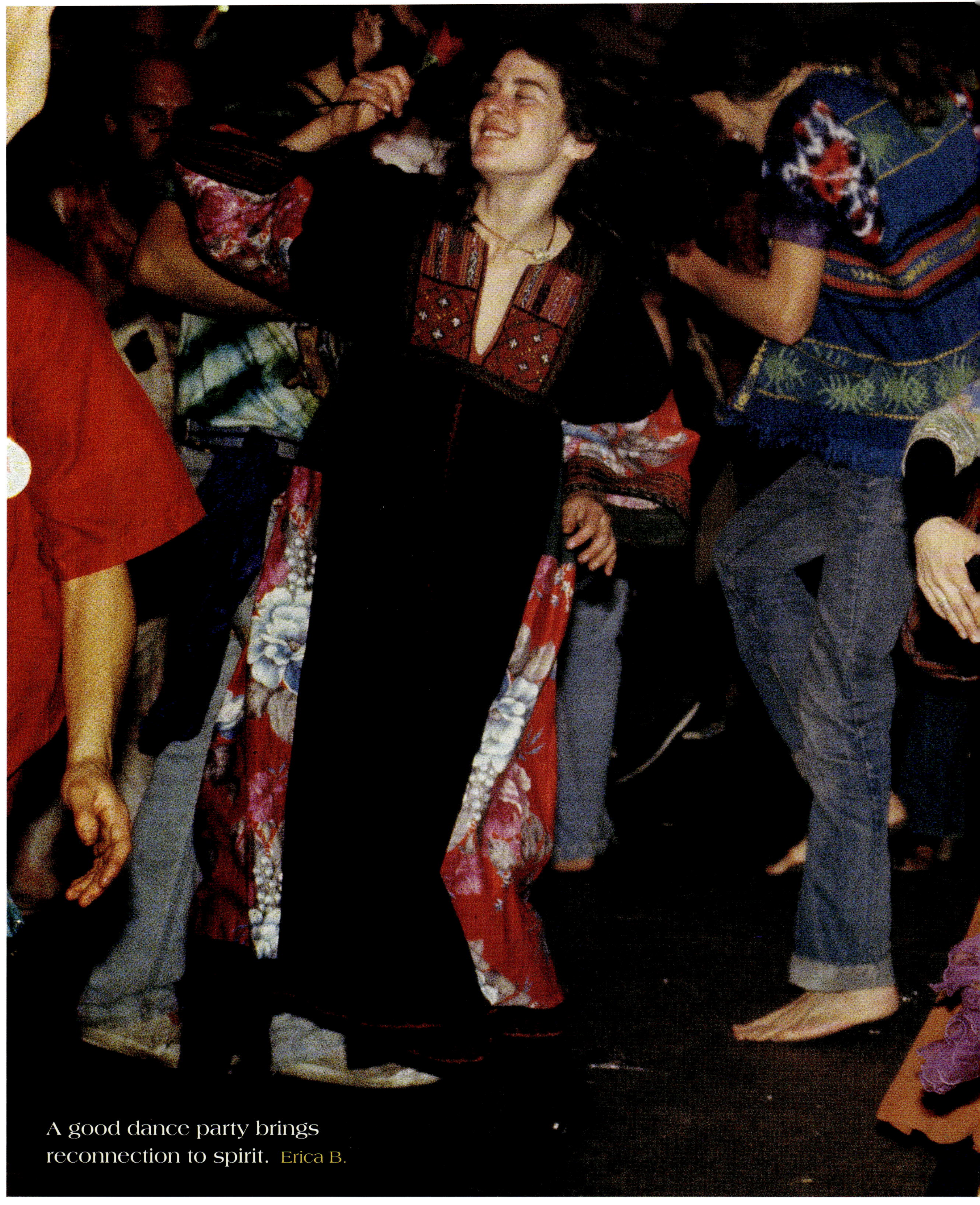

A good dance party brings reconnection to spirit. Erica B.

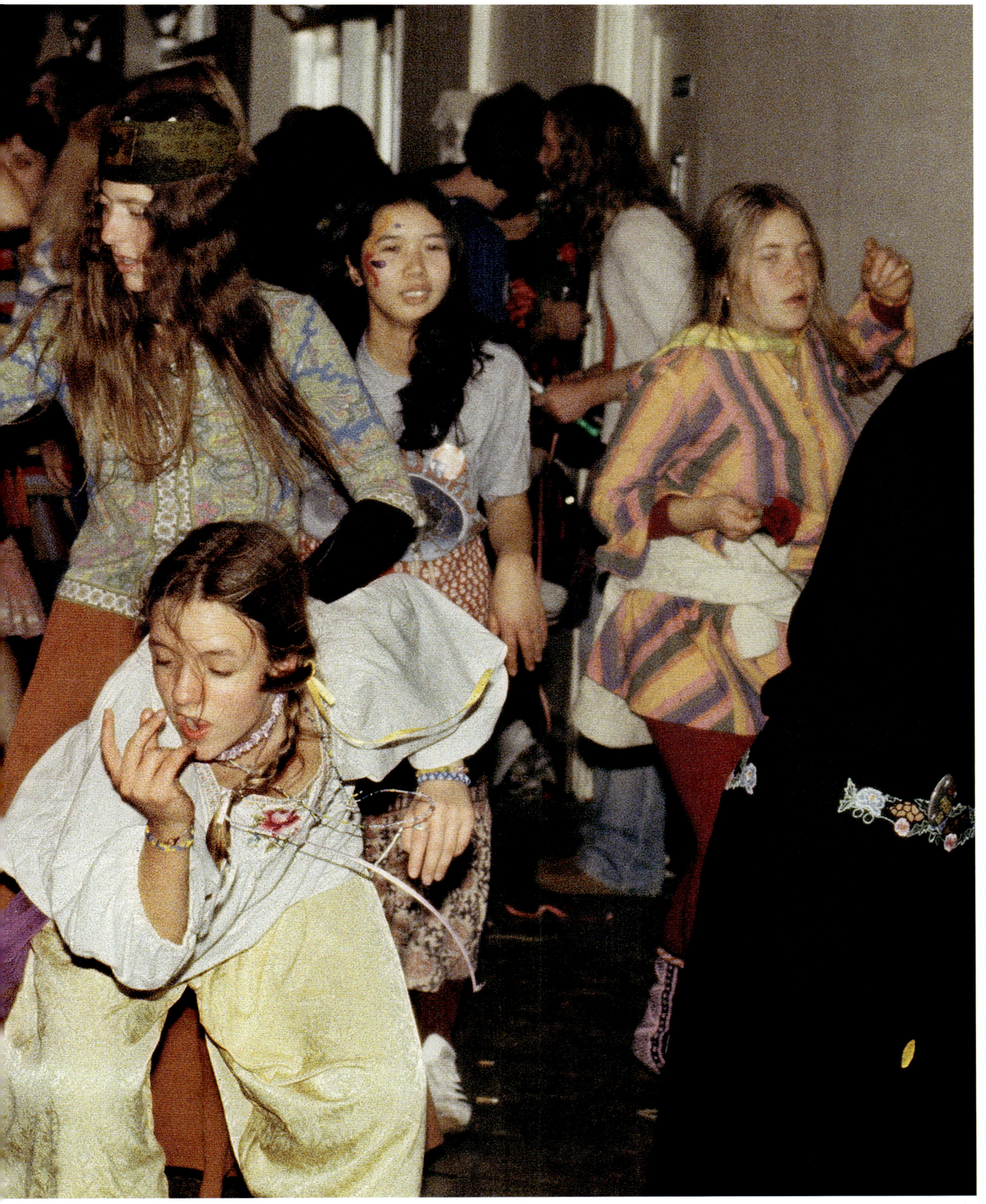

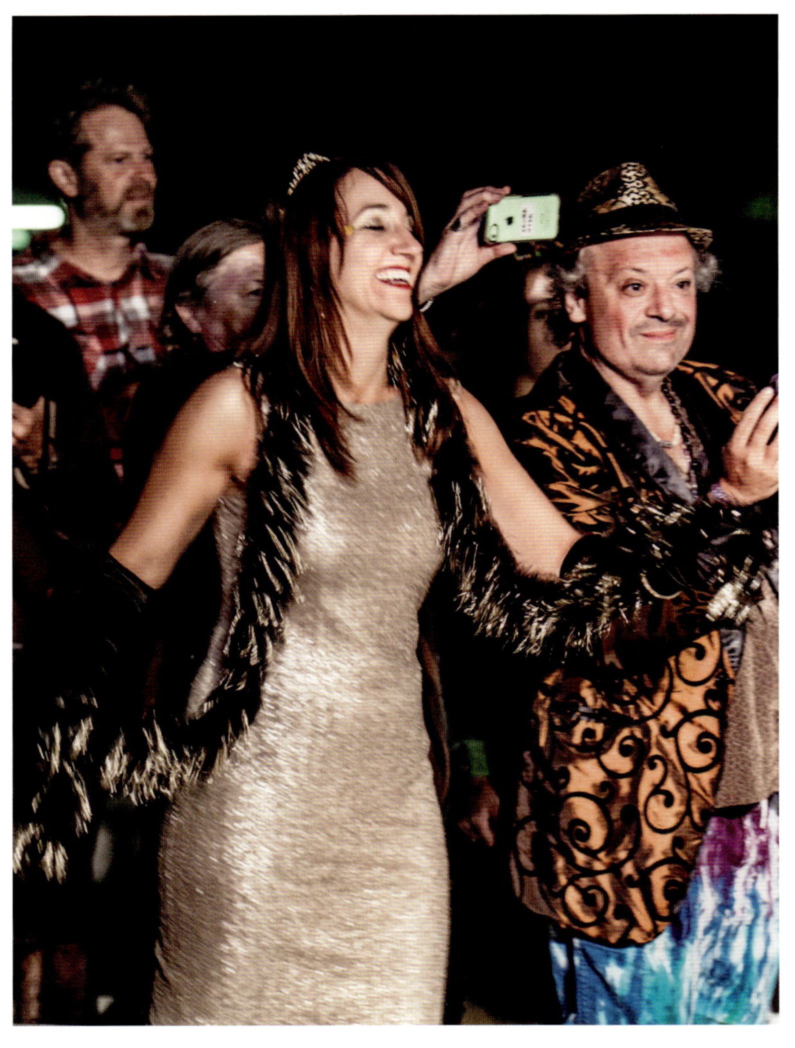

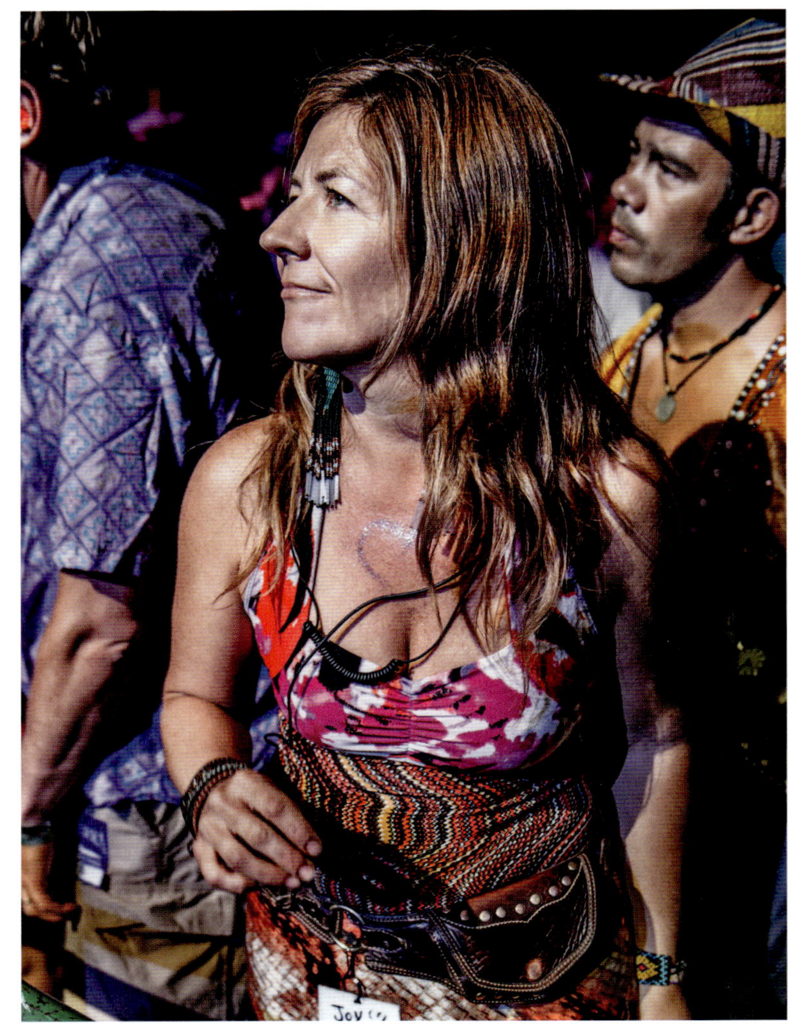

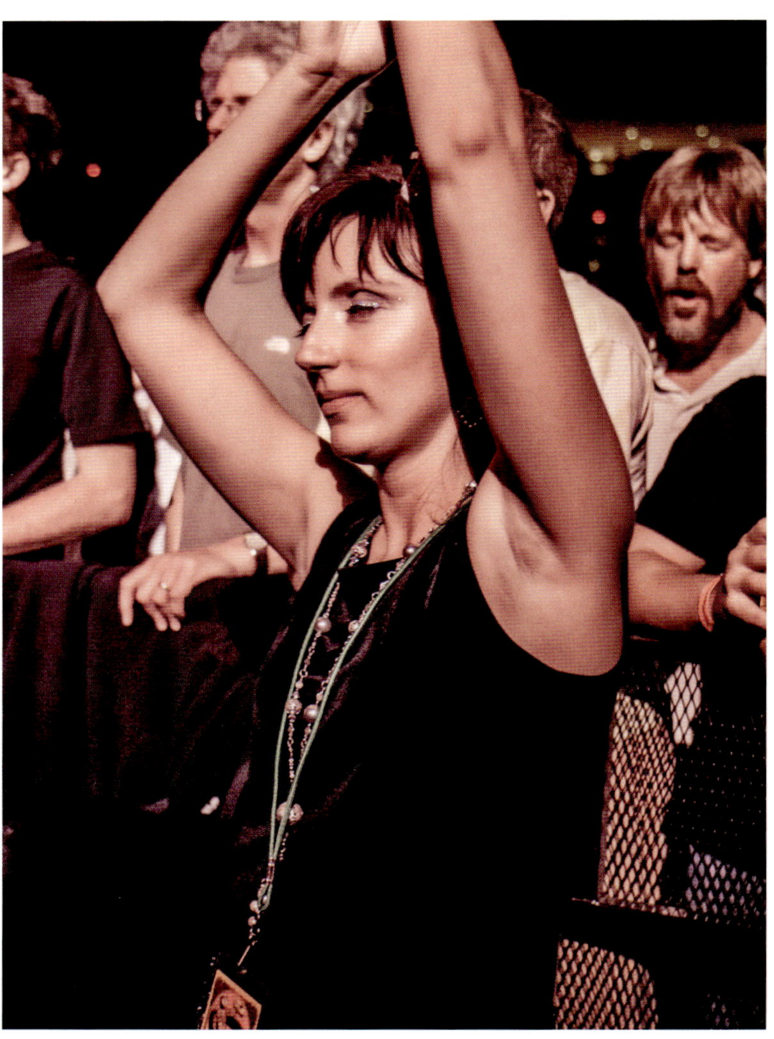

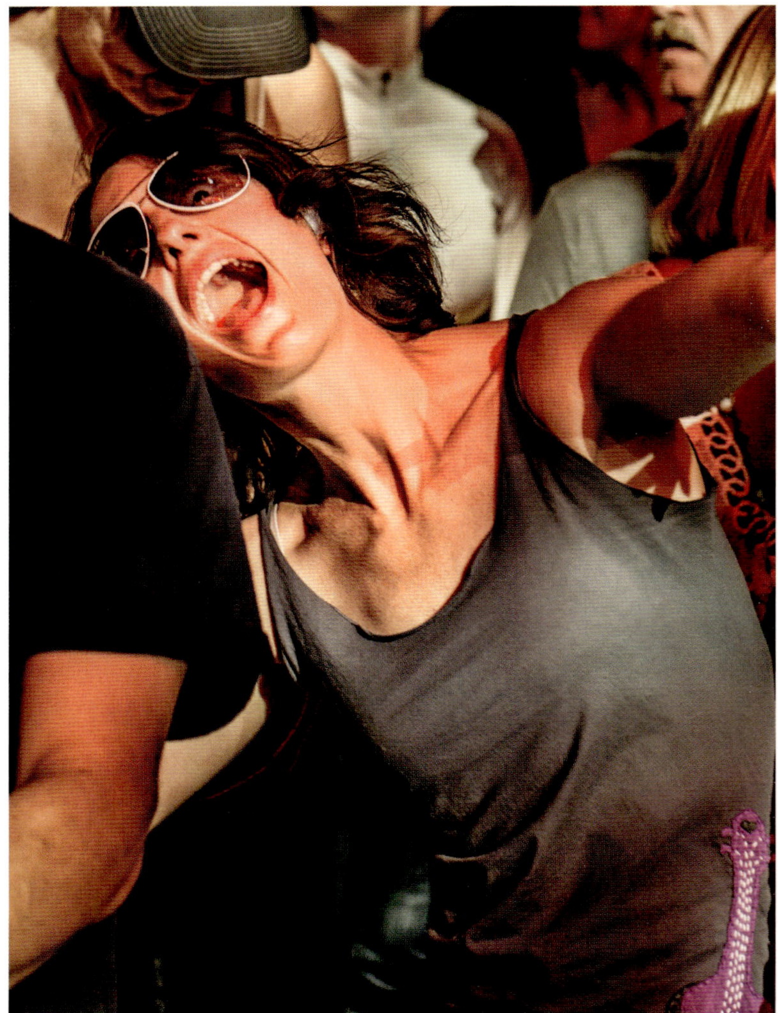

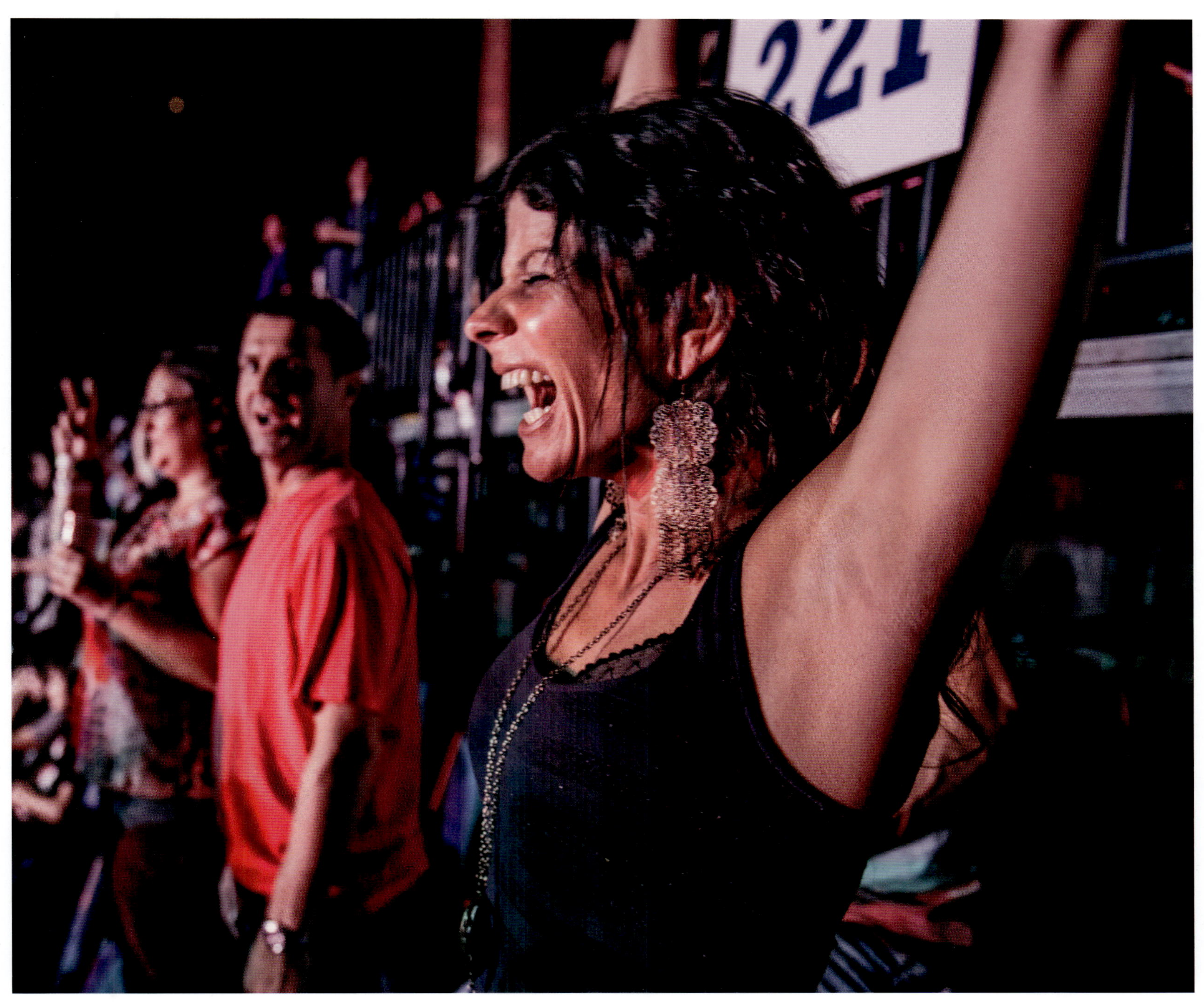

Music is my therapy, passion, and love; the deepest, most spiritual connection to myself and the universe. It allows me the strength to be my truest self, to live in the moment, completely free ... Robin A. (pictured)

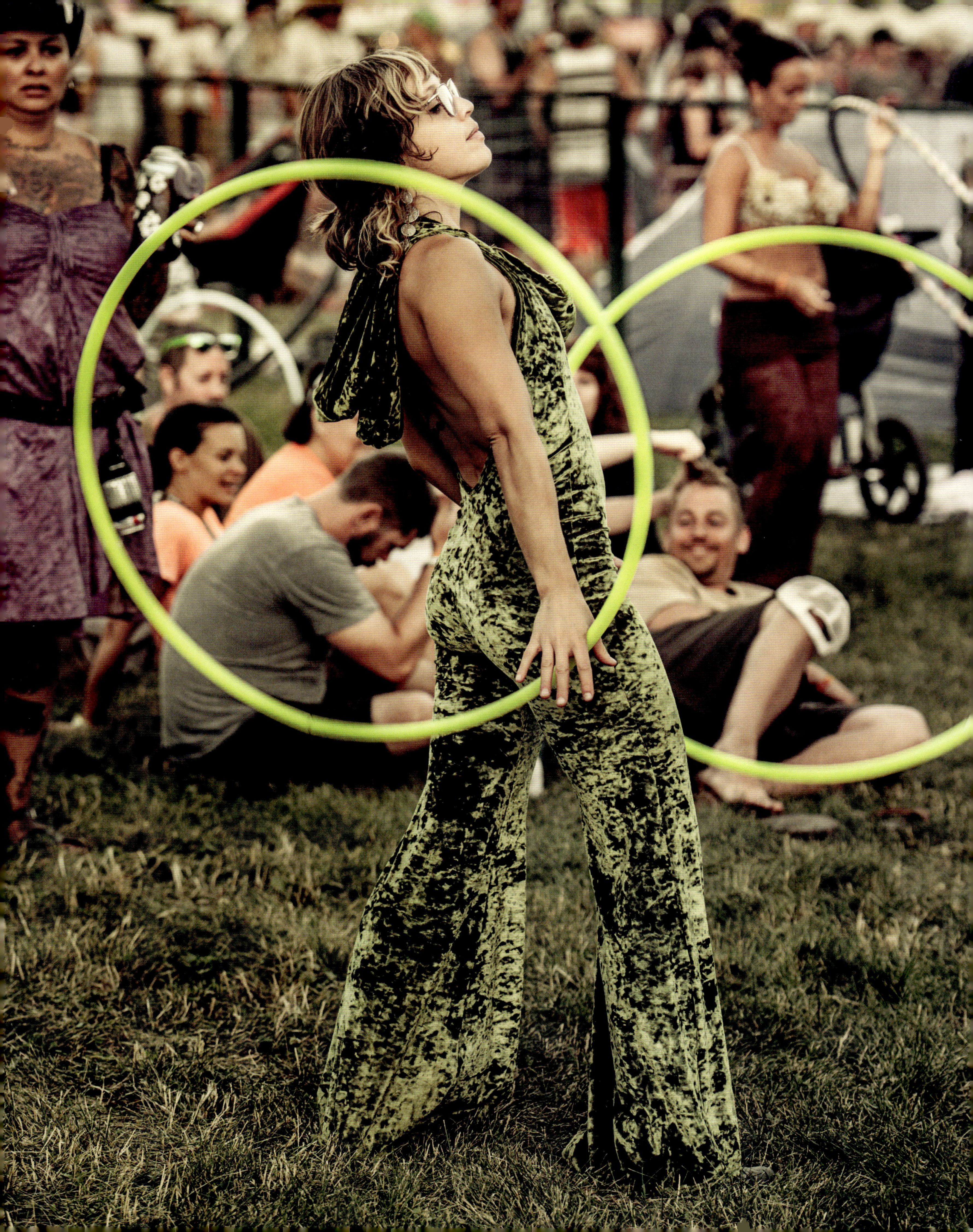

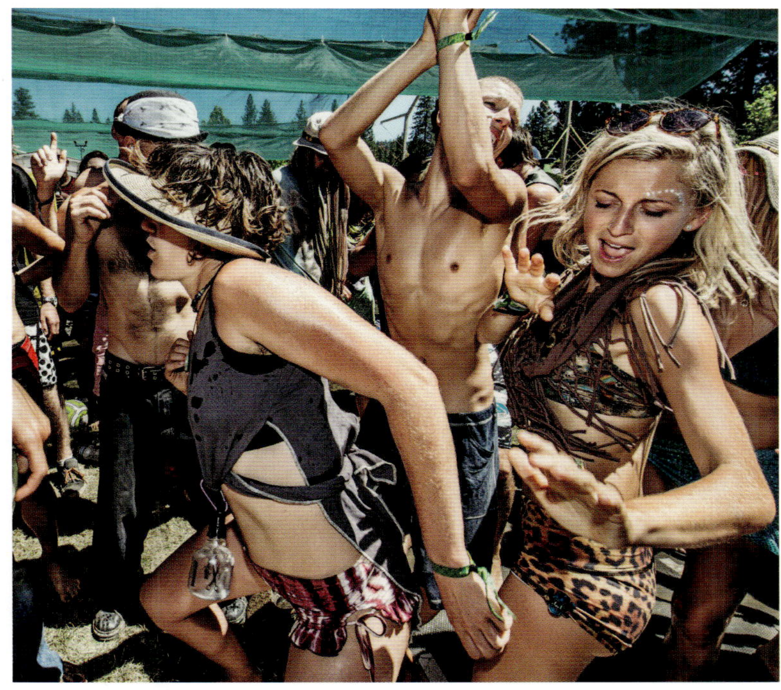

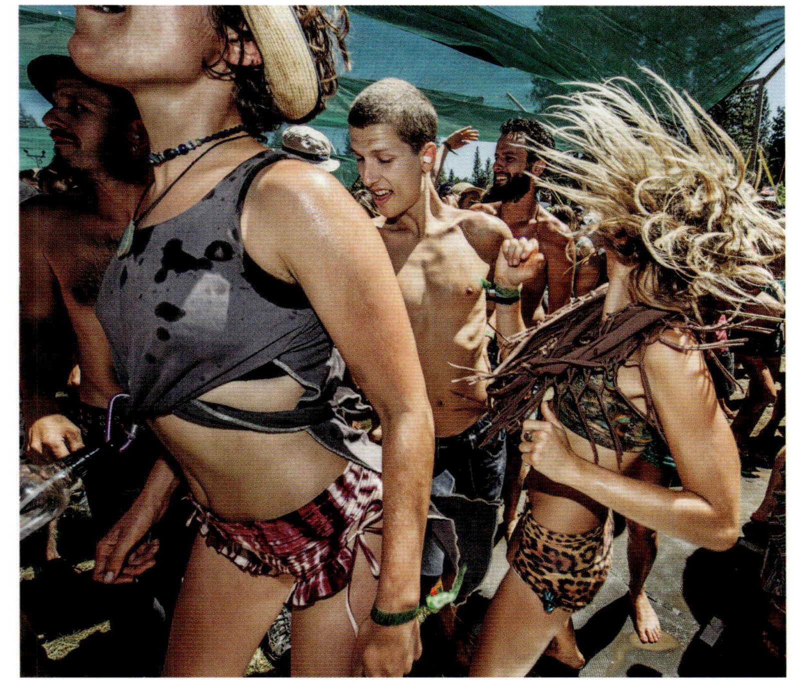

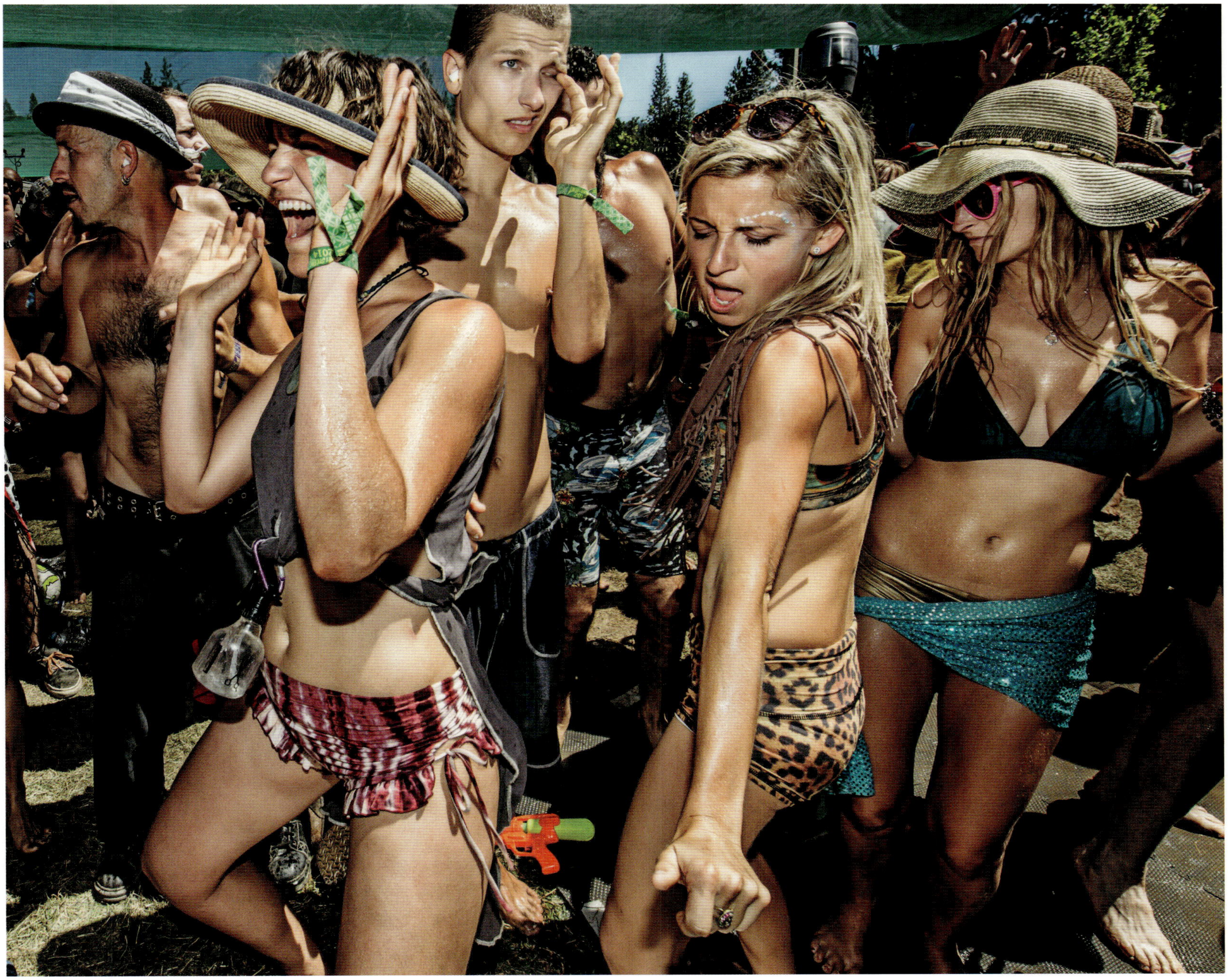

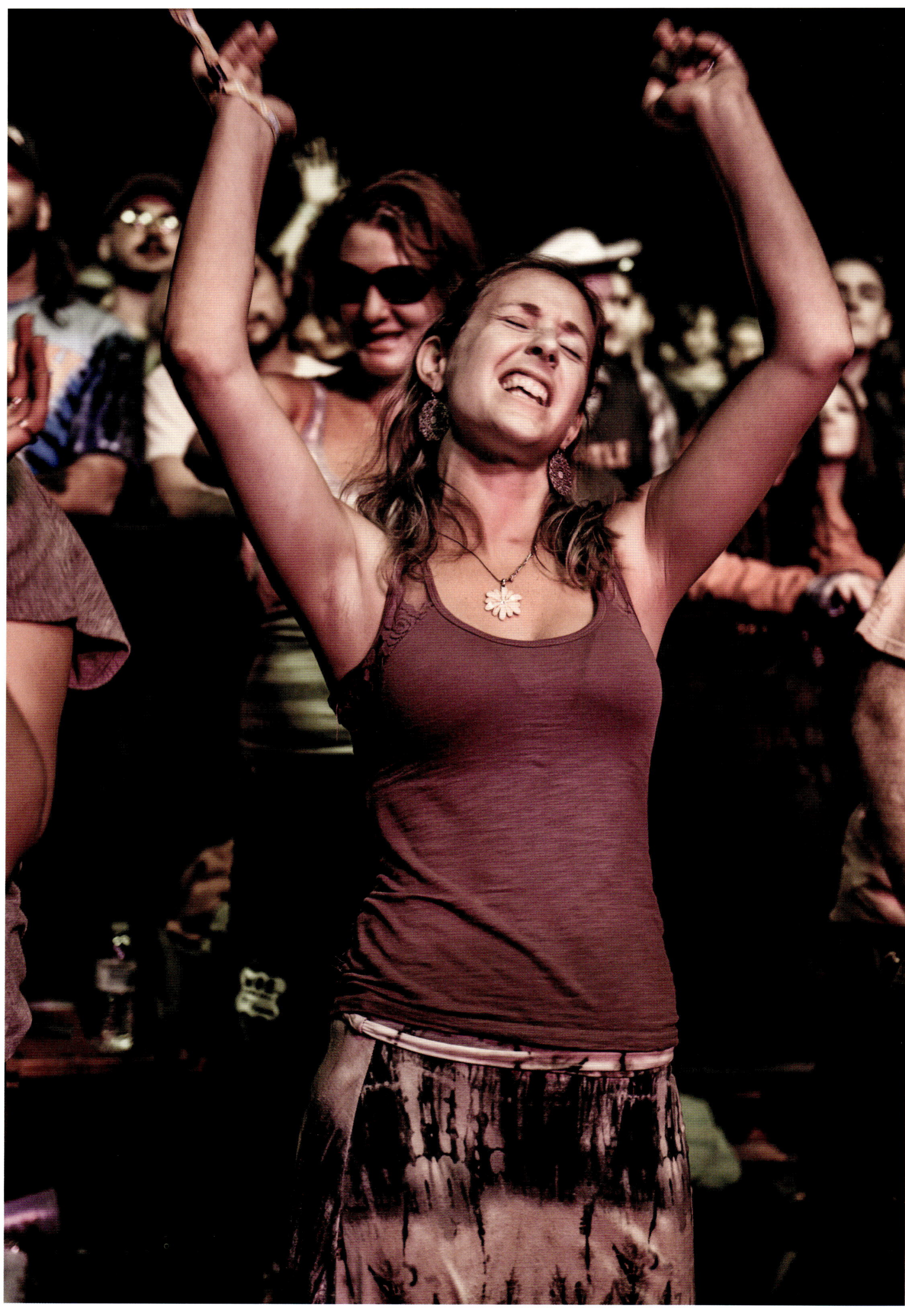

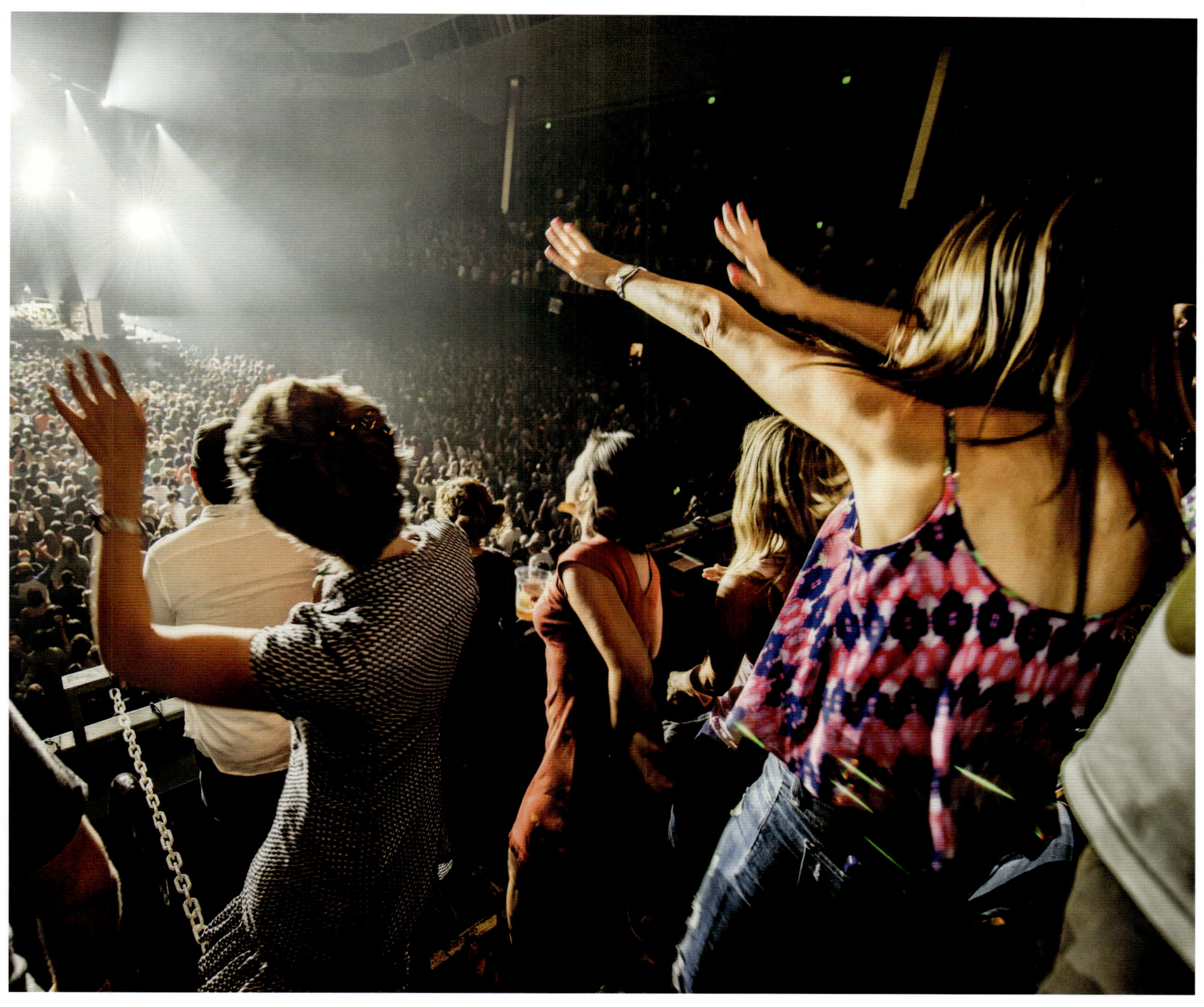

My personal inspiration is an infinite yearning to be around my people. Even if I wanted to go back, I could never. I am forever changed, forever grateful, forever on the road. Mary S.

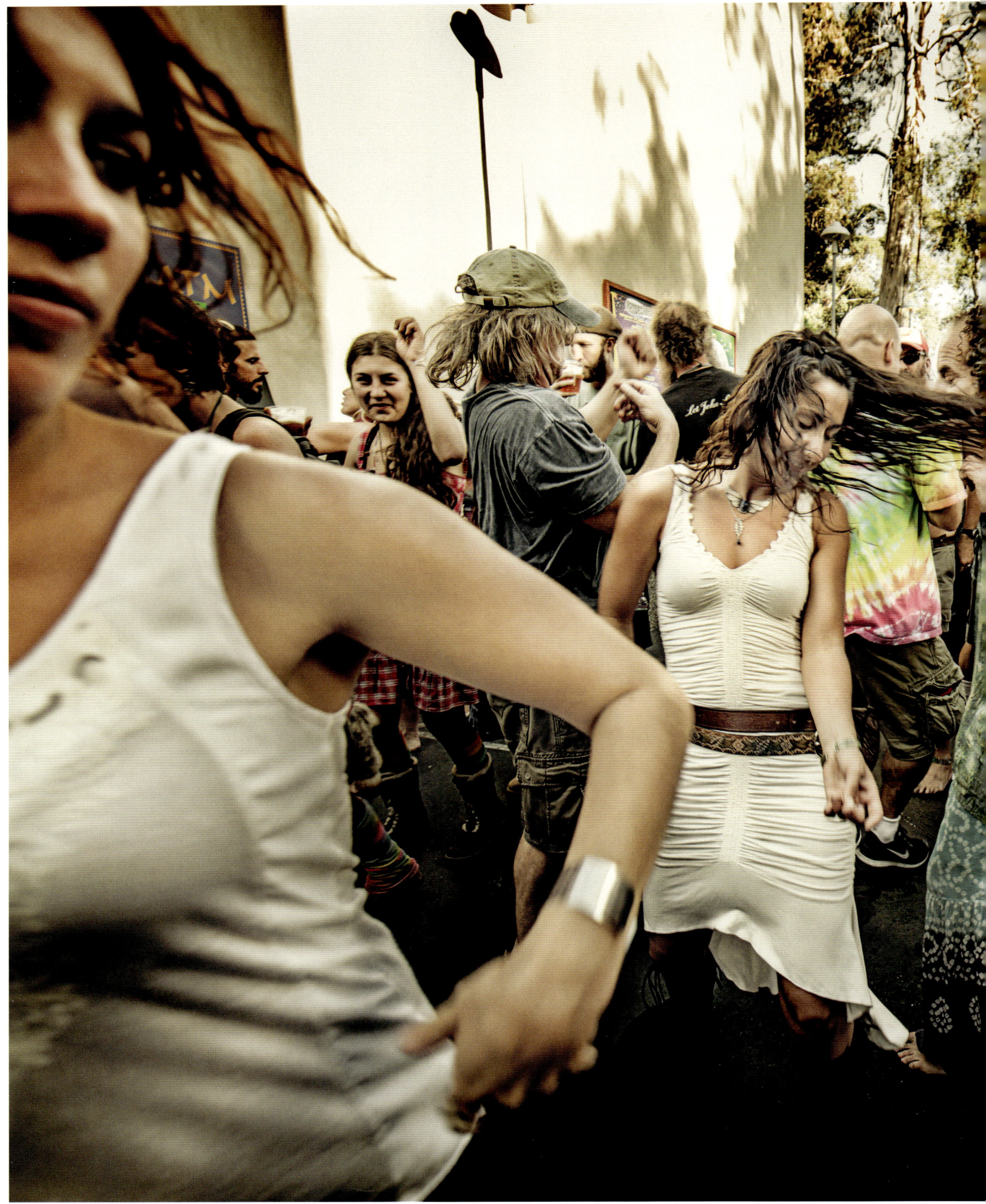

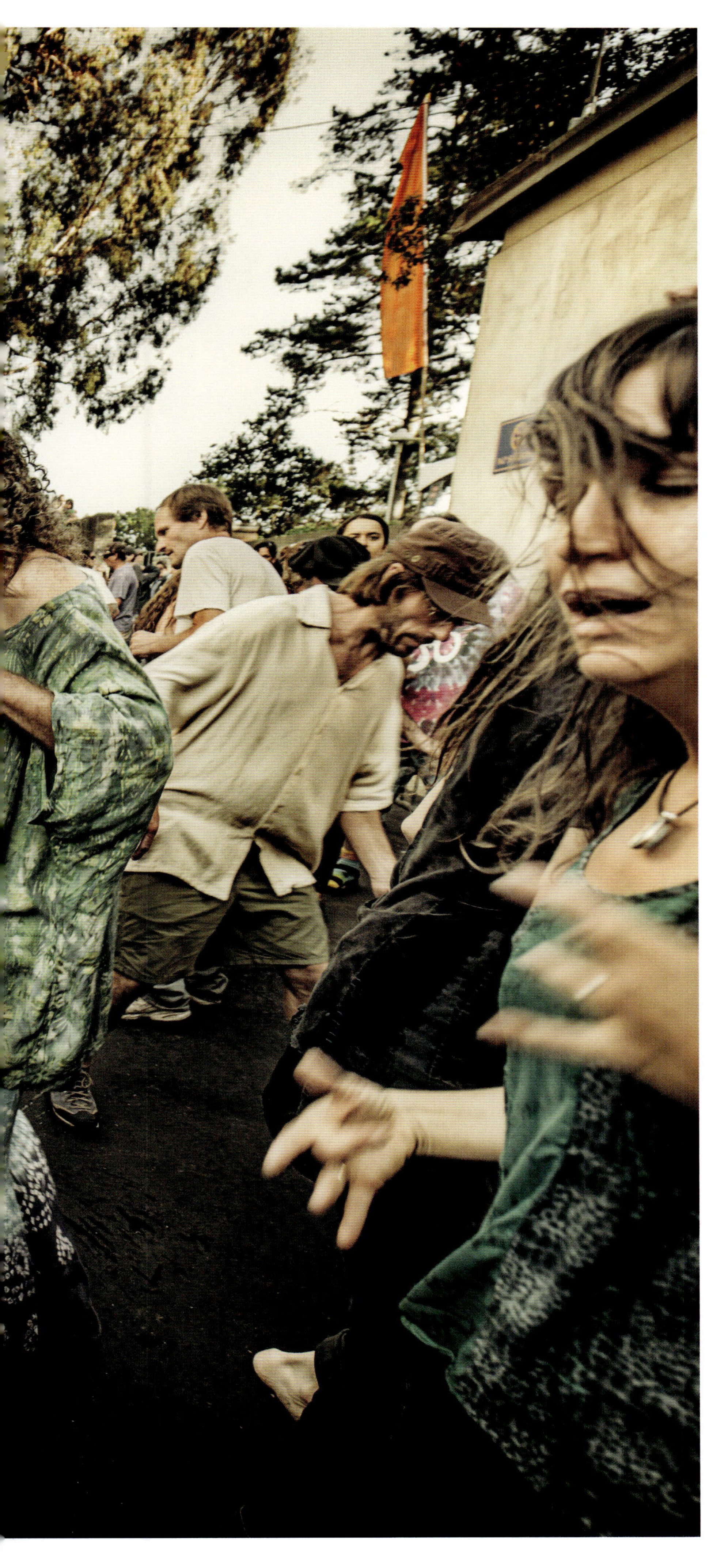

I love enjoying the vibrations of music while I'm underneath the sun.

Natalie N.

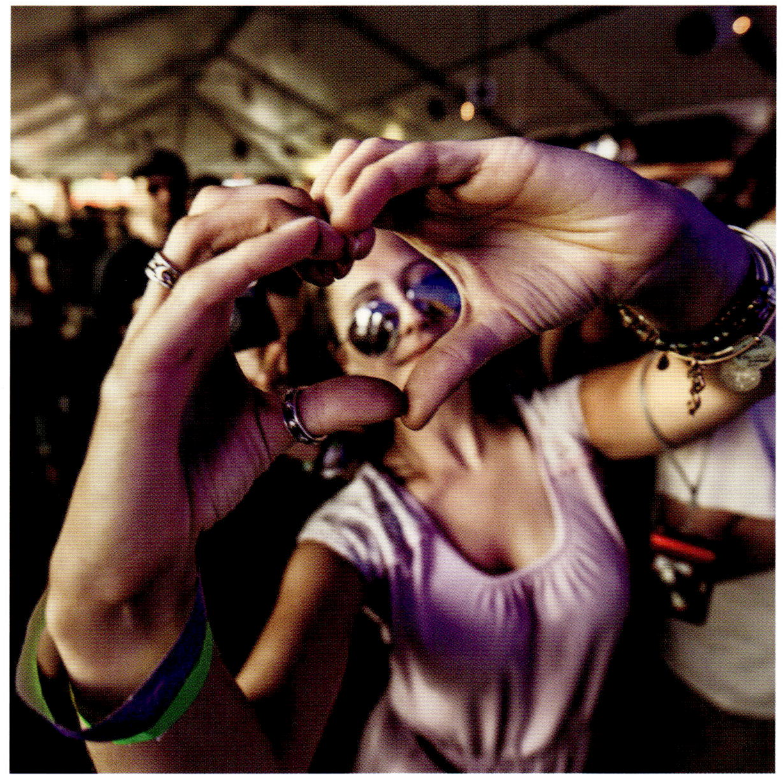

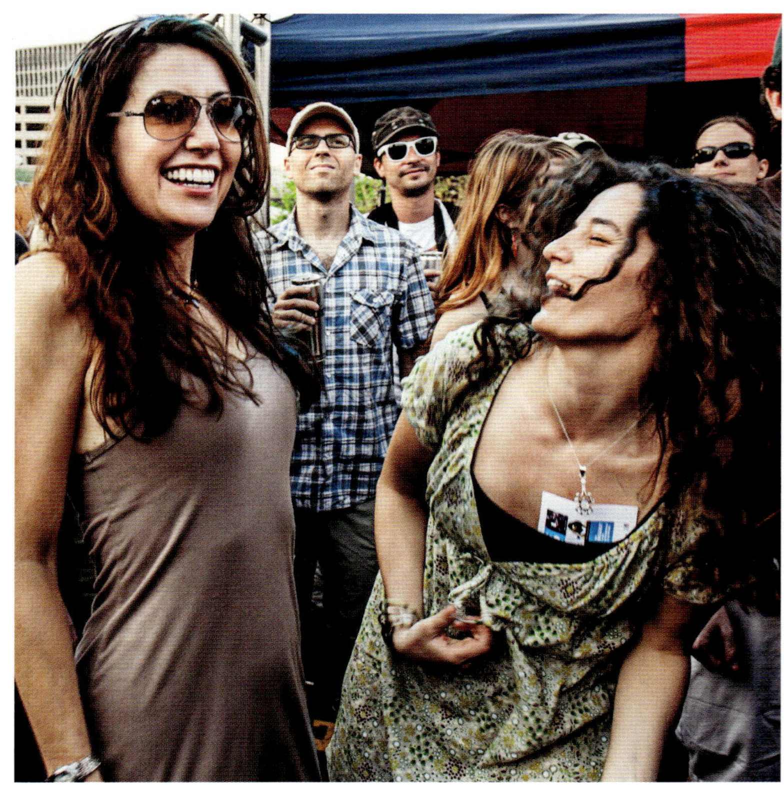

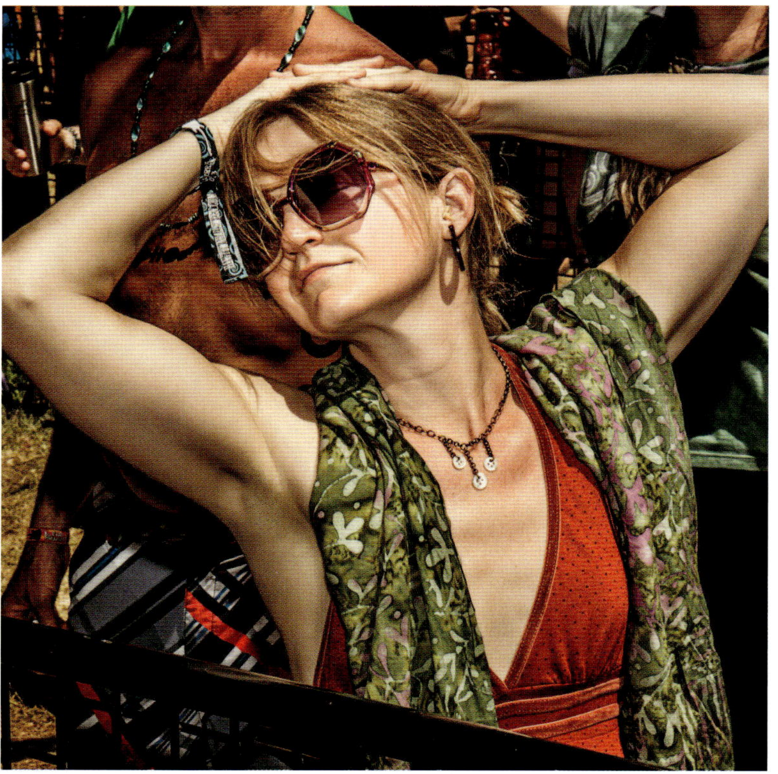

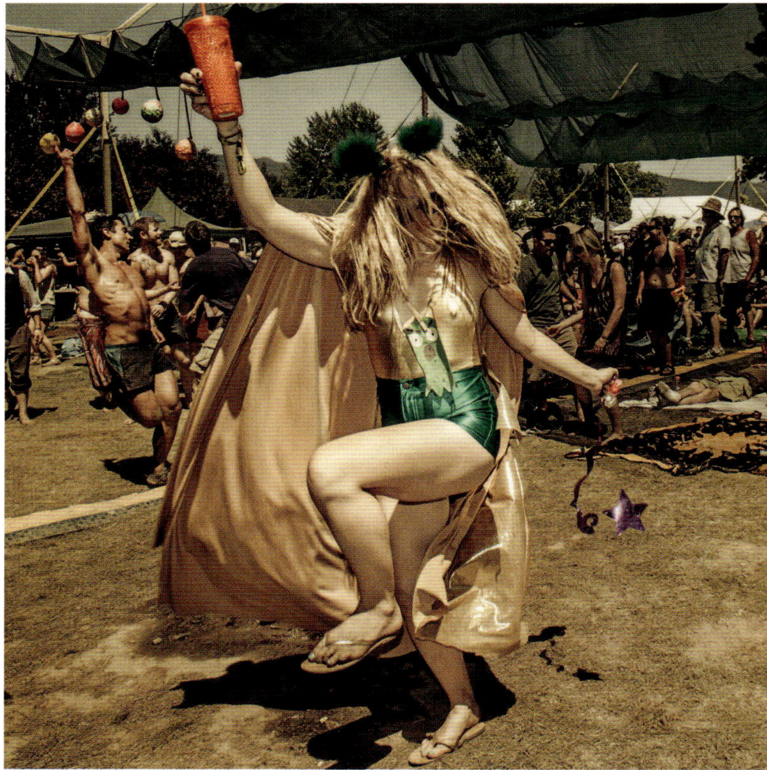

Live music for me is a magical, spiritual lava that rushes through my blood and wraps itself around my bones—a feeling of surrendering to the moment, becoming one with the music, and riding that wild wave. Jacqui I.

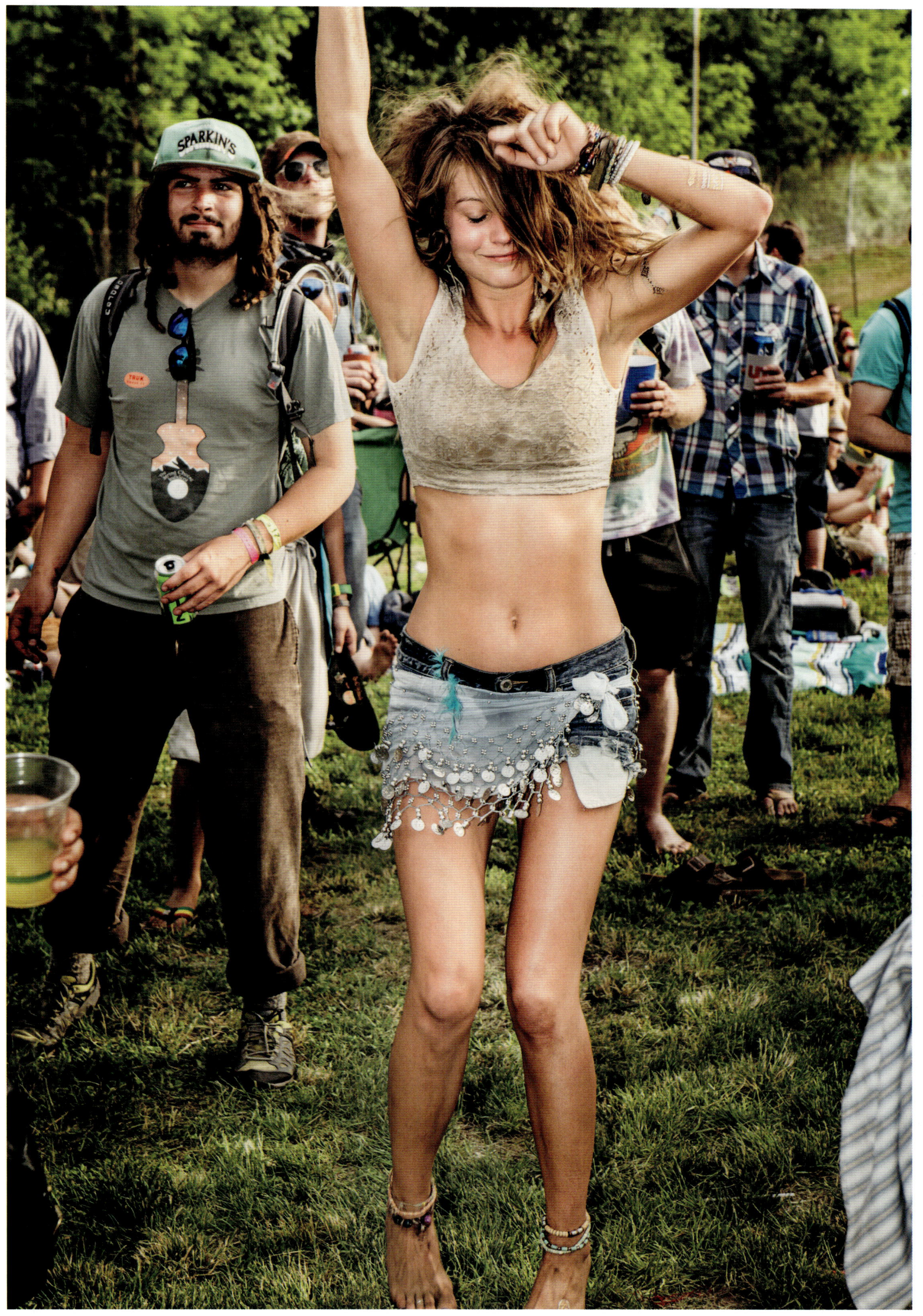
SPARKIN'S

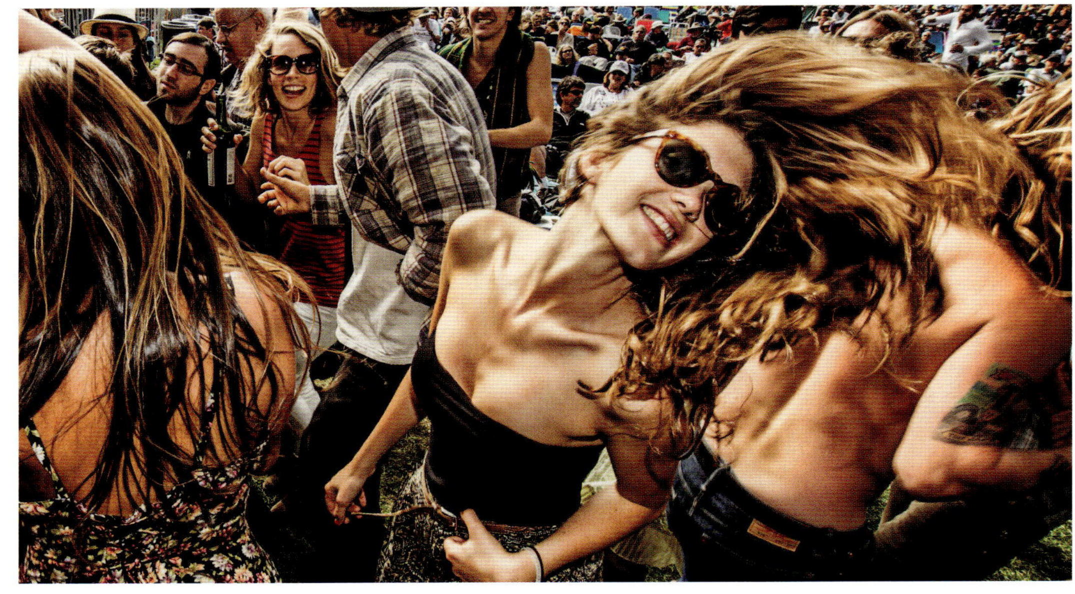
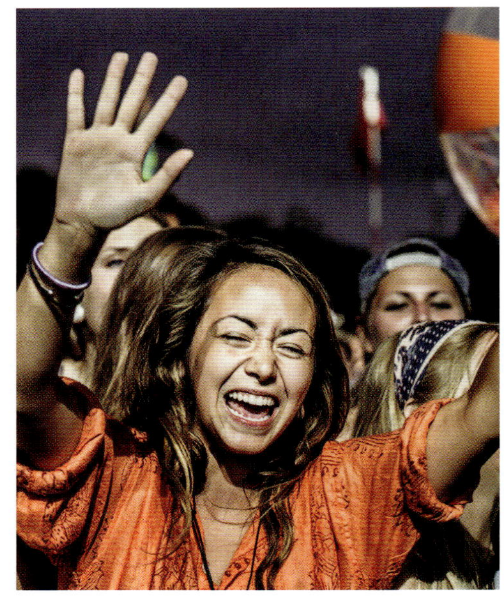
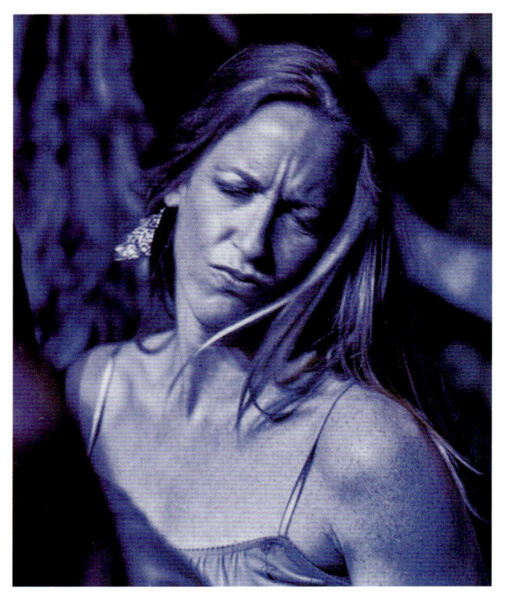
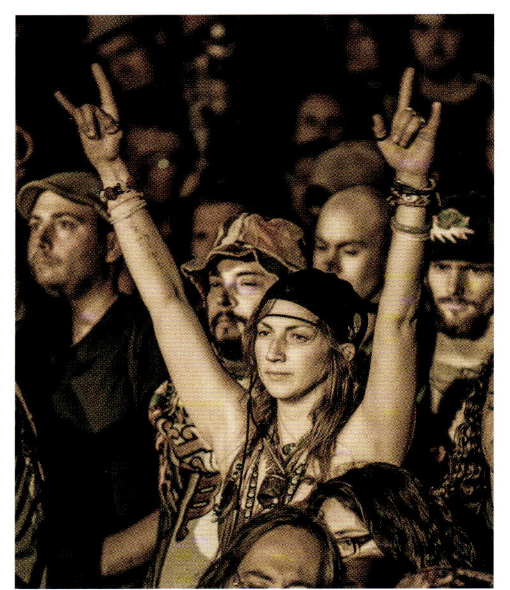
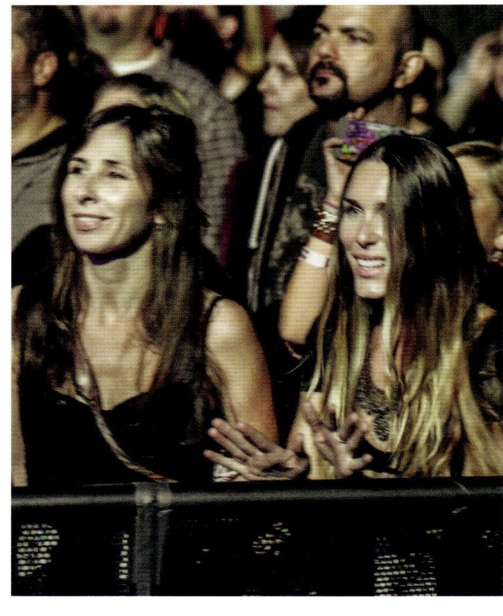
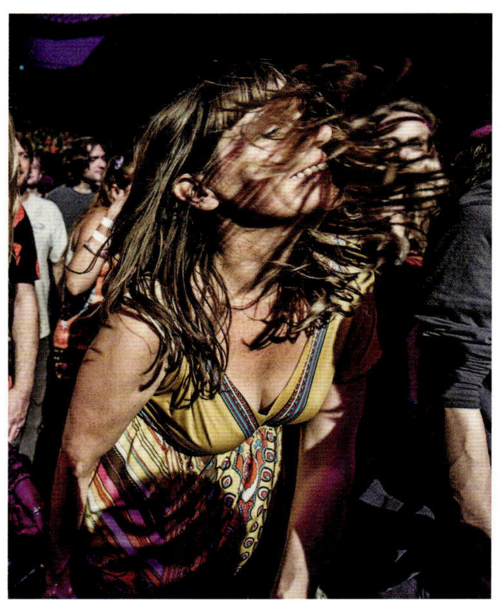
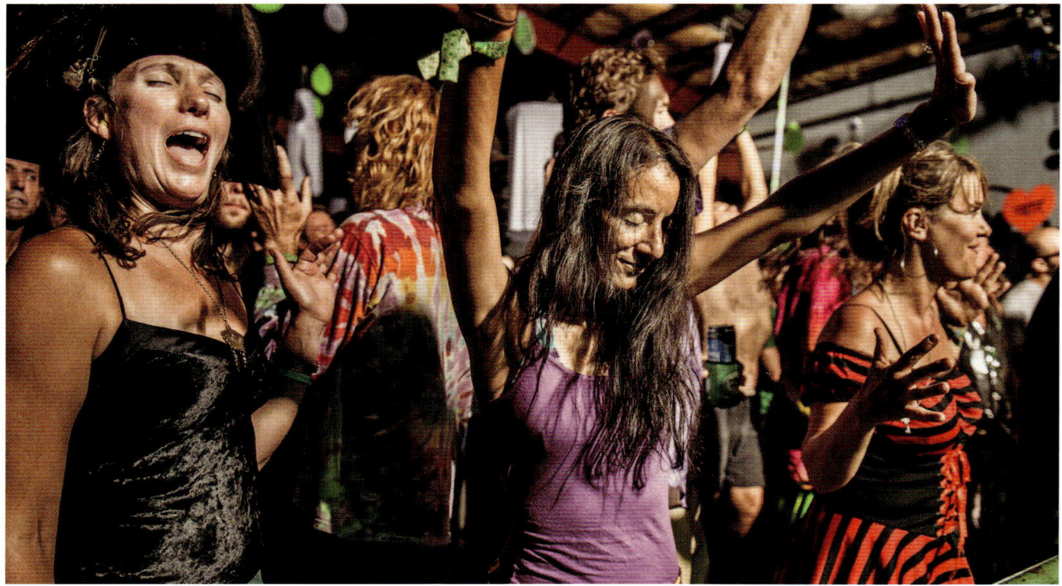

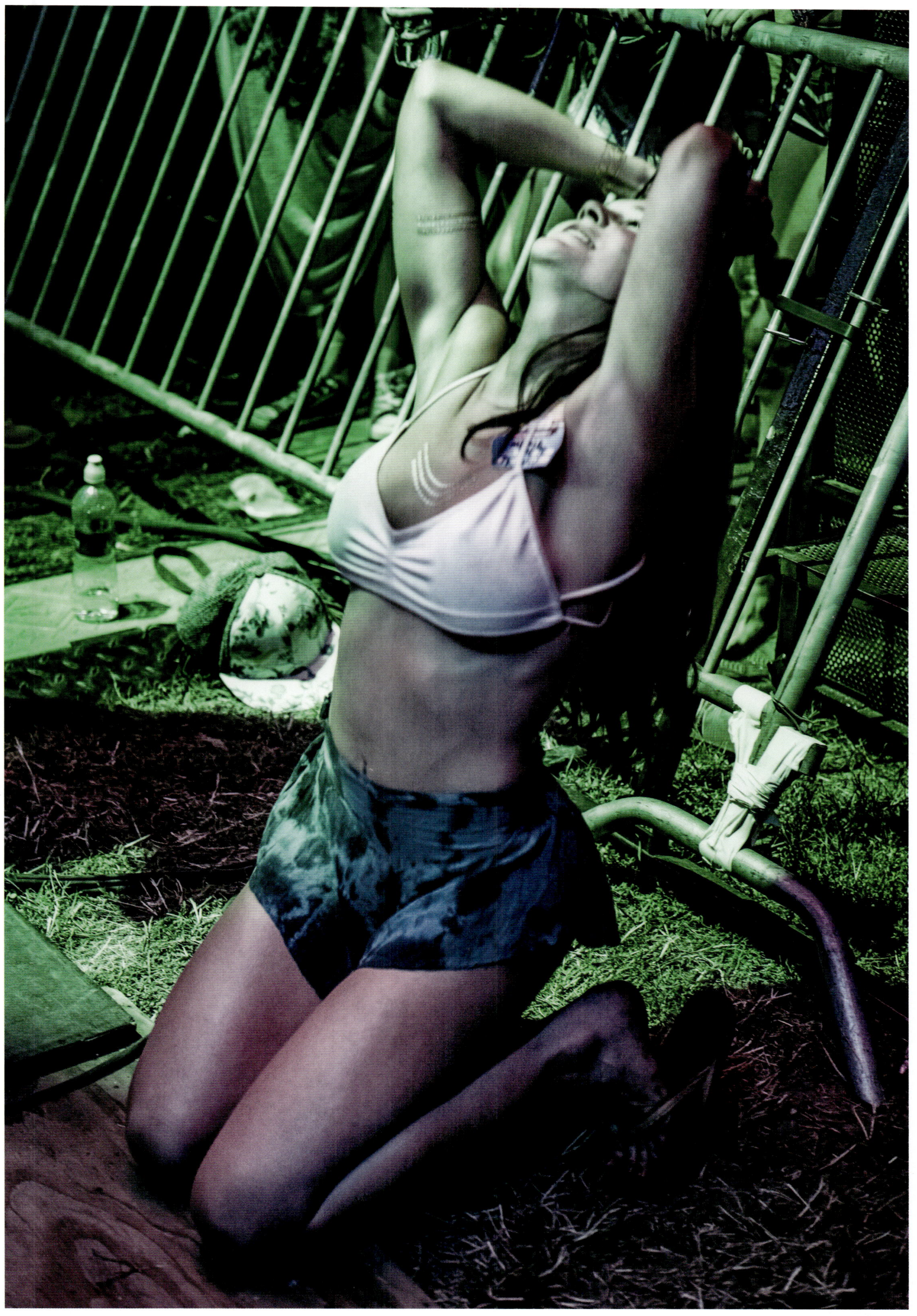

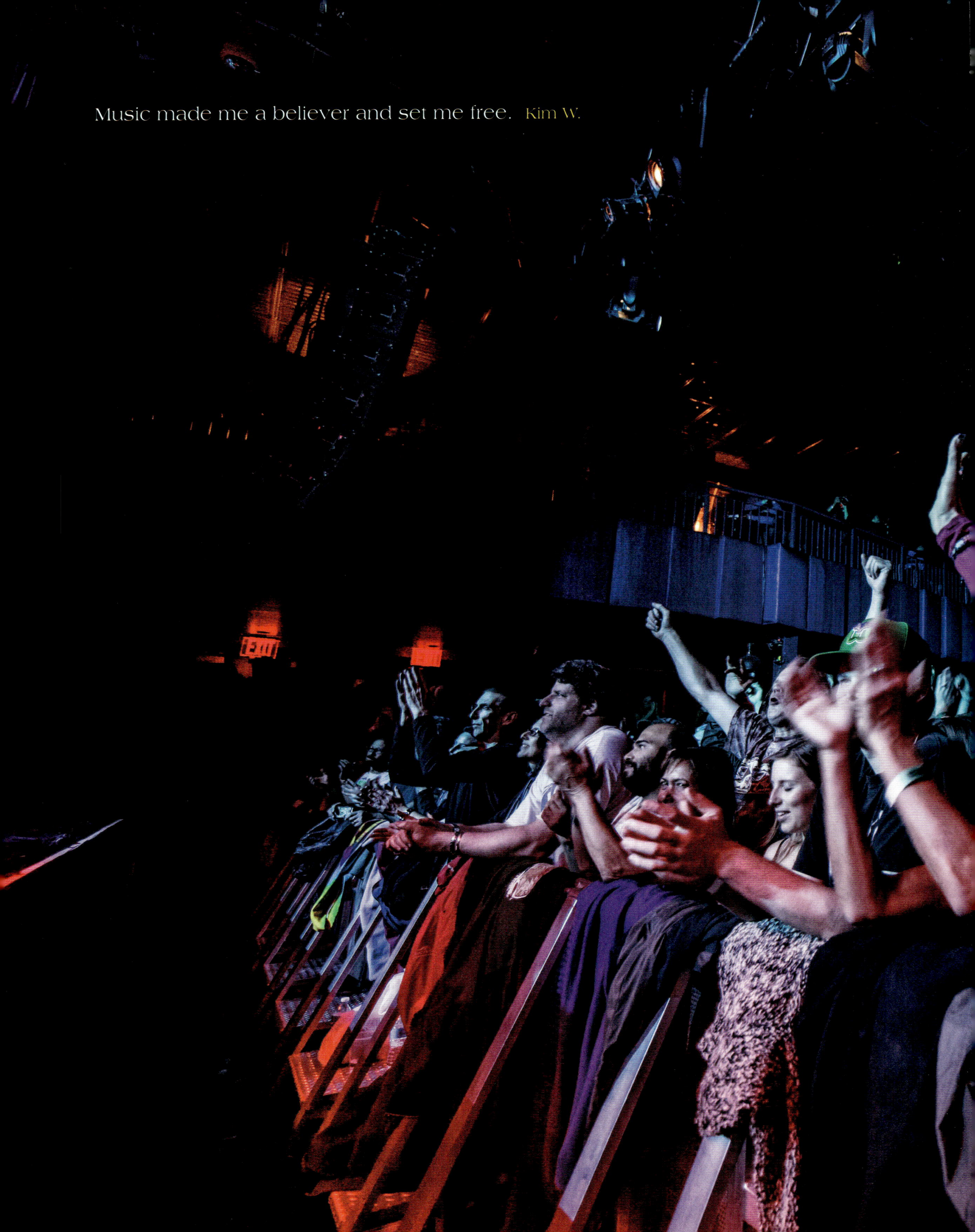

Music made me a believer and set me free. Kim W.

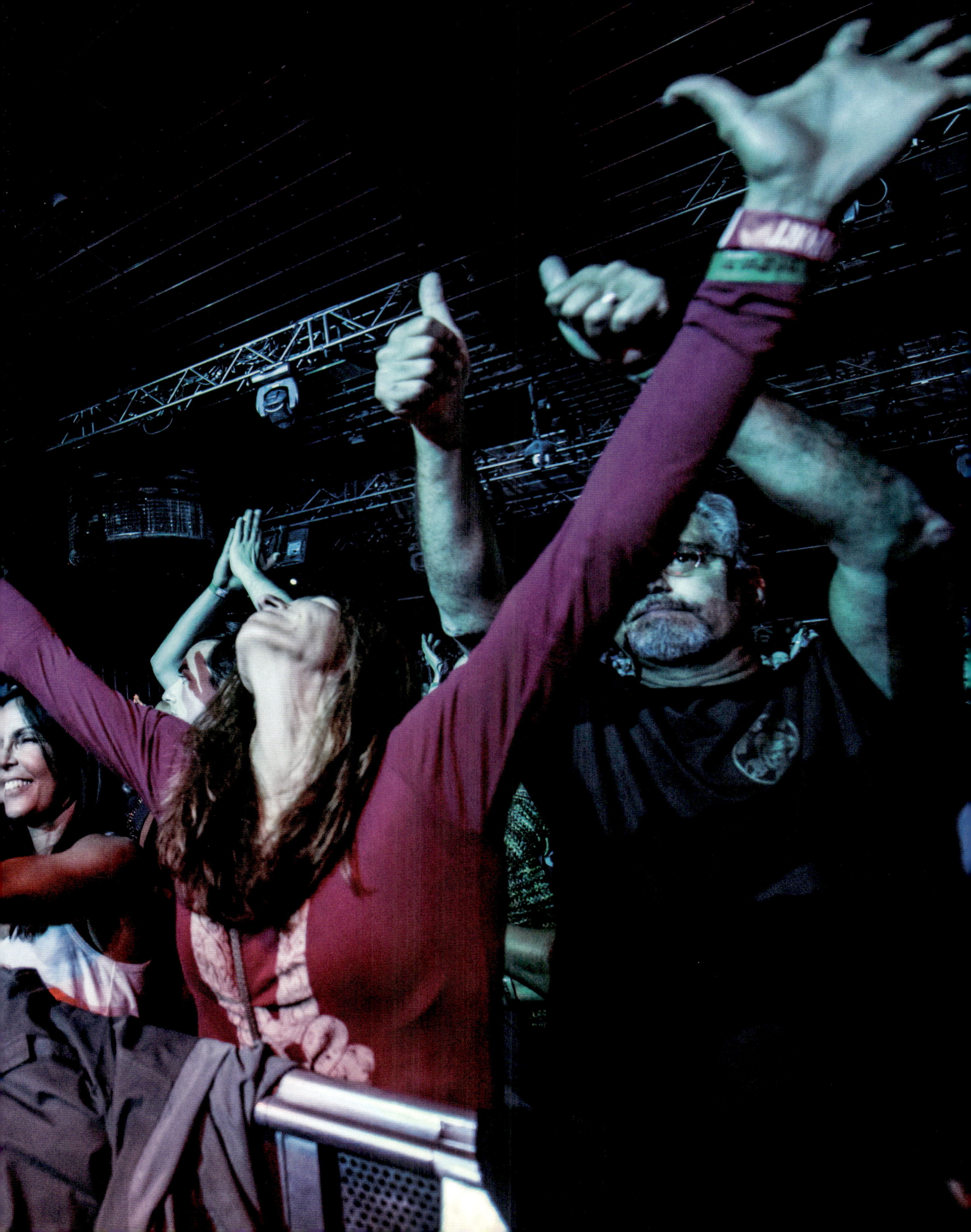

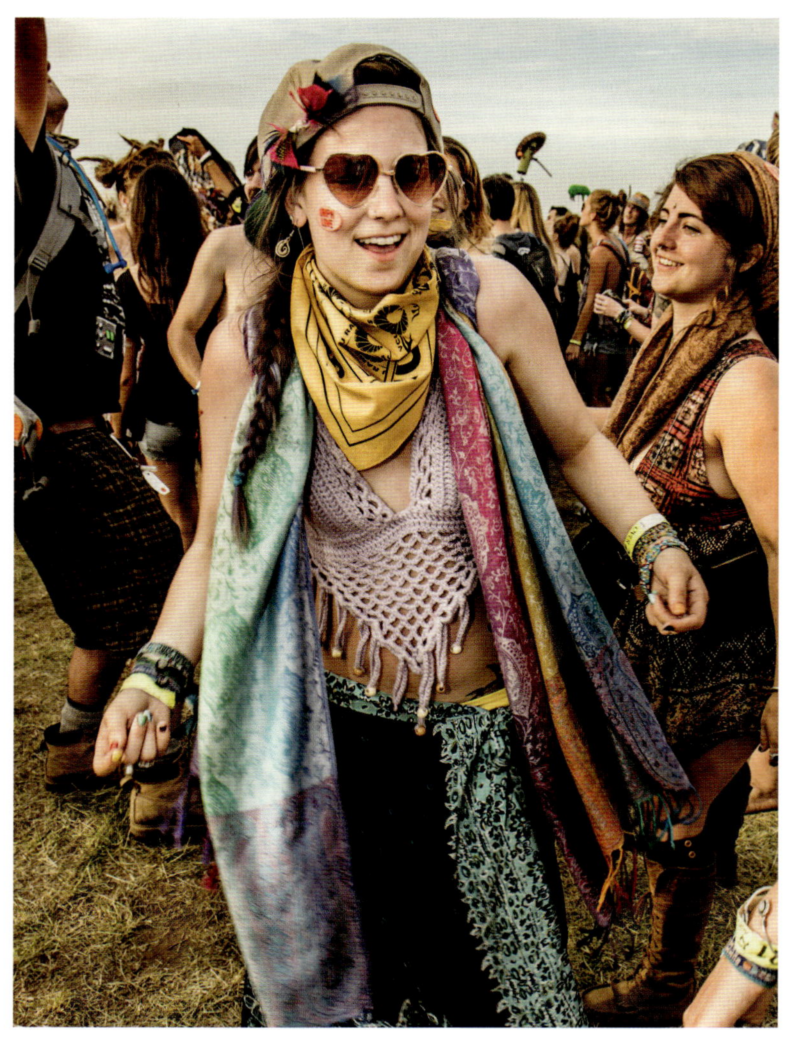

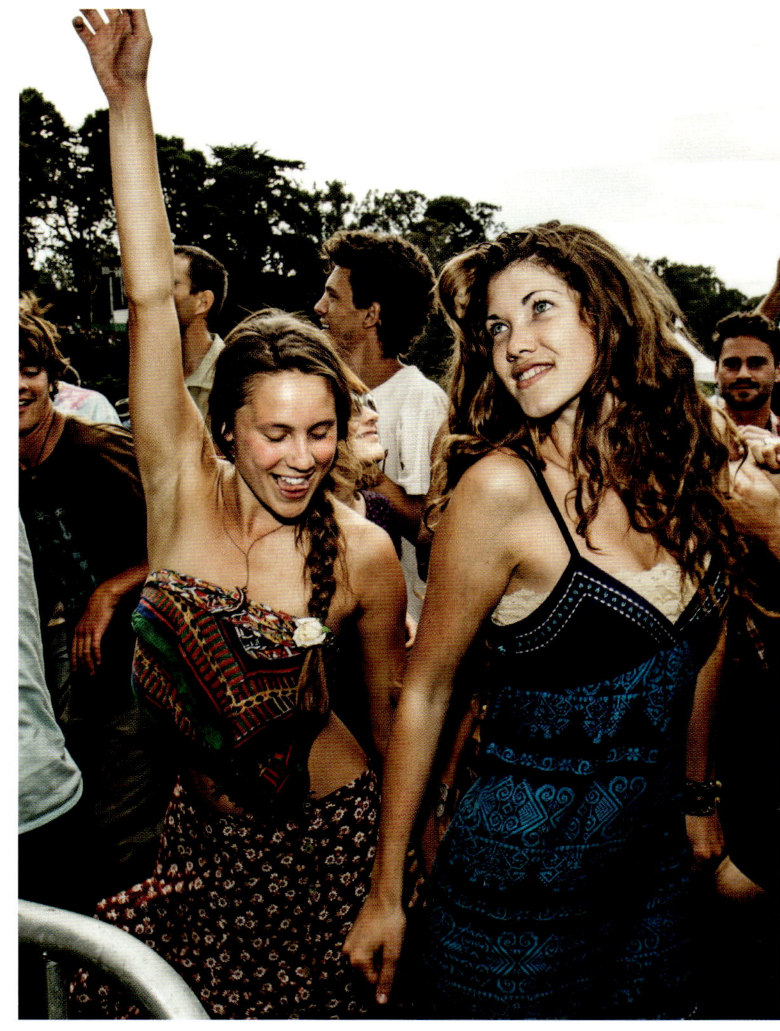

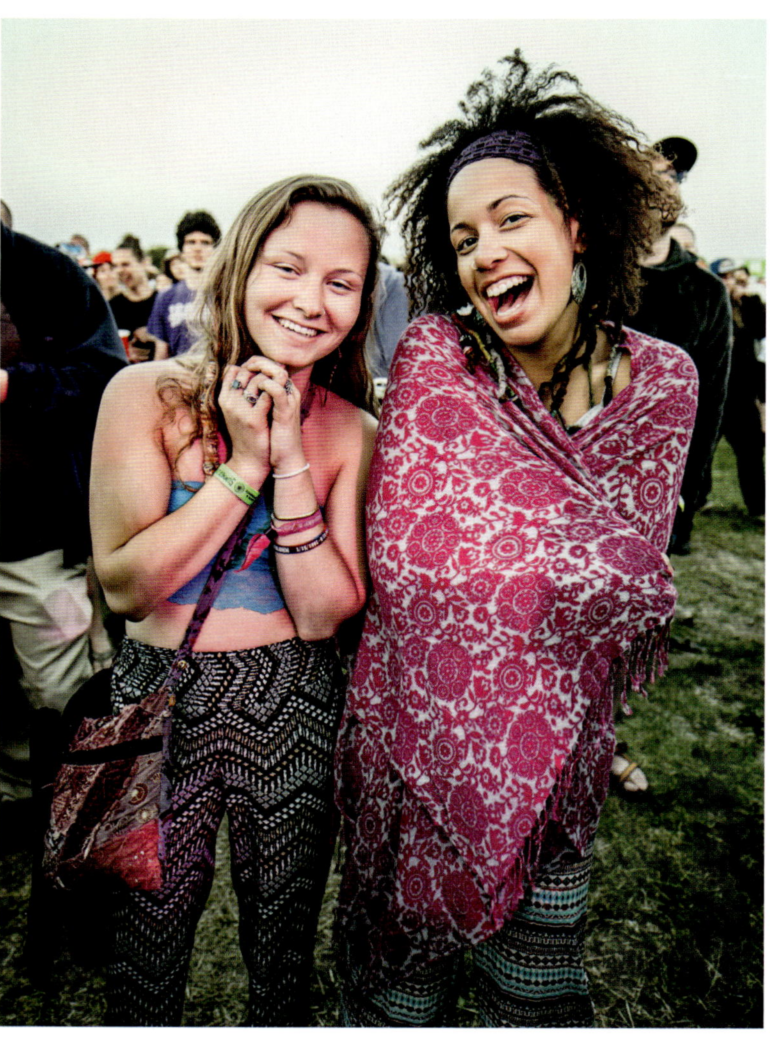

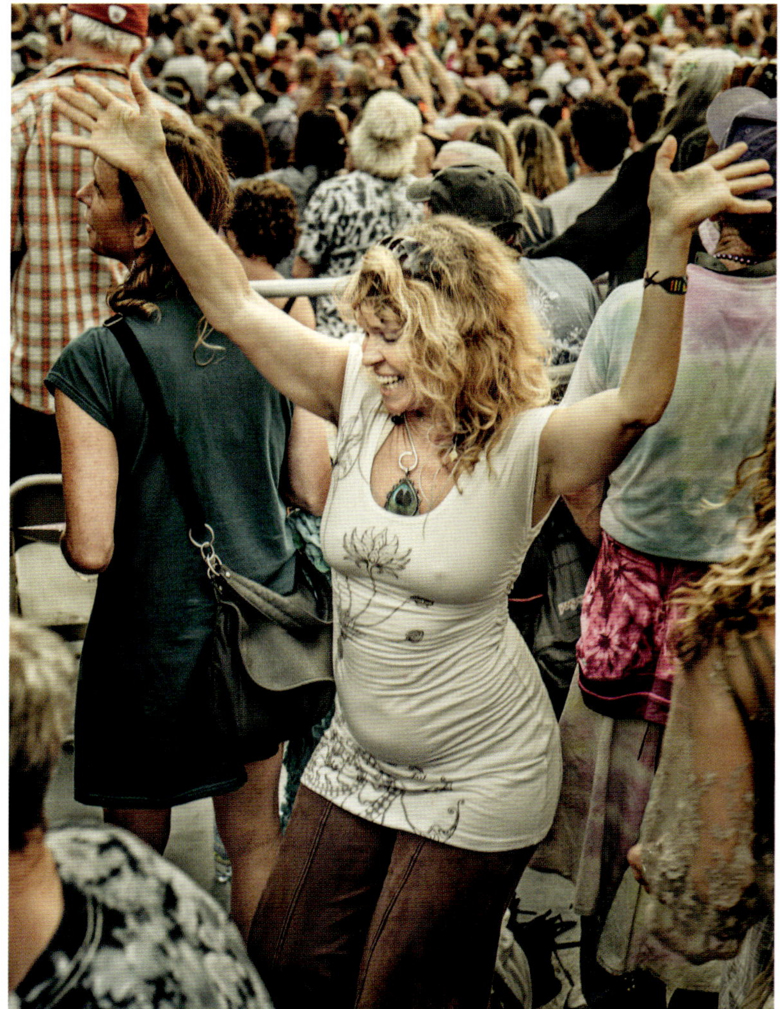

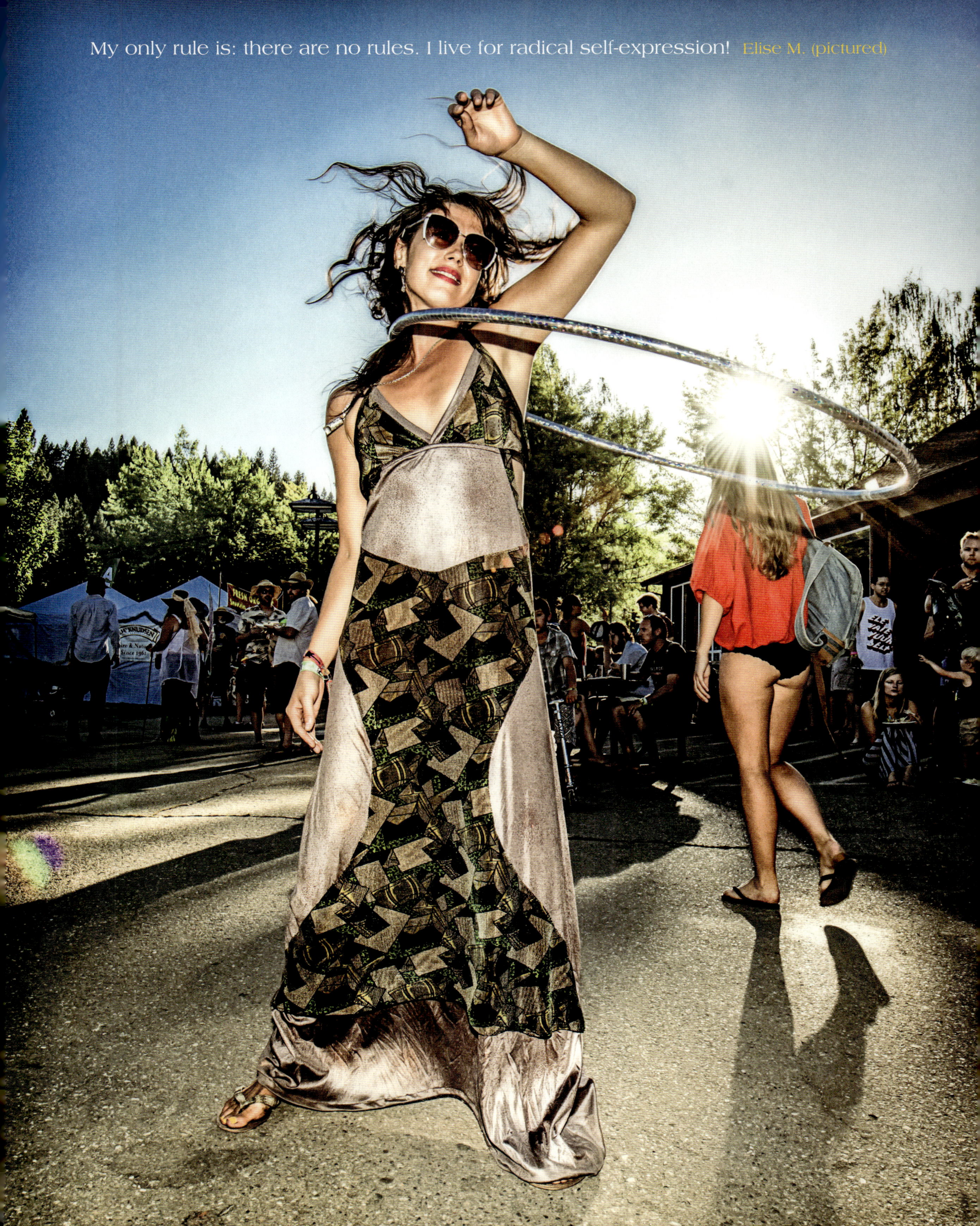

My only rule is: there are no rules. I live for radical self-expression! Elise M. (pictured)

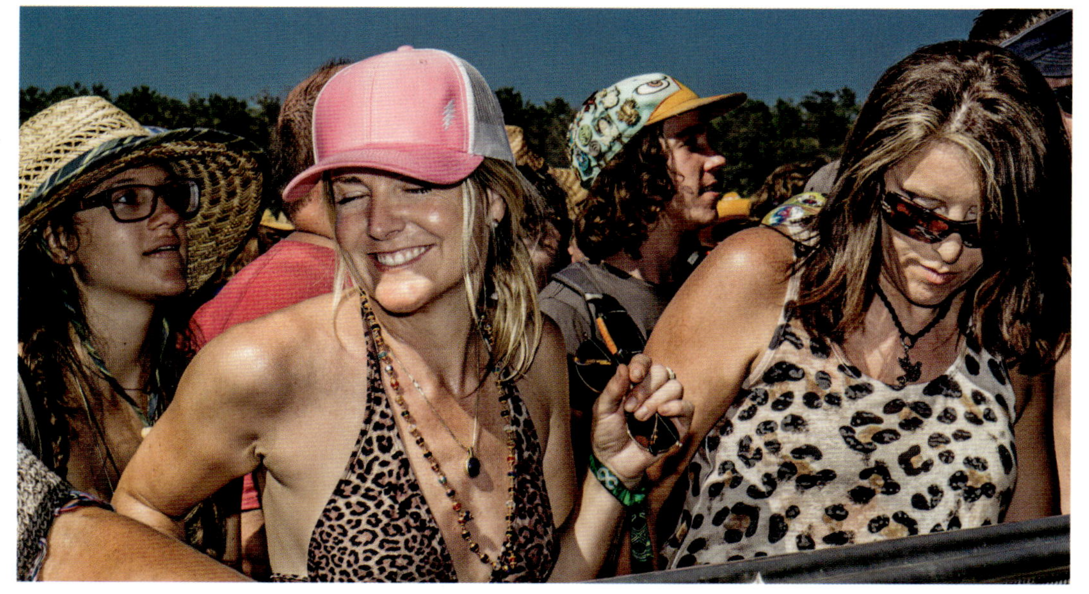
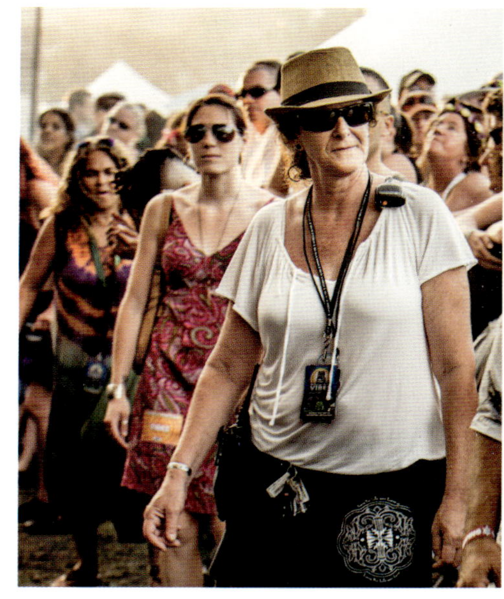
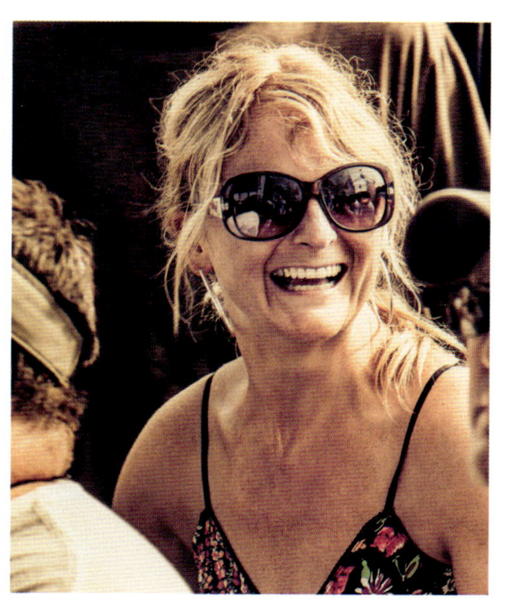
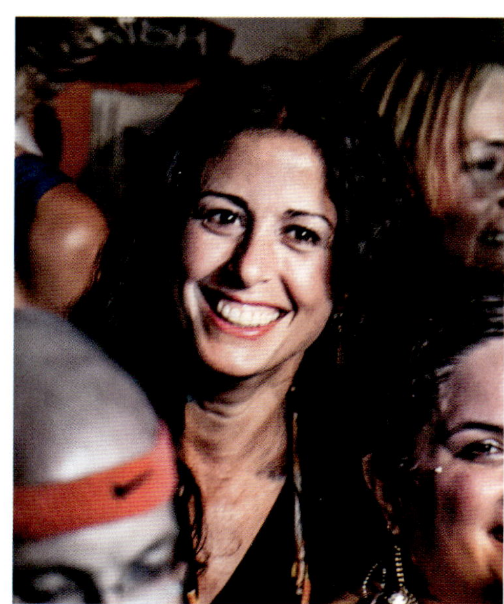
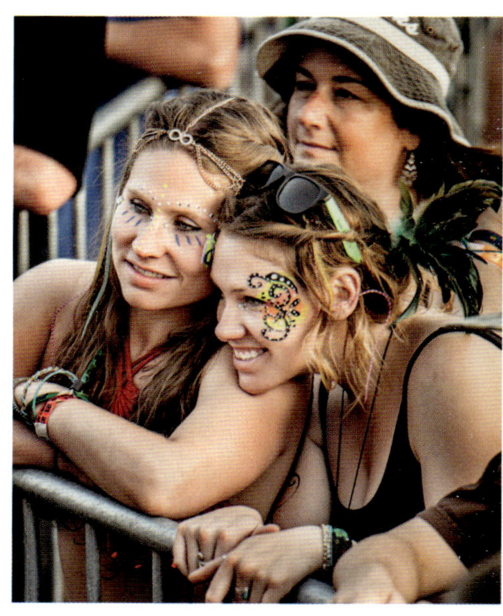
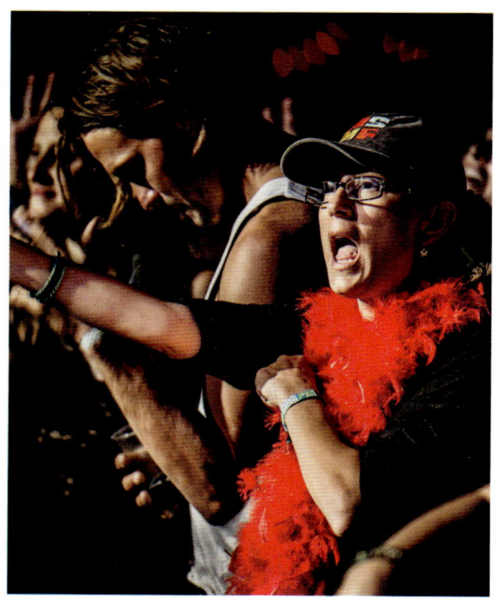
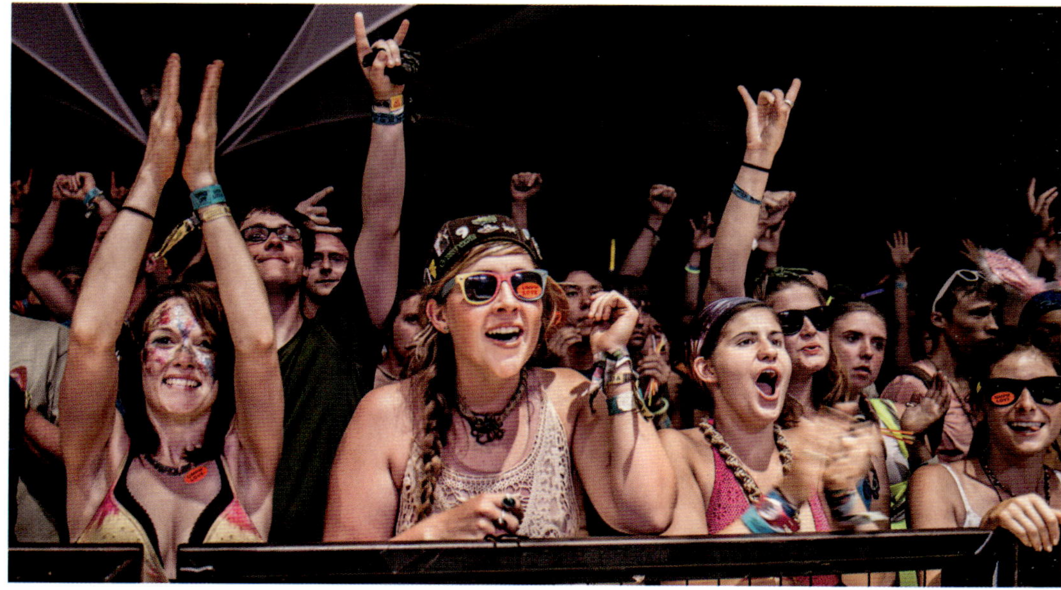

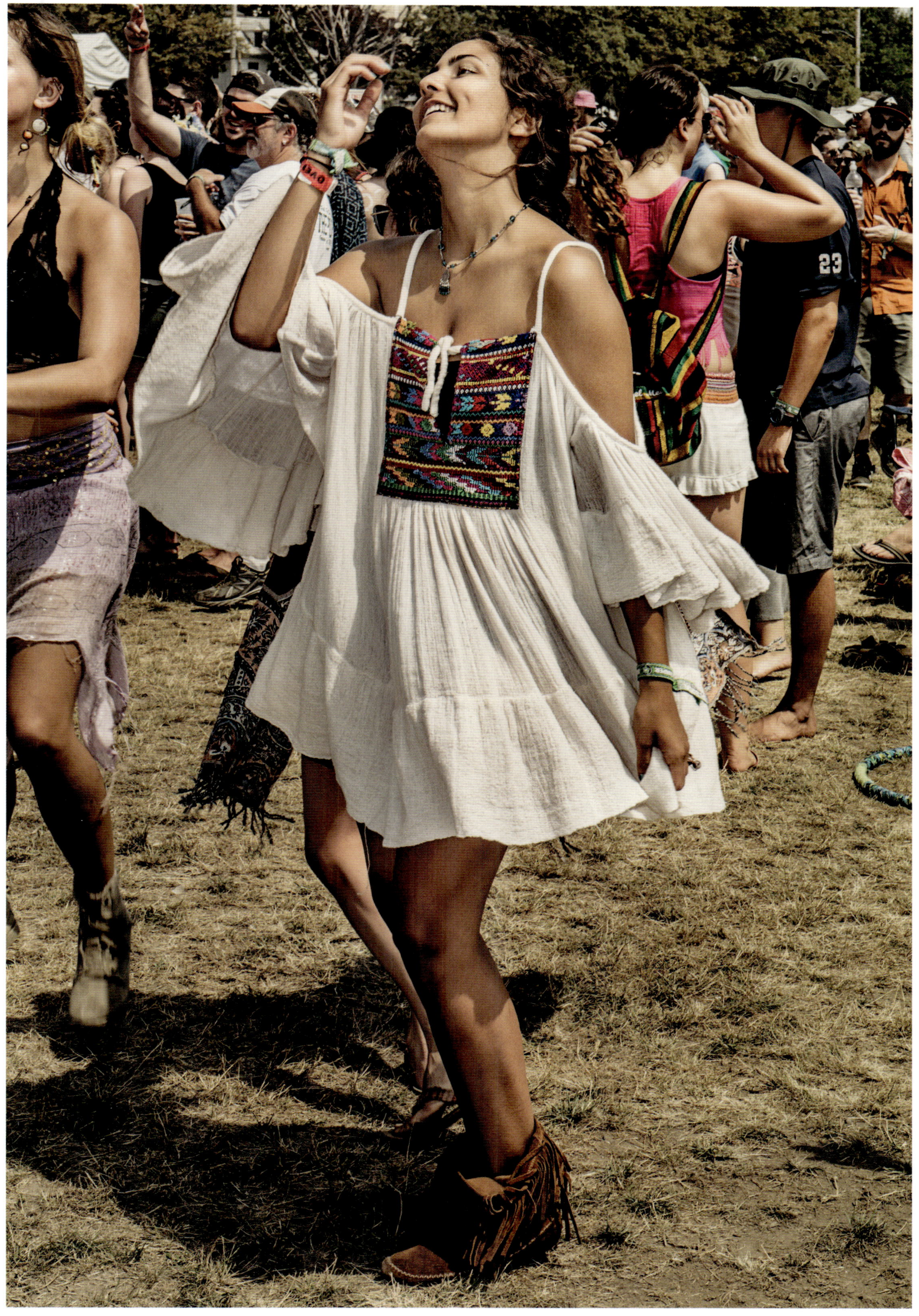

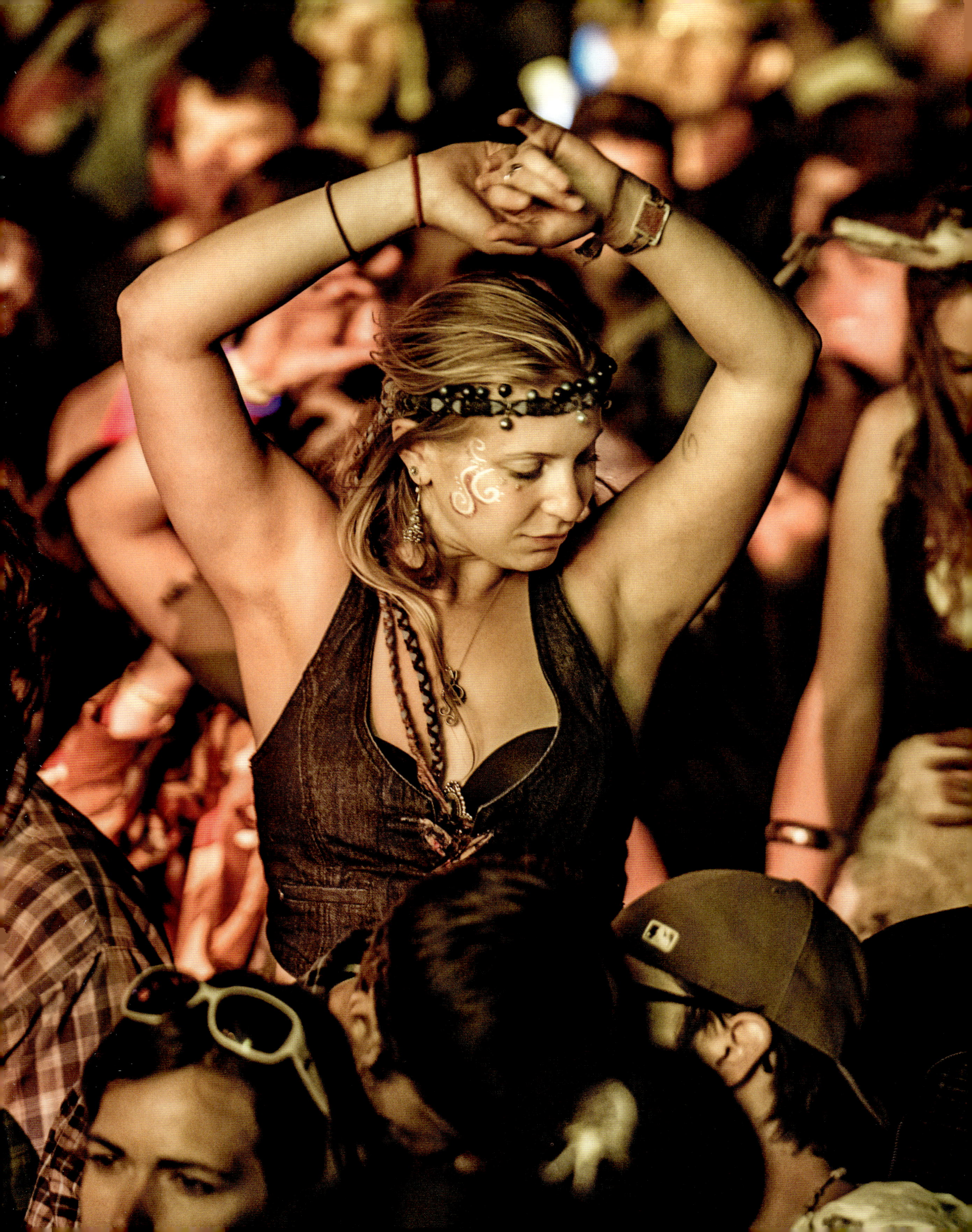

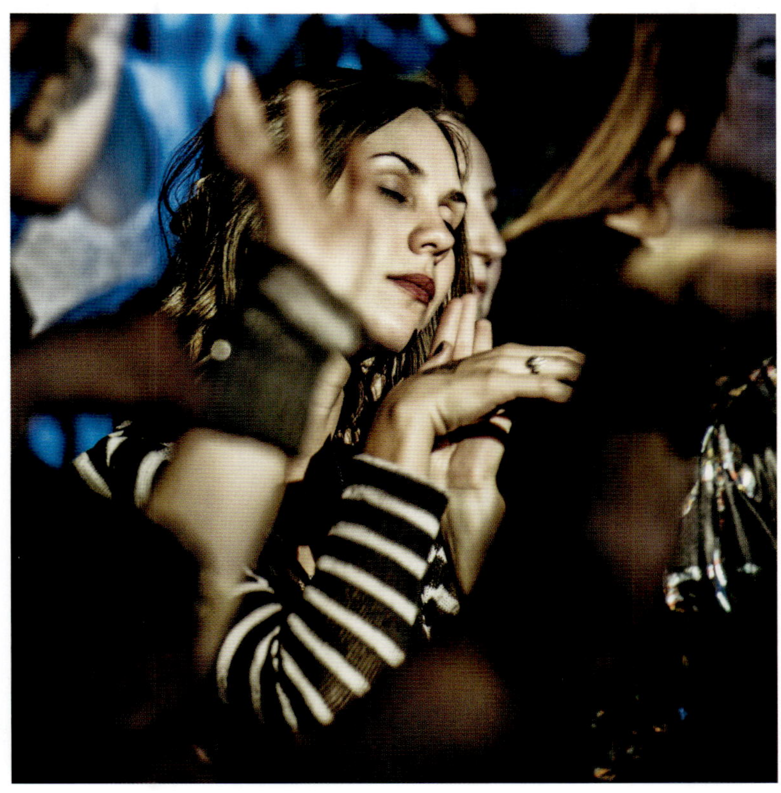

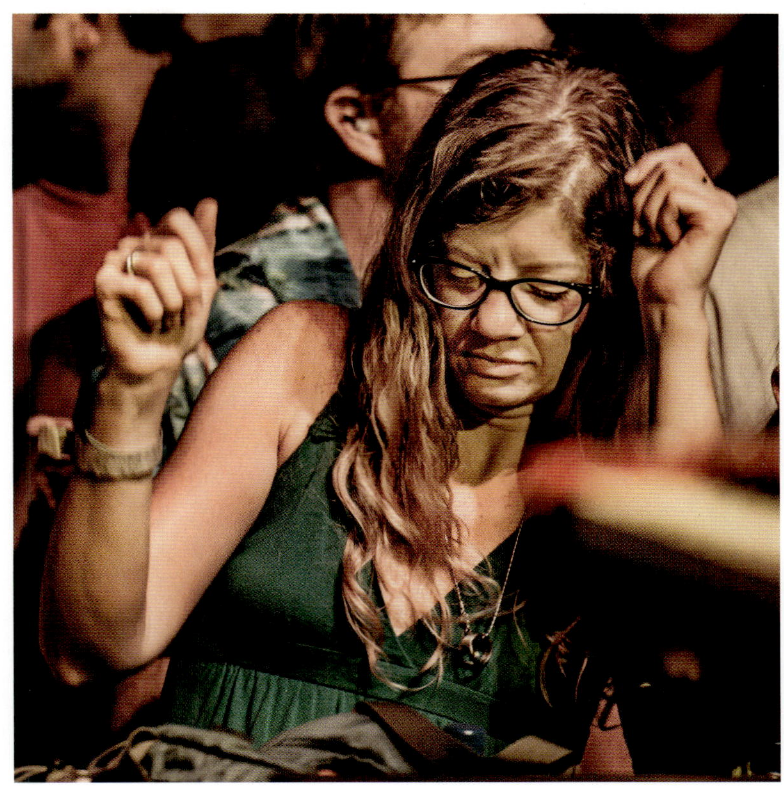

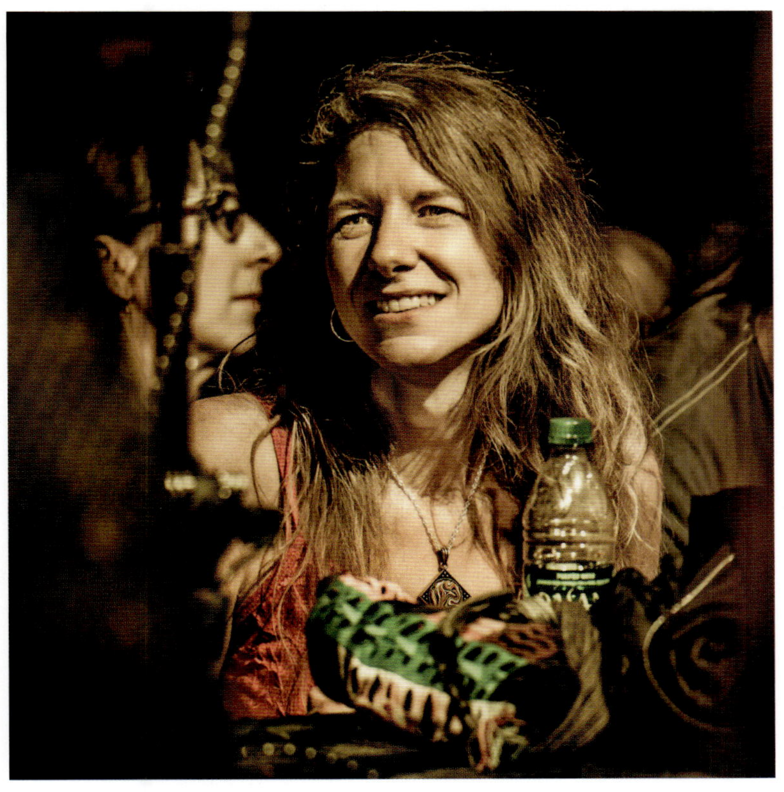

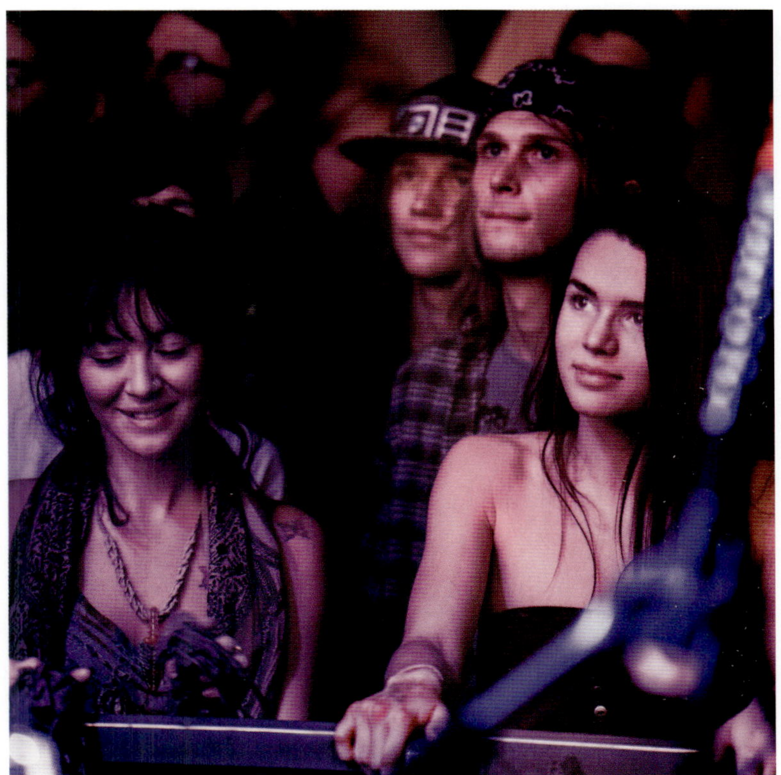

If it is good music that I really resonate with, I come away feeling refreshed, inspired, joyful, grateful, and in better alignment with all parts of myself. Kate F.

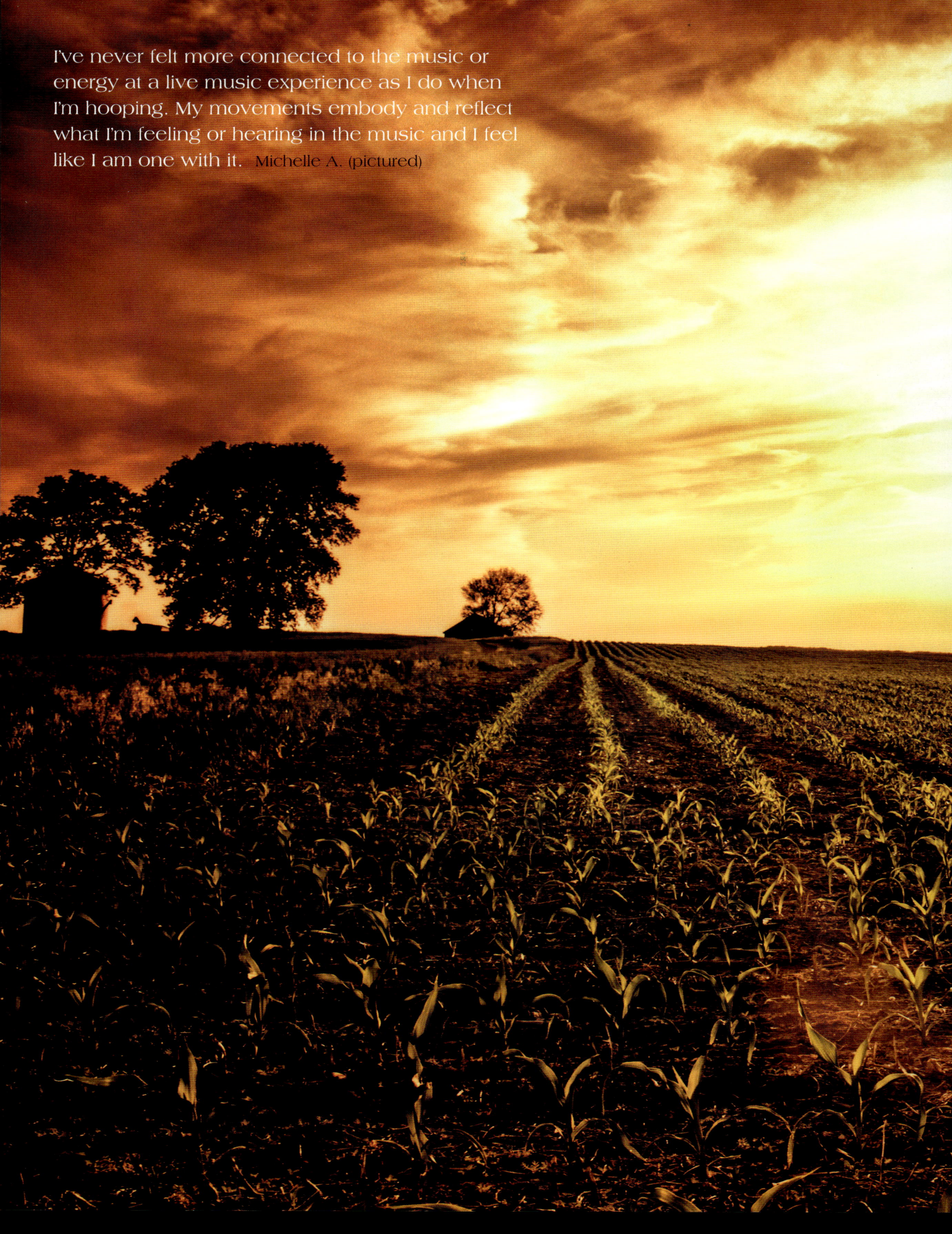

I've never felt more connected to the music or energy at a live music experience as I do when I'm hooping. My movements embody and reflect what I'm feeling or hearing in the music and I feel like I am one with it. Michelle A. (pictured)

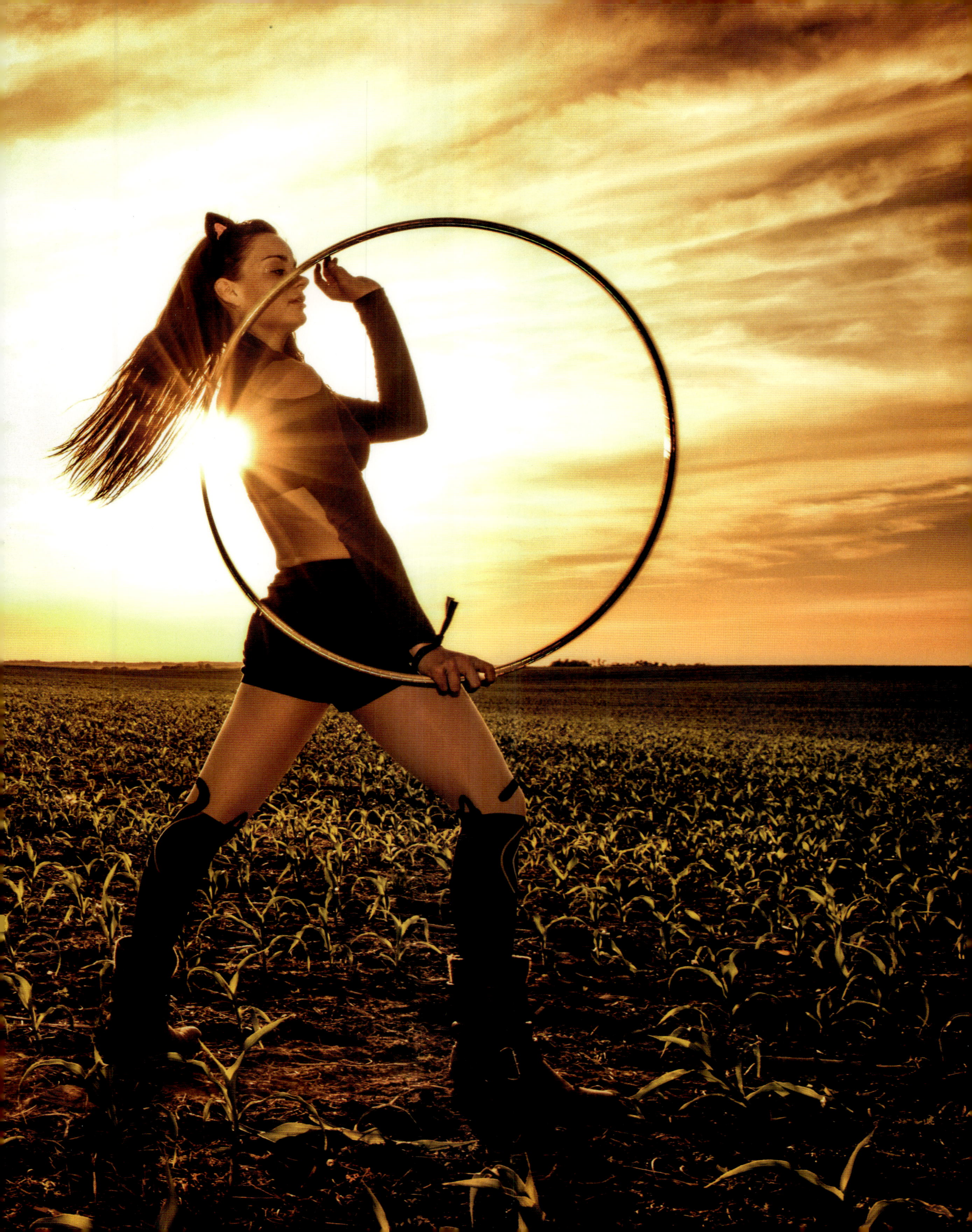

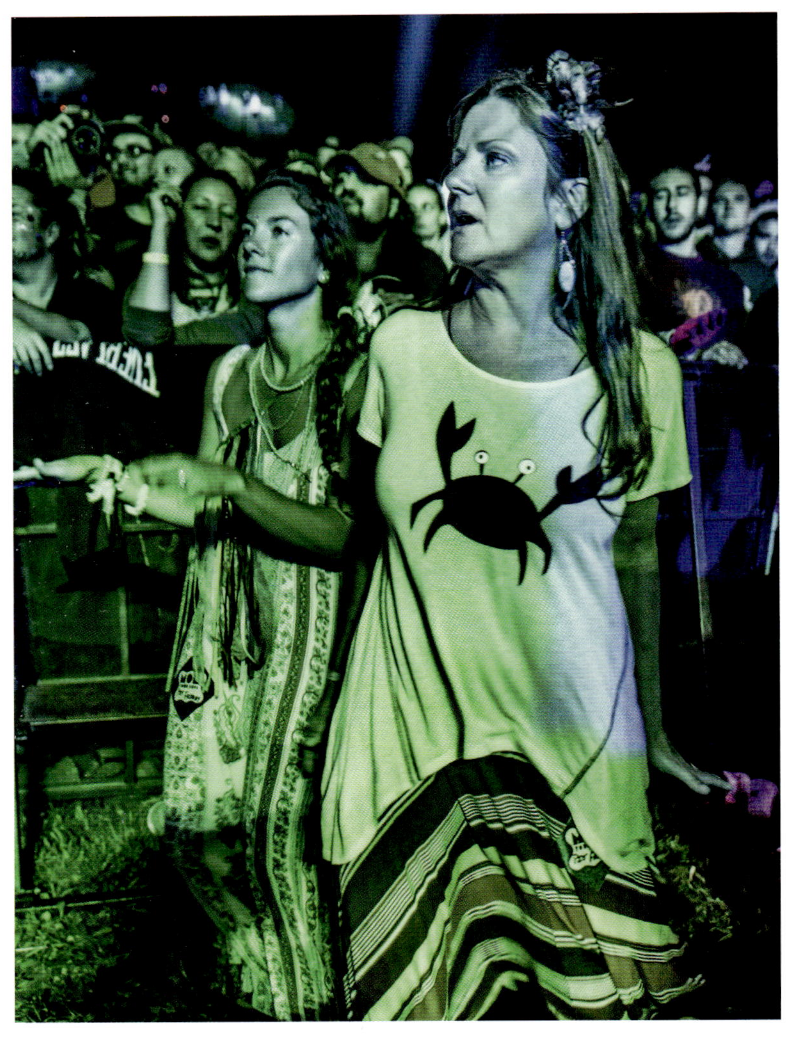

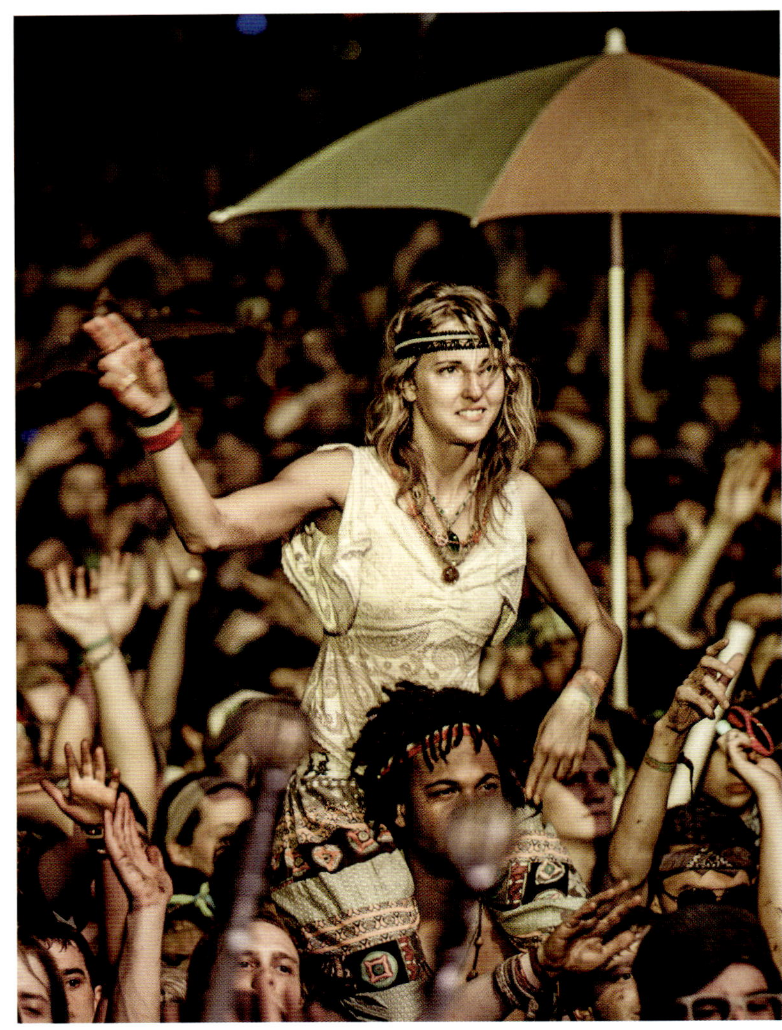

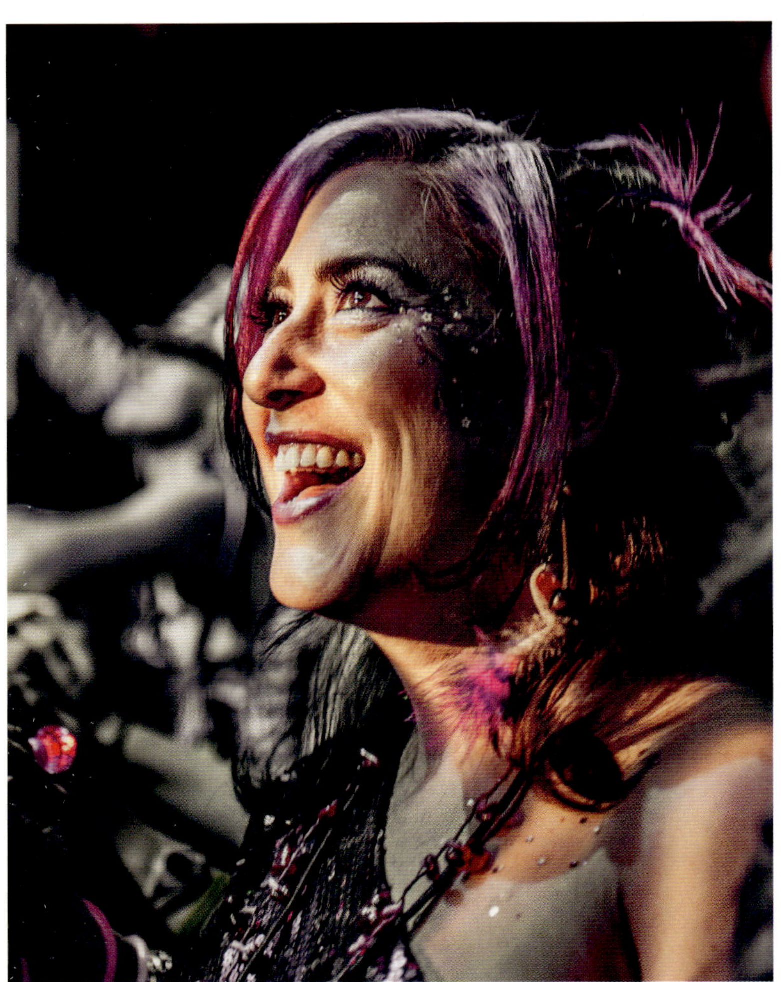

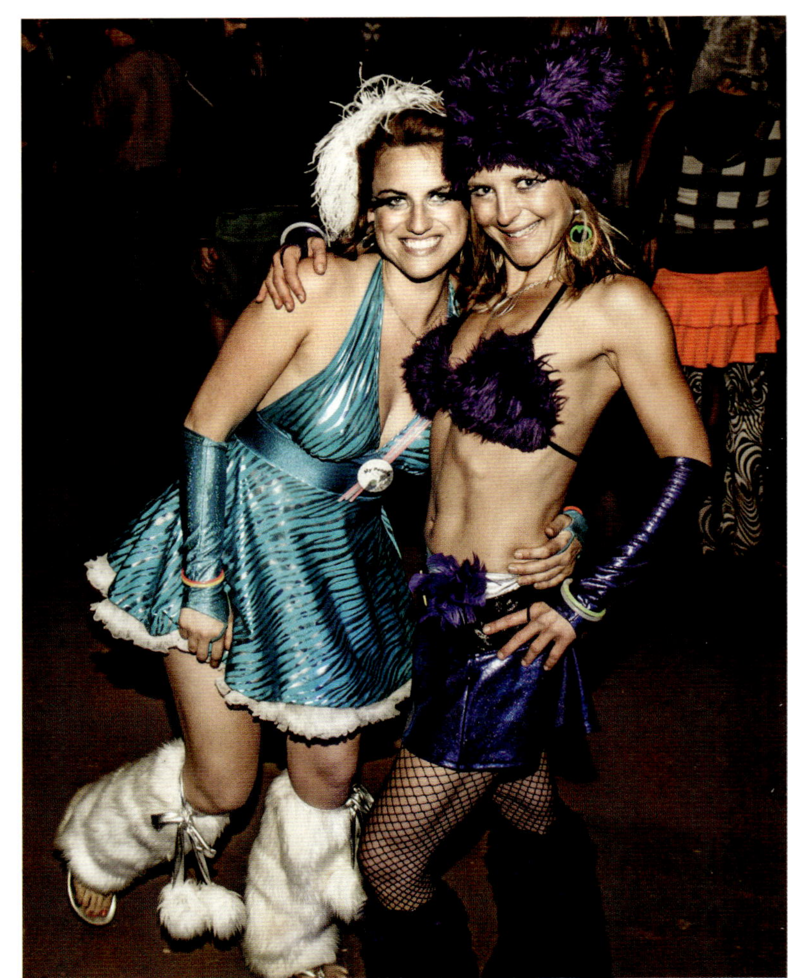

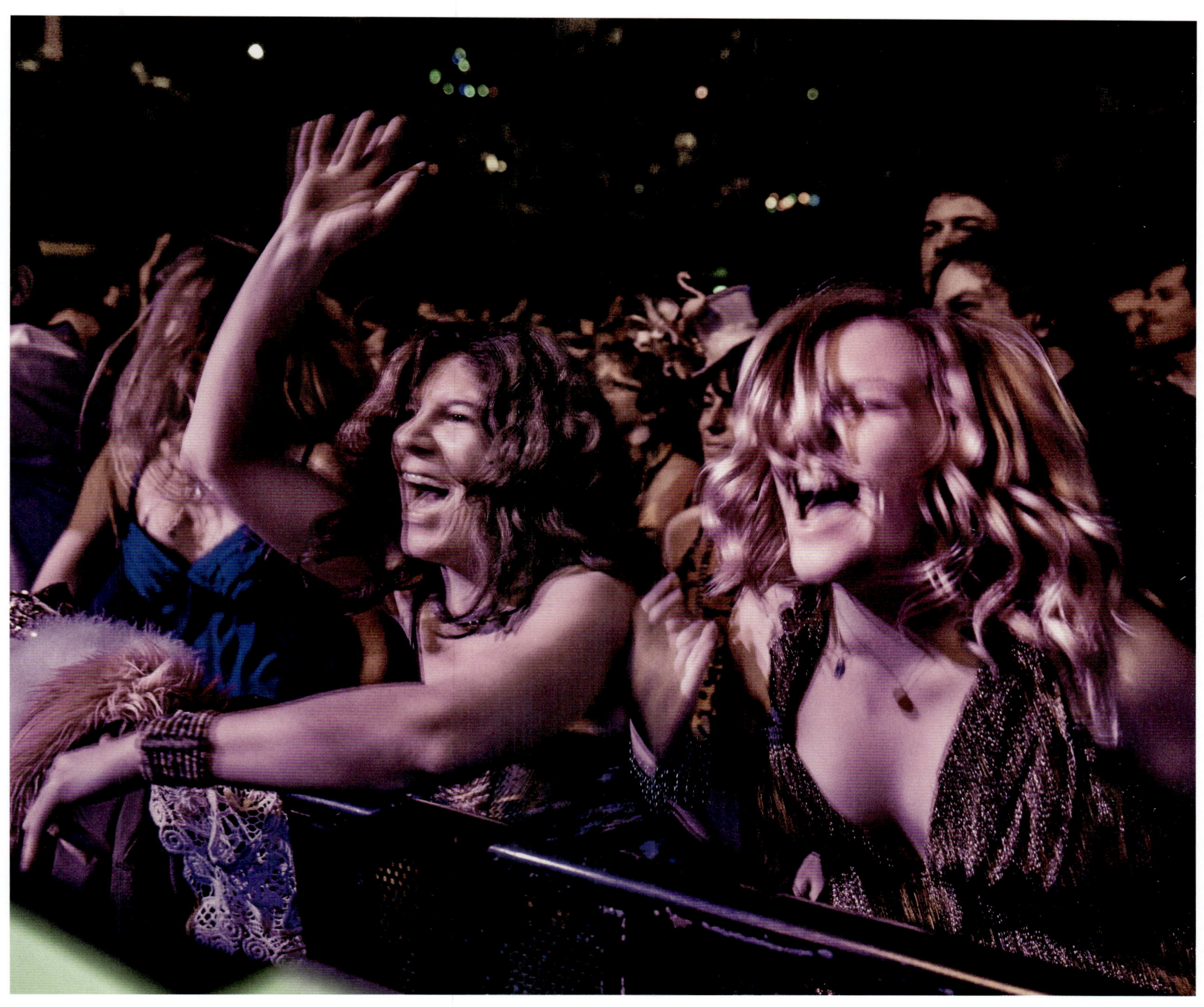

To be physically close to the creation of emotionally evocative music amplifies the joy and passion and thrill. It's powerful and sexy and transcendent! Jordan A. (pictured, right)

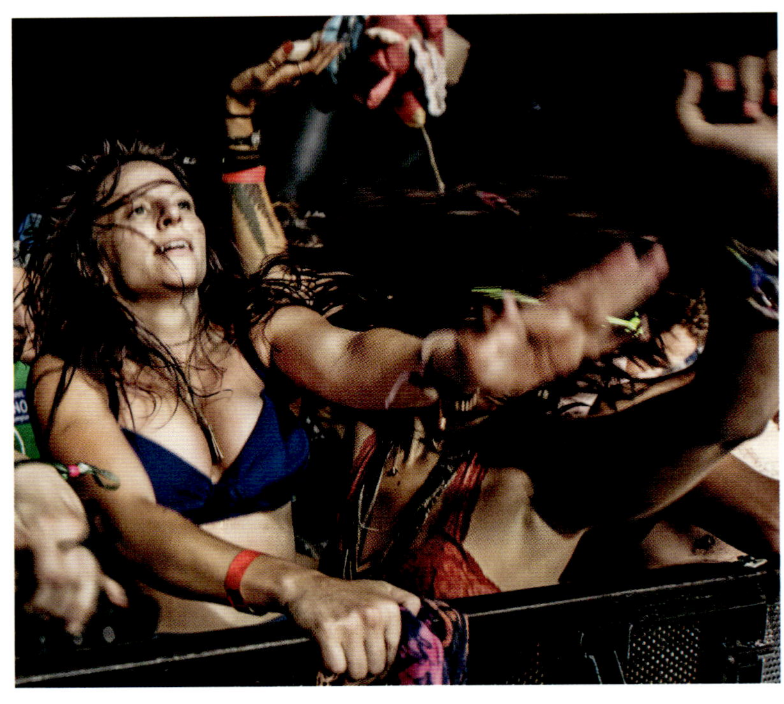

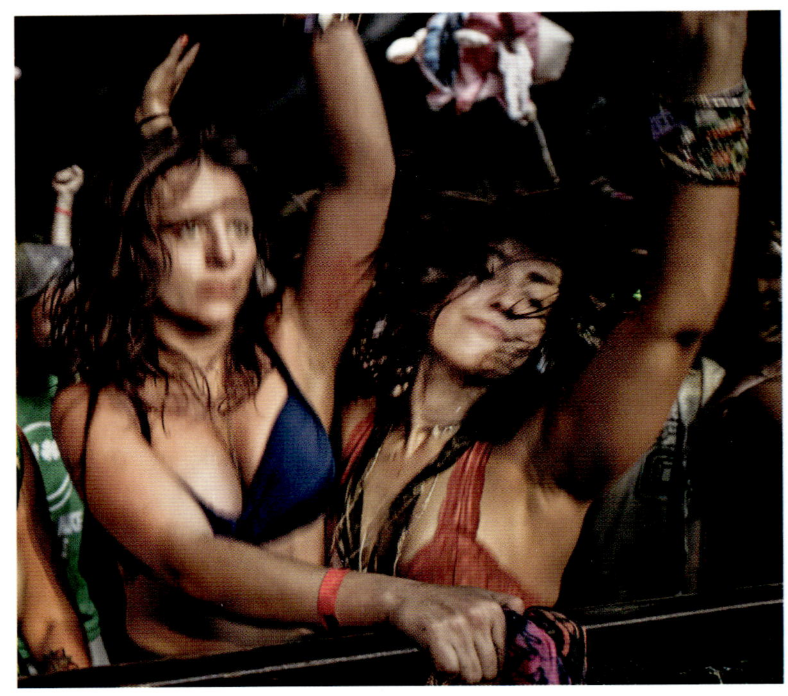

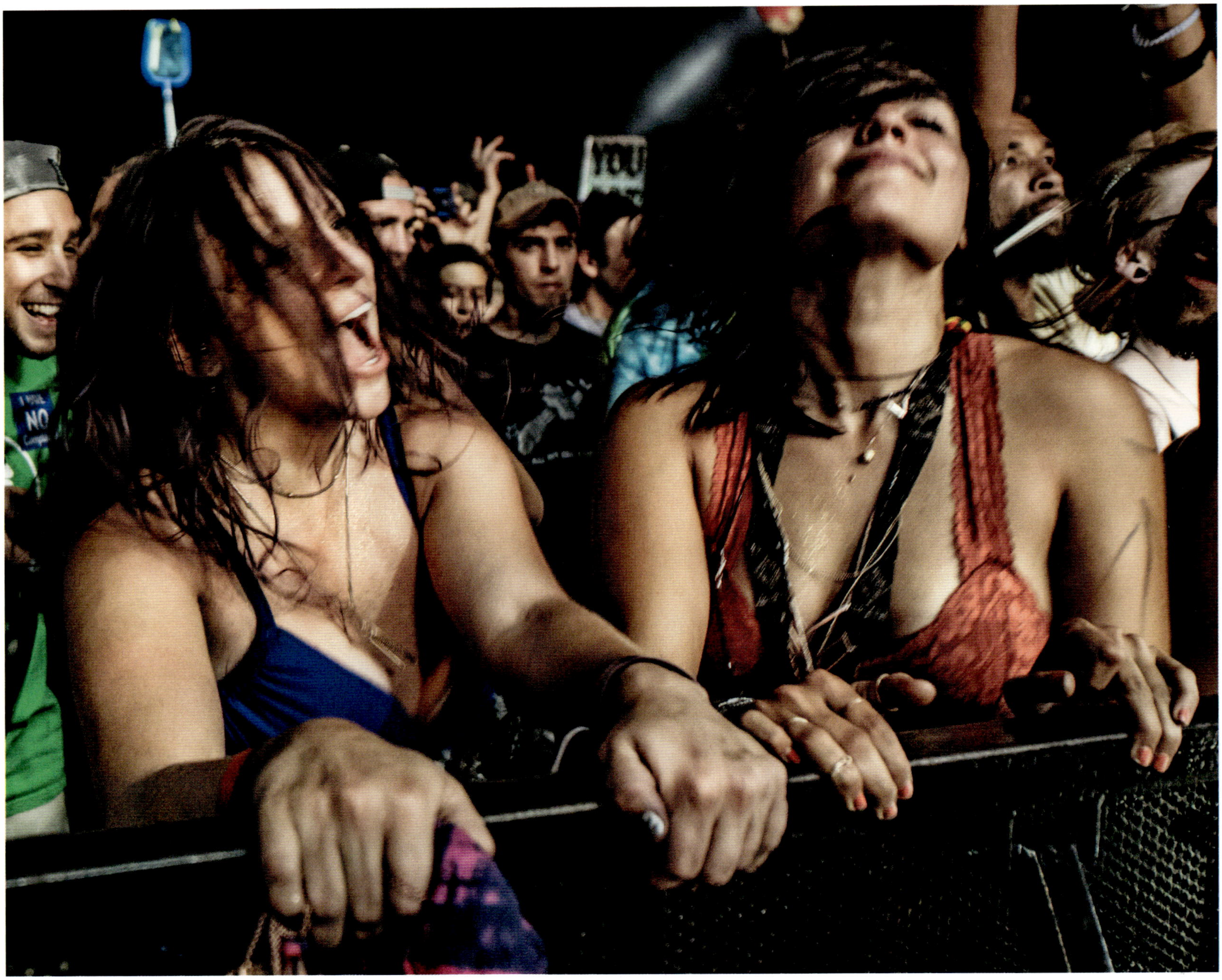

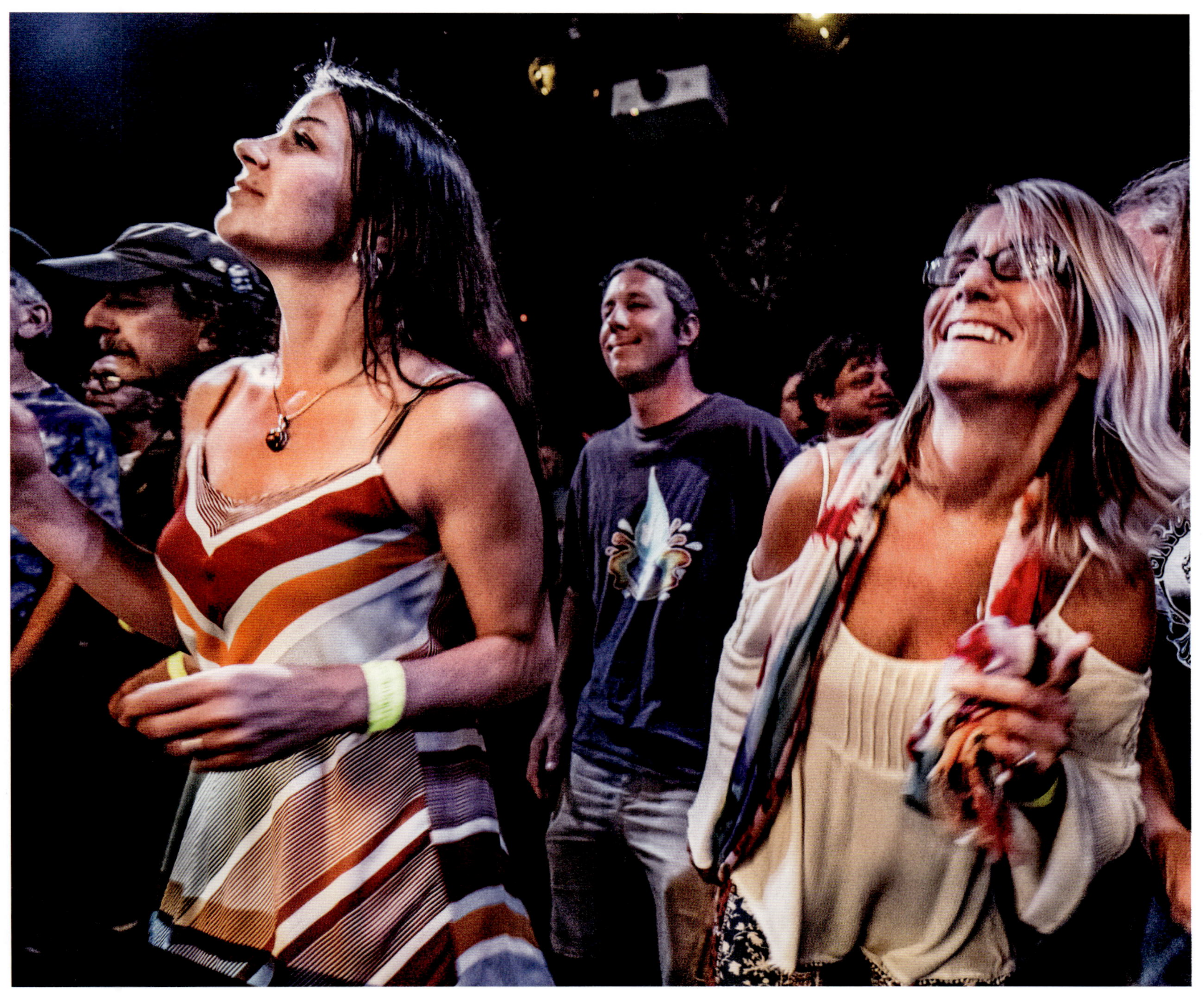

I love the front row! I like to be able to see the musicians, their facial expressions, their connection to their instruments ... and yes, even possibly make eye contact, letting them know just how much I am enjoying their music. Jessie T. (pictured, left)

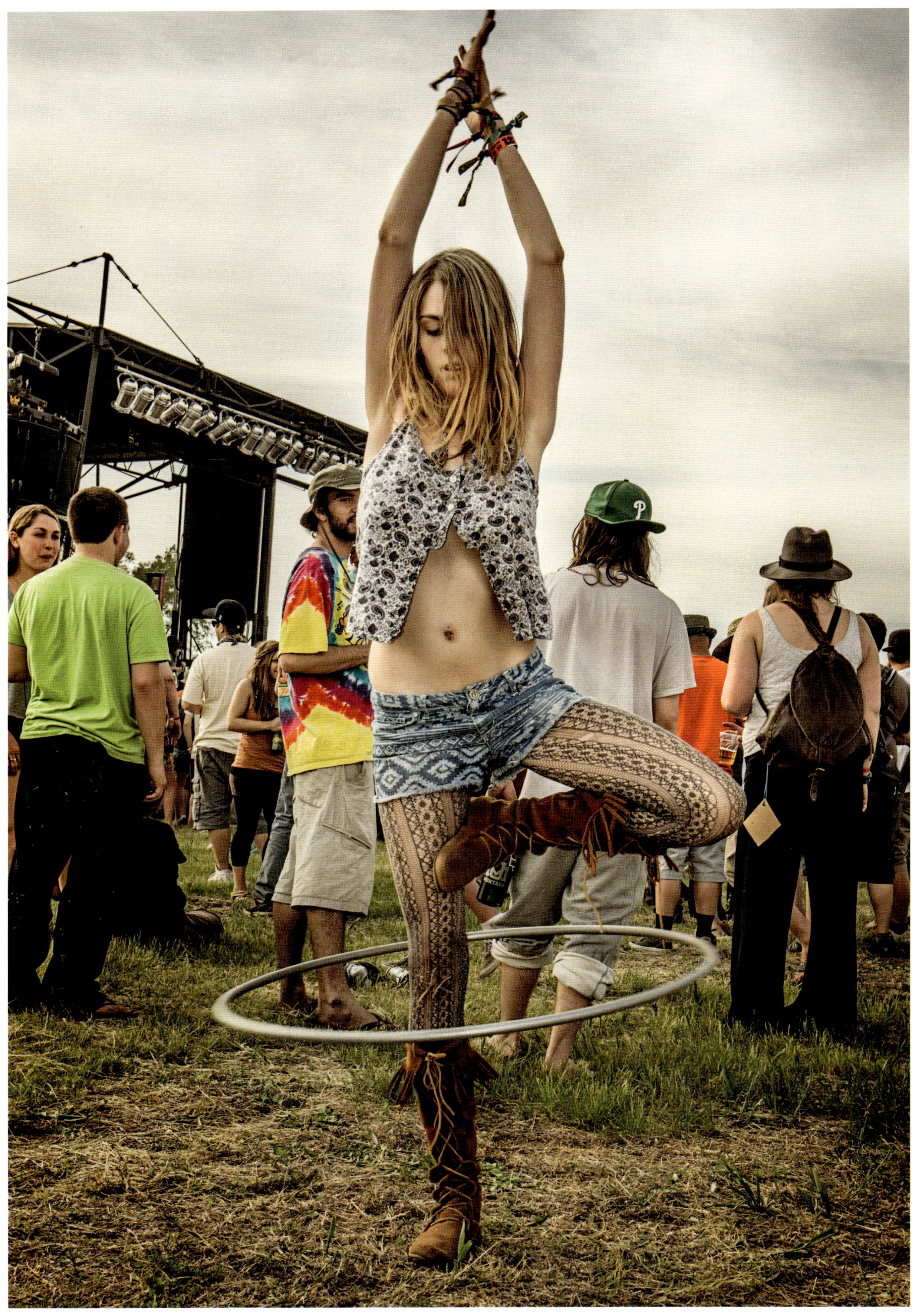

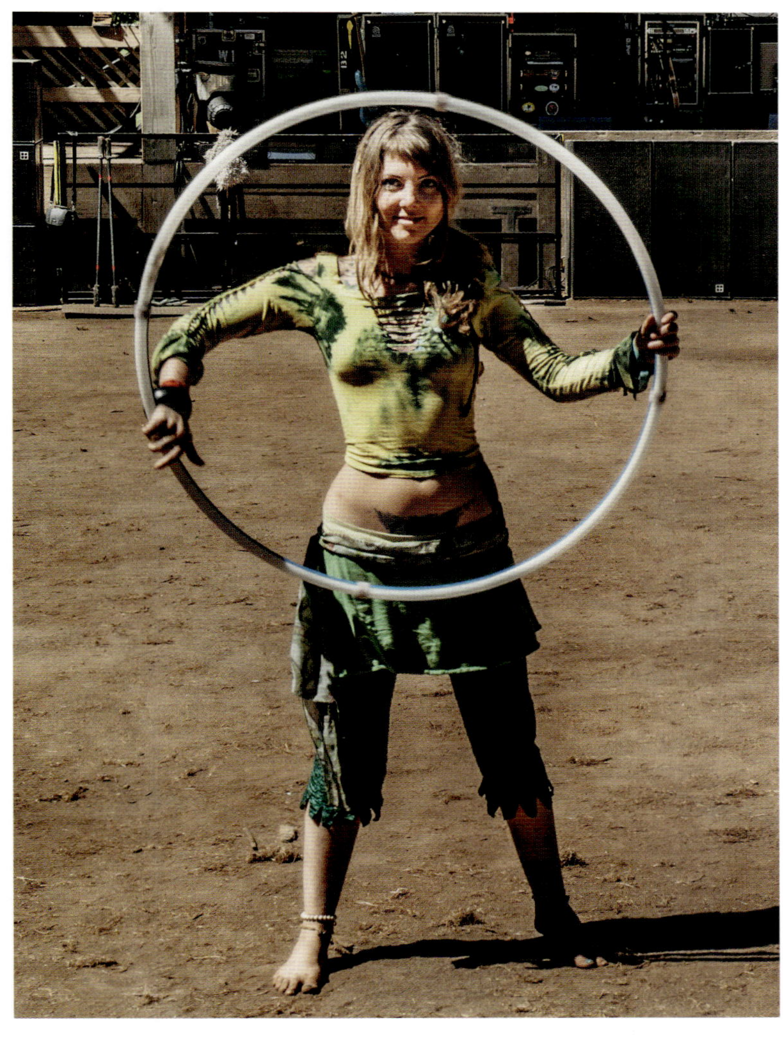
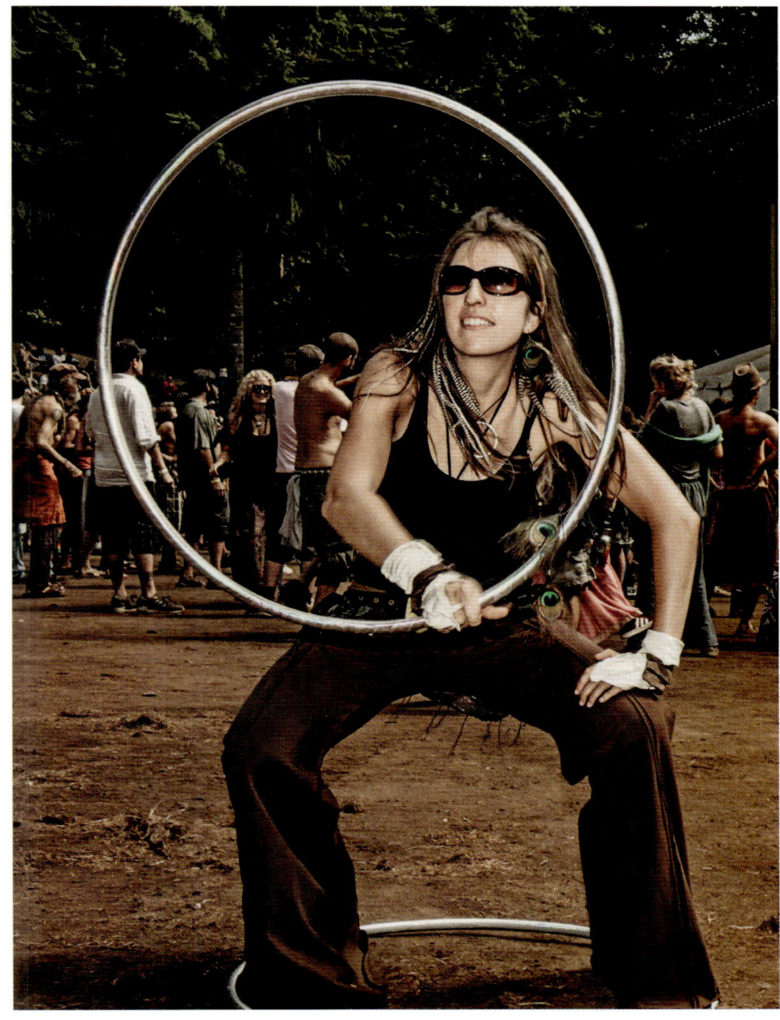
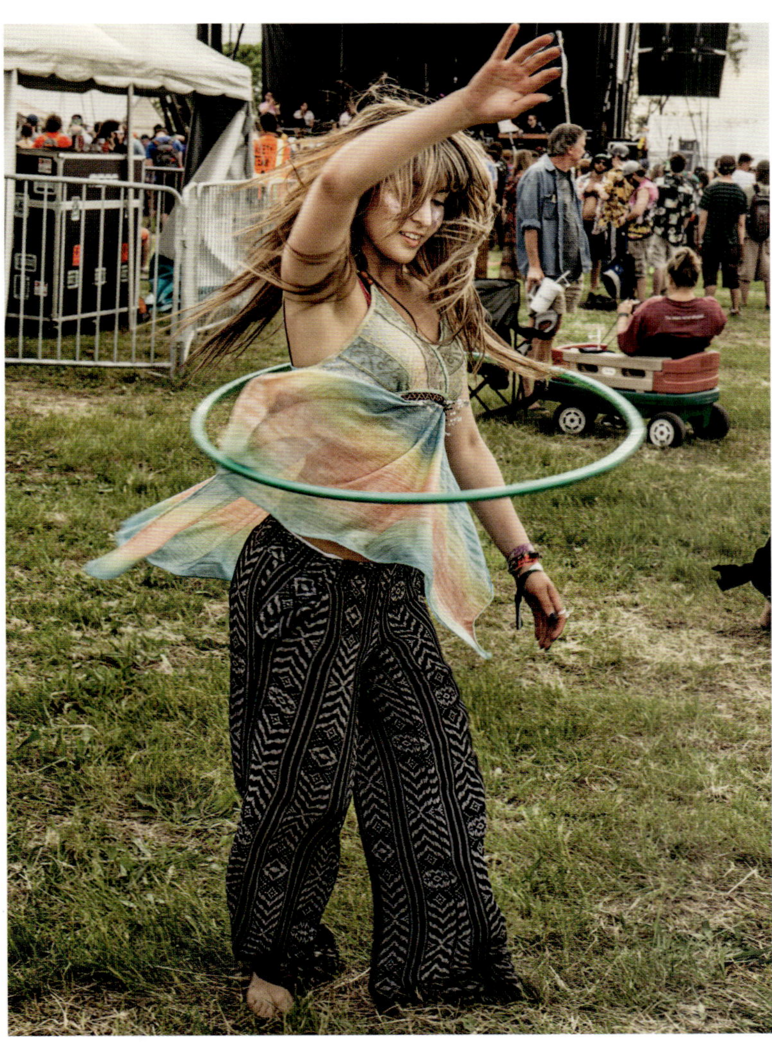
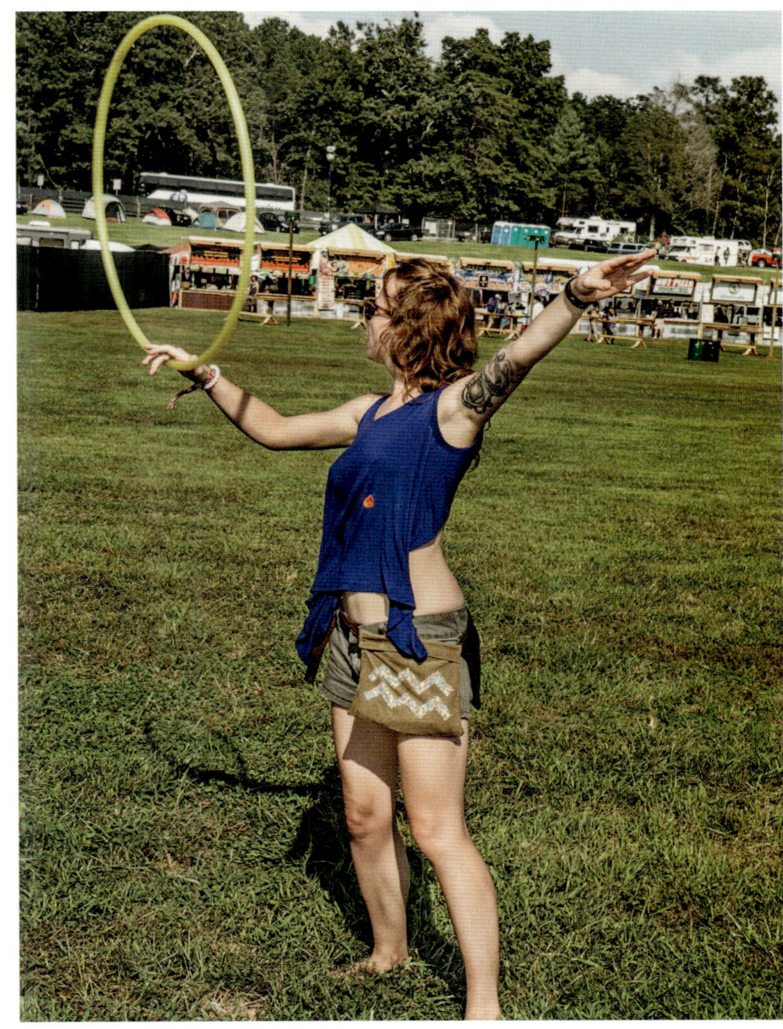

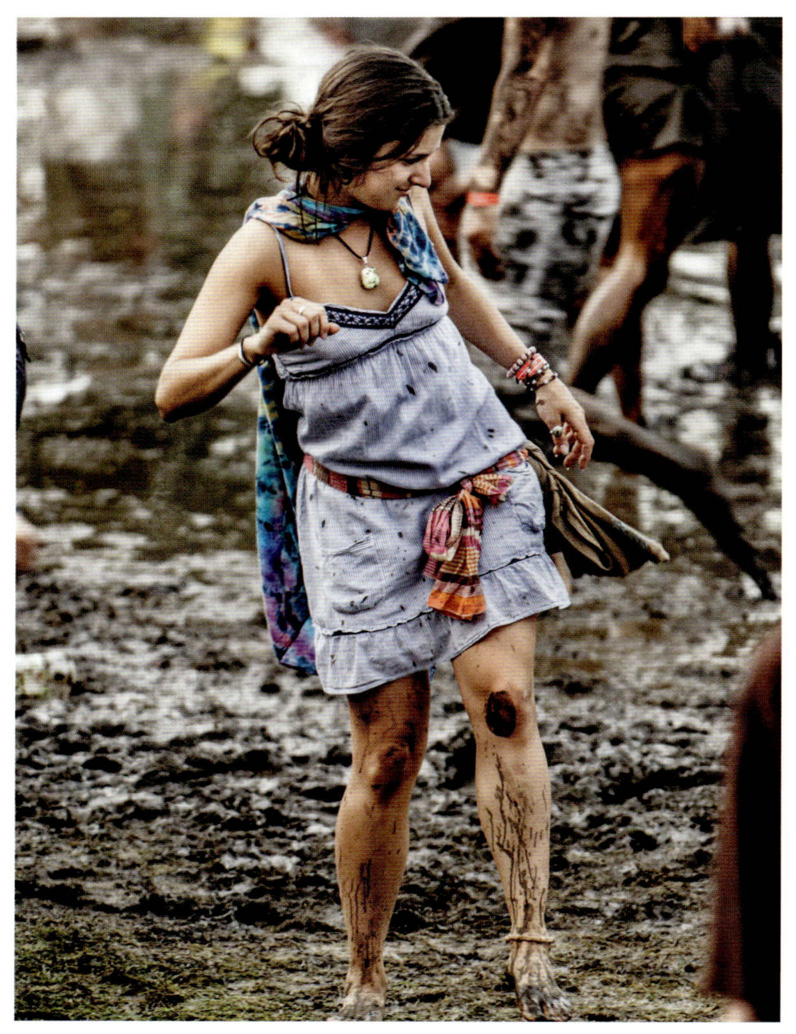

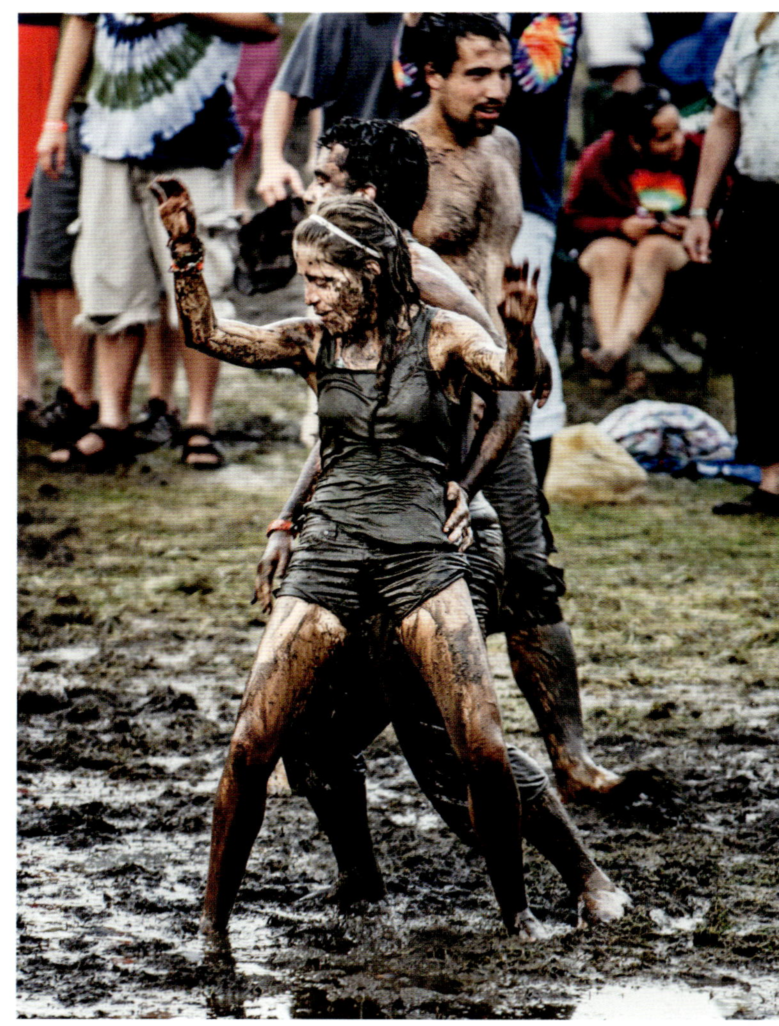

You come to festivals because you want a battery charge. You want to get around people that wanna just get down in the dirt with you and get dirty and weird and fun. Millie M.

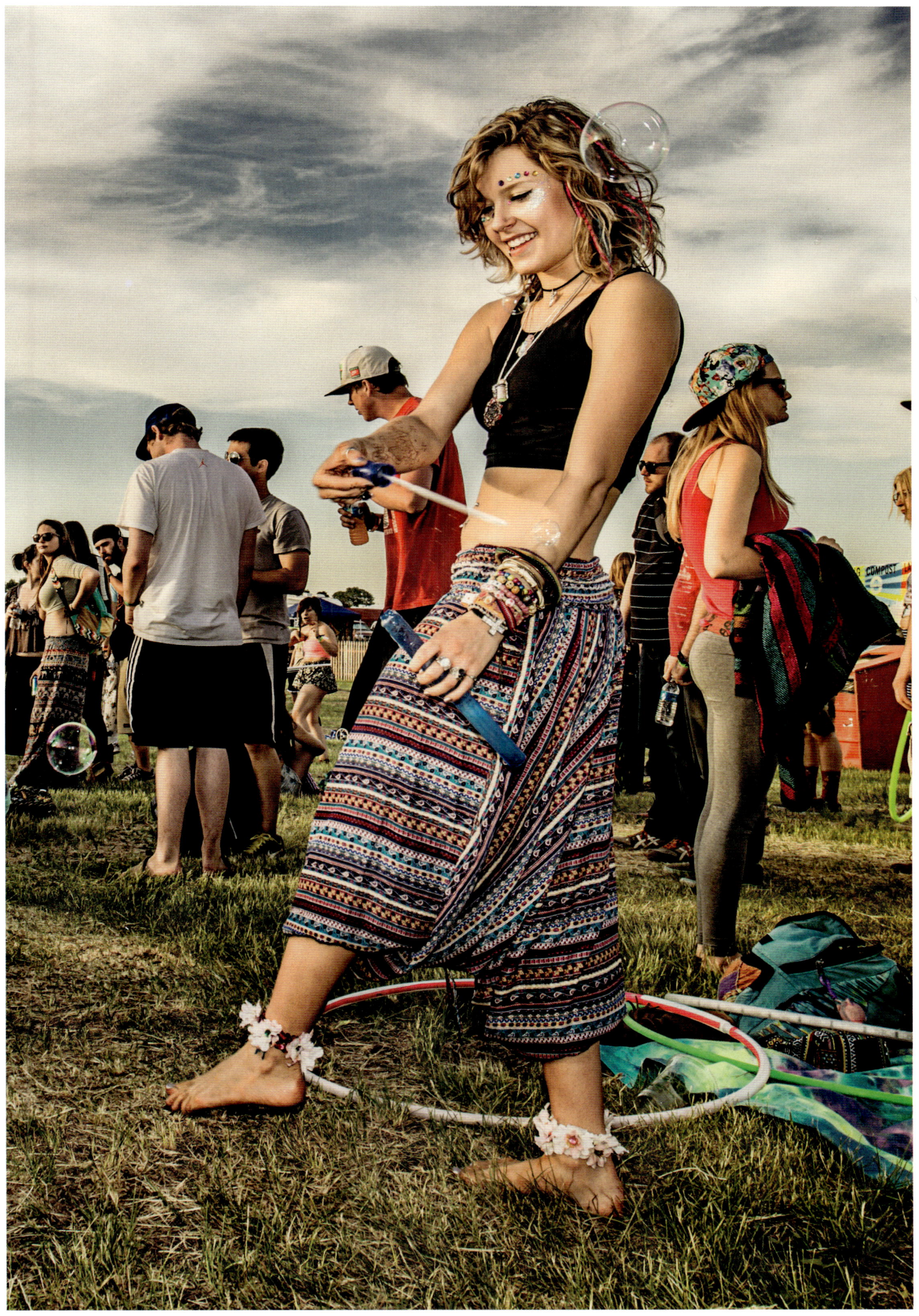
COMPOST

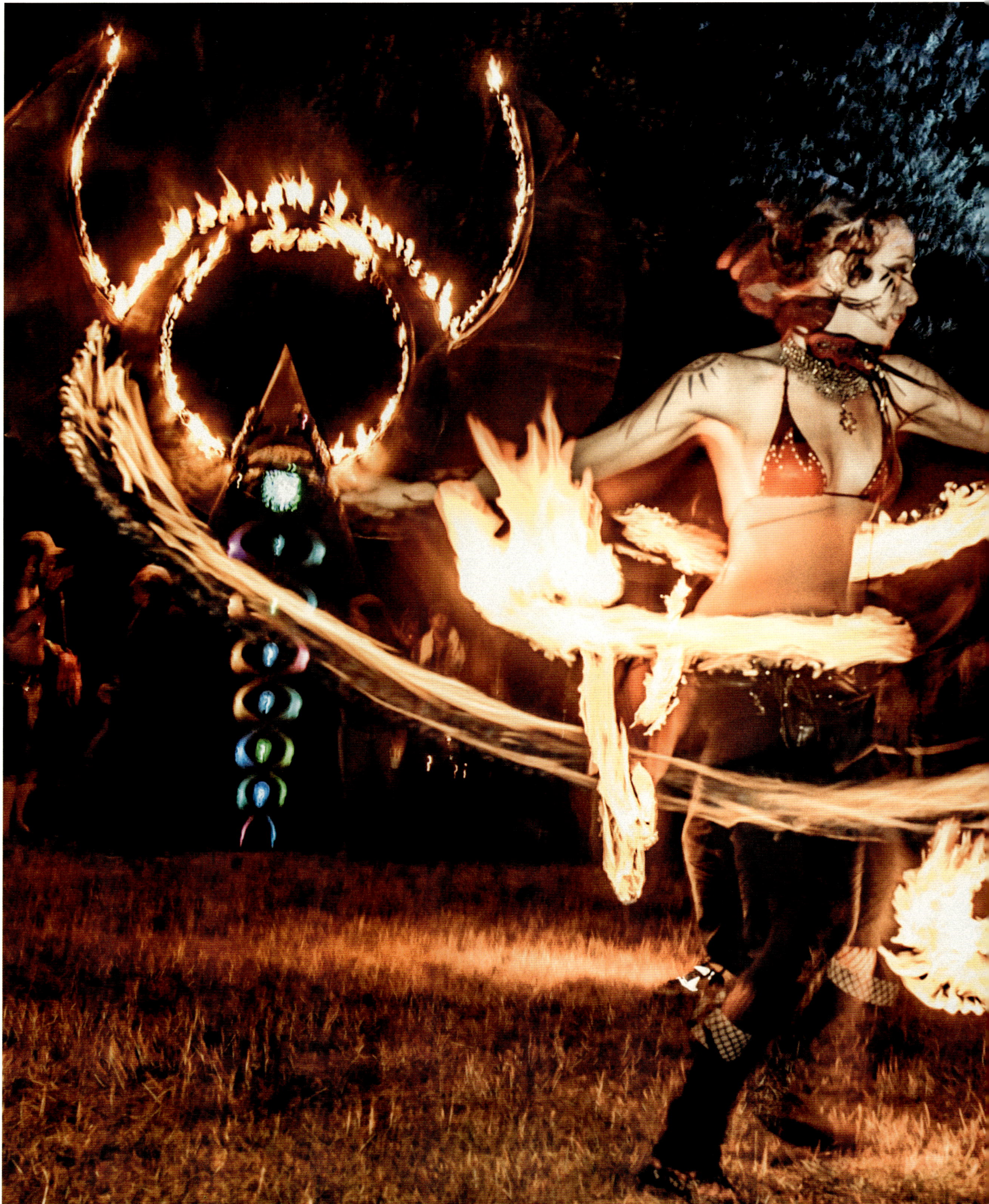

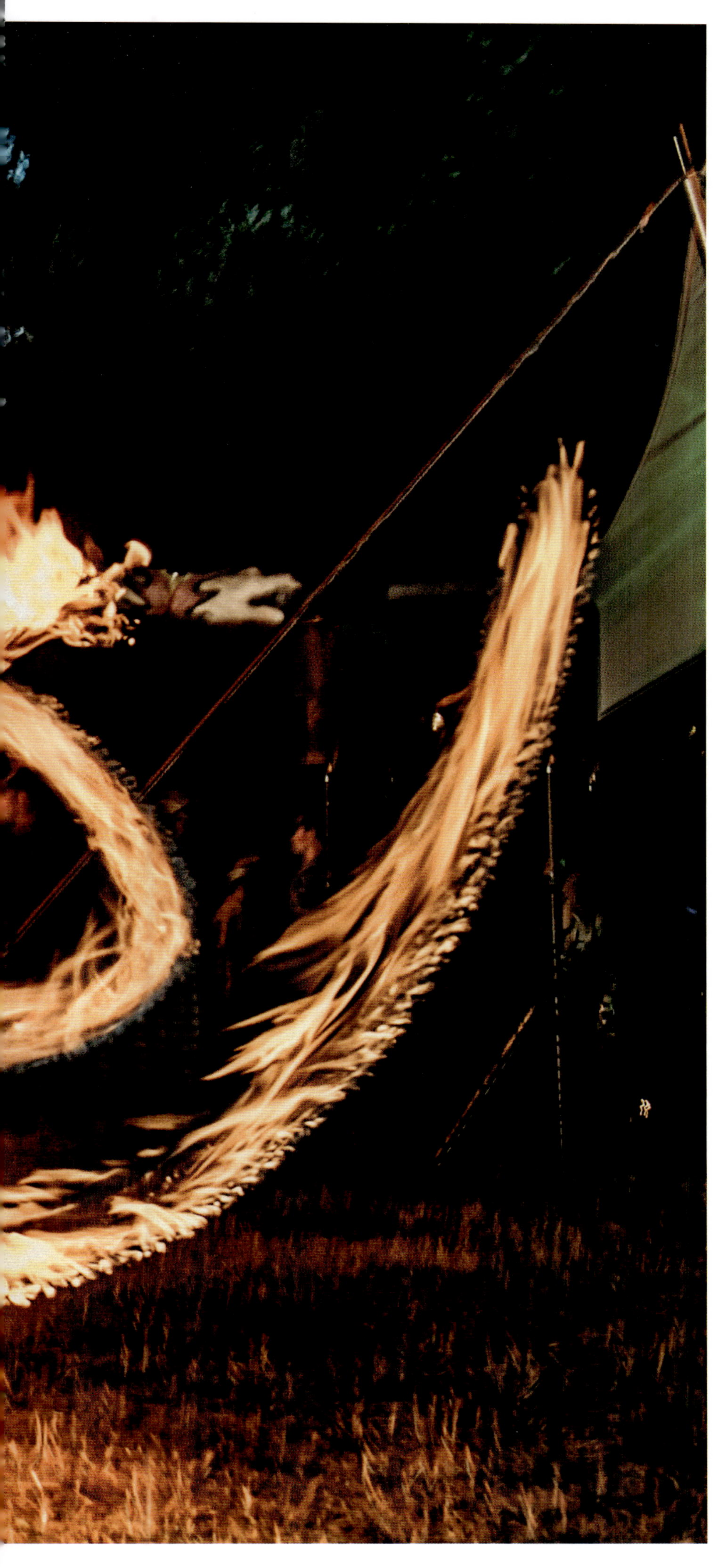

Dancing is beautiful—no matter who is moving, or how they are moving. Dancing is as close to God as this human body has ever known.
Molly N.

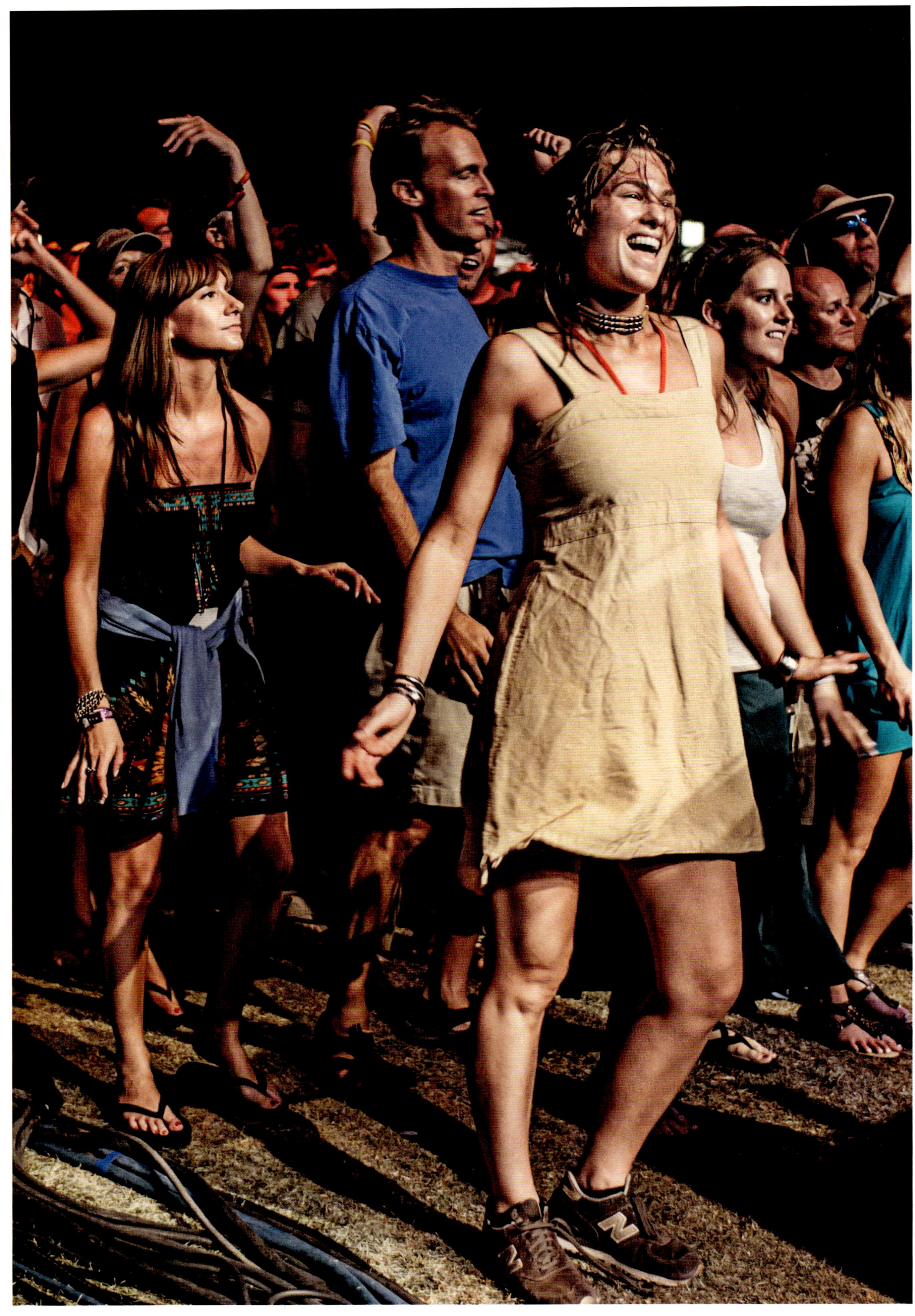

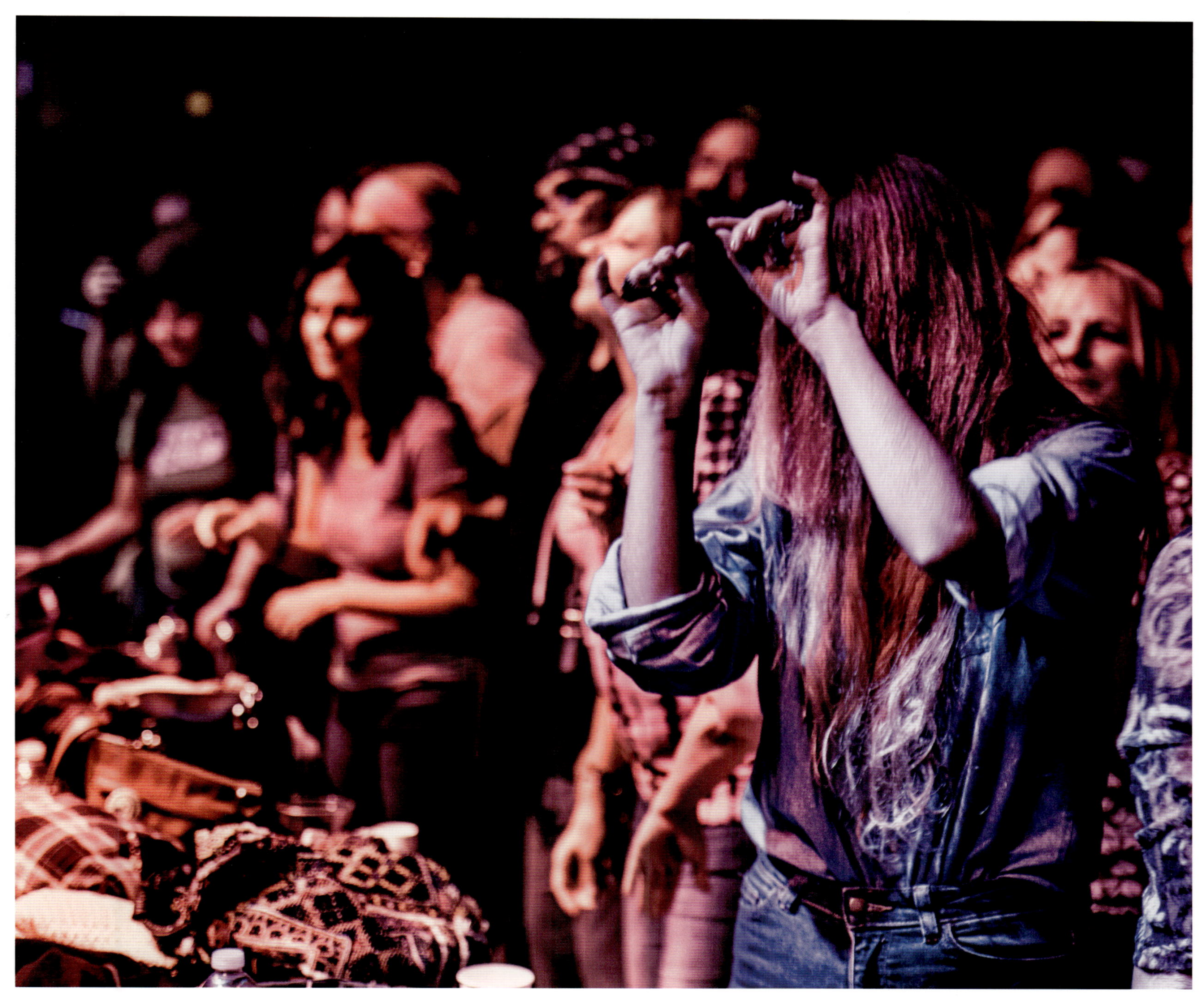

I really feel one with the music. I love the simplicity of my body and the music coming together. I open my heart and seem to be transported to a place of complete and total freedom for the soul. I wish that everyone on Earth could experience this feeling. Gretchen B. (pictured, facing page)

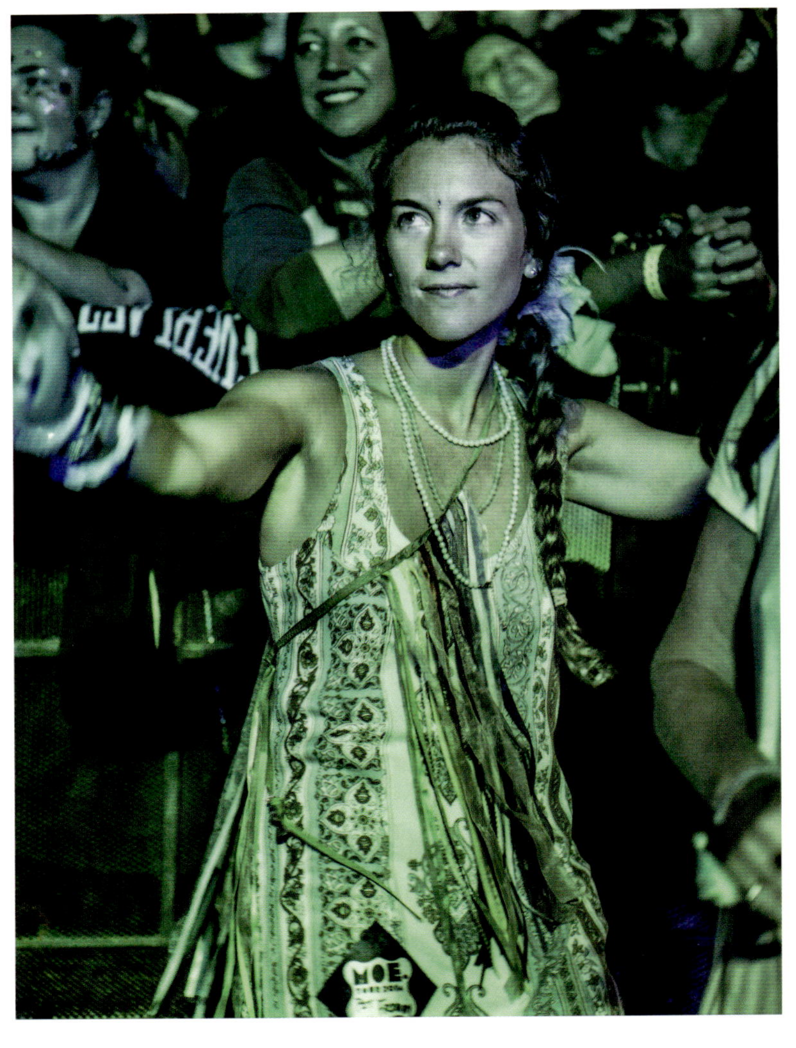
MOE.

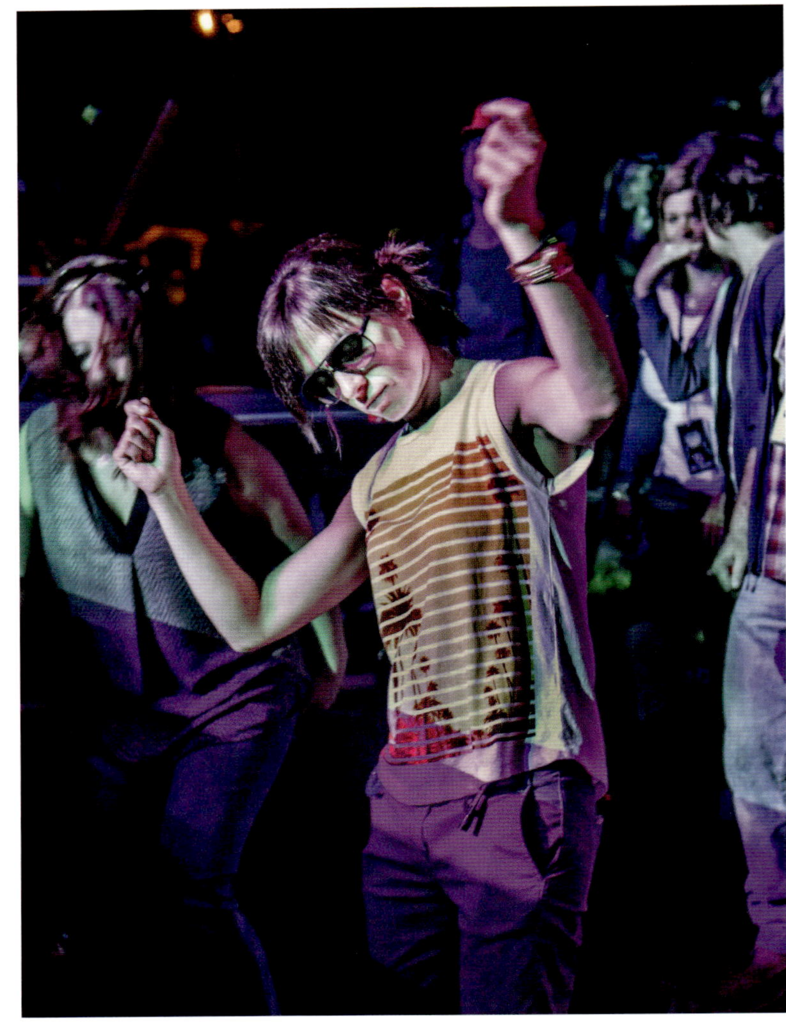

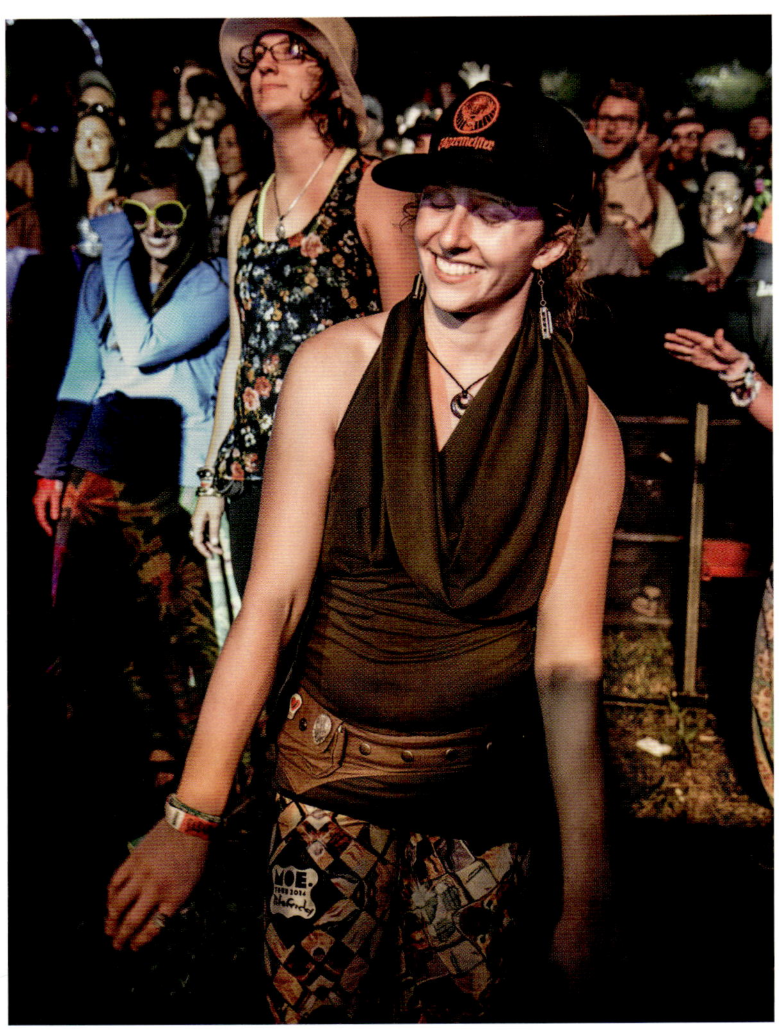
MOE.

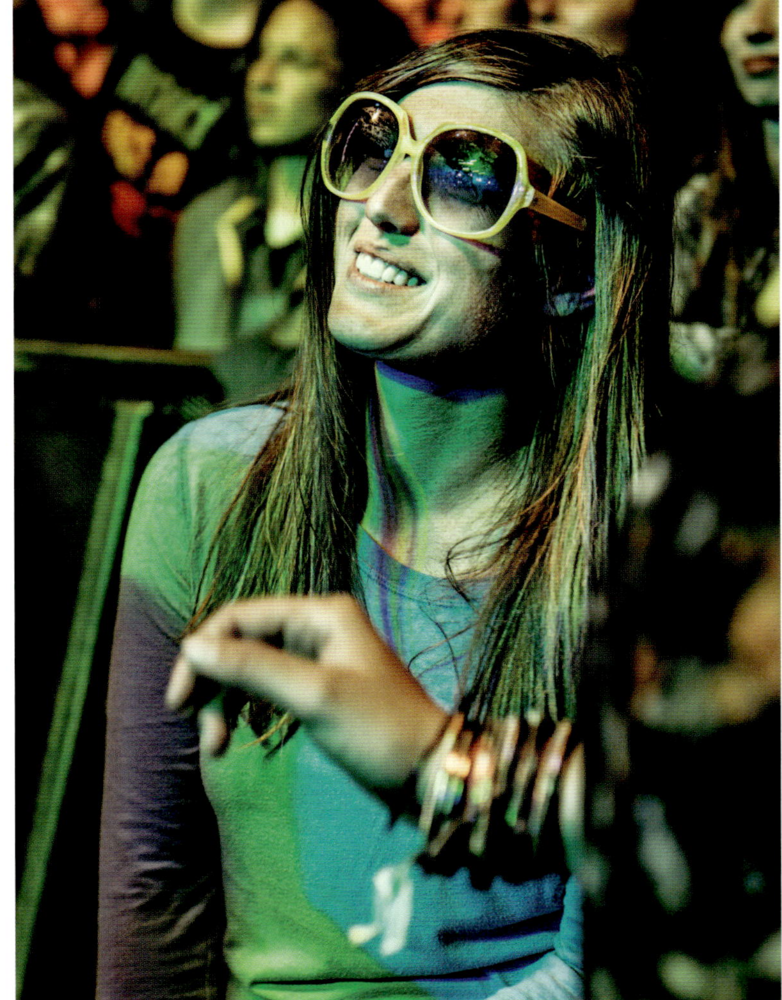

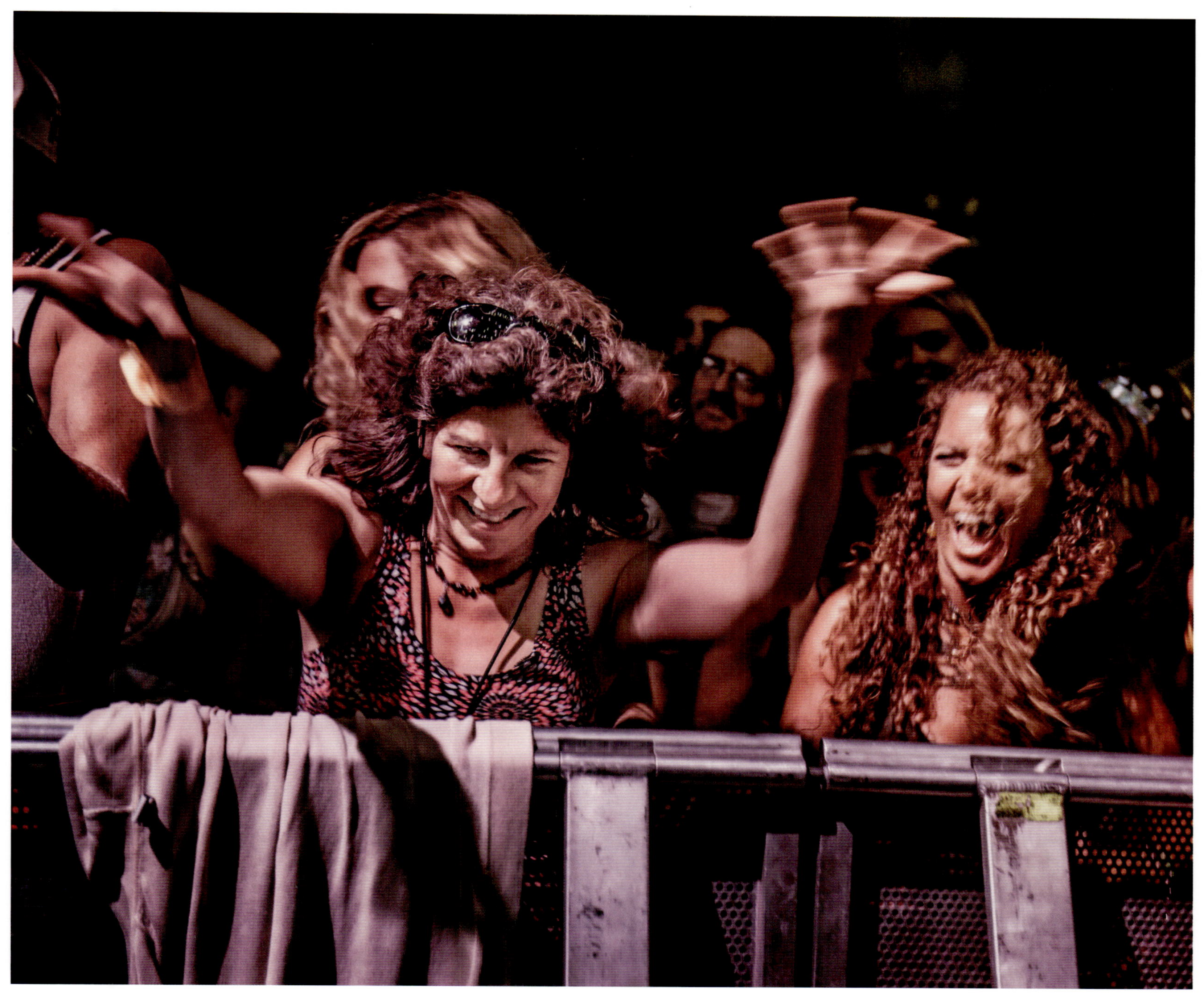

Live music is exactly that: ALIVE. I can't help but move when I'm around it and I love the feeling of dancing with abandon. Katy G. (pictured, left)

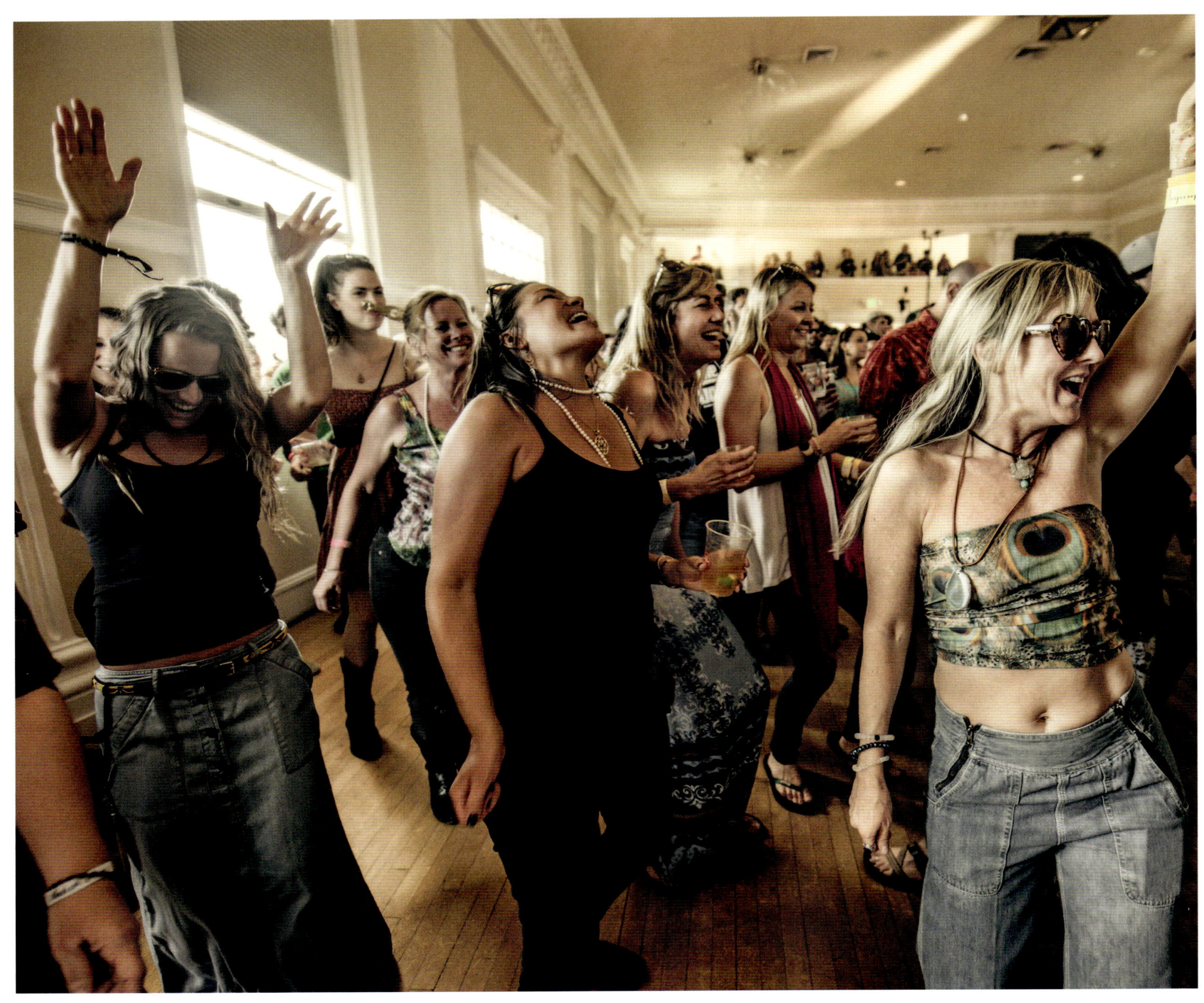

Live music can only be enjoyed in the present. Every note is fleeting. Here now, gone in an instant. You can't cling to it. After a while, this seeps into your bones. You carry it with you, this reminder about how to enjoy life: right here, right now. Cecelia G. (pictured, left)

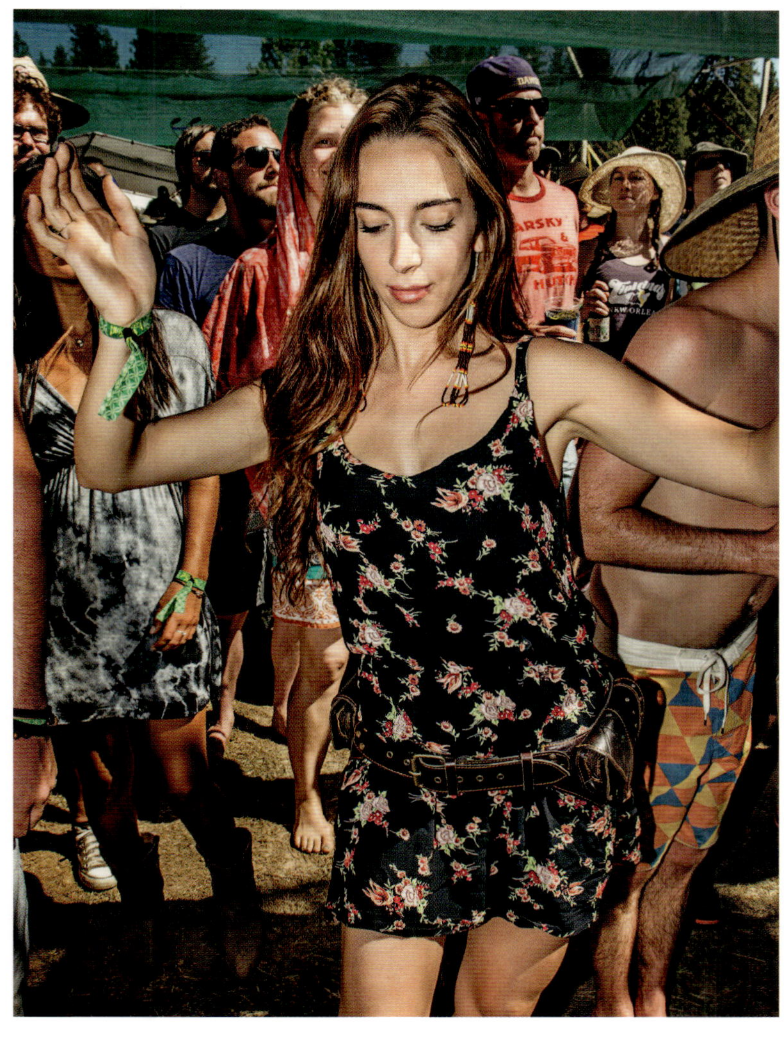

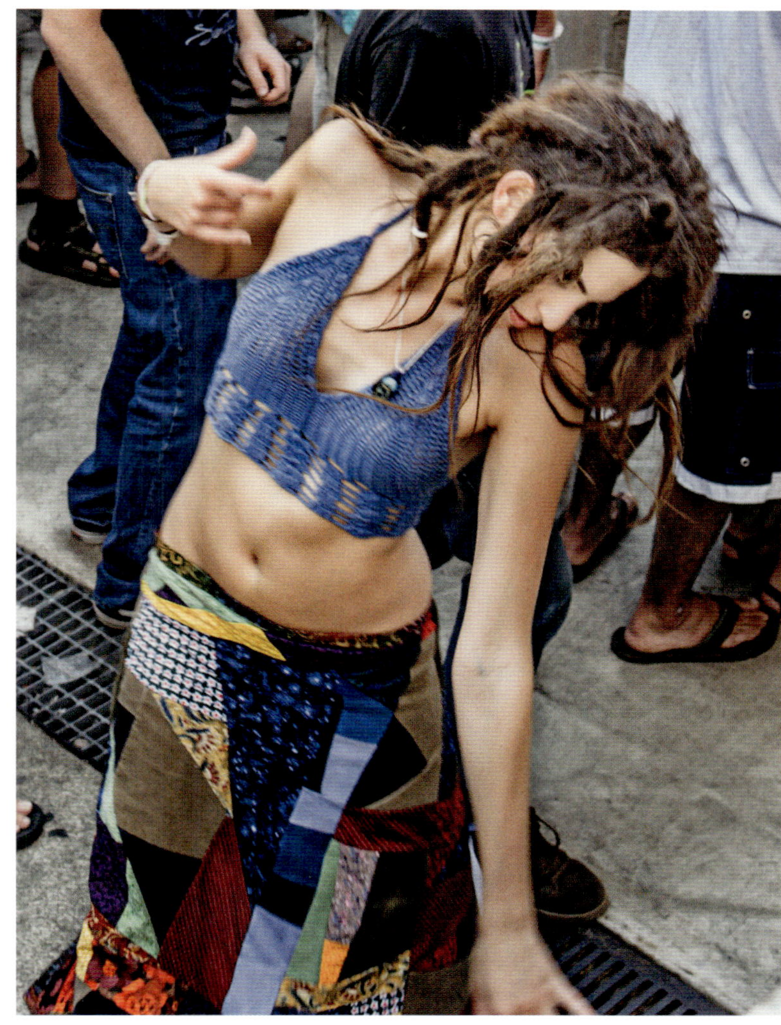

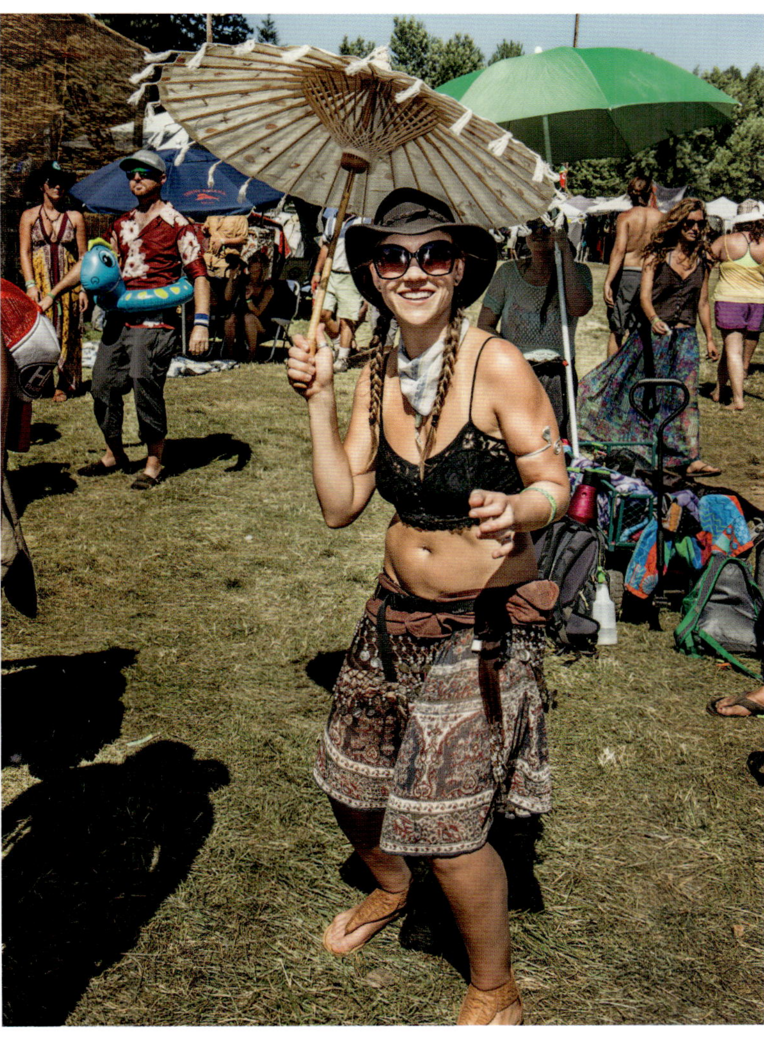

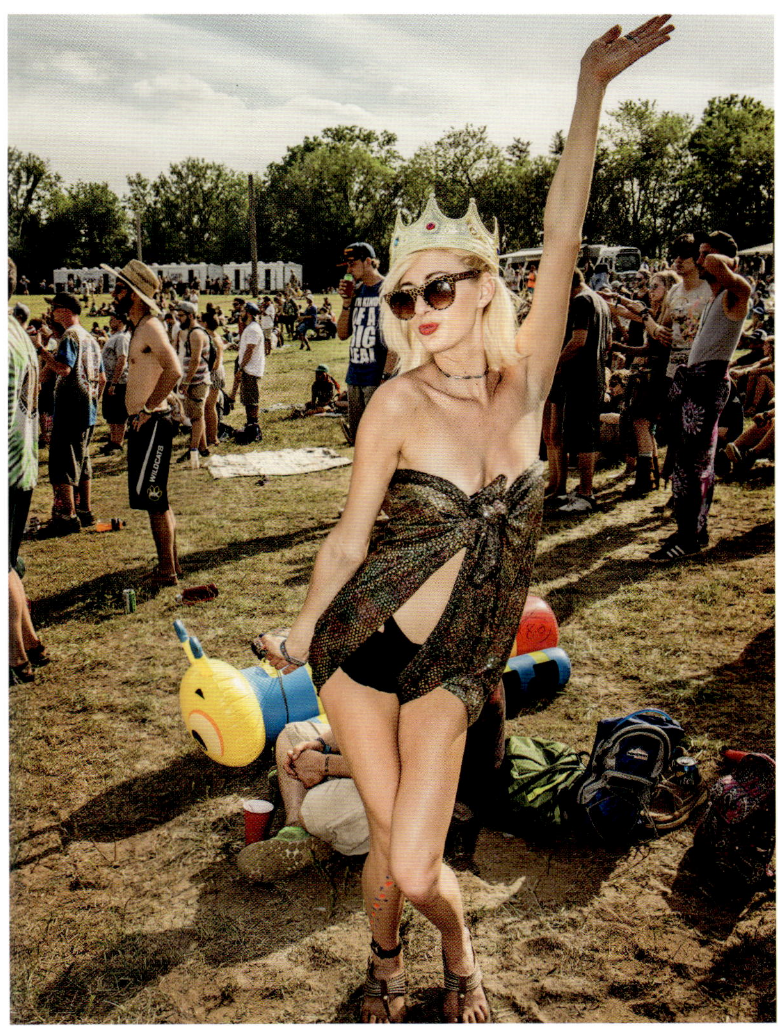

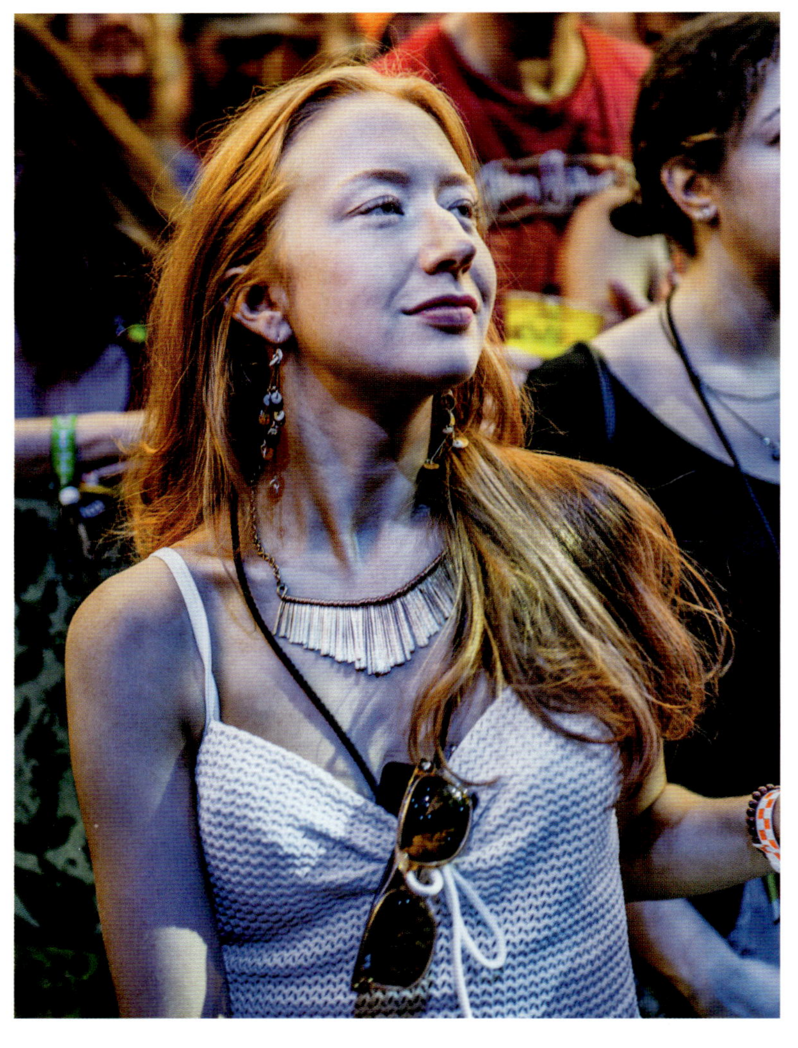

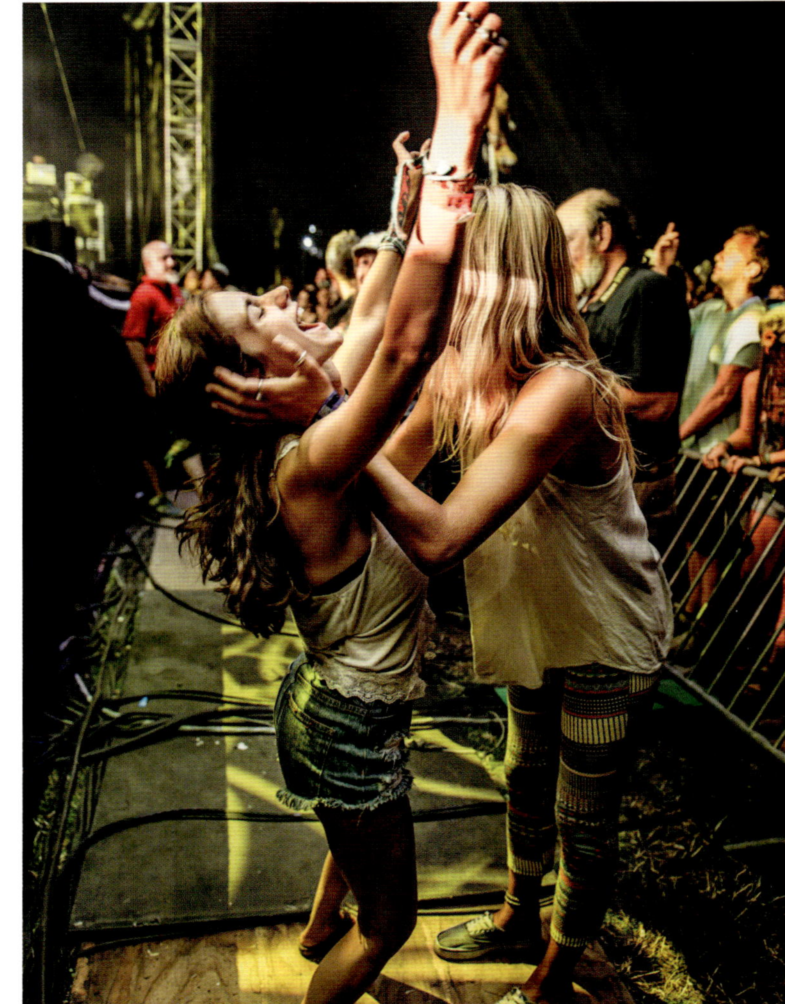

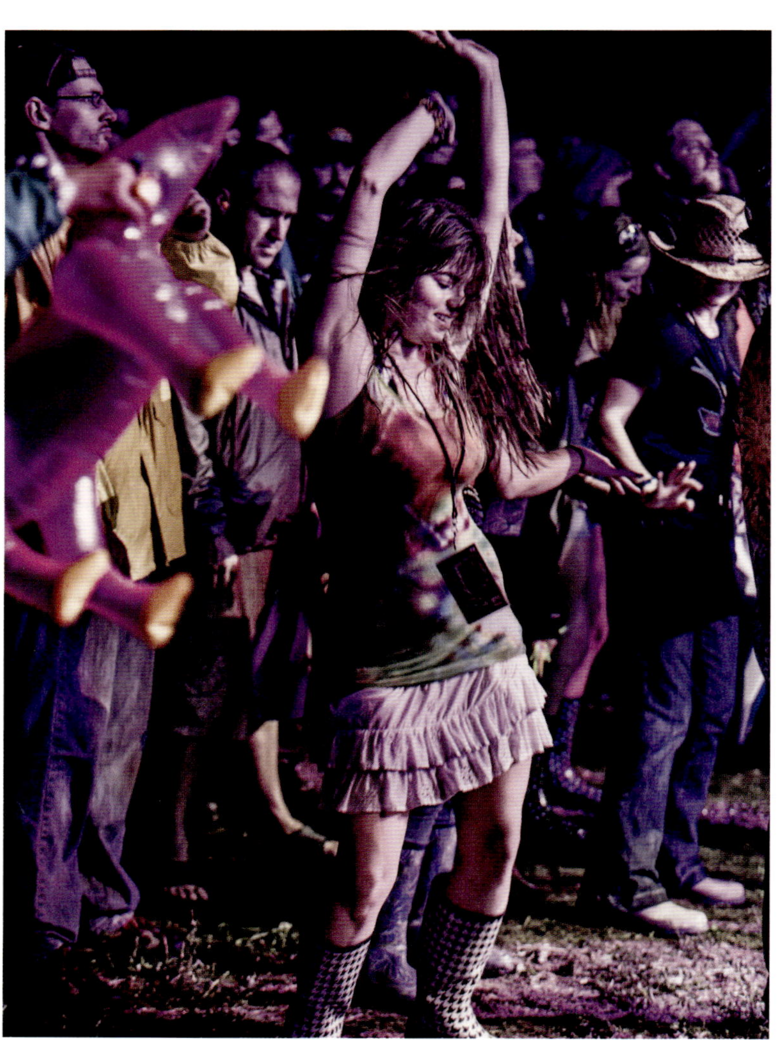

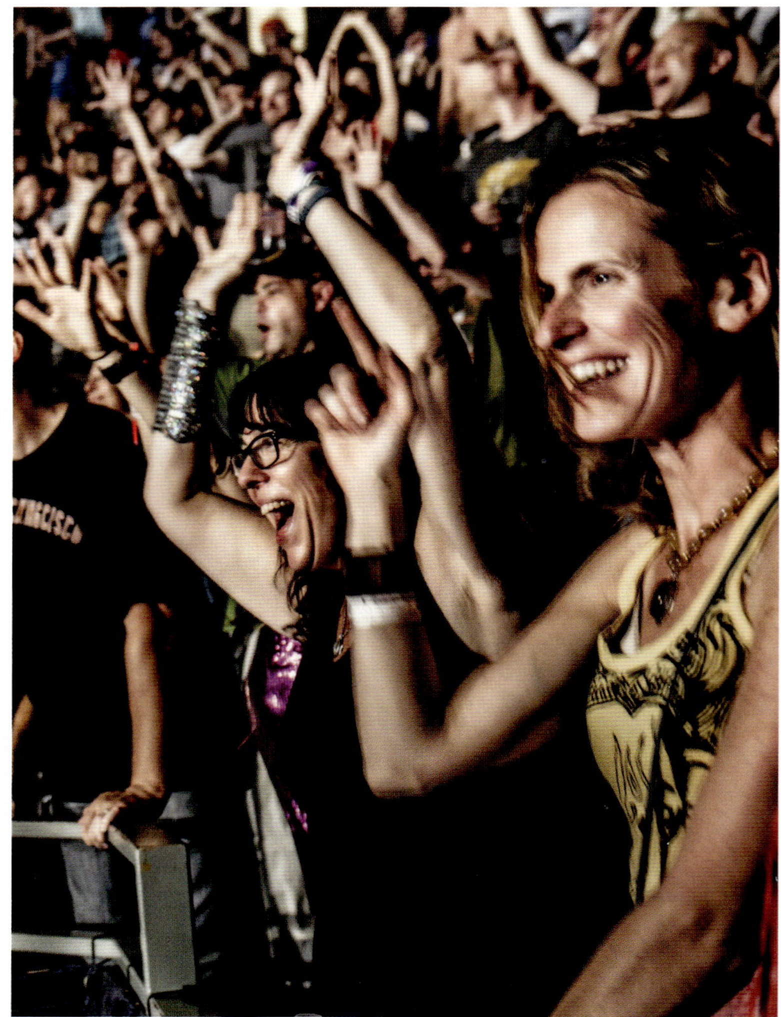

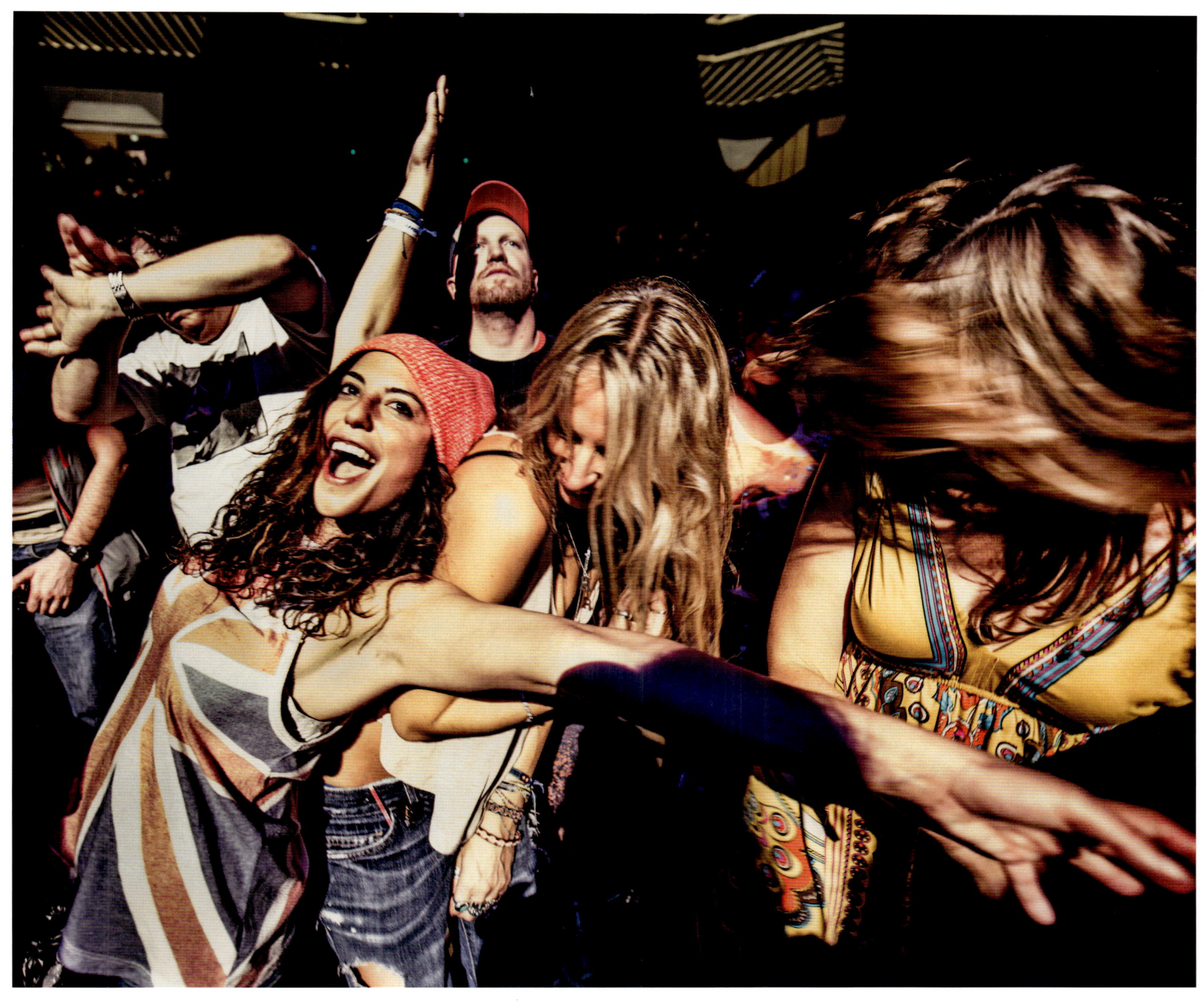

There is no better place in the world to me than being surrounded by good music, good people, and good vibes. Jacqui I. (pictured, left)

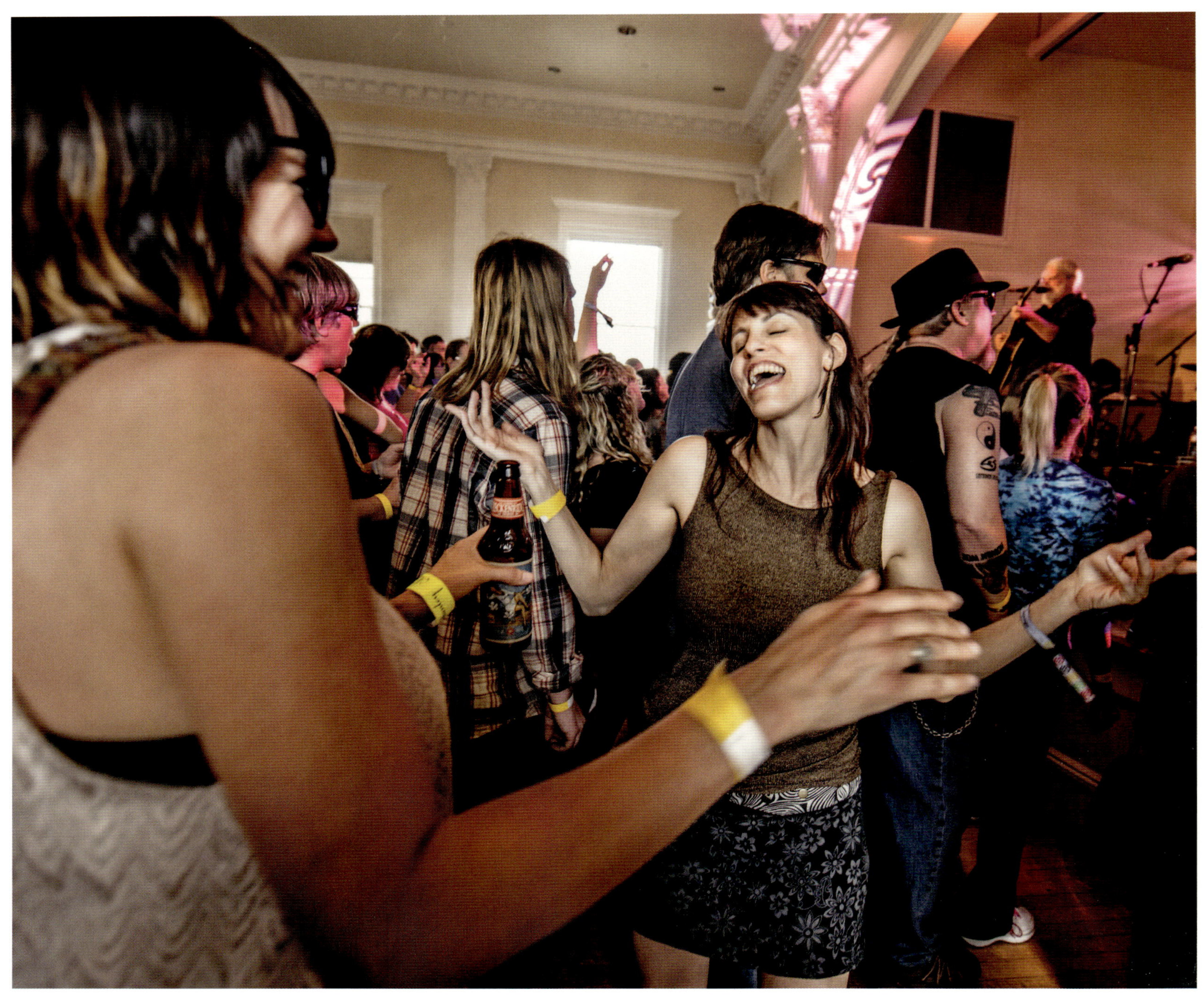

I love the feeling that live music can take you and have you soar to another plane and leave the rest of the world behind. Jennifer G.

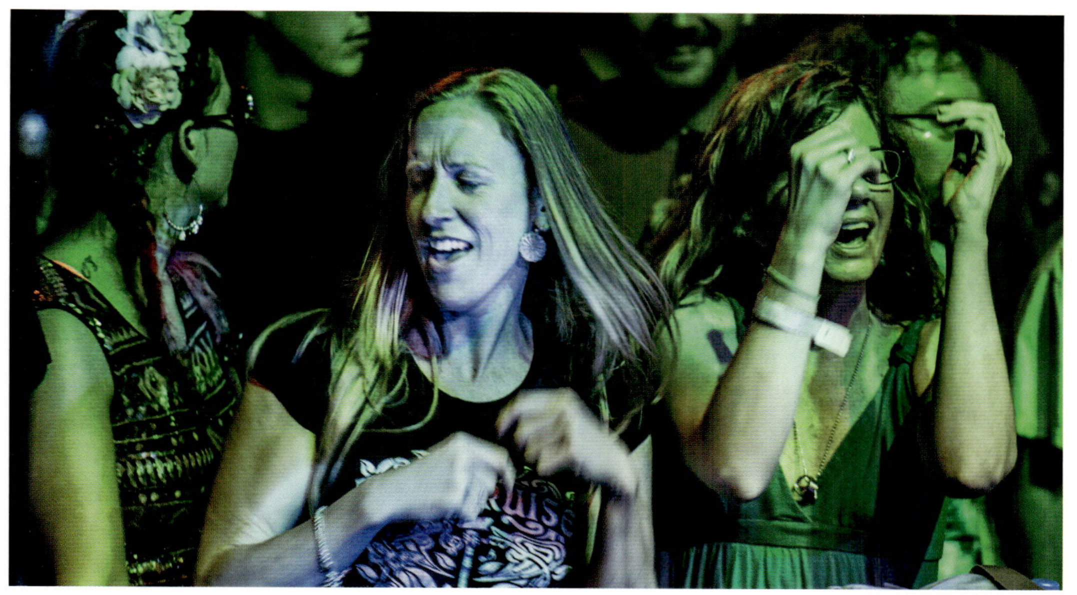
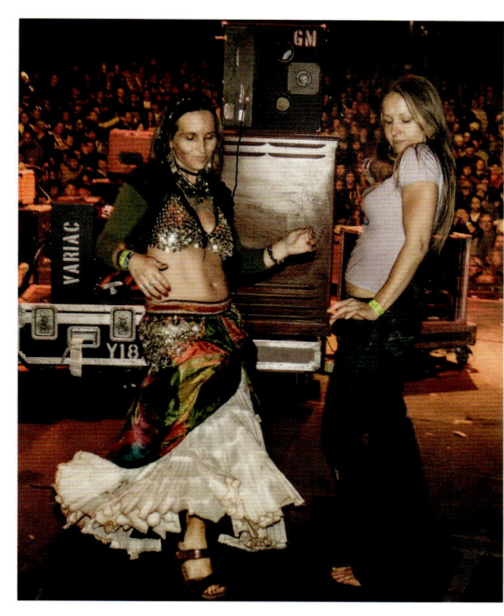
VARIAC
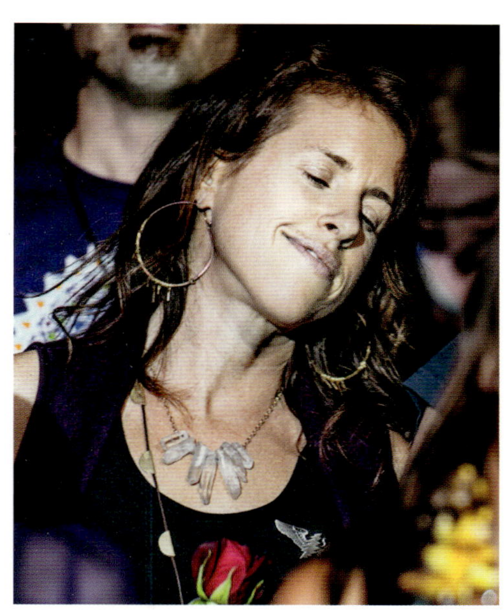
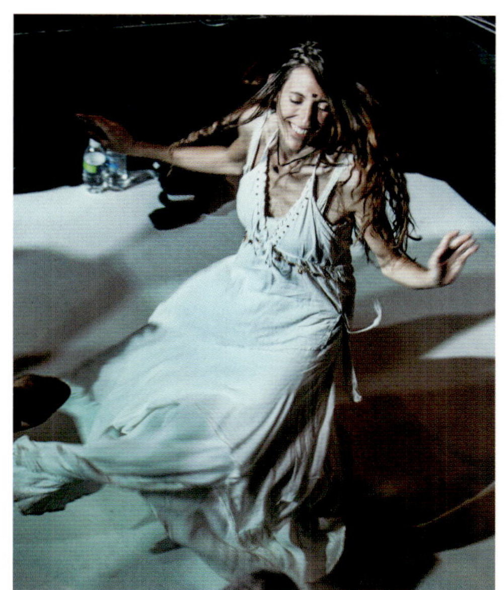
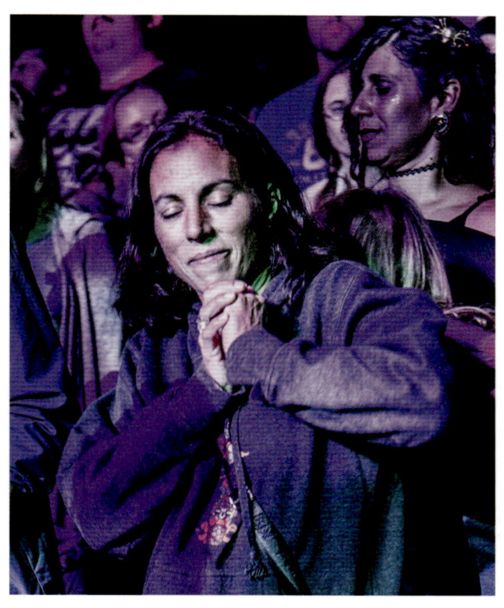
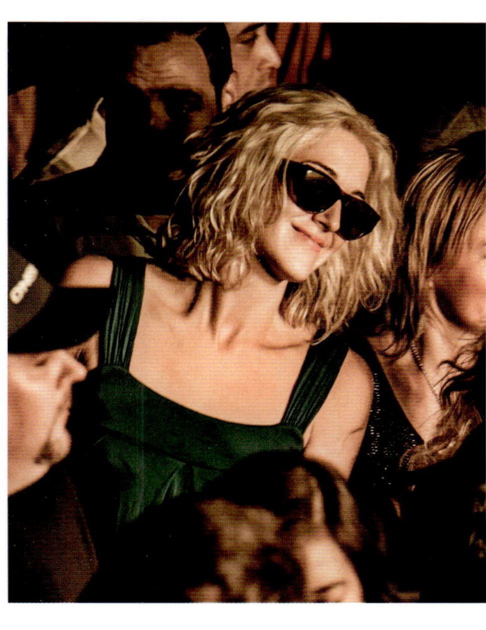
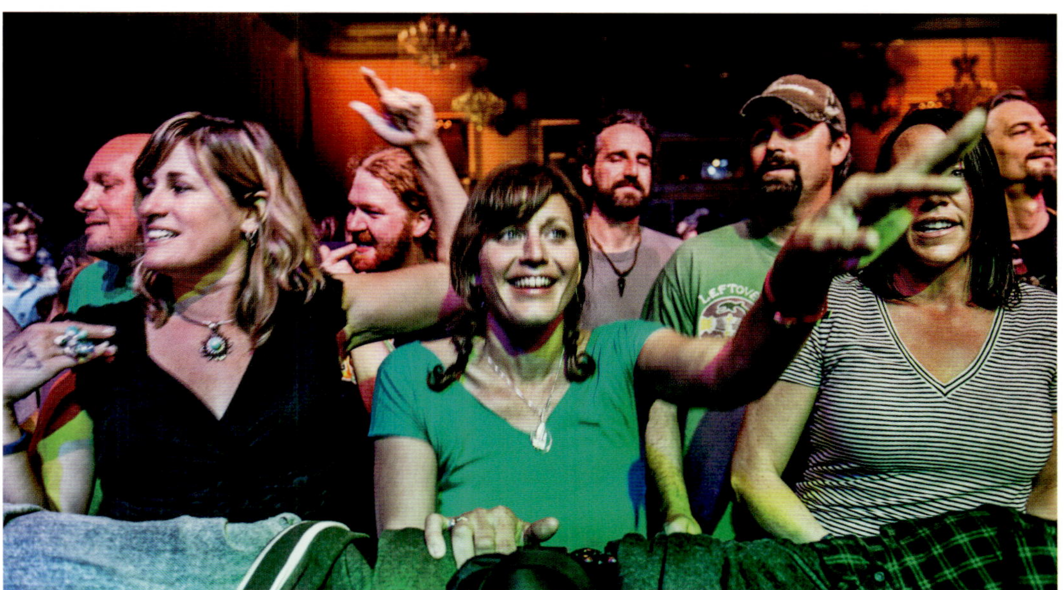

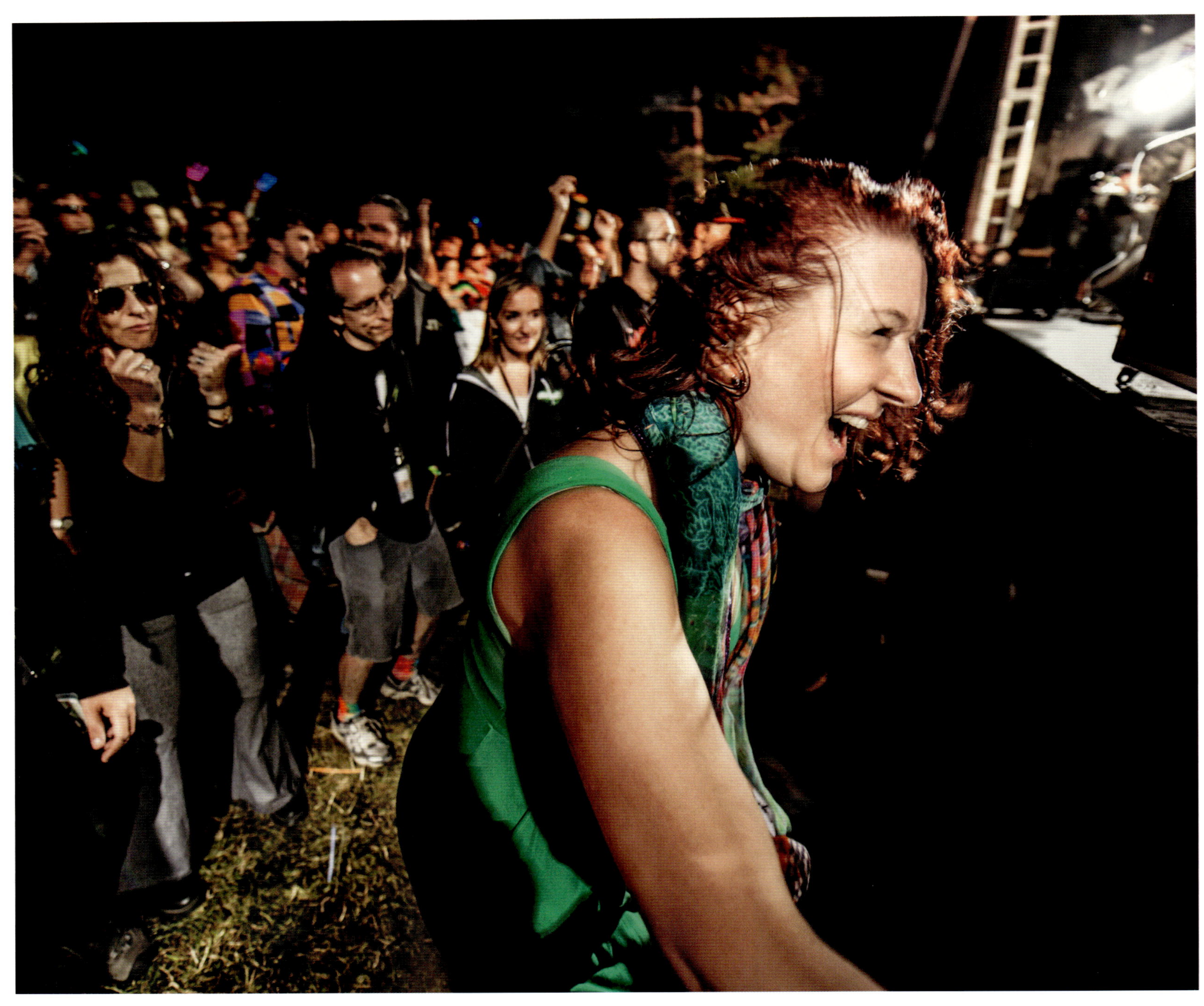

I see being on the rail or in the pit as a responsibility to be present; to take the energy and music they are sharing, to receive it, to lift it, to meet it, and push it and them to a higher, more massive space and sound. Jenn R. (pictured)

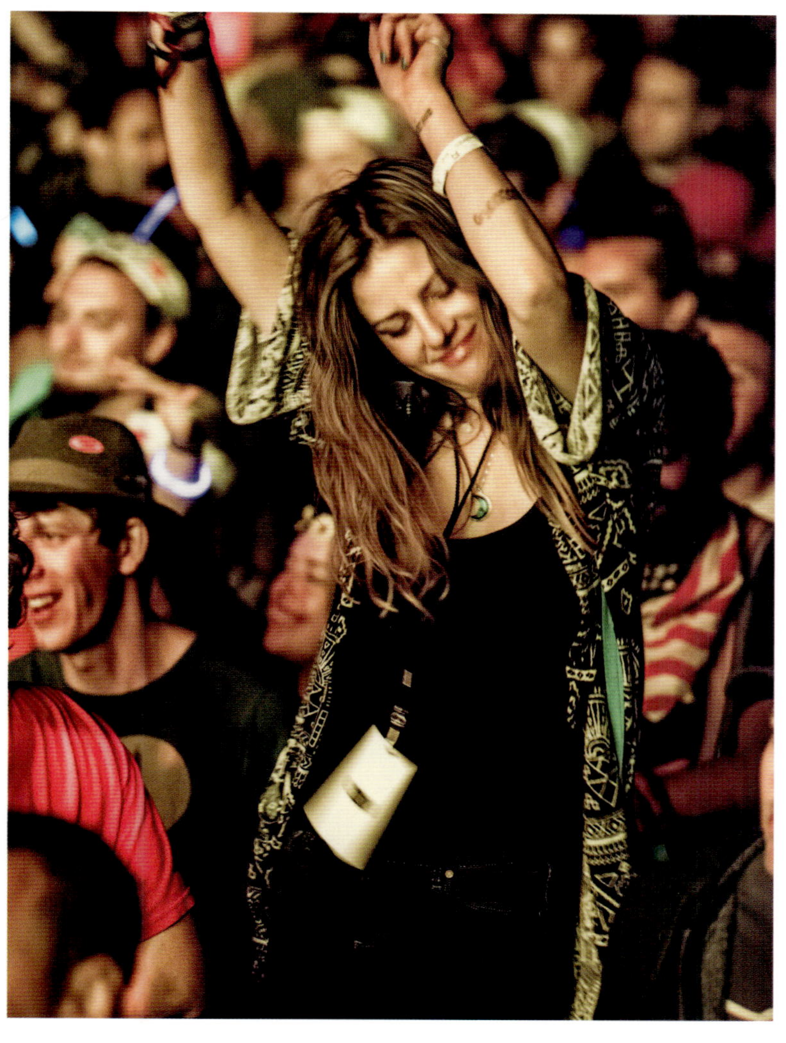
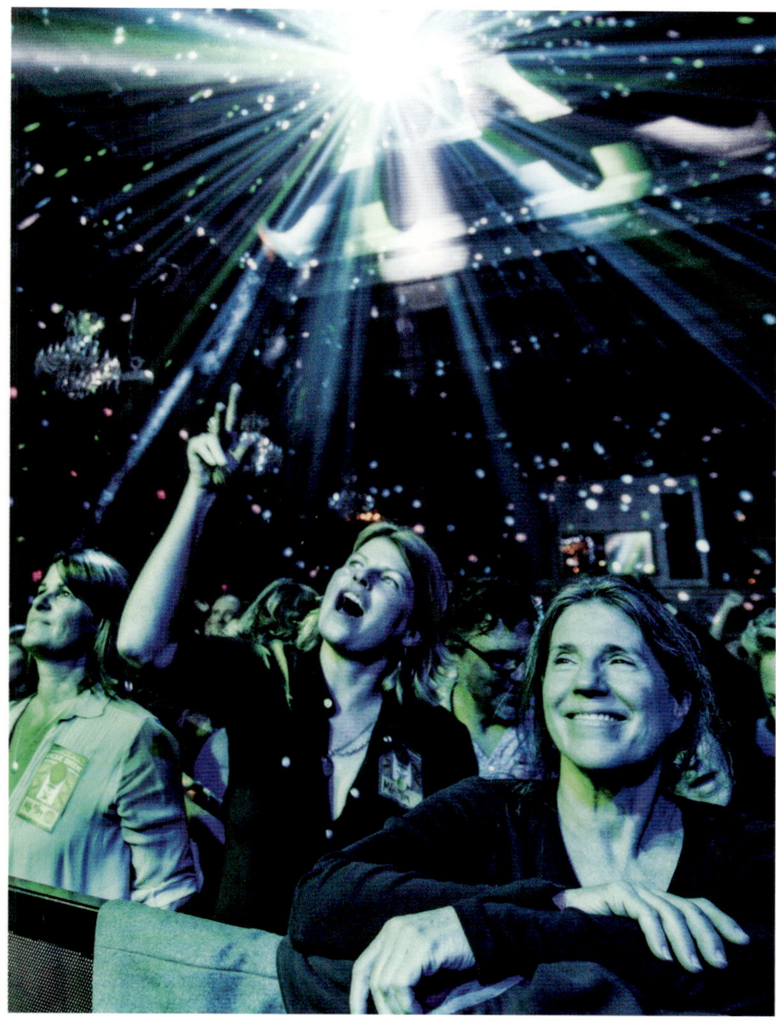
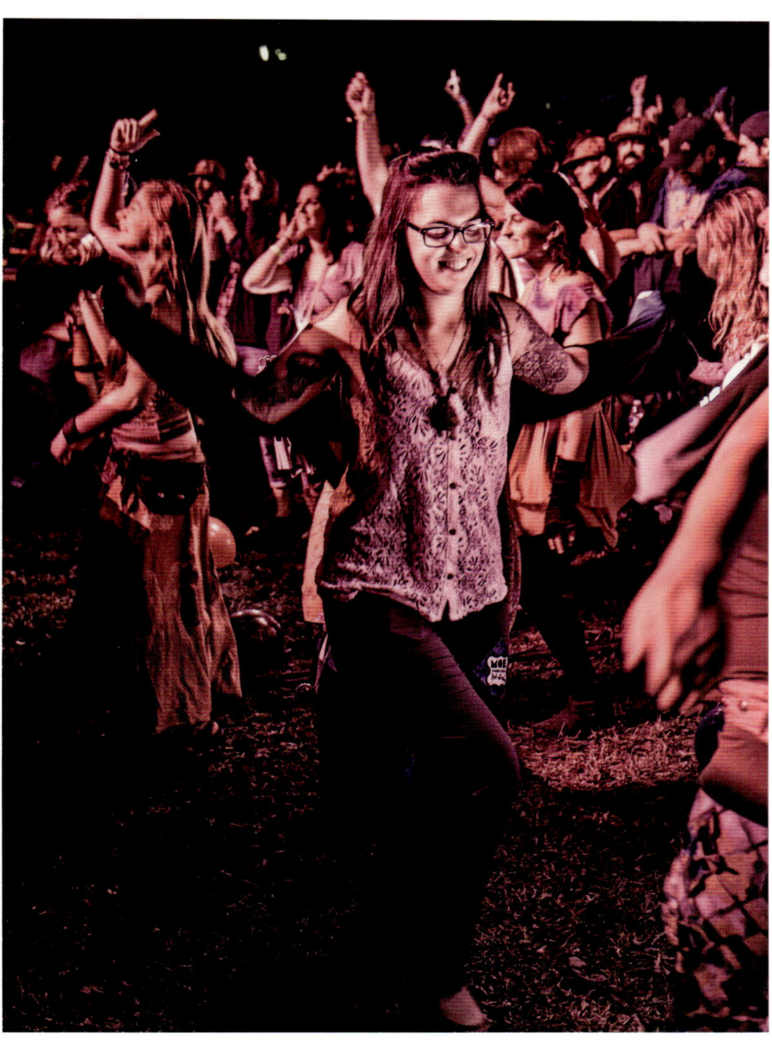
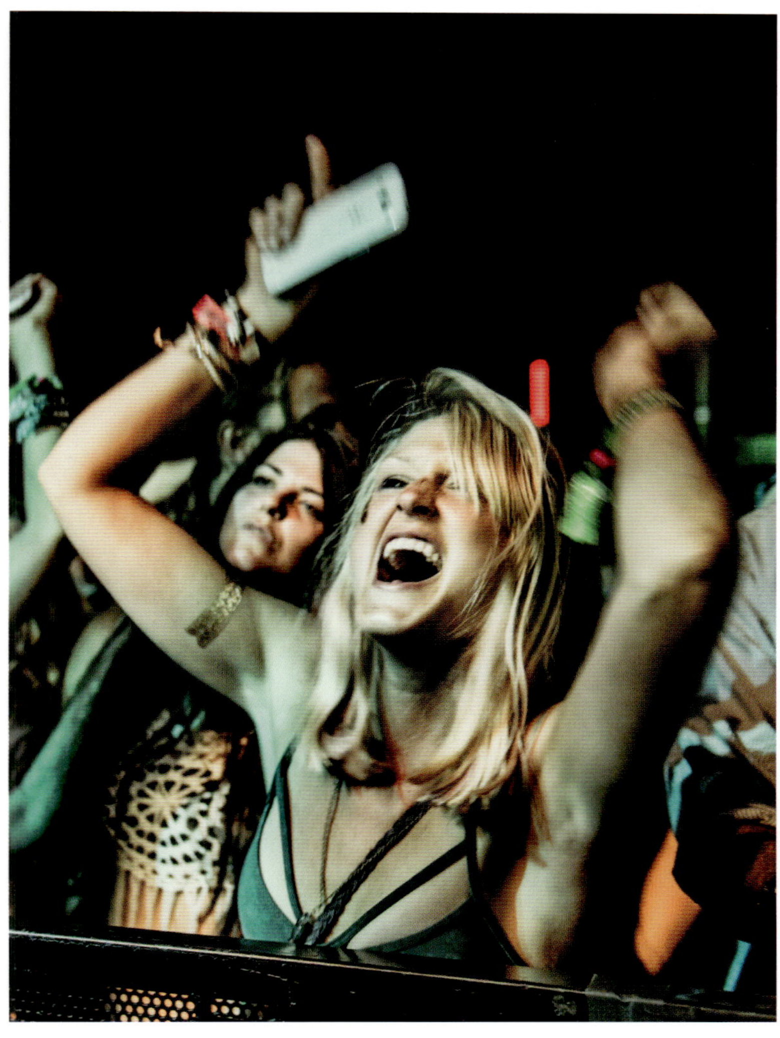

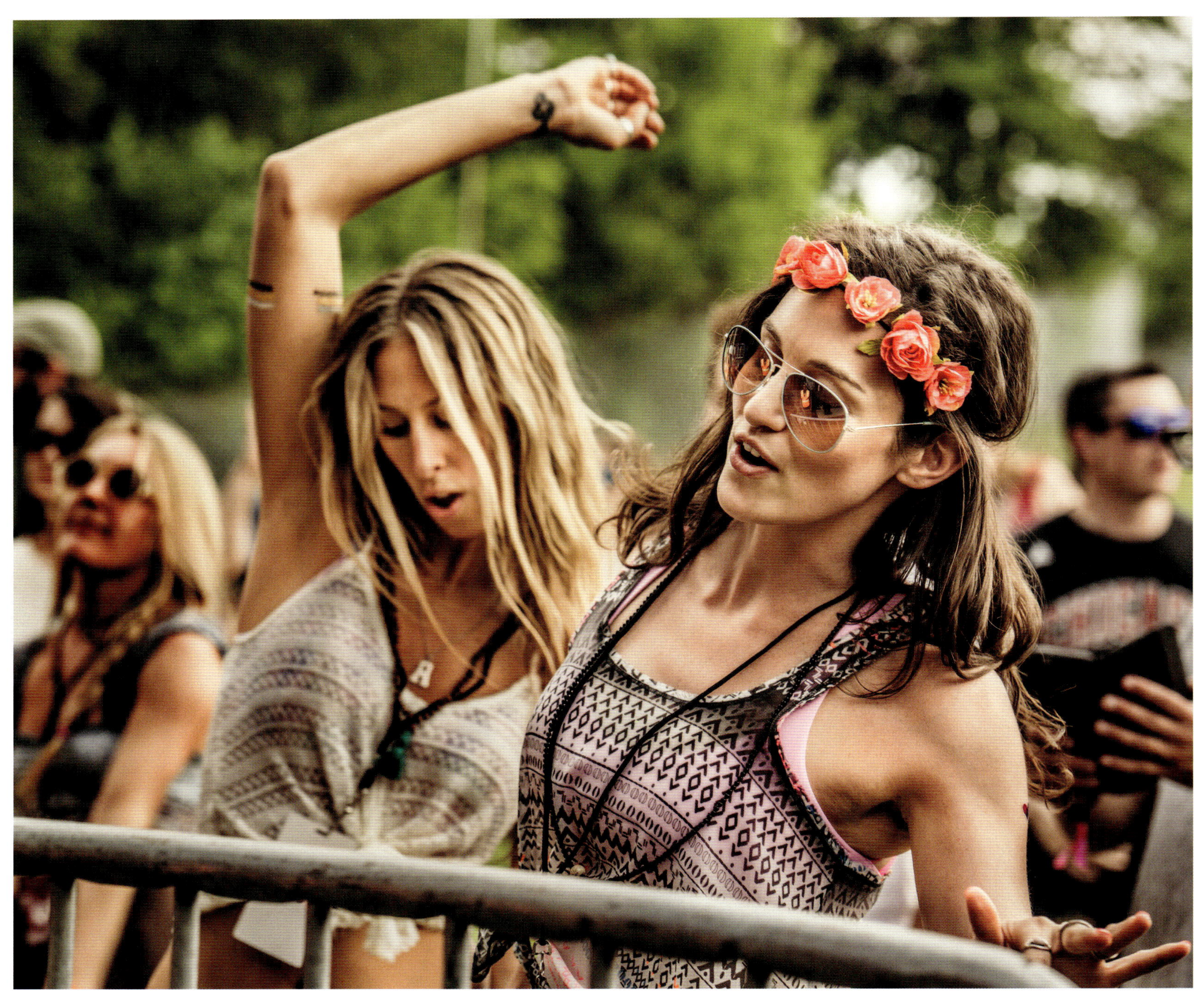

The music itself nourishes my soul. It's a part of who I am.

Dara K. (pictured, right)

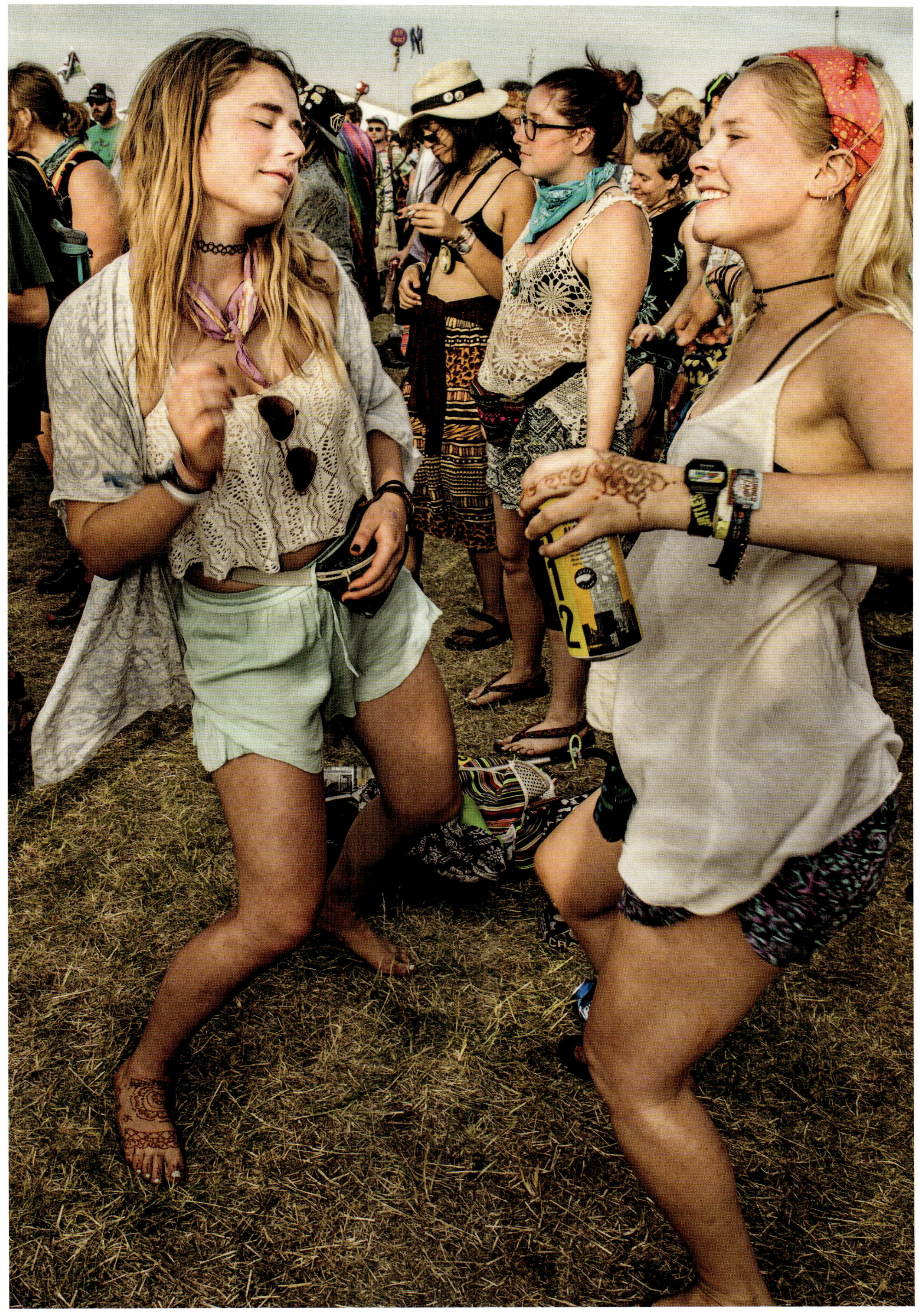

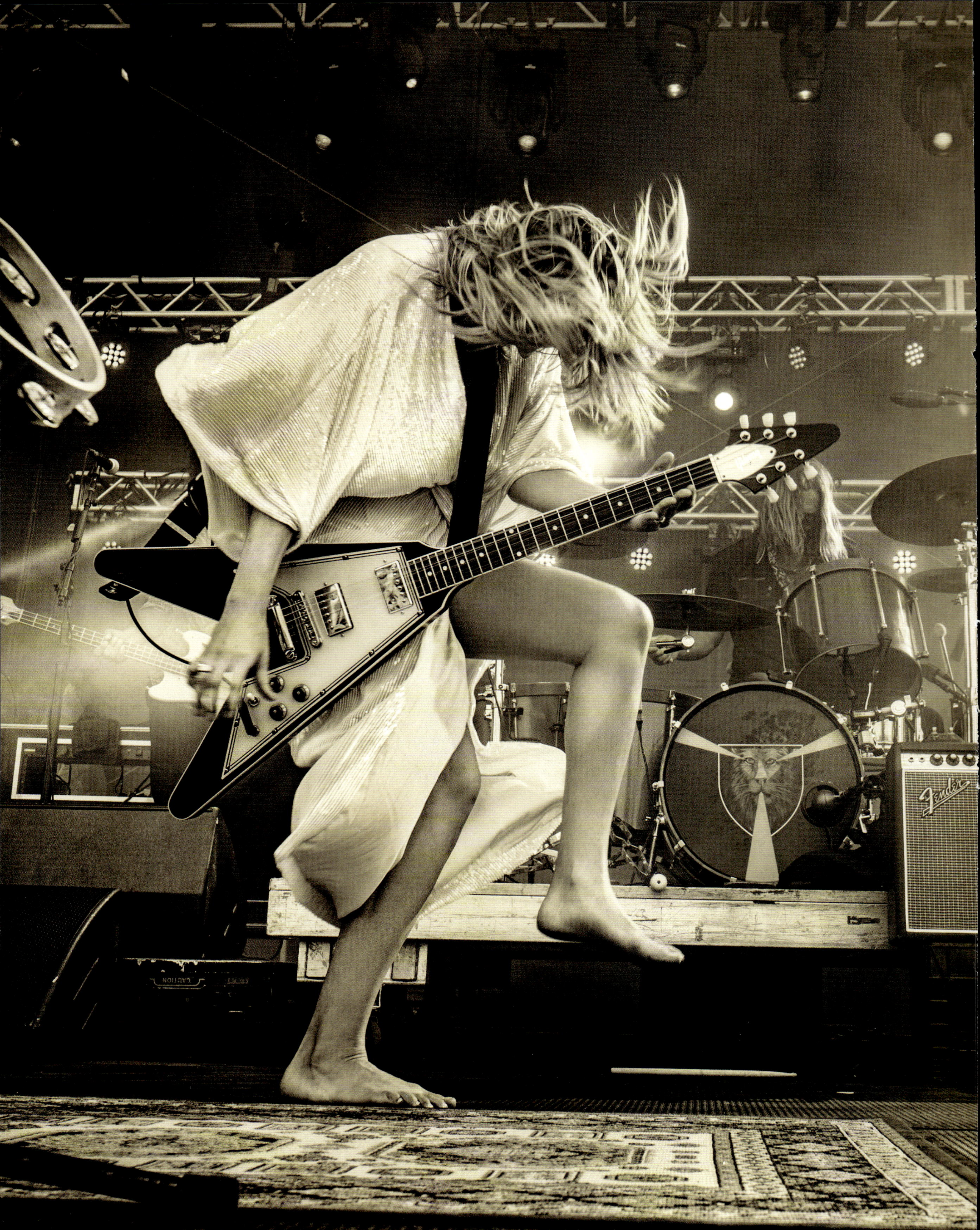
Fender

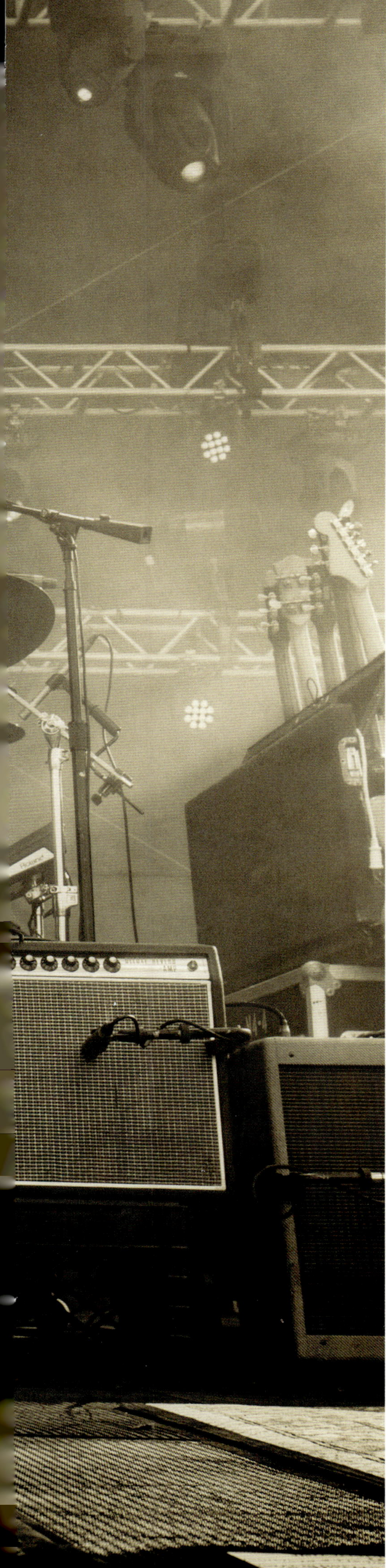

Afterword

by Grace Potter

What's in a name? Flapper. Beatnik. Hippie. The lines blur between definition, stigma, and myth ...

Hippie chick. Is this still a valid term for women of my generation? I've spent many a night in the hallowed campgrounds of festivals and late-night stargazer scenes. I've met women who can hold court with rugged prairie men, drinking moonshine and roasting venison over open fires and quoting Walt Whitman, all while tripping on more acid than every dude there. I've met women who walk down catwalks in nothing but a diamond encrusted merkin, basking in every moment of their sacred animal power, only to go home and study for the bar exam.

Duality. We own it. We share it. And when we are fully conscious of it, we need nothing in return.

We are not just the girls dancing in the front row at the concert. We are not just the wax figurine copies of our rebel ancestors. We are the living, breathing manifestation of every path they blazed, every war they protested, every song they loved—a strange transmutation of the original. Holy and grounded. Fearless and devoted. Messy and beautiful. Alive and well.

I have come to find that my fellow revelers and I are not far off from our mothers, but we are not the same. We need to pursue something beyond nostalgia. Are we mystics? Sure. Hunters and gatherers? Why not. But we're also builders and demolishers, scientists and magicians, engineers and dreamers—creating, emanating, overflowing, and containing ourselves only to overflow again.

My generation has reaped all the benefits of exploration, liberation, and empowerment that my parents attained, and now we need to apply that to our tempestuous, ever-changing planet. Whether we accept the label of hippie chick or not is irrelevant. But what we do with the power it represents is significant.

So, I ask you again ... What's in a name? As it turns out, quite a lot.

Let's keep digging.
Keep climbing.
Keep singing.
Keep finding ways to feed our head.

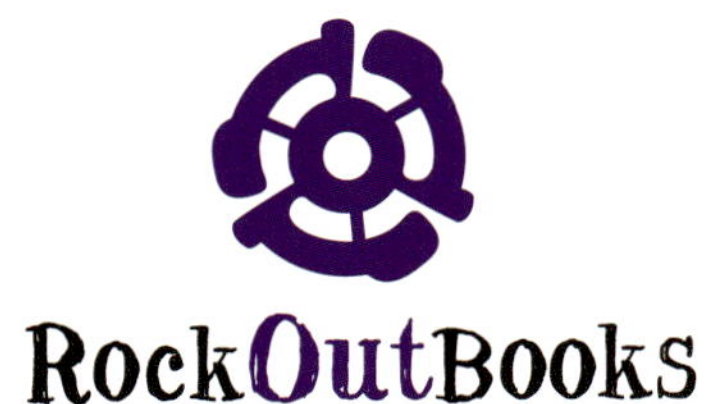

www.blakesberg.com
jay@blakesberg.com
ISBN 978-0-9844630-6-0
First Published, October 2015

Art direction and design by Frances Greene
All digital file preparation, re-touching, and pre-press by Ben Kautt
Graphics by Tracey Diamond Designs
All interviews edited by Edith Johnson
All text written exclusively for Hippie Chick

Published by Rock Out Books
P.O. Box 460054
San Francisco, CA 94146
Phone: (415) 239-2000
Fax: (415) 239-0900
Email: info@rockoutbooks.com
www.rockoutbooks.com

Distributed by SCB Distributors
15608 S. New Century Dr.
Gardena, CA 90248
310-532-9400

It's about freeing yourself. I think that's why people go to festivals. It's a slice of life they don't get to live every day. Abigail C. You can feel the music anywhere on the field—but the front row, that's where you can see the band pouring their hearts all over their guitar strings, on the piano keys, into the mic, and onto the djembe. That's where you can see the looks on their faces that tell you why they do what they do. Alysa O. It's an indescribable amount of joy I feel when the first note is hit at the first night of a festival. Ariel B. Dancing to music that I have a deep connection with allows me to truly let go and feel free. The music is the vehicle for that freeing feeling. Brigitte B. I was greeted with hugs from strangers, smiles from beautiful people, and marriage proposals from people passing by, all of which made me feel as if I were glowing from the inside out. Brittany F. The thing about live music that most excites me is the idea that, at any given show, I might be able to experience something that has never happened before and might not ever happen again. Dianna H. Since my first time being up front, I've never wanted to be anywhere else. There's just no going back. Elise M. If there is good, positive energy flowing from the front row to the stage, it can enhance everyone's experience. Elissa S. The rail is the closest I get as a fan to sharing the experience with the band; to exchanging energy with my favorites. It's a sacred space and I am grateful every time I get myself there early and hold down. Eliza J. In those high, pure moments, I lose track of exactly what is happening. I black out with bliss. I just AM. Everything just IS. Jenn R. It's the feeling of being completely disconnected from my real life, submerged into the music and surrounded by friends. Jennifer K. Music has always just been a way of life for me. It's almost like breathing. It's what I need to survive. Jenny D. It's all about music and art: inspiring, growing, helping, sharing, loving, caring. Showing what we can create. Learning from what others create. Sharing in the energy, love, and passion. Jessica L.